VIVIENNE LEE FRASER

This is a work of fiction. Names, characters, businesses, places, events and incidents are either the products of the author's imagination or used in a fictitious manner. Any resemblance to actual persons living or dead, or actual events, is purely coincidental.

Vivienne Lee Fraser
www.viviennelfraser.com.au

Cataloguing-in-Publication details are available
from the National Library of Australia
www.trove.nla.gov.au
ISBN: 978-0-6455157-8-7 (paperback)
ISBN: 978-0-6455157-9-4(hardcover)

Formatting and cover design by KILA Designs | www.kiladesigns.com.au

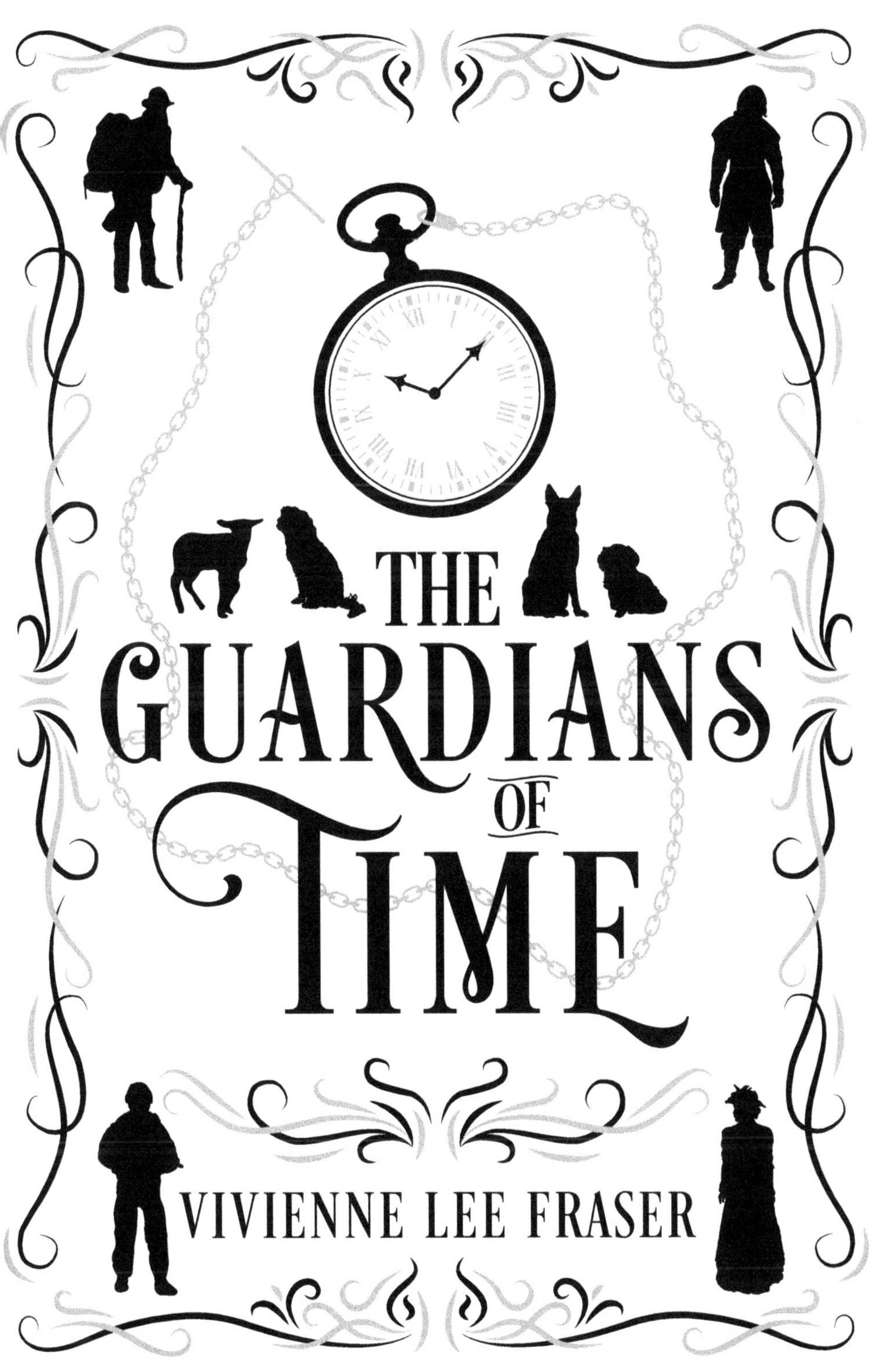
THE GUARDIANS OF TIME
VIVIENNE LEE FRASER

Thank you for the inspiration, Dad, otherwise known as Alain, Allan and Alan.

SWAGMAN
THE GUARDIANS OF TIME BOOK 1

PROLOGUE

EARLY AUTUMN SUNLIGHT dappled the forest floor as beating hooves sent the woodland animals scurrying for cover. Sounds of horses crashing through the undergrowth filled the air as the disturbance drew closer. The man glanced around, desperately searching for somewhere safe to hide. These forests were reserved for the royal hunt and, while no edicts had been issued to prevent the collection of wood from crown lands, no one had given him permission to gather there either.

Spying a clump of bushes close to a large tree, the man dragged his load over and hid himself, hoping the shelter would keep him safe from prying eyes and trampling feet. He took his place not a minute too soon. A stag crashed through the foliage, stopping abruptly in the clearing. Ears pricked, the animal stood quivering with exertion, listening for his pursuers.

For a second the woods fell silent. Droplets of blood dripped to the ground from a flesh wound on the deer's flank. The man knew the king and his cronies would not allow this creature to live. He surveyed the bushes. The slight movement of a branch here, and a crackle of leaves there, telling him men were moving into position to surround the injured beast.

Eyes swung in fear as the deer realised too late it was trapped. Stamping,

nervously seeking a way through the ring of men, its eyes found his. When recounting his tale later, he would swear the poor animal begged him for his life.

From his hiding place, the man observed the hunters reveal themselves. One by one they emerged from the undergrowth, standing silently, until the eerie quiet was disturbed by the twang of a bow string. A lone arrow sped through the air. At the last moment, the frightened beast stepped aside and the bolt whizzed past, finding its home in the stomach of the man standing opposite.

The corpulent target fell to the ground, and time stood still as the watching men collectively gasped. The thud when the body hit the forest floor broke the spell, spurring a frenzy of action. Forgotten, the deer made the most of the distraction and slipped quietly away, while frantic men rushed to their dying comrade. First to reach him, the bowman dropped to his knees beside the body.

'Sire. Sire, what have I done?' He wrenched the offending arrow from the prone figure.

As the other hunters drew forward, the injured man clutched at his stomach, as if to halt the flow of blood. Body shuddering, his arms fell to the ground and his eyes stared sightlessly at the canopy of leaves above.

'Tirel, you fool, you should have left well alone. Gut wounds are always tricky,' one of the hunters shouted as he reached the group. 'Here, let me look at him. My god, man, you killed the king.'

'But … but … you all saw I shot at the stag. It was an accident,' the stricken bowman wailed.

'We know, but others may not see it that way. Best you get away from here. Head to your lands in Normandie until we sort things out. Go on, quickly, before the rest of them catch us up.'

The pale killer tripped and stumbled in a daze as he left his fellow huntsmen. Seconds later, the sound of retreating hoofbeats confirmed he fled from the scene of his crime as instructed.

Realising he would not now be able to move until the hunters left, the silent witness settled in to observe the historic event unfold in front of him. Not knowing what to do, the men stood staring at each other, as if waiting for someone else to take control. More horses burst into the clearing. A dark haired, wiry man in royal purple dismounted and strode over to the body, whose lifeforce now mingled with the blood of the deer he had chased to his own death.

'The New Forest has claimed another of my brothers. Well, the monk did warn King William if he hunted today, he would not return home. The fool

should have listened. Come, our king is dead. There is much to do. When we reach the others, we will send a servant back to bring the body home.'

Leaving the dead king, the nobles of the land abandoned their monarch as if he were no more to them than the animals they chased and killed for sport. They made haste back to Winchester to begin their plotting and planning.

Once the woods were again free of the sound of hunters and horses, the elderly man rose, stretched out the creaks in his body, and walked over to the ruler of Briton. Though he tried, he could not summon pity for the dead man's fate. He had not been a good king. He had not been well liked. Even so, he did not deserve to end his days rotting in the forest, waiting for servants to come find him.

He retraced his steps until he reached his donkey and cart. After a short walk back to the forest glade, he threw the logs from his hiding place into the cart, where they clattered on top of those he had already collected that day. He moved them around to make a bed for King William Rufus' body. As a charcoal burner, he could not afford to lose any of his haul, even if his cart was to carry a king.

Making sure everything was secure, the man set off to find the servants from Winchester Castle. The woodsmen knew him and they would be pleased he saved them the effort of collecting the body, most likely even pay him a little something for his efforts.

In his bones he understood he was witness to a pivotal point in the history of this land. He decided once the body was delivered and the reward collected, he would find the apothecary Master Gavin. Together they might be able to do something to ensure the light shone more brightly in Briton after these dark days.

1

ONCE A JOLLY SWAGMAN

John stopped dead in the middle of the street as men, boys and a smattering of women continued to swarm around him, faces fierce and determined. As hundreds of feet kicked up dust, and hundreds of voices yelled and screamed and demanded attention, he wondered how the peaceful protest had so quickly turned into a full scale riot.

Turning at the sound of breaking glass, he spotted a group cheering as the window of a farm goods store cracked, then shattered to the ground. Spurred on by the violent act, others picked up stones and began pelting buildings along Main Street, uncaring whether the owners supported the landholders or them.

One storekeeper was foolish enough to come out to protect his property, but swayed and nearly fell as a stray rock opened a bloody gash on his cheek. John went to go forward and help, after all the man was one of the few in town who offered work to striking shearers from the camp, but the store keeper rushed back inside, firmly bolting the door.

Making his way back through the angry crowd, he marvelled how the men moved to let him past, like a river flowing around a rock. As the mob finally began to thin, he came upon a group of boys around his own age, surrounding a young girl and her mother, they were jeering and yelling insults. The woman

held her daughter in the protective circle of her arms, staring defiantly at their attackers, her trembling hands the only indication of her fear.

Blue eyes found his, and his anger was ignited by the plea she sent him. These boys must have mothers and sisters of their own. How would they feel if someone treated them this way? Besides, their argument was with the landholders and the wealthy townsmen who supported the cutting of shearer's wages, not women like this. Women had no more say in pay rates and working conditions than the men themselves did. In fact, many would argue they had even less.

Pushing his way through the group, he found the woman's hand and prepared to lead her away. Before he could, the circle closed back around them, voicing their protests at his interference.

'Hey, what are you doing?'

'You are meant to be on our side.'

'Class traitor.'

John glared at them, saying nothing but defying them to take him on. Something in his look caused the aggressors to pause, and he took the opportunity to break free, dragging the woman and her daughter behind him.

Slipping between two buildings, he led them through to a back street. It was deserted and seemed eerily quiet after the noise the striking shearers made. As he checked they had not been followed, the woman touched his arm and smiled gratefully at him.

'Thank you. Goodness knows what those boys would have done.'

'It was nothing,' John mumbled. 'I hope someone would do the same for my mam and sister. They would not have hurt you—I don't think they would have any way. They are just angry, and perhaps hungry too. They got carried away.

'If you head home through the back streets you should be safe enough, but lock your door when you get there, just to be sure.'

Bustling away, the woman glanced back over her shoulder before turning down a side street and disappearing from view. John continued watching long after they disappeared, listening to the sounds of unrest as they came from further and further away, as he tried to calm his nerves, and wondered what he should do now.

This was not what he had signed up for. Sure, he wanted fair pay for a fair day's work, and to be treated with respect. But he could not see how causing such a disruption and damaging property would achieve those goals.

As the noise of police whistles split the air, he made up his mind. He set his feet back towards the striker's camp that had been his home for the last

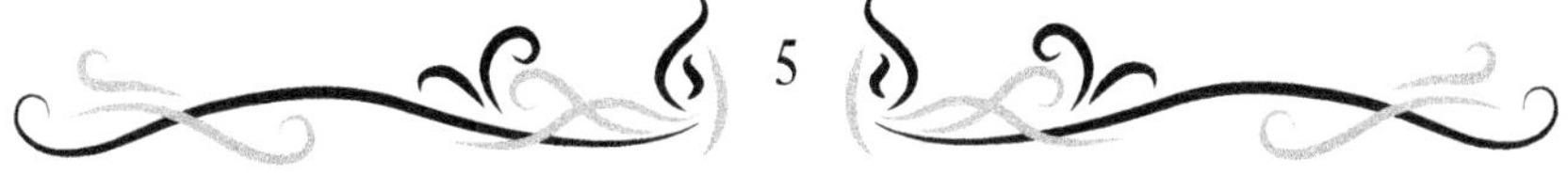

two weeks, ever since his shearing gang was thrown off their employer's property for refusing to work for less pay.

The camp sprawled out by the river, and was guarded by a few men who elected to stay behind to ensure they were not raided during the demonstration. In the midday heat the men gathered under a large tree, making the most of the shade. One detached himself from the group and followed John.

'You are back early, Jonno. How goes the march?'

Bill was a seasoned shearer from north of Brisbane, and had been the leading hand in John's gang. He frowned as he saw John rolling up his swag and stuffing his belongings into his pack.

'March? That is no march. It is a bunch of larrikins causing mayhem. The police came out as I left. They will all be locked up before sundown. There will be no one free to present our demands to the town council. It is a mess that will get us nowhere.'

'Ah, I did wonder… there were a few hot heads mouthing off before they even left camp. Sometimes they quieten down, other times they are egged on by the excitement of it all.'

'It was more than a few, Bill. Well, maybe it started off being just a few, but the others soon joined in. I couldn't stay. What will happen to my family if I get locked up? My mother would not be able to show her face around town, and they really need the extra money I bring in.'

'You did the right thing keeping out of trouble and coming back here, boy, but you are not planning to leave, are you? We still have a fight to win.'

'I do not see how we can win now. After today no one around here will take us seriously. And we do not have the numbers to force a change. I can see now we are not only taking on the landholders, but our demands threaten anyone who wants to hold onto their money and position.

'Besides, I cannot afford to stay. There are only a few coins left in my pocket, and after today, the few people who offered us work will be put off.'

'John you are a bright lad with a big heart, and we need people like you to balance out those stupid enough to believe a brawl in the streets will bring about change. Stay with us and help us plan our next move.'

'I cannot, Bill. I need to think of my family and how I can make enough money to support them through the winter. Maybe it is just not our time.'

'It will never be our time if good people walk away from the fight.'

Bill's words echoed in his head as he swung his pack over his shoulder and began the long journey home.

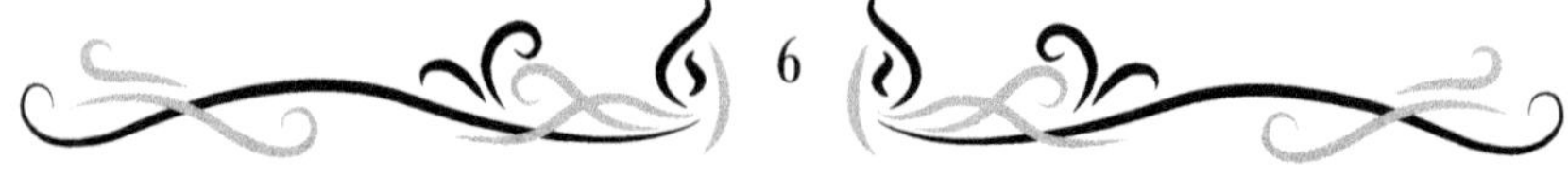

THE GUARDIANS OF TIME: SWAGMAN

DAPPLED SUNLIGHT PAINTED the dusty ground with light and shadow. John dropped his swag and bag, and flopped under the shade of the Coolabah tree by the edge of the billabong. Placing his bag in his lap, he adjusted the bedroll into a comfortable back rest.

'Matilda, we are a sorry pair.' He laughed to himself.

When had he started calling his swag Matilda like the older shearers? Snuggling into their bedrolls of an evening, John often smiled as they traded jests about sleeping in Matilda's warm embrace.

Rummaging around in his bag, his fingers searched for the little left of his meagre supplies. Only some hard travel biscuits. *Well, at least I have enough to drink* he thought as he filled his cup from the water hole in front of him. *Hopefully I can find berries tomorrow, otherwise I will soon be going hungry.*

Chewing on one of the dry wafers and sipping his water, he leaned back against the tree trunk and shut his eyes. After the harsh reds and ochres of the Queensland outback, the blackness soothed him. Even the water had a brown hue, rather than reflecting the brilliant blue sky. Weary through and through, and not just from another day's walking, he asked himself how fate managed to bring him to this point.

Dispirited and hungry, he was heading home with only a few copper coins in his pocket. Nowhere close to the amount he expected to give his mother to tide his family over through the coming winter. His forehead creased with worry. He needed to find some work near home or they would all starve.

Before making his choice to go back to the family farm he had considered all his options. With very little to show for his time away, he worried he would become a drain on his family's meagre resources. Perhaps the quarry would hire him. After his last growth spurt he was just about as tall as a grown man, and almost as strong. That hope alone allowed him to choose returning to his family over his only other option; heading to one of the bigger towns in the hopes of picking up some labouring work.

Cursing the unions for calling the men out, now he marvelled at how he ever believed they would improve his future. While working away, he witnessed daily how the landowners took advantage of their workers. Men who travelled far from home to shear sheep deserved better conditions and better pay than the bosses offered.

If they asked questions about falling wages, the shearers were subjected to tirades about unstable world markets, or lectures about money lost in overseas ventures. For all their grand words, employers lived in far better circumstances than those they employed. To John, it appeared in hard times unscrupulous bosses maintained their standard of living at the expense of the people who worked for them.

Sighing, he chewed thoughtfully on his biscuit. *What a mess this all is.* If only everyone would sit down and listen to each other. Yelling and fighting achieved nothing. A snap of twigs and a rustle of dry leaves interrupted his musings, and a lamb jumped out of the nearby scrub.

The animal took one look at John. 'Maaaaaaa.'

'I'm not your Ma.' John grinned at his own joke, wondering where his guest had appeared from. When he arrived earlier there had been no animals around.

'Maaaaaaa,' the young sheep insisted.

'I guess your mother must be around somewhere.'

Standing, he looked for the rest of the flock. There were no other sheep close by, and he could hear no drovers. This baby must be a stray. What should he do? Sheep stealing was illegal, yet if he left the lamb here it would surely die.

John scooped the animal up, choosing the lesser of two evils. Perhaps he would go home with something to show for his time away after all. Opening his near empty bag, he placed the lamb inside, then shoved the rest of his things around it.

He readied himself to leave, but paused as the sound of voices cut through the silence. Searching around, he found nowhere to hide. It was too late. Horses burst into the clearing and John turned to run.

'Hey, you. Halt in the name of the law.'

Hands held high, John swivelled on his heel to face the men, his back to the water. One wore military clothing, the other, from his dress, appeared to be a landholder. Both held guns aimed at him. Not knowing what to do, John began shuffling away. No shearer would be treated well by the likes of these two.

'Didn't I tell you someone had been helping themselves to my flock? And look, we caught one red handed.'

'I said stop,' the soldier commanded again. 'He will go before the magistrate, but it seems cut and dried to me. This boy will be a man before he sees freedom again.' As he smirked, John's stomach lurched.

Sheep stealing? Well, I guess I was, but I was really trying to save the lamb. They won't listen to me. Will a shearer receive an objective trial here? What about Ma? She

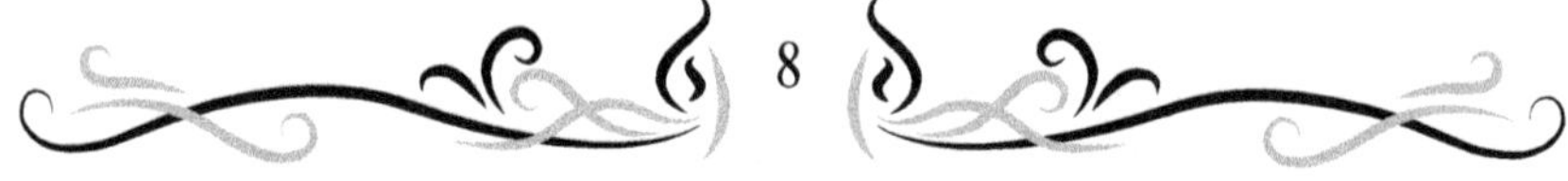

will be mortified. How will she ever face the neighbours at church?

Broken snippets of thoughts jumbled together in his head, making it difficult to think. Backing away from the danger, soon water lapped his ankles. There was no conscious decision to continue into the water, at least not one he could remember later, but that was exactly what he did.

As if in slow motion, the trooper dismounted, stowed his rifle and grabbed a coil of rope. Tying the reigns around some scrub, he walked towards the edge of the pond. The water lazily nibbled at John's knees.

'What are you doing?' the landholder yelled, turning red, his voice rising in anger. 'Come back here.'

The water gently caressed the bottom of his bag.

'Maaaaaa,' his new pet protested, but did not struggle for release.

'Do not go any further or I'll shoot.'

He pondered how the man with the rope would shoot him without a gun, before he stumbled and his feet struggled to find purchase. Falling backwards, he splashed downwards and disappeared into the cool depths.

Arms and legs flailed as he panicked, unable to swim. As he sank deeper into the inky cold world his head spun. He marvelled, drowning appeared like being dropped from a tremendous height, and was not at all as he imagined it would be. The thought barely entered his mind before he lost it as he blacked out.

2

HEAVEN OR HELL

'MAAAA.'

There are sheep in heaven?

'Maaaa.' Something cold and wet touched his face. Water? No, it was a cold nose.

'La… La…' He forced the words out of his parched mouth as he tried to sit up. The lamb peered at him with knowing dark eyes.

Hauling himself to his feet he surveyed the clearing he had landed in. The grass gently sloped to a narrow pathway. *So this is what heaven is like?* It was green and lush compared to the harsh, dry reds and browns of Queensland. He was surrounded by green leafy trees. Although he had never seen one, he realised he was in a forest.

Through the vegetation, he made out some odd shaped buildings. *Are there towns in heaven? How come I still have my Matilda and bag? Will I need possessions in the great beyond?* Urgently stuffing his hand into his pocket, he checked his coins were still there, just in case people used money here too.

Funny, he always thought heaven would be more white and floaty, like clouds. *Perhaps this is hell? Did I steal a lamb, and go down below instead? The preacher always told us thieves would burn in hellfire.*

Do not be so ridiculous.

'What?' John twisted around, searching for the owner of the voice. 'Who are you? Show yourself.'

'Maaaa.'

'La… La. You?' John's eyes widened as he looked more closely at the lamb.

'You call your lamb LaLa? How funny,' an amused voice intruded.

We will talk later, boy.

Again John glanced around, searching for someone to match to the new voice. Again he found no one. No one to match the mocking tones in his head, and no one to take ownership of the deeper voice in his ears. Heaven/hell was proving to be a frustrating place.

'Do you think he is dangerous?' A more feminine disembodied voice joined the conversation.

'He seems pretty harmless, and he has a name for his pet lamb. I am sure I would best him should it come to a fight,' the male voice boasted.

The undergrowth in front of him rustled, followed by some grunting, as two figures emerged through the greenery. A boy appeared first, as tall as John, but much broader. He stopped himself from laughing out loud as the lad wore a chainmail tunic and a sword belted around his hips. His clothes and swaggering stance might have leapt straight from the pages of his mother's book; *The Legends of King Arthur.*

Beside him stood a girl, hands on hips, staring down at him. He had to gulp back a laugh as she too was dressed as a character from the same stories. Wearing what appeared to be a long woollen apron over a coloured shift underneath, she was tiny, about the size of his twelve-year-old sister. However, the expression on her face and the confidence in her voice led him to believe her to be at least the same age as her companion.

Someone once told John when you drown, all the air is expelled from your body. The loss of breath must have made him light-headed, causing him to imagine things from the tales stuck in his head from days past. His mother had read to them from the well worn book of King Arthur stories every evening, and he often went to sleep dreaming he was a knight. Well, she used to, before his father died and she was too tired to do anything other than sleep after a full day's work.

'Do you think he is simple?' the girl asked her companion, not taking her eyes off him for a moment.

John heard her say the words, but her mouth formed all the wrong shapes

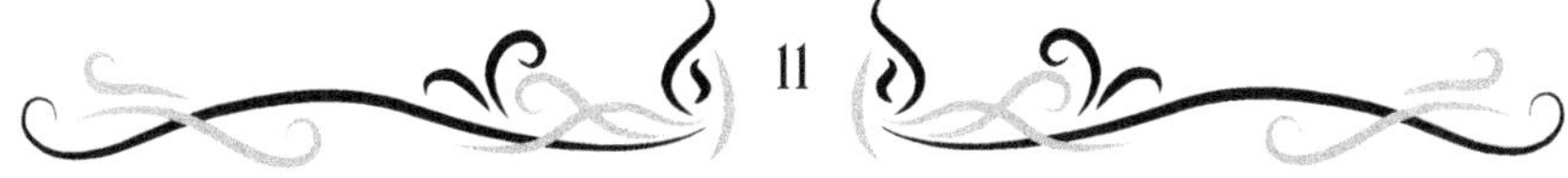

for the sounds coming out. He shook his head, hoping the action would bring everything back to normal.

'I am not sure. Is it possible he fell out of a tree and hit his head? You can easily scramble your thoughts with a good knock. Might take a while for him to come right if that is the case.'

John's eyes widened with disbelief. The boy's mouth moved, and words were coming out, but his words also did not fit with the shape his lips were forming.

I am translating for you. Speak normally and I will make sure they understand everything you say, and vice versa.

Astonished, John watched the lamb, who stopped chewing the grass on the side of the path for a moment to stare back. He then carried on eating as though his being able to ensure people speaking different languages could understand each other was nothing out of the ordinary.

'Perhaps we should take him with us. It will be night soon, and anything might happen to him in this state.'

The boy shook his head. 'I am not sure it is a good idea given what is happening at the moment.'

'But we cannot just leave him, Stanislaus.' Her face crumpled in to a frown as she turned to John. 'Where are you from, boy? Perhaps we can take you home. We might pass it on our way back.' She directed this last comment to the young knight.

'Queensland.' Able to ignore for a moment the odd way their mouths moved when they spoke, John actually managed to answer a question.

If they are not speaking English, what are they speaking? he wondered.

French. An old version, but it is French.

'Did he say Queen's Land?' The girl turned to the boy she called Stanislaus. 'Do you know of this place?'

The boy shook his head. John noticed his hand had not left his sword since they emerged from the undergrowth.

'I have no knowledge of a queen who names her land as her own.'

'Boy, this Queen's Land, where is it? Is it far from here?' the girl asked, taking pains to make her words clear as if she spoke to a child.

'I am unable to say as I would need some idea of where here is to answer that,' John admitted. 'But I can tell you Queensland is in Australia.'

'Aus...tray...lee…a.' The girl rolled the word around in her mouth as if it was a new treat to be tried out. 'Stanislaus, you are better travelled than me. Have you been to Aus-tray-lee-a?'

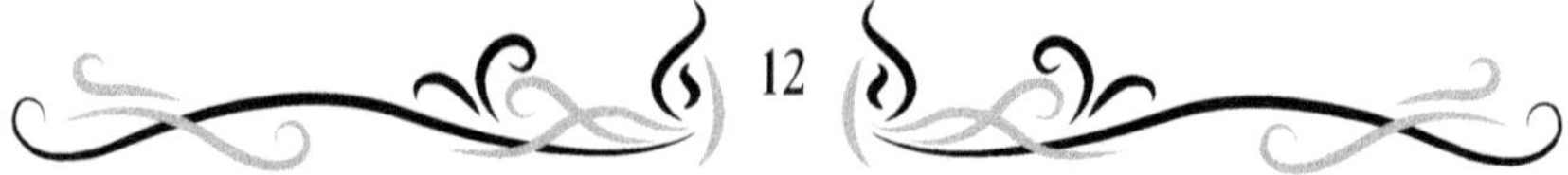

The boy's gaze swung skyward as he reached for his memories. 'No, it is new to me. This is all most strange. I think Prince Henry should be told of this. It may be a foreign plot. Or at least something to do with what happened today.'

'Or it may simply be a lost boy who has banged his head and scrambled his wits.'

'I *am* lost.' More troubled now, John asked, 'Can you tell me where we are?'

'Of course we can, dunderhead. We are in the New Forest,' the girl answered.

'New Forest?' John repeated. 'Where is that?'

'The forest is large, but this section is near Romsey,' she expanded her answer.

John searched his memory. He was quite sure there was no town called Romsey in Australia. Hadn't his mother talked about a place called the New Forest? No, this could not be the same one. The woodlands she spoke of were in her home country, England.

'Are we in England?'

'Yes, we are in Briton. Where else did you think we would be, silly?' Laughing, the girl placed her hand on her companion's arm. 'Stanislaus, I think he needs to come with us. His wits are addled. He cannot be left alone. If he died because we did nothing, well I do not want his death on my conscience.'

Still confused, John could not believe people in England dressed this differently to people in Australia. Then a thought occurred to him.

'What is the date?'

Stanislaus stood in silence for a moment before answering, 'The second day of August in the year of Our Lord, 1100.' The boy followed this with a decisive nod of his head. 'I believe you are right. If he does not even know the date, he must be very confused. He needs to see a healer at least. We can take him with us and ask Master Gavin to examine him when we get back?'

Without even asking for his input, the strangely dressed boy picked up John's swag and his bedroll from where they had fallen on the ground, and took him firmly by the arm, raising him to his feet. 'Come on, our wagon is this way. We must hurry, we are already late and our news is really important.'

'Oh, Stanislaus, quit complaining. It is hardly my fault the Mother Superior needed wood chopped. You should be pleased you could help.'

'You could have spoken out for me though. You could have told her we did not have time because we needed to get back and report to the prince.'

The boy's petulant tones barely penetrated John's thoughts as he pondered how he ended up in England, in the Middle Ages. For all he knew heaven/

hell might replicate something from your imagination so you did not feel scared when you arrived. Well, it wasn't working.

AS THEY WALKED along the path, John glanced over his shoulder to find his fluffy companion following along. With the boy and girl in front continuing their banter, he took the opportunity to test something.

Have you any idea where we are going? He formed the words inside his head, imagining speaking them slowly and clearly so he could be easily understood.

Of course I do, the voice in his mind projected disdain. *But you have not asked the right question.*

John shook his head, bemused not only by the oddity of talking to a lamb, but that the animal was instructing him. The right question? Was he to believe there was a right question in this situation?

Am I dead?

What do you think?

I fell into a billabong and I did not rise to the surface. It is not out of the question to believe I am dead.

I am disappointed. I searched long and hard for you. Well, a version of you I could use given the circumstances we are in. Unfortunately on first meeting I find you are not as intelligent and open minded as I anticipated. The lamb paused and looked up at him, as though assessing his worth.

He was not going to take being judged by a sheep of unknown origins without a fight. *I am disappointed for you, truly I am. Perhaps thinking of this from my point of view might give you some perspective. If I am not dead, then the only other option is I fell through water into Medieval England with a talking lamb, to be aided by a knight and a lady. Death or fantasy, which is more likely?*

I understand that where you come from, with your limited experience of the universe and all its permutations, your answer would be death. However, if you would open your mind a little and consider things from my point of view, the answer would be completely different. With these words the lamb obviously considered the subject closed as he continued on after the others.

Annoyed with what he considered to be an insult, but unable to think of a suitable response, John wandered along behind. When the group emerged from the forest path, he put his resentment aside as he dealt with the new situation.

Stanislaus dropped John's gear into the back of a rustic farm cart parked

beside the dirt track, and walked over to a draft horse picketed nearby, calmly eating grass. As the knight tethered the horse to the cart, the lamb roughly head-butted John's leg.

I am happy to travel in your bag.

Without thinking, John picked up the lamb and settled him inside.

'You can ride in the back,' the girl instructed as she climbed up to sit on the front seat beside Stanislaus. Once John had settled himself safely on board, the lamb snuggled in the pack beside him, the cart lurched forward and they were on their way.

As they travelled, John's thoughts once again focused on attempting to figure out what had happened to him. Which, unfortunately, meant once again talking to the lamb.

So, I am not dead? John asked.

No, you are most certainly not.

I am in Medieval England?

Yes.

How?

That is the wrong question.

John almost groaned out loud in frustration. *No, it is not. The answer is important to me.*

It does not help your situation knowing you fell through a time and place portal I created. You need to ask a different question.

Or you could just tell me what I need to learn.

Or you might think of this as a test. I want to observe how your mind works to be reassured you are up to doing this. Again the voice in his head sounded more like a teacher than a farm animal.

In his annoyance John briefly considered not asking the obvious question. His silence did not last long as he truly did want to find out what he was doing here. What was the right question to get the answer he needed? He fell through a thing called a portal to Medieval England. Ah…

Why? Why am I here, and what do you want me to do? Is that the right question? John grinned, sure now he was right.

Finally we are getting somewhere. I brought you here for a specific purpose. I cannot tell you exactly what it is because events must unfold of their own accord. For the moment though, while we assess the lay of the land, I need you to stop acting like a simpleton and start acting normal.

Frowning, John responded, *Yes, because it is so normal walking around in clothes*

from 600 years in the future with a sheep in tow.

Nearly 800 years, the lamb snorted. *And you may laugh about my form, but in this time, it is quite common for people to bring farm animals with them when they travel. They are way more valuable now than in your time. Besides, as a lamb people will take little notice of me, and I can better observe what is going on.*

John's stomach lurched as he remembered how he came to be in possession of the lamb. *Will people think I stole you? I mean, I did actually take you when we were in future Australia.*

His companion cocked his head to the side as he thought this over. *Actually, you did not take me, I took you. However, I guess we cannot totally rule out someone thinking I am stolen. Though you are well enough dressed for this period, so no doubt people will assume you can afford to own a valuable animal.*

Oh… umm. All right. If you are sure then. John was not fully convinced, but the lamb's voice was authoritative, and his travelling companions already assumed the animal was with him and raised no questions, so he decided he had far more pressing things to worry about.

If we are to be in whatever we are in together, I guess I should ask your name. Do you have a name?

Lala is as good a name as any.

Really? You do not think it makes me sound like a simpleton.

'Boy. BOY. Are you still all right? Stanislaus, he looks a little strange. Stop the cart, we should check on him.'

'No, I am fine.' Jolted from his internal conversation by the increasing volume of her voice, John answered then fell over as Stanislaus turned to check on him and the cart swerved onto rough ground.

'Stanislaus, watch where you are going. If you put another cart in a ditch you will not be allowed out without a driver again.'

From his place in the back, it sounded as though the girl was laughing, rather than being as distressed as her words made her out to be.

'It was not my fault, it was Alain's,' Stanislaus grumbled as he concentrated on his driving. 'He said turn left here, how was I to guess he meant at the crossroad ahead, not where we were? Surely I cannot be blamed for his poor directions.'

A snort erupted from John's mouth before he could stop it, and it soon turned into full blown laughter as he imagined the incident his driver described.

'At least you have a sense of humour, boy.' His reaction had gained the lady's approval.

'John. You can call me John,' he offered, tired of being called *boy* like

some servant.

'And you may call me Barabal. This big oaf is Stanislaus. Are you feeling better?'

Good, this is more normal. Do not muck this up, we need their help.

Shh, I am talking with actual people here.

'I am, thank you. The knock to my head appeared to be worse than I first thought.' Using the idea they had given him, he explained away his earlier behaviour.

'Do you remember where you are from yet?'

'It is funny, but I cannot.' Fortunately John remembered in medieval times Australia had not yet been discovered, but he did not know enough about the period to think up an alternative. In the meantime, losing his memory appeared to be the best option until he found somewhere far enough away to call home and not be caught out in a lie. As a bonus, if they thought he had amnesia there was a chance they would not ask too many questions.

'You can only remember your name?'

'Yes.'

'Not where you were going?'

'No,' John replied, wondering why Barabal was asking so many questions.

'Did you see anything odd on your travels?'

'Barabal, he cannot remember the day or how he fell, how would be remember that. Prince Henry will want to speak with him regardless of what he saw or did not see,' Stanislaus explained. 'Even if all this was not a little odd considering what has happened, he is bound to want to talk to any stranger who showed up in the area, today of all days.'

'We will take him to Master Gavin first though, will we not?' Although presented as a question, the tone implied it was more of an order. The other boy showed he understood it in the same way.

'Yes, ma'am.' The smirk in the knight's voice caused a smile. 'Anyway, Alain said he had something to show me, something about making a bang and breaking things. It sounds exciting.'

'I am not sure you two should be left alone together.' Barabal shook her head.

John's ears pricked at the mention of Alain, he was interested in meeting someone who knew how to blow things up.

And Alain makes four.

What do you mean?

Soon, my young helper, soon.

John dozed a little, the rocking of the wagon encouraging sleep. Having walked for most of the day, his body was tired when he stopped to rest under the Coolabah tree. Then being flung around in the water hole and thrown back in time to a country on the other side of the world had exhausted his last store of energy. His body craved a good night's rest.

The wagon came to an abrupt stop, jolting him awake. He forced his eyes open and found himself on the drawbridge of a real, live castle.

3

CASTLES AND WIZARDS ARE REAL!

STANISLAUS STEERED THE cart through the opening and into the castle's bailey, deftly moving around the people and animals milling in the courtyard. Everywhere John looked men and women rushed around. However, in spite of the frantic activity, the mood was sombre. Maybe in medieval England, people went round with long faces all the time, but this did not feel normal.

'See, I told you we would not be far behind the party accompanying the coal burner's cart.' Barabal turned triumphantly to Stanislaus.

'They obviously travelled more slowly to allow villagers to pay their respects.'

'Did someone die?'

As he considered the possibility a death would explain why people were so sad John fell, almost hitting his head on the seat in front as the cart lurched when his companions turned and stared in amazement.

'How can you not know?'

'Barabal, how would I have any idea who died? Many people die every day.'

'The king was shot with an arrow while hunting,' Stanislaus explained as he was called around the back of the castle towards what turned out to be a stable. In the cobbled space in front of a barn door, a boy took hold of the horse and waited for them to get down from the cart.

Is that why I am here? The king's death?

Partially, yes, but more because of the way he died. Pay attention and you will learn more.

'Master Black is not happy,' the boy holding onto the horse informed Stanislaus. 'He demanded an explanation when you returned. You were gone way longer than you said, and after last time…'

'He can take it up with Prince Henry,' Stanislaus retorted sharply, looking down his nose at the lad. 'After what happened to King William he sent us on an errand, and that took as long as it took.'

Without a backwards glance, the knight stalked away, with no offer of help and without further thought for the boy left behind to tend to his horse. His arrogance reminded John of the landowners in Australia, and he squirmed with discomfort as he followed behind the knight.

It is the way of nobility everywhere. Things can change if nudged in the right direction at the right time.

Looking down at the lamb he was carrying he thought, *Is that what I am doing here? Nudging things in the right direction?*

Only time will tell. The baby sheep settled more comfortably in the bag, closed his eyes and drifted off to sleep, if the sound of gentle snores were anything to go by.

The castle was a maze of wood and stone outbuildings, set around a central grand hall called the castle keep. Following Stanislaus and Barabal through the throng of people towards one of the larger dwellings attached to the keep, he shivered in the chilly evening air.

It had been warm in Queensland, and the day still had some heat when he arrived in this strange place. Now, with the sun's disappearance, the temperature had dropped considerably to a bone chilling level he had not experienced before. This weather was colder than a Queensland winter. Which was odd, as the leaves were still green, and the sun's heat during the day suggested autumn had not yet reached England.

As he walked through the corridor, John's nose creased in distaste as a horrendous odour hit him; a combination of damp wool, rotten vegetables and cooked meat. He had thought sharing a dormitory with shearers who seldom bathed was bad enough, but the stench assaulting his nose was overwhelming. He was forced to concentrate on keeping the contents of his stomach inside, where they belonged.

Finally they came to a small wooden door, opening into a room lined floor to ceiling with jars and bottles. The unpleasant aroma abated as he was

hit with the sweetness of fresh herbs. Searching for the source of his relief, John glanced up and saw bundles of plants drying in bunches hung from the roof. Stanislaus closed the door behind them, only for it to be flung open seconds later, nearly knocking them all over. A small man burst through the opening and dropped the basket he was carrying on the table before he realised anyone else was there.

'A… ah… Stanislaus, Barabal… and, umm… do I know you?' The man squinted at John as if trying to place where he had seen him before.

'Master Gavin, this is John. We found him on the road. He had a bit of a fall and cannot remember where he is from.' Barabal pushed him from behind. 'We thought you might check him over and do something to bring his memories back.'

Master Gavin frowned, peering closely at John. 'I can take a look Barabal, but it is generally only time that returns memories after a knock to the head.

'Perhaps someone local knows him and could help, although I can tell from the manner of his clothing he is not from around here. Maybe he is from across the sea? Squire Stanislaus, have you seen clothing like this before?'

Everyone appeared to treat the squire as the font of knowledge on things foreign. He shook his head.

'He is not from Normandie and he does not dress like anyone I have ever seen in my master's court, or anywhere else I have travelled.'

Gavin frowned more deeply, a furrow etching itself between his brows. 'You two had best be getting back to our future king. He has been asking where you are, and you know he does not like to be kept waiting. When you have reported, come back and I should be able to tell you more about your friend.'

Stanislaus headed for the door, but Barabal lingered a minute longer. 'You will be fine here. Master Gavin is the best apothecary for miles.' She gave a brief smile as she left for her important meeting with the future king.

'Put your bag down young man and let us take a look at you.'

The apothecary had a surprisingly firm grip as he took John's arm and led him over to a stool by the fire, where he placed the other hand on his shoulder, encouraging him to sit on a none-too-stable seat.

John dropped his bag on the rush covered ground beside him. Lala nuzzled his way out through the opening and stretched his legs, then ambled over to the fire, curling up in the warmth preparing to sleep. In reality, his black eyes watched Master Gavin with intelligent interest.

The master's examination consisted of touching all around his head,

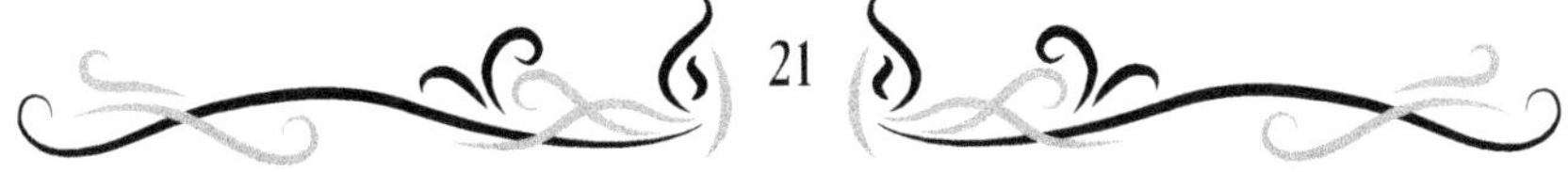

paying particular attention to the sides. He frowned and grunted as he went, but said nothing at all to John.

'Mmm,' the shorter man said under his breath. 'No lump. Unusual for a case of memory loss.'

He walked around John, and the boy turned to watch what he was doing, causing the stool to wobble. Medieval furniture was not suitable for someone of his build.

'Not made for one as big as you, eh? Now let us find the bump. Does it hurt anywhere in particular?'

John shook his head as the man's fingers began their search again, this time pressing a little harder. 'I cannot feel anything out of the ordinary.' The fingers on his head stopped moving and something warm trickled into his skull.

Throwing the hands off as he leapt to his feet, John gasped, 'What the…?'

Nothing to be worried about he was only checking inside your head.

But… but…

'Sorry, I forgot. I should have warned you it was time for an internal exam.' Master Gavin frowned again. 'Sit. Sit. I am almost done.'

John sat. A large rush of warmth encased him, and he realised he was unable to move, not even to wiggle a finger.

'What… what are you…' At least his mouth was still operational, even if his brain could not process what the man had done.

Gavin moved around to face him, hands on hips. 'I find nothing wrong with your head, and I suspect your memory loss is a ruse. I need the truth. These are troubled times, and we cannot tolerate spies in our midst.'

John stared warily at the man, whose eyes were now only slightly above his own.

'What have you done to me?' Shrugging and wriggling, he attempted to loosen the bonds holding him in place.

'Nothing harmful, just something to protect me while I find out the truth of you. Who are you and what are you doing here?'

'I will tell you what I told the others. I am John Smith, and I am from Queensland. They did not believe me, and I do not expect you to either. They thought I was insane, but they stopped fussing when I told them I lost my memory.'

Master Gavin stood still, the flickering of his eyes the only sign he was mulling over John's answer. 'Mmm, odd. Very odd indeed. I sense you are telling the truth, but this Queen's Land of yours is not a place I recollect. How did you get here? By ship?'

John paused before answering, wondering what to say. The truth would make him sound even more crazy, but the apothecary seemed to be able to tell whether or not he lied. Sighing, he decided to take a plunge and go with the truth.

'I am told I fell through a time and place portal. Apparently I am here to help events unfold in the right direction.'

John expected Gavin to laugh at the very least, or name him a madman at worst, but the man merely continued to stare at him, his eyes doing the strange flickering thing again. Finally the man's stance relaxed and the bonds around John loosen, but did not fall away entirely.

'I asked The Guardians for help to make sure this change goes well for the people of Briton. They suffered so under King William the Second, and deserve better this time around. Are you who they sent? How can you help us? You are but a boy.'

'I have no idea whether or not I can help you,' John admitted. 'I come from some time in your future where I jumped into a billabong—a pond—and I ended up here. Although I understand I am near the New Forest in medieval times, I am not sure I completely understand where *here* is. I can tell you though, if you need help and I can aid you, I will do what I am able to.'

'In what year did you jump into the pond with the funny name?'

Once again John did not know what to say. This whole story sounded absurd even to his own ears, he could only imagine what Master Gavin was thinking. If he told him the truth, the man would surely think him mad.

'Come, come boy. I am one of the few who is aware there are special people who can travel through time, so you can tell me. Although I must warn you to be careful not to reveal this to anyone else as they will think you addle-brained.

'You already said you come from the future, I am only asking how far into that future you have travelled back from.'

Still a little reluctant to answer, John realised as a captive he needed to say something. He opted for the truth again, and mumbled, '1890.'

'Good Lord! You came from that far forward? There are so many questions I need to ask you. So much you can teach me.'

It was the first time John had seen the man's face do anything but frown. His eyes glittered with excitement and his hands shook as he contemplated the possibilities a boy from the future offered.

No, you must understand knowledge of future events and inventions is not allowed.

John started. He had all but forgotten Lala was in the room. To his surprise,

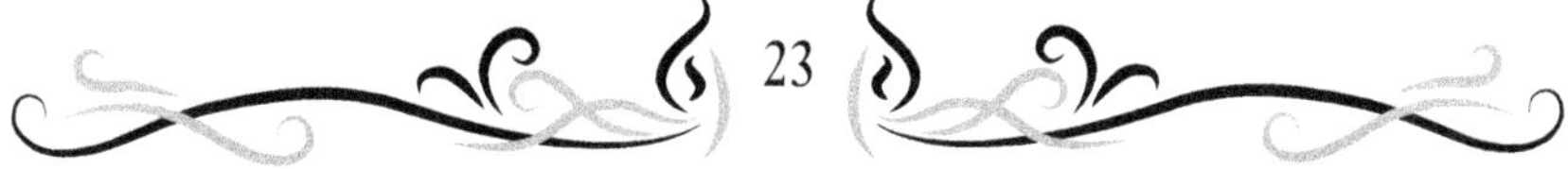

Master Gavin also appeared thrown by the interruption. Still only able to move his head, John looked at the lamb and raised an eyebrow.

Those with gifts can also hear me. Did I not tell you?

Clearly you did not.

'Who is talking in my head? It sounds like you, but your lips are not moving' he pointed at John. 'Someone else is here too.' He glanced around, his eyes coming to rest on the animal by the fire. 'Great One?' he asked in wonder.

You can call me Lala, as the boy does.

'Great One?' John asked.

'You do not comprehend the honour bestowed on you? You are travelling with one of the protectors of the earth. One of the Time Guardians.' Gavin was astonished.

'I do not know what one of those is,' John replied tartly, wondering what all the fuss was about.

In his time, they no longer remember the protectors of the earth. Although we are no longer revered we are still around, carrying out our work protecting the timeline. It will not surprise you to find they also lost the use of their gifts. If this one were born now, he would be an adept, perhaps stronger. As it is, he is the best I could bring to help you on such short notice. King William the Second was not meant to die this soon, and we were unprepared for the event when you called for assistance.

A long silence followed Lala's speech. Master Gavin shook his head, sadness and disbelief vying for rights to his face. Turning back to John, he waved his hand and the bonds fell away.

'I do not want to be told anything about your time. You do not revere the timeless ones who protect the world, and you squander the gift. Your time has no respect for the things I hold dear.'

Able to move now, John felt reluctant to stand. 'So you mean to tell me, not only did I fall through a time and place portal, but the lamb I fell with is some sort of special being? And I am also to believe you are what? A wizard?'

'I prefer Druid, if you do not mind.'

'I am beginning to wish I had actually drowned,' John said as his head sunk into his hands.

IF A LAMB could be said to laugh, Lala was definitely doing just that. His mouth was open and he was emitting a strange sort of bleating, choking

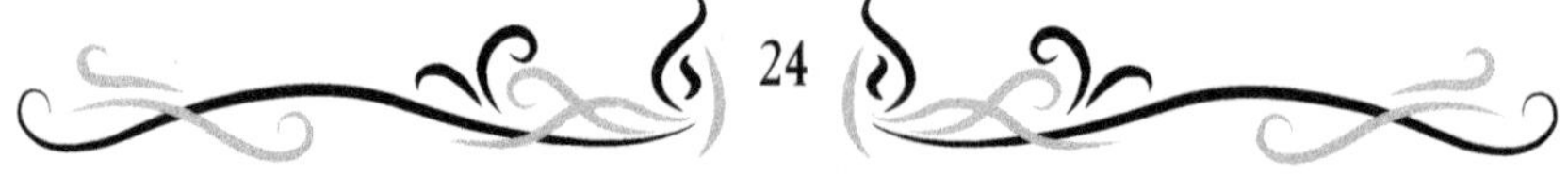

noise. Eventually he gained control of himself and was back to business.

Come now. There is little time and much for us to do. It is important we bring Master Gavin up to date on what is happening.

'Master Gavin? What about me? Surely I need to learn more about what is going on.'

That is simple. Today William Rufus, the second king of Briton by that name, was killed while out hunting. Those with him when he passed are being spare with the details of the event, consequently no one is saying whether or not it was an accident or regicide.

In fact, at the moment, no one is one hundred percent sure who sent the fatal arrow, and there are many potential candidates. He was not a good king and he had many enemies. His brother, Prince Henry, third son of William the Conqueror, is set to take over the throne, in spite of his older brother, Duke Robert Curthose of Normandie, having the stronger claim.

'And you want me to stop Prince Henry from stealing the crown?' John interrupted.

Master Gavin's head jerked up in shock. 'Good Lord, no. Tell me you did not bring him here to stop Prince Henry from taking the throne? That is not why I called for help. I want to make sure Prince Henry is crowned, anything else would be a disaster.

'The people want someone who is going to reduce taxation and strengthen the laws of the kingdom so the barons are kept in check. Henry is the only man who can achieve those aims. Many of the dukes and barons support that fat, lazy Robert Curthose. He would think nothing of bleeding us dry to fund his crusades and border disputes, while the barons run riot.'

'So if he is who the people want to rule them, why do you need me?' John asked.

Why? Because the people will have very little say in the transfer of power. Many of the barons want Robert Curthose to be king because he would not be able to control them, allowing them to do as they wished. Members of the Clergy would also see the disarray as an opportunity to snatch back power lost under King William the Second. The people fear this more than anything.

Then there are those who would prefer the return of an Anglo-Saxon King. Although there are no strong contenders, they would do anything to have one of their own back on the throne. A power struggle would also not benefit the people.

The future of Briton sits on a knife edge, and we are here to ensure a smooth transition for Prince Henry.

'If no one wants him to be king, why are we supporting him?'

In the original timeline, Prince Henry was acknowledged as King William the Second's heir before he died, and took the crown unopposed on the king's death. He is a learned man, and spent much of his rule establishing a new justice for landholders. Unbeknownst to him, he began the process of devolving power from the crown and the ruling classes to the people.

'If I am hearing you correctly, all the powers in the land want Duke Robert Curthose as king? I am but one boy. What can I do in the face of such opposition?'

Henry is moving fast to win over those who are against his taking the throne. He is talking to the Church, promising to give up the practice of appointing clergy to vacant post and returning this right to the bishops. This small concession of power, and income, will bring many over to his side. Lala paused to drink from a bowl Master Gavin placed in front of him, before continuing.

Some of the barons support him—those who do not want to see Briton fall into disarray, or be subjugated by a Norman prince more interested in the Crusades than his own lands on the continent. They fear Britain will be stripped of its resources to support his other interests. Those barons are working to win more of their colleagues over to their side, but Prince Henry will need to do more before he can be certain of their support. However, there is little we can do to help him in that area. We must rely on him being able to give them a little more independence, and perhaps forgive their debts to the crown, to achieve his goals.

The final prong to his campaign is where we come in. Henry aims to marry the King of Scotland's sister, as her Anglo-Saxon blood will swing many towards his side. Stanislaus and Barabal were assisting with this today. They went to visit the princess in Romsey Abbey. However, she will not wed unless he introduces a system of local courts they discussed when they first met, and he is not sure he wants to go this far with reform so soon.

We need to ensure Matilda and Henry pledge to marry, thus uniting enough of the ruling classes behind them for him to take the crown. This is the only way to ensure the first step in dispersing some of the royal power. Without Prince Henry on the throne, there will be no Magna Carta, no votes for all men and no votes for women. Lala stopped, placed his head on the side, and looked at Gavin and John.

'Firstly, we here in Briton know Princess Matilda by the name she prefers: Edith. If you call her Matilda, very few will know who you are talking about.

'Secondly, I only wanted to see Prince Henry crowned. I did not realise he was going to be so important for the future. Because of him, common men will get a say in government at some stage.' Master Gavin was wide-eyed with amazement. 'Votes for women though? Are you sure? In all honesty I do not think women choosing leaders would be a good idea. Their brains are not designed for making such important decisions as choosing rulers.'

'Tell that to my mother.' John laughed. 'She says she runs a farm just like

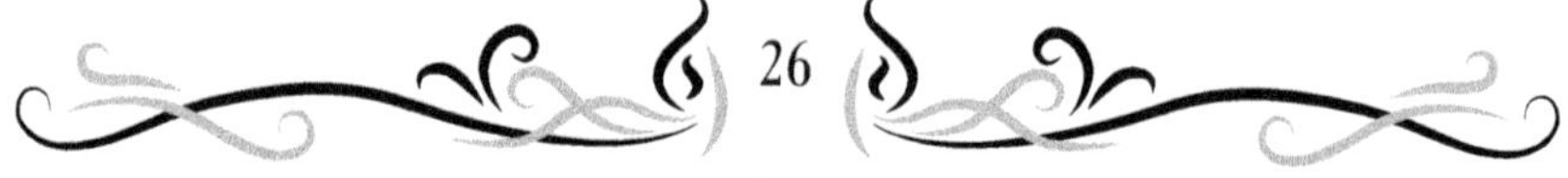

a man and yet has no say in choosing the government, or in how the taxes she pays are spent.'

Turning to the lamb he asked, 'Lala, how am I supposed to help with this? I could not do anything about the problems in Queensland caused by the strike.

'I ran away because, although I agreed with their aims, I was worried about the violence and how it would all end up. When I tried to talk to others about peaceful solutions, they did not want to listen to the lone voice of a mere boy.'

It is because you recognised violence was not the solution that you are perfect for this. There is a cost to change, there always is, but in the end peaceful change is more lasting.

'All right, suppose I am the right person, what can one boy do?'

Not one boy, but four people. Barabal and Stanislaus have been in contact with the future queen and are already working to bring Prince Henry together with his bride. You will join them and Alain to make sure Prince Henry is betrothed to Princess Matilda—umm Edith—then crowned.

'Do you not think it funny the future Queen of Britain has the same name as a swag?' Hysterical laughter bubbled up inside, bursting out before John could stop it. Amazed they could not see the joke, he attempted to appear more serious when he found Master Gavin and Lala observing him as though the strain had become too much, and he had lost his mind.

Swallowing his laughter, he said, 'Perhaps we should stick to calling her Princess Edith? If only because I cannot say her name without falling into fits of giggles.' When there was no response he asked, 'Have you any idea exactly what I need to do?'

No, Lala admitted. *Given the mix up with time, all I can be certain of is you need to be here to intervene in some way. I can only assume your role will become clearer the more we learn. Initially you can support Barabal, Stanislaus and Alain.*

'Alain? My apprentice? Are you sure? He is more often than not a little vague. Spends most of his time tinkering and inventing things. Not the type you would rely on to save the day.'

His unique way of looking at a problem will be essential if we are to achieve the right outcome for the people.

'I still do not understand why you brought me here from another time. There must be plenty of people around who can help the others.' Working through all the details in his head, John could not see why someone from the future was needed to resolve this problem.

You come from a time and place where the changes we want to occur are taken for granted. In fact, some might go as far as to say the basic tenets of fairness have begun to

be eroded by landholders, and that you and your shearing friends are fighting for fairness to be restored. Your passion and insight about what might be lost here may just be what is needed to tip the scales, and bring about the changes we need.

Now enough chatting, I think it is time you met the future King of Britain.

Lala stood on gangly legs and wobbled across the room, followed by Master Gavin and John.

'Will people not think it strange a lamb wandering the halls?' John asked Master Gavin.

'Would an animal in a dwelling be thought strange in your time?' The master raised his eyebrows.

'Umm, yes,' John answered. 'Especially in a palace.'

'Well, I never. Where do you keep your live stock in bad weather?'

'In the barn if we have a really bad storm, but sheep roam outside all year for the most part.'

Astonished, Master Gavin stopped still. 'You leave something as valuable as a sheep outside in the elements all year? How wealthy your land must be if you do not worry about your stock going missing.'

'I guess it is not so odd for a lamb to be here with me after all.' Once again reminded of the strangeness of this place, John followed Lala into the main hall where Prince Henry, the future king, was holding court.

4

MEETING THE FUTURE KING

GAVIN AND JOHN eased themselves in behind a group of men milling around in the packed great hall of the palace, ensuring there was enough space between them to protect Lala from stray feet. Nearly stumbling through the rushes strewn on the floor, Gavin righted John before he could fall into one of the richly dressed nobles. Wrinkling his nose as he regained his footing, he wished he had a handkerchief to press to his face like many of the noblemen were.

'Don't they believe in bathing?' he muttered under his breath.

Gavin leaned in. 'Of course they do, it is just when so many people are gathered together in one place it is difficult for servants to be able to accommodate regular baths for everyone, what with heating cauldrons over the fire, then carrying them to the bathing room. A court visit increases their workload, in fact they did not get around to changing the rushes on the floor in here today, I could smell the stench when I entered the building. No doubt they will not get an opportunity until the nobles are well in their beds.

'We are a sleepy little castle between royal visits. When the nobles roll into town the servants work dawn til dusk and beyond to ensure everyone's comfort as best as they are able.'

Suitably chastised, John attempted to hide his embarrassment by surveying

the room. He had not considered how people would bath without a tub and running water, nor how they would clean a castle filled to the brim with guests.

The druid had found them a position along a wall to the side of the room near the back. They had a little space and could see over the heads of the assembled nobles of the land to a platform at the other end. Winchester's great hall was a large, rectangular room with a balcony level running around the two long sides and across the back. Opposite them were other people in poorer dress, perhaps senior castle workers like Master Gavin, or lesser nobles. With faces turned towards the man standing in prayer on the dais directly in front of the door, they all waited.

As the man communed with God, John studied him. Shorter than most, he was slight of form but when he stood, he moved as someone confident in their physical ability. Although no one would call Prince Henry good looking, there was something about the dark haired man that drew you to him. Maybe it was the intensity and intelligence of his startling blue eyes. Flanking him were two men dressed only a little less flamboyantly than the prince himself.

'Robert de Beaumont, a supporter of the Prince's, and Ranulf Flambard, the late king's close advisor,' Gavin whispered when he saw the direction of John's gaze.

'There are an awful lot of noble looking people here,' he commented.

'Most of Briton's high and mighty came when King William Rufus called the barons to court. The hunt today was by way of a welcome. A feast had been planned for tonight… all that food gone to waste…'

'How very convenient for him to die with so many barons here to ratify a new king.' The words came out louder than he expected, and he was rewarded with a glare from the man standing in front of them.

'Your thoughts are not something I would voice out loud while suspicious rumours circulate about King William's death,' Gavin admonished.

'You don't mean…' John turned to look at the druid. 'You do not think that Prince Henry killed his brother?'

Lala answered, *Henry may be named Beauclerc because of his scholarly leanings, but make no mistake, the man can wield a sword and bow along with the best of them.*

John thought about his own family and could not imagine being able to kill any of them, no matter how annoying they were. 'I cannot believe anyone would kill their own family members,' he finally said.

Master Gavin drew himself up tall, and spoke in the same tone many of John's teachers had used when lecturing in class. *Brothers they may have been, but no love was lost between William the Conqueror's three sons. Why, King William the Second and Duke Robert Curthose joined together to throw Prince Henry off the lands in*

Normandie he had legally purchased from his brother with his inheritance. This detente between Henry and King William was a recent thing.

John interrupted, *Still, to kill your own brother, you risk burning in hell for all eternity.*

Lala answered, *True, and to be fair, Prince Henry is not the only man here holding a grudge against the king. Almost everyone in this room had a reason to want the man gone, especially as many believe this court was called for King William to raise another tax on the gentry. Now hush, I want to listen to the prince.* The lamb ended their conversation.

John turned his attention back to the stage, finding Prince Henry was waiting for quiet so he could speak.

'Dark days are on us when a king is felled by a stray arrow while hunting. I know many of you are calling this a judgement from God for the ungodly actions of my brother. Many of you are also alleging his death was not accidental, looking amongst our number for someone to cast blame upon. We detained the man who shot the fateful arrow. If we are to keep our country from falling into disarray, all speculation about events today must stop until we have had time to question him.

'Upon finding my brother's dead body, I realised we needed to move quickly. My first priority was to ensure the country stayed strong, and to prevent our neighbours taking advantage of the situation. I rushed back here to attend to matters of state. Then spent the afternoon ensuring our Welsh border was fully manned, and I want to thank those of you who escorted the king's body back for your thoughtfulness. It warms my heart to know he did not take that final journey alone.'

'Rushed back to secure the royal treasury more like,' the man in front of John whispered to his neighbour, who chuckled his appreciation.

'We have much to do over the next few months,' Henry Beauclerc continued over muttered comments from the floor. 'However, we are now in mourning for our departed king, and I would ask you to leave off your politicking until we bury my brother.' He half-turned and gestured to the body laid out on the long table behind.

'You will not have to wait long. Tomorrow will see him buried in the cathedral here at Winchester, as befits a king of our land.'

'Will we not wait for Archbishop Anselm to arrive to perform the service?' someone in front of Henry asked so all could hear.

William de Breteuil, one of Robert Curthose's men. John looked down to see Lala standing by his feet. *We need to be wary of him.*

'As you are all aware, we are in early spring so our days are warm, and my brother took an arrow to the gut. His body deteriorates as we speak. For our

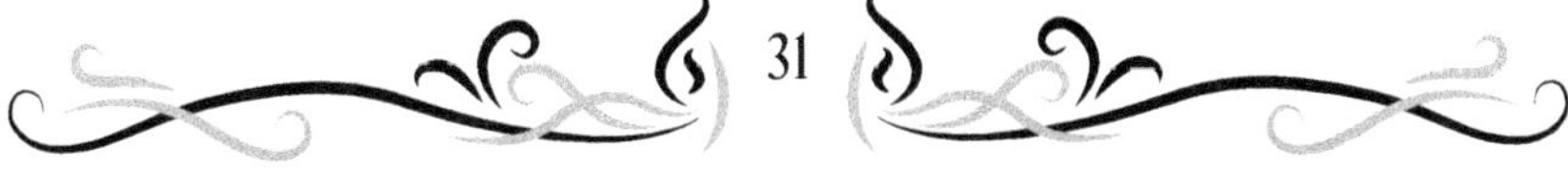

king's dignity, we cannot wait days until the archbishop arrives.

'Now, we are all weary and I would like some time to mourn my brother alone.'

A clear note of dismissal rang through his voice. Amidst grumblings and arguments, the assembled lords left the hall and headed to their accommodation in Winchester. A man in rich clerical robes remained near the front as the others departed. Handing him a small pouch heavy with coins, the prince invited him onto the platform to pray for his brother's soul.

MASTER GAVIN NUDGED John towards the platform where Barabal and Stanislaus stood waiting for Prince Henry to take note of their presence. Barabal smiled briefly at John as he came up behind them, but was then called to speak with the future king by the man Master Gavin had called Robert de Beaumont. Stanislaus' shoulders dropped as he remained behind with them.

'No one ever thinks I have anything to offer,' the young squire grumbled.

'Shh,' Master Gavin hushed him. 'I cannot make out what they are saying.'

Stanislaus glared daggers at the druid, but Master Gavin ignored him, turning his attention to the man he hoped would become the king of Britain.

'Ah, Mistress Barabal, did you find Princess Edith in good spirits?'

'She was well, sire, and not too saddened to learn of the death of your brother the king.' Barabal dropped into a curtsey as she spoke.

Henry Beauclerc laughed in appreciation. 'Please rise, Barabal, we are informal here. I will not trouble you to relay her message word for word, that lady made clear her opinion of my brother to all who would listen. So what about the matter I sent you to discuss with her?' A single eyebrow rose in query.

'Well… sire…' For someone who had previously had so much to say, Barabal now appeared lost for words, peeking John's interest. Was this a potential problem?

'You may speak plainly with me, Barabal, I will not punish the messenger if the message is displeasing.'

Barabal took a deep breath. 'Sire, the lady will consider your offer, after she receives the full details of your proposal.'

'What more is there to say?' Prince Henry was genuinely puzzled. 'I offer the lady the crown of Britain as my wife. How could I possibly make my intentions more clear?'

'Forgive me, sire, there is more to her message. The lady requires you confirm the vision you share and your plan on how to bring it to fruition, in

writing, before she will say yes.'

'Goddam the woman,' Prince Henry spluttered. 'How often have we spoken of our shared dream for Briton? Is it not obvious I chose her for my bride because she has been vocal in support of my ideals? Why must I put it down in writing to be believed?'

'If I may be so bold, sire?' Barabal interjected. 'Her exact words were, "If I am to leave a life of contemplation and learning and take up the mantle of Queen of Britain, I need reassurances I will have a true role in government and Henry has a clear vision of the first steps he will take to allow more localised self-government. I am sure he will be angry when you tell him this, but I am a mere woman in a man's world and I want contractual assurances".' Barabal shuffled uncomfortably after delivering Princess Edith's words, waiting for the prince's explosive reaction.

Laughter rang through the room. Deep, throaty, joyous laughter. 'And that is why Edith is the wife I need at my side as I take the crown of Briton. Not only will she bring me support from Anglo-Saxon dissenters, she will also back my changes allowing landholders a level of self-governance, which will bring better justice for all men. Best of all though, she is pragmatic and plain spoken. I really could not spend the rest of my life with a simpering fool, forever guessing what they want from me.'

Robert de Beaumont did not appear to be as happy about the situation as his friend. 'Henry, today you sent a letter to Archbishop Anselm offering a return of the allocation of clerical vacancies to the church in return for their support.

'I know the barons are straining under heavy taxation and you assured them you would wind down activity on the Welsh border. You even hinted at forgiving their existing debts to the crown. Then you let the barons know you were not against giving them back control of arranging marriages.

'Any one of these actions reduces the amount in your coffers, both now and in the future, while boosting the power of the barons and the church. You will gain many supporters as a result of those actions, so the cost is well worth it.

'If they then find you want to reduce their authority and income by allowing landowners to hold their own courts in the hundreds, you may lose some of them again. Is that wise?'

John watched Prince Henry as he stood, unmoving, stroking his beard.

Lala, I know of barons, but what are the hundreds?

They are smaller divisions of the land a baron controls, usually used for organising military contributions to the crown. King Edmund the First allowed local courts in the hundreds with a system allowing local landholders to administer their own justice. Prince Henry always talks about

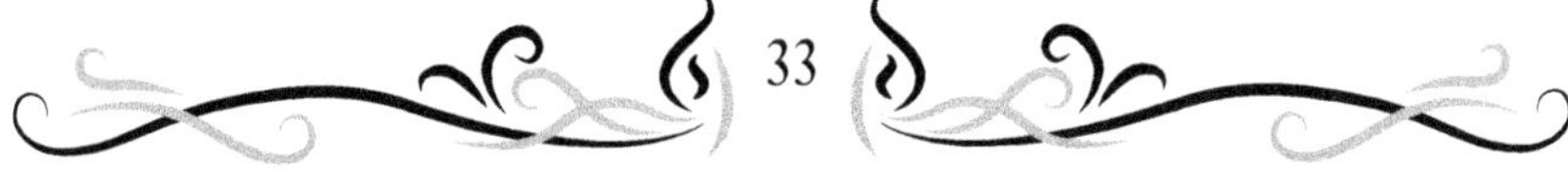

restoring that institution, and Princess Edith supported his view whenever they chanced to meet. The Scots have always been more progressive than the English when it comes to sharing power.

'Well, perhaps we do not need to tell them of that particular plan quite yet. We can wait until I have the crown placed on my head.'

'Umm... excuse me, sire, I have more.' Was Barabal blushing? 'The lady also said to tell you in return for your full restoration of Edmund the Confessor's legal system, she would bear your children, and agree to turn a blind eye to your other… umm… dalliances.' Barabal's face was now scarlet, and she would not meet the Prince's eyes.

What?

Our Prince Henry is a man who, let us say, enjoys the company of women. So much so he has not married for fear it would restrict his activities. Oh, he says he is still a bachelor because he is a pauper with nothing to offer a bride, but in reality, no good woman would put up with his affairs.

Oh. John felt the heat rising up his neck towards his face, and he sympathised with Barabal having to raise such a delicate topic.

Again Henry laughed. 'Edith knows me well. Robert, I must give much to gain the support of the barons lest too many of them decide my oldest brother is a better option for the crown, simply because they can run roughshod over him.

'This marriage though, this I do for myself and the Princess Edith. We both are better off not tied to anyone, but if we need to be married it should be to people who allow us to be ourselves. If the price of that is instituting courts in the hundreds, then so be it.

'Although, I do strongly believe landholders deserve the right to settle affairs in their local areas. Many of my brother's barons are getting fat off their lands, while their people suffer the consequences. Ruling as they see fit, without recourse to the laws of Briton, their excesses must be curbed. Once I have given them a little something at the top to sweeten them up, I will then take from the bottom to restrict their power and show my strength. It will keep them on their toes.'

Without thinking through his actions, John found himself stepping forward and interrupting, 'What about the men who own no land? Are they to be given any concessions?'

What are you doing? Lala asked as all eyes in the room turned to John. Master Gavin stepped away from his side, physically distancing himself from the boy's ill considered words.

5

CASTLES REALLY DO HAVE DUNGEONS

IN THE SILENCE, Henry's eyes bored deep into John's, the power in them almost forcing the boy to step back.

'Who are you to talk to your betters without invitation?' the prince asked as he advanced towards the edge of the dais.

'Begging your pardon, Prince Henry.' Stanislaus stepped in front of John, shielding him from the intense scrutiny for a moment. 'We found this boy on the road after he bumped his head, and he is still not in his right mind. He only spoke out of turn because he is addled-brained.'

Henry frowned, and started to turn away, but John continued.

'If you give this power to the landholders, they will use it to abuse the common man. And in the long run you will cause more trouble for those the barons abuse now.'

John, hold your tongue. You are fighting for something more than we need at this point in history. Lala's voice rang in his head, halting his outburst for a moment while he answered the lamb.

Lala, it is because the landholders are given such powers they think they can walk all over the shearers. Perhaps if all men are included in the court system now, we can avoid the shearer's strike in my time.

John had never experienced a silence like this, it was if the whole world had paused. Even Lala did not speak. The lamb's head tilted to the side, observing John's discomfort, but he said nothing. Prince Henry stopped mid-action, scrutinising John. Finally he broke the silence.

'Master Gavin, has this boy lost his wits?'

There was a pause before Master Gavin answered. 'I can honestly say he is a little confused, sire, but no, he is still in his right mind.'

'So, you lecture me on allowing the landless and uneducated to participate in courts when I struggle for support to extend that right to landowners. Only a madman would consider making such a move. Next you will want me including women in our government.' The prince laughed dismissively and started to turn away.

'That would not be such a bad idea.' The words slipped out, and all in the room except Prince Henry gasped. With a sinking in his stomach, the boy looked at his woolly mentor.

Sorry, I truly did not mean to say that. I do not know what came over me.

Henry swung back round and was about to speak when he was rudely interrupted.

'The boy speaks blasphemy!' The cleric who had been quietly praying in the background now rose. Shaking with suppressed anger, spittle flying from his mouth with the force of his words, he flung accusations at John. 'Seditious ideas spill from his mouth like water. Sire, you cannot allow such blasphemous words to go unpunished.'

Henry's gaze did not waver. Pinned by piercing blue eyes, John again resisted the urge to back away. Time seemed to slow down as the future king turned to the cleric.

'You are right, Friar Cedric, I cannot allow this. We are in a precarious situation at the moment. If rumours circulate I allowed a boy to discuss letting freemen and women take part in running the land, any support I gained amongst the barons will melt away like snow in the sun.

'Stanislaus, take this boy to the dungeons. Maybe a week in a cell will cool his hot head.' Prince Henry turned his back, dismissing them all.

'Sorry,' Stanislaus whispered to John as he took his arm.

Shrugging out of the loose grip, John turned to argue his point. Stanislaus shook his head, warning against such a move, and once again grabbed hold

of him. This time the grip was firmer and John allowed the squire to lead him out of the hall.

Master Gavin and Lala followed behind. As they walked, John tried to think of something to do to turn this situation around. Earlier he jumped in the billabong to avoid prison, and now he was headed for something potentially worse. In his mind, dungeons were dank, dark places where people were left to rot, forgotten by everyone.

Once outside, his head and ears were bombarded with voices. Although everyone spoke over top of one another, he gleaned they all asked some variation of what he thought he was doing speaking to the future king as he would do to a man of the same station? When the noise became overwhelming, Master Gavin held up his hands to shush them.

'Boy, you do not appear to understand, the king is the ultimate power in this land. He holds life and death over us all, with little to curb his power.

'Prince Henry is progressive, but he will not tolerate having his actions questioned by a commoner. You should be grateful he only sent you to the dungeons. At least your head is still attached to your shoulders. The best we can hope for is he forgets about you, then in a bit we can petition for your release.'

'But… I meant no disrespect. I only wanted him to consider the long term effects of his actions.'

'We cannot stand about talking. If he catches us out here you might get in worse trouble. Master Gavin, you will need to take the boy's lamb as he will not be able to stay where John is going.' Stanislaus tugged on his arm, pulling him towards a doorway.

I will think about what I can do to get you out. We do not have a week to wait for Prince Henry to cool down. Lala's voice followed him. *While you are in the cold and dark, I want you to think on this—I looked into the future and if the prince did as you proposed, there would be an uprising against him within five years. His brother takes the crown and all his changes are immediately reversed.*

From that time on, the barons hold sovereignty. They run their lands like petty fiefdoms and Britain falls into anarchy. There would not be another chance to start devolving power from the ruling classes in Britain for another 400 years.

Still, you would have stopped the shearer's strike because in your time there are no unions and non-landowners are little better off than serfs in Britain today.

Oh.

An inadequate response given the circumstances, but it was all he could manage as the heavy wooden door of the palace slammed shut behind them.

VIVIENNE LEE FRASER

'WHERE YOU COME from are you able to talk to your king like you would speak to a common man?' Stanislaus asked as he led him out into the courtyard, and across the open ground towards a dark wooden door set in the base of a stone tower. Their way was lit by torches placed at intervals around the walls.

'Where I come from, the king listens to councils of both the lords of the land and the commoners,' John said. 'I foolishly assumed it would be the same here. Obviously I was wrong.'

'Yes, you were very wrong. You need to understand here in Briton the un-landed serfs are little better than cattle. They have no learning and no thoughts beyond staying alive, and they are more or less owned by their masters. What good would it be to include them in government?'

John started to argue that perhaps they would then be treated better than animals, but stopped himself. His modern ideas had placed him in trouble once already today when he spoke before thinking. Instead, he considered the other boy's words, attempting to understand them in light of his knowledge of the time.

From school he learnt non-landholding classes would not have been able to read and write. In fact, although the Queensland government passed a law saying all children between six and twelve must go to school, many of the children he knew never saw the inside of a classroom because their family's survival meant they needed to work. And, even though school was free, many families could not afford suitable clothing for their children to attend every day, so they did not go at all.

In spite of this knowledge, when he studied history at school, he always imagined medieval farmer's lives to be much the same as tenant farmers in 19th century Australia. Now he was beginning to understand he had no idea how people lived their lives outside of the castle. Maybe he should hang back a little and think about following the lead of those who knew this time better.

Sighing, he answered the squire, 'Perhaps you are right. I am tired and far from home. Everything here is so strange, I just did not think. I hope Prince Henry will forgive me my outspoken thoughts, perhaps I should go and apologise.'

He turned to head back, but his captor roughly hauled him around.

'That is the last thing you should do. Prince Henry is very annoyed with

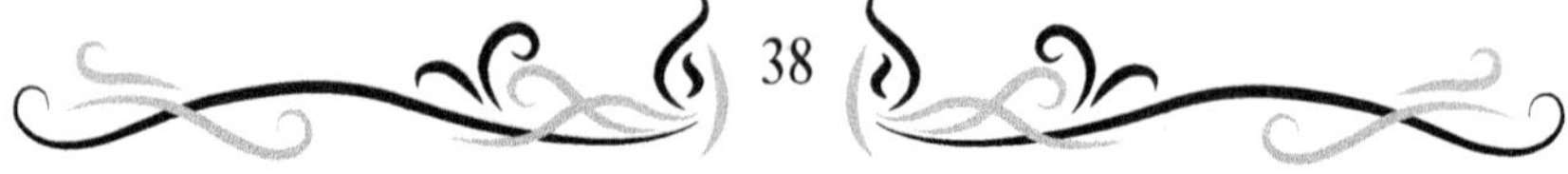

you, you need to let his temper settle awhile. Then you can apologise and hope he changes his mind about keeping you locked up.'

Another sigh escaped as they continued their journey to his prison. 'I will try to do a better job of keeping my ideas to myself.'

'Now that is a marvellous idea, a pity you did not think of it earlier,' Stanislaus responded as he pulled the heavy door open. Before entering he turned, wearing a look of sympathy on his face.

'When I came here from Normandie I found this place rather strange myself. The peasants are far rougher than at home, with much less education. I understand how odd it must be for you. I can only caution you to take some time to adjust. Until then best you learn to keep things inside. You do not want to be getting into any more trouble.'

'You come from Normandie? Where is that?' Although John asked in part to find out more about the boy, if he were honest, he also did it to delay the journey to the dungeons.

'Normandie is across the channel, in the land some call France. My father farms there, on a property given to him for his service to Sir Robert de Beaumont.'

John studied the boy as he stood in the dim torchlight. He was tall, as tall as John, which made him large for someone in medieval Briton. This he knew from the book of King Arthur his mother read. His hair was darker, and his complexion more olive than the servants here. His usual good natured demeanour changed to sadness when he talked of home.

'How did you end up here?'

'My father was a servant, but became a knight in Sir Robert's household at a young age when one of de Beaumont's men saw his potential with weapons. When he retired, he was given a grant of land for his services.

'He expected me to follow in his footsteps and learn the craft of fighting. So when Sir Robert offered to foster me in his household and treat me as a son, my father jumped at the chance. At the time I also thought the offer acceptable, although I was not asked. Sir Robert is a fair man and lives close by our family holding, so I was able to visit my parents often. Then we followed Prince Henry here.'

'Hold on. You have parents who are alive and love you, yet they sent you to live in someone else's household? That is a crazy idea.'

Stanislaus looked startled. 'You find such a practice odd? It is commonly done in Normandie, *and* here in Briton. It cements ties between the noble houses, and it is a great honour for someone as highly placed as Sir Robert

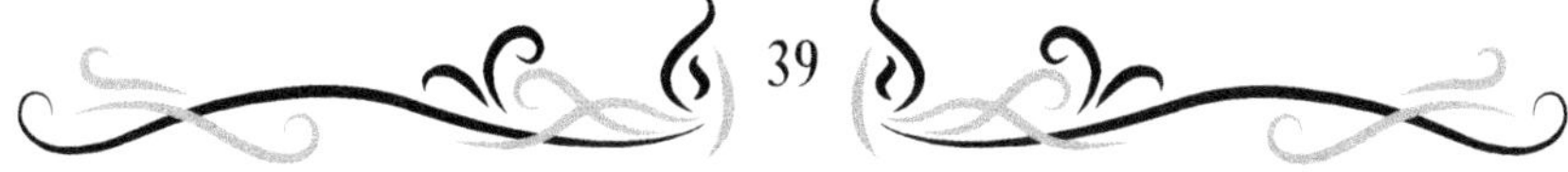

to take in someone like me. Although I suspect Robert de Beaumont and my father have an understanding I shall marry Elle, the eldest Beaumont daughter, when we are old enough.'

'Did I hear you correctly? Your parents are arranging your marriage?' John was sure the strangeness of this time was confusing him and he must have misunderstood the other boy.

Smiling, Stanislaus responded, 'Where you are from must be quite different if you think such things unusual. No one of the landed class or nobility gets to choose who they marry. Everything is arranged to make strong alliances and keep power within a small group of families.'

Amazed, John blurted, 'And you are all right with them organising your life like that?' So much for keeping his opinions to himself.

'Yes, of course. It is a good match, and at least I like Elle. Many of my friends are betrothed to people they have never met.'

While Stanislaus appeared to be perfectly happy that his parents planned his future for him, would the outspoken Barabal give in as willingly to the choice made for her? His thoughts then leapt forward a few centuries, and he wondered if this age old practice was why many parents in his time still thought themselves better able to choose partners for their children?

'Anyway, it is how things are done, I try not to think too hard about it.' Stanislaus's voice penetrated his thoughts, bringing him back to the present. 'I do miss home though, and if I am being honest, I miss Elle. We grew to be close friends before I left.'

'If you miss it so much why did you come here?'

'Well, Prince Henry had a falling out with his brother Robert Curthose, Duke of Normandie, and fled to England to ask for sanctuary with his other brother, King William. Sir Robert de Beaumont is one of Prince Henry's closest friends, and he felt obliged to escort him to safety. Now de Beaumont stays because Robert Curthose is unhappy with him, and he is waiting for the duke's anger to cool before we return home.'

'That explains why de Beaumont came, but not you.'

'Sir Robert could have ordered me to come, and I would have had no choice, but he gave me the honour of making up my own mind.

'It was a hard decision for me to make. Although my father is one of Sir Robert de Beaumont's vassals, as a Norman landholder he also owes indirect fealty to Duke Robert Curthose. I spoke with my father and he said as we made a promise to serve de Beaumont faithfully, and a man is only as good

as his given word, I should travel to Briton with him.'

As if Stanislaus suddenly realised they were dawdling, chatting in an open doorway, he tugged on John's arm, leading him inside.

The door opened to a candlelit stairway, going both up and down. His guard led him downwards, and John shivered as the stairs spilled them into a cold, dark corridor. Four wooden doors spaced evenly broke the stone walls, two on each side. An elderly man sat at a table placed in an alcove at the far end. He did not stop eating what looked like a watery stew until Stanislaus halted right beside him.

'We is a bit full young squire, this one will need to share, or you needs to lock him up elsewhere.'

'Prince Henry specifically asked for the dungeons. Can we put him with someone not too violent? He is a gentle soul, and I heard some real villains are held down here at the moment, horse thieves and the like.'

'We can put him in here.' The man laughed a hollow laugh. 'He might enjoy sharing with the gentleman brought in today.'

Completely missing the sarcasm, Stanislaus pushed John through the door the old man opened. 'Thank you, Tom. I will send someone down with food for him when I can.'

'Good luck to you, John.' His parting words were almost cut off as the door slammed closed behind him.

JOHN STOOD WHERE he stumbled to a stop, allowing his eyes to adjust to the inky blackness. He could not remember ever being anywhere so dark. Even though they were below ground, the cell had a single slit of a window high up the wall. It did nothing to let in any light though as the night was black as pitch.

Something scrabbled over his foot, and he bit back a scream. Deciding he would never be able to use his eyes to find his way, he reached out and found the edge where the wooden door met the stone wall. Inch by inch, he followed his hand around until he came to where two walls met.

Concentrating on breathing in and out, he attempted to calm his nerves as he stood in the corner, legs trembling. Although the rodents scurrying around the floor made him reluctant to sit, he was so bone weary he braced himself, and slipped down the wall until his bottom hit the rush strewn floor.

Trying not to focus on the fact he was in complete darkness, in a dungeon, with things running over his legs, in a strange country eight hundred years before his birth, he attempted to control his panic. At this point, he wished he had just gone along with the militia at the billabong. Prison in his own time would have been preferable to this.

'It takes a bit of getting used to. The darkness, I mean.'

John's heart jumped into his mouth at the sound of a voice from the other side of the cell. In his terror, he forgot he shared his prison with another.

'Wha… who?' he stammered, not quite able to get a full word out.

'Sorry, did they not tell you someone else was in here already?' Bitter amusement laced the words spinning in the darkness.

'No… yes… sorry, they did. I was thrown off a bit when they closed the door. The old man said something about a gentleman being in here.'

'So, they demoted me to a mere gentleman.' Defeat now joined bitterness.

Listening to the man, John started to worry. Why would they throw a noble into the dungeons? It could only be for something unforgivable, like, maybe, murder? What sort of world was he in where a gentleman murderer was considered less dangerous than a common horse thief? A clank followed by shuffling told him the man shifted position before he spoke again.

'You are lucky they did not shackle you,' the voice said. 'At least you can move out of the way of these blasted vermin.'

John let out a sigh of relief, if he stayed on his side of the room, he would at least be safe.

'Would they put me in chains for speaking my mind to the king?' John found himself again bewildered by this place.

A harsh laugh erupted from across the way. 'Lad, people hang for less than that. Well, unless someone with power speaks up for them. Hold on a moment, we have no king. Ah, you mean Prince Henry is exercising royal prerogative. Of course he is.'

Ironically, the voice in the darkness carried more weight than Lala's admonishments. It finally dawned on John he was in dire straits. The king had absolute authority here, and although Prince Henry had not yet been crowned, he was still in absolute control. He really might lose his life for merely speaking his mind.

As the coldness seeped through his thin shirt, he wondered at how he ever thought non-landholders were hard done by in Australia in the 1890s. Compared to here, they had it much easier.

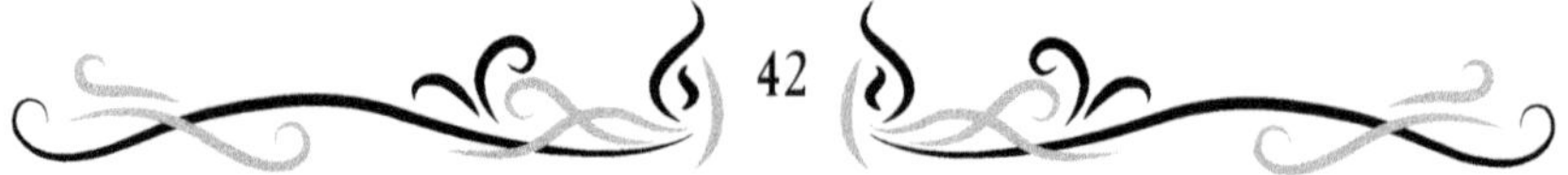

Stuck in this godforsaken hole, he finally realised the importance of these initial steps spreading the power downwards. How annoying to come to this conclusion now he was locked up and unable to help as planned. Grunting in frustration, he kicked away a rat as it attempted to nibble on his boot.

As he dwelt on his situation, he noticed the moon had risen, letting a watery light into the cell through the window. As his eyes adjusted, he could just about make out the shape of the man opposite him, leaning against the wall with his hands chained above his head.

'You must be uncomfortable.' He really needed to stop and think before opening his mouth.

'Yes, lad, more than a little. I stand and my legs ache. I sit and my arms ache. I cannot lie to sleep. I am sure though my comfort is not their main concern.'

'Why are you here? Do you mind my asking?' He added the last in case he appeared rude. His mother constantly told him off for being nosey and asking inappropriate questions.

'No, I do not mind at all. Talking helps take my mind off the pain. Besides, you may be the only person I get to tell my story to before they separate me from my head. I am accused of killing a man in cold blood.'

Frozen in place by the words, John did not know what to say next. The man he shared the dungeon with was actually a killer. Swallowing his fear, he reminded himself the other man was chained to the wall and not likely to be a threat to him. Though… he did not say he actually killed a man.

'Who do they think you killed?'

'The king, William the Second.'

'Wow.' The word escaped of its own accord. 'They did not like it when I spoke my mind to Prince Henry, I cannot imagine what they might do to you for killing a king.'

Again the other man laughed. 'Oh, they will behead me for sure. They need to ensure someone is blamed for King William's death, and I am to be the scapegoat. Just because I took the wrong track in the hunt, thinking I discovered a better trail to the deer. In the excitement, I loosed the first shot. Unfortunately, the deer moved at the last moment. The arrow sped through and hit the king, who happened to be standing behind the animal, opposite me.'

'So you are the man Prince Henry told everyone he needed to talk to about his brother's death,' John mused. 'I don't recall him talking about executing you though.'

Now the man laughed out loud. A harsh, grating laugh with no real mirth.

'You are a wet behind the ears one, truly you are. The prince has no choice but to kill me to appease the blood hounds ruling this land. When he rushed back here to get the key to the royal treasury from that bend'wi'the'wind Ranulf Flambard, he was followed by William de Breteuil.

'I had slipped back to my rooms to gather my belongings and that slimy toad de Breteuil found me. Stupid dolt! He will do anything to advance Duke Robert Curthose's suit for the crown of Britain. The man believes William the Conqueror, King William's father, made a grave mistake dividing his lands; giving his elder son the coveted barony of Normandie, and his middle son the crown of the lands he conquered in Briton.

'In the demented fool's head, de Breteuil thinks we would all be better off if the lands were again united under Robert Curthose. He believes bringing in King William's killer, and spreading rumours about my working with Prince Henry, will have the barons calling for Robert Curthose to be crowned. To be fair, I think he truly believes there was a plot to kill the king.

'One thing you can say for Henry Beauclerc though, he is smart and kept one step ahead of de Breteuil. When he turned up with me in tow, Henry thanked him for finding me, but said under his promise to the barons I would need to be accused and stand trial before all the nobles of the land. That could not happen until after the king was buried. With his clever words, he convinced the fool de Breteuil the best thing to do was to hold me here and keep quiet about my identity until after the funeral.'

For once in his life, John decided to think before he opened his mouth. Not from politeness, but because so much information swirled round in his head he was unable to tell truth from lie. The silence lengthened, and it soon became obvious his companion waited for him to respond.

'Ah, I see,' said John, though he really did not. 'At least you will get a chance to prove you are innocent and go free when you speak before the Baron's court.'

'My young friend, you are truly naive. No, I shall be beheaded. Unlike his father, King William the Second was not well liked. Oh, he was a great soldier, in battle he was magnificent. Sadly, he bled this country dry to pay for his glory, and made many enemies along the way. They are but a few of the reasons why many think his death must have been planned.

'The fact they would have liked to kill him themselves also makes it easy for them to believe someone actually went and did it. Even so, they will turn this country upside down to find his killer. And Prince Henry needs to

execute someone, lest they accuse him of plotting with the murderer.

'So here I am, having the misfortune of being in the wrong place at the wrong time, taking the fall to keep the kingdom stable. Yes, Walter Tirel will forever be known as the king's murderer, come what may.'

'But that is not fair. There has to be a trial. Surely the truth will come out.'

'I said Henry told Breteuil he would bring me before the Barons, but I am sure he will not. It is in no one's best interest for me to muddy the waters with my version of events. There were enough nobles with the king when he died to confirm the killing shot came from my bow. It will be enough for the barons to agree to my guilt. I will not even get a chance to speak.'

'That is wrong. You should not be judged by men who will gain from your conviction. They need to find someone impartial to decide what happened.' John was astounded.

'My, you do have some strange notions. I dare say if I had killed anyone but the king my family would be able to purchase a pardon, but no one has ever been pardoned for regicide.' Walter sighed and John watched as his body sagged against the wall.

'It's not right,' John said, not liking this glimpse of life in medieval Britain. It did highlight the need for Henry's proposed changes, letting leaders of the hundreds run their own courts. Although to him it first appeared to be a tiny step, he now realised what a leap forward it was. Closing his eyes, he sent a mental apology to Lala for reacting rather than thinking, and mucking up their chance to bring about change.

6

BARABAL TO THE RESCUE

AS STANISLAUS LED John from the Great Hall, followed by Lala and Master Gavin, the men on the dais appeared to forget Barabal's existence. Unwilling to anger her future king, she did not know whether to stay or leave. No one had dismissed her, but nor were they including her in their conversation. Shifting uncomfortably from foot to foot, she waited for someone to notice her presence, while mulling over the scene she witnessed moments before.

John was a strange one. He did not understand what a great thing Henry Beauclerc proposed to do should he become king. People like her father would no longer need to go cap in hand to their baron to request justice. Even though it was still likely money not truth would win the day, men would be masters of their own destiny. They would no longer be subject to the petty whims of those who ruled by right not ability.

John appeared unaware he placed something benefitting so many in jeopardy by proposing all sorts of extreme ideas. Prince Henry would find it difficult getting the barons to agree to his proposal as things stood, if they worried about more extreme changes, he would lose the little support he had.

'God's teeth!'

Prince Henry's explosion brought her attention back to the room. The men lent over the royal coffer, the key of which dangled from Henry's hand.

'Flambard, what is the meaning of this? What is in here is scarce enough to see us through to the end of this year. I understood this quarter's taxes had been collected.'

'Well… sire, the Welsh campaign nearly emptied the coffers, and… well to put it bluntly, your brother near bled the country dry to finance your older brother's crusade.' Ranulf Flambard stumbled over his words as he fumbled for an answer that might deflect the prince's anger. 'After paying the additional tax levy King William imposed, there was little coin left for last quarter's payments. Most barons sent in promissory notes instead.

'Why else do you think King William began selling rights to church lands and livings, and taking bribes to allow some unusual marriage alliances?'

'The vain, incompetent fool. He stripped the country of its resources all for his own ends, and to have something to hold over Robert Curthose,' Prince Henry spat out through gritted teeth, his anger barely contained.

'Our first act upon coronation will be to request my brother repay his loan. We need the money more than he does.'

'Are you sure that is wise, Henry? After all, he will not be happy at you usurping the crown he believes belongs to him. Asking for our money back will be like poking a bear with a stick. It will likely cause another war.' Robert de Beaumont counselled the future king.

'That lazy, good-for-nothing cannot keep his duchy in check, I will not allow him to destroy this country as well. Besides, he has no real claim on the throne. King William himself named me his heir. He had no queen, not even any bastard off-spring to raise to the throne. He knew he would die without a son, and he wanted me, not Curthose to rule in Briton.'

'I know, we were together when he proclaimed it, Henry. But as he did not put it in writing, Robert Curthose sees otherwise, and you know that. He, like many of the barons with Norman holdings, see Briton as a cow to be milked for their own benefit. I cannot imagine he will consider repaying the money loaned to him by King William, he will see it as his right to keep it. In fact, it is more likely he will raise an army to take the land from you. He will not let Briton go that easy.'

'By the time he stirs himself to move, the men of Briton will be united behind me. Once I am coronated, there is little he will be able to do,' Prince Henry boasted.

Frowning, Ranulf interrupted. 'If I can be so bold, sire, there are still those who prefer the idea of Robert Curthose's rule simply because he is so shiftless. They regard this as an opportunity to grasp more concessions than you are offering them.'

'Pah. A few men. Most support me now I have offered them some relief from their monetary problems.' The prince dismissed the idea.

'A few men, yes, but a dangerous few. I would not turn my back on them, de Breteuil especially,' Ranulf warned.

Closing the chest Prince Henry turned and caught sight of Barabal still waiting nearby.

'Is there something else, Mistress Barabal?'

Face turning red under the Prince's scrutiny, Barabal had never wished more to be able to control her blushing.

'Umm, begging pardon, sire, but I have not been dismissed.'

The prince frowned, and Barabal thought he would explode again. Instead he burst out laughing.

'Why, you are correct. That was remiss of me. I am sure I need not remind you what you heard here is private, and not to be discussed with the other servants.'

'Barabal was my wife's maid for two years, and we have always found her trustworthy,' Ranulf informed them.

'She has been looking after my wife since we arrived in Briton, and we trust her implicitly,' Robert de Beaumont added his support. 'In fact, I believe my wife asked her to return to Normandie with us.'

While Barabal felt a rush of gratitude for their kind words, she did not have the heart to tell de Beaumont she did not want to go with him and his family to a foreign land.

Prince Henry regarded her intently for a moment, then smiled. It was like a cloud had passed overhead and the sun suddenly reappeared.

'It is good you stayed behind. I need a letter taken to Princess Edith tomorrow, and you shall deliver it for me.'

Barabal frowned, wondering how she might be able to take advantage of the situation she found herself in.

'Is there a problem?' Prince Henry pursed his lips. 'Well, speak up, girl.'

'I cannot go alone, sire, I would need Stanislaus and John to accompany me for protection, and to help me into the Abbey without being seen. It is important to go undetected because people would comment if I were to meet with Princess Edith twice in two days. I am sure you would not like rumours

to spread.'

'Take Stanislaus by all means,' Robert de Beaumont told her, releasing his squire from his normal duties. 'But who is this John? Is he one of the Winchester guards?'

'The boy Prince Henry sent to the dungeons,' Barabal spoke quickly, hoping to gloss over the incident and have her master and the prince agree to John's presence without thinking too much about it. Her ploy was unsuccessful, Robert de Beaumont was far too shrewd to be taken in that easily.

'Take Alain with you by all means, if Master Gavin can spare him. That other boy stays where he is. He needs to learn to keep to his place.' Prince Henry commanded.

'Begging you pardon, sire, perhaps one night in the dungeons is punishment enough for such a misstep. He is not from around here and intended no real harm.'

'Barabal,' de Beaumont whispered. 'You worry for your new friend, but you must not harry Prince Henry on this. Leave things a couple of days and I will see what I can do for him.'

'Come to me in the morning at first light and I will have a letter ready for you.' Prince Henry turned away, the matter decided, and walked towards the private quarters at the back of the hall.

Barabal resisted the urge to stamp her foot in frustration, certain had she been a boy Prince Henry would have paid more attention to her request to release John. Her anger must have shown on her face as Robert de Beaumont stepped between her and the retreating prince.

'Go and eat some supper, then return to your mistress. We will talk about this later.'

Curtseying, Barabal backed away, annoyed her efforts to free John had been in vain. Well, there was more than one way to skin an apple. Foregoing supper, she decided to find Alain.

WAITING IN THE SHADOWS outside Master Gavin's rooms, Barabal formulated a plan to rescue John from his prison. All she needed now was to persuade Alain and Stanislaus to work with her. She knew she could twist Stanislaus round her little finger. Since she moved to Sir Robert de Beaumont's household they had become fast friends. However, for her plan to work, she needed Alain's help, and the other boy was an unknown quantity.

Since King William's court moved to Winchester less than a month ago, Stanislaus spent most of his spare time with Alain. Barabal only knew the apothecary's apprentice through the squire. Talking to him first was a risk, but without him her plan would have no chance of succeeding.

Her patience paid off, the door opened and Master Gavin emerged, followed by his apprentice. Deep in conversation, the master walked by the hiding place without even noticing her. As Alain passed, she reached out and touched his sleeve, putting the finger of her other hand to her lips. Jerking her head to the side, indicating the door behind, Barabal hoped he understood she wanted to talk to him in private. Fortunately the boy's serious green eyes flickered with understanding.

Catching up with the apothecary he said, 'Master Gavin, sorry, I forgot I did not properly store the elixir I worked on earlier. In all the excitement I left the stoppers off while it cooled and forgot to put them on later. I will go back, finish the job, then catch you up.'

'It could wait until after we ate, but I guess with that lamb frolicking around we do not want to risk an accident. I will meet you in the hall.' Master Gavin carried on, not wishing to delay his evening meal waiting for his apprentice.

Letting out the breath she held, Barabal followed Alain back into the apothecary's rooms, and waited until he closed the door behind them before speaking.

'Alain, I need your help. Stanislaus said something today. Do you… do you know how to blow something up?'

She rushed the words out, having previously decided a direct approach appealing to the boy's sense of adventure was the best way to attack the problem. Alain frowned at her and ran his hand through his curly midnight black hair while he considered his answer.

'Master Gavin and I have been experimenting with a little Greek fire he managed to buy from some pedlars,' he finally admitted. 'Why?'

How annoying, she grumbled. Used to dealing with loyal, steadfast Stanislaus who never thought to question her, she found this boy's curiosity irritating and time wasting. She chose to ignore his question.

'Would you be able to use it to, say, open a locked door?' She arranged her face to appear honest and as if she was a little in awe of Alain. This approach usually resulted in boys eating out of her hand, but not with this one. His frown deepened and she detected distrust in his eyes.

'I will tell you no more until you tell me why you want to know.' Crossing

his arms firmly across his chest, his gazed bored into her.

Barabal glared straight back, not intimidated by Alain in the least. Realising she had no other option, she shrugged her shoulders.

'All right. I want your help to break a boy out of the dungeons.'

'Do you have a plan?'

Barabal's eyes widened. She expected allegations of madness or worries about getting caught, but not this matter-of-fact question.

Alain chuckled at her discomfort, took her by the arm, and led her to the table. After she was seated, he picked up John's lamb from in front of the fire and placed the animal in his lap as he sat opposite her.

'Before going to dinner we spent time discussing this very problem,' Alain continued speaking once he was settled. 'But we were unable to think of a way to rescue John without Henry Beauclerc being able to trace it back to us. We thought something to eat may help fuel our brains, which was what we were going to do when I met you.'

Barabal smiled a genuine smile this time, pleased she no longer needed to play the simpering girl to get what she wanted.

'I think I may be able to help you. My plan means we can get away without being found out… hopefully.'

'Go ahead then.' Alain nodded encouragingly, and Barabal looked down to find the lamb watching her. If she did not know better, she would have sworn he too was listening.

'Prince Henry asked me to go to Romsey Abbey tomorrow morning to take a letter. You and Stanislaus are to come with me. I think if we time this right, I can pick up the letter, we can start on our way, then you two can double back, blow the lock on John's door and bring him along with us. That way no one will suspect any of us of helping him escape.'

Alain looked into the distance for a moment, then asked, 'What about the guard? How will we get past him?'

'You will not need to.' Barabal grinned, impressed by her own brilliance. 'I am sure you have observed the day guard is sweet on one of the kitchen maids.'

Alain's puzzled face told her he had not.

'Really, you have not seen how he follows her around with puppy dog eyes?'

Again nothing, and Barabal suppressed her sigh. She was constantly amazed men ever got anywhere in life as they did not seem to pick up on any of the little things happening around them. Consequently, they had no idea how such things might be used to their benefit.

'Anyway, he often brings his breakfast plate back to the kitchen, and lingers to talk with her. He normally stays about five to ten minutes, and returns via the privy.

'If we hold our departure until we see the guard take is plate to the kitchen, once we are out of sight, you boys can double back. You would have about ten or fifteen minutes to blow the door and fetch John, that is, if you slip in as the guard leaves.'

'That might work.' Alain drew his words out as if he were still thinking things through. 'The only problem might be the Greek fire. We are still experimenting with it. To say Greek fire is unpredictable is an understatement. A small amount might blow the lock, or it might take down half the building.'

'But worth a try?' Barabal asked impatiently.

A slow smile spread across his face as he seemed to check with the lamb on his lap, who looked as though he was nodding in agreement.

'Yes, we should definitely give it a try. Let us find Stanislaus and tell him what he needs to do.'

'Do you not mean ask him?' Barabal countered.

'I am sure you worked out long ago, things go more smoothly if you do not let Stan think too much about his role in a plan.'

Barabal laughed, realising she liked this boy. He was not threatened by how smart she was, and he treated her as an equal. A rare quality in her experience.

7

PRISON BREAK

JOHN CHANGED POSITION yet again. If he sat for too long his bottom hurt. If he stood, his legs soon grew tired. If he lay down, well he only tried that once—the rats swarmed over him. Now completely exhausted, still sleep would not come. Kicking his leg out, he dislodged yet another rodent before leaning back against the wall in the hopes he might find some comfort.

With his stomach growling his hunger, he tried to think of something, anything else other than food. Last night, sure Stanislaus would not forget his promise to send something to eat, he asked Walter when to expect supper. The man barked out yet another of his bitter laughs before answering.

'Sorry, lad, they will not waste food on those who are not long for this earth.'

That had not comforted him at all. After a restless night he continued to worry about whether or not they might still decide to kill him. He answered his own question. Yes, they might. In this time and place where one man made the laws, and where a person without land was little better than an animal, no one would stop Prince Henry doing whatever he wanted with him.

Sighing, John stood and stretched his limbs, wishing whatever they were going to do with him they would just get on with it and put him out of his misery. If they waited too long, these blasted rats would ensure there was nothing left of him to punish.

Reaching his arms up to stretch his back, John was thrown forward, almost losing his footing, then pushed backwards, slamming into the wall and ending up flat on his bottom, narrowly avoiding banging his head against the stone floor. An acrid smell filled the air. As his eyesight adjusted to the influx of light, he found the cell door now lying in pieces on the rushes.

'I think you used a little too much of the Greek fire.'

'Do you think?' A sarcastic voice responded.

Either the blast had damaged his ears, or Stanislaus was breaking him out.

Expecting his friend, John was bemused to find himself face to face with someone he had never seen before. The stranger studied the scene in front of him and finally fixed his gaze on Walter.

'Stan, did you not think it important to tell me he shared a cell with someone?'

Entering the room, Stanislaus' face split into a wide grin when his eyes found John. 'Oh, I forgot. When I brought him down it was a bit full so they put John in with someone else.'

'Dolt. Now we have to deal with a witness.' Frowning, the boy looked directly at John. 'Come on then. Don't just sit there, we are rescuing you.'

'What you mean "deal with him"?' Stanislaus asked, then his eyes widened in alarm. 'You do not mean kill him, do you? I am not sure I could do that.'

John rose to his feet while Stanislaus and the other boy discussed what to do with the man chained to the wall.

'Set him free.' John offered his opinion as he joined them in the still smoking doorway.

'What?' In unison the two boys turned and gaped at him.

'Has a night down here sent you even more mad? Who knows what he has done? It must be something violent, he is chained to a wall,' the unfamiliar boy said.

'According to him he did nothing, but they think he killed the king. Anyway, it does not matter what he did, you are both in danger if he tells anyone who rescued me.'

Ignoring Stanislaus' muttering, the boy stared at the ceiling as if the solution would appear before him, then spoke to John. 'What a brilliant idea. If we release him, they will think all of this was for his benefit. I mean, who would go to all this trouble to rescue a mere boy? No one will ever suspect us of being involved.'

'What?' Stanislaus shook his head in confusion. 'Alain, you mean to set

King William Rufus' killer free? If they capture him and he tells them about us, we will swing for sure.'

'But you will run like the wind, will you not?' the other boy, Alain, asked Walter as he fiddled for something in his pocket. 'Ah, here we are.' He pulled out a thin piece of metal and set to work freeing the noble from his chains.

'I have friends nearby, in Southampton, who will smuggle me out of the country. Briton will never see my face again.'

Walter Tirel forced himself upright and, before Stanislaus found his voice to object, he ran out the door, his footsteps echoing along the corridor as he escaped his prison.

'Look what you have done,' said Stanislaus in dismay. 'We only planned to help John. Now we will really be in trouble.'

'Only if they catch us.' Alain seemed to be relishing his adventure. 'Come now,' he grabbed John by the shirt and started pulling him towards the door. 'We must be gone before the guard returns.'

John followed him out. He stopped when he realised Stanislaus still stood in the middle of the cell, mouth hanging open as he tried to comprehend the enormity of what he had just been a part of.

'Stan. Stanislaus! Come on.' Alain urged him from the hallway. 'If you stand in the cell like a dolt you will get caught.'

As if in a daze, the squire turned and, dragging his feet with reluctance, left the dungeon. John and Stanislaus were still on the stairs when Alain stepped through the door into the courtyard, then immediately ducked back inside, forcing John to stumble back into Stanislaus.

'Up,' the boy said, darting up the winding stairway. The others followed, only stopping when the shadows hid them from anyone coming through the doorway below.

Seconds later, a whistled tune drifted up to them as someone opened the external door and headed downstairs. Stanislaus went to move, but Alain held his hand up, signalling for them to wait. A moment later the whistling stopped, and curses John had never heard before filled the air. A crash and a shudder as the door banged against the outside wall proceeded the announcement of their escape.

'Help! Prisoner escape. Ring the bells.'

'Now.'

Alain led the two other boys down the stairs and through the open door. Crouching close to the ground, they managed to make it behind a wagon

unloading barrels before the courtyard erupted with the sound of thundering feet and clanging metal. All other activity in the castle precinct ceased as everyone turned to the dungeons.

Holding his finger to his lips, Alain stuck his head out, attempting to gain a better view of the frantic activity. John searched for a better hiding place. Tapping Alain on the shoulder, he pointed to a gap under a lean-to close by. Alain nodded, then frowned as a man in the prince's colours wandered over to stand by the opening. As he watched the mayhem around him, he leaned against the wall, idly picking food from his teeth.

'Stanislaus, you need to go over and distract that man so we can hide properly. Then go and find Barabal and tell her the bad news. Tell her we will meet her when we are able.'

'But surely they will not think you or I are involved in this,' Stanislaus said, a worried frown creasing his brow.

'No, they probably will not. However, if we all stroll out of here someone might recognise John, and then all our good work will be for nothing.'

Stanislaus thought for a moment then, without even acknowledging his friends' words, he crawled backwards until he was able to stand without it being obvious he had been hiding. He sauntered across to the guard as if he had not a care in the world, and struck up a conversation. Moving around so the man had to turn to face him, the guard's back was now to the wagon allowing the boys to move without being seen.

'That is what I love about Stanislaus. Ask him to protect someone and he will do so without a thought for his own safety.' Alain's voice filled with pride for his friend.

'It is unlikely anyone will worry about trying to find you with Tirel on the loose, but we cannot be too careful. Prince Henry has a mind for detail and we cannot assume he will not remember you and wonder where you are.

'Are you ready? We will need to be quick and quiet. No, wait.'

The other boy sank back down and John caught a brief glimpse of Henry Beauclerc as he exited the palace, his face a picture of rage. Catching sight of Stanislaus in conversation with one of his men, he turned beetroot red and strode over to the pair.

'What are you two doing standing gawping? Stanislaus, you are meant to be with Barabal, off with you now. And, you there, whatever your name is, prisoners have escaped. You should be searching for them, not standing around chatting.' Striding off to the dungeons, the future king did not wait

around to see his orders obeyed.

Stanislaus risked a quick glimpse towards the wagon before heading off to find Barabal, and the guard marched behind the prince to the dungeons. As they disappeared from view, Alain tapped John on the shoulder and pointed to the lean-to. From where they crouched, they could just make out a depression in the dirt allowing access to a hiding place underneath.

'Run fast, keep low. I will make sure no one sees you.'

John shuffled passed the other boy, glanced around to make sure no one was watching, then made a crouching run for the dark space. As he neared the hole, he slid along the ground, reaching above to grab hold of a board to pull himself fully underneath. Taking a deep breath, he wriggled back to make enough room for Alain.

His heart raced and he tried to take deep breaths to slow it down, and to minimise the sound of blood pounding in his ears. It was so loud it drowned out everything else, preventing him from hearing what was happening outside.

'Alain. Alain, what are you doing sneaking around behind that cart? Trying to find out what is going on, no doubt. Are you not supposed to be going with Barabal and Stanislaus to deliver that message for Prince Henry?'

The unfamiliar voice had John inching forward until he had a clear view of the courtyard, just in time to catch Alain standing up and dusting himself off. From his hiding place all John was able to make out was the voice belong to someone wearing the leggings of a noble.

'Sir Ranulf, please do not say anything to the prince. Nothing ever happens here in Winchester. Now, with the prison break, it was so exciting I could not help myself.

'Barabal is perfectly safe with Stanislaus protecting her, in fact I am not sure why they asked me to go with her in the first place. I am pretty useless with a sword. Do you know what happened?'

John marvelled at how calmly Alain moved from conspirator to the role of young boy attempting to justify his skiving.

'Nothing for you to concern yourself with,' Sir Ranulf told him. 'You had best be on your way. Although you may think Barabal safe with one escort, Prince Henry specifically asked for you to accompany her. With the mood this will put him in, you would not like to be found disobeying his orders.'

'But...'

'No *buts,* you young scallywag, this is not the time for one of your pranks, or any high-jinx. Be off with you.'

'Yes, sir. My travel things are in my room. I will collect them and go find her immediately.'

'Be quick about it, and make sure you are gone before Henry leaves that dungeon. If he finds out you are still here, even my support will not save you from his wrath.'

The legs of the nobleman walked towards the dungeon door and, when he was far enough away not to hear, Alain whispered loudly, 'Wait here for me, I will come back for you in a moment.'

Once again John was left in a cold dark place, but not quite as alone as he thought. A rodent scrabbled over his leg and he suppressed a shiver.

THE BOARDS ABOVE John's head creaked and two legs dropped down in front of the hole.

'Psst, pull this on,' Alain shoved something through the gap.

'A skirt?' John questioned as he attempted to make out what the other boy had given him.

'Yes, and do not dally, it is getting busy out here.' Stifling his chuckles at John's discomfort, Alain continued, 'Once you are done, slide out. I will try and keep you covered, or at least distract anyone who shows an interest in what we are doing.'

John struggled in the confined space to pull the woollen skirt over his boots and trousers. With Alain's foot tapping impatiently, he fumbled with the unfamiliar article of clothing. *How do girls manage with this?* John thought as he tried to wriggle the skirt on over his hips, getting his feet tangled in the fabric in the process.

'Hurry up.' Alain's strained tones reached him.

'I am going as fast as I can. Wait a minute, nearly there.' John told him as his head popped out of the hole.

Alain jumped to his feet in a flash, a cloak held out for John to wrap himself in. It was huge. The original owner was around John's height, but more than three times his size. The shorter boy choked back a laugh as he tugged the hood up over John's head. Pulling himself together, he issued instructions.

'Do not speak. Follow a few paces behind me, and try to behave like you just happen to be going the same way I am.' Passing him a basket with a few items in it, Alain explained, 'Put this over your arm and you should look like

any goodwife going about her daily business.'

'Goodwife,' John spluttered. 'You are helping me escape by dressing me as a woman? Great!'

Closing his eyes to block out his embarrassment, he could only imagine what the men in the shearing shed would say if they ever heard about this. They would start calling him Matilda, and asking to snuggle up with him at night. Unable to stop his face flushing red with the image, he pulled the hood down lower, hiding in its folds.

'I cannot do this.' His mouth was dry with fear.

'If you want to get out of here with your head still attached, you need to try.' Alain was all seriousness now.

John gulped and said begrudgingly, 'All right. Lead on.' After all, what other choice did he have?

Alain turned and started off out of the castle bailey. Waiting a few moments, John followed, trying really hard to take smaller steps. He crouched down to appear elderly, hoping old age might explain his strange gait. It took all his concentration to make sure he did not trip over the skirt, so he did not realise they had left the castle precinct and entered the town until he bumped into Alain. Along with everyone else on the street, the boy had stopped suddenly.

Gazing from under his hood, John glimpsed a group of guards heading down the muddy street towards them. His stomach lurched. Had they found him already? Hoping to hide in the crowd, he joined the others moving to the side of the road making way for the guards. Staring at the ground, he tried to ignore the boots coming to a stop in front of him. All he could hear was a pounding in his head. His heart beat so fast he thought it might explode.

'Alain, there you are. Barabal and Stanislaus are waiting at the gates for you. Best hurry along or they will leave you behind.'

'I got held up in all the ruckus, I am on my way to meet them now.' Alain's voice rose above the general mutterings. 'Should I try slipping past the guards? Or should I wait until they pass by?'

'I would wait if I were you as we have some of Prince Henry's men with us. One of them may see you moving about and, not knowing who you are, might think you are hiding something. If you are detained for questioning, Barabal will be even more unhappy.' The owner of the boots laughed, as if sharing a secret with Alain. 'And I would not like her to take her anger out on me, or you for that matter.'

'Thank you,' Alain said to the retreating soldier.

John steadied his hands and took a couple of deep breaths to still his

nerves. That was a little too close for him. He sensed rather than saw Alain continue up the street towards the town walls. Lifting his head slightly to keep the other boy's back in view, John followed.

Hampered by his skirts and long cloak, he was unable to slip between people the same way Alain could, and he soon lost sight of his rescuer.

Had he turned off? No, the side streets were empty. Trying hard not to panic, he approached the city walls. The gate was guarded, but they were not stopping everyone, just the few they thought suspicious. John prayed like he had never prayed before.

Attempting to blend in with the people leaving Winchester, he drew level with the guards. As he did, Alain appeared from no where and sidled up to the soldier closest to John.

'Good morrow, Bran, I am supposed to meet Mistress Barabal by the gate this morning, but she is not here. Have you seen her?'

'Yes, and she is very unhappy. First Stanislaus was late meeting her, now they are both waiting for you. I guess you were delayed by the searches.'

'That I was, but if I am being totally honest, I did dally a little. There may never be another escape from the dungeons so I did not want to miss this one. I do not think Barabal needs to know that.' John overheard Alain as he passed through the town gate, and he imagined the boy's conspiratorial wink. 'I guess I had better go find her. Do you know where she is, by the way?'

'Yes, follow the path to the left. The cart is waiting on the road to Romsey. Do not delay any longer, you do not want to make her madder than she is.'

Overhearing the instructions as he was sure Alain intended, John turned left once through the gate. He followed the path around the walls as if he planned to go that way all along. A quick glance showed him a cart with two people waiting beside the dirt track everyone here called a road, parked near a conveniently placed hedge.

Ignoring Barabal and Stanislaus, he followed the shrubbery along past the horse and cart. When he found a gap, he took the opportunity to duck in behind the hedge, having first checked no one was nearby. Taking off the skirt and cloak he bundled them up and made sure they were well hidden under the hedgerow.

He did not have to wait long before the clip of a horse's hooves announced his ride was leaving. As the cart passed his hiding place he nipped out from behind the bushes. Making sure he kept the wagon between him and the castle, he rolled on to the back tray, slipping under a canvas cover, and waited for the shout telling him he had been spotted. When none came, he breathed freely again.

8

TO ROMSEY ABBEY

ONCE THE WALLS of Winchester were behind them, the cart slowed and Stanislaus came round back to let John out from his hiding place. In the light, the boy found he shared the cart with his pack, bedroll and, of course, Lala. He found the sleeping lamb curled up on a bundle of clothes.

'Not another dress,' John groaned and Stanislaus laughed.

'No. We thought it was time you changed from those strange garments you wear into something more local.'

Tipping Lala off his bed, Stanislaus handed the bundle to John, and pointed to a copse of trees close by.

Holding up the clothes, John was not convinced he would not be better off dressing as a woman. They expected him to exchange his trousers and shirt for what, in essence, were a long shirt and woollen leggings. The leggings appeared to be held in place with a draw string tie and bits of cloth criss-crossed up his calves. A leather belt would draw the shirt in a little at the waist and prevent it from flapping up.

'Are you sure you want me to wear this? My own clothes are more practical, and comfortable too, I am sure.'

Barabal turned around, brow creased in displeasure. 'We just went to a lot of trouble to rescue you, I do not want all our good work undone because

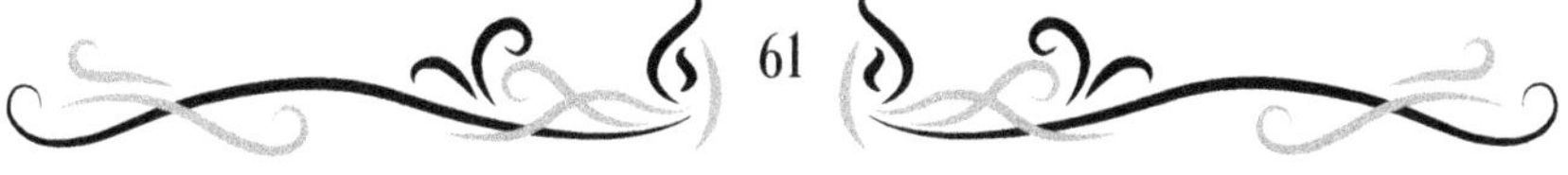

you stand out dressed the way you are. Now, go get changed and be quick about it. We are already late starting out.'

Stanislaus wiggled his eyebrows and wrinkled his nose as Barabal turned back around, causing the other boys to laugh.

'It is all right for you,' John told him. 'You at least get to dress as a fighting man. I will be dressing like a…' he could not find the words to complete his sentence.

'Like me, you mean,' Alain asked. 'I may not be able to wield a sword, but I was the one who actually rescued you, so do you think now is the best time to make fun of the way I dress?'

Sighing, John knew when he was beaten. He mentally threw daggers at the strangely quiet Lala, before wandering over to the trees to change. Taking off his shirt and rolling down his under clothes, he started to pull the woollen tunic on. He shuddered as the coarse, scratchy fabric brushed against his skin. Deciding he would keep his long-johns on for comfort's sake, he removed the shirt and pulled his under clothes back up before continuing to dress.

A few minutes later he returned to the cart, wearing his new clothes and feeling like a bit of a fool. Stanislaus handed him a pair of soft leather boots, no where near as sturdy as his own. Outfit complete, he rolled his own clothes up and tucked them inside his pack, along with his boots. His mother would skin him alive if he turned up back home minus his clothing and footwear. That was if he ever made it back there.

I hope you are happy now, he said to Lala. *I must look like a right odd-ball.*

The lamb stared back at him with unblinking black eyes. John wondered briefly if his companions somehow managed to mix his lamb up with another. Then a tingling sensation pierced his head.

Sorry, it took a lot out of me, enabling you to understand the language while you were not in my presence. I am sure you do not need me to tell you, no matter how uncomfortable you are, you at least fit in, Lala said as he curled up on top of John's pack.

'Are you ready yet?' Barabal asked without turning, her tart tone indicating she was still unhappy with him.

'I guess so.' John mumbled as he hauled himself up, leaning back against the side of the cart.

Stanislaus glanced over his shoulder to check he was settled, then immediately swung back around, eyes round with surprise.

'Has your hair grown?'

John reached up to find his hair, which had been getting a little long and straggly, was now well down below his ears. Frowning he wondered how his hair managed to

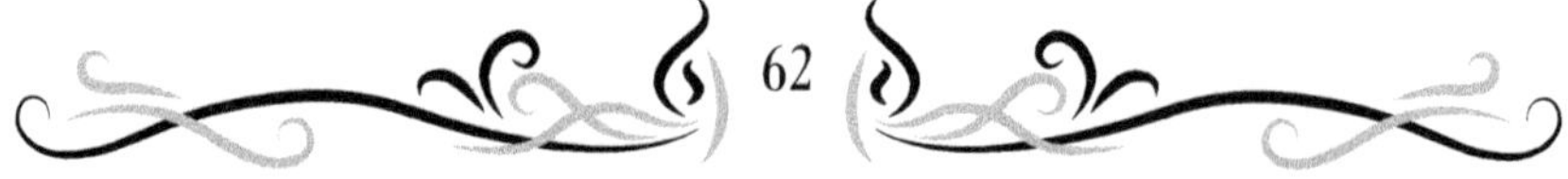

grow so much overnight. Wearily, his gaze moved to the lamb as he answered the boy.

'Ah, no,' he stuttered. 'It is the same length it was before, I have not had time to comb it today.'

Satisfied with his answer, the squire started them back on their journey. Losing his balance as the cart lurched forward, John righted himself and fixed his gaze back on the lamb.

Lala, what did you do?

The lamb opened a single eye, *I may have contributed a little to your disguise by helping your hair grow. Quit complaining. If you had not opened your mouth without thinking, you would not need a disguise. If you do not like it, think of it as your punishment.*

Annoyed, but unable to come up with anything else to say to the guardian, he instead turned his attention to more immediate matters.

'How long is it to where we are going?'

Alain answered, 'Romsey Abbey. From Winchester to there is about sixteen miles, so we should arrive late afternoon, if all goes to plan.'

'We would have completed our task and been on our way back if you boys had not wasted so much time this morning,' Barabal interrupted acerbically.

'We would not have taken so long if Stanislaus had informed us our prisoner had a cellmate, before we blew the door down,' Alain's tone sounded annoyed to John's ear.

'Maybe next time if you two think to include me in your planning I might remember to pass on all the important details,' Stanislaus added good-naturedly. 'Besides, we are all here now, can we not just enjoy the ride?'

'Thank you for getting me out of there.' John belatedly voiced his appreciation. Until now there had been no time to show the three of them his gratitude for ensuring he escaped captivity with his head still attached.

'We could not just leave you there. Who knows how long you would have been kept in that cell before someone remembered to let you out.' Barabal shifted on her seat so she could see him. 'Besides, I feel responsible for you, having saved your life yesterday. But please do not do anything that stupid again.'

'I won't,' John assured her. 'A night in the dungeon taught me to keep my mouth shut.'

Really?

Yes, really. John blushed. *I am sorry, but I did not realise how much of a change Henry Beauclerc was proposing yesterday. A night in the dungeons really did open my eyes.*

Compared to the time you live in, it must seem so very little, Lala conceded, not wasting energy to even raise his head as he mind-spoke.

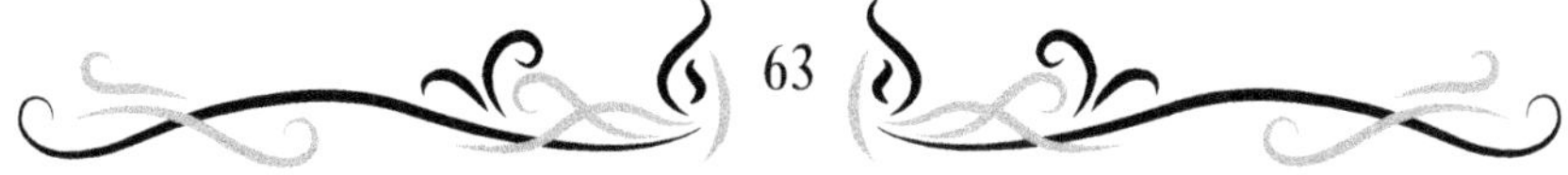

I had a long conversation with my cell mate last night. I came to realise most people have so few rights here a court in the hundreds would be an enormous change.

Silence followed his revelation, and John checked to make sure Lala had not gone to sleep. The lamb raised his eyes and met John's gaze.

It is possible I made a mistake bringing you straight to the castle. If we wandered through the countryside a little first you may have been better prepared for what you need to do. I will take that into account on my second mission.

Second mission? Is this your first time doing this?

No. Well, sort of. Of course I went out with masters to assist, but yes, this is my first time solo, the lamb eventually admitted.

Great. I am hundreds of years in the past, in a strange country, expected to ensure certain events occur so history can evolve without a hitch; and my guide is a lamb who is on his first mission. Could this get any better?

It could be worse, you could still be locked in a cell. Lala snorted and repositioned himself, back to John, showing exactly what he thought of his comments.

WITH THE SUN directly overhead, Barabal stopped them for a noontime snack. John blushed as he realised he had eaten a large portion of the food while the others looked on in astonishment. After he emptied his mouth, he explained he had not eaten since midday the day before. Embarrassed at forgetting to bring him food the previous evening, Stanislaus reached into the food basket and handed him another leg of chicken.

'I was saving this for later, but you need it more than me. To say sorry for last night.'

John was touched by the other boy's generosity.

Back in the cart, having not slept much the night before, he soon found the gentle rocking motion caused his eyelids to droop. Lying down, he followed fluffy clouds drifting slowly across the azure blue sky.

'John. JOHN. We are here.' Alain shook his shoulder none too gently.

Lift me down.

Blearily looking around, he found the cart parked by a stone wall. The crisp lines between the stones, and the lack of moss, indicated the wall had recently been erected. Sighing, he sat up to get his bearings, jerking at a cold nose on his hand. Glancing down, he saw Lala standing beside him expectantly. Without thinking, he picked the lamb up and placed him on the ground.

Lala promptly wandered to the grass verge and relieved himself.

Some water if you please.

Once again John automatically did as he was bid, putting some water in a pottery bowl he found in the back by the food basket. He grabbed a mug and filled it for himself from the water skin. The cool, fresh water contained none of the underlying hints of mud he was used to. Thirst quenched, the lamb wandered away and delicately nibbled on the grass.

'If you have quite finished…' Barabal stood in front of him, hand on hips covering his legs in shadows. 'We must get ready to go inside. We need to talk to Princess Edith before vespers.'

'Why? And what is vespers.' John asked, still not quite awake enough to deal with the oddities of this place.

'Vespers is evensong service, and there is no talking in the nunnery afterwards. If we do not conclude our business before then, we will need to wait until tomorrow.' The girl moved to the side inviting him to get down.

'Are we climbing over the wall?' John stared doubtfully at the structure beside him. 'It must be at least ten feet high.'

Barabal laughed, 'And give you boys a chance to look up my skirts? No, I have a better idea.'

Walking around the cart, Barabal reached over and opened what John had assumed was another basket of food. The lid dropped back to reveal swathes of black cloth. Pulling out the item on top and shaking it out, her plan became clear.

'No,' he sighed. 'I am not dressing up in skirts again. Once a day is enough for any red-blooded boy.'

Barabal stared balefully at him. 'Do not make me wish we left you behind.'

'I am happy to climb the wall if you need me to,' John volunteered.

'I would like you to tell me how you think you will be able to move around a Benedictine Convent dressed as a man.'

John's mouth formed an "O". 'When you said our destination was Romsey Abbey, I thought you meant a church.'

Barabal frowned. 'How can you not know that Romsey Abbey is a convent? Daughters of kings and nobles come from far away lands to study here. This particular convent is famous in all the known world as a place to educate young women. Even if you are not from close by, you should still have heard of the abbey.'

'Leave him alone, Barabal. Just because you always dreamt of being asked to attend the school here does not mean everyone else has heard of it.'

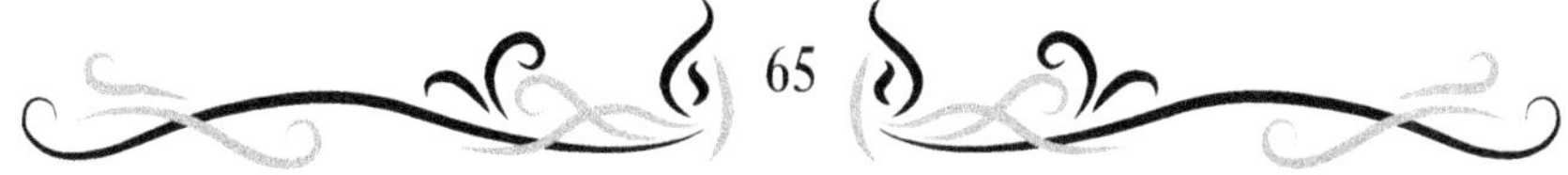

Stanislaus finished tying the horses to the stakes he and Alain had driven into the ground by the edge of the forest, and came to take the habit Barabal held out for him. Picking up another from the basket, he and Alain nipped behind some trees to change.

'You want to go here?' John asked.

'I want to learn more than how to write and do household accounts,' Barabal answered, a touch of sadness tinging her words. 'I want to read the writings of great thinkers and learn how the world works. However, although my father owns his own land, he could never afford the endowment for me to attend the Abbey.'

'Endowment?'

'Yes, to be educated here you must pay a fee. That enables the abbess and the sisters to teach rather than having to farm the land for their survival.'

'Oh. So if you are a girl the only way you can learn is to join a convent and take holy vows?'

If this was the case, he decided his mother's book on medieval knights had been sadly lacking in real information.

'No, silly, you are not expected to become a nun. Though you are required to live in the convent and follow their rules while you study here.'

Shrugging her shoulders, Barabal smiled, forcing the sadness from her eyes as her usual optimism returned.

'Come now, you must get dressed, we have not got much time here if we are to catch Prince Henry up on the road to London tomorrow.'

'London? We are going to London?'

She reached into the basket and pulled out some more black cloth.

'Yes, Prince Henry is taking the court there so he can be crowned in the great abbey. When we are done, we are to join him and attend the coronation.' Handing him the garments she turned her back to give him privacy and at the same time telling him, 'You do not need to take your clothes off, just pull this on over top.'

He dressed as per her instructions, as he did he asked, 'Do you think it wise for me to meet up with Henry? You know, since I escaped from his dungeon.'

Barabal snorted. 'There will be so many people travelling with the royal party we will be able to keep you well enough hidden. We can keep you dressed as a nun if it would make you any happier.'

'I think maybe I would rather stay here.'

Barabal turned to hand him the piece of black cloth. 'Your wimple,' she advised.

'Wimple? What...' John inspected the cloth as if it was some strange piece of equipment he needed to figure out.

'Here let me. You need to bend down,' she directed, taking the wimple from his hands. As he bent, she placed the cloth over his head like some kind of veil. It fell over his shoulders and down his front, hiding his hair and obscuring his face.

Barabal inspected him. 'I guess that will do. Best you keep your head down, like you are praying,' she said as she held up some rosary beads. 'Do you at least know how to use these?'

John nodded, thankful his best friend at school had been catholic and told him once the beads on the rosary were used to count the number of times you said a prayer.

'Good. You fix them like this.' Barabal reached around him and tied the beads like a belt, with the cross hanging down just above his knees. Job done, she turned towards the trees.

'Come on, you two, we have not got all day. It will be dark soon and we will be caught inside the walls for the night if we do not hurry.'

'Are you not getting changed too?' John asked as they waited for Stanislaus and Alain to appear.

'No, silly, women visitors are commonplace here.'

Her face crumpled into a frown as the other boys appeared from behind the bushes. She marched over and made them stand still while she adjusted their costumes to her satisfaction. Once they were dressed appropriately, she lined them up. With John walking beside her, and Alain and Stanislaus following behind, they were ready to go.

Walking around the wall, John spied a closed gate. It did not appear very inviting, yet Barabal strode over and thumped authoritatively on the wood. A small metal peep-hole opened and a face peered out.

'We are here to see Princess Edith.'

Without any verbal response, the door opened to admit the strange group.

'She is where you usually find her,' a female voice came from behind the wooden barrier.

Barabal nodded, and confidently strode ahead towards a side entrance in one of the stone buildings. John turned to catch a glimpse of the woman closing the gate behind them ,and was surprised to see Lala following Alain.

Lala, what are you doing?

Do you think I trust you alone after yesterday? the lamb asked.

A lamb cannot just go wandering about in a convent, John told him.

I think you will find that I am more welcome here than you would be if they found out you were a boy, the lamb chuckled as they reached the side door.

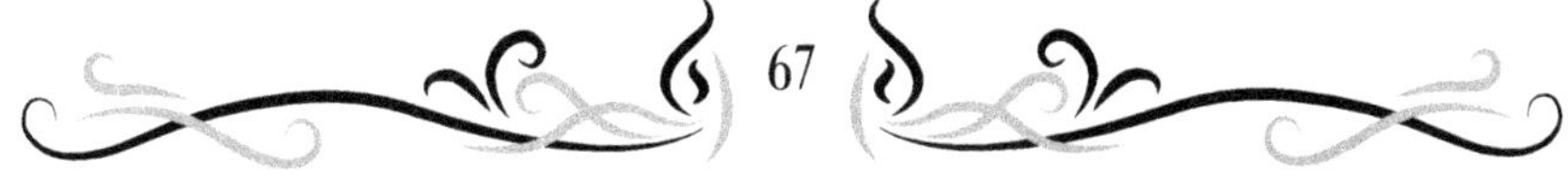

9

MEETING THE REAL MATILDA

JOHN KEPT HIS eyes on the polished wooden floor as Barabal led them through a hallway lined on both sides with closed doors.

'The sister's rooms.'

Although she whispered, Barabal's voice echoed alarmingly in the empty corridor. She huddled them close so she could keep the noise to a minimum before continuing.

'The library, where Princess Edith will be, is through the main vestibule and at the end of a corridor on the other side. Please do not gawp as we go through the entranceway, I do not want you doing anything to draw attention to yourselves. Things will go easier for us if we pass unnoticed.'

No one said anything in response as they returned to their earlier formation. Turning the corner, they proceeded down another door lined hall that soon opened into a larger area. Not wishing a repeat of the night before, John kept his head down as instructed until a commanding voice halted their party.

'You. Yes, you. What do you think you are doing?'

Reacting as though she spoke to him, John lifted his eyes to see a woman dressed all in black, wearing the most ornate cross imaginable around her neck. Idly wondering if the jewels were real, he dropped his head and waited

for Barabal to speak for them.

The green of her dress pooled around her feet as she curtseyed. 'Good evening, Reverend Mother. These sisters are escorting me to visit with your niece. I believe she is in the library.'

'I guess you bring with you another message from that young man.'

Her lips pursed as if she was sucking a lemon, making it obvious Princess Edith's suitor did not come high on her list of suitable husbands. John was just able to see her long elegant fingers tapping a rhythm on her thigh. The fingers ceased tapping.

'Hmm… well, I guess you had best deliver it. She would not thank me for holding you up.

'However, as the library is but a few paces away, you hardly need so many escorts. You two, the kitchen is short staffed this evening, you would be better employed helping with supper. Come with me.'

The tone of her voice brooked no argument, so Alain and Stanislaus meekly followed the imperious Abbess of Romsey. John raised his head in time to catch sight of the two boys disappearing down the passageway they had exited from moments before. Alain threw a stricken glance over his shoulder, while Stanislaus demonstrated his feelings on the matter by sticking out his tongue and mimicking being sick.

'What do we do now?' he asked.

Barabal rose, smoothed down the fabric of her dress and tidied her hair. Satisfied with her appearance, she continued on her way.

'We do what we came to do, and worry about the boys later.'

Before following, John had a quick peek round the room. On the walls hung tapestries rich with colour, depicting scenes from the bible. The surrounding alcoves contained panels of religious paintings even John could tell were valuable. A recess in the centre of the wall opposite the doorway, contained a huge cross those entering the convent would not fail to miss. John wondered if they positioned the artefacts to remind people of the house's religious nature, or to display its wealth. Realising he stood doing just what Barabal had told him not to, he sped after her.

The girl waited for him outside an open door, foot tapping impatiently. He glanced into a room with windows running down one side, filtering the last of the day's light. Bound leather books lined the walls. Sitting at a table by the windows was a diminutive woman, head bent, reading.

Her black hair was plaited away from her face to hang down the back of her sober grey gown. Neither handsome nor plain, John would not have looked

twice at her. That was until the disturbance in the doorway caused her to look up. Like her future husband's, her violet blue eyes were intelligent and striking.

'Stay here and make sure we are not interrupted,' Barabal commanded, before walking into the room alone.

Stopping in front of the woman she bobbed a curtsy, and waited to be acknowledged. The woman marked her place in the book with her finger before nodding for her guest to speak. Barabal pulled some parchment from her pocket and handed it to the lady.

'Child, you know animals are not allowed inside after vespers, and the bell is almost upon us. Best you take the lamb outside before the reverend mother catches you.'

So engrossed in the scene in the library in front of him, John had not heard the elderly nun come from behind. He literally jumped at the sound of her voice.

'Umm.'

Undecided what to do, John's head pivoted from the nun to Barabal, and back again. To his dismay, the girl was so intent on her conversation with Princess Edith she was completely unaware of anything else happening around her. There would be no help coming from that direction, John was on his own.

'Away with you now,' the nun instructed, her tone giving him no choice in the matter. Leading the lamb out the same way they had entered, John told his guardian, *I knew this would happen. You should have waited out by the cart.*

You had no way of knowing this would happen at all. Stop being so grumpy. There is nothing more you can do here. Barabal has delivered the note, you would not be able to influence the princess' response.

Resisting the urge to stomp his annoyance, he headed for the door, followed by the nun who was intent on ensuring he did as instructed. As he opened the external door, a bell sounded.

'Just put the lamb outside, it will find its way back to the others. We do not want to be late to vespers, do we?'

'Umm, no, I guess not.'

John attempted to make his voice sound as female and breathless as he could, but the nun still glanced quizzically at him. Dropping to the floor to assist Lala outside, he hid from her scrutiny.

Wait by the door, I will come back for you.

With no reply from Lala, John was unsure whether or not the lamb would be there when he returned.

Unable to delay any longer, he stood, closed the door, and followed the

woman back into the abbey. The elderly nun led him to an ornate chapel. He silently slipped into a pew beside her, behind rows filled with identical black heads. Someone turned as he sat. A glimpse of the face was enough to tell him Stanislaus and Alain attended evensong as well.

As he waited, the abbess walked from the back to the front of the Chapel. She blessed the nuns before thanking the Lord for the bounty of their day. The service was much like the one he had snuck into with his friend when he wanted to see how a Catholic Church differed from the Baptist one his mother made him attend. His mother had tanned his hide after, for consorting with the devil. How much more annoyed would she be now, knowing he participated in a full Catholic service?

A nudge from the nun beside brought him back to the present. Everyone was singing. In his church, songbooks were handed out to everyone as they entered. Here, it appeared the nuns were singing from memory. A frown from the woman told him not joining in was not an option.

Listening to the tune he realised he might cobble something together. He hummed while moving his mouth. The frown of displeasure left her face and she returned her attention to the service.

An age later vespers concluded, and the nuns filed out. His bottom numb from the prolonged sitting, his knees sore from all the kneeling, John creaked upright and followed the others out of the chapel.

Swept along with the crowd, he found himself in a room filled with long tables. Helpers distributed steaming baskets of warm bread and mugs filled with some sort of liquid.

When the others sat, he did as they did. They passed bread and he broke off a chunk, passing the basket on to the girl beside him. He drank what tasted like watered down beer while a nun read passages from the bible. No one spoke. When the reading finished everyone rose and left the dining room to go their separate ways.

Now free of his disapproving shadow, he searched for Alain and Stanislaus. He spotted them clearing tables under the watchful eye of the mother superior. No words were needed to communicate her displeasure at her charge's performance.

Sure that if he waited for them someone would decide he needed something to do to occupy his idle hands, he left the refectory. Striding purposefully to discourage anyone from stopping him, he soon reached the external door. Glancing around, he made sure no one was watching, then let himself out of the nunnery.

LALA'S WOOLLY WHITE coat shone like a beacon in the half-dark. Nestled under a tree, the lamb was curled up, sleeping. Deciding it would be a good idea to try and find Barabal, John was saved the effort by a jerk on his arm. He rounded to be confronted by the angry face of his new friend.

'What were you thinking, just leaving me like that?' She spat at him.

This appeared to be one of those statements Barabal presented as a question, as she did not give him a chance to answer before continuing her tirade.

'As if it were not bad enough those other goons being taken to the kitchen, you deserted me too. Honestly, I should have come alone, regardless of the danger a girl travelling by herself faces.'

Barabal paused to take a breath, and John took the opportunity to defend himself.

'Calm down, will you? While you met with the princess, a nun came along and instructed me to take Lala outside. She gave me no choice. As I released him, the vespers bell rang. I could not very well keep my cover if I missed evening prayers. After, everyone went to supper, so I went along too. There was no chance to slip away without anyone noticing until now.

'I found Alain and Stanislaus clearing down tables in the refectory. No doubt they will be along soon as well.'

'Hurmph.' Barabal folded her arms and glared at him, annoyed she was unable to continue letting off steam after such a reasonable explanation.

'You know the gates are locked at vespers.'

Having finished her rant, she voiced the real reason for her worry. As she spoke and he realised the impact of her words, John thought through their options.

'No, I did not know the gates were locked. Perhaps if you would wait here with Lala for the others, I will circle the walls to see if there is anywhere easy enough for us to climb over. It would be best if we left without having to disturb the good sisters.'

Barabal's only response was to sink to the ground beside Lala and lean back against the thick tree trunk, arms tightly clasped around her legs. John felt the need to do or say something to cheer her up, to try and remove the forlorn look from her face.

'Did your meeting with Princess Edith go well?'

Apparently it was the wrong question. Barabal dropped her forehead to her knees and did not answer. After a moment, she looked up, her face a

picture of consternation.

'I am not sure. The lady read Prince Henry's letter; sometimes frowning, sometimes smiling. After she finished, she gazed out the window for a long time. When she picked up her pen, she did not appear to know what to write. She restarted a couple of times, but once she got going, she wrote for ages. After a while, she stopped writing and sealed her letter with wax, before handing it to me. She bid me keep it safe and give it only to the prince himself.

'She gave me no idea of the contents, except to say people's lives would be in danger should it fall into the wrong hands.' Barabal sighed and dropped her head back to its former resting place.

'So we have no idea whether or not we have a new queen,' John said, feeling a little frustrated himself. He could not bear to see Barabal so deflated, so he added, 'Well, we did our best. Now all we can do is join Prince Henry as soon as possible.' A tentative smile rewarded his efforts.

With Barabal deflated and in no mood to lead, he decided it was up to him to find a way out. Walking around the back of the abbey, towards what he thought was an orchard and farm, he hoped to find an older section of the wall with a few broken bricks that would allow them to climb over. Or perhaps even a gap they might be able to slip through.

Sometime later, without having found what he was looking for, he debated whether it was quicker to turn back, or continue until he had circumnavigated the grounds. Then a thought hit him. Back tracking a few paces, he found what had sparked his curiosity—an old, gnarly tree with thick branches creating a perfect climbing frame.

It might be the answer to their prayers. Testing his theory, he ascended and leaned over the wall to survey the ground on the other side. A grassy bank grew partway up the old bricks, lessening the distance to the ground to around seven feet. If they held on to the top, lowered themselves down as far as possible, then dropped, they should be able to get over without injury.

Jauntily returning to Lala and Barabal, he found the girl pacing back and forth. When he asked her what was wrong, she replied Alain and Stanislaus had not yet returned. Gnawing agitatedly on her lip, she would not calm down no matter what John said.

Fretting about lost time, and worrying about how they would be able to catch up with the prince's party after such long delays, John did not help at all when he pointed out the darkness meant it would be too risky for them to begin their journey tonight anyway.

Ignoring his words, Barabal headed over to go and search for the missing boys when a small gap opened and two figures slipped out before shutting the door with a quiet snick behind them.

'Where have you…' Barabal stopped speaking when Alain placed a finger over his lips. He lent forward and pressed his ear to the door. Standing there for some time, the boy eventually straightened up and smiled.

'We finally lost her,' he announced jubilantly, and Stanislaus grinned in relief.

'I was sure we would be scrubbing floors on our hands and knees all night. We cannot help it if we are clumsy. If she had not stood over us watching every move, we would not have been so nervous,' Stanislaus complained.

'We were lucky to get away,' Alain told Barabal. 'The abbess really did not like us. We did not please her on kitchen duty, so she had us scrub pots and pans after dinner until they shone. When he put the pots away, Stanislaus knocked over a pail of milk, and we had to clean that up. We were fortunate someone called her away before we had finished, because scrubbing the rectory floor had been mentioned.'

'She spoke to you after vespers?' Barabal's amazement at such a flagrant disregard for the rules rang clear.

'Well, no,' Alain admitted. 'But she managed to communicate how unhappy she was with us perfectly well without using a single word.'

'Now we are all here, can we at least leave the grounds, have some decent food and a good night's sleep?' Stanislaus asked. 'Bread and small ale is not enough to keep a growing boy fed through the night.'

'Well, at least you have had something to eat. I sat here waiting for you for an age without any food at all.'

Before anyone else started another grumble, John told them his good news, 'I know how we can leave without waking the nun on duty at the gate. Come with me.'

Much to his surprise, they all followed him round to the exit he had found earlier.

'We climb up and drop over the other side. Of course, we will need to hang by our hands from the wall, or else the ground is too far away and we might hurt ourselves.'

The two boys surveyed the tree, then nodded their agreement to his plan.

'I will go last,' Barabal qualified her consent. 'I do not want any of you boys using this as a chance to look up my skirts.'

'I understand your concern, but I am not sure that is going to work,' John told her, earning a steely glare from the girl before he clarified. 'It is quite a

long way down the other side and you might need help to get there.'

'You are only saying that because I am a girl,' she stubbornly insisted, hands planted on hips.

'I am saying that because you are by far the shortest of us all.'

'I am more than capable…' she started to say before John blocked her words out.

She really has a thing about boys looking up her skirts, he complained to Lala.

I do not think you understand. Her underwear does not, umm, how to put this… Women's underwear in this time does not cover private parts.

Oh? Oh!

Appreciating the enormity of the problem, John had an idea. Cutting Barabal off mid-sentence, he said, 'I can climb up and help everyone over the wall. Barabal you can go last and no one will be standing below you on this side. I will lower you down as far as I am able…'

'… and you boys can all turn your backs when I climb down the other side. I am sure I will be able to manage without any further assistance.'

With no objections to his plan, John took off his habit and wrapped Lala inside, making a type of sling over his back. He climbed up the trunk, and straddled the wall.

Stanislaus climbed up next. The boy deftly swung himself over, grasped the top with his hands as he hung his body down. John glanced down and realised the wall was higher than he originally estimated. Before he could stop the other boy, he had let go and fallen to the ground. Rolling, Stanislaus regained his feet with a grin on his face.

'Piece of cake.'

'Right.' John glanced down and saw Alain climbing to meet him. The shorter boy looked over the wall and doubt crossed his face, but only for a moment.

John told him, 'I can hold your hands and lower you closer to the ground if you like.'

Moving himself into position so his stomach rested on the wall, Alain lowered his body. John grabbed his hands, lowering him an extra arms length. Grunting, as the slight boy was heavier than he looked, his grip was already slipping when Alain let go. He fell to the ground, collapsing in a heap.

Stanislaus rushed over to the boy and helped him up. After checking out all his limbs, Alain grinned back up at John.

'All good.'

'My turn now.' John twisted to see Barabal on the tree beside him.

'It is a long way down,' John warned her. 'You might want Stanislaus to catch your legs at the bottom. I am sure he will respect your… umm… privacy.'

The girl's eyes widened in alarm. 'I am not letting either of those boys stand under me. You can drop me like you did Alain. You there, turn away while I climb down.'

John watched as the boys folded their arms and turned until their backs faced the wall.

'Right,' Barabal said as she eased herself over. John grabbed hold of her hands and lowered her as far down as his arms would let him.

'Barabal, there is still quite a way to go to the bottom, are you sure…' Before he could finish, the diminutive girl let go of his hands and dropped herself to the ground.

'Aww.' Barabal's voice echoed in the evening air as she hit the bank feet first with an audible thud, and collapsed onto the bank. Alain and Stanislaus rushed over.

'It is my ankle,' she told them. 'It twisted as I landed.'

Alain was all business. 'Stanislaus, you go help John while I make sure it is not broken.'

The squire moved to stand by the wall. John lowered Lala still in his sling, and the other boy caught him. Then John launched himself over the wall, dropping to the ground without incident. By the time he landed, Stanislaus had freed Lala and was stripping off his own disguise. Bundling his and John's habits together, he stowed them in the nearby bushes, before joining John to check on Barabal.

'Just a sprain,' Alain informed them. 'She will need help back to the cart, but she should be able to walk on it tomorrow.'

John helped Barabal up while Alain went and put his habit with the others. When he returned, he replaced John as Barabal's crutch. As he was closer to her in height, it was more comfortable for her to have his help walking around to the waiting cart.

As they moved past the gate and rounded the wall, a movement caught John's eye. Stanislaus must have seen something too, because he held up his hand to stop them from proceeding any further.

'There are men in the bushes,' he spoke out of the side of his mouth.

'Can we run for it?' John asked, before mentally kicking himself. Of course they could not, not with Barabal's ankle. Besides, the horses were not attached to the cart, so they would not get very far.

The decision was made for them as they were surrounded by armed men.

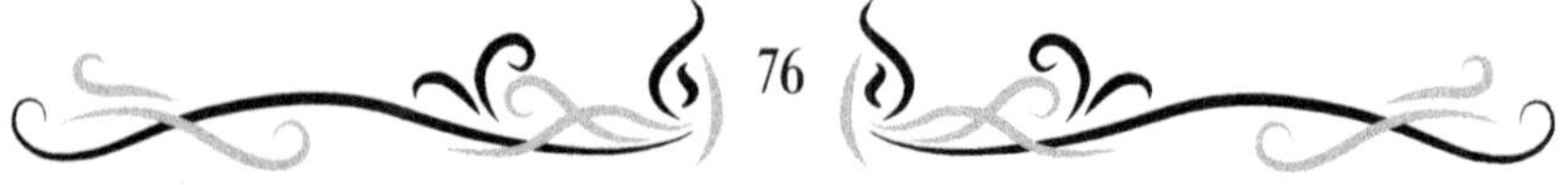

10

PRISONERS

'WHO HAVE WE here then?' A large man dressed in full chain mail sauntered over to them, hand ready on his sword should they try anything. His florid face sported an oily grin that went well with curly black hair that looked like it had not been washed any time recently.

'Just as we suspected—Mistress Barabal and young Master Stanislaus.'

Do not say anything.

How did Lala guess he had been about to object to Alain and him being ignored by their captor?

To William de Breteuil, and others of his class, if your family do not own land, you are beneath notice. Now please, hold your tongue and let Barabal deal with this.

That is William de Breteuil? He is not at all how Walter Tirel described him. He does not look like a fool, or anyone's pawn.

Tirel may be a little biased. De Breteuil is definitely no one's fool. What he is, is someone who holds true to his beliefs, so be very careful how you behave around him.

John slipped back behind Stanislaus to a position where he could watch proceedings, but hopefully go unnoticed. Barabal shrugged off Alain's supporting arm and stood tall, confronting Prince Henry's enemy. She would not be cowered by anyone.

'How dare you accost us like this. Let us pass and we will be on our way.'

His friend's courage was admirable. As her protector, Stanislaus attempted to make his way to Barabal's side, but the man next to him drew his sword and pointed it at the boy's breast.

'I am afraid I cannot do that until you tell me what you are doing here.' De Breteuil carried on as if unaware of the squire's discomfort.

Frozen in place, Stanislaus glared at the older man, as Barabal drew herself up as tall as her small stature would allow, and haughtily contemplated the noble in front of her.

'Sir, you are not in Normandie now. You have no right to question me here.'

'Know your place, woman, I will not be challenged by the likes of you,' de Breteuil sneered. 'I am an agent of the lawful King of Briton, Robert Curthose, and I will question whomever I choose in his name.'

The men behind them chuckled at Barabal's assertion of her rights being so easily dismissed by the arrogant man. John clenched his fists, wanting to punch them all for being so rude to her but, remembering his night in the dungeon, he held his temper in check.

Stanislaus, however, felt no such restraint. He knocked the sword aside and stood between de Breteuil and Barabal. Nearly as tall as the noble, he was not such an easy target.

'Sir William, as you and I both know, no king is yet crowned, so no one can claim to act on his behalf. Now, Mistress Barabal came to visit a friend, and our master bid me accompany her to protect her from attack. I suggest if you are unhappy with our actions, you should take it up with Robert de Beaumont. Regardless, I am sure he will want words with you about your treatment of those under his protection when we all get back.'

To give Stanislaus credit, he boldly stood eye to eye with the sword wielding lord, showing not an ounce of fear.

'I am unsure whether to be impressed at his gumption, or scared for his foolhardiness.' Alain's whispered comments echoed his own thoughts.

'Why climb over the fence if this was a simple visit to a friend?'

'Why, because these foolish boys got bored waiting for me and took it upon themselves to sneak into the abbey to look around. Not knowing the nunnery's routine, they did not realise the gate closed at vespers. Once inside, they found themselves unable to get out without letting the abbess know of their transgression.' Barabal attempted to lighten the moment.

'I would be inclined to take this on face value, except I am aware Princess

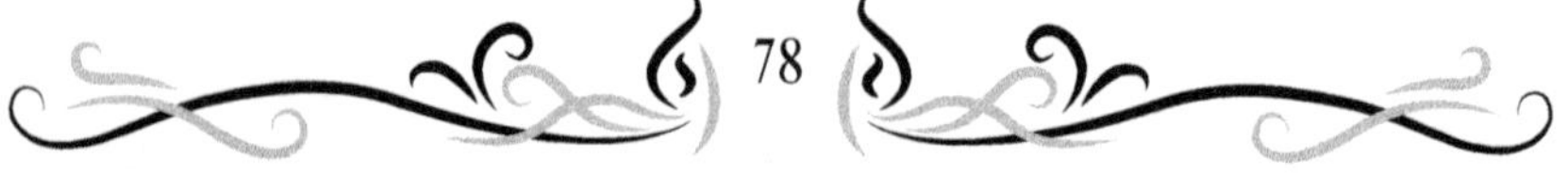

Edith resides within these walls. If she aligns herself with Prince Henry, he would have Anglo-Saxon support and there would be no stopping him from stealing the crown. If that happens, Norman influence in these lands would be severely reduced, and I can see no good coming from that.'

William Breteuil stroked his beard thoughtfully.

'Stanislaus, I am surprised to see you helping Prince Henry's cause. I know your master is a staunch supporter of his, but your father would no doubt be in support of his duke, Robert Curthose, being crowned king here in Briton. As a Norman, I am sure he would be in favour of consolidating our power base in Briton.'

Before Stanislaus could answer for himself, Barabal stepped forward.

'Please sire, Stanislaus is just here protecting me. He knows nothing of politics and intrigue.'

'Barabal,' Stanislaus stuttered. 'What are you doing?'

John made to move forward to join Stanislaus in protecting their friend.

Wait. Trust her. I am sure she has a plan.

'Ah, that makes sense. I was sure you would be no lover of the Britons.'

William Breteuil resumed stroking his beard as Stanislaus carried out a short, frantic conversation with Barabal. They spoke so quietly John could not make out a word they said.

Shaking his head, an obstinate expression on his face, the boy blurted out, 'No, my duty is to protect you, no matter what.'

'Enough.' De Breteuil had made up his mind and took control of the situation. 'Tie the others up. Stanislaus, come with me.'

'Why bother with restraining them? We can slit their throats and leave them here. Much less trouble.'

Their captor turned a stare on the man so cold it would turn water to ice. 'Have you no honour? I do not kill helpless children and servants. Do as I bid.'

Turning away in disgust, he took Stanislaus by the arm and dragged him off. The guard nearest to John grabbed hold and led him around the corner towards where they left their cart hours earlier. Alain and Barabal were pulled along behind, with Barabal biting back a yelp of pain as her ankle took her full weight. By the time they reached their captors' camp, her face was ash grey and covered in beads of sweat.

A fire treated them to the smell of a rich stew tended by one of the band's members, who had remained behind to feed his comrades. The aroma wafting from the pot reminded John he was still hungry. Unfortunately, no one

offered anything to eat before binding them to one of the cart wheels, and John's stomach grumbled its complaint. Attempting to take his thoughts off food, his mind came upon another problem.

'What happens if I need to relieve myself?'

'Best hope you do not need to,' Alain said.

'What do we do now?' John said as Lala curled up beside him.

'Nothing,' Barabal calmly answered. 'It is all in hand.'

'What?' Alain and John asked in unison.

'Do I need to do all your thinking for you?' Exasperation laced Barabal's words. 'Prince Henry is on his way to London to be crowned king. I told Stanislas to drop this piece of information into his conversation with de Breteuil, who will want to take his men with him to stop that from happening.

'Stanislaus will go with them because de Breteuil now believes he is on Robert Curthose's side. When he comes to say his farewells, I will tell him where I hid the letter from Princess Edith to Prince Henry. He can deliver it.' Barabal sounded smug as she whispered her plan.

'What about us?' Alain asked.

'For all he is supporting the wrong side, William de Breteuil is a godly man. I do not believe he will harm us. He just wants to prevent me from delivering Princess Edith's message. He may leave us to return home on foot, but we can manage that. The important thing is that the letter gets to Prince Henry.'

'I think you are putting a lot of trust in things going the way you worked them out in your head,' John told her.

'And even more trust in Stanislaus not mucking this up,' Alain chimed in.

'I do not see either of you coming up with a better plan.' Barabal turned away from them, well as much as she could within her bonds, showing her annoyance at their lack of praise for her quick thinking.

Lala, is there anything you can do here?

'Who is Lala?' Alain spoke in a low voice.

'You can hear me?' John's head swung round in surprise.

'Of course. All those with magic can hear mind speak if the speaker has not learnt how to, or does not care to, hide their voice.' Alain spoke as though this was something everyone knew.

Lala?

Sorry, I was distracted and let the shield drop for a moment. I guess there is no point putting it back up again now.

'Who is that talking? Are they near? Can they help us?'

'Umm, it is my mentor, and I guess you could say he is near. I was trying to find out if he could help.'

There is nothing I can do. In this form I am extremely limited.

This form? Alain asked

John nodded down at the lamb leaning against his leg and Alain's eyes widened in disbelief.

You call a Great One Lala?

You know he is a Great One?

Of course I do. We spent some time together during your little break in the dungeon. Master Gavin told me he was a Great One and we needed to take care of him. They spent some time talking together. I did not know I could talk with him as well.

Oh. All right. John half shrugged. *Anyway, he told me to call him Lala, so I have no idea what else to call him.*

Well, I guess it must be all right then. If he cannot help, I reckon it is up to me to get us out of this.

Alain leaned back against the wagon, eyes closed. Wondering how taking a nap would help them, John allowed his gaze to roam around the campsite looking for anything to assist their escape.

'What are you two whispering about?' While they were talking, Barabal had shuffled around so she was again able to see them.

John was prevented from answering as de Breteuil appeared by the fire.

'Right, you, you and you,' he pointed to three men. 'You are to stay here and guard the prisoners. Keep them here tomorrow and over-night again. The day after tomorrow set them free and let them walk home. That should prevent them getting the message to Henry Beauclerc, and buy us some time.

'The rest, come with me. You too, Stanislaus.'

'See,' Barabal crowed. 'I knew my plan would work.'

Stanislaus moved to say good bye to his friends, but de Breteuil stood in his way.

'Your friend will be cared for, and the servants will ensure she arrives home safely. You can ride one of your cart horses, I assume you can ride without a saddle?'

Stanislaus nodded and reluctantly allowed himself to be led over to choose the best animal from the two that had drawn their cart. De Breteuil paused by the fire on the way back.

'If anything untoward happens to your prisoners I will be most displeased. In fact, if they are harmed in any way, the same shall also be done to you. Understand?'

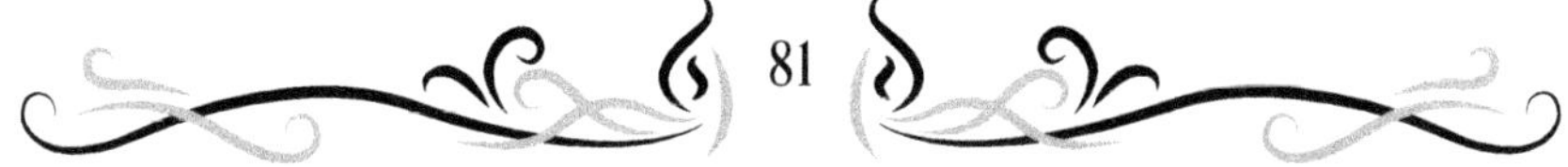

The men nodded, although one of them mumbled something under his breath as de Breteuil turned away, and the others sniggered their response.

As he prepared his mount, Stanislaus searched for opportunities to come and say goodbye, and to get Princess Edith's letter from Barabal. However, Sir William de Breteuil kept a close eye on him, and the boy had to be satisfied with a brief farewell wave as the men took to the road, chasing Prince Henry and his entourage.

'Merde,' Barabal exclaimed as they left.

Lala did not translate for him, but John understood the word did not mean anything good.

'What are we going to do now?'

Alain, who until then had appeared to be sleeping, slowly opened his eyes.

'I think I have a plan,' he said, turning his body away from the guards and holding up his unbound hands.

'HURRY UP AND untie us,' Barabal demanded.

Alain shook his head. 'We must be smart about this. Those men are bigger and stronger than we are. And you cannot run far with that ankle. We need to ensure they will not follow and recapture us.'

'So what is your plan?' John's interest was piqued.

Alain outlined his idea and what he wanted them to do to help. John had to admire his scheme's simplicity and deviousness. Barabal was not so happy, but not having a better alternative, she informed them it was worth a try, if only because her bladder was actually full to bursting.

'Guard. *Guard.* Please, I need to use the privy,' she wailed in a whiney tone that was not at all like her.

'Well, you cannot,' the guard closest to them responded, turning back to his meal.

'What, not at all? We are going to be here for another day. Surely you cannot expect us to go where we sit. The odour will get unbearable, not to mention we would risk getting sick. And you were told to look after us.' Barabal used her best wheedling voice, and the guard sighed.

'All right, but you can wait until after we eat.'

'I am not sure I can hold on that long.'

'For goodness sake, Pierre, take her now. I do not want my meal ruined

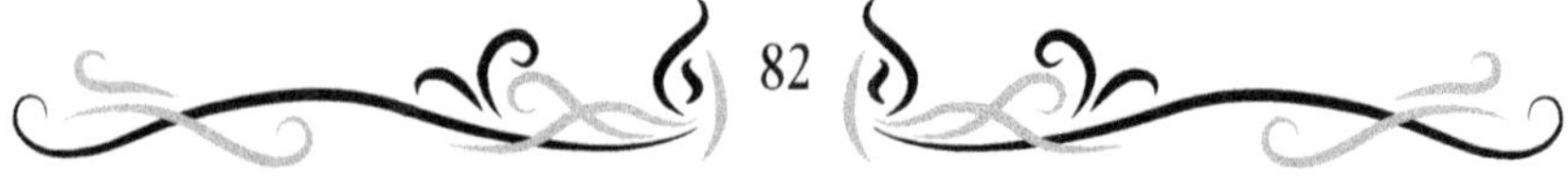

by her complaints.'

Sighing again, the guard lumbered to his feet. Now John joined in the ruse.

'If she gets to go, I want to go too.'

'I am not taking you both. Albert, you take the boy. I suppose you want to go as well.' Pierre nudged Alain with his foot.

'No, I am fine for the moment thank you.'

'Can you not take them both?' Albert asked. 'I do not trust Jean-Paul alone with the food. He will have half it gone before we return.'

'As if you would not do the same,' Jean-Paul retorted.

'Both of you come. This one is tied to the wagon, and if either of these two try to escape we will need an extra person for the chase,' Albert directed, taking charge.

He untied Barabal and John, and glanced quickly at Alain's bindings. Thinking ahead, the boy had wrapped the rope back around his wrists so it appeared he was still securely tied. The three men took the two captives round the other side of the wagon to the privacy of the trees.

Following instructions, John stayed in plain sight while he saw to the call of nature. One of the men went into the woods and found a suitable spot for Barabal. The man outside released her into the shelter of the trees, then both men allowed her enough privacy to complete her task. John took as long as possible, complaining to Jean-Paul having someone watch him put him off going.

Unsympathetic, the man told him, 'Go or do not go. Either way it does not bother me.'

Having delayed as much as he could, John turned to be escorted back to the wagon just as Barabal emerged from the trees. They arrived to find Alain exactly where they left him. Re-securing the prisoners to the wheel, the soldiers returned to finish their evening meal.

'Well?' Barabal whispered, and Alain nodded his head. 'So, what do we do now?' she asked.

'We wait.' A self-satisfied smile hovered around Alain's lips.

The three prisoners watched as the soldiers ate their meal and drunk from their water skins, not once thinking to offer anything to their charges, not that they would have taken so much as a mouthful.

'It is not working,' Barabal hissed.

'Just be patient,' Alain responded.

The minutes passed as though they were hours, and then one of the

soldiers, Albert, stood unsteadily. 'What was in that water you gave us, Jean-Paul?'

'It was just water. That skin flint de Breteuil took all the good stuff with him. I do feel a little light headed though, almost like we actually drank ale. Maybe the meat in the stew was a little…' Falling backwards before he finished, the guard appeared to be asleep.

'What? What is going on?' Albert turned and looked at the prisoners. 'What did you do to us?' He started to walk towards them, stumbled, righted himself, swayed, and crumpled to the ground.

Looking from one of his comrades to the other, Pierre seemed uncertain about what to do. Before he could take any action, he started to rock, then, in moments, was fast asleep like the others.

'How long before they wake?' John asked as he moved his hands for Alain to untie him.

As he worked on the ropes restraining Barabal, the boy said, 'Because I had to put the sleeping drought in their stew, I have no idea how much each of them took, or how long it will take to get out of their systems. I would guess about an hour, maybe two at the most.'

'Are you sure you did not kill them?' Barabal rubbed her wrists before adding, 'They are not moving.'

'I will check on them while you sort out the horses.'

Alain went over and leaned down to each man in turn, ensuring they were breathing and their hearts still beat strongly in their chests. He added some wood to the fire, and covered each of them with a blanket before returning.

'They will be fine. In about an hour or so they will wake up with a bit of a sore head, nothing I am sure they have not experienced before.'

'Right,' John said, already in organisation mode. 'I have saddled two horses. I will ride one and take Lala with me. Alain, can you ride? Can you take Barabal with you?'

'What do you mean "take Barabal with you"? I'll have you know I have been riding since before I walked. I will ride on my own, thank you.'

The diminutive girl stood, hands on hips, daring either one of them to disagree. Not willing to argue with her in the mood she was in, John turned to examine the horses seeing if he could find her a suitable mount.

'Their horses are warhorses, would you prefer to take the smaller cart-horse?'

Glaring disdainfully at him, Barabal rummaged through the back of the cart, pulled out some food and tied it in a bundle, then headed over to the

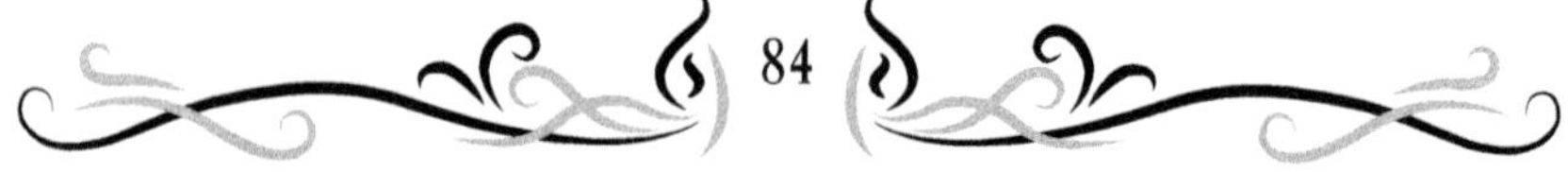

guards' remaining horse.

'This one will do. If one of you would saddle it, and give me a leg up, I will be fine.'

She proceeded to feed an apple to the brutish looking animal, and it nuzzled into her like a kitten.

Alain shrugged his shoulders and went over to help her while John pulled out his swag and bag. He sacrificed a set of his spare clothes to fit the lamb in. Slinging the bag over his shoulder, he walked over to his own horse, tying his bedroll behind before mounting.

By the time they were on their way, leading the cart horse behind them, John estimated they had used up around half of their hour head start. Reluctant to move at more than a walk in the moonlight, he prayed the guards had ingested more of Alain's sleeping draught than the boy believed, otherwise it was possible their captors could still catch them up.

11

GUILDFORD

AS THE SUN rose, turning the sky a dusky purple, the road they followed gradually became more visible. The three escapees urged the horses to a trot in an attempt to put some distance between themselves and the guards, who might already be on their trail. Not long after sun-up they stopped to allow their mounts to rest, and to eat some of the food Barabal had liberated from the cart.

Soon after, as they neared the turn off to Winchester, they set the cart horse free. They hoped it would make its way home, or at least find someone to take care of it. Now, able to maintain a steady pace, and with their captors not having caught them up, John stopped looking back over his shoulder. The day grew hotter, and as the sun reached its peak, John's stomach began to grumble.

'Are we stopping any time soon? I am beyond hungry, and I think the horses could do with a rest.'

'Boys are always hungry.' Barabal snorted.

'I am indeed proof of that, but I also really do need to eat,' John told her.

'I guess there is time to stop. I am to meet with Prince Henry in Guildford tonight. We should be able to make it in time, even with a break. These horses can travel almost twice as fast as the cart.'

They found a shady copse of trees near a stream. Tying the horses to tree branches, John removed their saddles and gave them a drink of water. He joined the others as Barabal was distributing the last of their food. They ate watching the horses nibble at the luscious green shoots by their hooves.

Appetite satisfied, John lay back, the soft grass cocooning him, the sun warming his face. Next thing he knew, Alain was shaking him awake. As he forced his eyes open, he realised the sun was no longer high in the sky. They had slept through the best part of the afternoon.

Rising swiftly to his feet, he found Barabal hurriedly packing up their belongings while Alain went to saddle the horses. Beside him, Lala stretched out lazily. John picked him up, shoving the lamb into his pack as he went to help with their mounts.

Aww, must you be so rough?

Stop grouching. We need to hurry. We slept away most of the afternoon.

John found grumbling without using words not nearly as satisfying as speaking them out loud.

Calm down. We are only fifteen miles from Guildford. We can make the town by sundown at a fast trot.

Not sure whether or not to trust the lamb, he asked Barabal, 'How close would you say we are to Guildford?'

Looking around, the girl checked her bearings before saying, 'I have visited only twice before, and only once coming from Winchester, but I would say if we keep a reasonable pace we should arrive by sundown.'

'Well, I guess we needed the sleep and the horses are rested, so not all has been lost.'

Rounding on him, Barabal opened her mouth to say something, then halted, as if she suddenly thought better of it. Her shoulders relaxed and she said, 'Yes, you are right. We might even be earlier than if our journey had gone to plan.'

Moments later they set out on their way to Guildford town. When they slowed the horses, giving them much needed rest, Barabal regaled them with tales of the great township. The town was built around a river crossing and was once called Golden Forde. It was named after flowers that grew on the river banks near the crossing. According to her, the only place in the world better than Guildford was the great city of London. John and Alain exchanged glances, not quite believing anywhere could be as fantastic as their travelling companion claimed.

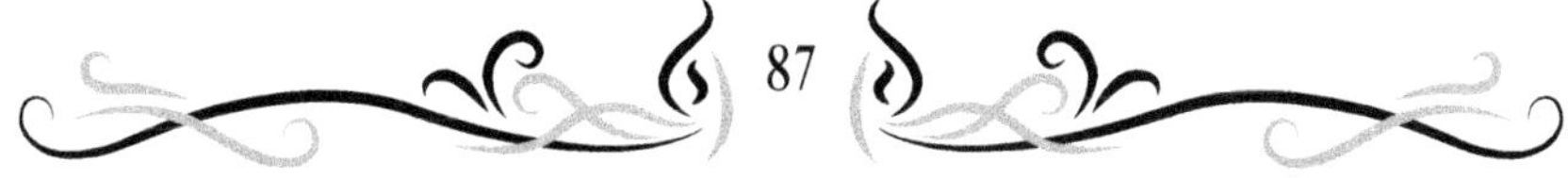

As the sun sunk low in the sky, they wearily approached their destination. Cresting a hill, they finally spotted the settlement below.

John laughed. 'Barabal, are you sure this town is the amazing place you described? Or do we have further to ride?'

'Well, I am pretty sure this is it,' the girl answered thoughtfully. 'Both times I came before was for the annual market fair, and it was much more festive than today.'

'Right,' John said, thinking from where he sat this walled town appeared far less impressive than Winchester.

Before they rode on, Alain held up a hand to stop them.

'We do not know what to expect when we show up, so it would be better to come in from a side road and approach the castle from behind.'

Barabal considered his suggestion, and shook her head.

'What ever happened between Prince Henry and de Breteuil today, both my masters will be here, and I trust them to protect us. Thinking on it, I believe I will feel much safer if everyone knows we have arrived. I do not think de Breteuil will do anything to us in front of witnesses.'

'I am certain that is true for you,' Alain grumbled. 'Much can happen to us common folk in the halls of a strange place, even in front of others.'

'I will speak to Sir Robert de Beaumont, and ask if he will let you two bed down with Stanislaus tonight. That should keep you safe. Right, shall we go?' This was one of her command questions, but John still did not move.

'Have you two forgotten something?' he asked when they turned to see why he was not following.

'No...' Barabal's brow wrinkled at his question. 'At least I cannot think of anything.'

'I think it has slipped your mind only yesterday you broke me out of a dungeon, turning me into a fugitive,' John patiently explained. 'I do not think it is the best idea for me to be anywhere near Prince Henry or his men at this time.'

'Oh, that,' Barabal waved her hand, swotting his concerns away like an irritating fly. 'You look like any number of commoners now, no one of any rank will take a second look at you. And if they do, I will explain how Walter Tirel's rescuers forced you to go along with them, then abandoned you on the road to Romsey. We found you and took you along to the abbey, meaning to turn you in when we caught up with the prince.

'In the end finding you was quite lucky, because we would not have escaped

from de Breteuil's men without your assistance. The Prince must forgive your outspokenness given you are the sole reason we were able to bring Princess Edith's letter to him.'

'Inside of you there is a plan for every situation,' Alain said, his tone suggesting approval of Barabal's quick thinking as he gazed at her in wonder.

'When you have so little control over your own life, I find it is important to manage the people around you,' she responded.

John had to admit Barabal did seem to be an expert at manipulating others. Although her proposal might work, he still was not convinced enough to bet his freedom on it.

'It is a big risk, I would rather not find myself in another dungeon because you misjudged things.'

You need to go with them, no matter your misgivings, Lala commanded.

But..., John started.

I cannot tell you any details. All I can tell you I do not see a dungeon in your immediate future. What I do see is failure should Alain and Barabal continue alone.

'John? Did you hear me?' Barabal brought her horse up beside his, and shook him by the arm, worry marring her face. 'Are you having another one of your turns?'

'No, no, I was just thinking. Do I truly look so different no one will recognise me?'

Realising he needed a reason for changing his mind so easily, having been so adamant just seconds ago, this was the best he could come up with.

'I do,' the girl said confidently. 'Well, at a quick glance at least. I will talk to my lord first thing when we arrive, and ask him to intercede on your behalf with the prince.

'Until then, Alain and you can wait in the kitchen. Boys always hang around where there is food, so no one will think twice about your being there. If you are lucky, perhaps they will take pity on the two of you and give you something hot to eat. No doubt you are both starving again.'

Still reluctant, John followed the other two down the hill towards the smokey haze of Guildford. As they arrived at the outskirts of the town, John chuckled. Alain had boasted about Guildford's size but, even by Australian standards, it was a country village.

The riders stood out among the locals going about their business, all of whom travelled on foot. How the trainee apothecary ever thought the three riders would have been able to sneak into town was a joke.

VIVIENNE LEE FRASER

THE STREETS THEY rode through were little more than mud paths, with the houses lining them built mainly of wood. Even the defensive castle they headed for was constructed mostly of timber. They did pass one ornate stone building, which Alain explained was a cathedral. It appeared the church had more money to spend on its houses than the crown.

The area outside the castle bustled with activity. A makeshift camp had been set up for Prince Henry's guards, and the castle servants rushed round ferrying food and drink, ensuring everyone had everything they needed.

'See, I told you. There is so much going on here no one has time to look at a common boy, let alone try and remember where they might have seen him before,' Barabal said as Alain helped her dismount.

John scowled at her, hating that she was right, but really a little in awe of her ability to read and manage situations.

'Alain, take the horses round to the stables. When you are done there, you and John should go to the kitchens. I shall go and report to de Beaumont and sort everything out, then I will meet you there.'

As Barabal turned to leave, Alain grabbed her arm.

'You may have been here before, but I have not. Which way do we go to find the stables and the kitchens?'

Releasing an exasperated breath, Barabal spoke slowly and clearly, as if she were speaking to a half-wit.

'If I needed to get to the stables, I would follow others leading horses because there is a high likelihood they are looking for somewhere to house their mounts for the night too.

'Then I would find someone delivering food to the guards and follow them back to where they came from, which is likely to be the kitchens.' Instructions delivered, Barabal yanked herself out of Alain's grip and hobbled slowly towards the castle entrance, her ankle still not quite healed.

'I dislike it when she does that,' Alain said, although his face showed admiration as he followed her retreating figure with his eyes.

'What? Tell you something you might have figured out for yourself if only you had thought about it?' John grinned.

'Yes, exactly that. Annoying, isn't it? Come on, we had best get these animals seen to.'

Following another boy around their age leading a horse, they found the stables. It was over-crowded and the harried stable master directed them round the back, to a field.

'You can unsaddle here, leave the tack there, over the fence, and someone will see to it when there is time. You need to take the saddle bags with you. Our storage space is full up. You can leave the lamb here, it will be quite safe.'

No, you most certainly cannot, Lala told him emphatically.

John considered ignoring the lamb and leaving him behind for some peace, then thought better of it. He still did not know his way around in this century, and Lala might be able to help keep him out of trouble.

'Ah, he is only young. It will be best if he comes with me.'

John picked Lala up and settled him in his bag.

'Fine by me. One less thing to worry about. Which lord do these horses belong to?'

John figured as they had to abandon their cart, they might need the mounts to return to Winchester. So he told the man, 'We are with Robert de Beaumont.'

'Right, the saddle and tack will be stowed with his, although I say this looks more like Duke William of Breteuil's marks on the leather.' The well-built man raised a questioning eyebrow.

'Your eye is keen, sir,' Alain was quick to respond. 'We were a last minute addition to de Beaumont's household, and de Breteuil offered to loan us mounts for the journey.'

'Mmm, all right then,' the man said skeptically as he wandered off. He had too many other things to worry about this day than to do more than ask the question about a discrepancy in markings.

Once again back in the courtyard, the two boys searched for someone serving food. When they arrived earlier, a number of people had been distributing bread and stew, now they were unable to find a single one. Alain's stomach rumbled in complaint, and John's responded in kind. They must have looked either quite forlorn, or likely to cause trouble, as they had not been standing around long when a group of guards wandered over to them.

'What are you young 'uns up to? Not causing mischief I hope.'

John was looking at the ground, trying to hide his face in a not-hiding-his-face sort of way, leaving Alain to speak for them both. Keeping his tone friendly and sticking to the truth, the boy answered.

'Our mistress, Barabal, instructed us to meet her at the kitchens after we sorted the horses, but we do not know where they are, and we have no idea

where to start looking.'

The man laughed. 'Normally you would follow your noses, but with the great unwashed camping out here in the courtyard you would never find your way.

'Tom, show the boys where they need to go, and do not be hanging around after trying to fill that bottomless pit you call a stomach. We are meant to be on guard duty, so meet us at the west gate when you are done.'

The guard nodded at the youngest of the group, a boy not much older than them. The young guard's expression changed to delight when he heard his new orders, then resignation as his commander's final words forestalled his chance for an extra snack.

'Come on,' he said. 'Kitchen's this way.'

Tom led them around the side of the castle, away from the stables, weaving so expertly between the crowd he had to stop a couple of times for the boys to catch up. Finally they walked through an archway into a courtyard, and on towards the castle's only stone building.

Through the doorway, John made out a cooking fire with a cauldron swinging over it. Even though the staff were busy clearing up, this one sight gave him hope he might still eat a hot meal this day. It had been so long since he had eaten anything warm; his mouth salivated at the thought.

'Kitchen's over there.' Tom pointed, and prepared to leave.

'Ah, before you go, can you tell us if Duke William de Breteuil has arrived, and where his men might be?' John asked.

'Most of the time I am not really interested in the comings and goings of the high and mighty.' The boy paused before continuing, 'but he created such a ruckus when he arrived today. He and his men rode in here not long after the prince, like the very devil was chasing them.

'Prince Henry was busy seeing to his men, but de Breteuil strode up and started haranguing him. Yelling at Prince Henry, he called him a cheat and accused him of killing the king. They almost came to blows, and their guards drew weapons. My master called in his men to keep the peace until they both calmed down.'

The delight on Tom's face as he spoke told them how much he enjoyed telling his story. Seeing this, John decided the talkative boy might be pumped for more information.

'Do you know where de Breteuil is now?'

'Yes, he took over some rooms in one of the towers. He posted a guard outside the door. Says he fears for his life with Prince Henry staying in the

same place, but he will be damned if he lets an upstart steal a crown that rightfully belongs to Robert Curthose. He is an odd one. My master would never let anything happen to any of his guests. Are you part of his retinue?' Thinking perhaps he might have over-stepped the mark, Tom looked worried.

'Sounds like he was in a state,' John said. Then quickly added, 'Do not worry, we are not his men.'

'We are castle staff from Winchester, we came here with Mistress Barabal.' Alain reassured the young guard. 'One of our friends travelled here with de Breteuil though, and we had hoped to find him this evening if possible.'

'I can take you to him,' Tom said helpfully. 'That is unless you planned to eat.'

'We want to do both,' Alain told him. 'I thought you might join us for a quick bite, and afterwards take us to find our friend, Stanislaus.'

Tom's expression changed from pleased to worried in a matter of seconds. 'I want to help you, but orders are to go directly back to my duties at the west gate.'

'It is all right, you can tell your captain that Mistress Barabal asked you to stay and help us get around. Believe me when I say your captain will be unlikely to argue with that particular lady, and she will be grateful for your help.' John hoped to persuade the boy to stay.

'If you think it really will be all right, I could really do with a little more to eat. Supper was over an hour ago.'

The guard's face brightened considerably as they entered the kitchen, the smell of food driving away all thoughts of duty. After he helped them wheedle some stew and fresh bread from the cook, the three boys took their meal outside. Finding a bench against the wall, they sat down to eat.

12

CONSPIRACIES AND CONFRONTATIONS

HAVING ALMOST FINISHED their meal of meat stew served in a hollowed out piece of bread, John leaned back and allowed his food to settle. Alain called the bread a trencher, and John marvelled at the useful invention. The bread mopped up the gravy, and you simply ate it when you were done.

Alain also said people fed it to the pigs once they had eaten what was inside, but John did not understand why you would waste such wonderful food. When no one was looking, he fed a little bread soaked in meat juices to Lala, who had curled up by his feet. The lamb immediately spat it back out.

It does not taste the same in this form.

You keep saying this form, does that mean you are not an actual sheep?

Of course not, did you truly think I was? Lala transmitted an impression of amusement along with the words.

Well, to be honest, I had not thought too much about it. On reflection though, I guess it is unlikely you would be. I imagine a Great One would be more like a god, having no body at all.

In fact…

'John, quit wool-gathering. Tom said he would take us to where Stanislaus is staying if we are ready.' Alain shook his arm.

'Oh. All right.'

John stuffed the last of his meal in his mouth and placed Lala securely in his pack. Following Tom across the courtyard, he soon found himself at a wooden tower.

'Is he in the dungeon?' John asked.

'No,' Tom stared at him like he was not quite right in the head.

'Not all castle towers contain dungeons,' Alain explained. 'Some house guards, or provide additional rooms used for guests.'

'Oh.'

John's anxiety disappeared as their guide led them up some winding stairs. Standing on the slightly larger step leading to a doorway, they were stopped by a burly man.

'What do you want?' the man asked gruffly.

'Ah, we just want to see if our friend is inside,' Alain said.

'Well, you cannot. Go away.'

John looked at Alain, who shrugged his shoulders. He too appeared unsure of the protocol in this situation. Before they could think of anything to say to change the guard's mind, Tom stepped between them.

'My lord asked me to accompany these boys and ensure they met with their friend. I am sure you do not want to disrespect his hospitality.'

The guard glared at Tom. Just when John thought they had no option but to leave, he reluctantly stepped aside.

'I guess a couple of minutes will not hurt. Keep the door open though, and no funny business.'

Opening the door for them, he ushered them through and half-closed it behind. Leaving just enough of a gap to make sure they behaved.

They found themselves in a surprisingly large room dominated by a four-poster bed. By the far wall sat a makeshift wooden pallet with a straw mattress and a thick woollen blanket. Stanislaus slept on top, mouth open, snoring.

'It must be so hard being taken captive by a noble man,' Alain whispered.

'Wha… what?'

Stanislaus half-opened his eyes, blinked, and peered blearily across the room at his visitors.

'Hey, Alain and John. You made it.' He swung his legs over the side of the bed, stood and stretched in a single fluid movement.

'When did you arrive? Have you come to take me back to Sir Robert de Beaumont?'

'Take you to de Beaumont? What do you mean?' John asked. 'We thought you sided with de Breteuil and so you are staying with him now.'

Looking to the open door Stanislaus winked. 'I am. He knows I am on his side over this thing about Prince Henry and the crown. I fully support his notion we Norman's should take back control of you Britons. I mean you had no real culture until we arrived. But he told de Beaumont I am his hostage. I think it is to make sure no one here attacks him.'

'Oh, well I guess you will not be leaving with us then,' John said.

At these words Stanislaus began making some weird movements with his mouth. Lala's translation magic did not appear to be working, because John could not make out what he was trying to say. Looking to Alain, the boy turned both his hands outwards in a "search me" gesture.

Lala, I need a little help here. Can you work out what is going on?

The lamb wriggled a little and his head popped out of the bag. He examined Stanislaus for a bit and snuggled back inside.

Well?

He is mouthing "get me out of here".

'Oh,' Alain said, and John realised Lala had decided not to shield this conversation.

He felt the bag settle as the lamb made himself comfortable again, having completed his task. John hesitated, allowing Alain to take control of the situation.

'Everyone is still eating in the hall, do you want to come down to the kitchens for some supper? You can be back here before de Beaumont sees you out and about without a guard. That way de Breteuil can keep up his little ruse, that is if you are truly not being held prisoner.'

'No, the man outside is for show.' Stanislaus went to the door. 'Hey, I am just nipping down to the kitchen with these boys for some food. I will be back before dinner in the hall is over, so no one will know I even left.'

The guard planted himself in the doorway, arms folded across his chest, blocking their exit.

'I do not think that is such a good idea.'

'Yes, it is. I am hungry and I would like to eat with my friends.'

The man mountain stood strong, not moving a muscle.

'You are behaving as though I really am a prisoner here…' Stanislaus

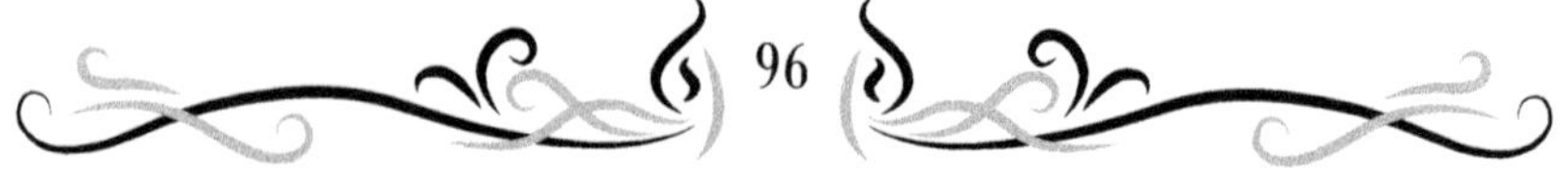

started only to be interrupted by their new friend Tom, who John had forgotten was in the room.

'And that cannot be, as my lord would need to be informed of what crime has been committed for one man to hold another captive in his house. Should I fetch him over so we can discuss the matter?'

'I think you had all best stay here until Sir William de Breteuil returns.'

'I am unable to do that, I am afraid. I was ordered to escort these boys to find their friend, then report for duty. I am late already. My captain will come looking for me any minute. So, while I would like to stay and enjoy your company, I am afraid I must leave.'

Tom moved, pushing the guard backwards into the corner. The boy then stood in front of him, making it difficult for the man to move.

'Run now,' the young guard instructed.

The others did not need a second invitation, they were out the door and off. As they exited the doorway of the tower they stumbled over a man about to enter, causing him to drop the bottle he held. Alain stopped to help him to his feet, and was distracted by the broken vial on the ground.

'Come on,' John tugged at Alain's arm while checking behind them to see how close their pursuer was.

'Wait a minute.' Alain turned back. 'Are you Master Bernard, the castle apothecary?'

The man paused, dusting himself off and stared at Alain. 'I am. Who wants to know?'

'Oh, pardon me, sir, but I am Alain, apprentice to Master Gavin of Winchester. I just wanted to apologise for causing you to break a precious glass vial. Can I replace it with something from my own stock?'

'Well, ah, thank you for your offer, young sir, but what Duke de Breteuil required is not something you would be carrying round on your travels.'

John noticed Master Bernard's demeanour altered when he realised he spoke to a fellow apothecary.

'Perhaps not the exact same cure, but maybe something else equally able to deal with his problem.' Alain continued to press, trying to find out what the other apothecary had been delivering to Prince Henry's enemy.

'Sorry, but Sir William de Breteuil specifically ordered some Fowler's Tonic, and an especially concentrated dose. It seems with all this travelling around the country he is not feeling as sprightly as he might. I brewed a double batch, and what he is paying will more than cover two deliveries and

two glass vials.'

No longer flustered, the elderly man busied himself sweeping the pieces of glass into the grass with the toe of his shoe, away from trampling feet. Meanwhile, John started edging Alain away as sounds from within the tower grew louder.

'Oh, well of course I would not bring anything like that with me. It would need to be stored separately, seeing as I would not want anyone to mistakenly take something so dangerous. And it has so few uses, it would just waste space. I am sorry again for causing your fall.'

'All is forgiven, I was a young boy myself once. I remember what it is like having a bit of spare time and a lot of excess energy.'

With the path now clear, the man bustled off, John guessed to go and fill another vial so he could over-charge de Breteuil. While watching Alain as he stared thoughtfully after the older man, John was hit from behind and stumbled before regaining his balance.

'Sorry,' Tom gasped. 'Run!'

The four boys took off just as Stanislaus' guard burst through the tower door. Running as fast as they were able, the boys followed Tom between the tents in the makeshift camp. Eventually they reached the west gate, and Tom skidded to a halt right in front of his captain. By the expression on the man's face, he was none too happy to see his errant charge. Anticipating a lecture, John came to Tom's rescue.

'My Mistress Barabal sends her apologies, sir. She asked Tom to help us out for a bit. He argued strongly he needed to return to his duties, but she is very persuasive. I am sure if you go to the palace early tomorrow, she will thank you for loaning us your Tom.'

The captain glared at John as though he wanted to say something. Expelling a deep sigh, his expression softened and he said, 'Who am I to question what my betters do? They do not care about any extra work they cause for us.' He spun on his heel, and Tom gave them a farewell wave and a grin as he followed.

'Thank goodness, it looks like our guard friend was put off by the presence of the Guildford men,' Stanislaus informed them when they were alone.

He an Alain checked the crowd to make doubly sure, but John stood his ground, sizing up the apprentice apothecary.

'So what was that all about?' John finally asked. 'The man we knocked down, something he said worried you.'

A shadow crossed over Alain's face. 'It might be nothing, but Fowler's

Tonic contains arsenic, and a strong dose will contain lots of it. It is not a well known curative, but the Roman's used it a lot. For the most part, it is used to restore energy, but too much can take a person's life. If anyone else ordered it, I would not worry, but…'

'… but it is de Breteuil, and you are worried he might use it on Prince Henry?' John finished and turned to Stanislaus. 'Do you know anything about de Breteuil's plans. Has he spoken of poisoning Prince Henry?'

'Not that I heard. But I am not sure he fully trusts me.'

'We need to find out whether or not he intends to use the tonic for himself,' Alain said. 'Stanislaus, I am afraid you must return to de Breteuil and keep up your pretence as a loyal follower.'

Stanislaus sighed. 'Must I really? He is so boring, always going on about God and doing the right thing, and how we Normans are far superior to anyone else. And his men do not appreciate a joke at all. Also, I think he might be holding me hostage, for real.'

Stanislaus was so downcast John considered telling him not to return. Fortunately, Alain displayed no such weakness.

'Yes, you must Stanislaus, you are the only one who can find out what he is up to. I am sure he would not hurt you as he would not want de Beaumont, or your father, as an enemy. I would not ask, but you can appreciate how important this is.'

'After running away, he will no longer believe I am on his side,' Stanislaus said hopefully.

'If you hurry, you may still get back before he returns. Tell the guard you just wanted a bit of fun. With any luck he will not want to admit you ever left the room because it might get him in trouble as well,' John told his new friend, not wanting to send the boy back to his prison, but also not seeing any other way to gather the intelligence they needed.

'It will be an act of sacrifice and bravery, and you will be a hero should we save Prince Henry from coming to harm,' Alain told him.

The idea of being the prince's saviour brought a smile to Stanislaus' face.

'Yes, I will be facing grave danger to save our future king. Of course I will be hailed a hero after he is crowned. Best I hurry back before anyone important finds me here. See you later.'

Without further thought, the boy sprinted away, hoping to be safely back in his rooms before the nobles of the land left the dining table.

'I sometimes wish it was not so easy to persuade Stanislaus to do what I

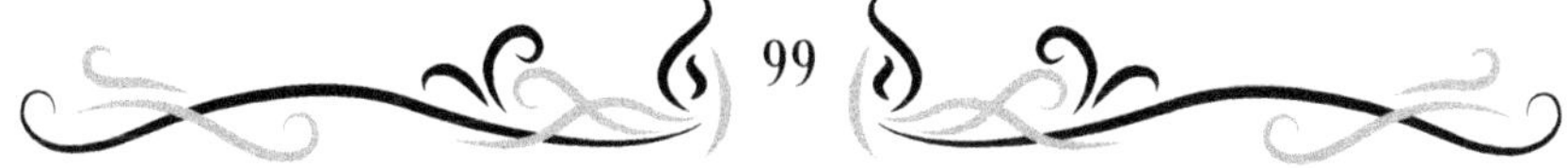

want. He is brave, and a skilled fighter with an enormous heart, but he is not one of the world's great thinkers,' Alain said.

'If we thought his life truly in peril we would not ask him to do this.'

John's attempt to raise their spirits after having returned their friend to the lion's den fell a little flat.

If it is any consolation, I do not see anything untoward happening to the boy in the immediate future. In fact, there is a potential promotion for Stanislaus if this all goes well.

Alain's eyes widened as Lala allowed him in on the conversation. 'While that is nice to know, I still feel like a louse,' he said. 'But it is too late now. Come on, let us go and find Barabal. She will be looking for us, and we need to tell her everything we found out.'

IT HAD NOT taken Barabal long to track down the prince's people. In the crowded dining hall, Prince Henry and his men were easily found as they sat on display at the high table. From the look of things, supper was not long over as half empty dishes still sat untouched. No one moved because their host still plied his high born guests with wine, and while he and the prince enjoyed a drink, everyone else must stay.

Standing in the doorway, she tried to attract her master's attention. Unfortunately Robert de Beaumont was so deep in conversation she was unable to do so. Vexed, because she could not just enter the hall and interrupt him or the prince, Barabal glanced around at the gathered nobles, trying to decide her next move. As her gaze swept the room, another pair of eyes met hers with surprise.

William de Breteuil elbowed his neighbour in the ribs, and they both stared towards Barabal. De Breteuil called for his squire, speaking animatedly to him, he gestured and pointed to the girl. This was not good. She could not let herself be caught before talking with the prince. As she went through her options, a serving girl entered beside her, carrying a pitcher of wine.

'Ah, the prince asked me to bring the next jug to his table,' Barabal said, grabbing the pitcher.

Expecting the girl to let go when addressed by her superior, she was surprised when the servant did not even loosen her grip.

'I know, I heard him giving the order. Now, let go and let me get on with my work.'

Haughtily, Barabal stared at the servant to no effect. At that moment, she realised the rather stunning girl hoped she might catch the prince's attention when she served him. He did have a reputation for enjoying the company of beautiful women, and he was generous to those he took a liking to while they were with him. With that mindset, she no doubt believed Barabal had the same interest in the prince and wanted to do away with the competition.

'Well, Prince Henry requested another pitcher a moment ago for my master, Robert de Beaumont,' Barabal improvised. 'I am to take this one to him, perhaps you could help me out and fetch another to take to the prince?'

Hoping the girl would be happy enough now she would be serving Prince Henry, Barabal glanced over the taller girl's shoulder to find William de Breteuil's squire close by. While the servant pondered her proposal, Barabal took a chance and grabbed the jug away from her.

'Thank you ever so much,' she told the stunned maid. Carefully carrying the wine so it did not spill, she walked up the middle of the room, certain the squire would not accost her in front of so many people.

She was wrong. The boy dodged the serving girl and followed closely behind. He grabbed her arm, halting her progress and sloshing wine on to the rush strewn floor. Luck was on her side though, as de Beaumont glanced up to identify the cause of the commotion, and frowned as he spotted Barabal being accosted.

'What is the meaning of this?' He stood as he questioned the pair.

'The wine you asked for, sir?'

Barabal hoped de Beaumont would understand her cryptic comment and come to her rescue. Her lord's expression changed from confused to angry as he realised his charge had been assaulted by the young man gripping her arm.

'About time too, mistress. You there, what are you doing man-handling my wife's companion like that?'

Placed in the spotlight by someone of superior rank, the boy let Barabal go and took a step backwards.

'Bring the wine up here, girl, and, you, return to your duties.' Sir Robert de Beaumont sat back down, expecting them to carry out his orders without further incident.

The squire sent a questioning glance to de Breteuil, who glared back. His annoyance at being thwarted written all over his face. Shaking his head in disgust, the baron beckoned the boy back over.

With her stomach still churning, Barabal walked with apparent calm up

to the top table and started pouring wine. De Beaumont ignored her as he would any other person serving at the table. Only the fact he watched Sir William de Breteuil over the rim of his goblet as he sipped his wine gave any indication this incident was more than it appeared on the surface.

As she served, she noticed one of the other guests leaned in and spoke to de Breteuil. Robert de Beaumont took the opportunity to speak to her while the man was distracted.

'Stay behind my chair with Squire James. I cannot leave while the prince remains, so we need to wait until after the meal for you to explain to me what is going on, and why de Breteuil's man attacked you in public.'

Trying hard not to let her emotions show, Barabal placed the wine pitcher down and took her place beside James. As she waited, she worried. Now the baron knew they had escaped his clutches, de Breteuil would send someone to find Alain and John, and she had no way of warning them.

Throughout the rest of the evening meal, she checked to make sure de Breteuil's squire remained behind his master's chair, awaiting instructions. A couple of times when she looked, Barabal found the lad staring angrily back at her, and she quickly turned away. Sure that while he remained the other boys were safe, she relaxed a little.

The head table continued to drink and talk, enjoying the evening. Although people were beginning to fuss and fidget, no one could leave until Prince Henry did. It did not help her temper any that her stomach was loudly protesting its lack of food by the time the prince stood, signalling the end of the meal. She did not know how the waiting staff managed to do this every night.

Stifling her sigh of relief, Barabal followed Sir Robert de Beaumont out of the hall and through the door into one of the castle's common rooms. As she passed the serving girl from her earlier altercation, she received a knock that almost toppled her off her feet. The maid was not pleased at having been bested.

While they waited for Prince Henry to deal with some other matters, Barabal took time to recount the details of their journey to her master. She left out the part where they rescued John before leaving. However, she did mention how they found him by the road on the way to Romsey and had brought him along with them. De Beaumont agreed he would talk to the Prince about allowing John to remain free in light of his help.

They continued their wait in silence as Prince Henry concluded his business with the other nobles. As they waited, Barabal's stomach rumbled and she coloured in embarrassment. Sir Robert asked James to fetch her some food.

A few minutes later she was seated in the corner with the squire, eating some bread and cheese. When the boy stole food off her plate, she pretended not to notice as he would not have a chance to eat until his master dismissed him.

Once finished, she drowsily closed her eyes, only to be awakened by a sharp kick to the ankle. Glaring at James with her most withering look, she realised the room had emptied and the prince and Sir Robert de Beaumont watched her, waiting for her to answer their question.

'Sorry, I must have dozed off. Can you please repeat the question, sire?'

'I hear you had quite a journey today.' Prince Henry smiled. 'I am not surprised you are exhausted. I asked if Princess Edith sent an answer with you?'

'Oh, yes, of course, sire.'

Barabal stood, reached into her pocket and handed him the letter.

'And William de Breteuil did not read this?' Henry queried her before opening it.

'No, sire, it did not seem to cross his mind to search me for a letter. From his words, I understood he believed I had a verbal message from Princess Edith, and by detaining me the message would not reach you.'

Henry laughed out loud, 'It probably never occurred to him a woman of your station, and an Anglo-Saxon to boot, was capable of reading or writing.'

Turning away from the others for privacy, Prince Henry broke the letter's seal and began to read. When he turned back, the smile on his face told Barabal whatever the princess said was to his liking.

Moving impatiently from one foot to the other, Barabal hoped the Prince would dismiss her soon. She wanted to find out if John and Alain were all right, but first she needed to find a privy.

DECIDING BARABAL MUST still be in the castle, John and Alain joined the servants cleaning up after the evening meal. They had just dropped a load of dishes back in the kitchens and were returning to the great hall when they came face to face with William de Breteuil. Turning to run, they found their way blocked by two of the lord's guards.

'Mistress Barabal's servants. I am surprised to see you here. You evidently have hidden talents.'

'Well hidden.' One of the guards snorted and earned a withering glare

from de Breteuil.

'Your mistress managed to make contact with the prince, in fact she is in with him now.' De Breteuil nodded towards the door at the back of the hall.

'Then you lost.' John finally found his voice, though his gut still churned with fear.

'The game is not over until Prince Henry wears the crown on his head, boy. This is a minor setback. There are other ways to stop the coronation.'

'Then why bother with us?' Alain had also found his voice, although it wavered a little.

'So you can pass a warning on to that little upstart Barabal. Stay out of the dealings of your betters, and stay out of my way. If you do not, I will be forced to start thinking of ways to sideline you… permanently.'

Poor Stanislaus, what had they let him head back into? John turned to Alain, who glared at de Breteuil.

'We Britons want nothing of your Norman Duke. If Prince Henry is made king, Saxon blood will run through the veins of the next King of Briton. That is something worth fighting for.'

John wondered where Alain suddenly got his courage from, but he had to admire the boy for standing up to the bullying noble.

'Bah, you Saxons were nothing until our great Duke William conquered you and became your first King William. We brought culture and discipline to this uncivilised part of the world. Without Duke Robert Curthose being crowned your next king, you will fall back into savagery and your civilisation will fall.'

De Breteuil stood taller, towering over Alain, who looked smaller in the larger man's shadow. The boy was undaunted, in spite of the physical intimidation.

'Robert Curthose cannot administer the lands he holds now, something you and the other barons are relying on. We will be a nation without a head, free to be pillaged by you and your Norman brethren. I think it is more likely Briton will fall apart under his rule than Prince Henry's, and there are many of us prepared to fight to prevent that from happening.'

Alain himself stood taller as he spat the words at the despised Norman baron.

'Bah, I do not have time to bandy words with a common boy. Pass on my warning to Barabal and the man she serves, Prince Henry's lackey. Come.'

The nobleman departed and, as suddenly as they had been accosted, John and Alain found themselves alone. Relief surged through his body as John leaned against the wall. Finally he stopped trembling and found his voice.

'Wow, Alain, I did not realise you felt so strongly about what we are doing.

I thought it was just a bit of an adventure for you.'

Alain, who had not moved a muscle since they first encountered William de Breteuil, turned and stared at John in disbelief.

'You must be joking. I risked everything to break you out of the dungeon, just because a Great One said without you Prince Henry would not be crowned king.

'Do you have any idea what it was like living under the Williams? My father lost his lands when William the Conqueror handed them over to one of his men, simply because my father supported his sworn lord against the Norman invasion.

'Then his son, William Rufus, ruined this country when he took the crown because he wanted to follow in his father's footsteps. Intent on expanding his holdings, he thought he could take the Welsh on and win. He lost time and time again. All those resources and men wasted simply so he could extend his power, while the people of Briton starved. Bring civilisation, huh? They stripped the country of everything good and tried to wipe out our Anglo-Saxon identity.

'While he is of Norman heritage, at least Prince Henry is offering to return some power to the people of Briton, and he will marry a Saxon wife. I would give my life for that. Barabal feels the same.'

'Oh.'

It was hardly an adequate response in the face of Alain's passion, but he was unable to think of anything else to say.

'Why are you doing this then? You are not from here, what have you to gain by helping us?' John opened his mouth to reply, but Alain continued speaking. 'Master Gavin assures me the lamb who talks to our minds is a Great One, one of the Time Guardians. Are you one of them too?'

John frantically tried to think of some believable story to tell, but stopped himself. Alain had been brutally honest with him, perhaps he deserved the same honesty in return, even if he was unlikely to believe it.

'Yes, Lala is a Time Guardian. I am not though. He transported me from a time in the future to ensure Henry takes up the crown and the Charter of Liberties is enacted. If your court system is not changed, the problems we face in my time will be far worse than they are now. So, I guess you could say I came here to fight for the future of my country and my people.

'Lately though, I believe Lala also might have brought me here so I could learn another way to bring about change where I come from.'

John expected Alain to at least laugh at him, or to call him mad, but the

other boy tipped his head to the side as he thought, then shrugged.

'That means we both have something to lose if Prince Henry does not become king. Come on, we still need to find Barabal.'

'What about Stanislaus? I feel very uneasy after that run in with de Breteuil. Should we not at least try and rescue him from the man's clutches?'

Now Alain laughed. 'That would be worse for him than leaving him there. William de Breteuil would know Stanislaus is only pretending to support the Norman cause rather than just suspecting it, and we would still be no closer to finding out what he has planned.

'Now, the one thing you can say for Stan is he has a knack for saving his own skin. He will be over convincing de Breteuil he is his new best friend. Stan may be an open book, and he may be readily talked into doing things he perhaps should not, but he is also cunning. And he has the gift to be able to talk his way into getting the best out of any situation.'

If Alain was not worried, John was not going to argue. After all, he had known the young squire longer.

At that moment, the door at the end of the room opened and a weary Barabal emerged. Her face brightened when she saw her friends. Prince Henry followed her out, and John's stomached lurched for a second time that evening.

'THERE YOU ARE. I thought I was going to have to hunt through every building and all the grounds for you both when James said he could not find you in the kitchens.'

Barabal had the ability to tell you off while making you feel pleased to see her at the same time.

'Our escaped prisoner has returned,' Prince Henry said looking at John and Alain. 'Mistress Barabal says I should thank you both for the letter from my future wife making its way to my hands.'

Learning from his last experience, John said nothing, and the prince laughed out loud.

'She is right, young John, you have learnt your place. Is she also correct when she says where you come from all may speak their mind to your leaders, no matter what their rank?'

When John did not answer, Prince Henry told him, 'I give you permission to speak freely in my presence.'

With the prince having given him leave to talk, John's words came tumbling out.

'My apologies for the other night, sire. If I had known more of your customs, I would have kept silent. I only spoke as I did because where I come from a person can disagree with our rulers and not be thrown into prison. That is unless they speak lies or untruths, then they might very well find themselves locked up.'

'What a noisesome place it must be. How can anyone rule if everyone must speak their mind before a decision is made?' Prince Henry rubbed a weary hand across his forehead as he considered what John had told him.

John said nothing. He knew giving away too much about the future could have unforeseen consequences, so he kept quiet.

'Master John, with everyone having their say, decisions must take an age to be made, but no country could be ruled that way. I think perhaps there is more to this system of government than you said. Is there more?' The prince pinned John with a steely gaze, and the boy wriggled uncomfortably.

Before answering he weighed up the consequences of giving Prince Henry more details over what he might do if John refused to answer. With Lala offering no advice, he finally decided he had no choice but to respond to the future monarch.

'It does not quite work like that, sire. In my country every few years we choose people to govern us, and to advise the king. Those people make the laws guiding our society by winning a majority vote. There are paid officials who ensure the rules are followed.'

Henry's eyes grew wider with surprise the more John spoke. When the boy was done, he stroked his beard as he wandered over to the fireplace.

'So, if we did that here, the barons and landholders would elect a council, and the council would decide what happens for all. I have never heard the like, but it might sort of work. Robert, imagine if instead of all the barons coming to court, they elected a few to represent their views. I would not be forced to listen to so many tiresome voices objecting to my every move.'

John held his breath, wondering if he had gone too far, expecting a lecture from Lala at any moment.

Sir Robert de Beaumont laughed before he weighed in on the conversation. 'I do see the appeal, sire, and it would be perfect if you could decide or influence who the barons would choose as their representatives.

'Imagine though, if they selected your most vocal enemies. Those men

might perhaps feel justified in opposing you more aggressively if they considered themselves having been raised in status by their peers.'

Prince Henry drew back as though he had been bitten by something nasty. 'You are right, Robert. I do not want any of that bunch to believe they have more influence than another. At least with all the barons here, I can look them in the eye as we make decisions. It is easy enough to identify those I need to bribe or bully to get what I want.'

Well done, Lala told John. *For a moment history stood poised to change, and not in a good way. Now everything is back running as it should.*

'Well, at least I now understand why you spoke out as you did, John. It is clear that landholders where you come from have more say in government than they do here. I grant you permission to do the same when we are in private, but you must keep to your place when other people are around.'

'Thank you, sire,' John answered, not correcting the prince's assumption he came from a higher station in life, not wanting to risk being returned to the dungeons.

'Now, since we are near to London, I suggest you come along with us. After I am crowned, you can head back to Romsey with Barabal. Princess Edith has requested Mistress Barabal be included in her retinue, and you might as well continue your duties as escort to her for the time being.'

His final command given, Henry retreated to his room and shut the door.

De Beaumont turned to Alain and John. 'Now you two have the look of boys who have been up to something. Tell me all the details.'

'Umm.' John briefly considered not saying anything, but de Beaumont forestalled that idea.

'You may as well tell me everything, no good ever comes from trying to hide things.'

'Oh, no,' Barabal cried. 'What did you boys do while you were out of my sight? Honestly, can I not trust you to keep out of trouble for even a short time?'

'Why do you always assume we caused the trouble?' Alain seemed more annoyed Barabal had jumped to conclusions than being wary of Sir Robert de Beaumont finding out what they had been up to.

'Because you have been running, and I know you did not wait in the kitchens as I asked because James did not see you there when he went to fetch food for me.' She stopped speaking as something dawned on her. 'Did you find Stanislaus? Yes, you did. Why is he not here? Did you lose him again?'

'Can she read our thoughts?' Alain asked John.

'It would appear so.'

Do not be so daft you two, she is an extremely bright girl with an aptitude for reading people.

'Come on, you two, tell me what happened.'

Barabal planted her hands on her hips, and John looked pointedly at Robert de Beaumont then at Alain, willing the boy to hold back key details of their evening until they were alone. De Beaumont intercepted the glance.

'I saw that, young man. I am not going anywhere until I have heard everything. So the sooner you start, the sooner we can all get some sleep before leaving for London at first light.'

The noble gestured to a table and, when they were all seated, he started.

'Well?'

Resigned to the fact they had no choice but to tell their tale, John let Lala out of his bag. The lamb wandered over to the fire and curled up. At first glance, anyone would think he slept, but John knew he kept a close eye on the door, ensuring their privacy. In the meantime, Alain had begun telling their adventures. De Beaumont sat back and regarded them both with a twinkle in his eyes, which changed to dismay when he heard about their run in with William de Breteuil.

'I do not know whether to be impressed at how much you learnt in such a short time, or annoyed at the havoc you caused in a delicate situation. I am leaning towards the latter, not least because you allowed my ward Stanislaus to return to a dangerous situation.'

'What about the fact de Breteuil is likely going to try and poison Prince Henry?' Alain asked. 'Surely that is important enough for Stanislaus to risk himself?'

Shaking his head, Sir Robert de Beaumont displayed his displeasure. 'Alain, all the royal family are aware of how easy it would be for someone to do away with them using poison. That is why any food served to the prince is tasted first.'

Alain remained unconvinced.

'The vial Master Bernard had contained arsenic. A big dose will kill quickly, but smaller doses over time can go undetected, and the prince would appear to become sick with a regular illness. If de Breteuil planned this well enough, we may not realise he was poisoning Prince Henry until it is too late.'

Robert de Beaumont considered this information but Barabal spoke up before he could answer.

'I agree de Breteuil might consider this if he had time. Alain, how long would this type of slow poisoning take?'

'Depending on how much he ingests, it might take weeks, or even months.'

'I think we can rule that out then. De Breteuil does not want Prince Henry to be crowned king, and the ceremony will happen in two days' time. He will need to go for a bold move,' Barabal informed them.

De Beaumont nodded his agreement. 'Barabal is right. He will need to kill Prince Henry as soon as possible, in a way that cannot be traced back to him. Especially so soon after one death in the family already this week.'

As he listened to the conversation something occurred to John.

'Umm, talking of murderers, did you recapture Walter Tirel?' De Beaumont looked up wearily, and John added, 'I shared his cell before he escaped. I thought him a good man. I just wondered what happened to him.'

De Beaumont considered John a moment longer before answering.

'We searched but could not find him in Winchester, so Prince Henry called things off. He was only locked up because de Breteuil was causing such a fuss, insisting he had proof Tirel plotted to kill the king. However, all those who were there agreed King William the Second's death was a tragic accident. In the end, Henry decided Walter Tirel's escape was the best way to end the matter.'

'Perhaps not his smartest decision,' Barabal said boldly, and de Beaumont raised an eyebrow at her outspoken comment.

'We may be speaking openly here, mistress, but do not take that as licence to say what you please. Calling the future king stupid is not wise any time.'

Barabal had the grace to blush, but she carried on regardless. 'I mean if Walter Tirel is on the loose, and Prince Henry dies before he can be crowned, then he would be a very useful scapegoat.'

'I am not sure that gives de Breteuil a free hand to murder Prince Henry,' Alain interrupted her. 'If the prince is murdered then Robert Curthose would be the one everyone suspected for both deaths, as he would be the only one to gain from them both. I believe many would only accept him as king if Prince Henry died by natural causes.'

'Prince Henry is a man in his prime and in excellent health. If he dies before being crowned, questions would be raised anyway,' John said.

'But if poisoning could not be proven, their suspicions would remain just that,' de Beaumont added. 'Barons do not like to delve too deeply into things if it is not in their best interests. If there was no obvious sign of foul play, they would be too busy jostling for position to think twice about Prince Henry's death.'

'All this talk gets us nowhere then.' John's exasperation spilled out.

'No, not quite,' Barabal said. 'Stanislaus is in the right place to help us, much though I dislike that we must leave him there.'

'And, in the meantime, we can keep an eye on the prince and anyone serving him,' Alain added. 'It is only two days until the ceremony. He should be safer once that is over.'

De Beaumont stood and stretched.

'Thank you all for your input, but I think what we need now is sleep. There is a tent set up outside for my men. You two boys can find a place to bed down there. I will sleep better myself if you are somewhere safe from de Breteuil's men.

'James will show you the way. Barabal, I will escort you to the ladies' chambers, they should be able to find you somewhere to lie. Tomorrow we shall all need our wits about us. So make sure you all get a good nights rest.'

Before leading Barabal away, Sir Robert de Beaumont ordered one of the servants to find his squire. As James arrived to take them to their quarters, John glanced over his shoulder to find a serving girl knock discreetly on the door to the prince's room. The door opened a crack, and Henry let the smiling girl in.

13

OFF TO LONDON

SO EXHAUSTED WAS he from lack of sleep the night before, John was snoring gently the minute his head hit the ground. Moments later, a cold nose pressed to his face, waking him instantly.

Did you forget something?

Oh, Lala, I am so sorry. I was so tired I forgot about you.

I would forgive you, but do you know how dangerous it is for a lamb to be wandering around a camp this size?

Dangerous, are you kidding me? John nearly laughed out loud. *With so many soldiers around, this is the safest place in the kingdom.*

I kid you not. Not everyone sees a cute animal as I wander passed. Some see their next meal.

John stopped laughing. He had not considered Lala to be a source of meat, which would put his life in danger anywhere food was scarce. If anything happened to Lala, not only would he lose a friend, he would also have lost his only chance of getting home. Feeling truly sorry, he opened his swag for the lamb to snuggle beside him.

I am sorry, Lala, I did not think. It will not happen again.

Do not fret, only the body I inhabit would die, but it would have been inconvenient

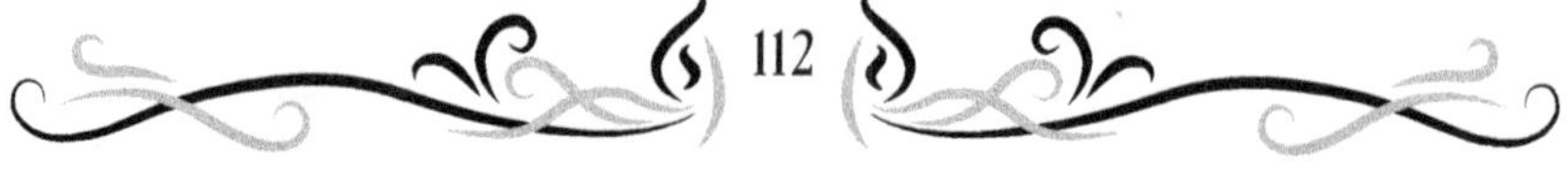

trying to find another way back here. I really must consider these things more carefully in the future.

The lamb curled up and promptly began snoring. John was not so lucky. Sleep now evaded him as thoughts chased each other through his head. *How do you stop someone from poisoning a person? Who was that girl who went into the prince's room? Would Stanislaus be all right? Would he ever get to go home?*

Hours later, snuggling into his swag, unanswerable questions still swirled in his mind as he fell into a restless sleep.

Awoken before dawn the next morning by the noise of breaking camp, John looked blearily over to Alain. Slow to wake, his companion rubbed his eyes as he sat up.

'You boys,' the captain who found them space last night stood over them. 'Roll up your beds, take some bread and a little cheese to break your fast. After, you best go and see to your mounts. We leave at sun up.

'Squire James said you are to ride with us today. So bring your horses back here. Seems you lads cannot be trusted on your own.' Amused, he barked out a laugh before going off to harass someone else.

Muttering under his breath, Alain began rolling up his bedding, and John followed suit with his bedroll. Then the two boys, accompanied by Lala, left the tent to grab some food and small beer from a passing servant before walking over to the stables. With so many people around, John thought it best to pop Lala in his bag, lest he end up in someone's cook pot.

The stable area was crowded, but the boys easily found their tack out by the field where they left their horses the evening before. Surprised de Breteuil had not reclaimed them, they nevertheless readied all three mounts and, leaving Barabal's horse tied to the fence, they led their own back to the camp.

They were early and had to wait while the guards finished packing up. John took the time to watch the others they would journey to London with. Differing uniforms highlighted the number of barons, each with their own retinue, preparing for the day's ride. John realised he had not seen a single noblewoman in the company.

'Where are their wives?' he asked Alain.

'They will be coming by cart, I suppose. If they left yesterday morning, by my estimate they will not arrive in London until tomorrow.'

Question answered, John searched for and found William de Breteuil's men. Stanislaus stood among them and, even though the other boy made a point of ignoring them, it was a relief to see him well and unharmed. John

felt a tap on his shoulder and turned to find a tired looking Tom.

'I finally found you. Your friend gave me a message. He said to tell you he is fine, but he needs to speak with you urgently. If he can sneak away when you stop for food at noon, he will tell you then.'

'Thank you, Tom, you have been more than helpful,' John told the young man.

'I hope you did not get into trouble for yesterday,' Alain said.

The boy's face broke into a grin. 'My captain was not happy and I kept waiting for him to give me a punishment. This morning, before we came off duty, your Mistress Barabal turned up to thank the Captain for letting me help you both. I have never seen anyone charm the captain like she did. He tripped over himself, offering to help with anything else she needed in the future. Made me feel quite sick.'

'That is our Barabal,' Alain said in an offhand way.

John turned and considered the boy. He was always complimenting Barabal. Was there something more to their friendship? As if the other boy sensed his interest, he cleared his throat and carried on.

'I am pleased you did not receive any punishment for helping us. Perhaps we can meet again on our way back through to Winchester and share an ale in the tavern.'

'I would like that. I must be off to bed now. I am working again tonight, I am afraid. Safe travels.' Tom waved farewell over his shoulder as he returned to the guard's barracks.

'Speak of the devil,' John said as he caught sight of Barabal leading her horse over to Sir Robert de Beaumont.

She now wore a type of divided skirt so she could ride along with everyone else without showing her legs. James helped her up as the rest of their party mounted. A cart loaded with extra bedding and some of the prince's own servants left the courtyard as more of the barons began to appear. As he moved out of its way, he noticed the pretty serving girl he saw with the prince last night sitting up by the driver.

'Who is she?' John asked Alain, nodding his head at the girl.

The boy turned from glaring at Squire James, who seemed to be taking an extraordinary amount of time getting Barabal settled on her horse, to study the girl John indicated.

'I do not know her. She is not one of the staff from Winchester, and to my knowledge she did not come with the royal party. Prince Henry probably picked her up somewhere. He does that quite a bit I am told.'

Losing interest, he swung his gaze back around to Barabal. John's focus, however, did not waiver. There was something about the girl he did not like. He could not say why, but he thought someone should keep an eye on her. He followed the cart out of town until a commotion by the stables caused him to turn away.

A squire, dressed in de Breteuil's colours, held onto a midnight black stallion, who clearly did not like being around other animals.

'De Breteuil always likes the showy one,' one of the men beside John muttered. 'A pity none of his people can control the beast.'

Horses near the stallion started stamping and shuffling nervously, then the unthinkable happened. The animal jerked his head and the lead rein slipped from the squire's hand. The animal reared up on its hind legs, causing a nearby horse to shuffle to the side, its rider barely able to keep his seat. Another horse bolted back towards the stables, still another bucked and threw his rider to the ground.

'Blast it, boy, what do you think you are doing?' William of Breteuil emerged from behind the building just as his horse's hooves hit the ground and he made ready to rear again. The baron cuffed his charge round the ears and grabbed the reigns before the stallion could make best use of his freedom. 'Get out of my sight, you useless good-for-nothing,' he yelled at the boy as he mounted the beast.

Dropping his head, embarrassed by his master in front of the gathered nobility, the squire went off to find his own mount.

'Poor lad, even the stable master had difficulty with that animal last night,' one of Robert de Beaumont's men commented.

'Not a very forgiving nature for a man of god,' his companion agreed.

The squire came back with his own horse, head still hung low. The noble's behaviour worried John. What if Stanislaus displeased him? Would he receive the same treatment as the squire—or worse?

'Alain, that guard called Sir William de Breteuil "a man of god", that is the second time I have heard someone call him that. What do they mean?'

Already in his saddle, Alain glanced down at John. 'Did you not know? De Breteuil is not only a baron, he is also the Abbot of Breteuil.'

'An abbot? If he is a clergyman he should not be so involved in worldly affairs and politics.' John pondered this new information as he hauled himself into the saddle.

'You do hold some funny ideas.' Alain laughed. 'William was made Abbot

of Breteuil because the abbey brings with it a sizeable income. Also the land the monastery sits on gives him considerable influence in the court in Normandie, and here as well.'

'Oh. Is that allowed?' John asked, thinking about the ramshackle house the priest back home lived in, and the time he spent helping poor people in the community.

'If you pay enough money to the right people almost anything is allowed, barring murder. Although, to be truthful, if you pay the right people even that is acceptable.' Alain turned his horse, ready to follow de Beaumont's guards out of Guildford.

John climbed into the saddle and followed his friend, thinking that medieval Briton was nothing at all like the fairy tale his mother read to him.

THE LONG COLUMN of nobles did not move as fast as they travelled the day before. Consequently, John found the trip, on the whole, boring. There were only so many fields and small villages you could go through in one day without wishing to see something else.

When they stopped at lunch, he and Alain drifted away and sat, backs against a tree, waiting for Stanislaus to join them. When it became apparent de Breteuil was intent on keeping a close watch on him, they tried to join the group. Any time they wandered near, guards stopped them and turned them away. Only when Stanislaus went to relieve himself behind some bushes and the squire accompanied him, did the boys give up trying to meet with their friends.

Barabal, likewise, was off limits. She sat with the prince's company, eating and laughing, behaving as though she did not have a care in the world.

The girl John worried about served the noon meal, along with the other servants from the cart. Through half closed eyes he spied on her until he realised she did not hand anything directly to Prince Henry. Instead she gave food and drink to a young man sitting nearby, who sampled everything before handing it over to the prince to eat.

'There is not any amount you could pay me to do that job,' John said to Alain.

'He is not paid exactly,' the other boy told him. 'He is a convicted criminal, sentenced to death. He would have been given the option to serve one year as a food taster for the prince, or be hung by the neck. If he survives the

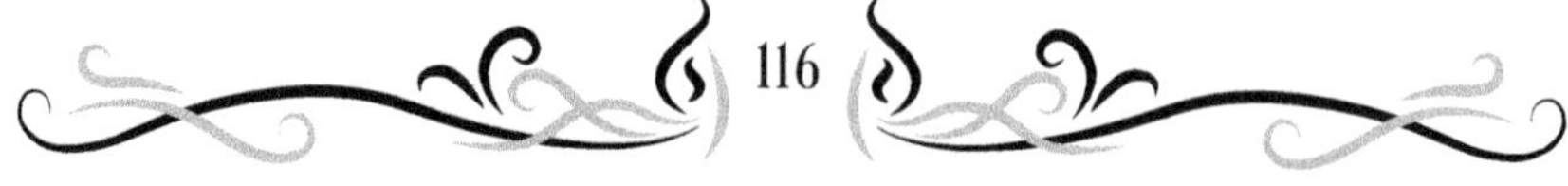

year, he earns his freedom and a purse of gold. If the prince dies from poison and he lives, he will be killed and his family will also be sentenced to death. So he chose to do this.'

'Not much of a choice though, is it?' John said, thinking this was just one more example of how barbaric this place was. 'I wonder what type of man would put his family at risk in such a way?'

'A man whose family will not survive for long if he is not around. It is truly a job for the desperate.'

When servants started packing up food, it acted as a signal for everyone else to mount up and continue on to London. John sighed, not looking forward to more hours in the saddle. As a boy, he dreamed of having his own horse and travelling the land. His dream would have been quite different if he had realised how boring and painful it would be.

On the other hand, Alain was terribly excited. He found joy in almost every new place they passed through. John tried not to dampen the boy's spirit, after all, he had never left Winchester before.

When John himself had first heard they were going to London, he too had been eager to go there. His mother always talked about the city as being magnificent, full of wonder and surprises. She had only visited it once on the way to Portsmouth from Northampton, but her time there had given her fond memories. From her description of England's capital city, John had pictured it as a place of excitement and lights and bustle.

The London he came upon at the end of a long day's ride was far different to the one his mother described. As he surveyed the city in the distance, he estimated it might be around the size of Brisbane, which he knew from school had a population of around eighteen thousand people.

Its dwellings clustered around the River Thames, including a large stone tower, a grand church and another palace made of wood. If forced to describe it, he would have said it was grey and smoggy, with not a sparkling light in sight.

'Holy Mother Mary,' Alain whispered in awe. 'Have you ever seen such a huge place? And look, there are King William the Second's masterpieces; The Great Tower, Westminster Cathedral and Westminster Palace. Although it is wrong so much of our taxes were spent to build them, I do feel a certain pride now I see how magnificent they are.'

Secretly, John thought Brisbane was more splendid. But he guessed for the time they were living in, and given the towns and villages they travelled through that day, it was a little impressive. His opinion changed as they road

through the streets on the south side of the Thames.

The smell overwhelmed him, and the filth littering the road turned his stomach. This place was a breeding ground for all manner of disease. Alain also wrinkled his nose in distaste, his view of London a little tarnished by this introduction.

As they passed by a group of beggars completely covered in rags, not a piece of skin showing, the column gave them a wide birth. This surprised John as other beggars on their journey had been given some coin, then were moved out of the way.

'What is that about?' John leant over to ask Alain.

'Do you not have lepers where you come from?'

'Lepers?'

'Yes, they have a disease that eats away at the body. It is passed on through touch, so few people want to go near any of the sufferers. I am surprised to find them begging for alms in a city as they tend to live in colonies, hidden away from the general population.'

'Is there no cure?'

'I guess if there are none where you are from there must be, it is just we have not found it yet.'

Soon after, the column came to a wooden bridge, where their progress slowed. The river crossing only took a few horses at a time, and they were at the back of the party. As the sun began to set over the Thames and the buildings of London, John had never felt further from his home.

Finally it was their turn to cross the water, and John did so with some trepidation. The gaps between the planks were wide enough for him to see the water rushing below. He marvelled that the gushing tide did not take this flimsy bridge with it. Like many others, he heaved a sigh of relief when he reached the other side safely.

Wearily, de Beaumont's group entered the precinct around Westminster. Many of the other barons and lords had left the group on the way, heading for their London houses. A few barons, including Sir Robert de Beaumont, Sir William de Breteuil, and Ranulf Flambard, elected to stay at the palace with the prince.

Servants appeared from nowhere to take care of the horses and escort everyone to the accommodation prepared for them. Alain spoke to someone and waved for John to follow.

As the servant led them through the grounds through a series of buildings,

Alain explained Master Gavin suggested he try to stay with local apothecaries where he could. They were like a brotherhood and would take care of their own.

'Besides, if we stay there, we can stay out of William de Breteuil's way, while still being close to the action,' the boy added.

They followed their guide through to a smaller courtyard containing a cluster of stone buildings. Making for the one on the far end, he lifted the latch and opened the door.

'Master Barwick prefers to stay at his shop unless he is called to the castle for an emergency, but he often has visiting apothecaries staying,' the servant said as he showed them into the dwelling. 'The work room is at the front, and the sleeping room at the back. Old Barwick is particular about his workroom, so I would not touch anything here unless you check with him first. I will ask one of the kitchen staff to tell him you are here when they go to the markets tomorrow.

'Perhaps you would like to take a look around the grounds until I can find a maid with time to bring you fresh linen. Oh yes, there are limited cooking facilities here, so you can take your meals in the kitchen with the staff.'

With those last instructions, the servant left in a rush, no doubt he had a lot of additional work to do with so many people arriving.

John surveyed the ill-kept rooms. The dried herbs hanging from the ceiling sported a thick layer of dust, as did the rows of glass jars arranged neatly on shelves. Even a small stack of books that had fallen over on a work desk under the window cried neglect. In front of them, a well worn work table with benches tucked underneath dominated the room. Behind it, in front of the fireplace, sat two threadbare, but comfortable looking chairs.

Alain entered and headed towards the back door, which led to the bedroom. He opened it to reveal an enormous bed with a rolled up mattress at one end. John joined him, and together they unrolled the pallet.

'What luxury,' Alain exclaimed when they realised the mattress was filled with sheep's wool rather than straw. 'Master Barwick must be a wealthy man if his shop accommodation is better than this.'

John privately thought he and Alain had very different ideas of luxury. His mother would be appalled to think her son slept on anything other than sheep's wool. Before he could voice his opinions though, a knock on the door admitted a maid carrying sheets and blankets.

'I am here to make the bed,' the middle aged woman announced. With her hair escaping her cap, and a blushing red face, she looked more harried

than the servant who escorted them here, if that were possible.

'Here, let me take that,' John said as he relieved her of her bundle. 'We can make our own bed,' he told her as he spotted Lala.

Having escaped John's bag, the lamb stared forlornly at the unlit grate.

'If you could send someone to light the fire that will be all we need, thank you.'

The grateful woman thanked them, and quickly departed. Alain and John made the bed and stowed their possessions in the bedroom, then looked at each other.

'Food?' they both said together, and laughed.

Lala, do you want to come with us? John asked.

No, I am fine here. The lamb bedded down on the rushes in front of the fireplace. *I do not think anything of note will happen today, and I have some thinking to do.*

'Come on,' Alain called. 'We want to get something to eat before they start feeding the nobles, otherwise we will have a long wait.'

14

UNCOVERING THE REAL ENEMY

JOHN AND ALAIN exited their quarters into the castle precinct, trying to decide the most likely location of the kitchen.

'Inside?' John asked.

'Are you mad? The palace is made mostly of wood, it would be too dangerous to house a large kitchen inside.' He surveyed the area and pointed to a young boy carrying a basket filled with logs. 'We follow him. That much wood must be for the kitchen fires.'

Shrugging his shoulders, John followed Alain, who followed the boy, who led them round the corner to a stone building that appeared to house the guard quarters. Thinking Alain had made a mistake, he turned and found another stone building behind them, snug up against the wall of the palace. With the double doors thrown wide open, framing two huge fires and showing a number of staff running around preparing food, it had to be the kitchen. He elbowed Alain, and the boy turned with a grin spreading across his face.

The two boys wandered over and looked around, trying to work out where the servants would usually eat. Unable to find what they were looking for, they approached the young boy, who was busy stacking his wood by the fire.

'Can you tell us where the staff table is?' Alain asked, and the boy glanced

up, bewildered.

'Whadaya want?'

A voice came from behind and they turned to find a huge man with meaty arms and clothing covered in grease glowering at them. With a wicked looking knife in his hand, and his unwelcoming stare, John was not sure he wanted to answer.

'We are looking for the servant's table,' Alain said, backing up a little from the rather threatening figure.

'Well you asked the wrongun. He cannot hear or speak. You arrived with the prince then?'

When Alain nodded, the cook asked, 'And you are?'

'I am Sir Robert de Beaumont's apothecary, and this is my helper.'

John had to admit he did not sound very convincing.

The man before him raised an eyebrow, folding his arms over his chest.

'Well, of course I am not a full apothecary yet.' The words tumbled out of Alain's mouth as if they had a will of their own. 'But my master trusted me enough to come here in his stead.'

The man laughed and his whole demeanour changed. 'We all start somewhere, lad, and if your master trusts you enough to come here by yourself, then that is good enough for me. Perhaps while you are staying you might take a look at some of the palace staff for us. Just some minor ailments, too small for Master Barwick to bother with now he has moved to town.'

Alain stood taller, changing from the boy he was, to the professional he would become.

'Of course I will. My supply of medicines is only small, but if Master Barwick will let me use some of his stock, I should be able to treat most common ailments.'

'I am sure it will be much appreciated. Now, I must return to my meat. It would not do to let anything burn with our guests being who they are. Take a seat and someone will bring food by-the-by.'

John started through the door the cook indicated, and found himself in a room filled with a square wooden table. Twenty people would comfortably find seating on the benches tucked beneath. On the other side of the table the wall was broken by another door.

'So staff can come and go as they are called to serve,' Alain explained. 'It will lead to the palace proper.'

As they were the first people to arrive for supper, it felt strange sitting

alone at one end of such a huge table waiting to be served. They had not been seated long when a kitchen hand rushed in, dropped some wooden bowls in front of them, and rushed out again. He returned with two pitchers filled with ale, spilling liquid on the table as he plunked them down beside some wooden cups, before bustling out.

John's mouth watered at the smells coming from the kitchen, but the boy did not return with food. They waited patiently, but no one brought them anything to put on the plates they had liberated from the stack. Alain had risen to go and find out what caused the delay, when the door from the palace opened.

Sitting back down, the two boys watched as the servants from Winchester who travelled with them to London entered and arranged themselves around the other end of the table. No one spoke. Silently they each took a plate from the stack, and one of them filled cups of small beer from the jugs or their group. They did not so much as acknowledge the boys. Alain glanced at John and smirked, ready to have some fun.

'So, Tobias, you wrangled yourself a trip to London.'

One of the oldest of the group peered down his nose at Alain, then turned away as if it was beneath him to answer the boy.

'In Winchester he ate with the servants in the hall. How it must gall him to be forced to eat in here with us. They will probably expect him to serve the nobility later. That will put him in his place,' Alain whispered to John.

'Mmm,' John answered, too distracted by the girl who slipped into Prince Henry's room the night before to pay full attention to Alain and his teasing.

As he regarded her, he caught her glancing back at him and Alain, trying not to be seen to be doing so. Her eyes met his as she reached for a drink, and he jerked back in surprise at the hatred they contained.

He wondered what he had done to earn that sort of response from a complete stranger. Before he could tell Alain, his attention wavered as a platter piled with steaming hot meat, and bread warm from the oven, was placed in front of him. His stomach's need took over and John pushed all thoughts of the strange girl to the back of his mind. Later, as he left the table, John tried to remember the last time his stomach had been this full, and could not.

'Agh, my stomach is like a drum. Maybe we should have a bit of a walk before heading back,' John suggested. 'Perhaps we will run into Stanislaus or Barabal and find out what they are up to.'

'They will be eating with the great of the land in the dining hall. We might take a wander past there on the way back,' Alain conceded.

They left the servant's dining room by the door into the palace. As they did, someone tightly gripped John's arm, pulling him backwards. He turned to find the girl glaring at him with such intense hatred he took a step back. Her grip tightened and her fingers dug into his arm.

'Tell your guardian to stay away. This one is already lost. If you continue to thwart me, I will make it my mission to ensure you and your guardian never leave this time.' She abruptly released his arm, turned on her heel and stalked off towards the hall.

Alain, realising John had not followed, turned around and stared in confusion as the serving girl passed him.

'What did she want?' Alain's eyes automatically followed the attractive servant as she strode away.

'I am not sure,' John said. 'I am pretty certain she just threatened me. We need to talk with Lala before we catch up with the others.'

AND YOU ARE SURE *she is not part of the Winchester staff?* Lala asked Alain again.

I told you, I never saw her before today, Alain answered, his tone petulant as he repeated himself.

I found her entering the prince's room last night, John said. *Then I saw her with the other staff from Guildford today, attending to the prince and his group.*

This is not good. Lala paced the room.

Why not? Do you not understand what she said?

Worried by the lamb's tone of voice, John knew the answer was going to be something he would not like. Lala did not answer immediately, which concerned John even more. Ignoring them, the lamb paced around the room for some time, before coming to a stop in front of the two boys.

With the unplanned turn of events around King William's death, we had not expected them to be here. At the very least, we did not think they would arrive so fast. Especially as in the grand scheme of things, this was such a small change to the course of history. The second King William would have died next month of a heart attack, so Prince Henry will only be taking the crown a month early. Lala paused before continuing.

I chose Henry's coronation as my first solo assignment purely because it should have been simple. Free from outside interference. Mmm, maybe it is not that they arrived so quickly, maybe they were here before us. That would explain it. Why did no one notice and send me a warning? Lala pondered out loud.

THE GUARDIANS OF TIME: SWAGMAN

Lala, who are they? John's exasperation at Lala's meanderings came through loud and clear.

They do not have a name as such, we call them the Time Wreckers. Lala sighed in John's head. *The universe must be in balance. Where there is good, there is evil. Where forces work to bring about harmony and progress in the world, forces working for chaos and regression will also be found. I believe your maid is one of them, one of the wreckers.*

John let loose with a string of curses that would have been right at home in a shearing shed. When he calmed down, he glared at the lamb in front of him and spoke his frustrations out loud.

'You bring me here with next to no information, to make sure something totally out of my control happens, forgetting to tell me this is your first solo mission. Now you inform me all along we had some other organisation working against us, trying to prevent Prince Henry from becoming king. Have you forgotten to let me know about anything else?'

Some part of John was aware Alain stared, opened mouthed, trying to take in what was happening between John and the Time Guardian. However, with all his energy focused on trying to deal with everything he had learnt today, John did not have the capacity to help his friend deal with this.

There is one positive thing to come out of this encounter. Lala's tone was conciliatory.

'Really? It had better be good, because at the moment I do not see how we can stop both the forces of chaos and a noble intent on Prince Henry's death, when we cannot even access two of our helpers to warn them of this new development,' John spat out at the lamb, his anger still not yet under control.

The universe places limitations on how we are able to affect events in other times, the lamb offered. *We cannot just turn up and kill someone to make sure an event does or does not go ahead. We also cannot initiate some new course of action a person from the time has not thought of themselves. All we are capable of doing is ensuring an existing plan moves things in the right direction.*

John paced the room, trying to digest this new information.

'Let me get this straight. Neither she nor I can take any direct action against a person in this time, we have to work with the people from here. That is why I am with Alain, Barabal and Stanislaus. So, it stands to reason she is working with someone else too.'

I believe so, or at the very least, she is searching for someone to work with.

John's thoughts were spinning out of control, and he was having difficulty wrangling them into a logical pattern. A random thought popped into his mind then out of his mouth before he could stop it.

'Hold on, what about when Alain and Stanislaus broke me out of prison and released Walter Tirel. In the other time line, did he escape?'

No, because in the original timeline Walter Tirel never shot an arrow at the king. The hunt was successful and King William the Second held his barons' court, imposing another tax levy. The barons did not take the additional monetary burden well. The stress this placed on King William, combined with the worry of trying to squeeze blood from a stone to keep his court running, placed too much strain on his heart. The fact he over-indulged his appetite cannot have helped either.

Lala froze, cocked his head to the side, then carried on. *Now I think on it, Time Wreckers may have worked to ensure Tirel's arrow hit the king, and they may also have been behind his capture. If they succeeded in having him tried for murder, and were able to link everything to Prince Henry, Robert Curthose would be crowned king unopposed.*

The funny thing is universal balance will be maintained, come what may. If they interfered beyond their remit, then the universe would work to rebalance everything. So it was perhaps no coincidence you were in Walter's cell, and that he escaped when you did.

John continued pacing until he calmed down, and things started to fit together in his mind.

'How could they make sure Tirel's arrow hit the king?'

Lala did not answer, he simply stared at John, as if saying "look at me".

'Ah, they could have taken the form of a stag and set everything up.'

Yes, that is certainly one possibility.

'All right, so they would have acted directly and put things out of balance. If I do something other than help, the universe will do something to place things back in balance too?'

Of course. That is why I counselled you to keep quiet and let things take their own course. I wonder if the universe conspired to have you and Tirel share a cell, and then be released together to realign things.

John thought some more, and paced some more, and then stopped in the middle of the room. Thoughts were still chasing each other inside his head, refusing to be tamed into a useful pattern. He was aware time was running out, so they needed to focus on things they were able to do.

'This Time Wrecker is likely to be working with someone else,' John said.

That is possible. And, if she is working with someone, we need to find out who.

'I believe we already know who it is. If Walter Tirel never killed the king, it is likely the person who captured him and proposed the idea of a conspiracy is the one working with the Time Wreckers.'

Pieces began falling into place for John, much like the old jigsaw he and

his brothers used to put together.

That is as good a place to start as any.

'Well, Walter Tirel told me it was de Breteuil who lay in wait for him when he returned to get what he needed to escape the country. I think it is safe to assume he is part of the same plot. Now we know who is behind everything, and who is going to administer the poison.'

'How did you make that leap?' Alain had closed his mouth and now tried to follow John's deductive reasoning.

'Prince Henry has an eye for pretty ladies and I saw that serving girl slip into his room last night, and none of the guards stopped her to check her over. What better way to by-pass the Prince's food tasters than using the woman warming his bed?'

Alain stared into the distance for a moment, brow furrowed in thought, then asked, 'Did you see her take in any food with her last night? Or witness the prince taking anything directly from her hand today?'

John considered the question for a moment, then shook his head. 'I am quite sure she had nothing with her yesterday, and she would not be foolish enough to feed poison to the prince in plain sight. I think we need to stop her from taking anything into the prince's room tonight.'

John felt much better knowing their task was not insurmountable. He and Alain needed to figure out how to watch the prince's bedroom without being moved on by his guards. As he pondered this question, the door to their rooms flung open and Stanislaus barged through.

'I have it,' he told them, his face breaking into a grin. 'De Breteuil bought poison in Guildford and a serving girl is willing to give it to the prince. She is biding her time, earning his trust, so she can slip it into his food when she joins him tonight.'

'We know,' Alain responded for them all, and Stanislaus' expression turned from pleased to crestfallen.

'If you knew, why did you make me stay with that prat?'

'We only just now realised, literally moments before you arrived,' Alain said. 'The serving girl gave herself away, and we only now worked out she is in league with de Breteuil. If she had not slipped up, you would have been the only one who knew.' Alain mollified his friend, and John could see Stanislaus perk up. 'At least now we know you do not need to return to de Breteuil's rooms.'

At that, Stanislaus looked sheepish. 'I could not go back anyway. I am

afraid I broke and told him on reflection I thought Prince Henry would make a better king than Robert Curthose. I mean, the man he thinks would be the best ruler for Briton is dull as dishwater. He has not got an original thought in his head. My father despises the man. De Breteuil turned beetroot red and told me to get out and never darken his door again.'

'Well, now we know what is happening, you are better off being as far away from that man as possible.' Alain reassured his friend. 'You are welcome to bunk here with us, or I am sure Sir Robert de Beaumont would be pleased if you returned to his service. We explained to him you had not actually joined with de Breteuil, but were spying for us. I am sure if you tell him what you told us, you will be welcomed back as the hero you are.'

How else were we going to explain how we made the connection? Alain responded to John's unasked question as they left the room in search of de Beaumont. *I cannot see the prince or Sir Robert de Beaumont believing in guardians and time travel, no matter how enlightened they both are.*

BARABAL MOVED THE food from her plate to her mouth without being aware of what she was eating, so intently was she watching the action at the top table. The serving girl she had taken the wine from last night was paying far too much attention to Prince Henry, and for some unknown reason that annoyed her.

It was not that she wished herself in the girl's place, attracting the attention of the future king for her own ends, Barabal considered that the wrong type of recognition. Although from birth girls were drilled to believe looks were important to attract a husband of the right type, no matter how beautiful a girl was she could not marry above her station. A prince would never marry someone who served him. Which meant the girl must be trying to attract his attention for other reasons.

What could the girl gain from a relationship with a prince? Prince Henry had a wandering eye, but he also had a reputation for leaving behind broken hearts, and often children in his wake. Lower bred mothers were paid off, and left in positions where they were despised by the other staff. It was only the women of noble birth who were looked after, and their offspring raised as nobles.

Sighing, Barabal admitted she was a little jealous of the regard that particular

serving girl received from the males in the room. Everyone from boys to old men followed her figure with longing gazes. Although she knew her own features to be pleasing, with dark brown eyes set in an oval face all framed by wavy brown hair, it was her body that did not attract the eye. Her petite, slim frame, showed little promise of gaining curves as she moved into womanhood, and would never be able to compete with someone like the maid.

Not only did the serving girl have midnight black hair and startling blue eyes set in the face of an angel, she also had all the right curves in all the right places. As she moved through a room, men stopped what they were doing and followed her with their eyes.

She shook the dark thoughts from her head. No use worrying over something you could not change. Instead she decided she may as well try and figure out what about the girl made her feel uneasy. What would she gain from this type of attention?

Leaning her head on her hand as she studied the girl, she earned a sharp reprimand for poor table manners from the lady sitting next her. Biting back a retort about how silly it was to worry about elbows on the table lest her bad manners be reported back to Sir Robert de Beaumont, she realised the object of her scrutiny no longer stood behind the prince. A scan of the room confirmed she had disappeared.

Politely excusing herself from the table, she slipped through the hall's side door. Upon finding the corridor empty, she quietly tiptoed down towards the entranceway. Peeking around the corner she found it empty. Drawing her head back, she caught a movement over by the door to the servant's dining hall. While wondering how she might get closer to overhear the conversation, her eye was drawn by a movement.

Risking a quick look around the corner again, she observed de Breteuil calmly walking out from the shadows. As he returned to dine, he did not so much as even glance her way. Still unnoticed, she decided to wait and find out who he was talking to. Her patience was rewarded with the sight of the maid entering the servant's dining room and shutting the door behind her.

Well, how interesting. All the pieces tumbling round in her head fell into place. That was how Sir William de Breteuil would gain access to poison the prince. Smiling to herself, she could not wait to let the boys in on her triumph.

15

STALKING THE PRINCE

THE THREE BOYS rushed to the dining hall, only to find they need not have hurried as the court had not long started dinner. Peeking through the door, they found Barabal sitting with some of the other palace women looking completely bored. Catching sight of her friends, she excused herself and exited the hall.

'You all took your time.' She grabbed Stanislaus by the arm and led them out into the courtyard where they could speak without being overheard. 'I have been waiting ages for you to come and find me. I think one of the serving girls is up to something. I caught her talking with William de Breteuil earlier. I want you to follow her and find out if she is in on their plot.'

'The dark haired one? She is, de Breteuil is plotting with her to poison Prince Henry before the coronation,' Stanislaus told her, pride sounding in his voice. 'I overheard them talking.'

Barabal's mouth formed an "O". 'You know already.' Deflated, she was quick to recover her poise as she instructed them, 'We need to stop her.'

'Of course we do,' Alain said. 'But how?'

'We should knock her over the head, tie her up and stick her somewhere,' Stanislaus announced.

His three companions glared at him, but the boy did not back down.

'It might not be the best plan, but it is a plan. And it will be pretty effective.'

Although he had some ideas of how they should proceed, John remembered what Lala said, and he decided the others should be left to come up with a way forward themselves.

'The wench wormed her way into Prince Henry's bed to gain access to kill him. Barabal, maybe you can oust her. You would be better for Prince Henry anyway.' Stanislaus' second plan was met with the same, if not more, disdain than his first.

'Are you mad?' Barabal's body tensed with suppressed anger. 'Is that all you think a woman is good for? Warming a man's bed? And do you think so little of me that you would ask me to use my body in that way?'

Rising anger caused her to run out of words, so she settled for clenching her fist and punching Stanislaus right in the stomach. The boy doubled over, looking sorry for himself.

'Barabal, my apologies, I did not think. Of course I would not want you to become Prince Henry's mistress, well, not unless you wanted to. You are worth more than that. I thought maybe he might fall in love with you and take you for his queen. You would be such a great queen.'

In the face of Stanislaus' boyish romanticism, Barabal's anger washed away.

'Oh, Stanislaus, you numbskull. Prince Henry brokered a marriage with Princess Edith. And even if he were not betrothed, he would never marry anyone as low born as me. Besides, when I wed, it will be to someone who treats me as an equal, not as something pretty to hang off their arm. I hope one of you can come up with a better plan.'

Directing her comments to Alain and John, she waited for them to answer. Alain remained thoughtful, but said nothing. It was left to John to outline the plan he and Alain discussed earlier. However, before he had a chance, Stanislaus showed he was not yet done.

'Why do we not just tell de Beaumont? He would then be able to keep the prince safe and we could enjoy the festivities.'

Barabal at least did him the courtesy of thinking his idea through before dismissing it, which showed John how much the girl thought of the squire.

'Stanislaus you were not there when Sir Robert de Beaumont assured us the prince had enough safeguards to prevent him from being poisoned. I really do not believe he will change his mind and talk to the prince. I can already hear him saying speculation is not evidence.'

Even though Barabal let the squire down gently this time, he still slumped his shoulders in defeat. John decided now was the best time to offer their alternative idea.

'Alain and I discussed this before, and we believe we only need to make sure the serving girl takes no food or drink into the room when she goes to meet with Prince Henry in private.'

'Sounds easy enough.' Barabal nodded. 'I think we can use an alcove not far from the prince's bedroom. If we watch the room, we can stop her from entering with anything in her hands.

'We will take turns. John, you and I will take the first watch after dinner. Alain, you and Stanislaus will relieve us after the three am bell is rung.

'Right, I best get back to the meal. I can make sure he eats nothing the others do not while I am around. John, wait outside the door and join me once the meal is over.'

Orders issued, Barabal swept past them and returned to the dining hall, not even pausing to check they agreed with her plan.

'I AM OFF to find some food, then to see if I can bunk in with James tonight,' Stanislaus told them, happy to be free from Sir William de Breteuil's clutches. 'Alain, come wake me at three.'

'I will need to, because you sleep like a log and will never hear the bell,' Alain said under his breath as his friend walked away. 'Wait up, Stanislaus, I might join you for some more supper. See you after three,' he called back over his shoulder to John.

With everyone else having something to do, John found himself at a loose end. Casually kicking at a loose tile, he decided he may as well wait for Barabal closer to the action. Snooping through the door he saw serving staff lined around the wall, waiting for instructions.

Guessing with this many new people no one would notice an additional face, he slipped into the room and made his way to a gap behind Barabal. The only sign she noticed his entrance was the way she deliberately glanced away as he neared her table.

After a short time, John's legs began to cramp from standing still for so long. He shuffled from foot to foot, while trying to keep an eye on the room. Compared to everyone else, de Breteuil and his retinue were sombre. Once

again they were not seated at the top table, a sign of disfavour for someone so high born, or so he gathered from the comments the boy beside him made when he caught John watching the nobleman. Given his objections to Prince Henry taking the crown of Briton, he understood the apparent demotion, but he did not share this with his informant.

Surveying the top table, he managed to catch de Beaumont's eye. The Baron tilted his head in acknowledgement, and returned to his conversation. However, John still could not find the one person he was looking for.

As servants placed yet another course of food on the tables, he finally found his target. The girl busied herself serving the prince, making a point of not serving Prince Henry himself, but placing the dish of steaming fish down in front of the poor condemned man to test before the prince ate. Almost as though she felt John's gaze, she raised her head and sent a look that could only be read as a challenge in his direction.

'Pretty, that Isolde, isn't she? I suggest you stay away from her though. All her time is spent trying to catch a prince, and she won't let anything get in her way,' his servant friend murmured.

John responded by shuffling his feet again, wondering just how long this meal would take.

'New to this?' his companion asked. 'There are still two more courses to go. It helps if you stand one foot flat, use the toes of the other foot to balance, then two feet, then the other foot. You will not fidget so much that way.'

'Thank you,' John whispered, and tried following his suggestion. Although still tiring, it was decidedly easier on his legs. Even so, his feet were nearly numb by the time the prince stood and ended the meal.

John slipped in behind Barabal as she left. The girl led them down the corridor to the sleeping quarters. When he caught her up, she was speaking to de Beaumont. She was explaining she needed an excuse to be gone from the women's quarters for the evening, an excuse that would not tarnish her reputation. De Beaumont thought for a moment before he responded.

'Perhaps I could take ill and send you to Master Barwick for a remedy. John and Squire James can accompany you. I will send James along to bring Master Barwick regardless. If something actually does happen to the prince, it would be best for a trained apothecary to be on hand. If he is not poisoned, I am sure Prince Henry would welcome him at the coronation tomorrow.'

'Excellent thinking, thank you, sir. Come, John, let us take our position for the night.'

'You told de Beaumont about the poison. I thought we were not going to?' he whispered as they left the baron behind.

'I had to tell him why I needed to be out tonight didn't I?' She said no more, clearly not feeling the need to explain herself any further.

Turning down another hallway, Barabal pointed to an alcove with a table.

'It is where the maids place dishes and bedding and the like when serving this far away from the kitchen and laundry,' Barabal explained. 'Here, give me a hand.'

John helped her move the furniture back into the corner. This made enough room for one person to sit on the table and another to stand beside without being seen, unless you specifically looked into the space.

They started with John sitting and Barabal standing, because she said she was too full after her evening meal to sit comfortably. They swapped places some time later. Then changed again, and once more, before anyone came down the corridor.

Remaining statue still as the prince passed by, flanked by two men and followed by two guards, the pair only relaxed when the group stopped by the prince's door. John knew Ranulf Flambard, but not the other man who wore the robes of a cleric.

'Archbishop Anslem,' Barabal mouthed.

'Everything is ready for the coronation in the abbey tomorrow,' the cleric told the prince. 'However I shall need the document containing your written promises to the church before we proceed.'

'My scribes are working on the final copy now. When I checked earlier today, they assured me they would be finished tomorrow morning. There will be ample time to peruse it before you place the crown on my head in the afternoon.

'Now Ranulf will escort you out, I need to get some sleep before meeting with the barons early tomorrow. They too want to finalise our agreement before the ceremony.'

The prince's tone was firm but polite, and John had noted a weariness around his eyes as he passed their hiding place. Three days of travelling took its toll on a person, and no doubt the prince had been working late into the night as well. John sympathised as he stifled his own yawn.

'Your Highness.'

The cleric bobbed his head as the prince opened the door to his room and closed it behind himself, ensuring the meeting ended.

'He is true to his word?' the archbishop asked Ranulf.

'Yes, I checked the document myself, and everything you asked for is included. He is perhaps the only one of William the Conqueror's spawn you can actually trust.'

'Perfect. Shall we seal this with some more wine?'

No sooner had their voices faded than new footsteps echoed down the corridor. They were lighter and quieter, and John guessed they belonged to a female. He confirmed his suspicions when he stepped out into the path of Isolde. Barabal moved in behind the girl, trapping her between them.

'More wine for the prince, I see.' Barabal spoke in her most polite, reasonable voice, the one John knew meant she was deadly serious. 'I think perhaps this is another pitcher I need to take from you, for very different reasons.'

'Just try it,' the girl sneered. 'I shall scream the place down and we will find out how Prince Henry deals with those who accost his favoured servant.'

'Go ahead,' John told her. 'I for one would be interested in his reactions when we tell him the wine you brought for your cosy evening together is poisoned.'

John had no way of knowing whether or not this actual jug of wine contained poison intended for Prince Henry, but, given the circumstances, he was happy to bluff. Isolde stared at him, weighing her options. Grudgingly she handed over the pitcher, and slipped past John. She took a single step, then turned.

'You cannot protect him all the time. You will make a mistake, and I will succeed.'

'We do not need to watch him every minute,' Barabal said as she slipped back into the alcove. 'We only need to be on the lookout when he has time to spend alone with you, and he will have little enough of that before he is crowned tomorrow.'

Isolde did not rise to the bait, instead she carried on towards her destination as though nothing had happened, tapped on the door, and the prince admitted her into his bedroom. John carried the pitcher over to an open window and poured the contents out. Placing the empty jug at the back of the table, he once again took up his position.

No one else used the corridor for some time, so they took turns napping until they were disturbed by thumping and laughing. A bleary-eyed Alain, followed by a still half-asleep Stanislaus, appeared in front of them.

'You look terrible,' Barabal told the boys. 'Even worse than we do, and we have not had any sleep.'

'Nor have I,' Alain said. 'I woke at every bell, worried I might miss out

hearing the three am one.'

'I slept fine, well until Alain came into my room and woke me,' Stanislaus cheerfully informed them. 'You had wine to drink? Alain, why did we not think of bring some with us?'

'No, you dolt, we took a pitcher from the serving wench. She is in with Prince Henry now,' Barabal informed them.

'Oh.' Stanislaus was crestfallen.

'I can test the dregs tomorrow if you can take the pitcher back with you, John,' Alain said as he peered into the jug to see how much liquid was left.

'Well, I am off to bed. See you later.' Barabal slipped off the table and waited for John to follow.

He picked up the wine jug and slowly dragged his body down the corridor and out into the palace precinct. Finding the door to his quarters he opened it to find an elderly man sitting in one of the chairs by the fire, with Lala standing in front of him.

'You are correct Great One, he is not much to look at, but you must work with what you are given,' the man said to the lamb. 'Come in and close the door, boy, no use letting all the warm air out. These old bones do tend to feel the cold a little more nowadays.'

JOHN SHUT THE door behind him, his tired brain trying to work out who this strange man talking to his guardian was. As he placed the jug down and walked over to the chairs, his over-worked memory dredged up the answer.

'You are Master Barwick. Sir Robert de Beaumont said he would send Squire James for you.' John sunk into the other chair, pleased with his guess, and happy with the way the evening had gone.

'Of course,' the rather portly, well dressed man confirmed, his blue eyes twinkling. 'Your guardian was just bringing me up to date with progress so far.'

John studied the man through half-closed eyes, thinking Master Barwick was nothing like he imagined when the cook had been complaining about the apothecary not tending to their illnesses. In his mind he had envisioned a thin, sour skinflint, not this kindly looking grandfather figure with white hair standing out in clumps from his head.

'Cook is right to complain. I used to tend the people here. When I became less mobile, I sent my apprentice down. Last fall he became a journeyman and set up his own business north of London. I do not venture out much nowadays, and I cannot summon the energy to train another to service the people here. I am so pleased your friend offered to help as the castle staff no doubt suffered because of my neglect. As I am here now, I may even stay a few extra days and give what assistance I can.'

'Did you read my mind?' Now wide awake and on his guard, John sat upright and glared suspiciously at the newcomer.

Master Barwick frowned, 'Why yes, did your guardian not tell you? Many guardian's assistants can tell what others are thinking.'

John stared at Lala. *What have you withheld from me now?*

'Oh, I pick up mind speaking too,' the man laughed. 'Not much can be kept from me.'

Master Barwick is a candidate for guardian. Each generation produces a person ready to be elevated to one of the twenty-four. He has special skills, and he knew when we arrived in London. I asked him to come here when I realised Prince Henry might be poisoned. When James knocked at his door this evening, he was prepared and ready to travel.

'And you did not think to tell me about him?' John asked.

You did not come back til now. How could I?

'Oh, I guess you could not really.' John had to concede the point to Lala.

'So they tried tonight?' Master Barwick asked. 'You stopped them though, good lad.'

'I really wish you would stop doing that,' John grumbled. 'As it turns out, we intercepted some wine, but except for drinking it ourselves, we have no way of knowing whether or not it was poisoned. Alain said he will try and find out tomorrow.'

'If you do not like people reading you, you need to learn to put up some walls. Honestly, Sigma, that should be the first thing you teach them. He must be broadcasting your plans to anyone with a little talent.'

I misjudged our entry a little, so training time has been limited.

'Sigma? Is that your name?'

Not my real name, my guardian name. We are all named after a letter from the Greek alphabet.

'Well, I think Lala suits you at the moment, so I shall continue to call you that. Can you really teach me to shield my thoughts?'

Yes, I can, and I will. Just not now. You are tired and should sleep. You need to be alert tomorrow, and it would not do for you to fall asleep while you protect a future king.

Feeling like a young boy sent to bed, none-the-less John admitted he

could do with a decent night's sleep, so did not argue. Wishing the others goodnight, he went next door, undressed and slipped into the bed still a little warm from where Alain had lain.

AFTER JOHN LEFT them alone again, Master Barwick turned his attention back to the lamb in front of him.

Sigma, are you certain this is the one who is going to save the timeline? A bit on the green side, in my opinion, and I cannot imagine his friends are seasoned fighters.

I was worried as well, Lala told the man in front of him. *But I found all the required signs; the beginnings of magical ability, a need to do what is right, and a stout heart. Circumstances forced me to bring him from earlier in his evolution than was optimal, but you know how the council likes us to solve two problems with one event. The time I took him from was the one in his circle of life that he would most benefit from learning about the Charter of Liberties, and what it took for the document to be produced.*

This devolution of power, and the resulting belief all people have some rights, are the lynchpin of the shearers strike in the far off land I took him from. Also, there is a lesson he needs to learn to be able to temper the radicals in his era to bring about real change.

I guess if the council approved it, this must be the right course of action. He just seems so young, and so impetuous, the apothecary commented.

As am I by Guardian standards. Lala sighed. *I guess we are well matched. Although, I was a bit surprised when he got himself thrown in the dungeon. That almost ruined my plans. Funnily enough though, it galvanised the team so it worked out well in the end.*

And do you think they will be able to combat a Time Wrecker now that we know they are here? It sounds as though they sent a seasoned operative, and I am afraid I am not mobile enough to be of much use to them. Master Barwick worried.

It is the one they sent that concerns me the most. I felt none of the ripples normally accompanying their arrival. The council did not know of a Time Wrecker present in this time either. I am afraid our enemy sent one of their best to deal with this situation. The lamb's face contorted in what Master Barwick took to be a frown.

I hope you have this under control, Sigma. I must come back to this time once our next mission is complete, and I do not want to return to chaos. At my age, I want life to become easier, not harder.

It will all turn out well, I am sure. And if it does not, you will not be back here for long. I sense the end of your natural life will be soon. Once your body passes on, your training as a guardian will begin. Anyway, I am confident we will thwart the wreckers' agent.

Although the lamb sounded unconcerned about how the wreckers might affect the time line, Sigma was unable to totally shield his fear from the elderly man. However, realising there was nothing else they could do now, Master Barwick decided to change the subject.

I guess I should trust you, and we both should trust in the Council. Have you heard any more from them about what is in store for us when your mission here is complete?

We will meet with them tonight, in fact, I hear them calling now.

16

THE PLOT THICKENS

JOHN AWOKE THE next morning to the sound of laughter next door. He stumbled about pulling on his clothes so he could find the source of the disruption. He found Alain and Master Barwick sitting on one side of the work table, and the meat cook sitting on the other.

'So my friend, my lame foot will not support my weight any more. The less I walk, the more weight I put on, with more weight, I can walk less. For me to even ride a horse now is difficult.'

'I wish you had told us. Your apprentice did not explain to us why he came instead of you. Sour puss that one. We were pleased to see the back of him,' Cook said before taking a sip of water. Thirst quenched, he continued, 'Anyway, we thought we were beneath you now you have a fancy place in town. If we had known about your condition, we would have sent the cart for you. We still can, and you could come down once a week like you used to. Join us for a hearty meal and some wine; catch up with your friends.'

No longer angry with the apothecary, cook welcomed his old mate back to the fold, and Master Barwick seemed pleased to be included once again.

'Now that would be grand. It gets lonely in my shop, only seeing those with ailments. So, shall we find out where Alain is with his learning. Boy, cook here has a sore back, it has been giving him pain for years, too much standing and lifting all those heavy carcasses. What would you recommend?'

John decided he best leave the others to their work, and crossed the floor to find Lala sound asleep. Thinking it likely the lamb and Master Barwick talked through the night, he decided to let the guardian rest and go feed his grumbling stomach. He took himself off to the servant's dining room, where he found Stanislaus wolfing down porridge with honey and nuts.

'Morning.' The other boy greeted him through a mouthful of food.

John helped himself to a bowl of steaming oatmeal and sat down beside his friend. 'Did anything else happen after we left last night?'

'Not really. The girl left before sun up. Glared at us as she walked past, saucy wench. Nothing else happened until Prince Henry went to breakfast. Sir Robert de Beaumont will be with him until the midday meal, sorting out a heap of documents, then Barabal said you guys would take over and watch until the ceremony.

'I am finishing up here, then I am off back to bed.' Stanislaus stretched and yawned before continuing to empty his plate.

Not wanting to spend the morning alone, John asked, 'Do you want to take a wander with me first? I need to find out if the wine we discarded last night killed anything.'

'I thought Alain was going to test the pitcher?'

'He is so caught up with Master Barwick and tending to castle staff's ailments, I doubt there will be time for him to do it before this afternoon's festivities begin.'

Stanislaus shrugged. 'All right. Although I am not sure what you expect to find.'

'Nor am I, but I will know it when I see it,' John admitted.

After returning their plates into the kitchen, they walked around, attempting to count windows to find the spot where John emptied the jug the previous night. The precinct was busy, and a couple of times they had to lie, saying they were on a mission for the prince, lest they be hauled into preparations for the celebrations.

Frustrated because the outside of the palace looked different to the inside, John was about to suggest Stanislaus go in, find the window and lean out, when the other boy stopped dead in his tracks and pointed. In one of the garden beds, a pile of dead rats spilled out on to the pathway. They might have been killed by anything, except there was a red wine stain on one of

the stones beside the bodies.

'Well, don't just stand there, boys, clean that mess up.'

A gardener pushed a basket and shovel at Stanislaus, who promptly dropped them and ran.

'Oops, I forgot, I am meant to be serving Sir Robert de Beaumont this morning, he will be annoyed with me if I am late,' he shouted back over his shoulder as he disappeared into the crowd.

With the gardener staring intently at him, John had no alternative but to pick up the spade and begin shovelling rodents.

'Odd this is, never seen so many dead rats in one place. They do like to rummage in the garden manure, so I find an occasional one when I am working. But this? I have not seen anything like it in all my years working here.'

After John finished, the man directed him to the dung heap, telling him to bury the dead rats deep down. As John left, he busied himself tidying the garden so no trace of the dead rodents would be visible to the gathering nobility. Job completed, John found himself with nothing to do until the noon meal.

He entered the palace through the servant's entrance and lurked in the hall. One of the maids told him Mistress Barabal attended the women of the household, working on the prince's coronation robes. John happened to mention Barabal might prefer to come explore London with him rather than spending such a beautiful morning sewing, and earned a cuff to the side of the head for his observations.

Sighing, he left the palace and made his way down to the Thames. The morning sun reflected on the muddy blue water, causing the tips of the waves to sparkle as the tide went out. Criss-crossing the river, boats brought produce to feed the population of the large city.

John sat on the bank, dangling his legs over. As he swung them back and forth, he gazed around the town he could only describe as grey, missing the reds and blues that reminded him of his Queensland home. As he sat wallowing in his homesickness, his eyes found a boat heading for Westminster dock. Idly he followed its progress, and as it drew closer, he realised he knew the passengers; Sir William de Breteuil and Isolde the maid.

Searching the dock area, he found some wooden crates stacked nearby. Trying to act casual, he walked over to them and secreted himself in behind, hoping to overhear a little of the conversation as the two passed him by. Luck must have been on his side that day, as the pair stopped by the crates to finish their conversation.

'I say killing him now is too risky. If those blasted children are on to you, we should cut our losses and give up the plan.' De Breteuil's tone was commanding.

'The risk is not with you,' the persuasive purr belonged to Isolde. 'They will look for me once the prince is dead, and I intend on being a long way from here when they find his body. That is, if they even realise he was poisoned. No one of importance has seen you and I together. Your reputation will be safe.'

De Breteuil grunted, not used to having his decisions questioned. Still, he did not walk away. Fingers tapped a rhythm on the wooden crate as the duke considered the servant's words.

'I am not sure.' The duke's tone was uncertain when he answered.

'Just tell me you still want Prince Henry poisoned, and I will do my best to see the job done. There is still enough of the tonic for one more attempt.' Isolde pushed her accomplice, not yet ready to give in.

'I do, damn it,' de Breteuil told her.

'Consider it done. I must away now before someone notices I am gone.'

A rustle of skirts was followed a few moments later by the thud of heavier footsteps. John popped his head over the top of the crates to glimpse de Breteuil's retreating back.

He slumped down again, back against the crates. Annoyingly he had not learnt anything new from the conversation, except de Breteuil's resolve wavered, but not enough to prevent Isolde from bringing him back into line.

Time was running out. And with only enough poison left for one last attack, this afternoon would be her last opportunity to try anything. Sighing, he stood and headed back to the apothecary's, hoping to talk to Lala and Master Barwick about the overheard conversation.

Approaching the rooms, he was surprised by a line of people snaking through the door and around the corner. Frowning, he pushed past the bodies and entered the workroom to find Alain with Master Barwick, both busy with clients. Alain was so engrossed in his work he did not notice him enter. Lala still slept by the fire, so John let himself into the bedroom and soon found himself drifting off to sleep.

No sooner had he closed his eyes than Alain was shaking him awake. 'Hey, how about moving over and giving me some room. I am completely done in.'

'Wha… what time is it?' he asked, bleary eyed.

'Almost time for noon meal in the great hall.'

John sat bolt upright and swung his legs over the side of the bed. 'I need to eat and prepare for guard duty.'

'Yes, you do,' Alain confirmed. 'And I need some rest if I am to attend the coronation as planned.

'By the way, Barabal called by, mumbled something about Stan having all the luck being included in the meetings today, then left instructions for us.'

Remembering how Stanislaus had been looking forward to a morning nap, he did not think the boy would consider his assignment as being lucky at all.

'Are you listening? She said to let you know you need not wait through the meal, just meet her outside the prince's bedroom. We are to relieve you before three to allow you both time to dress for this evening.'

John shook his head, trying to clear his sleep fuddled thoughts.

'Did you find out anything about the wine jug today?' he managed to ask.

'I did a test, but it was inconclusive. Although I am leaning towards some arsenic being there, I needed more wine to be certain.'

'Well, after the number of dead rats Stanislaus and I found outside a window near the prince's chambers, I think we can categorically say if he had drunk any of the wine, he would likely be dead by now.'

Alain's soft snores told him the boy had not heard a word he said. Leaving him to his rest, John opened the door to the workroom and silently closed it behind him.

In a comfortable chair by the fire, Master Barwick also slept, his mouth open and eyes closed. Lala, seeing the boy up and about, left his fireside bed on wobbly legs and walked to the door. Looking back at John, his intentions were clear.

He let the lamb out and followed him round to a grassy area at the side of the building. Walking to the other side of the lawn the lamb discretely relieved himself. On his return, the Lala started nibbling at tender shoots of grass. As his guardian ate, John told him about the meeting he had witnessed earlier in the day. Lala stopped eating.

Can you tell me the exact words Isolde used? he asked.

She said something along the lines of, "Tell me you still want the prince poisoned and I will do it", John told him.

Oh, that is close to shaping events, but I believe it is still within the boundaries. Shame. It would be easier if she had mis-stepped.

You mean you would be able to go before a judge or something, and they would tell her to stop?

John hoped the outside powers were poised to intervene, at least he would be able to stop worrying if they did.

Nothing that easy, I am afraid. How they would step in and realign events does not matter now. We need to ensure history follows the right path the old fashioned way. The lamb chewed a few more shoots of grass before looking up at John. *I guess you can let me back in now while you go and eat. Oh, and if you could bring back something for Master Barwick before you find Barabal, I am sure he would appreciate it. It is the least you could do given you slept in his bed while he took the chair.*

A COUPLE OF servants he had not seen before left the table as John arrived. They nodded hello as they departed. Left alone, he ate his meal in silence. Once he was done, he filled a plate with some cold meat, bread and cheese, then filled a cup with small beer, and took it all back for Master Barwick.

Walking back past the hall, he saw people still sitting around eating and drinking. Prince Henry appeared to be enjoying a joke with Ranulf Flambard. Isolde was nowhere to be seen. With nothing else to do, he decided he would go to the lookout early. Much to his surprise, he found Barabal sitting on the table swinging her legs and frowning.

'What is wrong?' he asked.

'You got to walk around London, Alain got to work with a renown apothecary, Stanislaus got to listen in on meetings of state. And what did I get to do? I got to sew flowers on a shirt.' She kicked her heel against the table leg, causing a resounding bang to echo around the hallway. 'Then, I had to unpick it,' she continued through gritted teeth. 'And re-sew it, because my flower was not deemed good enough for a future king.' The hall echoed with yet another bang.

'I am trusted to take letters to the future queen. I can do their dirty work for them. But as soon as I am no longer needed, I am relegated back to the sewing room.' Bang. 'It is so unfair.' Bang. Bang. BANG.

John hated to find his friend so down in the dumps, but he did not know what to tell her. His mother made similar comments over the years, and he knew over seven hundred years later, women were still not treated the same as men. All he could do was speak from the heart.

'My mother has run our farm and brought up three children without any help since my father died. And yet she is still not respected by the other local farmers because she is a woman.

'You, Barabal, are one of the most capable people I have ever met. Nothing I can say will make this right, or make you feel better. I do want you to know though, I believe you can do anything I can, and you can probably do it better. It is not fair no one recognises that, but it is the way life is.'

Barabal smiled sorrowfully. 'I know. It is so frustrating sometimes. Especially knowing that my only course of action is to marry and try and influence things through my husband. If I want to do anything at all, I need to work twice as hard as any man. Alain says I should try and affect change closer to home. Perhaps he is right.'

Barabal shrugged half-heartedly and John kept a grin in check, guessing Alain may have been thinking of a specific place close to home with a very specific person.

Outburst over, Barabal and John took turns pacing the corridor and watching the prince's room. It was not until well after one the meal in the main hall broke up. Barabal was sitting on the table dozing when Prince Henry passed and opened the door to his bed chamber.

A little while later, John nudged Barabal, and she took her turn watching the door. Worried if anything was going to happen it would be now, he slipped himself off the table and walked up and down the corridor, only to find Barabal looking concerned on his return.

'Did we miss something? Is it possible we both dozed for a moment and that girl slipped in?' Her fingers worried the fabric of her dress in agitation.

John replayed the short time since the prince returned from lunch over in his mind.

'I do not see how she could have. I think you are upset because you had a nap. Perhaps she is waiting until later, when the boys relieve us. She may think Alain and Stanislaus are easier targets.'

'Who thinks we are easy?'

The voice came from right behind John. Startled, he jumped and turned to find Stanislaus and Alain had crept up the corridor and now stood less than a few steps away from them.

'How did you do that? I did not hear footsteps,' John blurted out in surprise.

Stanislaus and Alain both held up their boots.

'We are practicing being extra quiet… and we may have taken the opportunity

to play a little prank.' Alain could not wipe the cheeky grin off his face.

'And it worked.' Stanislaus' face was plastered with such a broad grin even Barabal smiled in response.

'What did you do? No, wait, do I want to know?'

'We found Tobias asleep at the back of the hall. We tied his legging ribbons together so... well, you can guess. We took our shoes off and crept out so as not to disturb him,' Stanislaus told them while putting his footwear back on.

'Have your fun while you can, boys, we will all be working until late tonight. The festivities are planned until well into the wee hours of the morning, and we have been asked to help serve and clear up.'

'Do I understand from what we overheard that Isolde did not appear this afternoon?' Alain asked.

John and Barabal shook their heads.

'Good, that means we will be the heroes again.' Stanislaus' grin grew still broader. 'So, what are you two hanging round here for, trying to steal some of our glory?' He laughed.

'We might want to stay and see how to do things properly,' Barabal teased.

A door creaked open further down the corridor and a head popped out. 'You there, keep the noise down. Mistress Barabal, what are you doing here? I am sure Robert de Beaumont would not like to find out you are cavorting with boys in the shadows.'

'No, Sir Ranulf, I am on an errand and came across these louts lounging around. I am off to the women's quarters to change for this afternoon's events now.'

Barabal feigned contriteness, but Ranulf Flambard waited until she was well down the corridor before popping his head back inside his room.

'Well, boys, keep an eye out and I will see you at the coronation.' John said as he turned to leave.

'John.' Alain stopped him. 'Master Barwick needed some sleep, so he took the bed when I woke up. You will need to be quiet. I left some proper clothes for you over the chair.'

Sighing, John looked at the boys in front of him. Both wore embroidered tunics made of fine wool over soft woollen leggings. The clothing itself was not so bad, in fact, the material was of a finer quality than their everyday clothes, as were the colours.

Alain wore a green tunic with yellow leggings, and although Stanislaus' leggings were a more sober blue, his tunic was bright red with gold trimming. Wondering what delight they had left for him, he reluctantly left them to their duties.

17

HOW TO KILL A KING

JOHN WASHED HIMSELF all over, including his hair. Now sparkling clean for the first time in days, he changed into his new clothes, which were an unassuming mix of blues and greens. He then sat down in one of the chairs, closing his eyes for a moment, or so he thought. He awoke some time later to Master Barwick trying to move around the work room without waking him. Half opening his eyes, he realised the fire had gone out and Lala had curled into his body for warmth.

'Sorry, I am afraid I do not move as stealthily as I once did.' The apothecary placed a book on the table as he offered his apology. 'I guess you are still tired from your night's vigil, the bed is free now if you want to use it.'

John's eyes flew open. 'No, thank you, master. What is the time?'

'Oh, around three, or three-thirty, I think. The high and mighty are not gathering yet, there is still time for a quick nap.'

'Thank you but my stomach is doing somersaults, I think I had better go and find out how guard duty is going.'

He pulled on his shoes and darted out the door towards Westminster Palace. The palace precinct was still awash with people all going about their business. A coronation was a big event, and preparations to ensure the day ran smoothly would continue right up until the new king went to bed.

Dashing past palace servants and guards alike, he made it to the corridor where he found Alain sitting on the table, elbows on his knees and chin in hands, and Stanislaus propped against the wall, throwing a stone in the air and catching it.

'You two are keeping busy I see,' he whispered.

Remembering they had been told off once for making noise, he did not want to risk being sent away at such a crucial time.

'Since you left, no one of note came. Nothing at all interesting happened until the prince's squire brought some bathing water and a change of clothes just before you arrived. We made him drink a little to show it was not poisoned. We thought he might be annoyed with us for asking, but he said he is used to that sort of request so prepared the water himself.'

Stanislaus sighed, stood and stretched his limbs. 'Maybe they decided against killing the prince.'

Shaking his head, John said, 'No, I am sure they will still try. Isolde would not give up that easily.'

At that moment, the door to Prince Henry's room opened and he emerged looking refreshed and energetic, and only partially dressed for his big day.

'Have you boys nothing better to do than stand around in corridors killing time?' he asked them. 'I am sure my steward can find jobs for you all.' He laughed when their faces dropped. 'Be off with you and finish getting ready for today. I understand you are all to attend my coronation. You do not want to miss a moment of it, I am sure.'

'You knew we were out here?' John's eyes widened in surprise.

'Even a deaf man would have heard the noise you made last night.' The prince seemed in high spirits. 'It is almost the hour when I will be crowned, and I am safe and well. I am sure that is in no small part thanks to you all, but you can stand down now.'

At that moment, Sir Ranulf left his room. 'And here is Ranulf come to talk with me while I dress. I will be as safe with him as I would be with you all.'

The two nobles went into Henry's bed chamber and the door closed.

'Do you think he is right? Is he safe?' Alain asked.

'For the moment, I guess. We may as well go get something to eat while we can. I am told the ceremony will be hours long and I do not want to make it seem longer by being hungry the whole time.' John led his companions away.

As they walked passed the entrance to the hall on the way to the servants

dining room, Barabal accosted them.

'You left your post? Are you mad?' she hissed.

'Hold on a moment,' John told her. 'Sir Ranulf is in with the prince, so he will be fine. If you think he needs to be babysat, why don't you go and do it yourself?'

Barabal raised her eyebrows in alarm. 'You left him with Ranulf Flambard. Are you all stupid? Much as I like the man, he was loyal to King William the Second, and with rumours going around that Prince Henry was in league with Walter Tirel planning the king's demise, he is the last person you should trust with the prince's safety.'

With that, she flounced off, leaving the bewildered boys staring after.

'She is a force of nature,' Alain commented, the tone of his voice telling them he thought that was a good thing.

'Still, does she need to make us look stupid all the time?' Stanislaus asked.

'Maybe we were a little thoughtless,' Alain said as the three boys went through the door to the dining room. 'We should take something to go, then go and help her.'

They helped themselves to some bread and cheese, not knowing when they would be allowed to eat again that day. Before they could leave, they were forced to stand aside as the servants from Winchester entered. John watched them file in and chuckled as Tobias entered carrying his ribbons, leggings pooling around his ankles. As the man glared at Alain, he could not help thinking something was amiss. Then it struck him. Isolde was not there.

Pushing past them and through the doorway, he ran from the dining room with Alain and Stanislaus close behind. Not stopping to explain, he sped down the corridor, past the guards standing sentry duty as they did when the prince was in his room, and brushing past the prince's squire and a cloaked figure, who was forced to step out of his way. As she did, he found Barabal lying in a heap on the floor.

At the very moment he recognised the girl on the ground, he realised who he had run by. Looking up, he found Isolde boldly staring back at him.

'You are too late, it is done.'

She smiled triumphantly as she turned and walked away. John was torn. He wanted to go after her, she should not be able to get away with what she had done. However, Barabal and the prince were of more pressing concern.

'John, what is it?' Alain had caught him up, followed closely by Stanislaus.

Seeing Barabal on the floor, the apprentice apothecary dropped to his knees and began checking the girl out. As he felt around her head, she stirred

and opened her eyes.

'Isolde,' she said weakly. 'We must check on the prince.'

'Not yet.' Alain was suddenly in his element. 'Stanislaus, go tell Master Barwick we need an emetic.'

'A what?' Stanislaus looked confused.

'Just say these exact words: "The prince needs an emetic",' Alain ordered. 'He will understand.'

'Something to make the prince violently sick,' an exasperated Barabal told him as she sat up, now completely lucid. 'Help me to my feet, I will come with you to make sure you get it right.'

As Stanislaus helped Barabal down the corridor, Alain's gaze worriedly followed them even though she seemed as good as new. Once they were gone from sight, the boy turned to John.

'Are you ready to break into a prince's room and tell him he has been poisoned?'

BARABAL SPED AWAY from the scene, dodging between nobles and servants alike, focused on her mission to bring the apothecary to the prince as fast as humanly possible.

'Do you think the prince will be all right?' She asked worriedly as she slipped around a man carrying chairs.

Stanislaus, barely able to keep up with her as it was, said nothing, saving his breath for more important things. His companion stopped dead in her tracks and swung round to face him.

'So you do not believe he will live through this?' she demanded.

Catching his breath before he answered, he finally managed a, 'I do not know. I did not get a chance to even see him before we took off.'

'Then why did you let me think… oh never mind.' Spinning on her heel she took off and the boy, still not quite sure what had just happened, had no choice but to follow after. He caught her up outside Master Barwick's rooms.

Stanislaus knocked on the door while Barabal moved from foot to foot, then up on her toes and back down. Waiting clearly was not one of her strong points. Sounds of a chair scraping across wood came from inside, and he looked around the courtyard while he waited for the apothecary to shuffle across the room and open the door.

The yard was busy, full of servants bustling around finalising preparations

for the coronation, and the celebrations that would follow. He lost himself in the bustling activity until a movement by the castle caught his eye. He glimpsed a head of dark hair before the figure slipped behind a group of servants. Nudging Barabal, he pointed.

'Did you see that?'

'See what?' she asked without taking her eyes from the door.

'I think I spotted Isolde heading for the river.'

As the latch moved, Barabal turned to him. 'Well, what are you waiting for? Go after her.'

Master Barwick opened the door and glanced about in surprise as he heard the tail end of her words. Looking at Barabal, Stanislaus made sure she was not joking before he sped off through the crowd.

Unfortunately he was forced to pull up abruptly, as the cook chose that exact moment to lead a train of servants carrying tables out into the yard to be set up for the servants feast later that day. Eyes darting, Stanislaus searched for a way around the blockage. Not finding one, he ran, dropped to the ground and slid underneath a table, almost taking out the legs of one of the men carrying it. He was followed by a string of abuse as he regained his feet and took off around the edge of the castle buildings.

Pulling up short by some crates of chickens, he searched Westminster dock for any signs of his prey. She was not there but, perhaps more importantly, she was not in any of the boats leaving the castle either. That meant she was still on this side of the river.

Walking around crates and baskets containing food to feed the swelling number of nobles in London for the crowning of their new king, he made sure the serving girl had not secreted herself anywhere. Happy there was no sign of her, he considered where else she might have gone.

His roving eye caught sight of a black haired woman weaving her way along the river path against the run of the crowd. Picking up speed, he attempted to follow. However, the tall squire was not as small and nimble as the girl he chased. For every two steps he took forward, he was pushed back at least one by everyone heading to Westminster Abbey to find a spot to watch the day's proceedings.

Frustrated, he watched her move further and further away from him. In desperation, he engaged his elbows and started pushing people out of the way. He made some progress, and soon the crowd thinned enough for him to walk at a fast pace.

Just as he thought he might have a chance to catch her up, she glanced back over her shoulder and, seeing she had a tail, she slipped through the people beside her and into an alley. Overcome with panic, Stanislaus broke into a run, only to find himself flying through the air and landing flat on his face.

Turning to abuse whoever had tripped him, he found his legs tangled with a small boy wiping tears from his eyes. Overcome with guilt, he picked the lad up and handed him to his mother, apologising for his clumsiness. He received a glare in return, and he did not wait to hear the stream of angry words coming out of the woman's mouth.

By the time he made it to the alleyway, it was empty. Running to the other end, he frantically searched the street, but could see no sign of the girl who poisoned the king. Returning to the castle, head hung low, he at least consoled himself Isolde was free, but she was no longer a threat. After all, she had done what she intended to do. The only question now was whether or not she had succeeded.

JOHN HESITATED IN front of the prince's door. 'What happens if we barge in and there is nothing wrong with him?' he wondered out loud, not wanting to risk another night in a dungeon.

'Here, let me.' Alain sighed and knocked firmly on the wood.

'Come,' a voice spoke from the other side.

Alain opened the door and the boys came face to face with a prince dressed in all his finery, about to take a sip from a goblet. John acted on instinct. Rushing forward, he knocked the cup from Prince Henry's hand.

The prince's face darkened, like a storm cloud blocking the sun. His jovial demeanour of the morning disappearing as he became the imperious ruler.

'Boy, you go too far. You will be hung for daring to touch your king.'

John thought about telling the prince he was not yet king, but for once held his tongue.

'Begging your pardon, sire, but we believe your wine to be poisoned.'

Alain move beside John in a gesture of support, but stopped short of laying hands on someone of royal blood.

Prince Henry frowned. 'What do you mean? My squire brought this pitcher. Anything he hands to me has already been checked by my man.'

'Think, sire, please, it is important,' Alain begged him. 'Did your page hold the pitcher of wine, or was it in Isolde's hands?'

Prince Henry's frown deepened as he tried to remember exactly what happened. 'Isolde and my squire arrived at the door at the same time. While the squire cleared my room, Isolde suggested we… ah…'

'Celebrated your coronation early?' John helped the prince out in the interests of saving time.

'Umm, yes. I told her not now, but perhaps later… Ah, she handed me a jug and said it was a pity to waste it, perhaps this would help settle my nerves. But she would not have done anything so base as to poison me. I believe she truly cares for me.

'Besides… I heard Barabal on watch in the hallway. Surely she would have—'

'She was out cold when we arrived,' Alain said. 'She had no bump on her head, so I suspect someone used a special technique to put her to sleep.'

'Oh, she is all right,' John added when the prince looked concerned. 'But I am afraid the squire must be working with Isolde.'

'He has been with me since boyhood. He would never do anything to harm me.'

'Maybe not knowingly. A pretty face can be very persuasive though. Perhaps he thought he was doing you a favour, allowing your friend some time with you in private. They did not hurt Barabal, so no harm was done. He may not even have known what Isolde was up to,' John assisted the prince again.

'I am still not convinced she did anything at all, other than try and seduce me. I feel fine.'

Alain was suddenly all professional. 'How much did you drink?'

'A few sips, perhaps half a goblet while I finished dressing. I was about to drink another when you rushed in.'

The prince gripped the bed post, swaying a little, pinpricks of sweat forming on his brow. 'Perhaps I do not feel so well after all. I had put it down to nerves. Will I die?'

'Not if I can help it,' Alain answered. 'If it is arsenic, as we suspect, all we can do is try to stop it going through your system. Can you stick your fingers down your throat and make yourself sick?'

'Really? You cannot give me something to help with that?'

'Barabal has gone to get Master Barwick. He will bring something to help empty your stomach. In the meantime the more poison we can remove now, the better your chances. Sorry, sire, I would not ask this of you, but it is for your own good.'

The prince turned away from the boys and walked over to the window. Sticking his fingers in his mouth, he made himself sick. John felt sorry for anyone walking below, but he guessed manners were not the most important thing at a time like this. A little wine came out, but not much else.

'Did you eat anything at noon time?' Alain asked.

'Yes, I was ravenous, and I did not know when I would get a chance to eat again today, so I rather over-indulged.'

'Good, that might help slow the poison's effects, but I think everything needs to come up,' Alain declared.

As the prince turned back to the window, Barabal rushed into the room clutching a vial. She shoved it towards Alain. 'Here, Master Barwick said he should drink the whole thing. And he is on his way, he shall be here presently. Can I do anything else?'

'Yes,' Alain told her, seeing her embarrassment at being in the prince's rooms. 'You can go to the kitchen and bring a large pitcher of fresh water, and another of milk.'

Barabal seemed more than pleased to do something that would take her out of the bedchamber. When she had shut the door behind her, Alain took the vial over to the prince, who was still valiantly trying to bring up his meal.

'Here, drink this, every last drop.'

Henry took the top off, and the smell had him gagging. 'I cannot.' He shuddered. 'Wait, has my man tasted it?'

'Do you want to live?' Alain was firm.

'I have been poisoned once today, I think I am right to be cautious.'

'Here,' John grabbed the vial and took a sip. 'See, I am fine.'

John swiftly handed the medicine to the prince, hoping the cramps he felt starting in his stomach was the potion doing its work rather than a sign he had been foolhardy and would die in this strange land.

Prince Henry took a deep breath, closed his eyes and downed the vial of liquid. John estimated he had no sooner finished than his stomach decided to rid itself of its contents. Henry just made it to the window before his lunch reappeared.

Wave after wave of cramps went through the prince's body, and continued long after his stomach was empty. Exhausted, he finally slipped down the wall beneath the window, his face grey and his body shaking.

At a timid knock on the door, John opened it to find Barabal. She passed him a jug of water, and one of milk. 'It has been tasted,' she informed them

before moving out of the way to allow Master Barwick entry.

'I shall be outside if you need me,' Barabal said, once again closing the door.

John laughed, for such a bossy person she had some very strange scruples about being in a man's bedroom. He turned back to find Master Barwick looming over Prince Henry. The apothecary took the pitcher of water from John and told the prince to drink it all. From the look on the prince's face, you would have thought the water was toxic, but John guessed after throwing up his breakfast, the prince's digestive system would be none too happy.

Realising his presence was no longer required, and needing to find a privy as his stomach was threatening to relieve itself of its contents, John quietly slipped outside.

Barabal sat on the floor by the door, twining her fingers through Lala's wool.

'How is he, John? Has our work all been for nothing?'

'I do not know. I am not sure if there is a cure for arsenic poisoning, but Master Barwick is doing his best, with Alain's help.' Clutching his stomach, he was about to make a run for it when he noticed someone was missing. He clenched his jaw, holding everything in as he asked, 'Where is Stanislaus?'

'He thought he saw Isolde and went chasing after her.'

As she finished speaking, the door opened and Alain emerged. 'The master will stay with the prince a while,' he informed them. 'He said from the state of him, Prince Henry probably did not ingest enough of the toxin for it to kill him outright. Thank goodness we caught him before he had that second cupful of wine. Master Barwick praised me for my quick thinking. There is a slim chance the prince will survive without any side effects. Now we just have to wait and see.'

John knew he was not going to be able to wait with them, his stomach cramped again and he took off to find somewhere to empty it in private.

18

THE CORONATION

JOHN AND ALAIN waited in the apothecaries' rooms until it was time to leave for the ceremony. Master Barwick had not yet returned, and it seemed the boys would be attending the celebrations alone. The excitement of saving the prince had worn John out, not to mention the time he spent in the privy afterwards as a result of taste testing the prince's medicine. Wearily, John asked why they needed to go to the coronation at all, and immediately wished again he would learn to keep his mouth shut.

Lala decided to lecture them on being witnesses to events in history. *This is an important occasion and you have a unique chance to be at the true beginning of the devolution of royal power. You cannot miss it.*

'So, just because we can then,' Alain said as he put on his new leather shoes.

More because the new king asked you to, and you cannot give me a good reason why you should not, the lamb answered wryly.

John laughed and adjusted his clothes, then tied the yellow ribbons Alain handed him round the end of his leggings to keep them in place. Master Barwick had left them both with new leather shoes as a present, and John tried his on to find they fitted perfectly. By the time he applied the finishing touches to his outfit, he felt as trussed up as a Christmas turkey. His only

consolation being Alain looked more like a peacock.

Later, sitting at the back of Westminster Abbey, John felt a lot less unhappy with his attire. Most of the common people in the back rows were dressed as he was, but when the nobility began to make their way in, he saw his clothing was plain by comparison. He wondered how the boys were not fidgeting and uncomfortable under all the jewels and fancy stitching decorating their costumes.

John's eyes widened as William of Breteuil entered the abbey, followed by the men and women of his household. Surprised the duke would show his face after what had happened, John nudged Alain so he could share the spectacle.

'He could hardly not attend, could he?' Alain muttered. 'At the moment, only our word links him to the attempted murder of the future king, and we are not yet adult and so could not be heard in a court of law. To stay away would be admitting his guilt.'

If he felt any shame at all at his actions, he did not show it as he sauntered down the aisle, head held high, taking his place in the front row along with all the others of noble birth. Some of his household were also of high enough birth to take seats in the rows behind, but a few had to make do with trying to find space at the back, or standing along the walls.

Musing how lucky he was to have been offered a seat as the wait for proceedings to start was a long one, he was distracted by Robert de Beaumont's entrance. As one of Prince Henry's closest friends, he was one of the last to arrive, and he strode quickly to his position front and centre. His household followed at a more sedate pace.

Stanislaus strode into the hall wearing a heavy tabard, sporting what John assumed must be his family coat of arms. He held out his arm, and Barabal placed a hand on it, and they followed the de Beaumont family to their seats, which were only a few rows from where the Archbishop waited to begin proceedings.

The diminutive girl looked beautiful in a finely woven blue linen dress, over top of a fine white linen under-dress. Around her waist she wore a belt of gold. Her hair fell in dark brown waves down her back, held off her face by a circlet of fresh flowers. She looked amazing. Alain obviously thought so, as he gasped in wonder as she passed their seats, giving them a cheeky wink in the process.

The church was now full to the brim, and people shuffled in their seats as the Archbishop wrung his hands, anxious for the prince to arrive. Once everyone was seated, they all waited in anticipation, and waited some more.

'Are you sure Master Barwick actually saved Prince Henry?' John asked, only to be shushed by a haughty looking woman in front of them.

Alain glared at her, daring her to say anything as he answered. 'When I left, the prince was rather grey and not looking too well, but that was two hours ago. Surely there would have been a commotion if he had taken a turn for the...'

Trumpets sounded, blotting out Alain's final words, and the prince, resplendent in his coronation robes, stood in the doorway. He made a slow procession through the gathering, and only those close to him could see how pale he was as he made is way towards the throne. Most in the room would put his pallor down to the strains of the day, but John knew better. That man was lucky to be here.

Relaxing now their job was done, John and Alain prepared themselves for a long and boring ceremony.

THE PROCEEDINGS MAY have been more exciting if he and Alain were not seated so far back in the abbey, although John suspected not. Barabal and Stanislaus were closer to the action, but the amount of times the squire turned and caught his eye, led him to believe the coronation was not particularly interesting even when you were in the thick of it.

There was a short break in the speeches as the Archbishop called for the crown and sceptre, and they were marched down the aisle. Stifling a yawn behind his hand, John studied the crowd. Many, like him, spent their time watching others rather than the ceremony. As a few people moved in their seats, uncomfortable from hours of sitting, those standing round the edges shuffled to improve their circulation.

John's eyes pivoted back along the wall. Something caught his eye, but his brain had yet to process the information. All he knew was a deep sense of unease. There, one of the servants was inching towards the front.

Not quite sure yet whether it was anything to worry about, he attempted to stand to get a better view, only to find his tunic roughly tugged, pulling him back down in his seat.

'What are you doing, you fool? Do you want to end up back in the dungeons?' Alain whispered, drawing John's attention to the soldiers spaced around the room.

'But...'

Marshalling his thoughts without taking his eyes off the moving figure, he found the words he needed.

'Someone is moving through the crowd up the front. There is something about them, something familiar. Maybe the dark hair?'

At that precise moment Stanislaus turned, while appearing to follow the procession in the centre isle, he took the opportunity to grin at his friends. As he raised his arm to wave, John jerked his head to the side, attempting to direct the other boy's gaze to the figure now nearly at the front of the church. Just as the squire frowned quizzically, Barabal pulled his arm back down and said something, causing the boy to shrug.

Helplessly, John considered his other options as he watched Stanislaus' head bend down towards his companion. His lips and hands moved excitedly. John could only hope the boy had understood the meaning of his gesture. Ever so slowly, Barabal's head lifted and she looked towards John. He nodded towards the person slipping in and out of sight. She glared back at him.

'Oh, for goodness sake,' Alain said as he raised his arm and pointed to where John wanted the girl to look.

Barabal followed the line of his finger and he saw her jaw drop as she finally understood what worried them. In that split second John also realised why he was so concerned. Isolde had not finished with Prince Henry.

As he found the Time Wrecker again, he followed her progress as she slipped in and out of view, then finally ducked in behind the flowers decorating the alter. They had moments before she was able to strike at the prince. John did not know what to do. He was so far back in the cathedral, even if he yelled, they would not hear him at the front, and the guards would no doubt remove him before he could do anything.

He turned questioningly to Alain, only to find the boy was not there. Looking down, he found him using his smaller body to good effect, crawling underneath the pews towards the isle. While admiring his resourcefulness, John knew he would not be fast enough to stop whatever Isolde intended.

However, he need not have worried. Glancing forward, he found Barabal raising herself from her seat. Swaying slightly, she swooned gracefully to the ground. The prince rose from his throne and quickly made his way to their friend's side. At the same time Isolde emerged from behind the alter, knife raised.

The crowd gasped as Stanislaus launched himself towards the prince's would be attacker. Staring in dismay as all eyes in the church turned to her,

the girl darted past the assembled clergy. The determined squire launched himself at Isolde, managing to grasp her foot. Unfortunately he brought her to the ground just as one of the guards had been about to grasp her. The would be assassin crawled through the legs of the prince's men, and darted for the back of the church, Stanislaus in her wake.

As if unaware of what was occurring behind him, Prince Henry called for someone to assist Barabal from the church. Two guards gently escorted the girl out. Head down, she used a curtain of hair to hide her face from the gathering. Barabal's eyes widened as she reached the end of their pew and found Alain peering up at her. Stumbling a little, she raised her head slightly and grinned at John before being escorted out.

Henry returned to his throne. He must have said something to ease the situation, as people near the front tittered in nervous release. Robert de Beaumont glared at de Breteuil, while the duke studiously ignored his gaze, choosing to concentrate on the scene in front of him as the crown was lowered on Prince Henry's head, and he was finally declared king.

The sound of trumpets filled the church as Prince Henry, no, King Henry I, stood. Robert de Beaumont joined him and placed an ermine robe around his shoulders.

'Long Live King Henry.' De Beaumont raised his voice, and he was answered by the nobles of the land.

'Long live King Henry.'

Looking every bit the king he now was, the new monarch of Briton walked down the central aisle and out of the church to cheers from the crowd waiting outside. The nobility followed in his wake, creating a colourful parade out of the abbey.

John, with Alain now back by his side, slumped in his seat and congratulated himself for a job well done.

WHEN IT WAS finally John and Alain's turn to leave the church, the shouts of the people for their new king were still strong. The royal party paraded back to Westminster Palace for the celebrations, but many people mingled around out front, waiting for the crowds to thin before making their way to the banquet.

There was a bright spot in the day. Earlier, while they were dressing, a

messenger delivered an invitation from Prince Henry, requesting the two boys join the celebratory meal in the hall. So, instead of facing a night working, they would now be able to have some fun. While they waited for Barabal and Stanislaus to join them so they might all sit together, John passed the time people watching.

Sir William de Breteuil and his followers assembled with a group of men who did not look quite as jubilant as the rest of the gathered nobility. John imagined they still could not afford to absent themselves from King Henry's celebrations, lest they be associated with such a public attempt on the prince's life.

Before Alain had left Prince Henry that afternoon, he had requested they tell no one of the attempt to poison him. If it were known someone tried to kill him, he would be forced to find and punish everyone involved. When Alain asked why that would be bad, he had answered.

'After my brother's time as king, Briton needs healing, strong leadership and a chance to refill her coffers. A witch hunt for a potential killer would drain resources, and might potentially turn baron against baron. Not the best start to my reign.

'Besides, my guess is de Breteuil took part in this, and he will be heading back to Normandie after the ceremony, no doubt to report back to my brother. So, as it stands, I will have little time to prepare before facing my true opposition, and there are more important things to do than to waste what little time I have chasing down my poisoners.'

They all agreed to keep this attempt to themselves, and for their assistance Prince Henry issued his generous invitation, adding a special note saying he would like to meet with them all after the feast.

De Breteuil turned to head to the palace and caught John's eye, then attempted to walk around the two boys as if they were not there. John, unable to help himself, stepped directly into the man's path.

'So, both your attempts to kill Prince Henry failed.'

'I have no idea what you are talking about. Out of my way.' The duke pushed past John only to come face to face with Alain.

'Running home, tail between your legs, are you? We will be well shot of you and your Norman friends.'

Haughtily raising his head, de Breteuil's tone was strangely sad. 'Perhaps I did wrong, but I did what I did because I believed it was for the best, as did you.

'Yes, you will get your Saxon Queen, and your landholders will be given some governance over their own lands, but at what cost? Robert Curthose will not let this go. There is bound to be war, and that benefits none of us.'

The Duke strode past, and John stood statue still as the baron's words sunk in. Until de Breteuil had spoken he had felt proud of their victory, but he was having second thoughts. Now, at the very end of his mission he learnt there was no good or bad side, no true right or wrong. There were only people fighting for what they believed in. In that moment he realised he had learnt a great truth about the trouble in his own time.

'I guess you must be mighty pleased with yourself.'

John jumped as the person spoke close to his ear. He had been so engrossed in his own thoughts, he had not heard Isolde slip in behind him.

'Is it not dangerous for you to come back just to gloat?'

'The crowd is my friend today, helping me evade the guards. Their movement has brought me this opportunity to tell you, you may have won this round, but you cannot win them all. My time will come. Until we meet again, young Time Guardian.'

John swung around, searching for a guard, but there were none in sight. When he turned back, Isolde was nowhere to be seen. At that moment, Barabal and Stanislaus appeared, and John decided to forget about Time Guardians, Wreckers and politics for just one night.

19

TYING UP LOOSE ENDS

YOU DID NOT want to consider staying and accepting King Henry's offer? LaLa asked John as the boy changed back into his own clothes, packed his pack, and attached his swag.

'Being squire to a king would be exciting, and a great honour. However, if I stayed, I would be running away from my own life. I need to go back and do what I can in my own time to make sure the changes we started here will continue. Perhaps this time I might even be able to help people see things a little differently.'

I expected nothing less from you. Your sense of responsibility is one of the reasons you were chosen to help. LaLa sounded like a proud parent.

'And maybe also because I had a lesson or two to learn here?' John smiled.

I am surprised to hear you learnt anything at all, the lamb chuckled.

'Well, I did. Perhaps to maybe think before I speak.'

And…

'All right. I give in. I also learnt there is no absolute right and wrong in any argument, although I am not sure how I can use that when I get back.'

I am confident you will find a way.

'You are going to say good-bye to Stanislaus and Barabal before you leave, aren't you?' Alain asked as they quietly left the apothecary's rooms so as not to disturb Master Barwick. He was sound asleep in a chair by the fire, having indulged a little too much during last night's festivities.

John paused, wondering if he should rethink his earlier decision to just slip away. 'I am not sure how to explain everything to them. I think it is best if I just leave.'

Those two are not yet far enough into their cycle to understand why John is here, and where he has come from. Their time will come, LaLa told them cryptically.

John stared down at the lamb. 'I guess you are not going to explain that any further?'

The lamb cocked his head to the side. *Those who help guardians on their quests develop powers and understanding over many life-times. When they are ready, they learn more about us and they are asked to assist on a mission. Barabal and Stanislaus must gather more life experience and awareness before they become assistants.*

John shook his head. 'Interesting though all that is, it is past time I returned to where I belong. How do we do this?'

Follow me.

John and Alain followed Lala out of the castle precinct and down to the banks of the Thames. In the pre-dawn morning, only a few people were about. They were so busy clearing up after the day before, they paid very little attention to two boys and a lamb.

Where do you want to go back to exactly? I am assuming not to where I found you? Home perhaps?

Thinking for a moment, John smiled. 'Not to my home, and most certainly not back to the billabong. If you can manage it, I would like to go back to the shearer's camp. I think I need to return and work with the moderates there to bring about peaceful change. Put what I learnt here to good use.'

He turned to Alain. 'Thank you for your friendship, I will not forget you.' He hugged the other boy. 'Please tell Barabal and Stanislaus I shall miss them too.'

Alain brushed a tear from his eye. 'I will never forget you either. Stay safe and well.'

Come on, you two, there is no need for long goodbyes. You are destined to meet again, although not in this lifetime. Come on John, let us be off.

Alain and John frowned and looked at Lala as the lamb walked towards the gently lapping waters of the Thames River.

'Whoa, hold on there, I am not going in that water.' John's face twisted

in horror at the thought of entering the sludgy, sewer ridden river below. 'We might catch something.'

How else do you think you are going to get back? I need water to create a portal.

John swore the lamb smiled. Alain also appeared a little sick at the thought of anyone going in the water that was London's primary sewer outlet.

'Can we at least find somewhere cleaner, further along the river perhaps?'

We would need to go some way away to find anywhere less polluted. Besides, the magic used to create the portal will protect us from anything in the water. Do you want to go or not? I am happy if you want to stay here and take up Henry's offer.

'All right, we should go.' John took a deep breath, not sure whether he was more nervous about entering the water, or going back home.

Pick me up and walk backwards, just as you did at the billabong.

Picking the lamb up, John climbed down the slimy steps and on to the muddy bank. Trying to put thoughts of the scummy Thames water lapping at his ankles out of his head, he fixed his eyes on Alain and walked backwards into the river.

The water rose against the back of his legs, and as it did the current became swifter. When it reached his knees, he was swept off his feet by the incoming tide. Shuddering at the thought of any Thames water actually getting inside him, he firmly closed his mouth and eyes. As he did, he began to feel nauseous as he fell into a swirling vortex. The world went black, and the next thing he knew he was waking up with the scorching Australian sun on his face.

You will be safe from here, thank you for your help. Until next time.

John arose on shaky legs, happy to find himself in a familiar landscape.

'Is that it? When will we meet again?'

Suddenly reluctant to let his lamb go, John delayed the moment as long as possible.

I am afraid I must hurry back as Master Barwick and I have a very important appointment to keep, and the portal will not remain open for long. You will do well from here. I checked your future, and you have much to look forward to. Although I cannot tell you any details I can say your life will, on balance, be a happy one. Goodbye and live well John Smith.

The lamb blinked out of sight. Shrugging his bag over his shoulder, John headed down the road towards the shearer's camp, all the while thinking how much lonelier it was travelling without companions.

Whistling to keep his spirits up, he put his hands in his pockets and

touched something metal. Pulling his hand back out, he found two five pound coins; more money than he had ever held at one time in his short life. It was enough for him to survive for a few months without needing to work. Things were looking up.

A little while later he turned the bend, and he was back where it all started. Although he had only been gone a short while, the tents were fewer in number, and the camp looked tired and defeated. As he drew closer, he spotted a familiar figure packing up his swag and tent.

'Bill. Bill, what has happened here?'

'Why, young John, you are just about the last person I expected to see. Have you come back to join us?'

'Ah, yes, I had a change of heart. But what happened to the camp?'

'We are being moved on. After the riots the locals no longer wanted us hanging around. Most of the others have left, there are only we few stragglers now.'

'Oh.' John's stomach sank. 'I am too late then.'

'That depends on how committed to the cause you are.' Bill stopped what he was doing and looked up. 'A few of us are heading over to Brisbane. We are thinking about joining up with the general worker's union, and seeing if we can bring about change for more than just we shearers.'

John's mood immediately lightened. 'Do you think I could come along?'

'It won't be easy, you know. They arranged places for us to stay, and promised some work on the docks, but you might be able to get by and still send a little home to your family. What I am going for though, is the promise we will be able to join their union and help them bring about some changes. I am sure they would welcome a thoughtful young man like yourself.'

'I guess I could at least come along and see what it is like,' John told him, thinking maybe this was an opportunity to make a change for the better in Australia.

'Good. Good.'

'We are ready when you are, Bill.'

John turned at the sound of a new voice, and almost fell over in shock.

'Are you all right? You look a little pale there.' The boy reached out and grabbed his arm, as if to make sure he did not collapse.

'No, no I am fine. It is just you look very much like someone I know.'

'I guess introductions are in order, since we are all to be travelling together. John, meet Stan, the local constable's son. He joined us just after you left. He did not like the way the shearer's were treated after the riot, and decided to come to Brisbane and help us make some changes for the better.'

VIVIENNE LEE FRASER

ALAIN GAZED AT the Thames water lapping against the dock, pondering his friend's departure from London. He had watched John, carrying the lamb guardian, back slowly into the water. The river swirled around in a circle, and then they disappeared.

It was not until that moment he actually believed a talking lamb had brought a boy from the future to help make sure Prince Henry became king, and enacted his charter. Now he could not deny the evidence of his own eyes. He was unsure if Lala was coming back, not that he was waiting for him exactly, rather he was trying to decide what to do with his life from here.

Last night the newly crowned king gave them his thanks for their efforts. John had been offered a small parcel of land and a position of squire with the king, which he politely turned down, saying he thought it was time he returned home. Stanislaus agreed to join King Henry's personal guard as a captain, flushing with pride as he did.

Barabal had been a different story. At first the king offered to make her a good marriage to a kind man. Fortunately, she managed to contain her temper, although disdain was written all over her face. In the end she settled for an expensive piece of jewellery.

Alain had been amazed she accepted the necklace until Barabal explained her decision. If the king gave her property, title would transfer to her husband on her marriage. However, her jewellery would remain her own for ever. Personal wealth for a woman was a form of independence.

The king had not offered Alain anything, he merely told him to talk with Master Barwick, and if his future was not settled after, then King Henry had some ideas of his own on how to reward the boy who saved his life.

That evening, Master Barwick had offered Alain the position of journeyman apothecary. He had no family, and in time, he would pass his practice on to Alain. The master was most persuasive, but it would mean staying in London, leaving his family and, well, he had to admit he did not like the idea of leaving Barabal.

Then there was the conversation he overheard as they waited for the king. King Henry had received a report of an outbreak of St Anthony's fire in the New Forest, affecting much of the local community. They were petitioning for aid. Through the door they heard the newly crowned king tell his friend, Robert de Beaumont, he believed the New Forest might be cursed.

Having two of his brother's die in the forest, now this, he wondered out loud if his father had been wrong to place the land under royal charter. He spoke of removing the charter and washing his hands of the whole place.

Alain considered returning home. He had long wondered if it was something in the grain that caused the skin rashes, blisters and hallucinations of St Anthony's fire. He would welcome an opportunity to study the outbreak, and perhaps find something to cure it, or at the very least, relieve the symptoms.

Then again, if he helped with the outbreak, would King Henry still want to give the New Forest back to the people of Briton? In his opinion, the return of any land seized after the Norman conquest had to be a good idea. He thought perhaps he might even petition for restoration of the property stolen from his father.

As he mulled over his future options, he saw the water by the dock swirl and a lamb pop up. Lala walked across the water to the bank, and Alain wandered over to meet him.

Your musings can be heard a mile away.

'Well, I have a lot to think about.'

You think the New Forest should be for everyone? How would you feel if I told you it will become a national treasure to be enjoyed by all if you leave it as it is?

'And I should just take your word for that?'

Alain heard a sort of a buzz in his head, as if the lamb spoke to someone, but he could not quite catch the conversation.

Come with us. You can find out for yourself.

'Come where? With who? Oh, like John? You want me to go back in time and help you fix something.'

You are nearly right. I want you to come forward in time, and help us with a little problem Master Barwick and I need to deal with.

Alain stared at the lamb in wonder. So many things ran through his mind, but all he said was, 'Master Barwick?'

Yes, the master has helped us before. His scientific skills will be needed on this trip, but we are able to take you along too if you want to come. You might be of help to him, and you will be able to see how you work together before deciding on his offer.

'Umm…'

You might also learn some useful skills to help you with the outbreak of St Anthony's fire.

'I have to say, that is tempting.'

We can have you back before anyone realises you left.

'Please stop reading my mind. Where and when would we be going?'

VIVIENNE LEE FRASER

Alain was not sure why he was even considering the lamb guardian's offer, but he was.

Quite some way in the future, beyond John's time. Something strange is happening in the New Forest, and we need to find out whether the trouble they are having with dogs is more than it seems on the surface. That is why I need Master Barwick's skills. At the very least, you can see what becomes of the New Forest if King Henry does not touch it.

They started walking back towards the palace.

'And you are sure you can bring me back before anyone knows I am missing?'

Of course.

Alain followed the lamb back to Master Barwick's lodgings, deep in thought. A man carrying a barrel of wine bumped into him, pulling him from his reverie.

'Sorry,' the man mumbled as Alain stepped aside to allow him past.

As he did, he glimpsed the man's face and stopped dead in his tracks. With his dark hair and tall build, the boy looked very familiar.

'That boy looks like... Was that John?'

John? Of course not, he is back home.

'But he looks exactly like... never mind.

Well, w*ill you come with us?*

Alain paused, trying to appear to be considering the offer, but excitement wriggled in his stomach and he knew the decision was already made.

'All right, I will come.'

EPILOGUE

'THAT WAS A close call, perhaps a little too close,' Alpha admonished Beta. 'I told you we were too quick to raise Sigma to our ranks.'

Beta's life form thrummed with annoyance. This debate was not new. For some reason Alpha had taken a dislike to Beta's protege, taking every opportunity to belittle the new Time Guardian. At least this time he was doing it in private, not in front of the rest of the council.

Patiently Beta responded, 'There was no way of knowing the Time Wreckers would interfere with this little slice of history, let alone send one of their most experienced operatives. Anyway, it all turned out well in the end, with Sigma's guidance.'

'And now you want this new guardian to take a trainee and a helper into the mayhem that is twenty-first century England, to deal with perhaps one of the biggest threats to our timeline.'

'I think you exaggerate, Alpha. They go to investigate a problem with dogs dying, to assess whether or not this is part of a bigger threat in that time period.'

'There will likely be Time Wreckers there, either working with the instigators, or observing as we are. Will Sigma really be able to handle it? Or will we

have to pull them out, disrupting the timeline even more? Or worse still, losing Zeta's replacement while he is still only a trainee.'

Beta's life form darkened as he realised Alpha insinuated Sigma was not able to deal with events smallest of small problems. He had trained the boy himself, and knew he was more than capable of dealing with anything the timeline threw at him. Now, if only he would prove it to Alpha.

'We can only watch and wait. The council already approved this mission, and only they can decide to end it.'

'I will be keeping a close eye on the situation.'

I am sure you will be, Beta thought to himself as Alpha winked away.

ABOUT THIS BOOK

HOW MUCH IS fiction and how much is real?

On 2 August 1100, King William Rufus, William the Second, was shot in the New Forest. His brother, Henry Beauclerc moved swiftly to seize the royal treasury from its holder, Ranulf Flambard, on the very day of the king's death. On the 6th of August, a mere four days later, Prince Henry was crowned King in Winchester Abbey. He was supported by his close friend Robert de Beaumont and opposed by his brother, Duke Robert Curthose of Normandy, who was championed by William of Breteuil.

On the 11 November Henry married Princess Matilda, sister of the King of Scotland. That month he also enacted the Charter of Liberties. Before her marriage, Princess Matilda studied at Romsey Abbey, under the guidance of her aunt, who was the abbess.

William Tirel was accused of shooting the arrow that killed King William, but this has never been proven, nor does anyone know whether the arrow to the stomach was a deliberate act or, an accident.

The political details in this book relating to Henry's manoeuvring to gain the support of the barons and church are well documented, as are relations between William the Conqueror's three sons.

VIVIENNE LEE FRASER

In 1890 in Australia, shearers began a strike over pay and conditions. Banjo Patterson wrote the song Waltzing Matilda at the time of the Queensland shearer's strike, and this was the starting point of my story. Everything and everyone else exists only in my imagination.

AUSTRALIAN COUNTRY MEETS Medieval England - how this all came together.

As I sat with my father in his hospital room, listening to his country music (Banjo Patterson was a favourite), and reminiscing on the stories he told us as children, an idea came to me. I started telling my father a story about how the swagman did not die in the billabong, but fell through to medieval times (dad loved the Knights of the Round Table).

Then I wove in my father (Alain), and added a character representing all of his friends (Stanislaus). Some of the antics of my father and his friends made it into this book (the cart in a ditch and blowing things up, tying shoe laces), making it truly a story for my dad.

As I wrote and researched some more, I had a feeling this book was meant to be because everything fell into place way too easily.

When the swagman left Australia in the 1890s I wanted him to fall into Medieval England to a time when the supremacy of kings began to erode. I typed in a google question, as you do, and the first thing that came up was Henry I and his Charter of Liberties. I had expected hours of trawling to find a time in history to link with the ideals of the strike, and there it was in front of me.

Serendipity then kept giving. Henry's accession to the throne came with its own dramatic plot line. The unexplained death of a king, followed by a struggle for power. It would be difficult to imagine a plot line this twisted.

To top it off, King William the Second, William Rufus, died in Hampshire's New Forest, then was taken to Winchester. Only a few months, before I had been with family visiting the New Forest. I had started planning a story that linked the past to the present set in a town we visited. (This will now be book two in the Circle of Time Series).

The bow to wrap this gift came in the form of Henry's wife, who was coincidentally christened Princess Matilda, but more often called Edith. Amazing, as swagmen and shearers used to call their bedrolls Matilda, hence the song name Waltzing Matilda.

ALCHEMIST
THE GUARDIANS OF TIME BOOK 2

PROLOGUE

BETA GAZED OUT over the Ethereal City from his suite in the Council Tower, and marvelled at how the Time Guardians had built their home to replicate Earth's cities. Strange, really—how they were so reluctant to give up ties to their former lives. Their absence of a physical form meant they no longer actually needed buildings.

Sighing, he imagined himself standing and his ghostlike form complied. The Council meeting would start soon and he must prepare. No doubt someone would have questions about his protege Sigma's latest adventure.

'You're still set on sending Sigma to cover the New Forest situation?'

Beta hated it when Alpha spoke before he materialised. There was no time for greetings, and thus no time to prepare for the attack his fellow councillor would inevitably launch—not to mention that the very act of admitting himself without permission was intrusive.

'Must we go over this again?' Beta asked wearily. 'The Council believes his connection with the potential Time Guardians who will be in the area during the event make him the best suited for the job.'

'I hear he is planning to take Alain, the apprentice apothecary from the Middle Ages, along with him and Barwick. Is that a good idea? I mean, it's

Barwick's final test before he rises to our ranks, so it is doubly important for him—I would hate to think his ascension was to be placed in jeopardy.'

Alpha's rehashing of old arguments was another trait that annoyed Beta, but he felt compelled to answer anyway. 'Again, Alpha, the Council believes because this group have teamed up successfully once before, that outweighs any of the other concerns.'

Beta paused for Alpha to respond. When he was met with silence, he continued his argument. 'Sigma could have left the boy behind but his incarnation at this time is living on a different continent and we were not able to speed up his return to England. In any case, a council majority agreed the benefits far outweighed the risks.'

'I know, but ...'

'Besides, his being taken along has some benefit for us. At the moment he is all set to abandon his training and leave for the New Forest to agitate in favour of returning crown lands to their original owners. Given his recent assistance to Henry, he might well be listened to.'

'Henry would not be so foolish as to handover land his father confiscated less than a generation ago. After all, King William conquered so much of Briton, it would set a dangerous precedent. Not to mention the ramifications in centuries to come.' Alpha sounded so sure of himself.

'My point exactly. Unfortunately, at the moment he believes the New Forest is cursed—two of King Henry's older brothers lost their lives in the area. You cannot blame him for thinking the royal forest best be handed back. There is a real possibility it will happen after the Time Wreckers' interference with the timeline. Now he is even more convinced the forest is jinxed.'

'Would returning the land be so bad?' Alpha mused.

Beta gritted his teeth. 'You know it would. The ripples through time would cause enormous disruption. It's only because the forest was a royal preserve that it was saved from overdevelopment, giving southern England one of its few national parks, and an area of great natural power.'

It was too much to hope that Alpha's silence indicated this conversation was over, but Beta found himself hoping anyway, only to be disappointed when Alpha said, 'And I guess we still need to deal with the problem of the boy learning to think before he leaps. A little time in the field may teach him to consider his actions first.'

'Yes, Alain does need to learn to consider consequences. He is young, yet...' Beta was suddenly reminded of Sigma, who was very similar at the same age, and his voice drifted off.

'Anyway, we have no time for pleasantries. I have called a special meeting of the Council,' Alpha interrupted. 'I proposed your team be pulled out and a more experienced one inserted in its place.'

'Oh, and what team would that be?' Beta asked the question, but was already sure he knew the answer.

'I thought as Theta was free at the moment . . . ' Alpha confirmed Beta's suspicions.

'Of course you did, and it would just be a coincidence that she was your trainee.'

'I am not sure what you are saying.' Alpha frowned as he stared directly at his host.

About to shoot off a stinging retort, Beta paused as something occurred to him, then asked, 'Alpha, is there something you are not telling me? Have you found some evidence this is more than a quick investigation to rule out foul play by the Time Wreckers?'

The air around Beta changed, indicating a rising tension in his companion. 'Not exactly'

Ha! Seemed like the Time Guardian couldn't bring himself to lie. 'Alpha?'

'Oh. All right. On her last mission, Theta picked up chatter about something going on in 2017 in England. I am concerned this might be part of it, and I am not sure Sigma has the experience to handle a full-on Time Wrecker attack and manage two untrained assistants.'

Beta sighed. 'You are right; that would be beyond his current capabilities. King Henry's coronation had some unexpected activity and Sigma handled it well. I am not sure though that he would be lucky enough to thwart a Time Wrecker incursion a second time. Perhaps we should go and find out what the rest of the Council think.'

1

JOURNEY'S END

THE TINKLE OF the shop bell alerted the teenage girl to a new presence, and Jo raised her head from the book she was engrossed in. Jenna, dishevelled and looking every one of her fifty-plus years, bustled from the door towards the counter.

'Hi Jenna. Watch—'

The stand by the counter toppled as charms flew everywhere, eventually finding a place on the ground. Trying to step around them, the distraught woman knocked a pile of books arranged on the counter ledge to the floor.

'Oh ... sorry ... oh dear.' Jenna froze, then burst into tears.

No doubt drawn by the ruckus, Alice, the store owner and Jo's boss, popped her head out to see what was going on. Moving swiftly, Alice pulled out a chair by the counter and manoeuvred Jenna towards it, narrowly avoiding any further disasters as Jo went to clear up the mess.

Having picked up the stray charms from the floor, she placed them on the counter, re-stacked the books, then busied herself untangling the charms, leaving Alice to calm their visitor.

When the sobbing subsided, Alice said, 'This is so unlike you, Jenna. What has you in such a fluster?'

'It's Pepe. I have just dropped him at the vet. He came down with it this

morning. You know, the same thing as all the other dogs ... the ones who walk the New Forest tracks. I have to prepare myself ...'

'Most of the dogs recover well if they are caught early,' Jo reassured the woman. Working at the local vet, she had seen a few cases of Alabama Rot come through. Unlike other places where outbreaks had occurred, all but a couple of their patients had recovered.

'I know ... but he is so ill …' Jenna trailed off, clearly too upset to go on.

'Let me go and make us some tea,' Jo said, leaving Alice to comfort her friend.

'It must be difficult for you. Pepe is a great companion for you, especially with Bill travelling so much for work.' Jo overheard Alice say as she entered the back room.

'I'm not sure I could bear to be without him.'

'I am sure he will be fine.' Alice soothed Jenna. 'What did the vet say?'

'She said we caught it early. There's a good chance Pepe will be okay.'

'That's great, and as Jo said, not all the dogs who contracted Alabama Rot have died.'

'I know, but ...' Jenna hesitated, then blurted out, 'I was kind of hoping you might be able to do something.'

'Do something?' Alice's voice raised in query, and Jo turned the kettle off to better hear her boss's answer.

'You know ... do some of that stuff you do.'

Jo almost dropped the tea caddy. Alice was always complaining that in the ten years she had been running The Witch's Hat, her family and friends had studiously ignored the fact her store sold charms, trinkets, and all the items any modern witch would need to practice their art. If they mentioned the store at all, they described it as a tourist trap.

Was Alice's practical, non-believing friend now suggesting she use witchcraft to help with her dog?

Jo finished making the tea as quietly as possible, still listening to the conversation in the shop.

'Jenna, I am not sure what you think I will be able to do.'

Jenna sniffled before answering. 'I thought ... you know ... that you might be able to cast a spell or something to protect Pepe, or make him better.'

Jo almost snorted, unable to believe people really thought magic worked like that.

'Pepe is in the best place, Jenna. There are spells used in witchcraft that can certainly help channel healing energies, but they're no substitute for a good vet.'

'Are you saying you can't help me?' Jenna sounded defeated, almost as though she had written her dog off.

'Well, not exactly. There have been so many dogs coming down with this disease lately, more than in previous years. I've reached out to some, um ... friends ... who may be able to be of more help than me in dealing with the blight growing in our forest.'

Jo almost dropped the mugs in her hands. Who had Alice called to help them? And what would they be able to do that their own coven of witches could not?

'What will they be able to do that you can't?' Jenna asked, her voice sounding rather uncertain to Jo's ears.

'I'm not sure, to be honest,' Alice answered as Jo pushed her way through the curtain with three mugs of tea in hand. 'In this modern world we are so distanced from our ties to the land, the magic we can perform is limited compared to what it once was. I hope these people will have some ideas about how to, um ... help heal the land, I guess.'

Jenna sat forward in her seat. 'Who are they? Will they be here soon?'

For a person who was usually reluctant to acknowledge the existence of magic, Jenna was awfully eager to know more. Jo waited for Alice's response, but her boss was strangely silent.

Sometime later, once Jenna had finished her tea and left, Jo decided to ask her boss what was going on.

'I am sorry, Jo. I really don't want to talk about it. It was just something I tried on the spur of the moment—I am sure nothing will come of it. I only said it to boost Jenna's mood. If you wouldn't mind putting those charms back out for me, I still have some work to do in here.'

Sitting down at her desk, the shop owner turned her computer back on and straightened the pile of papers, ready to return to work. Having been dismissed Jo turned to leave, and knocked some files to the floor. She bent to pick them up and caught a glimpse of the spine of a book in amongst the paperwork—*Spells from Medieval England.*

As she replaced the files she slipped the book behind her back just as she was summoned by the shop bell.

ALAIN STOOD, WIPING off his leggings, and slowly turned to survey his surroundings. Morning fog rolled across the grass and swirled eerily

around them. The soupy substance was so thick the trees encircling them were merely ominous shapes.

'Are we there?' Alain asked through chattering teeth.

'Yes, I believe we are in the New Forest, although I have no way of knowing whether or not we are in the right year.' Master Barwick's answer was short and sharp as he rolled onto all fours in an attempt to get up. Alain reached down to help the rotund older man to his feet. As he did, a rumbling filled the pre-dawn air. Two glowing beams cut through the mist.

Whoosh!

Alain looked up in alarm. 'What ...?' His eyes grew round as the light swiftly drew closer, and there was another *whoosh* as a peculiar rectangular shape passed them by. The journey here must have scrambled his brain because he was sure he saw a face staring out of the contraption at him.

It was difficult to believe just seconds ago he had been standing on the wharf in front of Westminster Castle, his only concern whether to stay with Barabal or go home to Winchester. Now here he was, hundreds of years in the future, all because Lala had suggested this journey might be good for him to understand the importance of the New Forest remaining a royal preserve.

Now that very same Time Guardian was nowhere to be found.

Lala? Alain sent the thought out, hoping for some sort of a reply from the being who had brought them to this strange place.

'I can't see him,' Master Barwick grumbled as he turned in a circle. 'He must be here somewhere. He came with us through the portal in the Thames that brought us to this goddess-forsaken place.'

'Master Barwick, that is a little strong. We only just arrived, so we can hardly be judgmental.'

With his grey-white hair standing out in tufts from his head, and his robes damp and dishevelled, Master Barwick, apothecary to King Henry and part-time alchemist, glared balefully at the young boy.

'I may be having second thoughts about taking you on as an apprentice,' he said. 'Stop for a moment and really feel this place. Magic is weak here.'

Wrapping his arms around his shivering form, Alain calmed his nerves and allowed his senses to expand. He trembled a little, not from the cold—although it was certainly chilly—but from fear. Master Barwick was right. If he concentrated, he could just about feel a little tingle of magical energy. His whole life, magic had just been there; now, it was not. Its absence threw him off balance, reinforcing how far he was from home.

Master Barwick spoke into the silence.' The goddess holds no sway here. The people of this place no longer take care of the earth; the old ways have been forgotten.'

Alain was prevented from adding to the discussion as more lights cut through the air, and a rumbling drew closer. Moving slightly nearer to his master, Alain asked, 'What is that and how do we fight it if we have no magic?'

'Um, I don't think we will be required to do battle with the machines. I am not one hundred percent sure, but they are similar to something I saw on my last trip with Sigma—I mean, Lala—although these ones are larger and move more quickly. I am sure they are manmade contraptions used to move people around.'

'You can have a laugh at my expense, Master Barwick, as this is the first journey I have taken out of my time, but eventually you are going to have to tell me what they actually are.'

Frowning, Master Barwick shook his head. 'I am not jesting. I seem to remember they are called horseless carriages. They are not dangerous … well, not unless you stand on the tracks they run on, and one bowls you over.' Master Barwick chuckled. 'Come now. We need to find Lala. He has all the details of our mission, not to mention we cannot return home without him.'

Alain opened his mouth to voice his concerns about not being able to return to Westminster in time to say goodbye to Barabal, then he remembered how horrid travelling through the time portal had been and he shut it. When he had decided to slip away with the Time Guardian Lala, he had been so excited he had not thought about how they would be getting to their destination.

He had almost backed out when Lala had led himself and Master Barwick down to the water—the slimy, filthy water that ran through the city of London—and he realised how the Time Guardian was planning to transport them to the future.

Only an hour or so earlier he had watched Lala return John, a boy the Time Guardian had brought from Australia in the 1800s to help them save King Henry, home—through a swirling time portal in the same river he stood beside. Of course they would be travelling the same way.

Attempting to ignore the floating debris, Alain had taken a deep breath and followed Master Barwick and Lala into the icy-cold Thames. Concentrating on keeping his breakfast down, he'd been swept off his feet by a whirlpool of water as he fell into complete blackness, only to stop abruptly when his bottom hit the soggy ground of the field they now found themselves in. It

was not a journey he wished to repeat anytime soon.

If the Time Guardian wearing a lamb's body was to be trusted, they'd left London in November 1101, and were now in the New Forest, Hampshire, in the fantastical year of 2017. Having transported them nine hundred years into the future, Lala had then abandoned them to go and do ... well ... Alain was not sure what, but it wasn't very helpful of him.

'You should know better than to bring a boy out to play your stupid medieval games in weather like this—and without his coat too.' The shrill voice broke through the morning air. Dressed in some sort of unusual cloak, and wearing trousers like a male serf, a middle-aged woman leading a dog emerged from the fog and confronted Master Barwick.

'It is bad enough you men must play at re-enacting the past, but to drag your poor children into it as well is too much. Look at him; he is soaked through. Take him home before I call the authorities and report you for child neglect.'

Child neglect?

All right, his vision was somewhat obscured by strands of black hair dripping with water, and he had forgotten his cloak—but other than that, he was fine. Was this woman actually comparing him to the poor souls who hung about the castle kitchens, begging for scraps? How dare she compare him to those starving mistreated children.

He opened his mouth to give her a piece of his mind, then closed it. No one cared about the maltreated children in his time; no one in authority would even consider answering a call to help them. It appeared 2017 might take a bit of getting used to.

Lala must be close by because I can understand this harridan, Master Barwick spoke directly into his mind.

Huh? It took Alain a moment to comprehend what his master was saying.

Have you lost all your wits, boy? We need Lala to translate for us. English in this time is quite different from ours. He ensures we hear what people say in our tongue, and our words sound like modern English to them. Master Barwick's tone was impatient.

Lost my wit? Perhaps this is an everyday trip for you, but I have never time travelled before. Alain was quick to defend himself.

'Were you listening to what I said, or are you deaf as well as stupid?' The woman asked, her shrill voice pierced Alain's eardrums and he had to stop himself from putting his hands over his ears.

'I am sorry, ma'am, did you perhaps leave your manners at home this morning?' Master Barwick beamed, and his voice oozed with charm as he

traded insult for insult. 'The boy asked to come with me today, and his clothing is made of the finest wool so he is warmer than he looks. Besides he will be heading home just as soon as we find the animal we lost.'

The woman's eyes widened, then she pulled her coat more closely around her as she huffed. 'Well, I did see a stray Cockapoo—just over there. Similar colouring to my own Cherry, it was. Perhaps it is yours.'

Without answering, Master Barwick took off in the direction she'd pointed.

'Ah, thank you,' Alain said as he left the woman standing in the drizzling rain.

Within a few paces, they found a fluffy dog with long ears and sorrowful eyes sitting under the shelter of a tree. As they approached, it shook droplets of rain from its coat then settled down again as if waiting for them to approach.

'Is that a Cockapoo? I guess it has wool similar to Lala, but ...' Alain laughed.

I prefer the term Spoodle, and I could not go about in this time as a lamb. They are not exactly allowed in homes here, the dog sent to his mind.

Alain was distracted by rustling from behind him as the woman joined them.

'We have found our friend Lala. Thank you,' Master Barwick said politely.

'Lala. An escape artist like that is more aptly named Trouble.' The woman tossed over her shoulder as she stalked off. 'And he should be on a lead in this part of the forest.'

'Trouble.' Master Barwick's laughter filled the morning, and soon it turned into a splutter he was unable to stop.

You would not ... Lala protested.

I would and I am, Master Barwick said.

Impressive, Alain thought as he watched Master Barwick's shoulder shake with laughter. *How is he able to mind-speak while laughing so much?*

Practice, my lad, Master Barwick said. *And you need to practice shielding your thoughts from others.*

Shivering again, Alain was about to send a cutting response when he decided against it. He was keen to go somewhere a little warmer, complete their mission as quickly as possible, and return home. Lala had assured him he would be back in time for dinner, but Alain did not know just how accurate this time travel thing was, and he had promised his friend Barabal he would be there to say goodbye when she left to escort the new Queen to her wedding.

'Master Barwick, can we get going?' Alain asked out loud to reinforce the urgency he felt.

Master Barwick took a deep breath while the dog stared mournfully at

him. Catching sight of the dog again, he burst into fresh bouts of laughter as he choked out the word, "Trouble". The apothecary eventually managed to still his laughter to an occasional chuckle before saying, 'Righto, Trouble. What do we do now?'

If you don't want to call me Lala, use my Time Guardian name, Sigma.

'But you hate being called Sigma. And Trouble is a great name for a dog, and it is also an apt name for you, my friend.' Master Barwick smirked.

If I am having a name change, so must you. No one is called Master in this time, and Alain cannot call you Barwick as it would be disrespectful. You must be called by your Christian name—Barnaby, Trouble said.

'But I detest that name,' Master Barwick protested.

But you respond to it and that is what is important, Trouble's tone was matter of fact and Alain sighed with relief as their guide focussed on the task ahead.

'Humph.'

Trouble ignored Master Barwick's comment. *As you have already found, children are treated differently in this time. People cannot simply pick up a stray child and keep it.*

I am not a child. I am almost eighteen, Alain objected.

In this time in England, you are not legally an adult until you are eighteen. We could lie—simply tell people Master Barwick is your uncle, and he has taken care of you since your parents died. That way we explain why you have no family.

Sounds like a good cover story, Master Barwick agreed. *We also need to be from somewhere quite remote—somewhere no one has been—somewhere like the Scottish Highland.*

It was Trouble's turn to laugh, only it came out sort of like a barky snort. *I tell you things have changed a little since your time. People now actually live in the Scottish Highlands, and some even go there for holidays.*

Holidays? Master Barwick stroked his beard as he considered the word.

Yes, Barwick. That is when people take time off work to do the things they enjoy.

Master Barwick scratched his head. *Work is enjoyable. To not work? Now that sounds very stressful.*

Come on, you two. I am freezing here. Alain attempted to bring his mentor's attention back to the task at hand.

Spoilsport. Right, let me see. Perhaps you could be from an island in the Scottish Hebrides.

'So, Uncle Barnaby, we have travelled with our dog Trouble from the Scottish Hebrides, but where are we going to?'

Trouble stood and shook water from his coat, spraying his human friends

before walking over to a sign by the edge of the field.

That way. He pointed with his head.

As Alain passed, he read the sign—*Burley 3 miles.*

TROUBLE LED THE bedraggled group through the forest's back lanes until they reached the edge of a village. The fog was beginning to clear a little, and they were being passed by more of the horseless carriages, albeit going a little slower than they had been before. Still more of the four-wheeled vehicles were standing outside the enormous mansions they walked past.

'How do they work, Master Barwick? The horseless carriages, I mean. Is it by magic?'

The dog stopped and turned to face Alain, his head cocked to the side. *You need to get used to calling Master Barwick "Uncle Barnaby". And if you have questions about things in this time it is perhaps best you mind-speak them. You will appear quite odd to people if you voice these things out loud.*

'Sorry,' Alain mumbled. 'I will try to remember. You did not answer my question though, Uncle Barnaby.'

They have not been called horseless carriages for more than 100 years—they are called cars. They are mechanical contraptions, powered by petrol, one of the ingredients of your Greek Fire, Trouble answered before Master Barwick was able to.

Alain veered away from the "car" he was just passing. 'Don't they blow up?'

Trouble did that weird, yipping laugh again. *Good grief, no. There are so many of them; they're everywhere. This world would be very dangerous if they kept exploding all the time. They are perfectly safe to use—well, so long as they have a good driver behind the wheel. Come on, this way.*

The dog turned down a narrow alleyway, then stopped by a leafy green hedge. *We are here. You need to take the lead now, Barwick.*

'This is where we are going?' Alain whispered, his stomach clenching. He had managed to keep his fear of cars under control, but this was a step too far.

The two-storey house in front of them was painted white, and had more glass windows than he had seen in any dwelling other than Westminster Palace. Clearly the person living here was high-born and wealthy.

Looking around, he found the street to be full of similar buildings. It reminded him of the area in London where the barons and dukes had their city dwellings. Although he had spent time with King Henry, he was not

used to actually staying with nobility, and he was not interested in changing that any time soon.

'It's very grand. Are you sure we will be welcome?' Alain said, a little louder.

'Don't worry. We will be fine.' Master Barwick placed a comforting hand on his shoulder. 'Things have changed much since our time. The general population of England has a much higher standard of living, and I think you will find the people who live here quite ordinary.'

Taking a deep breath, Alain followed Master Barwick to the veranda and waited while the older man knocked on the door. The master waited a moment, then knocked again.

'Hold your horses, I'm coming,' a voice yelled from within, followed by the sound of feet slapping on bare floorboards.

The door flung open and standing in front of them was a woman who barely reached Alain's shoulders, with short grey hair and intense brown eyes. She reminded him of someone, but he could not place his finger on it. She slowly looked them up and down, her eyebrows rising quizzically.

'Can I help you?' she asked in a voice that told them she clearly did not think she would be able to.

'I think, madam, you will find it is we who have come to help you,' Master Barwick said.

Frowning, the woman glared at Master Barwick, then shook her head. 'I am sorry, but I am not into medieval re-enactments, so I am not sure how you can ...'

'Medieval?' The word slipped from Alain's lips. *Oops, I really must stop letting my thoughts escape through my mouth,* he admonished himself.

It is what people now call the time you lived in—the Middle Ages or the Dark Ages, Trouble told him.

Why the Dark Ages? Alain asked.

In later centuries, the so-called Middle Ages were seen as a time of artistic and intellectual decline, Trouble responded.

Alain snorted. *Dark Ages—well, that is downright insulting and ...*

... and not something you can do anything about, Trouble calmly informed him.

Still, I could name this period as dark given how much they have pillaged the land, Alain continued.

'Quiet. I am talking here,' Master Barwick admonished them.

'Well, I never —he only asked a simple question.' The woman placed her hands on her hips and glared at the man on her doorstep, then turned her

focus to Alain. 'It is just you are dressed in costumes from the Middle Ages, young man, so I assumed …' The woman stopped and stared at Master Barwick, who was blushing all the way to the tips of his wayward white hair.

Alain thought to himself, *How odd. She reminds me of Barabal—or maybe I just have Barabal on my mind.*

Wringing his hands, his Master started again. 'Please, this is not going so well. Perhaps we might start over. I am Barnaby Barwick, master apothecary and part-time alchemist. I have been led to believe someone at this address called for assistance from a group we believed long forgotten on this world.'

With her mouth hanging open, the woman swayed and clutched at the doorjamb before uttering, 'Oh my goodness. My spell actually worked? You are an actual guardian?'

'Well, no, not exactly. But I have been sent by them to help you out. Actually, we both have. This is Alain, my nephew and apprentice.'

'The guardians sent you?' the woman repeated. 'You're not having a joke at my expense?'

'Madam, I never joke.' Master Barwick pulled himself up to his full height and puffed out his chest. 'We call them the Time Guardians, and yes, they sent us. Do you still need our help? If so, perhaps we might come in out of the cold and talk about why you called for assistance. We have come a long way, and we didn't dress for this wet weather.'

There was a long pause as the woman stared blankly at Master Barwick, and Alain wondered if she might not be a little simple. Just as he was preparing to suggest they leave, the woman shook her head, and held the door open as she spoke. 'Yes, yes. Oh ... sorry ...please forgive me, it is just you took me a little by surprise. I didn't expect it to work ... oh, look at me ... where are my manners? Please come in.' She moved aside and ushered her guests past. 'Keep going down the hall. The kitchen is down the back and the Aga is on full, so you should warm up in no time.'

Alain warily followed Master Barwick in, but not before glancing behind to ensure Trouble was with them.

'The dog is with you? Is he okay inside?'

Looking down at the diminutive woman Alain frowned, not quite sure what she meant by okay. She had paused in the hallway, waiting for him to respond, so he said, 'Yes, he is with us and needs to come inside.'

'Good. I wasn't sure whether he was house-trained or not.'

Trouble humphed his displeasure as their hostess shut the door, then

escorted them down a narrow hallway. On the left was a room, and to the right were stairs to the second storey.

As he passed by a sitting room, Alain's eyes were drawn to a wall covered in books, showing how wealthy his hostess must be. Beside the books was a shiny rectangular black box on a table, and on the mantle next door was a gold pendulum clock. By the time he arrived at the doorway at the end of the hall, he was almost paralysed by the unfamiliar and expensive items on display.

The opening led into a kitchen which ran the width of the house. It was dominated by a wooden table that would easily seat ten people, and a huge stove to the left. The woman slipped by him and headed to the sink, which was under a window directly in front of them. She turned on a tap to fill a kettle before placing it on the stove. Alain's eyes widened—they had running water *in* the house.

To the right of the bench was another door with two rows of three glass panels at the top, framing a garden out the back. Nestled into the wall to the right was an odd white thing that gave off a faint hum. As he slowly moved inside the room, he bumped his hip against a floor-to-ceiling dresser with plates and serving dishes running along the wall.

Moving closer to Master Barwick, who had set himself by the stove, Alain enjoyed the delicious warmth encompassing him.

'You are both wet through, let me find you some towels to dry off. Where are your cases? Are they in your car? Perhaps you should get them and change into something dry.'

They must have looked confused, because she stopped and looked at them—really looked at them. Resting her chin in her hand, she circled them both, stopping when she came face to face with Master Barwick. 'Your clothes—they are not some sort of re-enactment garb, are they?' She reached out and rubbed the fabric at the bottom of the master's tunic between her fingers, then turned it inside out so she might better see how the garment was constructed. 'Your tunic is actually made of pure wool, and those seams are hand-sewn.'

When neither of them attempted an explanation, she said, 'When you speak, the right words come out of your mouth, but your lips are not making the shapes they should—it's like watching a badly dubbed movie. You have travelled from somewhere else entirely.'

How could he ever have thought this woman was addle-brained? Alain looked to his master, then at Trouble, wondering how they were going to

handle this situation.

What do I tell her? Master Barwick asked Trouble.

Barwick, I see no other way than to tell her the truth. Lies are too difficult to sustain for long, and I think you and Alain will need someone to help you both adjust to the strangeness of this time.

'Umm ...' Master Barwick started, but was quickly interrupted by Trouble.

Best you don't say anything about me for the moment. Time travel will be hard enough to deal with without introducing the idea of talking dogs.

'Um ... yes, you could say we are from far away—another time, in fact. Perhaps if you would not mind if we dried out, and maybe partake of a cup of tea once the kettle is boiled. When we are warm and dry we will tell you where we come from, and then you might tell us what is going on here and why we were summoned.'

The woman didn't move for a moment, then nodded once and swivelled on her heel. Over her shoulder, she said, 'I will get some towels. I think my husband's clothes should fit you, and I might find some of my son's things in the closets for Alain.'

She shut the door behind her. Alain soon heard footsteps on the stairs and the sounds of rummaging above. Wet and cold, they had little option but to wait for the woman who had called them to this time to return.

SOMETIME LATER, THEY were sitting at the table in the kitchen with Trouble curled up on a brightly crocheted blanket in front of the Aga. The clothes Alain wore felt strange. Alice, for that was the name of their hostess, had informed him the trousers were called jeans, and the warm top was a fleece. It was nothing like an animal fleece, but it was soft and warm, and cosy.

The clothes belonged to Alice's son, who was a soldier stationed in Afghanistan—wherever that was. His hostess was sure he would not mind Alain borrowing some of his clothes.

Master Barwick was dressed in something called corduroys, a shirt and a woollen sweater. They belonged to Alice's husband, who was on a business trip to another country called Hong Kong, and would not return for some weeks.

Warm, dry, and with their stomachs full, they were sitting with a cup of tea each. Alain rolled the tea around his mouth. It tasted different from the teas he was used to drinking. It was even more delicious when he followed

Alice's advice and added a dash of milk from the jug.

'Right, now we are fed and watered, it is time to get down to business. Let's start with your names again, and where you are from.' Her brusque and authoritative manner really did remind him of his friend Barabal, so much so it brought a lump to his throat.

'I am Master Barwick, apothecary to King Henry when he is in London.'

'King Henry? Henry the Eighth?'

'The eighth? No.' Master Barwick shook his head. 'My king is the only King of England to have been called Henry.'

'Oh my goodness.' Alice's hand flew to her mouth. 'You are from around the time of ... oh let me think …'

'We came from the year 1100AD,' Alain told her.

'Goodness, how strange all this must be for you.' Alice looked kindly at him, and he wanted to tell her how unsettling it actually was, and how much he wished he had not come. But she had been so welcoming, and she needed their help, so he mumbled it was not too bad, and carried on sipping his drink.

'How did you get here?' she asked.

'The Time Guardians can create time and space portals for travel,' Master Barwick informed her.

Alain waited for her look of confusion and some questions about how something like that might work. Instead, he was treated to a nod as Alice commented, 'Of course they would be able to do that.'

As Alain pondered what sort of world this was where magic was all but gone but time and space portals were treated as an everyday thing, Master Barwick continued to explain their current situation.

'We arrived with only what you see. As you can imagine, anything from our time would make us stand out, and we don't want that. So I am afraid we will need a bit of support while we investigate your problem.'

A frown furrowed Alice's brow before she launched into organisation mode. 'I have my niece and nephew arriving today, so things might be a little cramped. Let me see. You can have my husband's office over the garage. You did say you are also an alchemist. Well, he is a scientist and you might find his equipment useful. He also has a pull-out couch you can sleep on.'

Alain and Master Barwick exchanged glances. *Pull-out couch?* Alain asked and his master shrugged his shoulders.

'Bebe can sleep in the guest room as planned. Alain can share with Lee in my son's room—I think we still have the old trundle bed we used to use

when his friends came for sleepovers.'

Do not even ask. I have no idea about trundles and sleepovers, Master Barwick warned. *Trouble?*

The dog raised his eyebrows, but made no effort to enlighten them.

'Follow me. I will show you everything. Once you are settled in, we can talk about what drove me to ask you here. Will the dog be okay by the fire?'

I will be perfect, Trouble told them as he rolled on to his back, legs splayed.

ALICE LED THEM out through the back door and up the wooden stairs to the room over the garage. It was full of bottles, and burners and jars of powders and other things Alain was unable to name—everything any alchemist might ever want and more. While he and Master Barwick gawped, Alice apologised for the poor selection. 'I can get you anything else you might need,' she added

'No ... really ... this will be fine,' Master Barwick told her. His fingers were twitching so much Alain just knew he could not wait to get his hands on the toys on offer.

If the chemistry equipment was not enough, there was also a sofa, which turned out to be a comfy chair for more than one person. To their amazement, it transformed into a full-sized bed.

Am I in heaven? Master Barwick asked, the grin on his face emphasising his delight.

They re-entered the house through the front door, and their hostess led them up to a room which was obviously intended for sleeping, but contained some other strange items of furniture.

Retrieving something metal from under the bed, Alice asked him to help her pull out the legs. Once extended, it formed a kind of cot. So this was a trundle. Alice then led him to a cupboard in the hallway and asked him to pull a roll from the top shelf.

He unfurled the mattress out over the metal frame. Alice then passed him another mattress, called a topper pad, and some bedding. When he had finished making up the trundle, Alice came back with two pillows and a thick blanket she called a duvet.

'I am sorry. It is not the most comfortable of beds,' Alice said as he sunk down to test it out.

Expecting it must be as hard as a board, he found himself enveloped in the comfiest bed he had ever lain on.

'I would let you have the other one, but Lee is quite a bit larger than you, and I suspect this thing would not hold his extra bulk.'

'This is perfect,' Alain assured her as his eyes began to close and his mind drifted off, revisiting all the strange things he had seen so far that day. Alice's voice pulled him back to the room.

'Here take this.' She handed him some sort of fabric bag. 'Open it for me and I will put some of my Tom's clothes in here. That way, my niece and nephew will not suspect where you came from.'

Turning the bag over in his hands, Alain found the mechanism keeping it closed, but he had no idea how to open it. Peering over the pile of clothes she had taken from the drawers, Alice laughed.

'Sorry, I should have thought. This is called a zip,' she explained as she pulled at a metal tag, which moved smoothly down to reveal the inside of the bag.

Placing each pile of clothing inside, she named them for him. 'Jeans, T-shirts, sweatshirts, underpants, shirts and underclothes. Hold on a moment; I have an extra toothbrush here and some toothpaste.'

Alain's head swam. It was obvious what the toothbrush was used for. People here must use them instead of wooden sticks for cleaning teeth; but what on earth was toothpaste? His confusion must have been written on his face as Alice demonstrated how the paste was put on the brush and used with water to clean teeth.

It was all too much for Alain to take in. His head was spinning, and he was sure it would explode if he had to learn about one more thing.

'That's you sorted. Now it is your turn, Barnaby.' Alice handed Alain an oblong black box and said, 'Here, perhaps you could watch some telly while I sort him out.'

No doubt realising her mistake, she quickly grabbed the item back. 'This is difficult. This is a remote, it works the telly, or television, which provides entertainment.' Alice's hand swept towards the rectangular thing sitting on top of a dresser. It was a smaller version of the black box he had seen in the sitting room earlier.

Alain stared at his reflection in the shiny surface. How was this meant to entertain him?

Alice continued, 'It shows plays, and news, and, well, some other truly

dreadful stuff you should avoid if at all possible.'

Alain looked blankly at her. She sighed and ran a hand through her hair. 'Let me see. Do you know anyone who can scry using water?'

Alain nodded. It was an advanced skill some druids still practiced. He had only seen it once, but he was fascinated by the images they conjured.

'Good. Well this is like entertainment in a scrying bowl.'

Nodding, Alain watched as Alice pressed the remote. A buzz caused him to turn just in time to see the thin black oblong thing light up, and people appear. Alain's jaw dropped. this was more amazing than the transforming sofa in the room above the garage.

'Re-runs of *Emmerdale*. Perhaps not so good for your first day in our time; it might give you the wrong impression.' Like a blinking eye, the picture changed and some of the strange horseless carriages appeared in place of the people.

'You cannot go too wrong with *Thomas the Tank Engine*,' Alice said as she pressed another button and the sound of voices filled the room.

Alain jumped back. 'I can hear them speak.'

'Ah, yes. Think of this as superpowered scrying.'

Master Barwick and Alice left him alone, and Alain sunk on the bed, entranced by the modern scrying device. Once he stopped wondering how machines had evolved enough to speak, he lost himself in the story of *The School of Ducks*.

He marvelled at how the engines worked to help the children get home after their school building was destroyed. He learnt some useful concepts about this world. The first was, all children seemed to go to school, and they had a special name for making use of things rather than throwing them away—recycling.

Alain chuckled as the engines looked through the debris people had discarded—there was even a table with a broken leg. Back home, if a table leg broke a new one was made. Even the broken wood would be carved into a spoon. No one would consider throwing out anything as valuable as a piece of furniture—they could not afford to.

He was disappointed when Alice reappeared and turned off the telly and urged him to come downstairs as they still had things to discuss.

Alain reluctantly followed her back to the kitchen. 'Alice, I have a few questions I would like to ask Thomas and his friends. Is it possible to visit and ask them myself, or should I write them in a letter?'

Alice tripped on the stair and he prevented her from falling and helped right her before she answered, 'Oh Alain, that was a story. Engines don't talk; it is just a make-believe show for children to watch, sort of like a play.'

'But I thought you said it was a scrying machine, and you can only scry actual people and actual places.' This television thing was really confusing. Surely if Thomas was like a play then there really were talking engines.

'Oh dear. I see I am going to have to be very careful how I explain things to you. Perhaps we should steer clear of the television for a while.'

'So the engines aren't real?' Alain plonked down in the chair beside Master Barwick, shaking his head. 'Perhaps it was a mistake coming here. I don't understand anything at all and the machines …' he whispered to Master Barwick.

The older man squeezed his arm in understanding, then nodded towards Alice, who stood by the fire, ready to explain why she had called them.

'Before I start, I must address something. Perhaps your guardians were a little optimistic sending people from so far back in time to look into our problem. Since you arrived, I have found so many things that are new to you or that you don't understand. Modern technology and furniture aside, society has advanced so much you both stick out like sore thumbs.'

'We were led to believe there might be some sort of magical interference, and it has been a while since true magical practitioners walked the land in England, so what were the guardians to do?' Master Barwick countered on their behalf.

'I appreciate that, but your investigation might be hindered by your limitations in the modern world.'

I believe your skills far outweigh the disadvantages. Trouble raised his head and looked at them. *You just need to find a way to work around being in a different time.*

'Are you listening to me?' Alice asked, and Alain and Master Barwick turned to look at her.

'Sorry. We were thinking,' Alain explained on their behalf.

'I said, perhaps we tell the others Barnaby has come from somewhere quite remote to use Donald's equipment to run some tests on the problems we've been facing. I am sure you could play the eccentric scientist.'

Master Barwick nodded. 'We already thought of saying I live in the Outer Hebrides, and that Alain, my nephew, came to live with me as a small boy.'

'Good.' Alice nodded thoughtfully. 'If we explain how you homeschooled him because your island is so remote, and you never introduced him to technology because you don't believe in it—that will explain your lack of

skills. But why would you bring him here now?'

Alice drummed her fingers against her lips. 'I know. We have a good school nearby, the Ballard School. It is small and select, and is the perfect place to send someone to finish their A levels before heading to university—especially someone who needs to get to grips with the modern world.'

'That is a great story,' Master Barwick acknowledged. 'Can we tie any of this in with what is happening in the New Forest, so it sounds less like a story and more like what might have happened?'

'Of course.' Alice appeared shocked that he would question her ability to produce a believable cover for them. The more she spoke, the more Alice reminded him of Barabal—his friend had the knack of turning every situation to her advantage as well. He had never met Barabal's mother. She had passed away when his friend was not much more than a baby, but he imagined she would have been a lot like Alice.

It is not so strange that she reminds you of Barabal. Alice is a distant relation of your friend—a many times great-grandchild, Trouble informed him.

Hold on a moment. I might have plans for Barabal and myself. Does that mean she is a relation of mine as well?

I am unable to say, Trouble responded.

I won't be upset either way, Alain reassured the dog. *Well, not much ...*

No, I obviously have not made myself clear. If I say she is or is not, that tells you something about your own future, and therefore might change it.

'Alain. ALAIN!'

'Sorry, Barnaby. My thoughts wandered off on me,' Alain was still looking from Trouble to Alice, unable to get his head around the idea that this woman who was old enough to be his mother might actually be his many-times-removed granddaughter—or not.

'Please pay attention, Alain. This is important. Alice is ready to tell us why we have been called here.'

'I will start again so we are all on the same page,' Alice said, then waited as though she wanted to make sure she had their attention before continuing.

'For some time now, dogs in the local area have been getting ill. Many of them recover, but one or two have not pulled through. Local vets have not been able to identify the problem, but they have managed to narrow down the victims to dogs who are walked near here—in the New Forest.'

'Well that is a start,' Master Barwick commented.

'Yes, I guess it is,' Alice agreed.

'So, what are the symptoms?' He encouraged Alice to continue.

'The first signs are ulcers around the legs and chest, followed by lethargy and fever. This is as far as it goes for most dogs, but there are a few who advance on to renal failure—sorry, liver failure—and, in most of those cases, death.'

'Would you call it a mass outbreak, or an epidemic?' Master Barwick sat forward in his chair as he asked the question.

'No, not an epidemic. Well, not until recently. The number of incidents in our area have been growing exponentially compared to other places where the problem has been found. Still, I would not call it a full-blown epidemic, but I didn't want to wait until it reached that level before I called in help.'

Alain had been following along, and one question stood out, so he held up his hand to speak.

'You don't need to raise your hand; just ask what you want to,' Master Barwick told him.

'Alice, you said you called us here because more dogs are getting sick. Have there been any cases in humans?'

'Goodness no. Whatever this is only affects dogs.'

Master Barwick ran his hand through his hair, causing it to stand up even more. 'All right, now we have cleared that up, Alice you said local vets have been looking into the cases you have had?'

'Mm, yes.'

'Right. First off, what is a vet?'

Alice laughed. 'Of course in your time you probably treated both people and their valuable animals. Now, doctors who look after animals are called vets.'

'Ah, so the animal doctors are looking into this. If that is the case, why have you called for a more, shall we say, mystical form of help?'

Alice coloured a little, and seemed to be searching for the right words to explain herself. 'This might sound odd, and maybe like I am a little crazy, but I have walked the forest where many of the dogs walk, and it ... well, it feels a little off?'

'A little off?' Master Barwick asked.

'This is difficult for me. I am the wife of a scientist, and my family laugh at me for it, but I have always been able to sense the energies of a place. I can tell when something is in balance, and when it is not. In my own small way I work to bring the balance back.'

'You are a witch?' Alain asked in surprise.

'Well, yes. Perhaps not in the way you mean, but I am certainly a modern-day

witch. So when I say there are places in the New Forest that are "off", I mean they are out of balance with nature.'

'And you have not been able to fix it?' Master Barwick probed.

Alice frowned. 'No. I don't even know where to begin.'

I believe this suggests some sort of outside interference, just as the Council thought, Trouble said as he rose and moved to sit beside Alain.

Running his fingers through the hair on the dog's head, Alain attempted to sort through the information in front of him. 'Do any of your ... um ... vets know whether it is an illness passed from dog to dog? Or is it something from the earth or in the air?'

'They are not sure. Scientists are researching a number of theories on what causes the illness, but have not come to any conclusion. And, although they have found some animals respond well to blood transfusions, they have not been able to develop a cure.'

Before Alain could ask what a transfusion of blood was, Trouble provided the answer. *Modern man has found a way to replace a body's blood with blood from another like being.*

Oh, how exciting. I wonder if I could see them do that? Alain's curiosity was piqued.

With your penchant for blowing things up and pulling them apart, I do not think that is such a good idea. Trouble nudged Alain's hand with a cold, wet nose.

Yuck, what are you doing? Alain pulled his hand away.

A little scratch under my ears would be nice.

Alain obliged and returned his attention back to the main conversation. Master Barwick had already moved on.

'Right, I propose a three-pronged attack to investigate this problem. Firstly, we need to walk around the part of the New Forest you say feels wrong. Secondly, we need to take some water and soil samples from the area to analyse. Finally, do you have access to a diseased animal? Studying one would be useful.'

'By studying, do you mean cutting one open to see how the disease has affected them internally?' Alice's tone was matter-of-fact.

'Heavens no. What a barbaric thought.' Master Barwick blanched. 'I want to study the animal's behaviour, perhaps take a little blood or saliva, and maybe a scraping or two from one of the sores.'

Alice expelled a breath and smiled. 'Oh, that is easily arranged. My friend has a dog that's taken ill; it's at the local vets. I'm sure she wouldn't mind you having a quick visit with Pepe. I'll give her a call now and arrange it.'

Alice hurried from the room.

'Give her a call?' Alain asked. 'Does she live close?'

People in this time have a way of communicating that is similar to mind-speak over great distances, Trouble explained as they heard Alice talking in the next room. *Maybe not so much mind-speak; it's more like being able to project their voices.*

Moments later, Alice returned. 'Jenna said she will talk to the vet and see what she can arrange for tomorrow. Before we go, we can head into the forest and I will show you around.'

'Perhaps we should go now?' Alain said. The sooner they solved this problem, the sooner he would be home.

'I would love to. How long would we be?' she asked, checking the clock on the wall.

'That depends on what we find,' Master Barwick said. 'I would like to walk the entire area and collect samples to test. If the area is large we might be two or three hours.'

'We will need to wait until tomorrow then; I need to be back here in an hour or so. My niece and nephew are due to arrive from Australia, and I want to be here to greet them. In the meantime, perhaps you can make yourselves comfortable while I start on a meal for this evening—I think I can make what I have stretch to feed us all.'

Alain laid his head on his arm as Trouble wandered back over to his place by the Aga. Closing his eyes, he blocked out the room he was in and imagined himself back in the servant's hall in Westminster Castle and the tension immediately left his body. Why did I ever think it was a good idea to come here?

2

THE GANG IS HERE

TRACKING THE PATH of a raindrop down the car window, Bebe sighed. It reached the door and slid from view. Leaning back on the seat she thought of her friends, who would no doubt be down at the beach. Hold on—they would be tucked up in bed having spent the day sunning on the sand, while she was speeding along a motorway in dreary old England.

Half-turning in her seat, she glared at her brother, who was perfectly calm and relaxed beside her. Lee sat there, his shirt un-rumpled, his hair perfect, looking no different to when they had boarded the plane in Sydney thirty-six hours ago.

On the other hand, she was clothed in a wrinkled jacket and had dribbled coffee on the collar of her shirt at some stage during their journey. Nothing she could do about that. After touching her greasy hair, she pulled a hairband from her wrist and twisted it into a messy bun. Taking a discreet sniff, she cringed at her own smell before reaching into her backpack. She found her emergency deodorant and made use of it. There—that was the best she could do in the circumstances.

Rainwater swished up as the taxi changed lanes, and Bebe braced herself against the door. Why had her father agreed to take a new posting in Brussels now? Why had her mother decided to go with him to set up house? Why had they both thought it a good idea she and Lee go and spend the time after exams with their aunt in some tiny town in the middle of nowhere, England? She sighed again.

'Honestly, Bebe, it is not the end of the world. Burley is near Southampton, and there are trains up to London. It is not like we are going to outer Mongolia.'

'You sound just like Mum and Dad,' she snapped.

'Perhaps, but they were right. This could be a fun break for us.'

'Trust you to support them. We are not all followers like you. Some of us have minds of our own.'

The hurt in her brother's eyes tugged at her heart and she bit her lip, unable to take the words back. Their parents' last-minute decision to send them across the other side of the world wasn't his fault.

'Sorry,' she mumbled, slouching down in the seat. She couldn't do anything right.

'It's all right,' he said, placing his hand over hers. 'It's just I want to make the most of this holiday. These are my last few months of freedom.'

'You chose to join the army and go to the academy. You can't blame me if you're worried about giving up your freedom,' she said. 'Sorry, that was mean. I'm just feeling blah. School is over, and I don't have a plan like you. I should be spending this time looking at options for next year, not having a break.'

Instead of the sympathetic noises of support she expected from her brother, he burst out laughing. 'Come on, Bebe. We both know over summer you'd work in the ice-cream parlour or laze on the beach with your friends. Only when everyone started up at uni in the new year would you start seriously looking for something to do with your time. At least this way we can tour around England, and I can help you get motivated. Maybe together we can come up with some options for you.'

Although she hated to admit Lee was right, he probably was. Most of her friends had provisional acceptances into courses for further study next year; the rest had jobs. On the other hand, she had no idea what she wanted to do beyond not making ice-creams for the rest of her life.

To make things worse, her father had been offered the posting of his dreams just as they were about to finish their final school exams. He had spent most of his military career in Australia, taking local postings because it was better for his family. With both his children finishing school, he'd decided to put himself first and had accepted a post as liaison officer to NATO in Brussels.

Lee had congratulated their father. With his future sorted and his accommodation provided at the military college, he was hardly affected by the change at all. Already in limbo, Bebe found it harder to be pleased for him. At first, she'd thought she would remain in their four-bedroom house by the water while she sorted out her life. When she'd said as much, her mother had looked genuinely shocked.

'Bebe, honey, we are renting out the house and taking an apartment in Brussels.'

'But I don't want to live in Brussels,' she'd protested.

'Actually, darling, while you will be welcome to visit any time you like, we were not expecting you to come live with us.'

'What?'

'You don't speak another language, so working or studying in Brussel's is out,' her father interjected.

'But what am I to do?'

'We thought you might go and spend some time with your Aunt Alice in England. Her husband is away lecturing at a foreign university while he works on some sort of advanced research project. And her son is stationed away with the British army. Given the circumstances, she might enjoy some company. Lee can go with you if he wants to,' her father had said.

'Dad and I would join you at Alice's for Christmas before sending Lee off home to begin his studies and moving to Brussels,' her mother had added.

'And what would I do after Christmas?' Bebe had still been rather shocked at her parents abandoning her without a second thought.

'Well, darling, we rather thought you might like to stay on in England. There are way more opportunities for you to consider in the United Kingdom than here, and I am sure Alice would love for you to stay a while longer,' her mother had offered.

Bebe blushed with shame as she remembered the argument that followed; she was still embarrassed by her own behaviour. Worse still, in the two weeks that had followed, she still had not looked into a single option for her future.

On the night before she and Lee had departed, her parents had held a party to celebrate their eighteenth birthday. With exams done and summer break on the horizon, her friends had bubbled with excitement. They'd wanted to enjoy their time together before they headed off in different directions. She, on the other hand, had been unable to enjoy herself as she was not yet ready to leave her life behind.

She leaned her forehead against the window. Beside her reflection, the scenery passed by—grey houses and grey roads appeared even more dismal

in the drizzling rain. Smiling wryly, she considered how the day reflected her mood—dreary. How was she to find something to excite and engage her in a strange country in the middle of a winter?

Sickened by her own depressing thoughts, she asked, 'Do you remember Aunt Alice?'

'Not really. We were only about five or six when she came out to Australia for Grandad's funeral. I think I remember her face.'

'I don't even remember that. All I remember is Dad teasing her about selling magical things in her shop, but that may be from later conversations.'

'Yeah, that's strange. Here, look at this.' He passed his phone to her. He had googled their aunt's shop—The Witch's Hat.

Bebe took it and scrolled through the website. 'Oh my goodness. I thought it was like a touristy sort of thing, and some of it is. But see? It says the shop stocks everything the modern witch or wizard might need to practice their craft. Sounds like she must be pretty kooky—not like Dad at all.'

'I don't remember her being particularly odd; just sad.' Lee took his phone back as he spoke.

Staring out the window of the car as they left the motorway and headed into the New Forest, Bebe held back yet another sigh as the sun attempted to break through the clouds. The fields they drove through were green compared to her beloved Australia.

'Did you see that?' she exclaimed, pointing towards the forest. 'There are horses over by the trees, and they are not in a paddock—there are no fences to keep them in.'

'New Forest Ponies—they're a protected species.' Lee had an answer for everything. He would have thoroughly researched this place before they'd even set foot on the plane to get here. He leaned around her as if attempting to catch a glimpse of the native horses, and she sunk back into the seat so he could see better.

Only moments later, the taxi slowed down before pulling to a standstill outside a large, two-storey house. The door opened and a woman about Bebe's height rushed out to greet them, a large grin on her face.

'Welcome, welcome to Burley,' she said, pulling them into a big hug.

Bebe disentangled herself as soon as she could, observing the stranger who they would be living with for the next month or so. She glanced around the country lane that was so far from Sydney in summer. *Nice though all this is, at the moment I would rather be anywhere else than here.*

LAZING IN A comfortable armchair in front of a blazing fire, with Trouble curled up on a blanket beside him, Alain had spent a pleasant afternoon reading a book, much to his surprise. After lunch, Alice had encouraged him to search the shelves and find something to while away the winter afternoon. Shocked at such a waste of time, he had first offered to help Master Barwick go through the alchemical equipment in the office.

'I'm not sure what Alice's husband keeps in the garage, so I think I would rather look by myself and see if there is anything we can use,' his master said before heading out the back door.

He means without your constant questions, Trouble clarified, with a snorting chuckle.

Turning to Alice he had asked, 'Is there anything you would like me to do?'

She considered his question then shook her head. 'It is too miserable outside to do gardening. I cleaned the house within an inch of its life yesterday for my visitors—so not really. I am going to do some accounts. I guess you could help me with them if you have any experience in that area?' She raised an eyebrow in enquiry, and he grinned sheepishly in response.

'Accounts? Numbers aren't my strong suit,' he admitted.

'Well, I guess an afternoon with a good book in front of the fire it is then.'

After searching the bookshelves, he found a book on the modern history of England. The first few chapters had his head spinning—there was so much to take in. When he complained to Trouble, the dog told him no good ever came of learning about your own future and suggested he try a work of fiction.

Being compared to wealthy noblewomen, who were the only people he knew who had time to read story books, was plain insulting—as if he would be interested in romances anyway.

Perhaps Trouble was reading Alain's thoughts as he told him, *Don't be so quick to judge; some of those romances are great reads. However, times have changed. Books are now mass produced and affordable. Many people from all walks of life read for pleasure, and there are a wide range of options to choose from.*

Encouraged by his Guardian dog, he returned to the shelves and started reading the titles. Finally, he found one he thought he might enjoy—*The Lord of the Rings.* It was not the tale of noble doings he had anticipated; in fact, it was a fantasy book about elves and hobbits set in a fantastical world. Although the story was not what he'd expected, he was too comfortable to move, so he persevered.

Alice came in to place more coal on the fire, and he never stirred. Nor did he stop to drink the tea she placed on the table beside him, or raise an eye when she came to in draw the curtains in preparation of the coming evening drop in temperature.

'Oh, they are here!'

Alice's exclamation pulled him from the world of Middle Earth—that and Trouble stretching beside him. Master Barwick wandered in from the kitchen as Alice flung open the door and ran outside. Moments later she returned, leading a boy and girl into the hallway. Alain's jaw dropped. Standing in front of him were the two people he had left that morning: Stanislaus and Barabal.

Shut your jaw. You look like a half-wit, Trouble told him.

But ...

... I know. It is not by chance I asked you to come here. We thought getting the old team together might give us a chance to resolve this problem a bit faster.

They cannot be ... Alain stumbled

They are not, Trouble said, transmitting his impatience along with his words.

They are reincarnations?

Finally you get it.

'This is my friend Barnaby Barwick,' Alice said, and Master Barwick nodded hello. 'And this young lad is his nephew, Alain. They both arrived today as well. Alain, meet Bebe and Lee.'

'Hi,' the two newcomers said in unison.

'Hello,' Alain responded, still somewhat dazed.

'Alain, why don't you and Lee grab the suitcases and take them upstairs? You can show Lee to your room and settle in, then I think I will make some hot chocolate. Bebe, I will just go and put the milk on, and after I will show you where you are to sleep.'

Alice followed Master Barwick into the kitchen, and Bebe trailed behind, but not before shooting a bemused look at her brother.

'I hope you do not mind sharing with me,' Alain said as he grabbed a suitcase and started up the stairs.

A grin split the boy's face. 'No, I'm sure it will be fun. I don't know anyone here, so it will be nice to have someone to talk to.'

Lee's strong resemblance to Stanislaus dispelled Alain's fears about bunking with a stranger. It could have been awkward, but at the moment it seemed more like he was sharing with an old friend.

'You know, I cannot help feeling like we have met somewhere before,'

Lee said as they climbed the stairs.

'This is my first trip away from home,' Alain said. 'I live in the Hebrides—in Scotland.'

Lee shrugged. 'I've never been to Scotland, so I guess there is no way we could have.'

'No, I guess not ...' Alain said as he opened the door to their room. 'Here we are. Alice said you would need the bed, and I can see why.' The boy was well over six foot tall and moved confidently, like someone used to physical pursuits.

Lee dumped his case on the floor, turned around and grinned. 'Sometimes being this tall has its advantages, but we can chop and change if that bed is too uncomfortable.'

'No, it is not too bad,' Alain said, not wanting to lose his comfy bed to the other boy.

He popped Bebe's case outside the door to her room. As he returned, Lee was saying, 'I am not a big one for telly; do you mind if we put this in the wardrobe to make some room?'

'No, I'm fine with that. I had never seen one before today when I watched *Thomas the Tank Engine*, and I found it a little disturbing, so I think I'll stick to books from now on.'

Lee laughed. 'Well of course Thomas is weird—all those little talking engines. I could never understand why other kids didn't find it as scary as I did.'

He fiddled with some cords at the back of the telly, then carried it over to the wardrobe in the corner. 'Here, open this for me, would you?'

Alain held the door while Lee placed the telly on the ground in the closet, then closed it.

'So, is there anything much to do around here?' Lee asked.

'I only arrived this morning, but I was reading this good book …'

'Did you say "book"?'

Alain laughed at the horror on the other boy's face. 'Yes—*Lord of the Rings*. Have you heard of it?'

'Who hasn't heard of it? One of the best movie trilogies ever.'

'Movie?'

'Oh man, your island must be very remote. Didn't you have a cinema, or a hall to watch movies in? I will see if Aunt Alice has a copy on DVD, but perhaps you should finish reading it first. Friends of mine say if you see the movie before you finish the book it spoils it.'

Although the conversation was mostly going over Alain's head, he felt

more comfortable than he had since he arrived in this strange time. Like Stanislaus, Lee was open and friendly and easy to talk to.

Lee nudged his case under the bed with his foot, stretched and said, 'Come on. Aunt Alice mentioned hot chocolate, and although I think a coffee would help keep me awake for longer, I never turn down food. I wonder if we'll get cake to go with it?'

Yes, Alain thought. *This is exactly like being with Stanislaus.*

ALAIN WAS IN heaven. He had not imagined anything could taste as delicious as hot chocolate. Then Bebe showed him how to add little fluffy balls called marshmallows, and he almost groaned in ecstasy. So intent was he on savouring his drink and consuming some of Alice's gingerbread loaf he was unable to concentrate on anything anyone said.

'You guys came all the way down here to study some rare disease affecting dogs?' Lee asked.

'And to check out a school for Alain,' Alice added.

'Yes, but my point is, don't they already have people in Hampshire investigating the outbreak?'

'Well, um, yes they do,' Master Barwick responded, looking a little like an animal caught in a trap.

Alice came to his rescue. 'Barnaby's unique skills give him a different perspective from the other scientists.'

Perhaps because he was hungry, or perhaps because he thought he should help Master Barwick out of a sticky situation, Trouble chose that moment to join them in the kitchen.

'Oh, what an adorable dog,' Bebe said as she left the table and crouched down to scratch Trouble behind his ears. Trouble moved his head to the side to allow her to give the other ear the same treatment, and leaned into her in apparent ecstasy.

'What's his name?' the girl asked.

'Trouble,' Alain said, suppressing a smirk.

'Oh, no! You named this beautiful boy Trouble. I bet you are no trouble at all,' she crooned.

Trouble's liquid brown eyes turned to Master Barwick, and he said, *See? Someone understands and appreciates me.*

'And you would be wrong,' Master Barwick mumbled under his breath

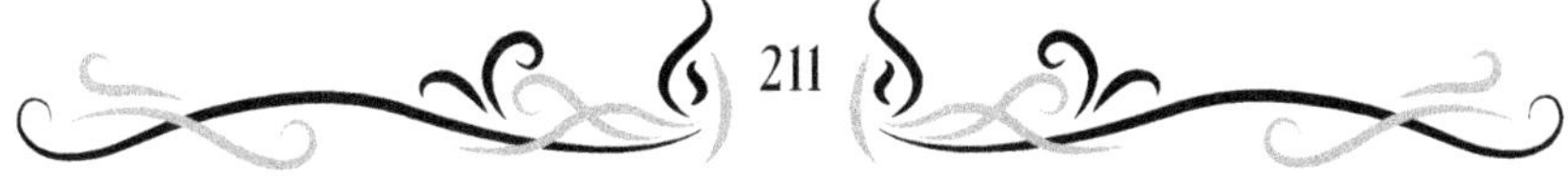

as Trouble wagged his tail while continuing to stare balefully at the alchemist.

'When do you start investigating? Can we help?' Lee asked, leaning forward and resting his arms on the table.

'Well, I am not sure what you can do …' Master Barwick started.

They are here to help, Barwick. I believe the old team will help us solve this more quickly, Trouble said.

But the old team isn't here; we're missing John, Alain told them, and he thought he heard Trouble say *yet* as he turned his attention back to the others.

'We could help you collect samples,' Bebe offered. 'It would be fun.'

'Fun?' Alain asked, unsure what was fun about running around in the middle of winter in a forest.

'And I can look things up on the internet,' Lee said.

Internet? Both Alain and Master Barwick thought together, but did not say anything as the others carried on sharing ideas. They were still in the dark as to what an internet was when a knock at the back door interrupted them.

Alice opened it to let in a girl about the same age as the others. She removed the hood of her coat to reveal spiky brown hair and thoughtful chocolate eyes. After hanging the outer garment on a hook on the back of the door, she rubbed her hands up her arms encased in a black sweater and headed over to the Aga to warm up.

Her bright colourful skirt swished as she walked past, revealing to Alain what looked like black leather work boots. What drew his eye, though, was the line of rings this newcomer had all the way down one ear. Once he managed to get past her strange manner of dress, he studied her face as she warmed herself, and realised she looked familiar—very familiar.

John? Alain asked Trouble, and the dog nodded.

John had been pulled from outback Australia in the 1880's into Medieval England, and he had quickly adjusted to the situation he'd found himself in—better than Alain was adjusting to modern Hampshire. So he had high hopes that this reincarnation of his friend would display the same no-nonsense attitude that made him invaluable to their team when they'd saved King Henry.

'Hi Alice. Just dropping your keys back. I locked the float and the takings in the safe. It was a slow day, so there wasn't enough to warrant dropping at the bank.'

'Thank you, Jo. What shift is your mum on today?'

'Afternoons,' the girl answered.

'Do you want to join us for some dinner?'

'Um …' She looked around the room as if she just noticed the other people. ‹It looks like your hands are full already. I'll head off home.'

'I made a big pot of spaghetti Bolognese, so there is enough for everyone here with some spare. There is enough for you to take home for your mum too,' Alice informed her.

'Well ... I guess I can stay. It beats warming up a frozen dinner.'

Alice turned to the others. 'Jo works for me in the shop. Her mother is a nurse at the hospital in Southampton, and she often shares an evening meal with me when her mum isn't home.'

They all made room at the table for Jo. Alice poured her a hot chocolate while the others carried on as if there had been no interruption.

'I will be collecting samples tomorrow morning, bright and early,' Master Barwick told them. 'If you want to come you best be up and ready. I will not dilly-dally waiting for you.'

Alain got the impression Master Barwick was only offering because he thought the young people would not want to join him on an early morning stroll.

'Most mornings I get up for a run before sunrise, so I will be awake,' Lee said, preening a little and looking at Jo, who seemed not to notice his antics.

'Won't you have jet lag?' Jo asked.

Jet lag? Alain repeated.

Shh, I am trying to listen, Trouble said, placing his head on Master Barwick's knee.

'Mm, that is true, so I will probably be awake much earlier.' Lee smiled.

'Then you can wake me,' Bebe said.

'No grumbling if I do,' Lee responded. 'I don't want a pillow to the head because you forgot you asked me to do it.'

Bebe laughed, and the two turned expectantly to Alain. 'Hey. I was already going. After all, I usually help Uncle Barnaby with his experiments and studies.'

Jo looked quizzically at them all, and Alice said, 'The pasta should be about done. Come and help me dish up, and I will explain.'

WITH SO MANY people sitting around the table talking and eating, Alain closed his eyes and was almost able to imagine himself back in the dining room at Winchester Castle. Well, until he took a mouthful of food. Although delicious, it was strange.

The long strands of spaghetti were difficult to wrangle into his mouth,

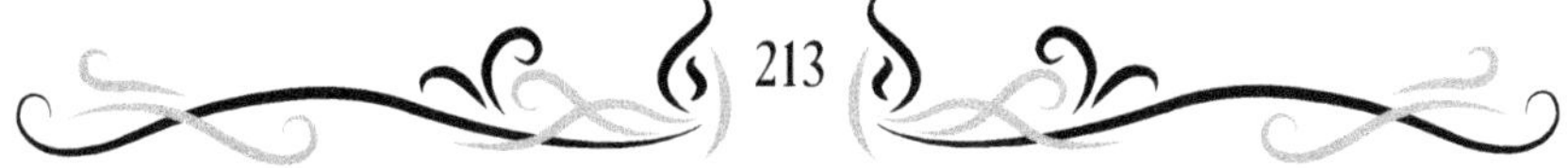

even after Bebe had given him a demonstration. He gave his full attention to each spoonful and so, rather than joining in the conversation as he would have done at home, Alain found himself becoming quieter and quieter. In the end, he was content to just listen.

As the twins cleared the table, Alice offered some of her "world-famous" carrot cake for dessert. Bebe and Lee yawned.

'I couldn't eat another thing,' Bebe said, stretching like a cat.

'And I can barely keep my eyes open,' Lee added. 'I think it is bed for me. Barnaby, what time would you like us up in the morning?'

'Don't forget I have to open my shop at ten,' Alice said.

'Ah, well, shall we say seven?'

Alice shook her head. 'It will still be dark. What say we get up at seven for breakfast and head out at first light?'

Having agreed upon a time, the twins rose to leave. As they did, Lee turned and said to Alain, 'Please try not to turn on the light when you come up. I'm a light sleeper.'

'I won't,' Alain quickly promised. There was no way he was going to touch the switch on the wall that made light appear using something called electricity—well, at least not until he figured out how it all worked anyway.

Alice told the others to make themselves comfortable in the living room and she would bring through coffee and cake. Alain warily followed Jo and Master Barwick into the other room, and sat on the sofa with Trouble half beside him and half in his lap. Patting the dog helped ground him, making this place seem less strange.

Are you all right, Alain? Perhaps my bringing you here was a little selfish. We could do with your help, but I think the stress of being in 2017 is getting to you, Trouble said as he dropped his head on Alain's knees.

'Who said that?' Jo looked at each of them in turn, then her eyes darted round the room.

'You heard that?' Master Barwick asked, head cocked to the side as he surveyed Alice's assistant, before turning to glare at Trouble. *You allowed her to hear you?*

The dog stared back, unperturbed.

'Yes, and obviously you did too. Is there some sort of speaker in here? And what did they mean about bringing Alain to this time?' Jo's eyes pierced Master Barwick's as if nailing him to a wall.

Please calm down, Jo. If you search your heart you will know who is speaking, Trouble

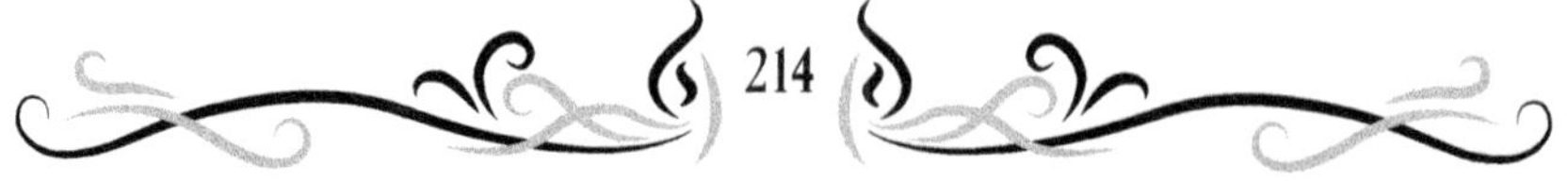

said, his voice low and soothing.

Before Jo could respond, Master Barwick said, *Trouble ... umm ... Sigma, is it wise for you to be activating Jo's memories at this time? She is not quite ready for true understanding of the roles and responsibilities of a guardian, so awakening this part of her mind will serve no real purpose.*

She is close enough, Barwick, and it would help us to have one more person totally aware of what is going on. Once she fully understands the situation she will be able to help us, and especially Alain, while we are here.

Unaware of their private conversation, Jo pointed at Trouble. 'You … you are talking into our minds. And ... we have met before, haven't we?' A frown drew her brows together. 'Not you and I, but ... Oh my, what did Alice do?'

'What did Alice tell you about us before?' Master Barwick asked, shooting a look at Trouble that screamed "don't interfere".

'Um, just that she called some friends to come and help with the dog problems around here. Oh, and that you came from somewhere far away, quite remote, in fact, and do not spend a lot of time with other people. She said I might find you both a bit odd.' Jo chewed on her lip for a moment before continuing. 'But I suspect you have come from quite far away—extremely far away.'

'Yes, we have, lass, from a time when our links to Mother Earth were much stronger than they are now. Being from the distant past, we bring unique skills to identify whether or not what is happening to the dogs is a natural occurrence, or something more sinister.'

Jo stared thoughtfully at the three of them. 'You're telling me you time travelled?'

'Yes, I am,' Master Barwick said.

Jo studied the three of them, and Alain squirmed under her scrutiny. She folded her arms. 'Can I assume that all dogs do not mind-speak in your time?'

'That is correct,' Master Barwick answered.

'Mm, so Trouble is not actually a dog.' The young woman's arms were still crossed as if they provided some sort of protection from this unusual situation. 'So ... who did Alice call to get you here? I thought she had phoned someone, but she didn't, did she? Ah, I know! She cast a spell from one of her books? One of the older ones? I found one on her desk.'

Phoned someone? Alain thought, then he remembered Alice talking to her friend before and he realised this must be quite a common activity in this time, and he chuckled at the thought of someone contacting the Guardians

in that way.

Yes, she invoked an old spell asking the Time Guardians for assistance. It is an ancient spell, one not used in generations, Trouble answered.

Jo laughed. 'Oh my gosh ... for real? Time Guardians? My mum used to tell me stories about the Time Guardians, ones her great-great-grandad used to tell his kids and grandkids. Do you expect me to believe they are real?'

After our meeting, John Smith kept an eye out for events the Time Guardians might have had a hand in, and he wrote them down as stories and shared them with his family, Trouble explained to Barwick and Alain.

'John Smith. You met one of my ancestors? The one who wrote the book?' Jo was incredulous.

'Yes, we all did,' Alain said.

'All did what?' Alice asked as she entered the room with a jug, some mugs, and plates heaped with generous slices of cake.

'These are Time Guardians,' Jo said, almost as though she could not quite believe she was saying the words.

'I know. I called them,' Alice said as she placed the tray on the table under the window.

Master Barwick cleared his throat. 'Strictly speaking, Sigma, or Trouble, as we are calling him in this form, is the only Time Guardian in our group. I am still in training, and Alain is only an assistant on this mission—although we will certainly be making use of his chemistry skills.'

'Sigma?' Alice asked.

'The dog,' Jo offered.

'You're kidding me. You're saying that the dog is in charge, not you?' Alice turned to Master Barwick.

'He speaks into minds,' Jo said.

'Not into mine,' Alice responded.

I can if I choose to, as you have a small magical gift.

Alice spilt the coffee she was pouring. Placing the pot down until her hand stopped shaking, she frowned at the dog in front of her.

I would appreciate it if you all do not go 'round spreading the fact that I am a Time Guardian. It makes my job harder, the more people know who I am, Trouble told them. *Not to mention the fact most people will think you are crazy.*

Alice stared at Trouble, her face an unreadable mask, before disappearing, returning a moment later with a cloth to clean up the mess. As she cleaned, she muttered, 'Talking dogs, people from the past, all from a simple spell ...

who would have thought?'

With the mess tidied, and Alice's composure restored, they all settled down with their dessert and the room was quiet for a while until Alice broke the silence.

'Has Trouble only just started speaking to us?'

'No. Well I don't think so because I heard him.' Jo frowned and turned to Master Barwick.

'Um … well …'

'How come Jo could and I couldn't?' Alice shifted in her seat so she could also direct her question to the apothecary.

'Ah, now that is interesting,' Master Barwick started as Jo sat forward as if eager to hear the answer. 'I believe we need to open our thoughts specifically towards you for you to hear mind-speak. Jo though is almost ready to begin her training as a Time Guardian so is more likely to pick it up unless we specifically shield ourselves.

'I'm to be a Guardian?' A grin split Jo's face.

'Yes, of course. I would say one or two more reincarnations should do it?' Master Barwick looked at Trouble.

I would say that is about right.

'What? I am going to get a chance to time travel and save the world? How cool!'

'Perhaps not you, as such, although who knows?' Master Barwick laughed. 'In the meantime, though, we need your help with our current investigation.'

'I would have helped anyway, even without the promise of future adventures. I would do anything to stop more dogs getting sick,' Jo assured the group.

'Jo is on a gap year after finishing school. She is saving up to go to university to study to become a vet,' Alice informed them. 'Not only does she work in my shop for extra cash, but she helps out at the local veterinary practice to get some experience. She is the one who will take you in to see Pepe the dog tomorrow.'

'I popped in to see Pepe before going in to work today. They gave him a transfusion this morning, and he was looking a little perkier,' Jo informed them as Alain took his first bite of cake.

'Oh, this is amazing.' Alain took another mouthful. 'With this and hot chocolate, I may never want to go home.'

After picking up the drink Alice had told him was decaf coffee, he took a mouthful. Expecting something sweet and beautiful like hot chocolate, he had

to stop himself from spitting the bitter liquid out. 'Argh. That is horrid though.'

'It is an acquired taste. Some people find a dash of milk and a little sugar help improve the flavour.' Jo sat forward and added milk to her own coffee to show him how it was done.

Following her actions, he tried the drink again, and found it more palatable. He ate a little cake, then drank some coffee. *Ah, apart one is too bitter and the other almost too sweet*, he marvelled, *but together they are perfect.*

Jo smiled at him. 'I think I am going to enjoy showing you around. Being with you is like learning about the world all over again.'

'Would you like some more?' Alice offered and Alain placed his plate on the table.

In spite of Master Barwick's disapproving stare, he accepted a second slice of cake and some more coffee. If he was going to be in this strange place for a while, at least he would eat well.

'Let him be,' Alice admonished Master Barwick as she returned to her seat beside him. 'I enjoy having someone with a healthy appetite in the house.'

'He won't be able to fit in to the house if he keeps eating like that,' Master Barwick said under his breath.

'Oh, there's Mum,' Jo said as a bright light penetrated a gap in the curtains. 'Thanks for the dinner, Alice.'

'Hold on a moment. I have some for your mother.' Alice disappeared into the kitchen.

Jo took the bag of food from Alice and waved goodbye to the others. 'I will see you at the vet tomorrow perhaps near the end of my shift—I finish around eleven. Come to the back door and I will let you in,' she threw back over her shoulder as she slipped outside.

Not long after Jo had left, Alice declared herself done in. Alain helped her take the dessert things back into the kitchen. After they had washed everything up, he followed her back out. While they were away, Master Barwick had made himself comfortable flicking through a history book.

'Are you not tired, Barnaby?' Alice asked, stifling a yawn.

'At my age, you do not need much sleep. Don't worry; I will lock up just as you showed me when I go to bed. And the key you gave me to let myself in tomorrow morning is quite safe,' he said as he patted a trouser pocket.

Creeping into the room he was to share with Lee, Alain stumbled over his bag and fell on the bed. Holding his breath, he waited for Lee to grumble his displeasure at being woken. His breathing remained steady and Alain

could not help but smile. Just like Stanislaus, Lee slept like a log.

Changing into his pyjamas, Alain thought about the day. Rather than being excited by all he'd discovered, he found the strangeness of life here made him miss the comforts of home. Not even hot chocolate and Lee could make up for Barabal and Stanislaus not being here with him.

When he had decided to go on this adventure he had not considered how much he would miss them. It made it all the harder because his last conversation with Barabal had ended badly. Hands clasped behind his head, he stared at the ceiling as he relived the scene.

'All I said was I was thinking about going home to Winchester to visit my family and to help ensure the lands of the New Forest are given back to their rightful owners.'

Barabal continued tossing clothes into her travel bag. 'What about your apprenticeship with Master Barwick, and taking on his practice?'

When Alain did not respond, she carried on. 'And what about ...' She stopped mid-action as if unsure what to say next. 'I thought we had an understanding that we would both be staying on here at Westminster.'

Alain's stomach had knotted, torn between committing to Barabal or going home to have his father's lands restored.

'Alain. Alain! Are you even listening to me?' Barabal stood in front of him, hands on hips. 'Will you be here when I get back from escorting the princess to her wedding?' Barabal demanded an answer, but he caught a look of uncertainty in her eyes. 'I have to leave in a couple of hours so I don't have time to talk this through properly, but ...'

'I just need some time to think, Barabal. I will let you know this evening before you leave—I promise.' Lala had assured Alain he would be home from the future before anyone noticed he was gone, so he should be back before dinner.

Lowering her troubled brown eyes, Barabal placed her chemise in the bag, then took her time doing up the straps. Meanwhile, Alain's stomach churned. He had not exactly declared his love for Barabal, and they were not betrothed, but the thought of hurting her made him feel ill.

'All right, I will see you before I leave. Best you go now. Master Barwick will be waiting for you.'

She would not look at him and he had departed, their unresolved issues lying heavy on his heart.

Unable to do anything about it now, Alain snuggled under the duvet and

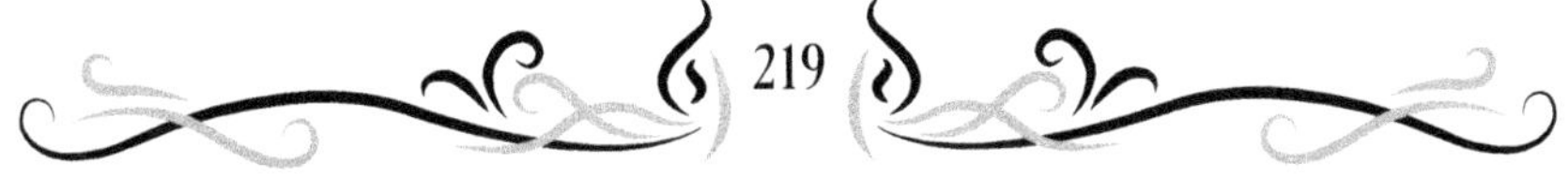

tried to clear his mind. Downstairs a door closed, followed by the crunching of gravel as Master Barwick retired to his room over the garage. A gust of wind caused a tree branch to scrape against the window and Alain rolled over, trying to get more comfortable.

Trying to relax, Alain found every time he closed his eyes his mind whirred with all the things he had seen, or some strange noise disturbed him. And Lee's snoring did nothing to help. It seemed like hours later his mind finally calmed down and he began to drift off to sleep.

3

ALABAMA ROT

A STRANGE GLOW lit the room when Alain opened his eyes the next morning. The night sky though the gap in the curtains was still dark, so he rolled over to find out where the light was coming from.

Lee was sitting propped up in bed staring intently at a thin, square, book-looking thing leaning against his legs.

'Morning,' he said, his voice creating mist in the air, causing Alain to crawl farther under the covers.

From his snug bed, he asked, 'What time is it?'

'About five-ish.'

'That's early. Couldn't you sleep?'

'Sorry, this jet lag thing has me all over the place. I have been awake for hours.' Lee spoke without taking his eyes from whatever was in front of him.

'What are you doing?' Alain propped himself up on his elbows.

'Searching Alabama Rot.'

'Alabama Rot?'

'Yeah, that's what they're calling what the dogs are getting.'

'And you are reading about it on that?'

'The Hebrides are the back of beyond, but you do have the internet, right?'

'Internet?'

'Yes, you know—a link from home to the network of computers all around the world,' Lee explained. 'Thank goodness Alice has decent Wi-Fi here. Life wouldn't be worth living if I couldn't plug in.'

The only word Alain recognised was the word plug, and he knew that meant something to do with electricity and stuff.

Not wanting to appear foolish, or give away their time travel secret, he attempted to be blasé and said, 'Actually, no. We didn't even have electricity, so what would make you think we had internet?'

'Come here and I will show you what I have been doing.'

Lee moved over on the bed, making room for Alain, who picked up his duvet and joined him. The thing in Lee's lap had a screen like a telly, but instead of pictures there were words, and he was using his finger to make the page move up and down.

'Okay, I swipe the screen like this, and it brings up a search engine—which is like a library catalogue. I type in what I want here—Alabama Rot—hit the search button, and it brings up everything it can find in books and articles all 'round the world.'

'Wow. You can get entire books on this thing? From anywhere you want?' Alain was impressed.

'And more—newspaper articles, blogs, scientific research papers. Most stuff has been made so you can access it on a tablet or iPad. It makes learning about things easier than going to a library.'

'That is amazing. What's this one here? "Man says Alabama Rot is God's Divine Curse".' Alain leaned over and pointed to the line that caught his eye. When he touched the screen it changed and went to another page, showing a picture of a man in front of a church with a grim, rather frightening face. Beside the picture was the headline again and some writing underneath.

'Ah, it didn't take you long to stumble on the curse of the internet. Anyone can write anything they want on whatever they want and publish it. That means every crackpot with a theory has a voice.'

'How do you sort what is real and what is not? It must be confusing,' Alain said.

'It can be.' Touching the top corner of the screen, Lee returned to the original page. 'See here? This one is like a sort of online encyclopaedia. It's updated by ordinary people and checked by them. You should always double check everything you find here, but it's not a bad place to start.'

'Sounds quite confusing. It would be nice to be presented with a single truth you could rely on,' Alain said, thinking back to the medical texts he had studied.

'Then you would not be able to form your own opinion. It's easy once you get used to it. You just need to make sure the authors or the publications have a reasonable reputation. If they don't, you pretty much discount them.'

'Still sounds confusing to me—almost like it shows you too much information to find out what is real,' Alain said.

Lee laughed. 'Sometimes, yes, but if you use your common sense you can find out almost anything. I like to be prepared, so I look heaps of things up.'

'Oh?' Alain did not quite know what to say.

'Bee …Bebe says it's because I can't think quickly on my feet, so I like to consider all options before I enter a situation. She may be right. I am not as smart as she is, but I am organised and I study hard.'

Not quite sure what to do with that revelation, Alain changed the subject. 'What did you find out on the internet about the disease affecting dogs?'

'Ah, well quite a lot actually.' Lee clicked a button and the screen went white, and Alain made out some scribbled lines of writing. Lee picked up a white pencil and pointed to a particular sentence. 'Alabama Rot has been found in a number of places around the world over the last few years. However, it appears that in spite of all the research carried out, and some promising initial findings, no one knows what is causing it or why some dogs become sick and others do not.'

'That is not very helpful,' Alain said.

'The recent outbreaks caused a flurry of new activity and some more research projects were set up. Quite a few people are interested because of the high level of activity around the New Forest recently—which we already knew—but it has scientists wondering if it has something to do with the waterways. Many of the dogs who have come down with the illness have been off-lead and enjoyed splashing in the streams.'

Alain nodded. 'I see the logic in that. We must make sure we get some water samples when we are out today. Did you find anything else useful?'

'I found a lot more, but I am not sure how useful it is seeing as I am not a scientist. Let's go downstairs and see if we can rustle up something to eat and I will show you the rest. Some of it is interesting.'

'Now you're talking,' Alain said as he rolled himself off the bed, stomach rumbling in anticipation of food.

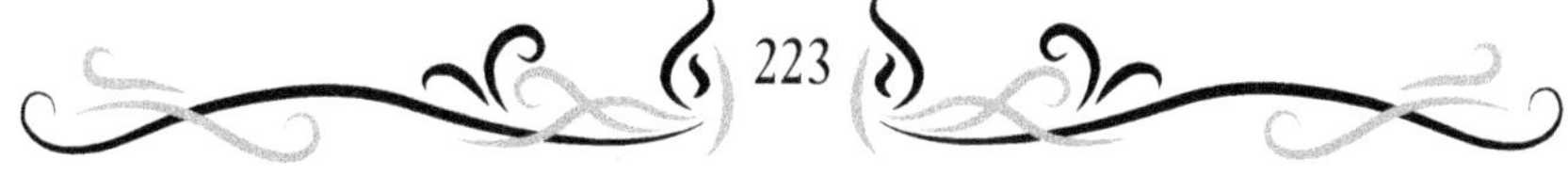

THEY WERE FINISHING up their toast and jam when Master Barwick ambled in. Moments later, Alice and Bebe joined the group and the quiet kitchen became a bustle of activity. While the others ate, Lee left them to it and headed upstairs to grab his coat.

'Oh, Alain, one of my son's old jackets is hanging up in the hallway near the door. It's the green one with fur around the hood. There's a larger black one belonging to my husband; it should fit Barnaby. If you wouldn't mind picking that up as well please.'

As Alain left in search of the warm clothing, he heard Bebe ask, 'Where are your own coats? Surely no one travels in England without one at this time of year.'

'Some of their luggage was lost in transit, so they have to borrow a few things while they are here,' Alice deftly answered.

When Alain returned to the kitchen, he hung the coats over the door handle. Sitting back down, he found Trouble beside him. When he had Alain's attention, he stared mournfully at his bowl.

'Oh dear, we've not fed you this morning, have we,' Alice said. 'I'm not sure I have anything in the fridge suitable for a dog. I used the rest of the mincemeat last night, and everything else is frozen.'

'Did his food get lost as well?' Bebe asked mischievously.

'No, smarty pants. He has eaten all Barnaby had, and we have not had a chance to go to the shops to buy more,' Alice said.

Bebe leaned over the table and fed Trouble some crusts from her toast. 'This will do him for the moment.'

'Bebe, don't feed the dog food from the table!' Alice's shocked tone stopped Bebe immediately, and she dropped her head, appearing contrite, but Alain was sure she winked at Trouble.

Pulling on a jacket from the hook over the kitchen door, Alice said, 'I'll pop next door and ask if they have something they can spare for this morning. Their dog is around the same size as Trouble.'

She opened the door and a cold blast of air swept into the room, causing Alain to shiver. He was not looking forward to a morning walk in the forest.

Trouble watched Alice leave, then turned expectantly to Bebe, who obliged him with another sliver of toast. They both made sure to remove all evidence

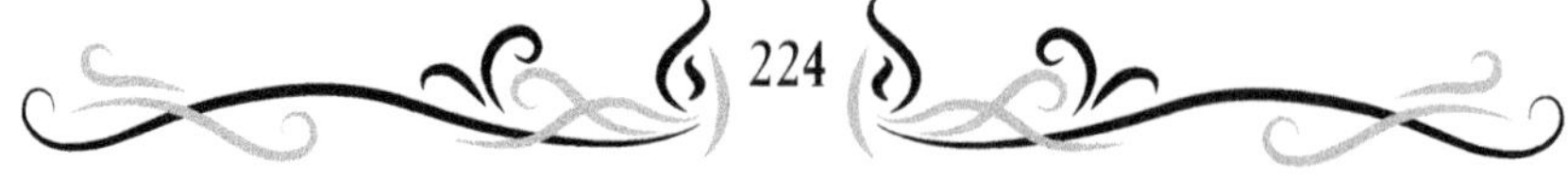

of their misdemeanour when Alice returned moments later with a bowl containing some small round things.

'Ellie said they have been tightening up the regulations about keeping dogs on leads since this latest outbreak of the rot. I know your dog is well-trained, but I think it best you keep Trouble on his lead this morning.'

Alain was about to say Trouble didn't have a lead when Alice held up a collar and some twisted rope with a link at one end and a handle at the other. The neighbour had obviously provided her with more than food.

After placing the lead over the back of the chair, she put the collar on Trouble, ignoring his sorrowful eyes. Finally, she put the food bowl on the floor and waited for Trouble to eat. He sniffed at the contents before raising his eyes, his expression even more doleful.

'This is not a restaurant,' Alice informed him. *You said we should treat you like any other dog in front of the others. Well, this is what dogs eat.*

Trouble huffed, then stuck his head in the bowl and began crunching through his biscuits.

'I am afraid we may have overindulged him by feeding him the same food as us.' Master Barwick raised his head from the book he was reading to explain the dog's behaviour before adding, 'He won't like using the lead either. He is very well-trained and we don't use one as a rule, but I guess if we must, we must.' A small smile played around his lips. 'If everyone is done we should be heading out.'

Picking up the lead, he attached it to the collar around Trouble's neck, then patted his head.

I hope you are enjoying yourself, Trouble said.

Immensely. Master Barwick chuckled as he left the lead on the floor. It snaked along behind Trouble as they headed for the door.

'You aren't taking him with us, are you?' Lee asked from halfway down the stairs.

'Yes,' Master Barwick informed him. 'I see no reason not to.'

'Should we really be taking him though?' Alain asked, suddenly worried for his friend.

'Yes. He could catch the disease,' Lee said. 'I mean, we are going to places where dogs have caught it before. It will be risky.'

'We will be careful with him. I promise,' Master Barwick said. 'We will keep him to the pathways and he should be fine.'

Trouble, you cannot catch this, can you? Alain thought to check with the dog.

No, I do not think so. I believe I am immune to viruses—one of the perks of the job. In fact, someone would have to inject me with something pretty toxic for it to affect me.

'Right, now that we have settled that, let's be off.' Master Barwick opened the front door and they all filed out after him into the chilly morning air.

CLOMPING THROUGH THE damp grass in a sturdy pair of boots, and wrapped in a warm coat, Alain found himself enjoying this walk through the New Forest more than he had the day before. Trouble trotted beside him, the lead hanging loose as they drifted behind the others. Alice led them down a lane and through some fields before nipping through a copse of trees.

'This is the path my friend always takes with her dog, Pepe, and it is where I feel a wrongness in the forest,' she told them as they followed the muddy bridle path by the fast-running stream.

'I doubt very much it is something in the water, as some have suggested,' Master Barwick said as they walked.

'What makes you say that?' Alice asked.

'Nothing lasts long in running water, and that stream is running particularly fast,' he answered. 'Still, I had best take a sample.'

He pulled a glass vial from the pocket of his coat and carefully made his way down the shallow bank. As he leant over the water, he pulled the stopper from the bottle, scooped up some liquid, and placed the top back on. He proceeded to pull a pen from his pocket and write something on the glass, waited a few moments for the ink to dry, then placed the pen and vial in his other pocket.

Walking a little farther on, Master Barwick asked Alain to use his containers to gather some dirt from the track and from the pasture beside them. He set Bebe to pick samples of each of the plants she found, and Lee was asked to take some water from a selection of the puddles on the path and by the side of the road.

About half an hour later, the path began to loop back towards Burley. Bebe declared she had not seen any new plants for some time, and almost all their glass jars were filled with specimens. Master Barwick announced they were done for the day, and he suggested a fast walk home when Trouble, nose to the ground and tail in the air, began to tug at the lead.

'Trouble, no,' Alain said firmly, but the dog merely planted his feet and

began pulling towards some trees a few paces from the path.

Trouble, what are you doing? Alain asked, but the dog ignored him and continued his attempts to get to the trees.

'It is not a good idea for him to wander,' Lee reminded them. 'We don't want him to catch anything.'

'I am trying my best to make him stay on the path,' Alain said as Trouble almost wrenched the lead from his hand.

Alain, there is something under those trees, Trouble eventually managed to get out.

Well, why didn't you say? Alain asked.

I got caught up in the scent. I had to overcome my dog instincts.

Okay. If I go and look, will you stay here?

Trouble humphed and dropped to the ground—head on paws, eyes focussed on the trees. Placing the lead beside him on the path, Alain told the dog to stay. He traipsed through the wet grass to the spot by the trees where something definitely glistened with dew.

Crouching down, he found a collection of items that at first looked like rubbish someone had thrown away, but on closer inspection he realised what they were—an altar. There was; a small bag of salt for earth, a glass jar containing water, some burnt sticks—possibly to signify air and fire—and a piece of string with three knots.

A shadow fell across the ground as Master Barwick leaned over and said, 'Mm, interesting, a magical altar. Someone has been casting, and, from the looks of it, not a spell to do good.' He reached over and picked up the knotted thread, then placed it in his pocket.

'Are you sure? I mean, all the elements for a spell are here, but they're ... well ... different.'

'Young man, many of the things we take for granted are not available to these people, so the elements to make a temporary altar to cast a spell may not appear as we would expect them to. Of course the magic created from these make-do items is not as strong as we are used to experiencing back home.'

'But ... if they have enough people casting a spell, they would increase the level of magic, wouldn't they?'

'They would indeed,' Master Barwick said. 'Perhaps you should have a scout around in the trees and see what you can find. I will search through the fields along the banks of the stream,' Master Barwick called back over his shoulder as he headed off by himself.

A few moments later, Alain joined the others on the path. He was in time

to hear Bebe say, 'You cannot be serious ... magic? I am sorry, Aunt Alice. Magic is something you read about in books; it isn't real.'

'That may be what you believe, dear, but there are still people who practice casting spells. And if Master Barwick said he found evidence of a casting here then I am sure he is right. After all, he should know.'

Bebe snorted with laughter. 'When you said Barnaby was an expert, you didn't mean he was a scientist; you meant an expert in witchcraft.'

'Of course,' Master Barwick said, as if it was the most natural thing in the world.

Bebe's tone was so much like Barabal's, Alain's stomach clenched in a momentary pang of longing for his friend.

'Technically he is both,' Alice added.

Changing the subject, Alain announced, 'I found two more altars.'

'And I found an additional two. Interesting—enough to form a pentagram. Someone was determined to ensure their spell was strong.' Master Barwick rubbed his chin thoughtfully, then abruptly turned on his heel. 'Well, there is nothing much more we can do around here. We may as well head back.'

Alain picked up Trouble's lead and they began walking behind the others. He asked, *How did you know?*

I didn't know exactly. I sensed something off in the air as we approached this field. A few moments ago, I caught a strong scent and, well, you saw the rest. Being a dog has its uses after all.

Are you sure this is related to what is going on? I mean, I cannot think of any magic able to do this type of thing. You know—cause a dog to get sick, Alain said.

Magic might not be the root cause, but if a person learnt the right spell they might help spread a disease. If that is what is happening, then this is far worse than the Council thought. I will wait until Barwick has a chance to look through what we found today, but I think I need to contact them. They may need to send in a more experienced team to deal with this.

As they plodded back towards Burley, Lee and Alain fell behind the others and walked in silence until Lee startled Alain by asking, 'Do you believe in all this magic being the cause of the illness in dogs? I mean, Barnaby does, but come on—supernatural powers? It's just stuff they put in movies.'

Alain took a moment to compose himself before answering. 'Those are two separate questions. Yes, I believe there are elements and forces that can be manipulated to affect our environment—call it magic, alchemy or science. Do I believe it is the cause of this disease in dogs? I'm not sure.'

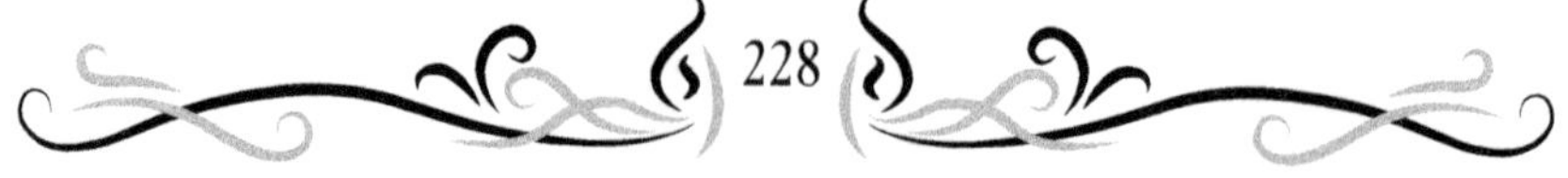

'You're saying it is magic?' Lee pressed.

'Barnaby and I both believe strongly in having proof before jumping to conclusions, but I wouldn't rule it out.'

Lee's eyes were wide in surprise. 'That's crazy. I mean you believing in the same off-the-wall stuff my aunt does?'

'I believe not everything can be explained away scientifically.' Alain wasn't sure how much to share with this boy. He trusted him, but his view on life was clearly very different from Alain's own.

'I am yet to be convinced,' Lee responded, which caused Alain to smile. At least his mind was open to the possibility, unlike his sister.

They caught up with the others to find their path had been blocked by a rather haughty-looking woman with steel-grey hair, and even steelier grey eyes that looked down her nose in disdain at them. 'Good morning, Alice. Out for an early morning walk?'

'Good morning, Tabitha.' The tone of Alice's voice did not invite further conversation, and she made to walk around the woman.

'You should not have that dog out here,' the grey lady commented as she moved to stand in front of Alice while looking directly at Alain. 'Not if you want it to remain healthy.'

'Leave the boy alone, Tabitha. His dog is on a lead, and not wandering off the path. He should be fine. Now, I must be getting on. It is almost time for me to open my shop.' Alice sidestepped Tabitha, and the others followed.

Tabitha made no attempt to move, and as Alain passed her, he heard her mumble, 'There is something about that dog. I am not sure what. But I will find out.'

And there is something about that woman, Trouble sent. *She is conflicted, but it is more than that. I sense something: disharmony and a lot of anger.*

As they reached the outskirts of Burley, Alain caught up with Alice and Master Barwick.

'She was part of our coven up until about three months ago. She and four others broke away, saying we were not daring enough for them and they wanted to try something different.'

'That does not sound good. Do you have any idea what they wanted to try?' his master asked.

'Tabitha was angry about a small business that opened up near her farm. They process hides for a very exclusive market. She complained that whatever they were using to treat the skins was affecting her horses. She wanted us to

work on a spell to bring ill luck to the business.

'As our coven's first rule is "do no harm"; we refused to help her. A couple of the newer members of the group agreed with her approach, and they broke away to set up their own community of witches.'

'Are they likely to do something like this though?' Master Barwick asked quietly, no doubt so Bebe and Lee, who had ranged ahead, would not hear.

'To be honest, although I never really liked the woman, I do not believe so. While she can be malicious to other people, she would never hurt a defenceless animal. Besides, not all of the attacks of Alabama Rot have been around the New Forest, so it is hard to imagine how they could be. Still, you never know ... she can be a little fanatical in her beliefs.'

Master Barwick rubbed his chin again. 'I agree it is unlikely someone who cared for animals would be a part of something like this. But if she were caught up with a larger group, she might be persuaded to do it. So, we cannot totally rule her out of the equation; nor can we ignore magical altars found in the area.'

Alice stopped dead in her tracks and Alain almost banged into her.

'A larger group? Do you believe this might be bigger than just a local break-out?' she asked.

'Um ... well ...'

Aware that Master Barwick was not at his best when confronted with emotional outbursts, Alain stepped around his hostess and said, 'I think what Uncle Barnaby was trying to say is, as a man of science he is not prepared to rule anything out. That does not mean he truly believes this might be part of a larger conspiracy. Right, Uncle?'

'Um, yes ... what the boy said,' Master Barwick muttered as he walked off.

You know there might well be others involved, Trouble said

If you mean who I think, there is no evidence they are involved in this. And until we have proof there is no point in worrying the others, Alain responded as he rushed to catch up with the rest of their group.

THEY REACHED THE house, and the group prepared to split up. Bebe decided to go spend the morning with her aunt in the shop, while Lee had offered to drive Master Barwick and Alain to the vet, which was in the neighbouring town.

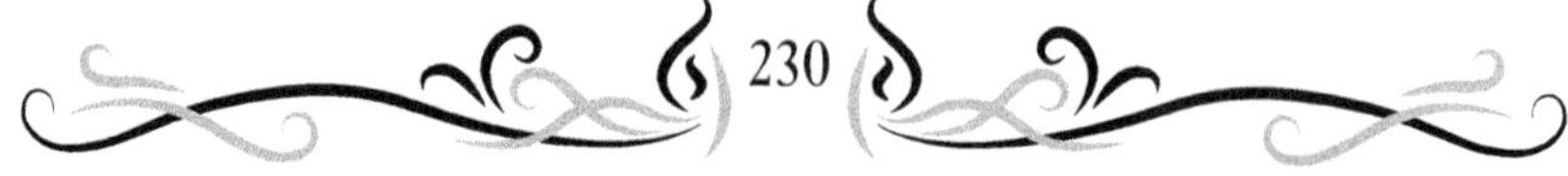

Lee pulled some keys out of his pocket and headed towards Alice's horseless carriage, which he called a car. He pressed something; there was a beep and the rear lights flashed.

'Jump in,' he said as he walked round the car.

Alain hung back. It wasn't like he was scared ...

All right, he was scared. His fear was partially due to the thought of travelling in this machine, but was mostly because he was not quite sure what to do when travelling in a car. Was it like being a passenger on a cart where you just sat there? Or was he expected to actually *do* something.

Master Barwick calmly walked forward and pulled the silver metal thing on the outside of the door, and it swung open. 'You had best take Trouble in the back,' he said as he slipped inside and closed the door behind him.

Suddenly wishing he had offered to go to the shop this morning instead, Alain walked tentatively towards the car. Pulling at the handle, he was pleased to find it opened for him just as it had done for his master.

Trouble appeared to have no fear of the vehicle. He jumped onto the seat and looked up at Alain as if to say, "What are you waiting for?" Taking a deep breath, Alain ducked down and joined the dog inside.

'Belt up,' Lee said as the car roared into life.

Lee pulled a long black piece of material out from the side of the car over his right shoulder, and a loud snick told Alain the metal end must have locked it into something. Master Barwick followed suit. Alain looked around and found an opening over his left shoulder and pulled at the silver metal. A belt sprung towards him. Placing it over his chest, he looked for where it was meant to go. Trouble discreetly put out a paw, showing Alain the opening the end would fit into.

Lee looked over his shoulder. 'All good? You had best hold on to Trouble. We don't want him falling off the seat, do we?'

Trouble obligingly draped himself over Alain's lap. Twining his fingers through the dog's hair helped soothe Alain's frayed nerves as they took off at speed out of Burley.

'Aunt Alice said we follow this road to the next town, and the vet is just as you go in. Should be a piece of cake.'

Lee might think the journey was simple, but after he had swerved to avoid a cyclist and had gone over yet another pothole at the side of the road, Alain realised that, like Stanislaus, he was not the best of drivers. In a horse and cart, ambling along like this was bad enough—but in a car that drove like

the wind, it was terrifying.

Master Barwick looked around over the back of his seat. From the look of pure joy on his face, he was finding the experience exhilarating. 'This is fun, isn't it?' he asked, confirming Alain's suspicions.

Please stop. You're hurting me.

Alain looked down to find himself gripping Trouble's fur so tightly the dog was looking over his shoulder at Alain's fingers entwined in his hair.

Sorry. Alain released his hand just as Lee said, 'Here we are.'

Lee pulled into a driveway so fast Alain found himself sprawled over the back seat. Only the seat belt locking up prevented him from squashing his travel companion.

Amazed they had not ended up in a ditch or a field, or driven another car off the road, Alain hauled himself upright, as did Trouble. He couldn't wait to open the door and let himself out. Trembling as he closed the door, leaving Trouble inside with Lee, he caught up with Master Barwick just as Jo appeared around the side of the building.

'This way. Jenna let the vet know she wanted you to examine Pepe, but the surgery opens soon so we don't have much time.' She led them around the side of the building and let them into a room lined with cages.

Though many of the inhabitants were cats and dogs, Alain was surprised to see a rabbit and a bright-feathered bird, and was that a ferret? Jo led them to the end-most cage and opened the door. The occupant was huddled in the back—a ball of white fur, its black button eyes widened in fear as Jo reached inside.

'Oh my lovely, no need to be scared.' Jo stood moments later cuddling the petrified animal in her arms. Placing him gently on a towel on the table in the middle of the room, the girl stroked the dog, all the while talking to him. 'You are a beautiful boy, aren't you? This man is just going to take a quick look at you.'

If Jo spoke to him that way Alain would just lie still and let her do anything she pleased. It had much the same effect on Pepe, who lay staring trustingly into her eyes. Master Barwick stepped forward and touched the dog's leg, carefully studying the angry-looking ulcer. The dog jerked away.

'You poor wee thing,' he said. He turned to Jo. 'I need to take a scraping from the wound, but I don't want to hurt him.'

'I thought you might need something to test, so I saved these.' Jo handed him a bag. 'We changed his bandages this morning, so the sample will be fresh.'

Master Barwick peeked into the bag, and nodded. 'These will do fine for what I have in mind.'

'Do you need anything else? A blood or urine sample?' Jo asked.

Master Barwick paused and stroked his beard before answering, 'Not with my current batch of tests. If they show nothing then I might have to reconsider.'

'All right. If you wouldn't mind helping me, I'll just put some more ointment on his sores then bandage him back up.'

Alain wasn't sure what help the girl needed as the dog just lay there while she dressed his wounds, and barely moved as she placed him back in his cage.

'Will he be all right?' Alain asked, worried that the animal did not have much life left in him. Tears welled in his eyes, and he brushed them away, knowing they would not change the dog's fate.

'The sores are healing, but it is his liver we are worried about,' Jo said. 'This disease causes liver collapse. Fortunately, Pepe is not at that stage yet. He had a blood transfusion yesterday and has perked up a little, but he is not out of the woods yet.'

Wow, if that is him looking better I hate to think what he was like before.

Jo continued, 'The vet will check him later and, if he is not improving, she may give him more blood. Apart from that and keeping him hydrated, there isn't much more we can do for him.'

Alain crouched and peered into Pepe's eyes. 'Hang in there, boy. We will help you if we can.'

'Thank you so much for this.' Master Barwick shook the bag. 'And for allowing us to study Pepe's wounds, but we should head back now so I can start my tests.'

'Actually, can I catch a lift to Burley with you? I'm finished here, and I'm supposed to be working a shift at the shop in half an hour.'

When Jo opened the door to the car, Lee blushed to the roots of his ginger-blond hair. Seemingly not noticing her new admirer, Jo jumped in on the other side of Trouble and put on her seat belt.

The ride home was less stressful, but was filled with chatter as Lee attempted to draw Jo out of herself. While the girl answered his questions, she asked none of her own, and it was clear to Alain she was being polite.

Back at Alice's place, Master Barwick gathered his samples and headed for the room over the garage, and Jo wandered off towards the centre of town to work.

As he locked up the car, Lee asked Alain, 'Do you think I have a chance

with her?'

'I'm not sure.' How could he tell the boy Jo did not seem remotely interested in him in that way.

Trouble snorted. *He has no chance. Jo's heart belongs to another.*

As they headed inside, Alain asked Trouble, *How can you be so sure of that, you have only just met her?*

Destiny.

Shaking his head, Alain closed the door. Removing his coat, he asked Lee, 'Do you want to come over and help Uncle Barnaby and me set up?'

'Not really my thing—chemistry, that is. Besides I want to check my emails and chats to find out what's going on with my friends.'

Not completely understanding what Lee was going to do, Alain left him to it, eager to help his master find out what was causing this disease. Not only to be able to return home, but also because they might find something to help the poor dog he had just left.

4

THE INVESTIGATION CONTINUES

MASTER BARWICK PLACED glass squares, glass containers, eye droppers and some things Alain had never seen before on the bench when he arrived. Unsure of what Master Barwick would want him to do, Alain leaned against the cupboards behind the workspace and watched before asking, 'If the scientists from this age cannot find a cure for Alabama Rot, how will you be able to?'

'Alain, remember we are not here to find a cure. Our job is to make sure this is a naturally occurring disease, not something caused by the Time Wreckers to serve their own ends. Once we confirm that, we can go home.'

'So we will not be helping Pepe?'

'Not as such. If we find something that might be useful we can tell Jo where to look, and that might save the dog from further discomfort. Here—can you mix this for me? The instructions are on the back.'

He handed Alain a bag. It appeared the powder inside would provide the perfect conditions to allow bacteria to grow. While he mixed the powder with water to create something called agar, he carefully considered his master's words.

'I don't believe the Time Wreckers would do something like this,' he said. 'I mean, don't they tend to concentrate on large-scale historic change?'

'Yes. They focus on bending major events to their own end, so this does seem a little small-scale for them. Which is good for us as it means we should be able to leave soon.'

While Alain wanted to get back home as soon as possible, something nagged at him. 'Master Barwick, Alice asked us here to help her sort out the problem in the New Forest. If we just leave, what will happen to the dogs? Will they still get sick and die?'

The elderly man stopped what he was doing and looked at Alain. 'Perhaps. If we find events are happening as they are meant to, we will leave and allow things to take their natural course.'

'Can't we …?'

'Time Guardians are not allowed to directly act to change history. Even if we find Time Wreckers are influencing this, we still cannot take direct action to stop them. We would merely be able to encourage and advise people living in this time on how they might counter the Wreckers' actions.'

'But …'

Master Barwick held up his hand to silence any protests. 'It is the hardest part of our job, but it is an important rule for us—it is the thing that makes us different from the Time Wreckers. While they feel it is their duty to change history to make a better world, we believe the timeline must be kept intact. However, that does not mean we can't do a little research and find out if we can offer anything new to the situation without becoming hands-on.'

Painting the agar gloop on the bottom of the flat, sterilised, round glass containers Master Barwick had set out, Alain said, 'It will be hard explaining that to Alice.'

His master was silent for a moment as he placed a small sample on the agar, then put the lid securely on top. He wrote on the container in pen, and moved on to the next sample before answering. 'Yes, it will be. We can only hope she will understand.'

For the first time since they had arrived, Alain hoped that something untoward was going on. Then there would be a reason for them to help Alice ... and Pepe.

When he'd finished putting agar in all the dishes set out on the bench, Alain washed his equipment and leaned his elbows on the counter. 'Master, how is it you know how to use all this equipment?'

'I told you how I travelled with Sigma a few times before. On one of those journeys I spent some time with a doctor in Scotland. He was an advanced

thinker for his time and studied what are called micro-organisms—things like bacteria.'

Alain nodded his understanding and Master Barwick continued, 'Although all this stuff is quite a bit more advanced, the principles are the same. Also, I spent part of last night reading the instruction manuals.' Tapping the book on the end of the counter, he said, 'And I read this text book to bring myself up to speed.'

After carefully adding the last sample to its own dish and closing the lid, Master Barwick stood and stretched his back. 'Right, over there are some glass slides and a bottle. If you could use the brush attached inside the lid to wipe some of the liquid on each of the slides, and place them along the counter, I will just put these Petri dishes away.'

Alain did as his master asked, setting up four slides ready for him to use. His teacher returned with the container of water they'd collected that morning and used a dropper to place a little on each of the slides. He reached under the bench and pulled out a tray of brown bottles with droppers for tops. He picked a few up and read their labels before selecting four and placing them on the counter.

With intense concentration, he added one drop from each of the bottles on one of the slides. Finally, he placed another glass slide over the top and put the bottles away. He turned to wash his hands in the sink before declaring that set of experiments done.

'What are they for?' Alain asked, curiosity getting the better of him.

Master Barwick sighed. Reaching under the counter once again, Master Barwick emerged with a strange-looking piece of equipment. 'This is a microscope. It is able to magnify things by an alarming amount. With this, I can identify any bacterial activity in the water.'

'And the stuff we put on the glass?' Alain chanced his luck, hoping the master was in a good mood.

'It fixes things to the glass. The liquid in the bottles helps identify certain micro-organisms.' Flicking through the book on the edge of the counter, Barwick found the spot he was looking for and turned it to face Alain. 'This explains it much better than I could.'

Alain took the book over to the couch and curled up with the tome in his lap. It was all so interesting, but he much preferred it when Master Barwick explained things to him. While he studied, his teacher labelled the slides.

He read the chapter as quickly as he could, then returned the book to the

counter. As he placed it down, he noticed a clean notebook had appeared from one of the numerous drawers and cupboards. Master Barwick wrote notes on each of his experiments before storing them in a cupboard under the bench.

'Ah, you are finished,' Master Barwick said. 'How about you head over to the house and get some food?'

The mention of eating pushed all other thoughts from Alain's mind. Not even pausing to ask Trouble if he wanted to join him, he dashed out of the room.

THE DOOR HAD barely closed when the old man slumped on the sofa beside the dog. 'This is not looking good, Sigma. There is more going on here than meets the eye.'

There was an odd feeling in that field today. I felt strong magic—too strong for this day and age. And it had an oily taint to it.

'No doubt we will learn a bit more once I finish these tests. The raw samples showed nothing obvious wrong, so all we can do is wait for the cultures to grow.'

When do you think you will have the preliminary results?

'This evening possibly … definitely by tomorrow. Alice's husband has an incubator, which should speed up the process a little given this cold weather.'

Trouble's head dropped on to his paws. *I can't wait until then to make my report.*

'I am going to study the water samples in more detail before I eat. Maybe I will find something, but it is unlikely as the stream was quite fast-running.'

I have been thinking on those altars and what about them smelled so off. I believe they reek of old magic, and that worries me. I think it might be best to contact the Council now.

Trouble took himself over to the blanket placed under the window by the radiator and curled up. He relaxed and closed his eyes, but the buzzing in his head told Master Barwick that rather than taking a nap, the Time Guardian was consulting his Council.

Turning back to his work, Master Barwick became so engrossed in the water samples and the superpowered microscope that it was a moment before he realised the dog had re-joined him.

I spoke briefly with Beta, Trouble said. *Something else has come up with this case and he was called to an emergency Council meeting. He will present our concerns and will tell us the outcome, hopefully sometime tonight. I get the sense our time here will soon be over.*

'What a shame. There is so much I would like to see and learn. Before you say it, I understand I cannot use any of it when I return to my own time, but still—there are so many new inventions here. It boggles the mind.'

Then you'd better make the most of the little time we have.

Trouble wandered back to the electric heater, leaving the alchemist to his experiments. Left to himself, Master Barwick picked up the first slide, noted its details in his notebook, then placed it under the microscope. He twisted knobs, looked through the viewer, then twisted the knobs again until what was on the slide came into focus.

'Mm, interesting.' He adjusted the microscope again to confirm what he saw.

He repeated the process with the other three slides, talking to himself as he did. 'Now, I did not expect that. Let me think.' He opened the text book and flicked through the pages until he found what he was looking for. He took some more notes. 'How curious …'

Taking another couple of slides, he put a drop of water from the stream on one with nothing else on it, pressed the other slide on top, and put it under the microscope. He studied it intently. The only sound was the ticking of the minute hand in the clock on the wall beside him.

'Ah, I found you,' he whispered to the slide, nodding in satisfaction. 'You are a wily wee thing, but you cannot escape me.'

He searched through the book again. Nothing quite matched the organism under the microscope. Shutting the book in frustration, he walked over to the bookshelf. Running his finger along the titles, he soon found what he was looking for—*Mutations of Common Organisms*. He took the volume back to the bench and continued reading and writing.

Sometime later, he shut another book with a thwack, rubbed his forehead and glanced around the room. It had turned dark outside, and the large hole in the bookshelf where he'd removed books during the afternoon stood testament to his hard work. He stared at the dog by the heater. Trouble raised his head sleepily.

Is that tantrum because you found something and are not happy? Or because you have not found anything and are unhappy?

'Humph.'

So, it is the latter, Trouble said as he dropped his head back on his paws.

Ignoring the Time Guardian, Barwick opened another book and flicked through the pages. 'Ah, well that is interesting.'

He turned back a few pages before slamming that book shut as well. 'But

not quite right either.' He added the discarded volume to the growing pile beside him, closed his notebook and leaned his arms on the counter.

'This is so frustrating. I found something in the water. It is not like anything I have ever seen before, so I thought it might be something discovered since my last visit forward in time. Only, just when I think I have found out what it is, I find a little detail that is not quite right.'

It must be frustrating, but not unexpected. Scientists have been working on this little problem for a couple of years now and have not found an answer.

'Nice to know you have so much faith in me, Sigma,' Master Barwick grumbled.

Barwick, if I didn't think you were up to the task you would not be here with me. But even you cannot expect to sort this out on your first day.

'Well, I didn't expect to,' he conceded. 'But when I found the organisms … well, I hoped …' Master Barwick stretched out his back and closed the other books on the bench.

'I am done for the day. Let's go and find the others,' he said to Trouble.

The dog stood, shook himself, stretched, then followed Master Barwick to the kitchen, wandering onto the lawn for a pit stop on the way.

BEBE WAS NOT sure what to make of her aunt's shop. Its mixture of touristy kitsch with *Harry Potter* wands, birthstones and charms was everything you would expect from a store attempting to fleece the tourists of a buck by making the most of the magical history of the area.

However, around the back Alice stocked serious books on the history of witchcraft and the practice of modern magic, along with pots and bottles full of all the accoutrements—everything the modern magical practitioner would ever need, or so Bebe imagined.

She spent the next hour unloading stock while her aunt served the few customers who wandered in. When the shop had been empty for a while, Alice checked outside to gauge the likelihood of potential customers before nipping out the back to make them a cup of tea.

Having told her aunt she took hers white with no sugar, Bebe idly cleared down the counter and tidied displays while she waited for her drink. The shop bell rang, and she popped her head around a display stand to find Jo had turned up.

With a quick 'hi', Jo slipped her backpack off her shoulders and headed out the back. She returned moments later backpack free, but with two steaming mugs of tea.

'Here, this is yours.' She handed Bebe a cup. 'Your aunt just left for the post office with the internet orders I packed yesterday. They are mostly in pre-paid bags, but as all the town gossip filters through the post shop, she won't be hurrying back and time soon.'

How many modern witches could there be? And how many ordered supplies from the shop? 'I knew Aunt Alice sold stuff online, but does she truly sell that much?'

'About twenty-five percent of our sales come through online. We are a little out of the way here, and most of our foot traffic is from tourists. So many of our less touristy items are mostly internet sales. Funnily enough, some of our best customers are from overseas. We even have one regular buyer from Salem in America.'

Jo laughed, seeming more amused than insulted by Bebe's questions. As they sipped their drinks, Jo leaned forward to better see the well-dressed, middle-aged woman entering the shop across the road. 'It's unlike Gladys to be arriving this late in the day. I wonder if her assistant opened for her.'

'Mm.' Bebe frowned and started over her cup at Jo. Why would she even be interested in what went on across the road, much less comment on it?

'They are our rivals. Well, not actual rivals. Gladys and Alice's friendship goes back years, back to when Alice first moved here with Donald. Although she sells some magical items in her store, Gladys sticks to local, handcrafted things whereas we do the touristy and the imported items. And, of course, all the local witches come here for their supplies.'

'Surely you do not believe in all that stuff? I mean, you're going to be a woman of science, a vet.' Bebe's tone invited Jo to agree with her.

'Actually, I do believe in it. I come from a long line of witches. I am part of the local coven. I also cast spells, most of which are successful.'

'What sort of spells? Love potions and things?' Bebe joked. She did not wish to offend Jo, but she couldn't get her head around all this nonsense about magic.

'Spells of protection and spells of remembering. Spells for a good harvest, or good health.' Although Jo did not appear to be upset by her questions, her voice had an edge to it as she took pains to add, 'I believe in science, but I also believe natural energies surround us that science cannot explain, and

I am happy to call on them to help myself and others.'

'Barnaby said something similar today when Lee found out he is not a man of science, but someone who studies and practices magic.'

Bebe had expected Jo to laugh, but she merely nodded before saying, 'Although Barnaby calls himself an apothecary, someone who deals in herbal medicines, I think you will find he is also an alchemist.'

'An alchemist? Do they really exist? Outside of fantasy novels, I mean.'

Jo laughed and explained, 'Alchemy is a term for anyone who mixes science with magic. In fact, I can probably find you a book on all the different types of magical practices if you like.'

'No, no, you're all right. I admit I don't know what I am talking about.' Bebe tried to laugh off her unease as she sipped her tea.

Placing her cup on the counter, Jo said, 'Alchemists were, and are, very real—as are witches. How come the subject of magic came up on your walk this morning? I thought you were just collecting specimens for Barnaby.'

'We found some weird things. Alain and Barnaby said they were altars for casting spells and were surprised to find five of them.'

Jo blanched. 'Five altars—the points of a pentagram. They meant business, whoever set them up. Can you tell me any of the other things found with the altars?'

Bebe frowned, trying to remember if she saw the men pick anything up. 'I am not sure I can. You should come 'round after work though. I am sure Barnaby will tell you everything. We found them just before heading home, and I was too busy at the time trying to stay warm to listen to what they were saying about them. Then one of Aunt Alice's friends arrived. She blocked our path and began acting kind of strange.'

'Oh? Who?' Jo asked.

'Some snooty woman named Tabitha. She was quite rude and, come to think of it, she didn't look dressed for a morning walk in the forest. I am sure her coat covered a suit, and she wore heels. Perhaps she was driving somewhere, saw us, and detoured to find out what we were doing.'

With her lip curling distastefully, Jo sneered. 'Nothing would surprise me with that woman.'

'You don't like her?'

'No, I do not, and I can honestly say, you should keep away from her.' Jo's aggressive tone took Bebe by surprise.

'I hope that is not me you are talking about.'

They looked around to find an attractive girl with wavy black hair and the most startling blue eyes Bebe had ever seen standing in the doorway. Strange, Bebe thought. I didn't hear the shop bell. The girl's lips curled into a supercilious smile. If Bebe had been a cat, her hackles would have risen, so intense was her dislike of this interloper, but for the life of her she could not tell why.

Jo, on the other hand, blushed, and the usually confident girl appeared nervous. 'Hi, Izzy. What can I do for you?'

The stranger's eyes twinkled with mischief. 'I can think of many things but, unfortunately, I've come across to beg some roll for the till from you. Gladys has run out.'

'Yeah, sure,' Jo said, knocking items off the shelf under the counter as she searched for the rolls.

'Here.' Bebe picked one up off the floor. 'Here you go.'

Izzy did not take her eyes off Jo as she took the item from Bebe's hand. 'Thanks. Perhaps I'll see you at the pub later.' She winked as she closed the door behind her.

Bebe turned to Jo. 'Who was that?'

'Gladys' new assistant. She isn't local. She arrived about ten or so weeks ago.' Jo started clearing up the things on the floor, and Bebe couldn't see her face.

'And you and she have a thing?' Bebe teased.

'What? No! I mean, I might have, but Gladys is a member of Tabitha's coven, and Izzy joined up soon after she started working in the shop. They are into some weird stuff—stuff most of us witches stay away from. So I'm steering well clear of her.'

'Still …' Bebe let the thought trail off.

'Mm,' Jo said. 'Still …'

Just as the conversation was getting interesting, the bell interrupted them and a couple of customers entered. While Jo helped one of the ladies select some tarot cards, Bebe assisted the other one in choosing a wand for her grandchild. She surprised herself by being able to remember the *Harry Potter* characters well enough to sell a wand belonging to the woman's granddaughter's favourite witch.

Thanking the shop assistants, the two women exited with beaming smiles just as Alice returned from the post office.

'Long queue, was there?' Jo smirked at her boss.

'You know full well there wasn't, you cheeky minx.' Alice took the ribbing

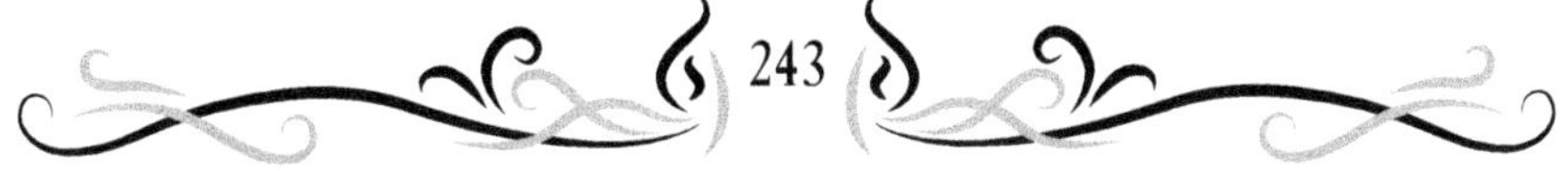

in good heart. 'Now if you two are all right here, I think I will go out back and catch up on my ordering.'

'We'll be fine. It isn't very busy. Oh, don't forget to put the new stock up on the website. With all of yesterday's orders I didn't get a chance,' Jo reminded her.

A steady trickle of customers visited throughout the rest of day. Around four it turned dark, and the small town was soon deserted. Alice popped her head out and said, 'Not much is going to happen now. You can begin packing up. Jo, would you mind doing the till while I finish off here?'

As Jo ran off the till totals and began counting out the float, Bebe tidied the shelves. The girls chatted, finding out a little more about each other.

Then Jo asked the dreaded question. 'So, now high school's over, what are your plans?'

Bebe's stomach clenched, and she attempted to sound nonchalant as she answered, 'I'm not quite sure yet.'

Jo's life was pretty much planned out, so Bebe tensed for a lecture on the importance of preparing for the future, but Jo surprised her by saying, 'That must be tough for you, especially with your brother having his next few years all sorted.'

'It is. I know what I'm interested in, but finding somewhere to channel it has been difficult.'

'Not so long ago I was in the same boat,' Jo said, and Bebe stopped what she was doing and reassessed the confident person she'd met only a day before. 'I can tell you're sceptical, but don't be fooled by what you see now. A couple of years ago, after my dad walked out, I was a mess. I was on the verge of being thrown out of school and was causing my mother all sorts of pain.'

Walking around the shelf she had been tidying, Bebe started sorting through the knick-knacks on the counter so she could watch Jo's face as she spoke. 'What changed?' she asked.

'The children's court sent me to a councillor. Ruth was amazing, although I didn't think so at first. I talked and she listened, and I told her of my passion—animals—and she arranged for me to spend some time at the local vet.'

'She sounds smart.'

Jo smiled. 'Yes, she is. My counsellor at school always spoke about my "feelings" and my "anger issues".' Jo used her fingers to make air quotes around the words to emphasise her disdain. 'Ruth found something I loved, and in turn talked me through what I would need to do if I wanted a future

as a vet. After a while, the vet offered me some shifts. It didn't pay enough for me to be able to consider university. Then Mum told me Alice needed help, so I started working for her as well.'

'Wow. You must have been busy.'

'Yes, with the extra work I took on at school, and with two jobs, I was soon too busy to be angry. After a while I started looking forward and not back, and the pain of my father leaving was no longer the driving force in my life,' Jo said as she closed the till and began putting the cash in a money bag.

'Do you ever catch up with your dad?'

Jo paused. 'This last year he got in touch again. He lost his job just before he left us, and things weren't great between him and Mum—hadn't been for a while. But he has sorted himself out now. It is hard, but maybe soon we can be friends again.'

Jo took the money out back while Bebe locked the door and pulled down the window blinds, before meeting the others by the back door.

During the walk home, Jo and Alice chatted but Bebe couldn't say about what. Her attention was on her conversation with Jo. Not on her story, but on the woman Ruth. She had helped Jo turn her life around, and the spark of an idea began to form.

'Bebe? Were you listening?' Jo's impatient tone interrupted her thoughts. 'What did you say about Tabitha today?'

'That she was rather snooty?' Bebe offered.

'No, the rest of it,' Jo prompted.

'Um, that she wasn't dressed for walking in the forest; it seemed more like she was heading somewhere else and came over to find out what we were doing.'

Alice paused for a moment. 'You're right. I was so annoyed at seeing her there, and with her arrogant behaviour I didn't even notice. How clever of you to work that out. I wonder what piqued her interest?'

As they continued their walk home, the other two chattered about what Tabitha's motivations might have been, while Bebe drifted back into her own thoughts. How was she ever going to flesh out what she wanted to do with her life in this backwater town where they believed magic was real?

CURLED UP ON the sofa, Alain once again lost himself in *The Lord of the Rings*. Seated in a chair by the fire, Lee was "looking things up on his tablet".

The fire crackled and the wind whipped around the windows as if trying to gain entry, but Alain hardly noticed, so caught up was he in his book.

'How can you read something that long and boring?' Lee peered over the top of his tablet at Alain.

'Huh?'

'I said ... how can ... oh, never mind.'

Holding his finger inside the book so he did not lose his place, Alain looked over and asked, 'What are you looking up now?'

'I am researching alchemists.'

Alain placed a slip of paper from the coffee table into the book and put it on the sofa beside him. 'Why didn't you just ask me?'

'What? You mean you're an alchemist too?' Lee swung his legs around so he was sitting properly in the chair, a glint in his eye.

'Almost. I'm an apprentice alchemist. Well, if I am honest, I am more of an apprentice apothecary,' Alain admitted. 'But Barnaby started to teach me alchemy so I can better treat my patients.'

'Alchemy has not been taught as a meaningful line of study for centuries, so I assume it's more of a hobby sort of thing?'

Alain's brow furrowed, suddenly wary of the boy in front of him. He came across as happy-go-lucky so it was easy to forget he was quite smart.

'In fact, it says here alchemy died out in and around the time of the Renaissance, when science took over,' Lee continued. He raised his eyes and pinned Alain with his steady gaze.

Shifting uncomfortably, Alain realised he may have given too much away. This version of Stanislaus was much more perceptive than the one he knew.

'Well, Barnaby is a bit old-fashioned …'

'Yes, but Medieval old-fashioned?' Lee pressed. Alain could not meet the other boy's eyes, and Lee smiled. 'I knew there was something odd about you two. It's all right. I won't tell anyone your secret.'

'What secret?' Alain asked in a last-ditch effort to throw Lee off the scent.

'That you two are not only not from around here, but not from this time at all.'

'Um, I am not sure I understand what you mean.' Alain fumbled for a plausible explanation.

'Come on. You two practice alchemy and magic. Then the way you behaved in the car today—it was as if you had never been in one before.'

'Your driving would do that to anyone who wanted to live,' Alain countered.

'Your reactions were too extreme for that. No, somehow you guys travelled

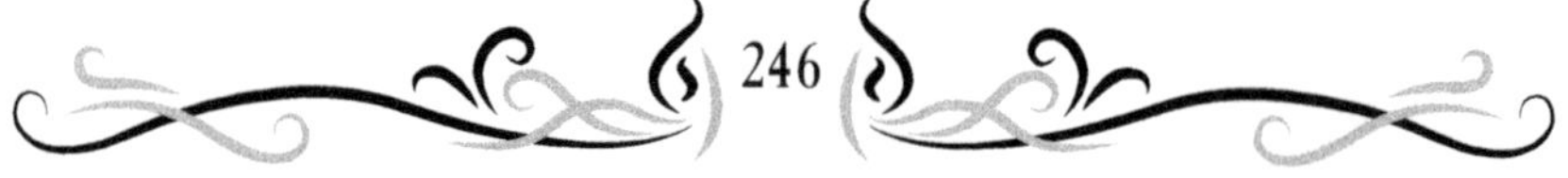

through time to be here.' Having presented his case, Lee sat back in the chair.

'Don't be ridiculous. Time travel isn't a real thing.'

'I think your being here is proof it is. Add that to the fact that some pretty knowledgeable scientists agree that in theory, travelling through time is possible, and —'

'Please, you cannot tell anyone. Master Barwick will be so disappointed in me for giving the game away,' Alain pleaded.

'I will make you a deal. If you tell me about some of your cool experiments, I promise not to let on I know anything.'

Alain pondered the proposal for a moment. Deciding it was the lesser of two evils, he reluctantly agreed.

He spent the next hour recounting some of his past antics: the experiments gone wrong, the diseases he'd cured and the tricks he'd played on others. Lee insisted on checking everything out on the internet.

When Lee showed him the screen, Alain was fascinated to find how things in the fields of chemistry and medicine had moved on from his time. Not so academically inclined, Lee showed more interest in the stories and the mayhem than letting Alain study drawings of the body, or allowing him time to read up on the details of new discoveries.

Saving the best for last, Alain told Lee about using Greek fire to blow up a door to break a friend out of a dungeon. The other boy was suitably impressed and they spent a little time researching Greek fire online. Lee then showed him how easy it was to make an explosion from everyday household items.

At the sound of footsteps in the hall, Lee turned his screen off, and the two tried to look innocent of any wrongdoing. Clearly, they were not successful, as Bebe stood in the doorway, hands on hips, and asked, 'What have you two been up to?'

'Nothing.' Alain's cheeks heated, finding it as hard to lie to Bebe as it was to keep the truth from Barabal.

'Mm.' She pursed her lips. 'Alice just put the kettle on and is warming some cottage pie for dinner if you would like to join the rest of us in the kitchen.' She turned on her heel and left the room.

'Remember, you promised,' Alain said as they followed her out.

'And I keep my promises,' the other boy responded. Then, under his breath, he said, 'Even though it might be impossible to keep this from Bebe. She always figures out when I am hiding something.'

'You've got to try,' Alain insisted.

'What did you promise?' The question came from behind, causing Alain to jump.

'Ah, Barnaby. I didn't see you come in,' Lee answered. 'I was just saying I promised Alain he and I would try the local ale one night soon—maybe tonight. Bebe and I turned eighteen yesterday and, because we were travelling, we still haven't had our first legal drink. He said you would probably not let him go, and I said I would speak to you about it. Would you let him come out with me? In fact, do you want to come along with us? We can make it a boys' night.'

Stopping in his tracks, the elderly man frowned. 'Why, thank you for asking, young man, but I am afraid my tavern days are long over. Besides, I want to spend some time checking my samples this evening. But you young ones go out and enjoy yourselves.' As he shuffled past them, Trouble in his wake, Lee winked at Alain. Just when he thought they had got away with it, Trouble turned and stared at him.

We will talk about what Lee found out later.

How did you know? Can you read minds? Alain asked, but the dog did not answer. He simply wandered into the kitchen, turned around a couple of times and flopped down in his place by the Aga.

5

NIGHT-TIME ANTICS

AS ALICE BUSTLED around busily preparing a meal, the others chatted happily drinking tea and spoiling their dinner by munching their way through a plate of home baked biscuits in the cosy warmth of the kitchen.

Alice placed a pie in the oven and started preparing vegetables. She paused mid-chop and turned around. 'Did you find out anything useful today, Barnaby?'

'Humph, not really. It was most frustrating. I did find some odd organisms in the water. They are not like anything I have seen before. If they are also in the soil or the puddles, we may have found our culprit.'

Alice paused for a moment. 'That's great, so why the long face?'

'Try as I might, Alice, I was unable to find any clues as to what it is. If Alain can help me go through some of your husband's books tomorrow, hopefully two eyes will be better than my poor old ones and we will find a name for it.'

'Of course,' Alain said. 'I am all yours.'

'Are you crazy?' Lee asked. 'It will take you hours to find something by going through books. I'll bring over my computer and we shall find it much quicker.'

Master Barwick raised one sceptical eyebrow.

'He is not joking, Barnaby. You should see the amount of information he can access on his tablet. If he helps I am sure our search will go more quickly,'

Alain confirmed.

'I guess it is worth a try,' Master Barwick conceded reluctantly. 'We may also be able to narrow down the search parameters if our samples grow overnight.'

'My computer can deal with an awful lot of information, so don't worry too much about that,' Lee said.

'And we can still take a quick look through your books if you like,' Alain offered in an attempt to reassure his mentor.

'So we haven't moved any further ahead,' Alice said as she took a seat at the head of the table.

'Well, Barnaby hasn't, but I think Bebe may be on to something with her comment about Tabitha,' Jo said.

Bebe shrugged. 'You think that's important?'

'Yes, of course.' Jo turned to face Bebe.

'All I said was, don't you think it odd she came to talk to you all when she wasn't dressed for a walk in the forest? I mean, what would make a person stop their car and traipse across the wet grass just to speak with you?'

'You raise an interesting point. Why would she do that? Probably to find out what we were up to …' Barnaby mused, then nodded. 'Maybe she knew about the altars and wanted to know if we found them?'

'Of course,' said Jo, banging her hand on the table. 'And the only way she would know they were there was if she and her new coven of witches were responsible for putting them there in the first place. They are probably up to their necks in this.'

'Hold on a minute.' Master Barwick help up his hand. 'Let's not get carried away here. It doesn't necessarily follow that those altars have anything to do with the disease affecting the dog community—the spell cast using them need not have been malignant.'

'There is only one way to find out,' Lee said. 'We need to break into Tabitha's house and see if we can find any evidence one way or the other.'

As Alain murmured his agreement, Alice exclaimed, 'You will do no such thing! Not only is breaking and entering illegal, but what would your parents say if they found out I let you do something so dangerous?'

'And stupid,' Bebe added.

'We will be in and out so quick it will be like we were never there—and our parents need not be any the wiser,' Lee said.

'No, and that is my final word on the matter. Let Barnaby finish his tests and things, then, if they prove those altars are somehow involved, we can

discuss how to approach Tabitha.'

Seeing Lee about to object, Alain touched his arm and shook his head. He had a better idea. 'Listen to your aunt, Lee. Besides you promised me a trip to the local pub tonight.'

Lee nodded, 'I did, didn't I. Is that all right with you, Alice?'

'Mm, I am not sure. You and Bebe have only just turned eighteen ... how old are you, Alain?'

'I am eighteen,' the lie rolled easily off his lips and he prayed Master Barwick did not rat him out. He was not eighteen for a couple of months yet, but it was clear that for his plan to work he needed to pretend to be a few months older than his actual age.

'Well …' Alice started.

'We will come with you,' Bebe jumped in. Lee opened his mouth to say something, but before he did, she carried on. 'Jo, you want to catch up with Izzy, and I would not mind meeting some of the locals.' Her eyes twinkled mischievously as she poked her new friend.

Lee winked at Alain.

Folding her arms and tutting, Alice said, 'You should keep away from that Izzy, Jo. She is bad news; I feel it in my bones.'

'You're worried because she's joined Tabitha's coven, but she's okay.' Jo defended herself.

Jo really seemed to like Izzy. Understanding washed over him, and he knew now what Trouble had meant by Lee not being Jo's "type".

'It's not just that ... I mean, something about Tabitha's new coven is definitely odd. I guess you are old enough to make your own mistakes though. Just be careful; that is all I ask,' Alice said as the oven beeped and she rose to finish preparing the meal.

'Shall we head down to the pub too, Barnaby?' Alice took a steaming pie from the oven as she asked the question, and so missed the worried glance Lee shot at Alain. In turn, Alain nearly cursed out loud. It would be difficult enough to lose the girls, but if the adults came too, a detour to Tabitha's wouldn't be possible.

'Uh, I guess we could, but I was planning to check on my experiments, and a couple of your husband's books looked very interesting. I want to flick through some more of them and maybe spark a new line of enquiry,' Master Barwick said.

Alice placed the meal on the table. 'Well, I am just as happy to curl up by the fire with a good book for the night,' she said, before serving the rest of the food.

The room fell into silence as they turned their attention to filling their stomachs.

Barwick, don't forget I want to meet with our friends tonight too. Do you want to join me?

What meeting was Trouble talking about? Alain glanced towards the dog, who appeared to be sleeping and did not even stir.

Is this something I should stay around for? he asked.

No, it is important, but we can update you on the outcome tomorrow. You go and enjoy yourself, but be careful.

Careful? Why would you say that?

You know why. The dog closed his eyes, ending the conversation.

As his attention returned to the meal, he found Jo staring thoughtfully at Trouble. Had she heard the whole conversation? Alain was pretty sure she had.

After the meal, the boys cleared down the table while Bebe and Jo washed the dishes. The two girls laughed and whispered as they worked.

Looking up from his phone, Lee asked, 'What's so funny?'

'Wouldn't you like to know,' Bebe tossed over her shoulder, causing another round of giggles.

Once the kitchen was cleaned and the dishes put away, they headed out to the living room. Alice and Master Barwick had settled in around the fire and were both engrossed in books. On the table between them sat a pot of tea and some of Alice's carrot cake.

Alice rose to escort them out, and as Alain passed by her she placed a hand on his arm. 'Here, you will need this if you are to buy some drinks. Although it might be best of you let the others buy them for you as you might need ID to prove your age.' She slipped some paper into his hand, which he assumed was what passed for local currency.

'ID?' Alain frowned.

'Yes. Something like a driver's licence or student card. You need it to prove you are old enough to purchase alcohol.'

Grateful for her generosity and advice, he bent down and gave her a quick peck on the cheek, and she rewarded him with a blush and a smile as she closed the door.

Now they were free how they were going to give the girls the slip, and how were they going to find out where Tabitha lived? He need not have worried. No sooner had the door closed than Jo said, 'C'mon, this way.'

'The pub is this way, isn't it?' Lee pointed in the opposite direction.

'But my mum's car is parked over here.'

Jo turned her head and motioned towards a dark green car parked a little way down the street.

Bebe laughed. 'A blind man could see you guys intended to drop us at the pub and disappear off to spy on Tabitha.'

'My mum sometimes gets a lift in to work and leaves her car here for me to drive home,' Jo said. 'We can all drive to Tabitha's, find out if we can get inside, rummage around quickly, and still have time for a pint in the pub before closing.'

'You are not coming with us,' Lee told them. 'It might be dangerous.'

Oh no, Alain thought. How could Lee be so clever about some things, and so dumb about others?

'All right, smart arse, how do you plan to get to Tabitha's?' Bebe glared at them, hands on hips, her face a mask of defiance.

'Come to think of it, do you even know where she lives?' Jo stood shoulder to shoulder with Bebe.

'And if it's too dangerous for us to go, the same could be said of the both of you.' Bebe leaned forward as she spoke, as if daring them to disagree with her.

Now they were playing tag team, and Lee simply crossed his arms over his chest and said, 'You're not coming.'

Sighing, Alain knew he was beaten even if Lee didn't. 'They're right, you know. We have no idea where we are going, and if Tabitha's place is not in walking distance …'

'… I thought we would take Alice's car,' Lee answered.

'If we sneaked the keys she would hear us leave, and if we asked she would want an explanation as to why we need to drive the short distance to the pub.'

Even in the face of such blinding logic, Lee would not budge.

Shrugging, Jo said, 'We don't need your permission to do anything and, unlike you two, I at least know where to go.' She turned and walked down the street. Alain and Bebe followed.

Glancing over his shoulder at Lee, who had not moved an inch, he said the words he knew would goad the other boy into joining them, 'Come on. You don't want to miss all the fun, do you?'

The look he got in return screamed "traitor", but Lee had caught them up by the time they had reached the car.

WITH LEE SAFELY in the back seat, his rigid stance emanating waves of disapproval, Jo pulled away from the curb. In spite of the tense atmosphere, Alain did not find the short drive to Tabitha's property too disturbing. It may

have been that he was getting used to travelling in cars, or perhaps it was because Jo was a better driver than Lee. She didn't launch them around corners at speed and when she parked the car a little way up a lane near their destination, she did not stop suddenly, flinging everyone forward in their seats.

They all piled out of the vehicle and milled around. Even from where they had parked they were able to see a light on at the back of the house.

'Looks like someone is in the kitchen,' Jo said.

'What makes you say that?' Lee moved beside her and peered over her shoulder.

'We used to come here a lot for coven meetings before ... you know ... she and the others broke away. The kitchen is at the back. It has French doors leading out to the back lawn.'

That wandered back to the corner, then turned down the road Tabitha's house was on. They kept to the shadows as they drew near to their destination, using the hedges lining the country lane as cover.

'I only saw one car in the driveway when we drove past, so there's a decent chance she's alone,' Bebe said.

'I would not be so sure of that,' Jo responded. 'Just over a month or two ago, not long after Izzy arrived, an American friend came to stay with Tabitha. It was the talk of the town, how this handsome, younger man came to live in her house, and with her husband working in London during the weeks. You know how gossip runs riot in small communities.'

'You say this happened about two months ago?' Alain asked. 'Around the same time the recent Alabama Rot outbreak started to get bad?'

'When you put it like that, it sounds suspicious,' Jo said.

'And that was around the same time Izzy showed up.' Bebe tapped her index finger on her lips, then raised her eyebrows.

'I am sure that is not related.' In the darkness, Jo's voice sounded unconvincing even to Alain's ears.

'So, let's just confirm the timeline here.' Bebe pressed her point. 'Tabitha left your coven, some guy shows up, then Izzy arrives and the Alabama Rot gets worse.'

'No,' Jo mumbled.

Wanting to soften his next words so Jo did not feel under attack, Alain placed a comforting hand on her arm before he spoke. 'Why don't you tell us what order things happened in?'

'Tabitha got angry and split the coven. Soon after, Izzy showed up. Gavin, the guy staying with Tabitha, came a week or so later.' Jo stopped, and was silent for a moment. 'We've had a few cases of the rot over the last couple

of years, but this bout started ... um ... when the weather turned ... around the beginning of September, I guess. But the cases started becoming more frequent later on that month.'

Aligning the times in his head, Alain figured out the likely chain of events, but wanted to double check. 'So, you had your first cases just before Izzy showed up. You think they got worse still later in the month ... Do you have any idea who this Gavin chap is? Because it appears the cases got worse after he arrived.'

As if he wanted to spare Jo any discomfort, Lee said, 'This is all very interesting, but it is only speculation. What we need is evidence. So, if we are going to check out the house we should do it now.'

'Oh, you're actually coming with us, are you?' Bebe teased.

Lee continued, 'I suggest you two girls take the front. Alain and I will head 'round the back and see if we can get a peek at what's going on in the kitchen.'

'Why do you guys get to go where all the action is? Is it because you are all manly and it's too dangerous for us mere females?' Bebe's lips curled into a sneer.

'No, my angry little sister. Because if someone catches us they won't know who we are or why we are snooping. We've a good chance of making up some story and getting away with it.'

'With Tabitha knowing Jo, it would be more risky for the two of you given she is more likely to be at the back of the house.' This time, Alain was able to support Lee.

'Oh ... right. That makes sense,' Bebe admitted. 'And I'm only five minutes younger than you, you know.' She punched Lee on arm.

'If that's all the questions, shall we go now?' When no one objected, Lee clambered over the fence, using the hedge bordering the property to cover his movements.

Alain followed him. Moving as silently as possible, he just made out the crunching of gravel as Bebe and Jo ran across the driveway. At the edge of the hedgerow, Lee found a wooden picket gate. He opened it quietly and held it for Alain to slip through before pulling it to. 'In case we need to escape quickly,' he whispered.

Keeping as much to the shadows as possible, they shimmied underneath the kitchen window, backs to the wall, then stopped short. Light spilled across the lawn from French doors leading to a deck and, worse still, the doors were open. Sitting at an outdoor table was a woman gazing out into the backyard as she sipped intermittently from a glass of wine. She was so deep in conversation with the man in front of her, she had not noticed them.

'Drop,' Lee whispered, as he sunk to the ground, trying to make his form as small as possible.

Alain was too slow. Before he could react, the woman looked up and stared him straight in the eyes.

'Who have we here?' she asked, rising to her feet. The man with her moved his chair to get a better view of what was going on, but his face remained in the shadows.

Alain decided the best defence was offence as he stepped into the light. 'Good evening, ma'am.' Politeness usually worked with strangers. However, Tabitha's steely grey eyes did not soften one iota.

'What are you doing skulking around in my garden?' After moving around the table to stand by her companion, Tabitha leaned forward, frowning slightly. 'Hey, aren't you one of the kids I met in the New Forest this morning with Alice?'

His brain felt sluggish as he searched for a plausible answer to both questions. Ignoring the first, he went straight to the second. 'Alice? Yes, my uncle and I are renting the room above her garage for a few weeks. She offered to show us a few of the local sites. Was that you she stopped and talked to?' He peered into the darkness as if trying to get a better look at her. 'Yes, it was. Hello again.'

The man beside Tabitha shifted in his seat, allowing Alain to see Jo had been right—he was about ten to fifteen years younger than Tabitha. An amused smile played around his lips, and eyebrows raised in query over his pale blue eyes. Rather than appearing amused by the situation, though, the play of shadows and light turned his chiselled face angular and sinister.

'You still have not answered my first question. What are you doing here?' Tabitha's impatient voice drew Alain's attention back to her.

'Well ... it's a bit embarrassing …' He stopped and looked around, hoping some excuse might present itself, then divine inspiration struck and he allowed tears to form in his eyes. 'I was out walking my dog in the lanes. He caught a scent of something and took off. I lost him in the dark and I've been looking everywhere. I'm sorry. I don't know this place and I stumbled into your backyard.'

'Yes, yes,' Tabitha said, turning her wine glass in her fingers. 'But that does not explain why you were walking a dog out here at night, or why you were lurking in the shadows.'

'Well ... when I arrived, you were having a private conversation, and my dog obviously isn't here—there's no way he would have been able to resist

coming up for a pat, and I didn't want to interrupt, so I was just going to sneak past ...' He trailed off when he realised Tabitha was glaring at him.

'Where is your lead?'

'Lead?' Alain had no idea what she was talking about.

'Yes, your dog lead,' she said each word slowly as if talking to a young child.

'Oh, that is the embarrassing part. I was daydreaming a bit and when Trouble bolted the lead slipped out of my hand. I was not quite quick enough to grab it.' He dropped his head as if trying to hide his shame.

'You call your dog Trouble?' The man laughed a great belly laugh, which sounded odd coming from such an ominous-looking individual. 'Seems like it is a very apt name for him. Come on, Tabitha, no harm done. Let the boy go find his dog. We should finish up inside anyway.' He stood and moved to go indoors.

Tabitha paused, tapping her wine glass as if considering what to do next, her eyes locked with Alain's. A crash from the back of the house drew her attention, and Alain took the opportunity to dart off towards the gate they had left open, then ran full tilt all the way back to the car.

Jo and Bebe were inside when he arrived, with the engine running and seat belts on. He opened the door, and moments later Lee pushed him from behind and he found himself sprawled across the seat, Lee on top of him yelling, 'Go!'

'Door,' Jo said.

Alain flinched as Lee's elbow pushed into the soft flesh of his stomach as he reached to comply.

Jo slowly accelerated and the boys scrambled to upright positions and belted themselves in. They crawled along the lane, lights off, until they reached the end of the road. Lee turned to check out the back window and confirmed they were not being followed.

The car filled with nervous laughter as Jo turned on the lights and sped up to the speed limit. Turning the car back towards Burley, Jo asked, 'Anyone else need a drink?'

They all agreed a trip to the pub was in order. As they pulled into the parking lot a few minutes later, Lee said, 'Did you recognise the man she was with? I would never have expected him to be that Gavin—not in a million years.'

6

ANOTHER PIECE OF THE PUZZLE

'ARE YOU SURE it was Gavin Vaughn?' Bebe asked.

'I said it was him a hundred times already.' Although Alain was unable to see Lee's face in the darkness, his frustration rang clear in the tone of his voice as it filled the pub car park.

Was he the only person who did not know who Gavin Vaughn was?

'Who?' Jo said.

Apparently not.

'You have no idea who Gavin Vaughn is? For real? He's only one of the world's most famous eco-terrorists,' Lee said.

'Otherwise known as Lee's hero.' Bebe feigned a swoon to add emphasis to her words.

'He is not,' Lee protested as Jo moved between them, pushing Bebe towards the pub door.

'What has he done that is so great?' Jo asked as Bebe reached for the handle.

As warm air carrying a hint of stale beer hit them, Lee answered. 'He started off with Whale Watch, interfering with whale-hunting. Then governments agreed to tighten regulations and he risked going to prison if he continued, so he moved to South America. He began sabotaging big corporations involved

in deforestation for profit. To keep big business happy, some governments put a price on his head, forcing him to flee. It looks like he ended up here.'

As they walked past Jo into the pub, Lee pulled his phone out of his pocket and showed Alain a picture. 'This was the man you spoke to, right?'

The man in the image had a beard, but the eyes were unmistakable. 'Yep, that's him.'

'What do you want to drink?' Jo caught them up as they searched the crowded bar for a free table.

Lee pushed past them and wiggled in between two guys leaning on the bar. 'Four pints of lager,' he demanded.

'Three and a bitters lime and lemonade, thanks Peter,' Jo called over his shoulder.

'What?' Lee turned to ask Jo.

'I still need to drive home, plus I start work early tomorrow morning, so I need a clear head.'

Lee shrugged. 'Okay, you guys find somewhere to sit and I'll bring them over.'

Alain and Bebe followed Jo to an empty table they spotted in the far corner. Used to the rather basic taverns in his time with sawdust on the floor and serviceable wooden furniture, Alain was pleasantly surprised by the modern equivalent.

Brightly coloured carpet covered the floor and a fire blazed in the open fireplace. Although the furniture was wooden, someone had spent time polishing it, and it was of a much better quality than those in the taverns he frequented. The only thing the same was the smell. The underlying hint of stale hops, smoke and unwashed bodies made him feel right at home.

Alain took a seat beside Bebe, leaving a space in between him and Jo for Lee. Putting the drinks down on the table moments later, Lee took his place and said, 'So, it is likely Tabitha is working hand-in-hand with an eco-terrorist. But why?'

Jo and Bebe shared a supercilious smile, before Bebe said, 'We may have the answer to that.'

'What did you …?' Lee started, but Jo spoke over him.

'Before we explain, let me tell you a little about Tabitha Synden-Moore.' Jo placed her drink on the cardboard coaster, then straightened it in line with the table before proceeding. 'She has been heavily involved in protecting the New Forest for years. From protesting against potential oil exploration, to lobbying against conifer tress being introduced, she is a strong advocate for leaving the forest as it has always been.'

'That may explain how she met this eco-terrorist,' Alain said as he tried to piece all the bits of information together. 'I mean, his being here now may just be coincidence. They do have common interests after all.'

'A nice thought, but Gavin Vaughn's tactics have become increasingly extreme over the past few years,' Bebe said, and Lee glared at his sister. 'Well, they have, Lee, and you know it. If he is here, something big is on the cards.'

'Anyway, there is more.' Jo intervened before a sibling squabble took over the conversation. 'Tabitha used to be an elected member of The New Forest Association, a group that basically runs the forest and surrounding area. It has a balanced government and elected officials. In the last round of elections hardly anyone voted for her.'

'I bet she was annoyed by that.' Bebe smirked before asking, 'Is there any particular issue or reason people stopped voting for her?'

'I believe so. She wanted to open the forest up to the public for only one month a year because she believes tourism is killing it.'

'Would that be so bad?' Alain asked. 'After all, perhaps the New Forest should be protected for those who live and work here, and for the future.'

Jo's hand stopped midway to her mouth and she glared at him. 'How can you agree with her? Many of the people who live in this area rely on tourist dollars to make a living. With fewer people coming in, many people would be forced to close their businesses and move away.'

'And there are other options. Something like turning the area into an environmental haven would achieve the same end, as well as teaching people how to respect the land,' Lee said.

Jo and Alain turned, surprised at his input. 'What? I am a great believer in saving our environment. Why do you think I even know who Gavin Vaughn is?'

'While this is all very interesting, can we just focus on the problem at hand?' Bebe pointed to Jo's phone as she spoke.

'So ...' Jo picked up where she'd left off. 'After she lost her position, Tabitha became more extreme in her ideas. She wanted our coven to not only cast protection spells for the forest, but to actually perform castings that might backfire and actually hurt people who did harm. That is not what we are about, so she took some of her cronies and left our group.'

'Do you really think the altars we found this morning might be theirs?' Alain asked, finally seeing the bigger picture she was painting.

Jo nodded, so he continued.

'You think they were casting a malicious spell?'

'I do, but I don't believe they have anything to do with the rot showing up in dogs. Tabitha loves animals. She would think nothing about hurting humans, but hurting dogs is a completely different matter.'

'But there is still more,' Bebe said as she took her phone from her pocket. Turning it on, she brought up images of typewritten documents interspersed with handwritten notes and drawings of buildings, as well maps. Placing the phone so Lee and Alain could see, she scrolled through the photos.

'Where did you get these?' Lee asked.

'We found an open window ...' Bebe started.

'You snuck inside? That was you making the noise that distracted Tabitha?' Lee clenched his fists. 'You fools. What if they'd caught you in the house? What if they had called the police? We wouldn't have been able to rescue you.'

'Keep your hair on,' Jo said. 'My foot knocked a book on the edge of a dresser as we climbed back through the window.'

'We didn't move anything else, and we left everything exactly as we found it,' Bebe added.

'And we hid behind the front hedge when the lights came on inside. Your friend Gavin rushed out the front door, and as he turned on the outside light, a cat took off from behind a bush. He cursed at it and went back inside. We waited a moment to make sure he wasn't returning before we ran back to the car,' Jo told them.

'Besides, it was worth the risk to take these.' Bebe raised her chin defiantly.

'What are they?' Although Alain could still understand everyone, his ability to read had left him. Trouble must be involved in something else, or perhaps Alain was too far away to benefit from the Guardian's full magical ability.

'They are planning documents from a local council.' Lee picked up his phone, typed into the screen, waited a few moments, then entered a number from one of the images. 'That is a planning application reference, and from what I can tell from the local council website, they haven't been made public. I'm guessing they are probably stolen.' Lee flicked through some more of the photos before saying, 'Did you read any of this?'

'Yes. I scrolled though a few of the documents while we waited for the two of you,' Jo answered. 'They propose ten thousand new houses be built in the New Forest over the next five years. This here is an impact assessment, and this one details new facilities that will need to be developed to support the population growth. This one in particular worries me—it is an impact assessment on the forest itself,' Jo said as she passed the phone back to Lee. 'The handwritten notes talk about how to "handle" the release of the details to prevent locals opposing the plan. The environmental impact will be devastating, and will change this part of the New Forest forever.' Jo's hand shook as she took her phone back.

'We should tell Alice and Barnaby about this,' Bebe said. 'It may not be related to what Barnaby is doing, but it is important. Though we can't say how we found it. Alice expressly forbade us from going to Tabitha's tonight.'

Used to getting himself out of tight situations, Alain's response was swift. 'We don't tell them … well, at least not yet. They are concerned about saving the dogs and what we found tonight isn't linked to that. I see no need to risk getting ourselves in trouble.'

As the others nodded their agreement, Lee said, 'That doesn't stop us from following up and seeing if we can find out some more about what is going on. I mean, this is so wrong. We can't just let the development go ahead.'

'Hello Jo. Don't you all look serious?' The voice coming from behind Alain sounded familiar, but he couldn't exactly place it, even though he had only spoken to a few people in this time. 'May I join you?'

Not waiting for an answer, the girl pushed past him and he caught a glimpse of dark hair and a leather jacket as she placed a chair between Lee and Jo and proceeded to sit. Lee went to object, looked at Jo then stopped and shuffled over closer to Alain.

'I never stood a chance,' he muttered under his breath, 'I'm not her type at all.' Lee stared morosely into his beer as Bebe looked on sympathetically.

'Are you here to catch up with me?' Placing her body to exclude the others, the newcomer was clearly speaking to Jo.

'Actually, I came here with my friends, Izzy,' Jo said, a blush rising from the neck of her T-shirt.

The dark-haired girl turned to study the group as if she'd just realised they were there, and Alain's breath caught in his throat as her violet-blue eyes slid past him, then back again. For a fraction of a second, Izzy looked at him as if trying to place his face before returning her attention to Jo, ignoring the rest of their party once more.

He'd come across Izzy before—only then, she'd called herself Isolde. *I must warn Trouble of this.*

Later, when Alain rose to replenish their drinks, Izzy followed him over to the bar to help. As they waited for the barman to fill their order, she leaned in close so no one else was able to hear what she said.

'What are you doing here?' she hissed.

'I could ask the same of you.' Alain attempted to calm his voice while his

stomach clenched in dread.

'You aren't here by yourself. Where is your guardian?'

Picking up the tray of drinks, he turned to face her, and with more confidence than he felt, he said, 'We beat you last time, and will do so this time as well, whatever you are up to.'

A smirk hovered around the corners of her mouth.

Damn, I gave too much away. Now she knows I have no idea what her plan is.

Then she frowned and looked back at the table. 'We? Jo is another John. That girl in the shop today ... she couldn't be ... so ... he is ...'

Ignoring her, he walked back to the table, not caring whether or not she followed.

AROUND NINE THIRTY Alice excused herself, saying she normally talked to her husband around this time every night. When Sigma heard the door close upstairs, he turned to Barwick.

I have been trying to get hold of Beta all night, but not a single one of my contacts is able to reach him.

Do you want me to stay up with you while you keep trying? Barwick asked as he stretched and yawned.

It's all right; no sense both of us losing sleep. Though I may come over and stay with you tonight just in case I need you.

Barwick mumbled his agreement, and Sigma followed him outside and up to his room above the garage. He waited patiently for the old man to pull out the sofa bed and make it. As soon as the bed was ready he jumped up, turned round a couple of times then flopped down.

He then proceeded to watch Barwick check all the cultures he and Alain had set up that afternoon. The alchemist nodded as he looked at each container, then smiled as he shut the incubator door before walking back to the bed. He undressed and crawled under the covers as Sigma settled beside him.

Sigma attempted to contact Beta a few more times before the warmth of the room, combined with a comfortable bed and an active day, caused his eyes to close. Soon he had joined Barwick, the two of them snoring soundly.

At some time during the night, the temperature dropped. Trouble rose, stretched and moved closer to the warm sleeping form of Barwick. As he did, the door handle rattled.

He jumped down from the bed and padded over to the room's entrance.

Sniffing the air, he then cocked an ear, trying to figure out what was going on. A scraping noise sounded. Was someone trying to pick the lock?

A growl formed in his throat, and he let it out. The scratching stopped, and a moment later there were footsteps on the stairs. Placing his nose to the floor again, Trouble had a good, long sniff and barked quietly as he placed the scent—she was here, in this time. Had she followed them, or had she come for her own reasons? His tail swished in irritation; either way, it was not a good sign. He humphed. There was nothing he could do about it in the middle of the night.

Confident they would now be left alone, he returned to bed but was unable to sleep. He was still awake when car engines started as Burley began to raise itself for the new day. He contemplated waking Barwick and asking to be let out into the garden when finally he felt the familiar tingle alerting him—someone from home was trying to contact him.

Sigma.

He relaxed. It was his mentor, Beta. If he was to be recalled, he would prefer the message to be passed on by a friendly face who would not rub his nose in the fact he had not been up to the job.

Yes, Beta, I am here.

Sorry to take so long to answer your calls. Things have been ... well, let us just say they are not good.

They are not good here either. Not only are there likely to be magical implications, but I think the Time Wreckers are here as well. One of them tried to break in last night, Trouble informed Beta.

I can confirm Time Wreckers are nearby, and are a part of what is happening. In fact, reports of their activity in your time are coming in thick and fast. We have had to send a couple of teams to other incidents. From what we can make out, something big is planned, and they are trying to divert our attention by causing as much noise as possible.

That does not sound good at all. Trouble sat up on the bed, trying to focus his sleepy brain.

Unfortunately we cannot tell whether your situation is a diversion, or the main event, Beta told him.

You are not calling us back, are you? Before this conversation started Sigma would have welcomed this news, seeing it as the council reaffirming their trust in him. Now, he was not so sure. *Beta, this is only my second solo mission. I am not ready to lead an assault against a full-blown Time Wrecker attack. Besides, I need to make sure Barwick and Alain return home.*

I understand all that, Sigma. Not only is there no one available to replace you, but

we believe Barwick's skill as an apothecary and alchemist will be needed in Burley.

But what about Alain? Sigma asked. *We might be placing him in grave danger.*

We cannot help that, I am afraid. Besides, I believe Alain's magic is stronger than Barwick's, and you will most certainly need him in the days to come.

Still ...

Tell me, did you get a sight of the Wrecker they sent to Burley? Beta changed the subject, and Trouble was sure it was a ploy to forestall any further arguments.

Realising he was not going to change his mentor's mind, Trouble sighed, then answered, *Not a look as such. More of a scent.*

See? I knew your penchant for taking animal rather than human form would come in handy. Who is it?

Isolde.

That news is not totally bad. She is a relatively new recruit, so if they sent her to Burley to disrupt the timeline then it is most likely a diversion.

Sigma considered his mentor's words, and he had to admit, he agreed. *She might only be a minor player, Beta, but Isolde does go off-script, sometimes in the most dangerous way. She might turn this little fiasco into a major incident whether the Wreckers intended it to be or not.*

Beta did not answer, and Trouble was about to close the connection when his mentor spoke again.

I agree. You need to be careful. This mission is no longer about fact finding. Your new instructions are to stop whatever Isolde is up to—no matter the cost. Good luck.

Before Trouble was able to answer, he sensed Beta drop their link. Although in dog form, the sinking of his stomach was no less disconcerting. He had some planning to do. First things first, though—he had more pressing needs. Stretching, he leaned over and licked Barwick's face.

'Leave me alone, you mutt,' the man grumbled and rolled away.

Deliberately targeting his bladder, Trouble climbed over the half-awake man and licked his face again. Barwick cursed and sat up as Trouble walked over to the door, making his intentions clear.

7

THE PLAN

SNUGGLING UNDER THE duvet, Alain imagined himself back home in his own bed. The thoughts comforted him until he noticed the mattress was too soft to be his. Concentrating on returning to his half-dream, he was unable to completely submerge himself as Lee's snores kept interrupting. They were loud enough to wake the dead. Unable to stand the noise any longer, Alain got up to use the toilet.

Heading back to his room, he banged into Alice—literally. As he attempted to sidestep around her, she moved in the same direction. He tripped, grabbed hold of the bannister, then righted himself.

Alice pulled the towel from in front of her face as she said, 'Sorry, Alain. I shouldn't be wandering around towelling my hair with others in the house. I am so used to being here by myself ... Were you wanting to use the bathroom? There is plenty of wat …' Alice stopped midway through wrapping the towel around her shoulders. 'Oh my goodness, I have just realised … I can't believe you have stayed two nights and I haven't …'

'At home I only bathe once a week,' Alain assured her. 'But if it's okay with you I would like to clean up a bit.'

'Have you used a shower before?' Alice had regained her composure and was back to her businesslike self.

'Is a shower something like a bath?'

'Ah, no, nothing like a bath. Here let me show you how to work it.' She led him into the bathroom and moments later Alain stood under a glorious stream of hot water, lathered in something called shower gel. As he washed, he attempted to figure out how this magnificent invention worked.

He could have stayed under the water for hours. Mindful of the fact others might want to use the facilities, he dragged himself out, dried himself off, and wrapped a towel around his waist. Opening the door he found himself face to face with Bebe, and automatically took a step back. Aware of his almost complete lack of clothing, his cheeks burned with heat as the girl stared at him, wide-eyed.

'Um, excuse me. I must, um ...'

Bebe was quick to compose herself. 'Ah, Alain, good thing I caught you. Jo texted me a couple of minutes ago. She wants to meet around ten in the cafe near Alice's shop to discuss our next moves. Can you tell Lee please?'

Not understanding why this news couldn't wait until he had dressed, Alain mumbled, 'Okay.' He slipped past the pyjama-clad girl, and almost ran to his bedroom. Shutting the door firmly behind himself, he leaned back against the wood.

'Wha …?' Lee spoke blearily from under the blankets. 'What happened?' Lee pushed himself upright. 'You look like you've seen a ghost.'

'Ah, I ran into Bebe in the hall. We are to catch up with Jo at ten for a planning session—at the café.'

As he spoke, Lee studied him carefully before chuckling to himself as he threw a shirt to Alain. 'You haven't got a chance with her, mate. Many a better man than you has tried and failed.'

'I wasn't ... I'm not … I have a …'

'Come on, get yourself dressed and let's get some breakfast while she's in the shower. Then we can get Barnaby's search set up before we need to get to the cafe.'

They rushed through their meal and had just finished washing up when Bebe joined them. Feeling his cheeks flush, Alain dropped his head as opened the outside door before stepping outside.

'We are going to help Barnaby with his research,' Lee told his sister as Alain beat his hasty retreat.

'Don't forget the cafe at ten,' she responded. 'We have some planning to do.'

Lee picked up the rectangular item he had brought downstairs and joined him.

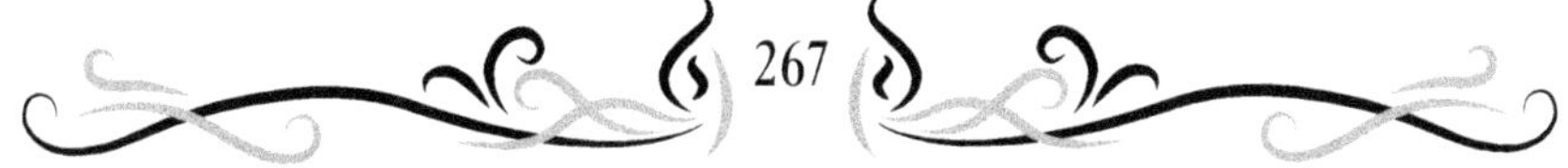

'What's that?' Alain asked to distract Lee from mentioning his hasty departure.

'My laptop. It's like my tablet, only on steroids.'

Alain nodded knowingly, not wishing to admit he had no idea what steroids were.

ALAIN FROZE AS the door to Master Barwick's room swung open when he raised his hand to knock. Tentatively, he stuck his head through the gap and found complete disarray. Lee pushed past him and surveyed the devastation.

'What happened here?' he asked. 'Where are Trouble and Barnaby?'

'Right here,' a voice came from below, followed by heavy footsteps on the wooden stairs.

'What …?' Barwick halted when he spied the state of his room over Alain's shoulder.

He pushed the boy out of the way and rushed to the bed. Leaning over, he pulled something out from underneath and heaved a sigh of relief. Alain frowned, unable to comprehend why the dog bed Alice had borrowed for Trouble was so important.

As Master Barwick lifted the cushion out of the bed, Trouble said, *We had a visitor last night, so when we went for a walk after breakfast we hid the samples.*

In the dog bed? Alain shook his head in wonder.

It was all we were able to think of at the time. You couldn't tell anything was in there once we put the pillow back on top.

'Who did this?' Alain had forgotten Lee was with them. 'We should tell Aunt Alice and call the police.'

'There's no harm done,' said Master Barwick. 'No use getting the authorities involved. Give us a minute to clean up and it will be like nothing ever happened.'

'Are you completely mad? We need to catch whoever broke in.' Lee swept out an arm to indicate the mess. He pulled out his phone. 'What do you call for the police here? Nine nine nine?'

'We already know who it was.' Alain grabbed Lee's phone as he moved into the room. After placing the mobile on the bench, he began cleaning up.

How do you know? Trouble and Master Barwick asked together.

I met Isolde at the pub last night. Turns out she is Jo's friend, Izzy, Alain explained.

Lee had made his way to the bench and picked up his phone. 'What is

going on here? Who broke in? And Why? What's more, why do I keep hearing a buzzing in my ears? And why do you keep looking at the dog as though you're expecting him to answer?'

Alain took the phone and placed it back on the counter. 'We believe it is Izzy because we foiled her plot to kill King Henry. She was definitely working against us then, and I believe she is now as well. And I keep looking at Trouble because, believe it or not, he is the brains of this outfit.'

Alain! Master Barwick and Trouble both shouted in his head as Lee burst out laughing.

'You've all lost your minds.' He grabbed for his phone again, but Alain beat him to it. 'Give that back. I am calling the police.'

Holding the phone away from Lee's grasping hand, Alain appealed to the others. 'Guys, Lee already worked out we came from another time. He can almost hear mind-speak, and maybe he would be better able to help us if he knew the whole story.'

Sigma? It's your call. After all, you are the brains of the operation. Master Barwick's mouth twisted into a wry grin.

Thanks for that. Trouble turned to Lee. *I am a member of an organisation called the Time Guardians. We are tasked with ensuring history unfolds as it should.*

'What? For real? Why are you here?' Lee asked.

Your aunt called us here to investigate whether or not other forces were at work in the New Forest causing dogs to become ill.

'What sort of forces?'

Unnatural forces, or perhaps mystical ones.

'And you all think there are? Don't you?'

Yes. Isolde, Izzy, works for an organisation called the Time Wreckers. Their agenda is different to ours. They seek to cause chaos and confusion. It was she who broke in here last night. I can smell her scent all over the place.

When the dog finished, Lee sank onto the bed and still did not speak. The others watched him for a moment, but as his silence continued for a number of minutes, they returned to tidying the room. When Master Barwick needed to fold up the bed, Lee stood as instructed then sank back down on the sofa.

About half an hour later, once Master Barwick returned to fiddling with his experiments, Alain and Trouble wandered over to Lee and sat down beside him.

'The dog spoke to me in my mind,' Lee whispered.

'Yes, he did.'

'We had a conversation about weird organisations, like one good and one evil.'

Alain tried to lighten the mood. 'Yes, he did—although why your mind is sticking on that and not the time travel bit I will never understand.'

'And they are here in Burley?' Lee continued as if Alain had not spoken.

'Yes.'

'And someone sent you to fight them?'

'Yes, and I believe it is likely you are here for that reason too.'

'What?' The glazed look left Lee's eyes and he turned his startled gaze to Alain. 'You can't be serious.'

'Okay, let me ask you a question. When did you make plans to come here and visit your aunt? I mean, was it planned a long time ago, or did something come up suddenly?' Alain asked.

'We booked our flights last week after Dad got a last-minute job offer. Dad had to use his influence to get our seats.'

'So … it probably isn't a coincidence that you are here now with us.'

If I may? Trouble butted in. *Lee, this is not your first time confronting the Time Wreckers. An earlier incarnation of you and Bebe worked with Alain and Jo to defeat a plot to stop Prince Henry becoming King Henry the First.*

'Trouble, did you have to tell him that? He was barely coping with talking dogs and secret organisations—now you've thrown reincarnation at him.' Alain worried for his friend, but he need not have bothered.

'Funnily enough, reincarnation is the one thing that is not odd about this. I always believed our spirits would be reborn into another body after we die. I also kinda thought we would keep meeting up with the same people. Time travel is also logical. Well, it's based on pseudo-science . It's the talking dog and the good-versus-evil thing. I feel like I am in a Marvel-*Secret Life of Pets* mash-up.'

'Marvel? *Secret Life of Pets*? Mash-up? What on earth are you on about?'

Lee laughed out loud, and it seemed to dispel all the tension in the room. 'If you are truly from the time of Henry the First, then being here must be weirder for you than me getting my head around this. If you can put that aside and get on with the job, I guess I should step up and do the same.'

Picking up his laptop, Lee walked over to Master Barwick. 'Okay, Barnaby, let's see if we can't find this organism you've been talking about.'

Lee and Trouble wandered over behind him. Barnaby pointed to the four slides he had prepared for the microscope the day before.

'I have chosen samples of the same life form in four different stages of development.' He pointed to the slides. 'What I am not sure of is how your

computer can help identify them. I spent hours looking through your uncle's books, and I cannot find anything useful at all.'

'Fortunately for you, I was talking to my uncle a couple of weeks ago about his new piece of equipment, and I did some research online about,' Lee said as he pressed the power button on his laptop.

While the screen flickered away, Lee pulled a plug out of his back pocket and connected it to a point in the back of the microscope. He plugged the other end into a hole in his laptop. He turned the microscope on, then fiddled around with something on his computer.

'All right, we are ready.' He placed one of the slides under the microscope, adjusted the lens, pressed some keys on the keyboard, and adjusted the lens again. 'Ta-dah.' He held his hands out in a flourish.

They others shuffled around behind and looked at the screen. In front of them, in glorious detail, was the image of the organism on the slide.

'Amazing though that is, I do not see how that helps us identify it,' Master Barwick said.

'Watch and learn.' Lee touched a couple of buttons on the keyboard and the computer made a *snick* sound. He followed the same process with the other three slides. When he had finished, he played around on the keyboard again, and the others crowded closer to see what he was doing.

'Right, I saved the images to the hard drive.' He showed them the pictures from the slides on his laptop. 'This programme here will search all the images on the internet and find any that are similar. I just need to load our pictures into the programme and start it up.'

He pressed a few more keys, checked the screen, and finally looked up. 'There, done. Now, I am setting the parameters to find an eighty percent match, or greater. That way we should be able to find any similar organisms and that may give you some idea on how to deal with this disease.'

Master Barwick leaned over Lee's shoulder. 'And this, um, programme, looks through hundreds of images to find a match?'

'Hundreds of hundreds of thousands,' Lee said.

'How long will all this searching take?' Master Barwick asked.

'Well, I am running four images against the billions and trillions of images available on the internet looking for a near-perfect match. So about four—'

A grin split Master Barwick's face. 'Four days! That is faster than I imagined. Still, it will give me some time to run other tests to see if I can identify ways of slowing the growth down, or perhaps killing it.'

'I was going to say four hours, give or take an hour.' Lee laughed.

'Oh.' Master Barwick froze mid-movement, and turned back around and stared at the laptop and nodded. 'I shall wait then.' Master Barwick settled with his elbows on the counter, watching the screen displaying the number of images checked.

'You won't be able to see much until the process is finished,' Lee said. 'There is still plenty of time for you to do some tests or check on your other samples.'

'Yes, true. I might try and work some more on a cure.' The older man stood and began clearing the bench, stopping every now and then to check progress on the screen.

'Will you be using magic?' Lee turned as he spoke, his eyes following the alchemist's movements. 'Can I watch?'

Master Barwick chuckled. 'Lee, I am first and foremost a man of science and healing, so I will be trying standard tests first. If that yields nothing, only then will I turn my focus to magic. All I will do after is test whether or not the elements were manipulated by magic to alter what is found in the natural world.'

'Cool, so you can do alchemy and magic?' Lee's eyes widened in fascination.

'I am not sure whether or not I will actually be able to do much in this time. Humans' link with the natural world has grown weak as they moved to cities and stopped tilling and caring for the land. Magical power is so weak here, so the tasks I am able to perform are severely limited,' Master Barwick said.

Deciding now was the best time to interrupt and ask a question that had been on his mind since last night, Alain said, 'Master Barwick, is it possible for the other coven to have had something to do with the development of this organism?'

'I spent hours teaching you the basics of alchemy, so you obviously realise a large part of it is the practice of transmuting elements into something else by combining them, or using heat, cold and the energy of the world to alter it. If you consider it in those terms, how do you think the coven might be involved?'

Alain disliked it when Master Barwick turned questions into teaching moments. It slowed everything down while he considered his answers, which in turn impaired his ability to take action.

Sighing, he sorted through the little he had learned about alchemy as opposed to his trade as an apothecary before he responded. 'Well, I guess if

they found an element to alter bacteria or a virus they could make it more lethal, but you would not really need magic to do that.' Master Barwick nodded encouragingly, and Alain thought about the first lesson he had in basic alchemy, helping plants to grow. It was as though a light had come on in his head. 'Some growth spells might be able to be applied to a virus or an organism to speed up its development.'

'Yes, that is a definite possibility. But there is no evidence to say whether or not that has been done—yet. Now, do you want to stay and help me, or have you two got other plans?'

'If it is all right with you, we arranged to meet the girls for tea at the cafe, but I can stay if you need me to,' Alain added, hoping Master Barwick had not planned this morning's work as a lesson for him.

'No, no, you run along. I need to make sure I have all the things I need for my tests. When I'm finished, I'm going to do some more study and it may throw up some more things we can test later.'

'You really don't need us?' Lee was partway to the door as he spoke.

'No, but if you can arrange to be back here later this afternoon when the results come in—both of you? I will need some help with this computer thing.'

Alain headed for the door, and Trouble made as if to follow.

'Sorry, Trouble. Dogs are not allowed in cafes here.' Alain stood in the doorway, preventing the canine from joining them.

Trouble sat and cocked his head to the side as if pondering something.

And why do I think that is precisely why you are all meeting in a cafe? What do you not want us to find out? Maybe something to do with what you uncovered on your nocturnal activities? Trouble raised his eyebrows.

Um ...

Don't bother making up a lie. Simply promise me you will think before you act, and be careful.

THE CAFE WAS buzzing with people when Lee and Alain arrived. It seemed the cold weather had encouraged most of Burley into the warmth of the local meeting place. Jo waved them over to a table near the window, miming she had organised drinks for them all.

After they peeled off coats, scarves and hats, the boys sat down in the two vacant seats. Alain took a sip of his warm, milky tea. It was just as he

liked it, and he looked over the rim of his mug to find Bebe smiling at him. It warmed his heart that she had remembered what he liked, and he immediately felt disloyal to Barabal, even though they had no formal arrangement. Feeling heat rising from his collar, he dipped his head and took another sip of his drink before asking, 'What is so important that we had to meet here today?'

Jo grinned. 'I spoke with Mum last night and she let slip Tabitha invited her to a coven meeting tonight, hoping to poach her.'

'You talk as though she is being asked to turn to the dark side.' Lee snorted.

Jo flashed him a disdainful look before continuing, 'Of course, Mum is not going, but she did say she regretted missing out on Tabitha's carrot cake, which means the meeting will be at her place.'

'How did you come to that conclusion?' Alain tilted his head to the side as he tried to follow the logic.

'Tabitha only goes to the trouble of making her famous carrot cake—which she swears is far better than Alice's—when the meetings are at her's.'

'You think we should go and spy?' Lee's cheeky grin was replaced with a glint of anticipation.

'Goodness no. I was thinking I might talk Izzy into taking me along. Make out I am getting a bit bored with the inactivity of my coven. I could be our insider, so to speak.'

Bebe's eyes widened in surprise. 'Jo, I really do not think that's such a great idea. If they are trying to stop the development, with Gavin involved, it might be quite dangerous.'

With Isolde involved, and with her knowing who they all were, Alain was not keen for them to do anything that would be seen as confrontational either. 'There must be another way—one that doesn't put you at risk.'

'If we skulk under windows again and listen, we might pick up something. But I don't think we will find out as much as we would if I attended the meeting,' Jo said.

Alain had to admit her idea had merit. Attending the meeting was a great opportunity to find out if Tabitha's actions to stop the New Forest development were connected to the outbreak of Alabama Rot. Hopefully, though, it would be a typical coven gathering and they would be able to discount the coven's involvement.

Lee, who had started scrolling through things on his phone when he realised they were not going to plan another group spy mission, now leaned forward. 'What about a compromise? How about Jo does what she proposed,

but we also go along and wait outside. One of us can act as a watcher, and two of us can be prepared to create a diversion should Jo need to escape.'

The determined set of Jo's jaw told Alain trying to talk her out of going would be a waste of time. Perhaps they should explore Lee's compromise. 'What sort of diversion did you have in mind?'

'One of the stories you told me yesterday has given me an idea. We might need to rummage around in Alice's garage to find what we need, and we still have to meet with Barnaby and help him interpret the data from the search, but there should be time to build the diversion I have in mind before tonight's meeting.'

'Lee, what are you up to?' Bebe stared intently at her brother.

'Never you mind,' he said, tapping the side of his nose.

Jo said, 'Look, I'm sure this is going overboard. I know these women. Even if there is something going on, none of them would ever hurt me. But I guess if I do not go along with it you will just turn up anyway.'

'Yep,' Lee agreed.

Sighing, Jo stood. 'All right then. The meeting is set for seven. You guys will need to be in place well before the start. Do you remember the way?'

'Yes,' Lee and Bebe said together.

'And we will be in place early—you won't even notice we're there,' Lee told her.

'You don't want to tell me what the diversion will be?'

'No, you need to be as surprised as everyone else. Otherwise they will suspect you are a part of it.' The grin on Lee's face as he said this worried Alain, especially as he had an idea of what his friend had in mind.

Jo tilted her head to the side and frowned at Lee. 'I thought the diversion's purpose was to give me a way out should I get into trouble.'

'This is even better. It not only gives you an escape, but because you will also be surprised by what I have planned, they won't link you to it. Just be ready to leave when something unexpected happens.'

Alain was sceptical, and Jo's frown had not disappeared—in fact, if anything, it had deepened. Even so, the girl pulled on her coat and said, 'Well, I hope I don't see you tonight.'

Lee and Bebe laughed, but unease churned in Alain's stomach. Any way he looked at it, this was a bad idea.

8

A STEP FORWARD

'SO, WHAT EXACTLY are we looking for?' Alain's voice echoed in the empty garage as Lee turned on the light.

'Here.' Lee passed over his tablet.

Alain studied the screen and a grin spread across his face. 'Oh, I like it.'

They spent half an hour or so finding what they needed, then another hour assembling the items in a container.

Lee stood back and admired their work. 'Right. We just need to put on some twine.'

'Shall we tie it on?' It was not the best option given the shape of their creation, but Alain saw no other way to attach the string.

'No. We glue it.'

'Glue? We don't have time to make it. Besides, it wouldn't have time to set by tonight.'

'Surely you've heard of super glue? No, of course not.'

Lee opened a drawer and rummaged around, eventually pulling out a tube about the length of a finger. After removing the top, he placed a small amount of clear liquid on the container and pressed the twine on a spot near the bottom. Alain noticed he took care not to get his hands anywhere near

the glue. A minute or so later, he announced, 'There, it's done.'

Alain didn't believe any glue was able to dry that quickly, or that such a small amount would hold the twine in place. But he gave the thin rope a tug and almost fell backwards when the container slipped off the workbench to hang from his hand.

'Amazing.' A smile worked its way to his face as he considered all the possible uses for a fast -acting glue. As Lee tidied up, Alain palmed the small tube of super glue, knowing exactly how he would use it later.

Hiding their efforts under a cardboard box, they grabbed a quick sandwich for lunch before heading up to Master Barwick's room.

THE ALCHEMIST MUMBLED to himself as he peered into the microscope and scribbled notes.

'You can record what you are doing on the computer and attach it to images and the like,' Lee said.

Master Barwick glanced up, blinked rapidly a couple of times, then focussed on the boys. He frowned as he said, 'No, no. That would not be useful at all. Writing things down helps me think. Besides, your computer has been making funny noises—beeping and such. I think it might be broken.'

'Excellent. That means the search is complete.' Lee picked up his laptop and sat on the sofa. Alain joined him, glancing over his shoulder at the results on the screen.

'Oh, this is interesting,' Lee said, his eyes glued to the computer.

'What did you find?' Alain looked at the information. 'It says you did not get a one hundred percent match on any of the images. How is that interesting?'

'It is because it tells us something very important.' Lee paused while Alain considered the data.

'It does tell us something quite important.' Master Barwick sat on the other side of Lee so he too was able to see the result. 'It tells us that although there are other cases of this disease around the world, our current outbreak does not match any samples taken in those investigations. That is, if I understand Lee correctly, and his programme checked images taken from all those outbreaks.'

'You are correct,' Lee said. 'They don't even match previous instances in the New Forest itself. We found some similar-looking organisms though, which may help you.'

'Are you not going to give us an analysis of those results?' Alain teased, and Lee tensed beside him.

'I know I'm not the sharpest tool in the toolbox, but you don't have to point it out all the time.'

Alain frowned, unsure where the comment had come from. 'Hey, I didn't mean that—I think you're smart. I ... I don't know what to say.'

Lee coloured. 'Sorry, sore point. I'm not as quick as Bebe and a lot of our friends, and they tease me about being a dumb grunt because I'm joining the army—even though it is officer training. I like the idea of structure and knowing what is expected of you, as well as being able to help people, of course. They still think it is a cop-out though.'

'From what your aunt tells me you're attending a very prestigious army college and will be taking a degree in Computer Science,' Master Barwick added.

Lee shrugged. 'I am good with computers and better with math. My brain seems to be able to put those things together easily enough. I struggle with any other subjects though, and I'm very good with abstract ideas. I am also bad at adapting to new situations, so I like to prepare.'

'You seem perfectly fine to me,' Alain said. ‹You accepted us, and you have been a great help finding information on the internet—you always manage to come up with what we need. I'm not sure how well I would have survived here without you.'

Again, Lee coloured. 'I spend a lot of energy and time learning to cope with change, and to hide my nerves. Now I research and find things out so no one realises I see things differently to them.'

'That in itself is a type of smart,' Alain said, admiration welling for Lee. Perhaps he could learn something from the way his friend studied and planned before he acted.

'Maybe it's best if you look at the full results. Here. You use this to change screens or to move the information up and down.' Lee handed the laptop to Alain, and sat on the floor beside Trouble, running his fingers through the dog's hair.

It takes a very evolved person to appreciate their own limitations and work with them, Trouble told Lee, bringing a wan smile to the boy's face.

Alain scrolled through the pictures and the information in the image-matching programme, clicking on links like he had seen Lee do, and reading everything there before returning to the initial report. After about half an

hour, he had pulled together some sort of a potted outline not only about Alabama Rot but their localised version of the disease as well.

'Do you want to read this, Master Barwick?'

'No, no, you summarise it for me and I will follow up on anything I find interesting.'

'All right. Firstly, Alabama Rot is more accurately known as Cutaneous and Renal Glomerular Vasculopathy—or CRGV for short. The closest thing the search showed to its makeup is E. coli, like you find with food poisoning, or aeromonas hydrophilia, a bacteria found in fish. The current belief is it is a form of bacteria found in water or mud.'

'Mm, that is interesting,' Master Barwick said. 'It's a bacteria rather than a virus, which at least tells me I was heading in the right direction. My research this morning led me to believe this was bacterial as the cells changed when I added certain oils like garlic, cloves and oregano. If I added some goldenseal or echinacea, the change was more marked.'

As Master Barwick spoke, Lee pulled out his phone and began tapping away. 'That is interesting. The internet said both garlic and cloves are used in fighting E. coli-type diseases.'

'Yes, they can be most effective in helping bacterial infection. It also explains why blood transfusions help some animals. It breaks the bacterial growth cycle and allows antibiotics and such to work,' Master Barwick said.

'Antibiotics?' Alain asked.

'Ah, yes, of course. They are a fantastic invention,' Master Barwick started but Lee interrupted, handing his phone to Alain so he could read up on the drugs.

'Wow, that is amazing,' he said handing the phone back before continuing. 'Another important fact is the bacteria is only found in dogs. It has not evolved or mutated enough to be able to spread to humans or other animals.'

'That at least is a blessing,' Master Barwick said. 'What I find more interesting though, is my attempts at finding a cure would get to a certain point, then either fail completely or make no further progress. I managed to interrupt the growth cycle. I mean, the disease stopped replicating, but I was unable to find a way to break down the bacteria and clear it up. This seems to be the point where other researchers have failed as well.'

'Don't lose hope Barnaby. Our samples are slightly different to the other images of CRGV, so maybe you can find something they haven't,' Alain said.

'What do you mean?' Master Barwick leaned forward.

'I mean, this programme says the fully developed bacteria is only a ninety

percent match. If a sample had been brought over from, say, America, and the coven had done something like accelerated its growth using magic, that could alter the bacteria or how it grows,' Alain said.

He looked through the images again, finding the closest match for each one. 'Look at this.'

Alain swivelled the laptop around to show everyone the screen. 'This shows our first slide has a ninety-seven percent match with early CRGV; our second is only ninety-five percent compatible, and the third drops to ninety-three. As our version of the bacteria grows it gets further away from the parent sample. If someone altered it magically early on to grow faster it would stand to reason the difference would accelerate.' Alain presented his case.

Master Barwick smiled. 'I knew there was a reason I took you on as an apprentice. I believe you are quite correct in your assumptions.'

But as an investigator you need to come up with evidence. We need to find out who is doing this and why.

Lee physically jumped as Trouble entered the conversation. 'I had almost forgotten you could do that,' he said, laughing.

'Well, we know Tabitha and her coven are up to something; I reckon it's them,' Alain said.

Master Barwick's eyebrows rose. 'And just how do you know that?'

Realising he had let something slip, Alain looked to Lee to bail him out.

'We may have found some evidence last night,' the boy said.

'At the pub?' Master Barwick pressed.

'Um, well ...' Lee stuttered.

'No, we took a bit of a diversion on the way there,' Alain admitted.

'What sort of a diversion?' Master Barwick held up his hand. 'No, don't tell me. I don't want to know. I only came here to work on the infection. I have no interest in becoming involved in anything else.'

Given our new orders are to stop the Time Wreckers, I am happy for you to follow up your lines of enquiry, Alain, Trouble said. *So long as you share everything with us, and, it goes without saying, you will be careful, won't you?*

'Of course we will be careful,' Lee said.

And one more thing. You found something at Tabitha's place and you are all excited about it, but she is not the only person who has an axe to grind around here. You might need to cast your net wider.

There was a moment's silence while Alain thought through the pros and cons of telling Trouble about the information they had picked up. Finally,

common sense won.

'At the moment, I believe she is our strongest lead, even if she is not the only suspect. We found out Tabitha is working with an international eco-terrorist, and they are doing something about a planned housing development in The New Forest.'

Trouble cocked his head to the side as though thinking about the implication of this new information. *Is Isolde working through Tabitha or this terrorist?*

'What do you mean by working through?' Lee asked.

'Oh, Time Wreckers cannot directly involve themselves in events; they can only encourage people to act. If they act themselves, time will find a way to balance things back to the way they were. We operate under the same constraint,' Alain explained.

'Oh,' Lee said. 'This is beginning to sound like a *Doctor Who* episode. How does Master Barwick coming up with some sort of a cure fit into the balance? Might he not just cause a rip in time?'

'*Dr Who?* Is he someone who might help us?' Master Barwick asked.

Lee chuckled, 'He is a character, like in a play, Barnaby.'

'Um … yes …well as to your question about my potential cure poses an interesting question. How does that fit in with the rules?' Master Barwick looked to Trouble for an answer.

Normally it would not. You would need to have someone like Jo find the information to create a cure. Then it would be up to her to actually work on producing it, Trouble said.

'Perhaps Lee using the computer programme to find the mutation has been enough to meet our requirement not to interfere in events so far,' Alain said.

'You may be right.' Master Barwick nodded, then ran his hand through his already messy hair. 'I am a little worried about how close we will be coming to breaking the rules if we use that information and succeed in making a cure—then if we use it on an animal ...'

Mmm, we would be walking a fine line. I think if this form of bacteria was the result of Time Wrecker interference, we should be all right identifying something that will help with the New Forest cases only, Trouble offered.

'Or I might be able to come up with something to slow the mutation down enough to allow the current treatments to work.' Stroking his beard, Master Barwick wandered back over to his workstation.

'Do you need any help?' As silence followed his question, Alain assumed Master Barwick was deep in thought, and he turned to Lee. 'What's is our plan for the rest of the afternoon?'

'I think we should get some more food in our stomachs if we are going to be out before dinner,' Lee said, his mind, as ever, turning to eating.

I shall come with you tonight, Trouble announced, following them out the door. *I want to see what is going on myself.*

'Are you sure?' Alain asked. 'We shall be doing a lot of hiding. It is only Jo who will be in amongst the action.'

Then you shall take me to Alice's shop and I will go with Jo tonight.

Trouble would not be talked out of his plan, so Alain reluctantly set off to The Witch's Hat, with Trouble walking jauntily beside him, while Lee went to organise their food.

ALICE HAD TAKEN a little convincing to loan them her car when they asked at afternoon teatime. At first, her main concern was their driving in the dark in a strange place. Then she said the pub they were going to for dinner was not really a place for teenagers.

'The crowd who hang out there are known to be a bit rough.' Alice's brows drew together in a frown.

'But Jo recommended it because the food is meant to be fantastic,' Bebe said. 'She told us we would not get a better beef and Yorkshire pudding anywhere.'

'If you are worried, perhaps you and Barnaby should come with us,' Lee said, and Alain threw him a worried glance—what happened if they said yes?

Master Barwick hastily declined. 'There's some more work I want to do on my experiments; I am at a crucial stage.'

Perhaps his mentor had declined because he knew full well they were not going to the pub at all, but Alain thought it more likely he was just so engrossed in his work he could not even contemplate a night off.

'What about you, Alice?' Bebe asked

'Well, much as I would like to, tomorrow is a work day. Besides, I don't want to miss my call with Donald. But you go and enjoy yourselves.'

Having gained the permission they required, the three went upstairs to dress for the evening. 'What were you thinking?' Alain asked Lee. 'What if they had said yes?'

Lee stopped outside their room and smiled. 'Why, I would have had Jo text us to cancel the pub meal and invite us 'round to her place instead.'

Bebe punched Lee playfully on the arm. 'That is a tactic worthy of me, bro.'

'It so could have backfired,' Alain grumbled as he followed Lee through the door.

When they returned downstairs, all three of them dressed in black, Alice tutted disapprovingly. 'I appreciate it is the fashion, but I don't like all this dressing in dark colours,' she told them. 'It makes you all look so old.'

'I guess that is somewhat the point,' Master Barwick said from his chair by the fire.

'Perhaps you're right. Still …' Alice said as she handed over the keys to Bebe, who had offered to be the sober driver. 'Behave yourself while you are there please. I don't want to be called to come and get you—well, I wouldn't be able to come anyway because you will have my car. And don't be too late home.'

'We promise to behave ourselves.' Bebe smiled.

'And don't forget to swing by Jo's and pick up Trouble on the way back. The goddess only knows what those two have been up to today, but I think it would be best for him to come home tonight as Jo's vet shift begins early in the morning.'

Alain started—it was odd to hear the goddess spoken of in modern times, even though he knew witches still revered her now as they had in the past.

'We won't forget him,' he promised as he closed the door.

Although only just past six o'clock, it was dark outside and the street was deserted, as was the village they drove through. Jo had suggested they drive a little beyond where they'd parked the night before and head a little way up the side road. Waiting there would mean they would not be seen by anyone arriving at Tabitha's, no matter which direction they were coming from.

Lee and Alain headed back along the hedgerows until they reached Tabitha's house. Once they arrived, Lee leaned out to make sure no one was about, then they crossed the driveway to hide behind the hedge on the other side of the drive.

They crouched and listened before moving again. Certain the only sound in the night was their own breathing, Alain stood lookout while Lee placed their device in the letterbox. He then gently closed the door, leaving a thin piece of twine hanging out.

A few paces beyond the property line, they both stood and started walking back to the car as though they were two people out for an evening stroll.

As they walked, Alain's stomach dropped and he grabbed his companion's arm. 'Lee, we need to go back. We forgot the matches.'

'No we didn't.' The other boy's teeth flashed white as he grinned. 'I have a lighter.'

'A lighter?'

'Here. I'll show you.' Lee pulled something out of his pocket. There was a snick in the darkness and a small flame appeared in his hand.

'That is amazing.' Alain grinned.

'That is our own brand of modern magic.' A mocking tone coloured Lee's voice.

As they reached the corner to return to their car, they just made out the silhouette of another vehicle coming along the road. Once it passed them they turned in time to see the brake lights go on—the first person was arriving at Tabitha's.

As they walked, another vehicle's lights swept along the road. They waited in the shadows of the hedge, eyes following the car as it turned into the driveway, before they continued back the way they had come.

'We cut that a bit fine.' Lee laughed and Alain joined him, releasing some of the tension in his body.

The boys met Bebe back at the car, where they waited until about ten past seven. Jo had informed them one of the coven members always arrived around five minutes late, so they gave her a bit more time before they headed back and took up their positions.

The boys kept to the shadows along the road while Bebe cut across the fields. At Tabitha's house, they took their positions: Alain behind the hedge on the far side of the driveway, Lee on the nearside, and Bebe at the corner of the house under a window, listening so she could signal the boys if they needed to activate their diversion.

'I really hope we didn't go to all that trouble today for nothing,' Lee whispered.

Alain's agreement was blocked out by the sound of a car speeding along the lane. A screech of breaks sounded followed by the crunch of tyres on gave. The offending car came to an abrupt stop not far from their hiding place.

'We're only late because you felt it necessary to convince me not to come,' Jo said as a door slammed.

'Our coven really isn't your sort of thing. You should just wait in the car.' Izzy's weary voice was less clear than Jo's in the night air.

Alain peeked around the hedge just in time to see Trouble's rear end as he followed Jo and Izzy inside. Crouching back down, he made himself comfortable, preparing for a long wait.

THE GUARDIANS OF TIME: ALCHEMIST

The freezing air fingered its way through Alain's clothing, and he shivered as he watched and sat tight. His mind drifted and he shook his head, trying to keep his focus. Why they had ever thought waiting outside for an indeterminate amount of time in the middle of winter had been such a good idea, he would never know. Oh yeah—something odd was going on, dogs were getting sick, perhaps because of magical spells, and they were the only ones who knew. Alain's body trembled, and this time it wasn't from the cold.

9

FOLLOWED BY A LEAP BACK

THE WARMTH OF Trouble lying on her feet comforted her as Jo sat back and observed the other members of Tabitha's coven. At first, they'd been suspicious about her presence, which she fully expected because in the past she had spoken out against their extreme ideas on magic.

They believed she was now doing a complete about-face. They were sceptical of her motivation, not fully buying her speech about not being sure where her heart lay after talking things through with Izzy.

'Like you all, I am worried about what is happening in the New Forest. At the vet, we treat many of the dogs who are getting sick and it breaks my heart. I believe we must do something more to protect our heritage and our animals. I'm not sure my coven will be able to do that. Besides, I would like to be with a group closer to my own age.' She smiled coyly at Izzy, hoping they might believe she'd come to the meeting because of their obvious feelings towards each other.

After about twenty minutes, the other members relaxed and appeared to accept her presence, although every now and then she would raise her head to find someone glancing surreptitiously at her, as if gauging her reaction to one comment or another.

'As there has been no change in public opinion since we started our last campaign, I suggest we move to phase two.' Tabitha's announcement brought Jo's attention back to the meeting.

The stricken looks on the faces around her had Jo thinking they did not feel the same way as their hostess. Even Izzy wriggled uncomfortably in her chair.

'It's a little soon to take such a drastic step,' Ruth said as she reached for her cup of tea. 'After all, we only set our plan in motion a month ago when we cursed the first site. And we only cast our second spell last weekend. We should give everything a little more time to work.'

Tabitha's lip curled in distaste. At Alice's coven meetings, the woman had not taken kindly to anyone who disagreed with her. The chilly look she threw at Ruth caused the other women to shuffle nervously in their seats, and told Jo she was still the same old tyrant.

'Well R-u-th,' she drew out the annunciation of the protestor's name in a patronising way. 'That would be an option, except I found people rummaging around near the site of our last working. I haven't had an opportunity to go back and check if our altars are in place. If someone moved them, that means the magic we invoked will not be as strong as we expected, and it will not last nearly as long.'

Ruth was not daunted but rather took Tabitha's words as a challenge. 'That may be so, but let us not throw out the baby with the bath water. We can reinforce that casting, or we can recast the spell in a new part of the forest—perhaps somewhere with more foot traffic to see if it will have more effect.'

Tabitha and Ruth glared at each other from opposite sides of the room. Izzy winked at Jo, obviously enjoying the battle, and the other three found themselves suddenly very interested in the plates of carrot cake they held.

'Yeee-ss, that is an option … but why do that when we can move forward.' Tabitha's tone sounded reasonable, but past experience told Jo she was preparing to strike.

'Why take a leap forward when we haven't exhausted all our options with this spell?' Ruth countered,

'It is that sort of talk that led us all to leave our old coven. Our new, brave group of talented witches is prepared to take on the world to save our New Forest.' Tabitha's oily smile did not reach her eyes, causing a shiver to run down Jo's spine.

'You are proposing an extreme move here, Tabitha,' Izzy intervened, and all heads in the room swivelled to watch her. 'Do you not want to perhaps continue our current work in and around the forest, expand it to more areas, and monitor the effect on public opinion before you take such a drastic step?'

Trouble believed Izzy was the brains behind Tabitha's plan. Yet here she was, if not quite counselling caution, at least getting Tabitha to think about how she moved forward. *Is this some sort of reverse psychology, do you think?* Jo asked Trouble.

Shh, I am listening, the dog replied.

Out of the corner of her eye, Jo caught Izzy's questioning glance before the girl turned her gaze to Trouble and tapped her chin thoughtfully. Oops, she must not speak to Trouble or she would give his identity away, Jo thought as she caught the end of Tabitha's response to Izzy's comments.

'... besides, Gavin and I discussed our situation, and we believe only a much bigger threat will force people to appreciate that overdeveloping our natural environment places the whole world in danger,' Tabitha argued.

Ruth placed her teacup on the table, only the rattle of the china giving away her anger. She stood and held Tabitha's gaze as she spoke. 'Are we a coven of witches, or the puppets of some smooth-talking man? Are we saving our forest or supporting the agenda of a foreign interloper?'

'How dare you!' Tabitha glared over the table at Ruth.

Izzy swiftly stood and moved between the two women. 'Come now, ladies, we are a coven, and we make up our own minds. I am sure Tabitha was just voicing an opinion. Shall we sit down and take a vote on the matter?'

The two women sat, although they did not break eye contact. Izzy remained standing. 'Shall I do the honours and outline the motion?' When no one spoke, she continued, 'The decision each of you must make is whether or not to continue spreading our little concoction through the New Forest to force a change in decisions relating to increased use of the land, or whether to ...'

'They are spreading Alabama Rot. Wait until the others find out,' Jo muttered under her breath. The room went quiet. Everyone had heard her. She froze, unable to move as her mind went blank.

I see some things never change. You open your mouth before thinking even in this reincarnation. Trouble rose to his feet, readying to leave.

'I knew you were not to be trusted.' Tabitha turned her anger towards Jo. 'You are here to spy for the others, you traitor.'

'She's heard too much. We cannot let her leave.'

Almost every head in the room swivelled towards the doorway where Gavin leaned casually, staring intently at Jo—everyone except Izzy. She

looked at Trouble, a finger thoughtfully tapping her lips.

Jo's stomach dropped, and she felt sick. How could she have been so stupid? Not only had she not heard Plan B, but because of her words, Trouble had mind-spoken again. Now Izzy's earlier suspicions had been confirmed and she knew Trouble was a Time Guardian. And if all that wasn't bad enough, Jo's mind was still not working. She had no idea how to extricate them from the mess she'd created.

Tabitha smiled at her, and Jo felt like a fish caught on a hook. Ruth moved in front of a snarling Gavin, her eyes filled with concern. No one else moved; it was as if time had stopped for them.

BOOM!

Everything in the room shook.

Run, a voice said in her head—and it was definitely not Trouble's.

PIECES OF LETTERBOX exploded into the air around him, and Alain's face broke into a grin. His and Lee's handiwork had performed beautifully. As he stood watching the devastation an outside light flicked on, just catching Lee and Bebe as they sped up the road, followed by angry shouts and footsteps across the gravel. Trapped, Alain wiggled backwards into the hedge, hoping no one would look his way as they chased his two friends.

Luck was with him, or so he thought until a voice came close to his ear, 'Shall I call my coven members back?'

His heart sunk. 'Izzy, you found me. Are you going to turn me in?'

He couldn't make out her expression in the shadows, but he hoped the fact they were talking meant he still had a chance to escape unnoticed.

'I should do, but no, I won't. But only if you promise me you will not let Jo do anything that stupid again.'

'Huh?' Alain wasn't sure he understood. 'Do you mean spying on the coven, or giving herself away?'

'I assume you all got together and cooked up the plan for her to attend the meeting tonight, to find out what was going on?'

'Uh, no, that was all her own idea. Besides, you could've stopped her when she asked to come with you. You can't tell me you believed she wanted to join the coven.'

A low chuckle escaped from beside him. 'I tried to talk her out of going, but you know Jo—or, should I say, you knew John. Once they set their mind to something, stopping them is impossible.' Izzy sounded almost as though she was as attracted to Jo as the other girl was to her.

Shaking his head, Alain attempted to focus. 'You're right; there is no arguing with Jo. So I could promise to keep her away from danger, but you and I both know that would be a lie—as if she would listen to me.'

Izzy sighed. 'Look, you clearly think I'm the bad guy here, but I'm not—I only want what is best for humanity, and Jo. To demonstrate this, I'm going to tell you something I shouldn't. I am not in control of this pony show.'

Alain snorted his disbelief.

'I mean, I was. I had Tabitha right where I wanted her. All up in arms about developments in the New Forest with a plan on how to spread a disease amongst dogs to cause outrage and stop the travesty of overdeveloping a natural resource—something I think you would be able to get on board with, given your connection to the area. Didn't your father once own land around here?'

'He did, and I am passionate about the New Forest. But supporting anything that would harm animals goes against everything I believe in.'

'We will have to agree to disagree on that point then.'

'So what went wrong?' Alain asked, changing the subject.

'That American showed up, licking his wounds from a fight in South America somewhere. Tabitha thinks the sun shines ... well, let's just say she admires him. She rebuilt his ego, and now he feels like he has to prove something, and he wants to hit back at the world for mistreating him.'

'So how is he planning to do that?' Icy fingers of fear worked their way down Alain's back, and he shivered. Izzy sounded scared, and anything that scared the girl who'd attempted to kill a king at his coronation had to be bad.

'He and Tabitha found a way to modify the CRGV bacteria so it can jump species.' She paused for a moment.

Her words slowly sank in and Alain froze, almost too scared to say the words. 'To humans?'

'Yes, to humans,' Izzy confirmed his fears.

'Isn't there anything you can do to stop it?'

'It is almost done.'

'What do you mean?' Alain clutched her arm, digging his fingers in so hard, she groaned and pulled away.

'They tested a small sample on an elderly aunt of Tabitha's yesterday. The woman had spent the last few years in a coma. She died suddenly this

morning—everyone else believes from natural causes—but I know better.'

'But ... that's murder.' Alain's voice was not much more than a whisper.

'And that's not the worst of it. Tonight they will take a vote on whether or not to cast the spell that will spread the new bacteria in one of the busier tourist spots in the forest. Then all they will need to do is wait until the next full moon to say the spell that will cause untold devastation.'

Initially, Alain was speechless, then he latched onto his one remaining hope. 'Perhaps they won't agree to do it.'

Izzy snorted. 'Oh, the coven is against it, but I am sure Tabitha will convince them over the next day or so, if not tonight. They will all turn up on Saturday night to do her bidding.'

'Hold on, Saturday night? That's only two days away.' Alain swallowed the fear threatening to choke him.

'I know, so you had better hurry and find out a way to stop them, or chaos will be released into the world.'

'Hold on, aren't you Time Wreckers supposed to foster chaos?'

Alain waited while the silence drew out. He thought she wasn't going to answer, but it seemed she was merely choosing her words carefully. 'That is not all we are. We intervene in different eras for different reasons.'

'Why in Henry's coronation then?'

'Because the Norman system of government was stifling the people. We believed if we brought chaos to England, the common man would throw off the yoke of Norman control and live free thereafter.'

Alain considered her words and strangely saw sense in them, but her explanation left out one important detail. 'But at what cost?'

'You cannot make an omelette without breaking an egg,' she replied. 'Besides, Henry was no saint. I can personally attest to that.'

He shook his head, unable to reconcile the way she casually spoke about death with her desire to save the world. 'And why are you here now? What do you hope to achieve?'

'I am sure your guardian told you we are targeting this time to bring about massive changes. We have co-ordinated a number of activities aimed at highlighting how greed and avarice is killing the planet—and people are not slowing their consumption in spite of the warning signs.'

'If I take that explanation at face value, then why are you against having CRGV move to humans? Surely that would be a much stronger message than killing pets.'

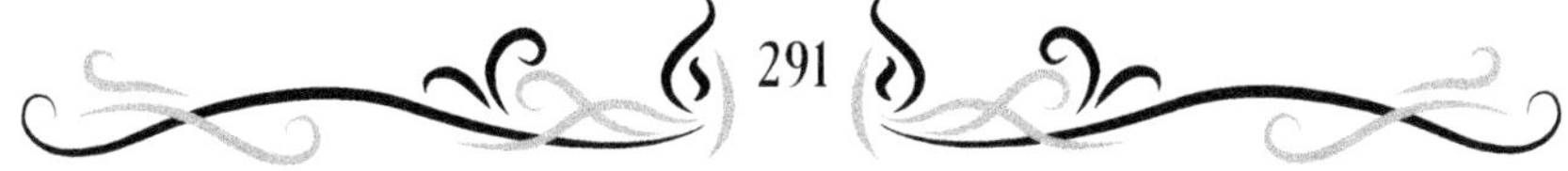

'You must really think me evil.' Izzy's voice carried a sadness as she said the words. 'Truth be told, I was not happy about hurting animals, but I saw it as the lesser of two evils. Though I am against allowing the bacteria to move to humans because if you introduce a new organism to the world, you cannot control it. If it sets off a worldwide epidemic, millions might die—it may even wipe out most of the human race.'

'They could simply start again—make a better world. Isn't that what you want?'

'I don't want humanity to end, and I don't want them so caught up in fighting an epidemic they forget the issues we are trying to highlight,' Izzy said.

'If you feel so strongly about it, why don't you just stop them yourself?'

'I can't. Not only would history find a way to counterbalance my actions, I would also be expelled from the Time Wreckers. Where would I go then? Even talking to you like this will earn me a sanction.'

'Why are you doing it then? Talking to me, I mean.'

'Because I started this.' She spoke the words so softly he almost did not catch them.

'What do you mean?'

'I showed Tabitha the spell to mutate bacteria to make it grow faster. She then added that to another spell, which mutated the cells again, enabling them to infect humans.'

'How could you do something so stupid?' Alain clenched his fists to stop himself from reaching out and shaking the girl. Was she mad?

'I wanted to save the New Forest, save the world. I acted without thinking. Can you not see how someone might do something in the heat of the moment then regret it later?'

'Yes,' Alain said; he could see exactly how it might happen. However, not wanting to let Izzy off the hook that easily, he asked, 'What, and now you want to roll back time?'

'Yes, I do, or at least try to undo a little of what I set in motion. Will you help?'

Alain didn't know what to say. He was so angry with Izzy he wasn't thinking straight. Besides, he had no idea whether or not it was against the rules to work with a Time Wrecker or not.

Luckily, the sound of footsteps on gravel saved him from answering—the coven members had returned. Izzy stood and strode away.

'Where were you?' Tabitha spoke brusquely.

'I went 'round the other side of the house to check,' Izzy glibly explained herself.

'Good thinking. Look at my poor letterbox,' Tabitha complained. 'It was

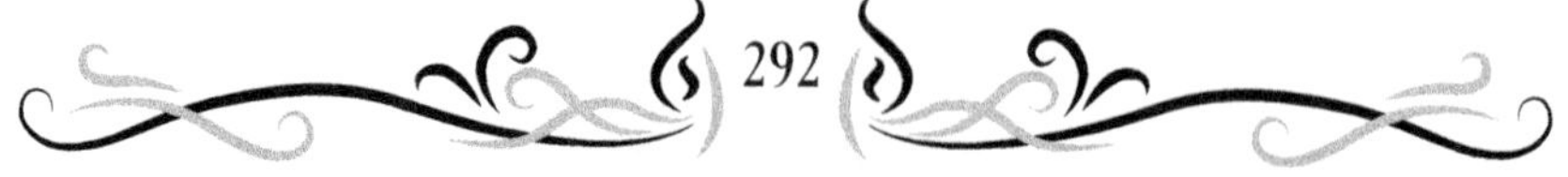

a one-off I had commissioned for the house. They destroyed a work of art.'

'Do you think it was pranksters?' One woman's plaintive tones irritated Alain.

'Or do you think someone suspects what we have been doing?' Another frightened woman voiced her concerns.

'Oh, quit it, Beth. I put up with these things all the time. It is the result of being outspoken. It was just a prank. Did anyone see what happened to Jo?'

'Oh, she took off when we all rushed outside. Her dog tried to escape too, but I gave him a little dose of something special to warn her to keep quiet.' A male voice sounded sinister in the darkness.

There was a yelp and a crunching of gravel, and Trouble's nose peeked around the hedge, but he stopped, making no move towards Alain.

'How will it get home?' Beth asked.

'I don't care,' the man answered. 'Come on inside, ladies. Now the interloper has gone I am sure you will want to finish your meeting. You have a vote to take, after all.'

THE FRONT DOOR closed, plunging Alain into darkness. He reached for Trouble. *I am here*, he sent

I know. I can smell you. Trouble moved closer and leaned against Alain's leg.

Are you all right?

No, not really. The dog settled more closely against him.

What did they do to you?

That man, Gavin I believe, grabbed me as Jo and I tried to escape. I told Jo to run on. When we were alone, Gavin took me into the laundry and injected me with something. He told me this would teach Jo a lesson she would never forget. He laughed, saying I would be gone soon and there was nothing she could do to stop it.

I thought you said you couldn't contract the disease. Alain tried to soothe the shaking Time Guardian.

True, but I think what they did to the original bacterial infection to change it allowed it to attack me—that and the fact he injected it directly into my bloodstream. I feel kind of odd, as though something is moving through my veins.

Do you hear that? It is a car, I think. Maybe we can catch a lift back to Alice's and let Barwick take a look at you.

As the light shone on his crouched figure, Alain shaded his eyes. It looked like Alice's vehicle, but he was not totally sure when he waved it over. His stomach clenched as it pulled up behind them. What if it was one of Tabitha's coven? Then the door opened and Jo leaned out, Alain sagged with relief. She signalled for them to climb in as she scooted across the other side of the seat.

As Lee pulled the car away, Jo made sure Trouble was comfy, while Bebe turned in her seat to find out what all the fuss was about in the back.

Once they were underway, in the lights from the dashboard Alain noticed Trouble's breathing was laboured. Placing his hand on the dog's chest, he found his heartbeat was faster than normal. Alain's hand trembled and Jo reached across and took hold of it.

'It will be all right,' she said, but he wasn't sure it would be.

'They did something to him, didn't they? I will kill them all if they have hurt Trouble,' Bebe threatened.

'I think they injected him with the disease, from what I overheard,' Alain said to explain how he knew for Bebe's sake.

'All right. Lee, turn here, then take the first left. We're taking him to the vets.' Jo dialled a number on her phone and spoke to someone on the other end, asking them to meet her at the surgery.

'Wait. We should take him to Uncle Barnaby,' Alain protested.

'He needs a vet,' Jo said. 'She can stabilise him, then we can get Barnaby involved.'

The others agreed with her, and Alain was too worried to argue. He gently stroked Trouble, trying to calm them both. When they pulled up outside, Alain went to pick up the dog, only to have his arm pushed out of the way by Jo.

'Leave him to us. We will work more quickly if we don't have to worry about you. I promise we will do the best we can for him. You will be more help going back to Alice's and finding out if Master Barwick has come up with a cure yet.'

Alain grabbed her hand as she reached for Trouble. 'Will he be safe here? I mean, what if they come for him again?'

'The building is secure, and Susan, the vet, will be here soon. Besides, I think they have done their worst; they are unlikely to give him a second thought.'

'I can't leave him alone with you,' Alain insisted, tears welling in his eyes.

She bent her head close to him and whispered, 'Yes, you can. Master Barwick may need you to help with developing a cure. You do realise if something happens to Trouble you may be stuck here for a while. He is the Time Guardian,

after all, so I suspect he is the only one who can take you home.'

Alain's heart nearly leapt out of his chest at Jo's words. She was almost right. Although Trouble's body could die, the Guardian would not. But it would be some time before his spirit was recharged enough to take another form and return to them. Meanwhile, he and Master Barwick would be stuck here not understanding a word anyone said. How would they survive, let alone deal with the threat they faced?

He let go of Jo's arm and watched as she carried the dog to the surgery. The door opened and she disappeared inside. He told Lee to drive, and for once was grateful the boy saw speed limits more as a suggestion than a rule.

10

A TESTING TIME

ALAIN FLUNG OPEN the door and jumped out before the car came to a complete stop. After running up the stairs to the room above the garage, he flung open the door only to find Master Barwick wasn't there. As he descended the stairs, the back door to the kitchen opened, flooding the backyard with light.

'What is all the noise about?' Alice asked.

'Where is Master Bar … Barnaby?' Alain spoke so fast his tongue stumbled over the words.

'I am here.' The master's voice came from behind Alice. 'What is so urgent you had to call me away from my dinner?'

'It's Trouble. He has the disease ... and it's bad.'

'I thought he said he was immune,' Alice said.

'What do you mean "he said"?' Bebe joined them by the open door.

'I mean, well, I just assumed he wouldn't catch it, otherwise Barnaby wouldn't have taken him into the forest the way he did.' Alice recovered herself.

'Gavin injected him with the bacteria,' Alain explained. 'So not only does he have it, but it's working faster than it does in other dogs.'

'How did he get injected? Was it at Jo's, or did you take him to the pub with you?' Alice's eyes narrowed with suspicion.

'No time to discuss this now.' Master Barwick pushed past Alice and headed towards the stairs. 'Alain, we need to get to work. I am so close, but perhaps with two minds working together ... well, we might be able to produce something in time to help Trouble.'

'What do you want us to do?' Lee's hand rested on Alain's arm, causing him to pause.

'You won't be much help with our work. I suggest you eat and be ready to take Alain where he needs to go when we are done.' Master Barwick spoke as he ascended the stairs, bundling Alain in front of him.

As they climbed, Alain heard Alice say, 'But I thought you went out for dinner. Why would you need more food now?'

Shutting the door behind them, Master Barwick started firing off questions. 'Tell me exactly what happened tonight, and don't leave any detail out.'

Alain sunk down on the sofa, and dropped his head into his hands. 'Bebe signalled Jo was in trouble, so we blew up Tabitha's letterbox.'

'How did Trouble get hurt?'

'In the confusion, the eco-terrorist grabbed him and decided to teach Jo a lesson for spying. He injected Trouble with a fast-acting high dose of the bacteria.' Telling the story to Master Barwick caused Alain's stomach to clench all over again, and he wrapped his arms around himself.

Master Barwick took a seat beside him and patted him on the shoulder. 'And how is Trouble now?'

'By the time we dropped him off at the vet he was not in a good way.'

'I am sure we can ... hold on a minute, you blew up a letterbox?'

Alain glanced sideways at Master Barwick. 'That's what you are focussing on?'

'Greek fire? That's some dangerous stuff. It can't have been easy to get.'

Alain sighed. 'We didn't. Use Greek fire, I mean. Lee and I found a recipe to make a homemade bomb on the internet, and we whipped one up this afternoon. It worked amazingly well. I think I might be able to replicate it when we return home.'

'Excellent.' The older man's eyes sparkled in anticipation.

Not willing to allow him to be further distracted, Alain held off telling Master Barwick about the wonders of super glue.

'Right, let's get moving.' Master Barwick took charge. 'I know Sigma cannot die, and he would return to us as soon as possible. However, with everything that is going on I would not like to be long without his skills, and particularly his link to the Council.'

'Me neither,' Alain agreed.

'Now, the good thing is I think I've almost found a cure. It's a combination of the natural extracts I spoke of earlier. I used a little magic to make their molecules resonate faster and it began reversing the effects of the infection. If it were to be combined with the treatments the vets have been giving the animals, I think it gives the dogs enough of a chance to fight off the infection and make a full recovery.'

'But Gavin seemed certain that what he injected Trouble with would act faster than the other one—what if it was a super-charged version? Would your cure still work?' Alain asked.

'Let's be clear. I am not one hundred percent sure it will work at all—it hasn't fully eradicated the bacteria in any of my tests, and it hasn't been tried on an animal yet. However, I am thinking that with two of us working on a growth spell we might double the effectiveness, and it might work well enough.'

'Really?' Alain was too scared to be too hopeful.

'I said think, young man. As an apothecary, there are no guarantees a cure will be successful. There are fewer when we are forced to rely on our alchemical skills as well.'

'I guess we can only try,' said Alain. 'The alternative is to do nothing, and that would be worse.'

'Right. If you're ready, let's go. You read through my notes while I assemble everything we need.'

Deciphering Master Barwick's handwriting was difficult at the best of times. Reading it when upset was almost impossible. Seeing his master had started measuring ingredients into a beaker placed over a single-flame burner, Alain skipped the section on how to concoct the potion and went straight to the spell.

Having memorised it, he moved on to the potion itself. Reading the alchemist's handwritten recipe, Alain was surprised at the quantities. 'Will that be enough?'

'Of course, it expands a little when heated, and a little more with the spell.'

Once all the ingredients had been added, Master Barwick stirred them together before holding the beaker up and assessing the murky brown liquid. Shaking his head, he swirled the contents, then checked again. It was now a lighter brown.

Seeming satisfied with the results, he returned the beaker to the rack over the flame, and the two of them stood and watched as the liquid came to a simmer.

Using tongs to remove the glass container, Master Barwick placed the potion on a wooden board before turning off the burner.

'We need to let it cool for about ten minutes before we cast the spell,' he said.

'But we may not have much time,' Alain protested, anxiety causing his voice to rise a little.

'If we do not allow it to cool a little and we apply magic the liquid grows too fast and explodes, along with the beaker.' Gesturing to the almost overflowing rubbish bin in the corner, Barwick said, 'Believe me, this is truly the least amount of time we can wait without having to potentially start again.'

Alain huffed, then busied himself cleaning up. Every couple of minutes, Master Barwick touched the outside of the glass and shook his head. Full of pent-up energy, Alain tidied the bookshelf and made his master's bed. He was just reaching for the bin to take it outside to empty when Master Barwick said, 'It is time.'

Joining his master, Alain started the routine he had been taught to follow before using magic. He closed his eyes and cleared his mind. Then he reached out until he found the gentle hum of magic present in all living things. It was not strong in this world, but if he supplemented it with a little of his own life force he might be able to gather enough to cast the spell.

'I am ready,' he said, placing his hand over the beaker.

Master Barwick wrapped his fingers around Alain's. 'Remember, this spell not only requires the words to be spoken, but also for you to visualise the elements in the potion working together to grow in strength and size.'

'Right,' Alain said, and he imagined how the liquid would change as he and Master Barwick recited the words of the spell:

'In my mind thee doth see,
hastily grow at a rate extreme.
Bring my thought-form to life this night,
and fight evildoing with all thy might.'

Opening his eyes, Alain found the liquid was now inky black and appeared to be moving in the container. At fist the movement was gentle, but it sped up until the potion was sloshing up the sides.

'We are done.' Master Barwick sighed as he opened a drawer. After removing two glass vials, he decanted half the liquid into each one. 'Now all we can do is pray to the goddess.'

CARRYING ONE DOSE of the new potion and another of Master Barwick's original formula, each vial wrapped in its own handkerchief and stowed safely in his jacket pockets, Alain returned to the kitchen. He opened the door to find Lee asleep, head resting on his arms on the table, and Bebe staring at something on her phone.

She raised her head when Alain entered. 'Have you done it? Have you and Barnaby come up with something we can try?' she asked, unable to keep the hope from her voice. Her phone pinged. 'Oops, let me just say goodnight to Mum, then I'm all yours.' Her fingers began moving over the screen as she spoke to him.

Alain smiled. She reminded him so much of Barabal, and in the midst of tonight's trauma he missed his friend so much he ached. 'Yes. One for Trouble and, if that works, one to try for Pepe.'

'Excellent. Come on.' She finished typing then she stood, sweeping the keys up from the table.

'What about Lee?' Alain asked, and a look of fierce determination appeared on Bebe's face.

'I am just as capable as he is,' Bebe huffed as she pulled on her coat. 'Are you coming or not?'

Alain followed her out the door. 'I didn't mean anything by what I said. I just thought Lee might like to come with us.'

'He'd be grumpy if we woke him. It's better for all of us if we leave him be.'

He opened the door and slipped into the front passenger seat, escaping the chilly night air. Bebe started the car. She didn't speak and the silence was uncomfortable. He began to wonder if she expected him to say something, and he was trying to decide what when she spoke.

'Sorry for jumping down your throat. It's not anything you said—it's me. Lee is so focussed and organised, and everyone loves that about him. Adults always ask him to do things because he is so dependable.'

When Alain didn't respond, she continued. 'Me? Well, I don't know what I want. I don't even know where I'll be living in a month's time. People never ask me to do anything. They always assume I will muck it up—as if not planning my future makes me incompetent in some way.'

Bebe paused, one hand on the steering wheel and the other covering her mouth. 'Goodness, I did not mean for all that to come out.'

The silence lengthened as she concentrated on the road. Alain tried to think of something to say. The atmosphere in the car was becoming more unbearable the longer he didn't say anything at all.

'I'm sorry if you thought I didn't trust you. I didn't mean it that way.' The air in the car lightened.

'It's okay. I guess it was on my mind because Mum just asked if I'd had

any more thoughts on my future.' Bebe chewed on her lip. 'I had to tell her no. I mean, we've all been caught up with what is going on ... I need time to prepare what I'm going to say.'

In the couple of days since they'd met, Alain had grown to like Bebe. He felt closer to her knowing she'd offered to drive him tonight in spite of her own troubles. Perhaps it was only because she was so like Barabal he felt compelled help her—but what advice could he offer?

Alain smiled to himself—of course. Bebe was like Barabal—perhaps he did know a way to help her out.

'I have a friend. She's a lot like you. Her options for the future are more limited than yours, and most of them revolve around making the right marriage. She also finds it frustrating trying to carve out a place where her talents can be used.'

'That does sound familiar,' Bebe acknowledged. 'Well, except for the marriage thing.'

'I think that may have more to do with where she lives than what we are discussing. Anyway, one of the things she is passionate about, is finding ways to make it easier for other girls to contribute more by being a role model, and by pushing at the boundaries of what is considered acceptable. She believes everyone has something unique they can contribute to the world—they just need to find it.'

Bebe chuckled. 'I think I would like your friend. I understand what she's saying. It's easy to do what others expect of you, and do it in the same way women have done for centuries. When I look around, there are so many options to choose from, but there's a lot of pressure to meet everyone's expectations as well.'

'She may have fewer choices than you do, but she doesn't let that stop her. She excels at finding workarounds.'

'My father would like nothing better than for me to follow in his footsteps and join the army like Lee. He tells me a brain like mine can be put to good use in the military, but women in the army are still treated differently, no matter how much he wants to deny it.'

'I can't imagine you being good at following orders.' Alain laughed at the thought, and Bebe joined him.

'Me neither. I think I would hate being told what to do and how to do it. My mother, on the other hand, thinks my empathy would be best utilised following her into psychology.'

Alain had no idea what psychology was, but he didn't want to let on to Bebe so he nodded, hoping she wouldn't catch on.

'I want to help others, but I am not sure that is the way for me to go. The thought of delving into people's deepest emotions makes me ... well, to put it bluntly, it sounds boring. Please don't tell my mother I said that.'

'I'm hardly likely to ever meet her, so I don't think that will be a problem.' Alain laughed. 'But seriously, I can see you helping others. Are you sure psychology can be ruled out?'

'Yes. I want to do something that is a little more proactive and practical.'

'What about becoming a healer, or a teacher ...?' Alain trailed off, not knowing what other options were available for women in this day and age.

While he waited for Bebe to answer, he remembered his own parents' reactions to his wanting to become an apothecary. Although they didn't understand why he'd wanted to do it, they had been nothing but supportive, urging him to follow his heart. Then again, they'd been landless after William the Conqueror had dispossessed them, and were grateful their son had found a future for himself.

'In my experience, parents just want their kids to be happy. Perhaps yours are happy in their work, so they are offering their jobs as examples for you,' Alain finally said.

'I'm sure you are right and Mum and Dad are just trying to help. Ignore me. I'm only taking advantage of this journey to have a whinge.'

Alain chuckled. 'We all need to do that sometimes. But do you have to make your mind up now?'

'No, I guess not. Mum and Dad would be happy enough if I took a year off to decide what to do, just as long as I can support myself.' Bebe was quick to defend them.

'So, what's the rush?'

Bebe chewed a little on her bottom lip. 'I guess, when you put it like that, the pressure is coming mainly from me. Taking a year off to make a decision is such a waste of time.'

'All right, if that's how you feel, perhaps we should make a start in the few minutes before we get to the vet. What do you like to do?'

'Read—but you cannot make a career from that. I like sports and I really enjoyed coaching a junior netball team this year.'

Alain wanted to ask what on earth netball was, but he forced himself to stick to the point. 'What was it you enjoyed about working with teams?'

Bebe didn't answer immediately. She gnawed on her lip for some time before answering. 'I like finding the best position for each girl, developing their skills, and helping them work as a team.'

'See? Just like my friend, you want to find out how to bring the best out in people,' Alain said.

'But I can't be a professional mentor or netball coach. I'm not good enough for that.'

'You are a smart girl, Barabal ... sorry ... Bebe. Those are not the only options open to you.' Alain hoped he had covered his slip.

'Is that your friend's name? How pretty. You must miss her a lot.'

'I do, but don't change the subject. There must be other things you can do.'

'Yes, of course. I looked into teaching, but I don't think it is for me.' She opened her mouth as if to say something, then shut it again, before pressed her lips together and focussing on the road.

'Go on. What is it?' Alain prompted.

'Well, Jo talked yesterday about a time when she was younger. After her dad died, she got into a bit of trouble and turned quite wild by all accounts. Her mother tried everything to help. Eventually, the courts sent her to a counsellor who worked with her to target her energies towards something she loved. She always felt comfortable with animals, so they found a vet who would let her help out after school. That was when she decided what she wanted to become, and she knuckled down and started studying for her future.'

Alain waited for Bebe to continue, but she remained silent. 'And ...›

'Well, last night I looked up some courses on the internet. The University of Southampton offers one that leads to that sort of a counselling position.'

'There you go. You do have some idea of what you want to do next year. Why didn't you tell your mum?'

'Because I need to wait until my exam results come in before I apply. Also, it is a popular course and rejection rates are quite high, and they show a preference towards candidates who can demonstrate experience working with children. And I also need some endorsements from someone who already works in the field.'

'That doesn't sound too bad to me,' Alain said.

'Perhaps not, but the course doesn't start until the new university year in the United Kingdom, which is September—almost a whole year away.'

'That sounds like ...'

'... excuses. I know. Alice would put me up, and help me find a part-time

job, and might also have some people for me to contact about volunteer work with children. And I can work on everything I need to do to apply while waiting for my results.'

'Mmm, and you said Lee was the planner in the family. Still, why didn't you tell your mum when you were texting her?'

Bebe sighed. 'I guess because I want everything in place before I can prove I can do this by myself. And with everything going on, I haven't had a chance to talk to Alice, let alone follow up any other leads.'

Bebe slowed the car and pulled up in front of the vet. 'Here we are. Thank you for being my sounding board. Especially when you have so much on your mind with Trouble being sick.'

Alain opened the door and turned to look at his driver. 'No, thank you for taking my mind off my worries, and for reminding me there is more to life than this crazy situation we've found ourselves in. Are you coming inside with me?'

'Thanks, but I think I will wait here. Maybe do a little more research on my phone and finish off talking with my mum.'

ALAIN RUSHED TO the door Jo had taken Trouble through and knocked. He waited, stamping his feet to keep warm, then knocked again. His stomach clenched as all his fears about Trouble returned. As the wait lengthened, he imagined all the reasons why Jo had not answered immediately—the foremost being they were trying to revive Trouble after some seizure or other.

Just as he raised his fist to knock again, the door opened and Jo's annoyed face confronted him.

'Are you trying to wake the whole neighbourhood?' she whispered furiously.

'Um, ah ... when you didn't answer the first time I got worried.'

'I was in the toilet.'

'Oh.' Suddenly, Alain had nothing more to say.

'Well, come in.' Jo held the door open to allow him past. 'Bebe not coming in?' she asked as she waved to the girl in the car.

'No, she is talking to her mum. She seems to want some privacy.'

Jo closed the door behind them and led him through to the room containing the crates for animals staying overnight.

In a panic, Alain looked around for Trouble and found him lying on his

side in a cage. Rushing over, he opened the door and patted his head. The dog looked up with liquid brown eyes clouded with pain. Jo leaned in beside him and gave Trouble a gentle pat.

'Are you here alone?' Alain looked around for signs of anyone else.

'Yes. When it was clear I was going to be here for a while, Susan, the vet, went home for some dinner. She'll be back in about half an hour though.'

'Why? Is something wrong?'

'No, nothing's wrong as such. We stabilised him, but Susan is worried because he should be improving by now. She is coming back to give him a blood transfusion and some intravenous antibiotics.'

'Oh, that is good.' Alain wasn't sure it actually was, but he felt obliged to say something.

Not so good for you, I am afraid, Trouble's voice was a mere whisper in his head. *I heard them talking, and they are going to give me anaesthetic while they do the blood transfusion so I do not move about.*

That is good. You won't be in pain anymore.

Trouble looked at him, as if the effort to talk was too much.

Jo touched his arm. 'What he is trying to say is, he provides some services for you and Barnaby while you are here. I've allowed him to continue to do so until now, but he won't be able to translate for you once he is under anaesthetic. I also advised him to stop until he is well on the road to recovery. He needs all his energy to beat this.'

Alain opened his mouth to object, then paused. His main concern about the guardian's death was being stranded here and not being able to communicate with people. Having that situation come about while Trouble was being treated highlighted how unworkable his death would have been, especially when they still had to stop Tabitha and her coven. Still, it was more important for Trouble to rest and fight the organism invading his body than to support them.

'Don't worry. It's night-time. Go straight to bed when you get home, and do not get up until I come for you in the morning. Hopefully no one will notice anything is wrong before then, and you and I can concoct a story as to why you can't speak—a sore throat, perhaps. All you need to so is smile and nod at anything I say.'

'Um, okay.' Alain was still a little in shock. 'He will be all right though, won't he? Is he in any pain?'

They gave me lovely painkillers ... and ...

'... and they are making him a little spaced out. As to whether he will pull

through, a lot will depend on how he reacts to this treatment and, of course, whether or not Barnaby was able to come up with something to help fight the infection.'

When Alain did not respond, Jo held out her hand. 'Do you have anything for me?'

Alain shook his head and concentrated on what Jo was saying. 'Oh, yes. Of course. That's why I'm here.' Alain reached into his pocket and handed the vials to Jo. 'This is the best we could do on short notice. Master Barwick believes in conjunction with the other treatments, this should wipe out the infection. The blue label is a stronger one for Trouble, and this is for Pepe.'

As Alain handed over the second vial, Jo's face fell. 'Poor Pepe passed away this afternoon.' Her eyes welled with tears and Alain was suddenly hit with the realisation that Trouble was in real danger, and that what happened in the next twelve hours would affect them all.

As he patted the dog, the silence lengthened. How would they get by without him? 'If something happens to Trouble, Barnaby and I will be left facing this threat to the world on our own—our link to the Time Guardians would be severed and with it, all our support.'

'Then you best let us get on with it.' Jo's matter-of-fact approach was reassuring.

She allowed Alain to pat Trouble one last time before closing the crate. As she opened the door to let him out, she placed a hand on his arm and said, 'I will not let anything happen to him. I promise.'

Alain looked back over his shoulder at his sick friend. *Take care, Trouble. You have to recover from this. Not just because I will miss you, but also because we all really need you.*

Trouble raised his head slightly, and Alain left, brushing unshed tears from his eyes.

WHEN ALAIN RETURNED to the car, he found Bebe dozing, her head leaning against the window. She awoke as he slammed the door shut.

'How is Trouble?' she asked dozily.

'How quickly can you drive us home? I need to talk to Master Barwick.'

Alain was so focussed on his need to talk to his mentor before the vet began Trouble's procedure, he did not realise he was being rude until he saw

the hurt look on Bebe's face as she did as he requested.

'I am sorry, Bebe. I know it's no excuse, but I am worried about Trouble, and I need to check something with Master Barwick for Jo. It may be important to the procedure Trouble is to undergo soon.' He didn't like lying to her, but he was unable to tell her the truth.

Bebe glanced at him out of the corner of her eye, and sighed. 'You are right; it is no excuse, but I can understand how worried you are. So I will forgive you ... this time.' She smiled, and when he didn't smile back, her face transformed with a worried frown. 'Is Trouble worse?'

Pain radiated through Alain's hands, and he looked down to find them clasped together so tightly the knuckles had turned white. He shook his head slowly. When did I do that? Unclasping them, he turned and tried to focus on Bebe.

'He's not in a good way. The vet managed to stabilise him and are going to give him a blood transfusion this evening. We hope that the cleaning of his blood, combined with the antibiotics and Master Barwick's tonic, should start to reverse the effects of the bacteria. In order to help that happen, they are going to put Trouble to sleep for a while.'

'Oh Alain, I am so sorry. You must be devastated.'

Bebe's empathy opened the floodgates, and Alain let the tears roll down his cheeks unchecked. He had been so intent on doing something—anything—to save Trouble that he'd held his emotions in check. Now there was nothing to do but wait, and worry overwhelmed him.

How would they cope with the threat to humankind without Trouble's guidance? Did the Council know about this turn of events? Alain looked down to find his fingers once again had wound around each other, and he concentrated on stretching his hands to release the tension.

As they pulled into the driveway minutes later, Bebe said, 'You go talk to Master Barwick. I will update the others so you don't have to. I'll leave you a chamomile tea on the table for when you come in. It might help you sleep. Would you like my phone so Jo can send you updates?'

Although heartened by Bebe's support, he answered, 'No', knowing that in a few minutes he wouldn't be able to understand anything. 'If you do not mind, I would rather hear any news, especially if it is bad, from an actual person.'

Bebe placed a comforting hand on his arm. 'Sure, I understand. Now go and see Barnaby.'

She left him to climb the stairs as she headed into the kitchen.

Before he reached the top, he noticed the light was off. Either Master

Barwick was asleep or he was in the house. Turning, he saw Master Barwick exiting via the kitchen door and hurried to meet him in the middle of the lawn. In hushed tones he gave the older man his update.

'I know in my heart this will not kill Sigma, but I do hate for my friend to suffer so.' The older man tugged at his beard.

'He has the very best care, and Jo said she will stay with him tonight,' Alain attempted to console his master.

'He will also be worried about us. I wonder if he managed to speak to the Time Guardian Council and warn them? He might not have been able to; they are extremely busy with all that is going on at the moment. They have been out of contact a bit.'

'All that is going on?' Alain's head jerked up at the comment. 'Izzy mentioned a few Wreckers are here. What do you know about it?'

Master Barwick ran a hand through his hair, causing it to stand up more than it normally did. 'Only a little. Trouble has not told me all the details—only that a number of Time Wrecker attacks are planned. Most are diversions, but one of them is going to have a massive impact. The Council is spread pretty thin covering everything, and they instructed us to get on with the job here by ourselves.'

Alain had thought this night couldn't be any worse, but he had been wrong. 'So we have to assume the Council don't know the coven are planning to release the infection on humans?'

Master Barwick's hand stopped mid-run through his hair. 'I am sorry. What did you say?'

'I said Izzy told me the coven—well, Tabitha and Gavin really—developed a strain of the virus for humans, and they were taking a vote to decide whether or not to release it in two days' time.'

'The night of the full moon,' Master Barwick said distractedly.

'Yes, and I'm not sure we can handle this ourselves.'

'You're right.' His hand moved from his hair to tug at his beard, and his eyes unfocussed. Then he took a deep breath. 'This is way worse than Sigma and I thought—an attack on humans with a new form of bacteria ... I do not even know where to start.' He stood staring into the night as his hand again worked through his hair. 'It is late; there's not much more we can do now. Let's sleep on it, and regroup in the morning.'

Frowning, Alain said, 'You are to be a Time Guardian—can't you speak to the Council? You need to warn them of the danger.'

'Only one initiated as a Guardian can make the connection, and I am a little way off from that. They can contact me if they cannot reach Sigma, and we must hope that will happen sooner rather than later so we can pass on your news.'

Still not ready to let it go, Alain persisted. 'If we wait until tomorrow we will not be able to speak with anyone here, except in a limited fashion. We will be completely isolated.'

Placing his hand on Alain's shoulder, the older man stared deep into his eyes. 'We can spend all night worrying about what might happen tomorrow, but these things are now out of our control. It is time to get some sleep so we can keep up our energy. Worrying about things we cannot control does no one any good. In the meantime, perhaps a prayer to the goddess, or even the god of this time, will help.'

When Alain did not move, Master Barwick pulled him into a gruff hug. 'We have each other, and Jo and Alice, and the Time Guardians will not abandon us, no matter what. Now, would you like to sleep upstairs with me tonight?'

Alain shook his head, and his mentor released him. 'I will be okay. And you are right; we should worry about tomorrow when it comes.'

Turning away, Alain let himself into the kitchen and smiled at Bebe's thoughtfulness when he saw a cup of camomile tea sitting on the table. He carried it upstairs and found Lee asleep in his bed, the light of the reading lamp he had left on for Alain casting him into the shadows.

Relieved he didn't have to try and talk to his roommate, Alain quickly changed into his nightclothes before propping himself up with pillows and sipping his tea. Picking up his copy of *The Lord of The Rings*, he found his ability to read was already gone.

He attempted to pick up some words from chapters he had read before, hoping to improve his grasp of modern English. However, the words appeared to be swimming across the page, so he put the book on the floor before reaching over to turn off the light. As he snuggled down under the duvet, waves of homesickness washed over him and he wished with all his might to be somewhere—anywhere else.

11

FIGHTING BACK

STRANGE NOISES WOKE Alain early the next morning. Hiding under his covers he listened, trying to work out what had awoken him. When he did, he gulped in a snort of laughter lest Lee realise he was awake and try to talk to him.

His roommate crept around in the dark, searching for something and cursing under his breath when he couldn't find them. In his attempt to be considerate, he managed to make twice his normal noise.

As Lee pulled on his jeans, he lost his balance and banged into Alain's bed. Alain considered sitting up and putting him out of his misery, but it was too entertaining. Finally, his roommate closed the door behind himself and Alain relaxed, happy to be left alone.

Leaning over, he picked up *The Lord of the Rings*, immediately confirming his worst fear from listening to Lee—it was gibberish. Trouble was not yet awake and back to normal. Dropping the book to the floor, he rolled to his back and stared at the ceiling, hands clasped behind his head.

The overwhelming despair from the night before had morphed into resolve. Trouble's absence did not mean work had stopped. They still needed to move forward. Shaking the sleep from his head, he focussed on coming up with a plan of action.

Firstly, they needed to find out the results of last night's coven vote. If they'd voted yes to distributing the bacteria tomorrow, he and Master Barwick needed to find a way to stop them. If they'd voted not to, there was time to work with Jo, Lee and Bebe to find a way to destroy the new people-friendly bacteria.

Right, time to visit Master Barwick and find out where they stood. He swung his legs out of bed and started to push himself up when a noise on the stairs stopped him. Rolling back over on his side, he pulled the duvet up so it covered his face. In his hiding place, he froze as the door creaked open, admitting Lee and Bebe in the midst of an argument.

'See? He is still asleep,' Bebe whispered. 'Just leave the food, Lee.'

'It's late. He can't sleep all day. Besides, I want to find out what happened last night, and he might enjoy some company.'

'If he wanted company he would be downstairs already. Jo hasn't called, so we've nothing new to tell him. Just put the food down and leave him be.' Bebe's tone was insistent.

Well, that was what he imagined they were saying from the fragments of words he understood. There was a clatter of dishes and the click of a door closing.

All right, perhaps finding out about the coven was not the first thing he needed to sort; his inability to understand what anyone was saying was far more pressing. Leaning over, he saw a plate of toast and a cup of tea on the dresser and his stomach grumbled, reminding him he was ravenously hungry.

After wolfing down the food, he felt a little better. Once again, he studied the ceiling as he wondered how Master Barwick was doing. Had he ventured into the kitchen or was he avoiding everyone as well? Closing his eyes, Alain attempted to mind-speak with the other man. Either the distance between them was too far or Trouble had been assisting them with their usual connection because he got nothing.

Whether from boredom or stress, Alain dozed off again. When he opened his eyes he found light streaming into the room from the window. Someone had opened the curtains and taken his empty dishes away. The position of the sun told him there was little left of the morning.

Come on, sleepy head. Get yourself dressed and come down here. There are things we need to discuss.

He sat bolt upright, suddenly wide awake. *Jo? But how ...*

Yes, it's me. I am about to call Barnaby. Get yourself down here.

But... but I cannot understand the others. They will notice, he said.

I found a solution for that. Please trust me and come down. The voice in his head

was impatient, and it left as abruptly as it had entered.

Standing in the shower a few moments later, he realised he had not asked Jo about Trouble. He sent his mind out to her, but she was no longer there. Then he laughed; there was only one way Jo would be able to talk to him mind-to-mind like that. *Trouble? Trouble? Are you there?*

Still, nothing.

Somewhat bewildered, Alain tramped down the stairs and entered the kitchen. To his surprise Izzy sat at the table with Lee and Bebe. As he entered the room, Jo was placing a large teapot on the table. He caught Jo's eye and she opened her mouth to speak, but was prevented by the noise of Master Barwick opening the door and joined them.

At the sight of Izzy sitting at the table, he stopped and glared. Shutting the door, Jo moved her body to force him into the room. 'Ah Barnaby, good timing. Please come in and take a seat.'

Pulling out a chair for him, Jo waited patiently while he made up his mind to stay. As Alain took a seat beside Master Barwick, he realised he had understood Jo. Once again, he searched around for Trouble. Unable to find the dog anywhere he raised a questioning eyebrow in Master Barwick's direction. The old man shook his head and shrugged.

AFTER SHE FINISHED pouring everyone tea, Jo sat beside Izzy and took the other girl's hand. A quick glance around the table showed Master Barwick was not the only one staring daggers at the Time Wrecker. Bebe glared at the girl over the rim of her teacup, and Lee sat back arms folded, his eyes challenging Izzy. She lounged back in her chair, appearing unconcerned, but the frequent eye contact she made with Jo told a different story.

'Alice took my shift at the store because I worked late at the vet's last night,' Jo started. 'After talking with her, I decided rather than rest I should bring you all here so we can work together to resolve things with the other coven. She agreed with me, so long as we do not make any firm plans without running them by her—especially you two.' Jo stared directly at Lee and Bebe.

Jo, how is Trouble doing this? I cannot reach him, Alain sent

It's not him, you dolt. It's me.

Alain's eyebrows almost flew off his head. *Izzy?*

'When I left Trouble early this morning, he was doing much better,' Jo told them, seeming undisturbed by the second conversation going on in her head.

'Excellent. When can he come home?' Alain asked. *Why? Why are you doing this, Izzy?*

'He is not out of the woods yet. They are keeping him sedated until lunchtime today to give his body a chance to heal. Before they wake him, they will do some more tests, but they are hopeful he is over the worst of it.' Jo's words warmed Alain's heart and everyone murmured their gratitude and relief.

Because I can. And ... well... what is going on is too wrong for me to stand by and do nothing. We have to stop it. This is not the right way to fix the ills of the world, Izzy sent.

'Sadly, two more dogs came in last night with similar symptoms. The numbers are on the rise. Susan, the vet, let me try Barnaby's cure on one of them–with the owner 's permission of course. They are both at the same stage of the diseases development, so we should get an idea of whether or not the cure helps.'

I do not trust you, girl. You are a Time Wrecker. Master Barwick cut into the second conversation, and at the same time he responded to Jo. 'I can make up some more if it helps, for the other animal, but I am pleased they let you test it. '

Time Wreckers is the Guardians' name for us. We call ourselves the World Fixers, Izzy told them.

Bah, semantics, Master Barwick dismissed her.

'Let's not get ahead of ourselves,' Jo said. 'It will take twenty-four hours before we know whether or not it helps. Remember, Trouble had an accelerated dose of the bacteria '

'Yes, one given to him by your friends,' Bebe spat the words out as she pointed at Izzy. 'You almost killed him.'

'Bebe!'

The hurt in Jo's voice did not deter Bebe. 'I know you like her, Jo, but that does not change the fact she is part of Tabitha's coven, and therefore is responsible for what happened to Trouble in the first place.'

Tears welled in Izzy's eyes. *It is not semantics; it is name-calling. The Time Guardians want time to flow exactly as it always has, without change. We want to fix things that are setting the world on a course for destruction. Who is to say whose approach is right or wrong?* Izzy defended herself against Master Barwick. At the same time, she turned and faced Bebe. 'I would never hurt Trouble, and I would never let anyone else either. In fact, I am here because I think my coven is going too far. Making a few dogs sick is one thing, and even that got out of hand. Giving this disease to humans is a whole other proposition—one I can't support.'

Bebe's jaw dropped, and Lee put down his phone.

In all the furore over Trouble there had been no opportunity to tell them about what Izzy had said last night. She resolved that problem by outlining the coven's discussions from the night before.

Throughout, Master Barwick was strangely silent. He stroked his beard and gazed thoughtfully at Izzy. She pretended not to notice, but Alain watched as she glanced at the alchemist through her lashes every now and then, as if watching and waiting for his next attack.

'So, what did they decide after we left?' Lee's question brought Alain's attention back to the matter at hand.

'Tabitha managed to persuade most of them to go ahead with the plan tomorrow night—the plan to release a new version of bacteria that can infect humans.' Izzy's voice was barely a whisper. 'That was why I searched out Jo this morning—to tell her everything in the hopes you can stop them.'

'Why can't you stop it?' Bebe turned on Izzy again.

'I would like to. In fact, I tried, but Tabitha is no longer listening to me. I cannot prevent the spread of this abomination alone—I need your help.' Izzy's gaze did not waiver as she admitted she needed them.

You cannot influence anyone else to act against those you've been helping, can you? Master Barwick asked. *But as we are already actively trying to stop the spread of bacteria, you can nudge us in the right direction?*

Correct. My Council will pull me out of here before I have time to convince anyone to oppose Tabitha. However, they cannot watch every move I make, and they are aware of my relationship with Jo, so they will be expecting me to be in contact with her, and they are a little distracted at the moment …

So I heard, Master Barwick said dryly.

Izzy ignored the comment. *I told the coven last night I will use my friendship with Jo to spy on what you are doing to ensure you do not get any whiff of their plan, so they won't be too suspicious. Now I can tip the scales in your favour when I am able—without being obvious of course.*

This is a dangerous game you are playing, missy, Master Barwick said, frowning at her.

There is no other way to stop this abomination, she declared.

'Izzy suggested she spy on us for the coven, when in reality she is keeping an eye on them for us,' Jo informed the group.

'How do we know you are not playing us both?' Although it was Lee who spoke, he asked the obvious question.

How do we know we can trust you? Alain added.

'You don't,' Izzy said out loud, answering both questions. 'In fact, I'm not sure that if I were you, I would trust me either. But what choice do you have? Can you do this without me?'

'Perhaps,' Lee said.

'But it would be harder,' Izzy told him. 'All I can say is, we cannot let this abomination be released. I will undertake to tell you where they are planning to spread the bacteria, and I will tell them I convinced you nothing is going on, or that they will be at another location. It is up to you how you stop them.'

'Are we going to wait until they are actually spreading the disease? Isn't that risky?' Bebe asked.

'Yeah, it would be better if we destroyed the bacteria before it got to that stage.' Picking up on Bebe's question, Lee proposed the beginnings of a solution.

Izzy sighed. 'Don't you think I haven't already thought of that? The vial containing the bacteria is locked in Tabitha's safe. I tried to break in, but it's state of the art and impossible to open for all but the most talented safecrackers.'

A slow smile spread across Lee's face. 'Alain and I are very good at blowing things up.'

'Honestly, Lee, I sometimes wonder if you still have the brains you were born with. If you blow up the safe with the bacteria in it, you risk releasing it into the world anyway,' Bebe said, shaking her head.

'Oh, yeah.' Lee laughed wryly. 'Perhaps not my best plan.'

'That's not such a bad idea,' Master Barwick mused. 'A small, local release of the bacteria might be able to be contained and dispersed harmlessly using magic. I am assuming the release is timed for tomorrow night so that your coven can use magic to ... um... accelerate growth perhaps, so it can multiply faster and spread further.'

Izzy nodded.

'So, let me summarise our two options. The first is Lee's: to steal the vial now, which would possibly result in a minimal release of the bacteria. The second is to stop the coven at the site of the dispersion. This course of action also has risks. We might cause the same bacterial spread as option one if they release it and our counter measures are not strong enough. Or, if they disperse it before we get there, the impact may be larger.' Master Barwick's gaze swept around the table as everyone seemed to confirm their agreement.

Everyone except Alain nodded. 'There is a third option. Izzy, do you

think the coven would go ahead without their full contingent?'

Izzy seemed to consider his words. 'I am not sure. I think if it were Tabitha. Or perhaps Ruth, a couple of the others sympathise with her and they might develop cold feet and refuse to go through with the plan.'

'So if we stop one of them from getting there we might be able to prevent the spread happening tomorrow, and that would buy us some more time.' Alain picked up her idea and took it to the logical conclusion.

'All these options are short-term,' Bebe said. 'If we destroy the bacteria, what is to stop them making more? And if we stop them tomorrow night, the coven will simply wait until the next full moon to try again. What we need to do is choose the one that gains us the most amount of time to come up with a long-term solution.'

'And don't forget, we still need to talk to Alice and get her agreement,' Jo added.

Master Barwick frowned. *If Sigma was here, he would be able to sense the possible futures and tell us which one would give us the best result.* He looked at Izzy. *Can you do that?*

Izzy shook her head. *Only our most senior agents are granted that ability, and I'm not at that level yet. If this mission had been successful I might have been promoted, but now who knows?* She sounded a little sad as she spoke of what she was giving up to help them.

The others waited for Master Barwick, the only adult in the room, to provide guidance, but he seemed reluctant to make a decision.

Maybe we should wait and see how Trouble is this afternoon before deciding what to do. Alain tried to help out his mentor.

Delaying doing anything in itself is a risk. There are times to wait and think, and times for action. I believe this is a time for action, Master Barwick was decisive. *There are a lot of things we need to take into account though.*

'All right. Bebe and Lee, how about you go to your aunt's store and search for anything on how to stop growth spells? Bebe, please also bring her up-to-date on everything we discussed this morning. And Lee, would you be able to spend some time on your internet thingy researching safe cracking?' Master Barwick took charge of the situation. *That also means they are out of the way when Izzy leaves and we can no longer understand their language.* He smiled.

Good thinking, Alain sent.

'Will do,' Lee said as Bebe nodded.

'Jo, do you think this Ruth person might listen to reason if you spoke to

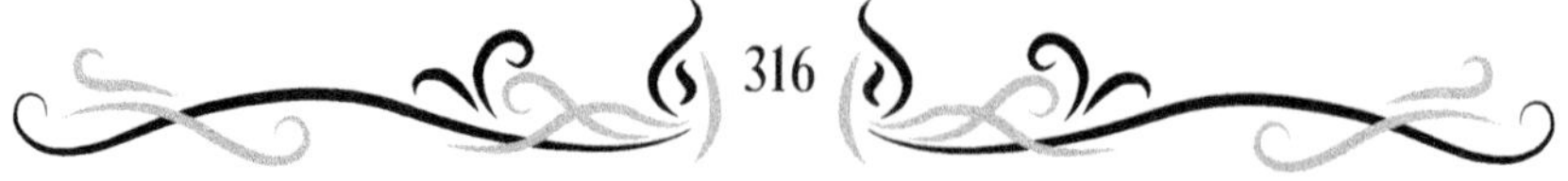

her today?' Master Barwick continued.

Don't you trust me to do it? Izzy asked.

'I am not sure, Barnaby, but it's worth a try.' Jo shrugged.

Jo is a better choice because of her history with Ruth. Alice tells me they are close, Master Barwick responded.

'I can go with her and tell her about what happened to Trouble last night,' Alain offered.

And how would she understand you? Izzy asked.

'And would she believe you. I mean, she doesn't know who you are,' Jo tried to dissuade him, and given Izzy's comment, Alain was reconsidering his offer.

'I should go too,' Izzy said, and the others looked at her in surprise, but it was Alain who spoke.

'How can you keep up your ruse if you are seen with us?'

How will you be able to understand what she is saying, or she you, if I am not nearby? Izzy mind-spoke. Out loud she said, 'If I look like I am wavering in my support of Tabitha, it might help to change her mind. And if she stands firm, I can find some way to let her know I am only with you because I need to stay in good with you guys to find out what you are up to.'

'Man, you are good.' Bebe's admiration at Izzy's plotting skills made Alain laugh.

Ignoring the girls, Lee turned to the alchemist. 'And what will you be doing, Barnaby?'

'I shall be here working on cooking up a new batch of the cure for the dogs, and seeing if I can figure out how they might mutate the bacteria to affect humans. If I can do that, I might be able to come up with a vaccination or a cure.'

'Do you need me to stay and help you?' Alain asked. *If you do, Izzy and I can stay behind. She can help with any books you need to read.*

'No, no, I am fine. You go with Jo. I will work faster alone.'

Master Barwick clasped his shoulder. *I will be working from my notes mostly and ...*

... and he still does not really trust me, so he wants me far away from his work, and he wants you to keep an eye on me, Izzy finished.

'Right, everyone has a job to do. Let's go,' Master Barwick dismissed them, and he used the hand on Alain's shoulder to help himself up.

And let's do Trouble proud, Alain added to himself.

THE STRAINED ATMOSPHERE in the car during the journey to Southampton was uncomfortable to say the least. After a whispered conversation during which Alain gleaned Jo had not wanted Izzy to come with them, the car remained silent until Izzy turned on the radio. However, the music she finally settled on did nothing to mask the tension between the two girls.

Jo concentrated on driving. Izzy sat beside her, glancing at her friend every now and then. A couple of times she moved as if to say something then, catching sight of Alain in the back, she stopped herself.

Watching the countryside speed by, Alain continued questioning his decision to come along. Maybe he'd read Master Barwick wrong. Maybe the alchemist had suggested he come not to keep an eye on Izzy, but merely to give him something to do other than fretting about Trouble. If that was the case, he could have stayed behind and helped Master Barwick, even if only to clean up a little, and avoided the argument brewing in front of him.

The scene outside the car changed from country lanes to a main road with houses on either side. The number of cars and houses and people overwhelmed Alain, making him feel very small and insignificant. Southampton was even bigger and busier than the London he'd left a couple of days ago. As they entered the city proper, Jo followed the blue signs directing them to the hospital. Upon entering the grounds, she found a place to park the car and they all piled out.

'You cannot possibly think you are coming in.' Jo turned to Izzy in astonishment.

'I most certainly am.'

'I can handle this. Ruth and Mum have been friends for years, and she and I ... well, we have a history.' Jo stood in front of Izzy, blocking her way forward, hands on hips.

'I am well aware of your history. We discussed it at the meeting in detail after you left. Tabitha believes Ruth is protecting you because of it. But that's not why I am going with you—I am going to give Ruth cover if she needs it. When we ask her to stay away tomorrow, if she thinks another coven member is prepared to try and thwart Tabitha's scheme then she might be more likely to consider it.'

'"We" ask? See how easy it is for you to slip into talking about you and I as

a team? What if you let slip you told us about the bacteria skipping to humans?'

'I wouldn't,' Izzy protested.

'It is too risky. You should stay here.'

Unwilling to become involved in their quarrel, Alain moved away and surveyed the car park. In his wildest dreams, he would never have imagined so many cars in the world, and this was only a small number compared to those they had passed on the journey here.

When he closed his eyes, the air filled with the sounds of their movements. Taking a deep breath, he coughed as his lungs filled with unclean air. He imagined if you lived in Southampton, the smell and noise from cars would be a constant backdrop to your life. He was beginning to appreciate why Izzy fought so hard to save the world form this sort of thing.

Jo sighed a loud and exaggerated sigh—she must have realised she fought a losing battle. She swivelled on her heel and walked off towards the closest building. Izzy stalked after her, leaving Alain behind. Had they even remembered he was there?

As they approached the building, Alain read the sign by the door, "Adolescent Behavioural Support Unit", and he realised how Jo knew Ruth—she was the person who'd guided her back on the straight and narrow after her father left. This meeting was going to be way more difficult than he'd first imagined.

Alain trailed after the others through a maze of corridors. If he got lost, he would never be able to find his way back out alone. Finally, they reached a door with the name *Ruth Claremont* on it. Jo stopped and raised a hand to knock, but stood frozen as the door opened before she'd had a chance to complete the action.

'Oh, Jo. Was I expecting you?' A tall woman in a white coat stood in the doorway. Perching her glasses on the top of her head, she glanced past Jo and saw Izzy. Her eyebrows raised questioningly. 'And Izzy is with you too. So, is this a social call, or something more?' Her eyes met Alain's. 'And who are you?'

'I am very uncomfortable at the moment, and not quite sure why I am here.' Alain shrugged, and caught a playful glint in the other woman's eyes as her lips turned upwards.

'I bet you are. But what can you expect when you spend time with such ... shall we say ... mavericks.'

'Ruth, Alain. Alain, Ruth. Now we have that over, Ruth, do you have time for a chat?' Jo asked.

'I was just on my way to the cafeteria for lunch if you want to join me.

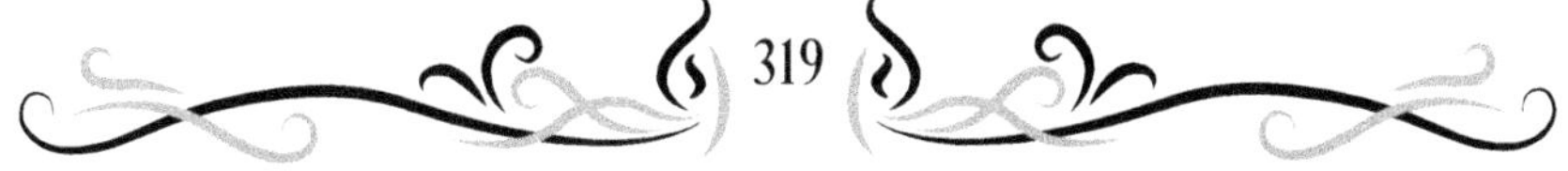

My schedule is pretty full this afternoon, so this is my only free time for the rest of day.'

The two girls looked at each other, and then nodded as if they shared a single thought. Minutes later, Alain found himself once again trailing behind the others with no idea where they were going or how to find his way out if he got lost.

The cafeteria was a large room full of tables. There appeared to be a rush for lunch, leaving only a few vacant places. On one side ran a self-service counter facing a wall of picture windows that framed the grey day outside.

Jo ordered teas for them, and they followed Ruth to a table by the window. Once seated, Ruth began eating her pie as if they weren't there. Alain watched as the two girls stared at each other, Izzy nodding towards Ruth, encouraging Jo to take the lead.

'Um, it's about Tabitha, and her scheme.' Jo opened the conversation.

Ruth smiled, tucking a strand of greying brown hair that had escaped its bun back behind her ear. 'You do surprise me,' she said before carrying on eating.

Alain grinned—he liked the woman sitting in front of him. She was not only confident and self-assured, but she was enjoying the awkward situation they found themselves in. That very fact relaxed him, and for a moment he forgot his worries about Trouble and the bacteria while he enjoyed the show.

'Well, I saw at the meeting you were not happy with her escalating things, and I wondered if you would consider returning to our coven.' The last words rushed out of Jo's mouth as if they had a momentum of their own.

Alain smiled at the look of shock on Izzy's face. This was not what they had agreed. Had she done it to show Izzy was not really privy to this?

Ruth laughed. 'Is this coming from you, or Alice?'

'I didn't tell Alice I was coming.' Jo raised her eyebrows defiantly as she answered.

'Mm, interesting,' Ruth said, pausing with her fork halfway to her mouth. 'So, the coven has not changed its stance; they will not take any action to preserve the forest beyond their growth and energy spells?

When Jo did not answer, Ruth ate another mouthful of food, then turned her attention to Izzy. 'And what is your role in this? You did not speak out against Tabitha's plan last night, but you clearly were not comfortable either. Have you left our coven?'

'I am considering it.' Izzy's voice sounded uncertain even to Alain, leaving her motivation open to interpretation. 'Okay, I don't want to. But I have

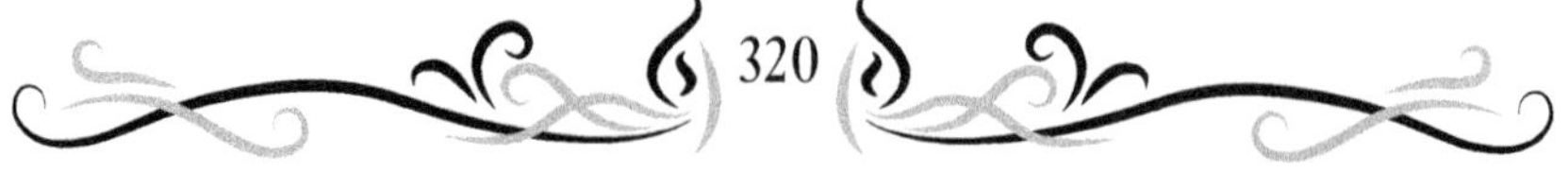

thought things over and I'm not really happy taking part in what is essentially the murder of animals,' she added hastily, clarifying her position.

Sitting back in her chair, Ruth regarded her three guests through hooded lids before leaning forward and resuming her meal. As if unnerved by the silence, Izzy spoke to fill it, and Alain saw how Ruth might work as a therapist.

'That wasn't our intention when we started this. We thought a few more dogs might become ill, forcing people to think more about protecting the forests. But you've seen how the virus works, what it is doing to dogs, what it could potentially do to—'

'Come on, Ruth. I can't believe you think hurting people's pets is the right way to go about changing things.' Jo spoke before Izzy could let on she had told them about the new bacteria that would kill humans. 'It breaks my heart when they come in to the surgery with this illness. If you saw them too, I know you'd change your mind. Perhaps if I pick you up and take you to the vets after work tomorrow.'

Nice, Alain thought to himself. You hid the fact that Izzy told us the whole plan, and you have given her an excuse not to go tomorrow.

Although Jo offered her an out, Ruth was not taking the bait. 'I am sorry, Jo. I am busy tomorrow night. Perhaps we might do it on Sunday.'

'I guess so, if the dogs are still alive then.'

'Jo!' Ruth's tone held a definite warning note. 'You are well aware of my feelings on emotional blackmail. I said I will catch up with you when I have some free time.'

Alain sensed Jo bursting at the seams, wanting to talk Ruth out of supporting Tabitha's scheme. Unfortunately, if she pushed any harder Ruth might guess they knew the truth. Alain held his breath, willing Jo to let it go. Finally, her shoulders slumped in defeat.

'Well, if you are certain you will not let me convince you, I guess we should leave you to finish your lunch in peace.' Jo stood and pushed her chair back, scraping the legs along the floor.

The girls' disappointment seemed to be the only thing that got a reaction from Ruth, but Jo turned away before she could see the conflicting emotions cross her mentor's face. As Alain stood to follow Jo, Ruth gabbed Izzy's arm. Izzy sat back down and he moved until he was out of Ruth's line of sight, but close enough to overhear their conversation.

'After our meeting last night, Tabitha's friend Gavin visited me. He informed me I should be careful because accidents can happen to anyone at

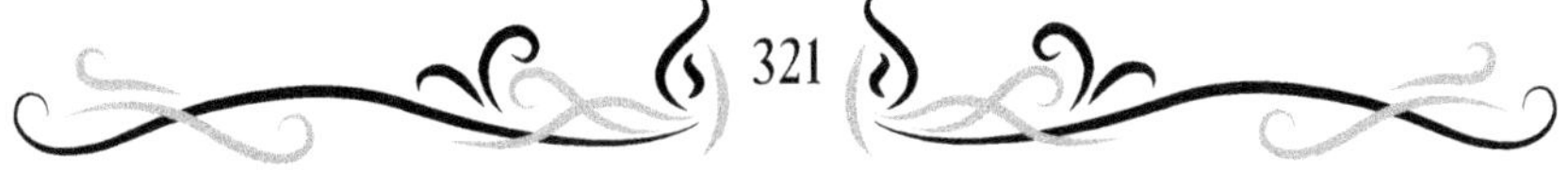

any time, and if I wanted to stay safe I should stay close to our coven. I can't tell if you are playing along while you spy on Alice's group, or if you are wavering from Tabitha's plan. Either way, I would be very careful if I were you. I don't think this guy fools around.'

Izzy whispered, 'Do not fear. I am only keeping in with Jo to find out what her coven is doing. I will be there tomorrow as planned.'

Alain headed for the door before Izzy was out of her chair, but she rushed to catch him up.

'I guess you heard that?' Izzy said

Alain nodded.

'She is really scared. There is no way we are going to be able to stop her or any of the others from going tomorrow night.'

'I know. We need to think of something else.'

By the time they reached the car, Jo was already in her seat and buckled up ready to go. Tears rolled down her cheeks and she gripped the steering wheel so tightly her knuckles had turned white.

'I cannot believe it,' she said. 'I just cannot believe Ruth is involved in hurting animals and is considering doing something that will hurt a lot of people.'

Izzy placed a hand on her arm. 'To be fair, Ruth argued against hurting animals, as did Gladys. They suggested we cast spells to make people uneasy when they visited areas of the forest being considered for development. I thought it was rather a good idea, but Tabitha wanted something more extreme. The others went along with her, so I agreed as well. Now Gavin is threatening Ruth, and she feels she has no choice but to go through with this.'

'But she cast the first spell without him bullying her into it.'

'Yes, she helped cast the spell. Beth always finds an excuse not to be available, and I pretended to be sick because I could not be involved, and Ruth had to fill in to make up the five. Then when we saw what was happening to the dogs, and how more than normal were dying, even Tabitha wanted to stop. But Gavin stepped in and convinced her to carry on.'

Rather than calming Jo's fears, this news made her cry all the harder. 'Ruth will never forgive herself if she casts the new spell. We have to find some way to keep her from participating.'

Taking a deep breath and wiping the tears from her eyes, Jo started the car. 'Let's head home. We have some more planning to do, and I want to ring Susan and find out how Trouble is.'

12

SOLDIERING ON

ALTHOUGH NO ONE spoke, the journey back to Burley was a little less tense than the one to Southampton had been. As the car pulled up outside Alice's house, Alain leapt out. He wanted to get away from the others and clear his head. Heavy with fatigue, his shoulders slumped as he let himself in through the back door.

Lee and Bebe sat at the kitchen table with a distraught Master Barwick. Wearily smiling his hellos, he noticed Bebe's hands trembling, and he froze as he attempted to work out what was going on.

Alice paced back and forth in front of the bench while Lee sat beside his sister, arm wrapped along the back of her chair. Master Barwick glanced up as he entered, his hands clenched and his brows furrowed.

Thank goodness you're back. Now I might be able to work out what is going on. Please tell me Izzy is with you.

Jo and Izzy bundled Alain through the door and went to stand in front of the Aga to warm up.

Alice stopped walking and stood with her hands on her hips, glaring at Master Barwick. 'Are you silent because you think I'm over-reacting? I might be, but I really want to hear what you think.'

'On the contrary, my dear, you may well have every right to be angry. How about you sit down and recount your story for the others, and we can all decide what to do together.'

Alain admired Master Barwick's handling of the situation. No one would ever have known he had not understood a word Alice said up until their entrance.

Jo pulled out a chair for Alice to sit on and placed a hand on her shoulder. 'Tell us what happened,' she encouraged.

'We were in the shop—the twins in the book room doing some research and me by the counter—when I heard the screech of tyres. Thinking it was just some young kids letting off steam, I looked out the window to find out who'd done it in time in time to catch the back door of a car open. A man half reached out and threw something, and next thing my small plate-glass window was in pieces. As I rushed over to inspect the damage, the car door closed and the culprits took off.'

Alice clasped the mug of tea in her hands, the tremors causing her to spill a little on the table.

Lee picked up the story. 'Someone threw a brick. It hit a stand on the way through, which fell on Bebe, cutting her face.'

On cue, Bebe pulled her hair back off her face, revealing a dressing. 'Only a small cut,' she said. 'No concussion, and the doctor told me to go home and drink heaps of sweet tea.' She pointed to the cup in front of her. 'And I always follow doctors' orders.' She smiled wanly at them all.

'It could have been much worse.' Lee's voice belied his barely controlled anger.

'Yes, we should be thankful it wasn't.' Alice said, patting him on the arm as if to calm him down. 'What was more disturbing, though, was the note tied to the brick.' Alice indicated the crumpled piece of paper in the middle of the table.

Jo leaned over to read it. 'Keep your nose out of other people's business. You have been warned.' Moving back to the heat of the Aga, she said, 'It's like something out of a bad seventies cop show. Did you recognise the car, or the person who threw the brick?'

Alice looked at Izzy as she answered, 'No, I didn't. But I can hazard a guess at who the message is from.'

Izzy shifted in her chair, but her chin lifted as she met Alice 's gaze. 'After what I heard today, I suspect you may be right.'

'You are part of the coven, so you are responsible for their actions,' Alice shot back.

'Hold on you two,' Jo interrupted what had the potential to turn into a major argument. 'Izzy's been helping us this morning, and she is as concerned about the way things are going as we are. I, for one, do not believe she supports any of the threatening activity going on.'

'You mean there has been more?' Lee asked, and Izzy recounted her conversation with Ruth.

Sighing as if the weight of the world was on his shoulders, Master Barwick leaned his arms on the table. 'If the one person who stood up to Tabitha is too scared to oppose her, then we have no hope of changing anyone else's minds.'

'I just want to clarify, it was Gavin who threatened Ruth,' Izzy said.

'But it is Tabitha who has the power to put a stop to this,' Alice said.

Alain intervened before things got heated again. 'It doesn't matter who is leading the coven. We need to change our tactic, as it is unlikely we will be able to prevent members from going along with the plan if they are too frightened to protest.'

'Hold on,' Jo said. 'We might not be able to talk Ruth into voluntarily boycotting tomorrow night's activities, but there are other methods of keeping her away. I would like to try them if only because I get the sense she does not want to be involved in this any more than Izzy does—but she is too scared to say no.'

Lee sat forward in his chair. 'You mean something like kidnapping her? How cool.'

Master Barwick held up his hand. 'Now Lee, I don't think we need to go quite that far. Not only is it illegal, but it might also be very dangerous.'

'More dangerous than facing a terrible epidemic if they succeed tomorrow?' Lee was ready to argue his point further, but Alice put a quick stop to the potential solution.

'Barnaby is right,' she said. 'Your parents would never forgive me if I allowed you to do anything that might jeopardise your future career.'

'But ...' Bebe's face wore the same expression as Barabal's did when she was scheming. '... if we managed to figure which tourist attraction the coven are targeting, we might be able to work out the route Ruth will take. Then we could block the road, force her to stop, and delay her long enough so she misses everything all together.'

'Why a tourist attraction?' Alice asked.

Jo's face lit up. 'Because they will attract the greatest number of people this time of year.'

'Of course.' Alice nodded. 'Most of the roads around the forest are so small, if someone broke down ... say with a flat tyre ... they could block the

way, and she would not be able to drive past. Also, Ruth is basically a good person. She would not leave anyone stranded on the side of the road.'

'It would have to be …'

Before Izzy finished her thought, Alice's phone rang. She took a quick look at the screen and picked it up. 'Sorry, I need to take this. It's Donald and he never rings at this time of day unless it's important. I won't be long.'

Once she left the room, Izzy continued, 'As I was saying, Ruth will recognise you, Alice, Alain and I, so it has to be Bebe or Lee.'

'Leave it to us,' Lee said. 'We would have to hire a car though, because Ruth must have seen Alice's and Jo's mum's cars before. We would also need a good idea of which way she is travelling to make this work.'

'I can arrange car hire,' Alice said, returning to the room and putting her phone back on the table.

'Is everything ok with Uncle Donald?' Bebe asked.

'What? … Yes.' Alice was running the charm on her necklace back and forwards along the chain. I have a friend in Southampton who owes me a favour or two and will do me a good deal on a car.'

Bebe frowned at her aunt, and looked as though she was about to say something when Izzy spoke. 'And knowing which way she will go should be easy to work out. There's a meeting this evening to finalise plans, so I should be able to give you the location,' Izzy said.

'I hope you all understand, removing one of the coven may not be enough to stop the ceremony from going ahead,' Master Barwick said once they finished planning Ruth's diversion.

They nodded, and Bebe said, 'We're not going to stop looking into other options, but this may be the best shot we have.'

'So long as you know,' Master Barwick said before moving on. 'Lee, did you manage to find out any safe-cracking methods that might help us break into Tabitha's tonight? '

'No. I did a web search, but everything mechanical required some technology that is not available in local stores—in fact, we would need to send overseas for most of it.'

'What about the old-fashioned ways?' Jo asked.

'Yep, I did some research on that as well. I watched a few online videos and it would take weeks, even months to develop the techniques to a level to be able to open even the simplest safes, and we simply don't have that much time.'

'Sound like your day was a complete bust,' Jo said.

'Not exactly. We did find a protection spell in one of Alice's books that might work for us. Alice checked her stock and she found everything we would need to cast it.' Bebe nudged Lee, who leaned down and pulled his backpack out from under the table. He rummaged inside before producing a book from its depths.

'It is an ancient rite that prevents anyone from casting a spell with malicious intent in an area,' Alice told them all. 'Do you think it might help, Barnaby?'

Lee pushed the book on the table over to Master Barwick, who opened it at the marked passage and read.

'Yes ... oh, this is good. If we were able to cast this in the same area the coven plans to work their magic it should be enough to stop them from being effective.' Master Barwick tugged at tufts of hair as he read some more. 'We need enough for five people. Did you take that into account?'

Lee pointed to a box on the bench. 'Already sorted.'

'I thought as Tabitha's coven were casting in a pentagram formation, to effectively counter then we would need to do the same. I believe we are prepared,' Alice said.

Alain, are you there? I cannot reach Barwick.

Trouble?

Yes, it is me. A weak groggy voice answered, but it had never sounded better to Alain.

Master Barwick is a little busy at the moment. I will explain later. How are you?

Better, still a little tired, but I can no longer feel the bacteria eating away at me.

Alain smiled; things were looking up. *Rest a while. Things are under control here for the moment.*

Returning his attention to the conversation, he found himself in the midst of a debate over who should make up their pentagram. Alain, Master Barwick, Alice and Jo were a given. Alice seemed to favour asking Jo's mother, but Jo wanted to leave her out of it.

Can Trouble cast a spell? Alain asked Master Barwick.

Yes, if he were well enough.

'How about we wait until tomorrow to decide who will be the fifth,' Alain suggested.

Jo eyed him suspiciously. 'Why?'

'I just thought of someone else, but I need to check if they can be available,' Alain responded.

'Wait a moment—even if you find someone else, we might still need your

mum as a backup, Jo. Donald called to tell me there is a delay with getting some equipment for his project and, as classes are finished for the year, he is coming home until after Christmas. He is waitlisted for a flight and might be here as early as tomorrow.' Alice dropped the news in ever so casually into the conversation.

'Would your husband forbid you from helping us?'

The others around the table tensed at Master Barwick's question, their eyes fixing on anything except Alice. Having been out and about a bit more than his master, Alain realised that women were no longer subjugated by their husbands, and could do as they pleased.

Fortunately, Alice took the question in good humour, ignoring everyone else's discomfort. 'Goodness no. It is just, well, getting him up to speed on this hours after he has arrived home might be a bit much. Jo, perhaps you might have a word with your mother—just in case. '

Jo was still staring at Alain, then it was as though a light clicked on.

'Oh, oh, of course you have someone else to help, and yes, Alice, I will talk to Mum tonight. Can she call you if she needs to? Because this all sounds a little kooky, and I'm not sure she will believe me.'

'Of course. I might give her a call later anyway,' Alice said.

'Okay. If we are finished then I'd best go and ring the vet to check on Trouble. Izzy, shouldn't you be getting back to work? You don't want Gladys to become suspicious—otherwise your coven may decide to expel you, and you'll lose your chance of finding out where they are going to be tomorrow night.'

'You are right.' The other girl followed Jo into the hallway. *And I must ensure my council does not suspect I am helping you and pull me out—or worse still, send someone else to finish the job.*

'And I need to return to the shop to see how the window repairs are going, and organise a car for tomorrow,' Alice said, rising and grabbing her coat from the back of the chair in a single motion.

'Now that we have a plan, Alain and I need to prepare the casting.' Master Barwick picked up the book and stared at Alain, waiting for him to move.

'Hold on, I've something that might help you in our room. Alain, can you give me a hand?' Lee said, standing to leave. Alain followed him out but stopped in the doorway and looked back over his shoulder—Bebe had not moved.

'What are you going to do?' he asked her.

'Oh, sorry. I was miles away. I have some things I need to look into—on another matter.' She winked at him and he grinned back, then turned to go after Lee.

As he walked up the stairs, he could not help but overhear Jo and Izzy in the lounge.

'Please Jo, there is still time to back out. I am scared of Gavin, and I couldn't bear it if he hurt you.'

'But you are still going to go to this meeting and place yourself in danger?' Jo's voice was angry.

'I am, but you know I have other commit—'

'No buts. I am prepared to fight for what I believe in, the same as you are. If you care for me as you say you do you should try to understand that and support me.' Jo stormed to the door, flung it open and ran out.

'I do support you,' Alain heard Izzy mutter. 'I am just not sure I could survive losing you again.'

Alain tried to figure out what Izzy had meant but, not knowing the pair's full past, he decided to ask Trouble about it later, and continued up the stairs.

'Quickly. There isn't much time before Izzy goes.' Lee handed him his laptop in the hallway. 'If I have worked things out right, Izzy has been allowing you to understand us when she is here. That means you cannot study the book without a translator. I set this programme up to change modern English into old English. It may not be perfect, but it should help you keep working.'

The door slammed below.

'Thank you,' Alain said, but the confused look on Lee's face told him Izzy was no longer working her magic.

IZZY PULLED INTO Tabitha's drive. The number of other cars already parked suggested she was almost the last to arrive—only Beth's vehicle was missing. She sat for a few minutes to gather her thoughts. What was she doing? She was throwing away everything she had worked for. No, she could not doubt herself now—there was a line between right and wrong, and the coven were about to cross it.

The door creaked as she opened it, and she slipped out of the car. She reluctantly made her way inside, not quite knowing what to expect.

She knew immediately that Ruth had told them of her visit today.

'I was not sure you were going to join us this afternoon.' Tabitha's voice was syrupy sweet. But Izzy knew from experience this was Tabitha at her

most dangerous, and she prepared herself for the strike.

'I am not sure we should allow her to remain.' Gavin sat in an armchair, watching proceedings, no longer hiding in the shadows.

'You allowed a man into our coven,' Izzy spluttered, diverting attention to buy herself time. Although, to be fair, she was a little surprised at Tabitha so openly acknowledging Gavin's role in the coven's recent activities.

'I invited him to attend. With his international experience, he brings a different perspective,' Tabitha said, her hard face daring anyone to object.

'What? Even if he was not a man, we haven't inducted him into our group.' Izzy attempted to suppress her anger and fear by arguing points of order.

'He has as much of a stake in this as we do—he stays. What I am not so sure about is whether we allow you to.' Tabitha's voice was like steel. 'Ruth said you attempted to convince her not to turn up to tomorrow's casting.'

Izzy glanced behind Tabitha to find Ruth at least had the good grace to appear ashamed at having ratted her out.

'I did, and I would have reported that to you when I updated you of Alice's coven's activity, if you had given me the chance. May I remind you, you all agreed to me using my connection to Jo to spy on her group to make sure they don't find out what we are doing. '

A couple of the women nodded in agreement, and this gave Izzy the courage to go on. 'If I had not gone along with Jo today she would not have believed I was truly with her. However, if you no longer trust me, I will leave.' Izzy's stomach fluttered as she wondered if she had overplayed her indignation, and if they might allow her to actually walk out.

'Come on, Tabitha, she is part of our group, and we did support her offer to spy on the others.' Mona, one of the quieter members of the group, spoke out in support.

Tabitha's index finger tapped her lips as she stared directly at Izzy. 'All right, you can stay. But you best have some good information for us to make this all worthwhile.'

As she took her seat, Izzy attempted to hide her relief, but noticed Tabitha look towards Gavin in the corner as if to confirm she had made the right decision, telling her once and for all who was really in charge now.

'As you heard from Ruth, Jo and her friend Alain and I went and visited her today. It was Jo's idea. After last night, she wanted to save Ruth from herself.'

From the corner of her eye she caught Ruth squirming in her seat, and she was not the only one. To her amazement, Tabitha blushed, then seemed

to cover it by taking a long drink from her coffee cup.

'Jo also asked me what else we were into, and what the vote to escalate our campaign was about. I said it was for the same—spreading the bacteria in more places—but it didn't matter as the vote failed. She didn't believe me. Even though I had her convinced I wanted to join their coven, she was sceptical about me giving up our secrets that easily.' Izzy sat back in her seat, attempting to appear more relaxed than she felt—would they buy her explanation?

'That sounds like Jo,' Ruth said. 'I am sure she wanted to believe you, but she would not like you so much if she didn't think you had integrity.'

'She is so worried about your involvement in this, Ruth.' Izzy turned slightly to better read the other woman's face. 'She could not believe you would be happy about hurting animals, no matter how much you wanted to save the forest. She was sure she could talk you out of supporting the coven, and I went along to talk with you to prove myself to her.'

Knowing how much the morning's meeting had upset Jo, Izzy took a certain amount of pleasure from Ruth's discomfort at her words. As she looked around at her fellow coven members, few of them would meet her eye. Only Rosalind appeared defiant. It caused her to wonder how many more of them Gavin had threatened, and how far this man would go to enact the final step in his plan.

'So they guessed about our involvement in the dog disease, and Jo confirmed it, but have no actual proof?' Tabitha asked.

Izzy nodded.

'Do they know anything about tomorrow night?' Gavin said from the sidelines.

Izzy hesitated before answering, giving herself away. Gavin sat forward, bringing his face into the light.

'Come on, girl, spit it out,' he commanded, and all pretence of Tabitha running the meeting evaporated.

'Well, it is a full moon, so they suspect we will be doing something, especially after the Jo being here last night.' Izzy had a brainwave. 'Then when Jo asked Ruth to visit the dogs tomorrow with her and Ruth said she had something on, it made Jo even more suspicious. I assured her we had no plans but, once again, I don't think she believed me.'

Gavin's face drew into a snarl. 'We need to make sure they do not interfere.'

Tabitha stepped in between Izzy and Gavin. 'Come now, we need not do anything hasty that might draw the wrong type of attention to us. We were lucky Alice did not involve the police today after that ... um... hasty move of

yours, Rosalind.'

Gavin stood and moved beside Alice. 'I agree. Stupid things like that draw unwanted attention to the area just when we need to be most careful.'

Rosalind's lips drew themselves into a snarl. 'I can't believe we are still afraid of that woman and her group. She needs to learn to keep her nose out of other people's business.'

'Is this really to do with the work of our coven, or is this payback for Alice telling her son you were not as devoted to him as you made out—that you were also seeing that drummer in Southampton?' Gladys, who did not often speak at meetings, locked eyes with the younger woman as though daring her to continue.

'It doesn't matter why she did it,' Tabitha said, bringing everyone's attention back to her. 'What matters is that we cannot tolerate anyone else here going off and doing their own thing.'

There were mumbles of agreement, and Rosalind huffed, 'Whatever.'

'Okay, from Izzy's report we can assume Alice and her coven are steps behind us. She is still trying to find out what we are planning to do, and we can take measures to ensure she never does.' Tabitha's shoulders relaxed a little as she spoke.

'Who is the boy? The one who went with you to Ruth's office.' Gavin was not yet ready to give up.

'He's a new boy in town. He and his uncle rented a room at Alice's—Jo's taken him under her wing. I think he has a bit of a crush on her.' Izzy improvised, and she must have been convincing as the others settled back down. Even Tabitha's stance was more relaxed. However, Ruth eyed her sceptically, and Gavin still glowered at her as he returned to his seat.

'Now that's all sorted, let's move to the plans for tomorrow.' Tabitha paused a moment, but no one had anything to add, so she continued. 'We will meet at The Sir Walter Tyrell pub near Lyndhurst at nine thirty—do not, under any circumstance, be late. With Beth in London helping her sister with a new baby we need all hands on deck. Also, our spell must be cast as the moon reaches its zenith to ensure we maximise its effectiveness.'

'Are we going to do the spell in the car park? With everyone watching? I thought we would stay anonymous.' Mona, often called Mona the Mouse behind her back because people tended to forget she was there, seemed confused—then, she often was.

'No, Mona, we are meeting at the pub. We'll travel to the site Gavin and I have chosen together. This is just a precaution so no one can let slip where

we will do the casting.' Tabitha stared pointedly at Izzy.

In response, Izzy tried to appear nonchalant, containing her disappointment. Not knowing the location in advance would make things harder for the others.

'I also want everyone there. We only need five for the casting, but with Izzy being sick the last two times we cannot be too careful.' Turning to Izzy again, Tabitha said, 'I hope you don't feel anything coming on this time. '

'No, I am fine. I'll be there.' In an attempt to appear nonchalant Izzy leaned back in the chair, but unfortunately heat in her cheeks probably gave her discomfort away.

Having scored her point, Tabitha smiled and expanded her gaze to include the entire group. 'Okay, on the table is a list of what you are to bring—take one as you leave. Please make sure you are prepared and that you memorise the spell. Any other questions?'

When no one spoke, she declared the meeting closed, and the coven could not leave the house quickly enough. It was not a good sign that the witches did not linger for their usual after-meeting chit-chat.

As she fumbled in her bag for the keys to her car, Izzy felt a presence behind her. After opening the door, she turned and found Gavin looming, a shadowy figure standing just out of reach of the light spilling from the car. Standing taller, she tried not to let the knot of fear in her stomach show.

'I hope for your sake you turn up tomorrow ... alone.'

'Of course,' she said, slipping behind the wheel. She resisted the urge to lock the doors, not wanting to show the man how much he rattled her. Her hands shook so much it took two attempts to put the key in the ignition, and the tyres screeched as she took off. She swore she caught a glimpse of him laughing in her rear-vision mirror as she exited the driveway.

STUDYING THE SPELL they needed to do tomorrow night was slow-going with having to type each phrase into the programme, wait for it to translate, then put it into a document to be read later.

As he worked, a thought occurred to him. 'Master Barwick, magic is stronger in our time than in this one. Would it create a stronger spell if we spoke it in our language?'

'When Trouble translates for us, we are speaking as normal in our language—others just hear us differently. You do realise that, don't you?'

Alain considered his master's words a moment before answering, 'Huh? ... I never really thought about it before. Now you have said it, it is so obvious.'

'The lack of magic in this time is to do with the decrease in people's connection with nature. In fact, population growth and overdevelopment means very little land remains in its natural state. Each time a town expands, or a farmer clears a field for planting, humanity distances itself a little more from the earth and some magic is lost. That is why we require five magicians in a pentagram formation to cast a spell that in our time, you or I would be able to do alone.'

'Oh.' Alain went back to his study, all the while thinking he could not wait to go home where things were in a much better balance.

Then he shook his head. Back home, people died of many things able to be cured now. Fewer people starved in the winter here and most people had access to education, meaning they had a better standard of living. And the food was delicious. It was one thing he was going to miss when he returned to his own time.

Oh no, was he really prepared to sell out the earth and the magic it created for creature comforts? Or would he choose his home with all its failings but an abundance of magic? Ah, so maybe that was why the Time Guardians preserved history—because no one person had the right to decide which direction humanity moved in, and that was what they were fighting for.

The Time Wreckers had no right to give Gavin and Tabitha the ability to wipe out a large number of people simply because they believed the world was heading in the wrong direction and needed to be saved.

Staring at the wall, he stilled his mind. These problems were too big for him to deal with. Besides, he still had to face his own ones. When he returned home, would he stay in London and study with Master Barwick or go back to the New Forest and fight for it to be returned to the people?

When they'd left London, the decision was difficult as the urge to return the land to the people William the Conqueror stole it from was strong. Now he had seen how the forest had flourished because of its royal protection, his decision was even more difficult.

Shaking his head, he laughed at himself. He need not decide now. Firstly, Trouble was in no fit state to take them back. And secondly, Trouble had achieved his goal by bringing Alain here—he was now thinking through the consequences of his actions rather than reacting to situations. That dog certainly was smarter than he looked.

Returning to his work, he typed in the next line of the spell instructions and began copying out the translation. Both copies looked the same—he

had obviously been working for too long. He shook his head, then blinked a few times. No, it still looked the same. That could only mean one thing.

Dropping the computer on the sofa, he flung the door open and dashed downstairs and into the kitchen. Jo had her back to him and was placing something in front of the fire.

'Trouble?' Alain rushed forward and knelt beside the dog bed. Trouble raised his head, then his eyebrows as he looked at Alain.

'Susan said he made a miraculous recovery—he's almost back to normal. He is still very weak, and a bit dopey from the anaesthetic, but he is clear of bacteria and on the mend.' Jo gently scratched Trouble under an ear.

'Thank goodness. Does he need anything? Water? Food?' Alain stood, ready to do the dog's bidding.

I am just here, you know.

'Trouble, I warned you.' Jo frowned at the dog, then pulled Alain away for an explanation.

'On the way here, I struck a deal with Trouble. He can translate for you when Izzy is not here so long as he stops when you go to bed so he gets some rest. No mind-speak unless it is urgent, because it is even more tiring than translating. We can reassess the situation tomorrow when the anaesthetic is out of his system and he has rested. And yes, he would like water and food. I think Alice mentioned some leftover chicken breasts in the fridge, which should be perfect.'

'Thank you, Jo, and thank Susan the vet for us. I am kind of fond of this mutt.'

Mutt?

'Trouble!' Alain and Jo admonished together as Bebe appeared through the door from the hallway.

'Trouble, you are back.' She dropped down beside the dog and scratched him under his ears. Leaning his head into her hand, Trouble looked up at Alain, and Alain could have sworn Trouble was saying, "See? Someone truly appreciates me."

Bebe stood, walked over to the fridge and opened the door. 'Let me get out the meat Alice left for him. Ah, and here is the lasagne she asked to be heated for dinner.'

As Bebe pottered around the kitchen looking after Trouble and preparing a salad, Jo put the kettle on and busied herself making a pot of tea. With nothing else to do, Alain made himself comfortable beside Trouble and ran his hands though the dog's fur, not sure whether he was comforting the dog or himself.

Closing his eyes, he was enjoying a few minutes of calm when the sound of thundering footsteps came from upstairs, and he opened his eyes to a kick as Lee stumbled over his outstretched legs. Quickly recovering, and saving his tablet from the hitting floor, the boy exclaimed, 'Dude, do you have to sit right in the doorway?'

'What's the rush?' Bebe asked as she joined Jo at the table.

'Someone's attempted to assassinate David Cameron.'

'What?' Alain said, just as Bebe said, 'Who?'

'Bee, for someone who is very smart, sometimes I wonder where your head is at. David Cameron is the Prime Minister of Britain.'

'Oh.'

'Don't worry, Bebe. I didn't know who he was either. Lee, why would someone try to kill him?' Alain said from his seat on the floor.

'Brexit,' the others spoke in unison, which was kind of scary.

'And Brexit is ...?'

'David Cameron and his government called for a referendum on whether or not the United Kingdom should leave the European Union. It is all anyone is talking about. Both sides feel very strongly about leaving or staying, so the country is getting to vote on it,' Jo explained.

'Why would someone try to kill the Prime Minster though?' Bebe asked. 'His only sin is avoiding dealing with the issue by calling for a referendum.'

Panic and disruption at a critical time in the country's development. This must be Time Wreckers, as an attempt on the Prime Minister's life runs contrary to history. Trouble's head dropped back to his paws as if speaking the two sentences had tired him out.

'Disruption,' Alain said.

'Yes,' Bebe acknowledged. 'His death now would not only cause a lot of unrest, it would also bring other elected representatives to the forefront of the debate, whether they wanted it or not.'

'Dinner is ready,' Jo said as a buzzer sounded moments before the front door opened. 'Ah, that must be Alice. Alain, can you please go and call Barnaby so we can eat? Tomorrow's a big day, so an early night would benefit us all after last night's drama.'

13

PREPARATIONS

SITTING ON THE drooping bed with her arms leaning on her thighs, Izzy clenched her hands into fists to stop them from shaking. Taking some deep breaths, she attempted to calm her scrambled thoughts.

Standing, she paced around the small bedsit she rented above Gladys' shop. Thanks to the bed, chairs and side table in the room, the space available for her pacing was almost non-existent. A wry smile crossed her face. Thank goodness the bathroom in the shop and the small kitchenette downstairs meant she didn't have to squish anything else into her living space.

When she'd arrived in town and offered to do a few shifts in the shop in return for a place to live, she'd assumed the upstairs quarters were an actual flat. When she saw the room she almost backed out, but then she would have had to find another way to meet Tabitha and be invited to join the coven.

As she circumnavigated her sleeping quarters, her mind searched for solutions to her current problem. She didn't believe the Council would support the extreme measures Gavin and Tabitha had put in motion, but it was difficult to be certain about that in the current leadership vacuum.

During their last contact, her mentor had let slip the number of operations going on in this particular time had stretched their resources to the limit.

Even so, it was unusual for someone new to the team to be left to their own devices for so long.

Then again, lack of contact was a good thing. No doubt the Council would stop her working with Jo and the others, not only because of the prohibition on working with Time Guardians, but also because of her's and Jo's past.

Before she left for this mission, her mentor had expressly forbidden her from making contact directly with Jo, especially after the debacle Isolde caused at King Henry's coronation. But she had not been able to stay away. There would be a price to pay for spending time with Jo, let alone assisting the group in their plot to stop the spread of the bacteria Tabitha and Gavin created. Sighing, Izzy lay down on the narrow bed, hands clasped behind her head.

Should she attempt to contact the Council again and risk being pulled out of this time, or should she carry on with her own plans? As the tension of the day got the better of her, she drifted off to sleep.

She slept restlessly that night and woke early. She made her way downstairs, and got herself a cup of coffee and dressed while it cooled. With nothing left to do, she sat at the table and stared at her phone. In her heart of hearts, she knew the decision was already made—she would use any means necessary to stop Tabitha and Gavin.

Picking up the phone, she texted Jo.

ALAIN STUMBLED DOWNSTAIRS in the half-dark to the front door. As he started to open it, Jo pushed her way in.

'Why aren't you dressed? We need to get a move on. There's so much to be sorted before this evening.'

Shoving past him, Jo headed for the kitchen. The sounds of the kettle being put on filled the house as he shuffled after her.

'What time is it?' Alain pulled out a chair as he spoke.

'Six thirty already.' Jo took cups out of the cupboard and banged them on the table.

'Jo, the coven are not gathering until tonight.' Alain ran a hand through his hair, making it stand upon end.

'Izzy just texted me. She told me where they are meeting but not the actual place of the ceremony, so we will need to get together and try and figure as best we can where they are going.'

'Still, it is very early.' Alain yawned and stretched.

Jo sunk into a chair, almost as if the air had been punched out of her. 'Once I got the text, I couldn't sleep. I am full of energy and need to be doing something—anything.'

'Couldn't you do that something at your place?' Alain asked, barely able to keep his eyes open.

Trouble stretched himself out and wandered over to Jo. He nudged her hand with his head and sat, looking expectantly at her.

'My mum is on nights. She'll be home around seven and my moving around would keep her awake.'

'And perhaps you did not want her asking questions because you would tell her everything and then she would offer to help tonight? And you don't want her involved?' Alain suggested.

'She would have to change shifts and … well I'd just feel better if she wasn't involved in any way with Gavin.'

Jo's smile was wan as Trouble reached out a paw and dragged at Jo's hand.

'I think Trouble wants your attention.' Alain smiled.

After absent-mindedly looking down, Jo's face brightened when she saw the dog staring back at her, tail wagging in great sweeps across the floor.

'Wow, you look great this morning. The anaesthetic is mostly out of your system and you look—well, you look almost normal.' She smiled a sheepish smile. 'Of course, you can tell me yourself. How are you? Do you feel better?'

I am much better, and ravenous. Thank you for asking.

She stood and walked to the fridge, and pulled out some food for the dog. As she worked, she told him, 'Given our job tonight, I think it best you stick to resting today. Later on we may need your help, so we do not want to tire you out before then.'

As Jo placed the bowl of food in front of him, Trouble's tail wagged so much it turned full circles and he almost hit himself in the face with it.

The sound of something hitting the floor drifted down from upstairs.

'We must have woken the others.' Alain rose to make him and Jo some toast as he spoke.

As he placed their plates on the table, Bebe appeared, followed closely by Alice and Lee. Turning to her nephew, Alice said, 'Can you please go and call Barnaby? We need to plan out our day, and he should be here to help us.'

Muttering curses under his breath, Lee left the warmth to fetch the alchemist. When the two of them arrived, the kitchen was a bustle of activity,

and it was some time before anyone spoke.

'Jo, I know you are an early riser, but this is extremely early even for you. What's up?' Alice looked over the rim of her teacup at her assistant.

'Izzy texted me this morning. They are meeting at The Sir Walter Tyrell pub at nine thirty tonight, and they will go on to the actual site from there. We need to check out all the tourist spots within a thirty-minute-or-so drive from the pub to work out where they might be going.'

'Only thirty minutes?' Alice asked.

'Yep. Jo says they need to be in pace ready to cast when the moon reaches its zenith.'

'All the places?' Bebe grimaced. 'There could be hundreds. How are we going to cover all of them?'

'We can narrow it down, I think. We are looking for areas of high tourist activity even in winter, that are still within the forest, and are sheltered from the road,' Lee said.

'We should concentrate on sites with magical significance, so that cuts out a few of the more popular attractions,' Alice said.

While the others discussed how to frame their search, Alain was chuckling to himself.

Jo glared at him. 'I don't see what is so funny.'

'They named a pub after Tyrell, the man who killed King William Rufus. You must find that funny,' Alain said.

'They only think he killed William,' Jo said.

'No, he definitely shot the arrow that killed the king,' Alain told her.

'How do you know ... oh.' Jo's eyes grew wide.

'Yes, how do you know?' Bebe asked.

Deftly changing the subject, Alice explained, 'The Sir Walter Tyrell is quite appropriately named since it is not far from the Rufus Stone.'

'The Rufus Stone?' Alain searched his memory for a stone named after Willian Rufus.

'Yes. Centuries ago, the people erected a stone marker on the spot where William Rufus died,' Alice said.

'How close is the stone to the tavern?' Master Barwick asked, stroking his beard.

'Less than five minutes' drive,' Alice answered.

'Then we need not waste our day looking for the site of tonight's rite. What place in the New Forest will have stronger magic than the spot where

an anointed King of England spilled his blood?' Master Barwick delivered his verdict, then carried on eating as if the subject were closed.

'Are you sure? It is almost too obvious a place when Gavin and Tabitha are being so secretive.' Jo twiddled a knife in her hand as she spoke.

They are going to hold the rite at William Rufus' place of death. You and Alain need to convince them of this, Trouble spoke to Barwick.

Why don't you? Alain asked. *Bebe is the only one we haven't told that you are a Time Guardian and can speak. Would it not be easier for everyone if we just came clean and told her the truth?*

She is not yet ready. It would do her soul more damage than good if she knew. Trouble slumped back down on his bed, head on his paws, his soulful eyes regarding Alain.

'Alice, you know the New Forest. What do you think?' Alain asked.

'There are places in the forest that are great for magical spell casting, depending on the spell. Given that this one is going to spread an evil disease, I believe a place of death would provide the perfect energy. Barnaby is correct; they will likely go to the Rufus Stone site.' She held up her hand to prevent Jo from objecting. 'We could debate this for hours and discuss options like following one of the coven for confirmation, but we need to make a decision quickly so we can prepare. If you have a better idea, now is the time to speak.'

Jo opened her mouth as if to object, then closed it. 'It would be just like Tabitha to tell everyone they would be travelling to another site, then go just a little way down the road. Perhaps you are right.'

'So where will we set up to waylay Ruth?' Lee asked.

'If we look at a map we might get a better idea about that.' Alice stood and opened the bureau draw behind her. Rummaging around, she eventually found a tourist map for the New Forest. Opening it up, she placed it where they all could see. As she spoke, she traced the roads she talked about. 'Here is the stone, and here is the pub.' Alice pointed them out, and Lee reached behind her. After pulling a pen from the drawer, he circled the two points on the map.

'Everyone coming from Burley will take the A31 and turn up this lane to get to the meeting place. In fact, to go to The Sir Walter Tyrell they will pass the Rufus Stone car park.' Alice traced the route on the map with her finger.

'Ruth's youth support group is today,' Jo said. 'That means she'll be coming from Southampton.'

'How do you know that?' Lee capped the pen and placed it down on the table.

'Because she used to attend, nosey.' Bebe punched her brother on the arm.

'She often used to give me a lift home, so I think it is likely she will take the same route she used when dropping me off—the A336 through Netley Marsh, onto to the B3079 and B3078. The road goes on to Frogham, where Ruth lives, so it is the way she is most familiar with.'

'And that helps us how?' Alain's attempts to follow the road numbers on the map confused him, and he really couldn't understand how knowing her route would help them.

Lee smiled. 'Because, due to the lateness of the hour, Ruth will no doubt want to drive a familiar route. She will approach the pub from the other end of the lane off the B3079.' He pointed to the place on the map for emphasis. 'That means Bebe and I can set up our ruse around nine fifteen.'

'Ah, I see. If we wait in the car park by the Rufus Stone, and you and Bebe are at the other end of the road, and we are wrong about the stone being where they are heading, we will be perfectly positioned to find out which way they go from the tavern.' Alain grinned, feeling pleased with himself.

'Yes,' Lee said. 'Although we are almost certain they will be going to Rufus Stone, just in case they aren't, we need to be able to follow them and find out where they end up.'

'This all sounds fine, but what if someone else stops to help us?' Bebe managed to tease out the holes in a plan just as Barabal did, and Alain smiled.

'Good point,' Lee said. 'And it doesn't take long to change a flat tyre anyway.'

'Maybe if you hide the jack somewhere, that might buy you some time,' Jo said.

Bebe nodded. 'Good idea, Jo.'

To Alain's ears it was as though they spoke a foreign language, so he kept silent.

'We will need to make sure our car is well hidden,' Alice said. 'Tabitha and Gavin are already suspicious. We don't want to make them more so by telegraphing our presence, especially as Tabitha knows my car.'

'That reminds me. Gavin and Tabitha are wary of Izzy at the moment, so she is going to keep away from us today,' Jo told them.

'Then that makes it all the more important that we go about our day as if we suspect nothing untoward is happening,' Master Barwick said. 'We don't know who might be watching us, and after yesterday ...'

'You're right, Barnaby, and I am already late for work—must dash.' Alice rose as she spoke.

'Ah, just one more thing, Alice,' Master Barwick said. 'Your husband—have you a time for his arrival today? Does Jo's mother need to be alerted to be on standby?'

'No, no, I shall be fine. There was a flight due in this evening, which would have had him home about eight, but it was full and he couldn't get a seat. He won't be here until tomorrow morning now.'

'Excellent.' Master Barwick smiled. 'It looks like we are all set then.'

'I will leave you kids the keys on the dresser by the door so you two can drive to the station in Brockenhurst when you go to pick up the rental car,' Alice said. 'The rental place is about five minutes' walk from Southampton Central. Directions are on the dresser. Jo, don't forget your extra shift today to do the internet orders. And you can take me to the station at closing so I can pick up my car.'

'A whole day with nothing to do.' Lee sighed. 'How can we make it look like we are doing something?'

'I have an idea,' Bebe offered almost tentatively. 'We have to pick the car up in Southampton, and I am supposed to be looking for something to do next year ...' Rather than meeting Lee's eyes, Bebe followed her finger tracing the grain on the table.

'Come on, Bee. If you've something on your mind, just spit it out.'

'After we pick up the car, we could head to the main campus of the university and get some information on courses,' Bebe said.

Lee turned to his sister. 'On any one course in particular?'

'Maybe.' Bebe may have been coy with Lee, but she winked at Alain as she stood. 'I'll just go and get my things.'

Lee rose to follow Bebe out. 'Alain, are you coming with us?'

'No, I have something I have to do.'

Once the others had gone, Alain turned to Master Barwick. 'I have an idea for a Plan B for Ruth. Do you fancy helping me make a sleeping draught?'

ALAIN WAITED FOR the others to leave before rummaging in the kitchen for the things he needed to make his draught. In the fridge, he found some lettuce leaves, and the store cupboard yielded some vinegar, but Alice's pantry would not give up any of the other ingredients he needed.

'What a noise. I am sure they can hear you all the way in Southampton,' Bebe said.

Alain jumped at the sound of her voice and hit his head on the shelf. 'Ouch'

'What on earth are you looking for?'

'Opium, or poppies.'

The girl's eyes widened in surprise, and she took a step back. 'I didn't realise drugs were your thing.'

Alain frowned. 'What? ... No. You think I want opium for me? To get high?' He laughed. 'No, it's for a sleeping tonic.'

Still keeping her distance from him, Bebe moved to the opposite side of the table. 'A sleeping tonic? For whom?'

'Ruth. It's my Plan B.'

'Still, you can't use opium or poppies in it. They're illegal.'

Dwale was so readily available in his own time he had not even considered he might not be able to find all the ingredients. Suddenly, Master Barwick's job of trudging the lanes to find hemlock and henbane did not seem so bad.

'What exactly do you need opium for?' Bebe's tone was still wary.

'The opium makes the person sleepy, detached.'

'Oh, well there's codeine in Alice's medicine cabinet. That is a manmade substitute, and it is perfectly legal.'

'Mmm, it might work. Let's take a look.'

Bebe returned a few moments later, a white packet in her hand. Having read the ingredients on the back of the box, Alain decided they might still be able to make the brew. If he used the standard adult dose of the codeine-based drug, it should be enough. Maybe he would put an extra tablet in for good measure.

When Master Barwick returned, they would dry the henbane and hemlock in the oven. Once it was done they would grind it down. All he needed now was the agent to help the body absorb the tonic. As if reading his mind, Bebe said, 'Do you need anything else?'

'Just one more thing—sow's bile.'

'You're kidding, right?' Bebe's laughter was nervous, as if she were afraid he might not be.

'Um ... no. Actually, bile from a gall bladder helps the draught act more quickly. Obviously being from a female animal will make it stronger.'

'Yuck, this is going to be foul. You might need something to disguise the taste. How about star anise? I think I saw some in the cupboard.'

'Are you kidding? That would counteract the bile—that is, if I can find some.'

'What about spearmint?'

Alain considered this for a moment. 'Yes, that might improve the flavour and it would not affect how the tonic works.'

'Good, because I put some packets of dried leaves away in Alice's shop the other day. Actually, now that I think of it, I also saw some dried ox gall bladder. Could you use that for the bile thing?'

'It might do at a pinch. These ingredients are all a little different to the ones I normally use, so I'm not sure how well they will mix together.'

You should check with Master Barwick when he returns, but if all the ingredients are as you described, then it will work in a fashion. Perhaps I would err on the side of caution with the codeine though—maybe don't use that extra tablet you were planning on.

He had forgotten the dog sleeping in front of the Aga, and started at the sound of his voice.

Thanks.

'Alain, are you listening to me?'

'Huh?'

'I said Lee and I are off in a minute if you want a lift?' Bebe asked.

'Ah, no, I should be fine walking.'

Bundled in his warm jacket, Alain trudged up the road towards the Main Street and Alice's shop for the final ingredient for his tonic. As the icy wind slipped through his jacket, he wished he had taken Bebe up on the offer. Checking for traffic, he crossed the road and entered Alice's store. She was standing behind the counter reading a book when he entered.

'Hi Alain. What can I do for you?'

'Do you stock dried spearmint and perhaps some dried sow or ox gall bladder?'

'Ah, you are making a tonic then,' she said as she emerged from behind the counter and headed towards the back room, then returned with two packets for him.

'Here you are. The gall bladder is powdered, so I would use about half of the normal amount. It does dissolve better this way though.'

Alice popped them in a bag and was handing them over when the door opened, and a cool rush of air entered the shop.

'Good morning, Alice.'

As the customer spoke, Alice dropped the bag on the counter. 'Tabitha.'

'Ah, hello boy. Did you ever find your missing dog?'

Surprised Tabitha recognised him, Alain went on the defensive. He was unsure what she had managed to piece together about his involvement in recent events—like, for instance, did she know it was his dog her friend had

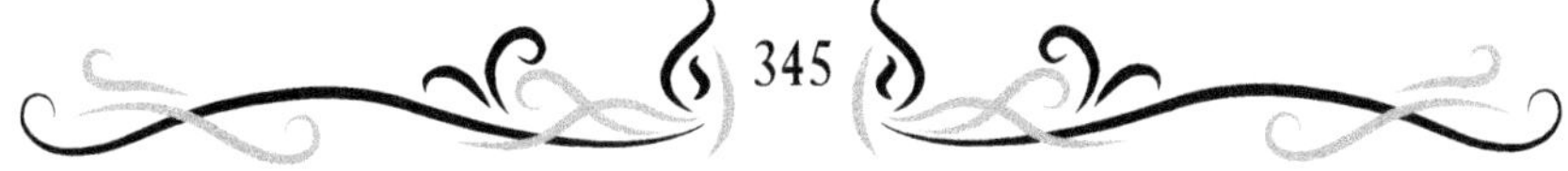

almost killed?

He masked his anger as he replied. 'Thank you, yes I did.'

'Not too busy today I see, Alice.'

'Not in the shop, but we are coming up to Christmas and internet sales are crazy. Jo is coming in later to help me with those so I can get them to the post office for last pickup.' Alice's tart tone did not invite further conversation, but Tabitha ignored it.

'Nice to find our local businesses doing well even though foot traffic is generally quiet this time of year.' Tabitha picked up a deck of tarot cards from the counter display and turned them over in her hand. 'I suspect after that you will be able to close early.'

Alice frowned at Tabitha as the woman replaced the cards. 'What a nice thought, but some new stock arrived yesterday and it won't process itself. Just because there are no customers does not mean I have no work to do.'

Tabitha opened her mouth to continue the conversation as the door opened again, and Jo entered bearing two takeaway cups of coffee. On seeing who was in the shop, she stopped. Her eyes widened like a deer caught in the headlights. She looked from Alice to Tabitha.

'Come in, girl. You're letting out all the warm air.'

Alice's fingers tensed into a fist as the other woman ordered about her staff in her shop, but she bit her tongue. 'Can I do something for you, Tabitha? Only I must be getting on with those orders.'

'Well, yes, you can. I'm looking for some purified rock salt. I need rather a lot—around ten packets.'

Alain held his breath, hoping Alice would not refuse to sell her the salt. That would only make Tabitha suspicious, and if Alice didn't sell her the ingredients she had plenty of time to drive to Southampton and buy her supplies before this evening.

'Of course. Let me check my stock. Do you need it for anything in particular?' Alice said as she moved from behind the counter.

Tabitha's laugh grated as she assured Alice she was working on a new spell. 'It's not quite perfect yet, so I want enough on hand to cover any mistakes.' She followed Alice into the back room.

Jo poked her tongue out at Tabitha's back as she walked past, and said under her breath, 'How can Alice be so pleasant to her?' She placed the coffees on the counter. 'Sorry, Alain. I didn't know you were going to be here so I didn't get you one.'

'That's okay. I should be getting back soon anyway.'

'You have plans for today?' Tabitha said, coming around the corner laden with bags of rock salt. 'Anything interesting? Perhaps taking in some of our local sites?' Tabitha's eyebrows raised in query.

'Um, no ... not really. It's just ...'

'... his uncle will wonder where he is,' Alice finished for him. 'Barnaby is not well today, and Alain just popped in for some ingredients for a tisane.'

'Oh, I am sorry to hear that,' Tabitha said. 'That reminds me, Alice. Have you heard anything about Jenna's Pepe?'

'He died,' Jo said bluntly.

Tabitha's face blanched, and her voice lost some of its false friendliness when she spoke 'Oh, I am sorry to hear that. I thought he was on the road to recovery.'

'He was, then he took a turn for the worse. The poor old boy just had no fight left in him and ...' Jo glared at Tabitha.

The other woman pulled herself upright and her face became impassive as she looked down her nose at Alice. 'I will pay for the salt on Visa,' she said as she turned away from Jo and put the bags she carried on the counter.

' … and it's your fault,' Jo finished.

Alain held his breath, waiting for Tabitha to explode. However, she ignored Jo's words, finished paying for her goods, then packed her bag with controlled, deliberate movements. As she reached the door she turned slowly and said, 'You should be very careful flinging around accusations like that Josephine Brown. You could land yourself in very deep trouble—trouble there is no way out of.'

Before anyone could react, she was gone.

14

OPERATION DIVERSION

LEE BENT OVER the tyre and attached the deflator tool he'd purchased from the hardware store in Southampton. The salesman had said the process was quick, but it seemed to him it was taking forever. A noise in the bushes beside the road caused Bebe to turn, redirecting the light from her phone.

'Bebe!'

'What?'

'Pay attention. This is England, not Australia—there's nothing in the bushes that will hurt us. I need the light over this way so I can see what I am doing.'

'Lee, it doesn't need to be completely flat—just flat enough to be unsafe to drive on. You do realise that, don't you?'

'Uh? No, I didn't think of that.' He looked down at the tyre. Was it deflated enough to be a hazard? 'What do you think?'

Bebe kicked the tyre and her trainer toe sunk into the rubber. 'Yeah, that's enough.'

Lee took the tool off and stood, stretching his back as he did. 'All right, where's the bag?'

Bebe handed it to him and he placed the deflator tool inside. After walking around the back, he opened the boot and removed the jack. The cheap gym bag sagged as he carefully placed it in. Zipping the bag up, he walked to the edge of the road and shoved it behind a tree, covering it in debris from the forest floor so it could not be easily seen.

'How are we going to remember where it is?' Bebe asked.

Lee looked around, found a branch and leaned it against the trunk. Wedging it securely, he turned around, dusting the dirt off his hands.

'Good. Can we get set up now? It is gone quarter past.' Bebe tapped her foot.

'Gosh, you are impatient.'

'Time is ticking and we need to be ready for when Ruth arrives.' Bebe was in bossy mode. Being scared did that to her. Choosing not to respond, Lee eased himself behind the wheel and waited while she walked around the car to the passenger seat. Once they clicked on their seat belts, Lee started the engine and eased the car forwards a little before quickly accelerating and turning the wheel to make it appear he had lost control and ended up half in the shallow ditch and partway across the road, taking care to ensure there was not enough room for another car to drive around them.

'Right, showtime,' Bebe announced.

Opening the door, she took some cases out of the back seat and flung them on the ground behind the car, creating more of an obstruction. In the meantime, Lee opened the boot and proceeded to take out the spare tyre. He had just wrestled it to the ground when car lights swung along the road.

'Here we go—showtime,' he said, mimicking Bebe as he mimed looking for the car jack.

As the lights hit them, Bebe leaned against the rental car and averted her face. Lee shaded his own eyes from the glare and tensed as the person pulled over, hopefully to help.

'Dammit,' Lee said under his breath. 'The driver is a male.'

'Need a hand?' The man asked as he got out of his car. His tone was clipped, and his accent sounded like the ones they heard on BBC news bulletins.

'Um …' Lee couldn't think what to say. Fortunately, Bebe took over.

'We just picked up this rental today, and I can't believe it—it's got a flat tyre. And what's worse, we can't find the jack to change it. Do you keep it somewhere different over here?'

'I don't believe so. Here, let me look.' The man walked purposefully towards them.

Lee tensed, wary of letting a strange man help them out. But out of the glare of the headlights, the man appeared less threatening. He was medium height

and with a slight build. The silver hair cut close to his head placed him perhaps in his fifties. His twinkling blue eyes were friendly enough so Lee relaxed.

'These rental companies charge the earth and they don't care for their vehicles,' the man said as he leaned over to search the boot.

As he rummaged around, another set of car lights turned down the road, lighting his view.

'Yep, you definitely are short one jack. I'll just get mine, and we'll have you on your way in a jiffy.'

The second car stopped and a tall woman with wild curly hair half-stepped out. Lee relaxed a little, she was exactly as Jo described her.

'What's the hold up?' Ruth's impatience gave her voice a sharpness in the evening air.

'Rental car company stiffed these poor kids. Gave them a car with no jack and a flat tyre,' the man answered on their behalf.

'Will it take long to change it, do you think? I am running late for a meeting.'

Lee glanced at his watch. It was nine twenty-five. They only needed to delay Ruth for another fifteen or twenty minutes for their plan to work, but he estimated the job would take way less than that.

'Sorry, I lost control on the narrow road. I don't know whether I punctured it when I spun, or whether I lost control because the tyre was flat.' Lee's apology was not only genuinely polite, but also a way of playing for time. While they talked, tyre-changing activities stopped.

'And I guess you are not used to these narrow lanes.' Ruth's voice was a little more sympathetic. 'Do I detect an Australian accent?'

'Yes, ma'am,' Lee said. 'And you are right. Our roads at home are nothing like this. If we were there you'd be able to whizz past us no problem.'

The man returned with his jack. 'Is there a wheel brace in the boot? I didn't think to grab mine.'

Lee took his time in the boot, rummaging around, and stood with the tool in his hand. 'At least they left us with something,' he declared.

Lee and their rescuer placed the jack under the car and began the process of changing the tire. Out of the corner of his eye, he watched Bebe move around the front of their vehicle. In the meantime, Ruth returned to her car and turned on the headlights. Initially, Lee thought she was doing it to help them; instead, she walked around the rental car, using the light to work out if there was any way she could get past.

She drove a four-door hatchback, and from where he crouched, he guessed

she could just about squeeze by them if she wasn't too worried about scratches to her paintwork from the bushes on the other side of the lane.

His car was now off the ground, and Lee attached the wheel brace, making a show of attempting to loosen the first nut. At the same time, he looked over to Ruth's car. It was well tended to, and he hoped she would not want to risk damaging it.

'Would you like me to give it a go?'

Lee had almost forgotten about the man who was helping him. He leaned over, clearly thinking he could do a better job of removing the wheel.

'No, it is all right. Dad insisted we learn how to do these things ourselves. It is just the initial loosening that is taking time.' He gave a good heave and the first bolt popped loose. 'See? This one's done.'

Three more to go, he thought to himself. He checked his watch; it had only counted down ten minutes. This would be close, and they were relying on Tabitha getting frustrated with Ruth's delay and leave without her if she were late. What if she didn't?

While he worked on the second nut, he listened as Bebe and Ruth discussed the possibility of getting her car by them. He could see Bebe fingering the vial Alain gave her in her pocket as she tried to discourage the woman from attempting the manoeuvre.

'We won't be long. I am sure whoever you are meeting with will understand why you are late,' Bebe said, using her most reassuring tone.

'That's just it—I'm sure they won't understand in the least.' Ruth's voice sounded fearful and her pacing was becoming more agitated. 'I think I will walk.' She turned on her heel and headed back to her car.

'Are you sure that's wise?' Bebe followed her. 'I mean, it is pretty dark. Other cars on the lane may not see you. Do you have a torch or something?'

Ruth got into the driver's seat, backed her car over to the side of the road and turned off the lights. Opening the rear door, she removed a leather backpack and slung it over her shoulder before locking her car.

'I can use the one on my phone.' Taking her phone out of her pocket, she turned the light on. 'Why tonight of all nights?' She switched it off. 'Less than twenty percent left on my battery. It can only be ten or fifteen minutes' walk up the road and the traffic down here is pretty light mid-week. I should be fine.'

'Wait a moment,' Bebe said. 'Lee, I am going to use my phone to help this lady to her meeting. It is the least I can do after we held her up. Can you pick me up after you've changed the tyre?'

'Fine,' Lee said, loosening the third nut. 'We should only be another ten minutes though. Wouldn't it be quicker, and safer, to wait?'

Ruth's phone pinged and her eyes went to the screen. 'No, I don't think that is the safer option at all,' she said as she typed something and started walking.

Bebe grabbed a bottle of water out of the car, drunk some until about a quarter remained, added the contents of Alain's vial of sleeping drought, and jogged off after Ruth.

Knowing it was now up to Bebe, Lee sped up changing the tyre so he could catch her sooner rather than later.

IN MOMENTS, BEBE caught Ruth up and turned on her phone light so they could see where they were going.

'I am Bebe, by the way. Sorry we put you out. We always thought England was so built up we could never get into any trouble, but here we are, caught out on our first day of touring round.'

'I am Ruth. And I am sorry, but I think you should go back to your brother. It's not far to the pub, and I really don't need the light or the company.'

'But I feel so bad that we put you out. Please let me try and help you.'

'It is one of those things—you need not feel guilty. And I'm sorry, but I can't chit-chat—I have to get to this meeting.' Ruth's tone was dismissive as she stalked ahead.

'I don't want to be nosy, but are you sure you really want to get to where you're going? I mean, I don't know you or anything, but you sound scared.'

Ruth stopped mid-stride and turned to look at Bebe, a frown furrowing her brow. 'Who are you and who told you about us?'

I guess we will find out if all those times I twisted the truth to my own benefit will come in handy now. Bebe smiled her most open smile and calmed the butterflies in her stomach before she spoke. 'As I said, I am Bebe, and I am spending some time in England with my brother before our parents join us here for Christmas. He is off to university in the new year, and I guess this will be the last holiday we spend together for a while.'

Ruth relaxed, seeming to take Bebe at face value. She asked, 'And you? What are you doing next year?'

'I am hoping to start university in Southampton. I took a tour today. My application is completed and ready to post in; I just need to talk it through

with my mum and dad when they arrive here. Well, that and I need to find some work for the next six months, and some work experience for my course to ensure I can get entry.'

'Oh, and what course are you looking at doing?'

'A degree in psychology, with a major in youth issues,' Bebe said

'How strange. I work in that field. Maybe our meeting tonight is not such a coincidence. Perhaps the fates brought us together.' Ruth reached into her bag and pulled out a card. 'When you are settled somewhere, give me a call. I may be able to arrange work experience for you.'

Bebe took the offered business card, certain it was a waste of time because once Ruth found out about their delaying tactics she would want nothing to do with Bebe. Then again, perhaps they had delayed Ruth for long enough for the coven to have left without her, and she would be so relieved at having missed the casting she would forgive them.

As the thought entered her head, Ruth's phone rang. She turned away to answer it, but Bebe strained to overhear her side of the conversation.

'As I said, there was a car blocking the road ... I am walking up the lane now ... All right, I will run if that is what you need me to do. I mean, for goodness sake, I am only fifteen minutes—twenty minutes late.'

Ruth removed the phone from her ear, punched at the screen with her index finger, then shoved the phone into the pocket of her bag. Turning back to Bebe, she said, 'Sorry. Look, I have to rush. You should head back to your brother. The people I am meeting may not take kindly to your presence.'

Bebe caught the fear in Ruth's voice and felt sorry for the woman. 'If it is dangerous, please don't go.'

'Thank you for your concern.'

Bebe made a snap decision. Stopping Ruth was more important than her future. Her gut told her the woman did not want to be involved in tonight's activities, and she wanted to keep her out of them if she could. Holding out her water bottle to Ruth, she said, 'Here—you may need this more than me. It is water with a little tonic a friend makes for me. It calms my nerves and gives me focus.'

'Thank you, but I am fine.'

Bebe would not give in that easily; the others were relying on her. Playing on Ruth's need to keep her safe, she said, 'Please. I will feel better returning to my brother if you drink it. It is only herbs and the like. Look, I'll take a sip to show you it's okay.' She opened the bottle and took a small mouthful before handing it to Ruth.

'If I drink this, you will go back to your bother?' She frowned and looked skeptically at the bottle.

Bebe nodded. Ruth took the bottle from her hand and downed the liquid, her face screwing up at the bitter aftertaste. 'Uh, what was in that? No, don't tell me. I don't want to know. Now go back to your brother. And don't forget to give me a call when you're settled.'

Bebe promised and walked back towards Lee. As she did, the sound of a car engine coming from the other direction filled the night. Looking over her shoulder, she saw red taillights speeding down the road. The car stopped by Ruth and a door opened.

'Get in.'

Ruth clambered into the back and Bebe sighed as the car sped off—there was nothing more she could do.

WITH TIME TO kill before the meeting, Izzy headed to the pub. She had ordered a bar meal and a pint and taken herself off to a seat by the fire. A few locals had come and gone, and she'd spent a pleasant evening until it was time to leave. With great reluctance, she'd pulled herself out of the chair, paid her bill and walked the couple of blocks to her car.

As she drove past the turn-off to the Rufus Stone, Izzy glanced into the car park but was unable to see much of the area. Although she knew the others would keep a low profile, she felt nervous not knowing for certain if they were there.

Her eyes drifted to the clock on the dashboard. It glowed 9:35 in the darkness. Her tardiness demonstrated her doubts about attending tonight's meeting, and she still had no idea how she was going to get out of taking part in the casting. She let out a long sigh when, moments later, she pulled into the car park of The Sir Walter Tyrell.

Tabitha accosted her before her door was even closed. The woman grabbed her arm and almost dragged her away from the vehicle. Izzy stumbled, and Tabitha's grip tightened.

'You're late. Can none of you keep proper time?' Tabitha said as Izzy wrenched her arm back and returned to the car to gather the rest of her things.

Another vehicle pulled up beside them. Through her car's passenger window, she caught Beth emerging, and the woman sent her a wry smile before locking her vehicle. It seemed Izzy was not the only one who didn't

want to be here. Surreptitiously, she searched for Ruth's car, and heaved a sigh of relief when it wasn't there.

'Come on, the two of you. We're over here.' An exasperated Tabitha herded them towards a seven-seater van. It wasn't her normal car; she must have rented it for the night.

Gladys, Mona and Rosalind waited inside. Izzy glanced around, searching for Gavin. Through the windows of the rental she found a similar-sized vehicle parked next door. The American sat behind the wheel. Six burly men who looked as though they would not take any nonsense filled the rest of the seats.

'Ah, you spotted out security detail.' Tabitha almost purred. 'Gavin thought it would be a good idea for them to come—just in case.'

'Just in case of what?' Izzy's stomach tensed with nerves, and she thought she might throw up.

'Interruptions.'

Goddess, Izzy thought. We did not plan for this. I need to tell the others.

Reaching into her bag, her fingers searched for her mobile phone. As she pulled it out, Tabitha held out her hand.

'Thank you—you just reminded me. I am taking care of all phones until after the casting. We don't want anyone interrupting us at a critical time.'

Izzy handed over her device, and Tabitha popped it into her bag before turning to the others and asking for theirs. Izzy slumped in her seat.

'Agnes, where is Ruth?' Izzy whispered.

'Someone broke down on the road and she can't get past. Tabitha is beside herself.'

They waited, and Izzy glanced at her watch. Almost ten and Ruth was still absent. Maybe this would not go ahead tonight after all.

A car door slammed, and moments later Izzy started as someone thumped the side of the vehicle. Tabitha got out and followed Gavin a few steps away, no doubt so they wouldn't be overheard. Gavin's head dropped down to Tabitha's as they spoke.

The conversation started out cordially, but Tabitha's lips began to tighten as Gavin interspersed his words with sharp gestures. An agitated Tabitha pulled a phone out of her pocket and stabbed her fingers at the screen.

She spoke briskly to whomever she called, and returned the phone to her pocket. Under the car park light's, Tabitha's face turned angry. She exchanged a few words with Gavin and he growled something in return before stalking away. Walking back to the car, Tabitha opened the driver's side door and

jumped in.

'Make sure you are belted up,' she ordered. As she turned the key in the ignition her hands were shaking, whether in anger or fear Izzy had no way of knowing. The car started and lurched away at speed towards the car park exit.

As they turned towards the Rufus Stone, Izzy released the breath she had been holding. Obviously Lee and Bebe had managed to waylay Ruth; they would be one person less.

Her victory was short-lived.

Tabitha was not a great driver at the best of times, and driving backwards down an unlit country lane in the dead of night could in no way be described as the best of times.

'Tabitha, what are you doing? You'll get us all killed,' Mona squeaked.

'Ruth is behind us, our destination is in front, and I can't turn this blasted car around on this narrow lane. Now shut up and let me concentrate.'

Along with her companions, Izzy grabbed whatever she was able to and held on for dear life. It was a good thing they did because moments later, Tabitha brought the car to an abrupt stop, almost giving everyone whiplash.

'Open the door.' This was no polite request; it was a command.

Izzy leaned over the seat and slid the door open, letting a rush of cold air into the warm interior as she did. A startled Ruth peered inside the vehicle, giving each of them a onceover as if trying to work out who they were.

'Get in,' Tabitha spat at the woman. 'Don't make us any later than we are.'

'Don't worry. We all arrived a little tardy tonight,' Izzy whispered as she helped the rather dazed woman into the car.

As they drove off, Ruth's eyes glazed over and she lay down on the seat. Within moments she was quietly snoring.

15

THE SPELL IS CAST

ALAIN AND THE others ducked down low as headlights swept the car park at the Rufus Stone. Popping his head above the seat in front, he watched as the vehicle pulled up under one of the security lights. The driver got out and checked the surrounding area.

'Looks as though we guessed correctly; they are going to use the Rufus Stone's power to augment their spell,' Master Barwick said.

'Phew. I wasn't looking forward to following them all over the New Forest,' Alice said.

'It is as we thought. Gavin is here directing things,' Alain informed the others. 'No, wait a minute.'

He peered through the windscreen into the darkness. The other passengers appeared more heavyset than a group of women would be. Alain sucked in a breath as the doors opened, and a group of large, burly men spilled out.

'Oh no. We didn't plan for that,' he said.

Trouble placed his paws on the front seat beside him to get a better look at the group taking position around the perimeter of the park.

Looks like he has brought some hired muscle along, the dog said.

As the men spread out with almost military precision, Alan silently

congratulated Alice on having the forethought to hide the car in the trees. After parking, they had placed a couple of loose branches over the windshield just to be sure the car couldn't be seen from the car park.

'What do we do now?' Alice asked. 'We cannot take them on as well as the coven, but nor can we let the ceremony go ahead.'

'The coven is not here yet,' Master Barwick said. 'Perhaps we should just wait and see what happens before we decide our next move.'

As he spoke, another car pulled into the almost deserted car park, coming to a stop beside the first vehicle. Moments later, the coven bundled out and huddled in a nervous group, glancing wearily at their protectors.

'I spoke too soon,' Master Barwick said.

'Oh no,' Alice wailed. 'Ruth is with them. Their full coven is here.'

'Wait a moment. She is leaning heavily on Izzy and is none too steady on her feet. Perhaps she ingested some of my dwale,' Alain said. 'It will be a while before she is able to help them. That gives us a little time to plan.'

Tabitha handed out baskets to the other witches. Ruth dropped hers, and in her attempt to pick it up almost fell face first on the ground. Her lips pursed and her brow drawn into a frown, Tabitha grabbed and wrapped Ruth's hand's around the handle before letting go.

'We use similar baskets to carry our mobile altars,' Alice said. 'It looks as though the others will cast the spell while she supervises.'

'But Izzy can't,' Alain said. 'She is not allowed to act directly.'

'She will find a way around it.' Master Barwick's confidence in Izzy being able to do what she needed to calmed Alain.

As the coven organised themselves, the hired muscle continued moving around checking their surroundings. One stopped almost in front of the car, his back to them. Alain was sure he saw a bulge in the men's jackets as he passed in front of them.

'I am not sure we can do this,' he said to the others. 'I think they may be carrying weapons of some sort—this has all gotten so much more dangerous.'

'I believe at least one of them is carrying a gun—a handheld weapon that fires projectiles.' Alice added and looked at Alain and Master Barwick. 'Perhaps we should call in the police,' Alice said. 'We can't tell them the truth about what is going on, but if we report strange men in the area almost certainly carrying weapons, I'm sure they'll come.'

That is a very good option, Trouble said.

'And that will meet our objective here?' Master Barwick said.

No, I did not say that. In fact, we are at one of those points in time where the future is murky. I cannot make out the outcome of any particular course of action.

'I think we should stick with our original plan. If it fails we can always call the police as a last resort.' Until that moment, Jo had been silent. 'Our best bet is still to get to the stone before them and protect the area, right?'

'You are correct. And they are almost ready to go, so we'd best move.' Alain made a grab for the door handle.

'Wait,' Alice said before he could open it. 'When we open the doors, the central light will come on. We aren't camouflaged enough to hide that.'

Reaching up above them, she fiddled with something. Moments later, she held up a bulb. 'Now we should be okay. Open the doors away from the car park. Do not bother with shutting them; just push them to.'

'You are quite good at this.' Jo voiced her admiration.

'The product of a misspent youth.' Alice chuckled.

Everyone remain alert, Trouble warned them. *Bebe and Lee haven't made it here yet, and I don't see them being able to sneak through that ring of guards. That means we have no lookouts.*

'All right? Let's do this.' Jo reached for her door handle and opened it as quietly as she could. Still, the small snick it made echoed through the night and they held a collective breath as the closest guard peered around, as if searching for the source of the sound. A few seconds later, his stance relaxed, and so did they.

Jo slipped through the opening, followed by Trouble. Alain reached into the seat well and passed out five bags before sliding over the back seat and joining her outside. Master Barwick and Alice appeared to be whispering. Alice reached down, and Master Barwick disappeared from sight. Next thing, Alain saw his master's butt raised in the air as he crawled up the passenger seat and over to the back of the car.

After the alchemist's awkward exit, Alice reached over and restored his seat before disappearing from view herself. Her departure from the car was even more awkward than his master's, and Alain wondered if it was less noisy than opening a second door. However, frequent checks of the guards told him the babbling voices of the women in the car park more than drowned out any noises they made.

Just as he thought they had managed their escape from the car undetected, Alice lost her footing, pushing the door open and rolling onto the ground.

The guard's head swivelled, and he reached under his jacket. They all

froze, unsure whether to run or hide. Before they could decide, lights illuminated the car park, and the guard looked towards the entrance.

The car stopped at the beginning of the driveway, then obviously thought better of continuing, and backed away.

Another guard ambled over and sniggered, 'Bet they thought this was a good place to make out or smoke up. We ruined their plans by being here.' They both laughed as the original guard moved back towards the cars.

They waited until the new guard had taken a wide-legged stance, back towards them, before moving as quietly as they were able through the woods. Even so, the debris of the forest floor crunched beneath their feet and Alain's heart leapt into his mouth at the noise.

Don't worry. I cast a spell to mute the sound, Trouble sent.

And you couldn't have used that before now? Alain asked in frustration, his ankle twinging as he nearly missed a step.

I cannot influence man-made objects—only nature. Trouble sent, his tone suggesting Alain should have known this fact.

'All right, ladies, let's get moving.' Tabitha's voice rang out in the night.

Oh no, their route is shorter than ours—they will beat us to the spell site, Trouble sent.

'What shall we …?' The sound of another car pulling into the car park muffled Jo's words.

A door opened and a new voice said, 'Why hello, Tabitha. I didn't expect to find you here.'

'Donald?' Alice gripped Master Barwick's arm, halting his progress. 'What is he doing here?'

I don't know, but he has provided a diversion. Come on, let's go, Trouble sent.

'But ...'

Jo took Alice's arm. 'At the moment, they haven't discovered our presence. We'll only make it worse if we go to his rescue. Let's hurry and do this, then we can make sure Donald is okay.'

Jo led Alice forward, and the older women moved with them, but kept glancing back over her shoulder long after they couldn't hear the conversation in the car park. She relaxed a little when she heard the sound of a car engine, and Alain hoped that it signalled Donald's departure.

In less than ten minutes of creeping through the forest they found the Rufus Stone. Alain surveyed the clearing as Jo assessed the best places for them to position themselves to form the pentagram needed to increase the spell's intensity. They had to be able to see each other so they could cast the

spell in concert, but remain hidden from the coven.

'Do not forget, the spell must be said in Latin for depth, followed by English to tether it to the here and now,' Alain said as he handed out the pre-made altars along with copies of the words to speak. 'Jo, don't forget to flash us with your phone light when we are to begin.'

'Yes,' the girl said. 'All right, Trouble, you stay here by the roadway and save your energy for the spell. Alain will be directly across from you in those bushes over there. Master Barwick, as the strongest of us, I will put you at the point of the pentagram by that tree. Alice, you and I will be the two lower points, behind those two bushes.'

Having been assigned their positions, they dispersed to set up their altars. Placing the candle in the middle, Alain waited for Jo to give the first signal before lighting it, moving his body into position between the clearing and the flame. Moments later he caught sight of the second flash—time to recite the spell in Latin.

IGNE IGNIS EFFULGENS

Ego autem in eaque lucerna lumen est

Sequelae flammae gramina pastus, incultisque rubens pendebit

Alain lit a bunch of dried hawthorn in the candle's flame, and recited the last line of the spell.

Stringesque tunicam ex terra ignis praesidio

As he readied himself for the signal to begin the English version, the sound of gravel crunching disturbed the night. He could just make out figures entering the park surrounding the sacred stone. Torchlight scanned the area, before falling on the lone dog standing by the edge of the road.

'Are we to be forever plagued by dogs?' He heard Gavin exclaim as he handed the torch to Tabitha.

Strangely, Trouble moved forward to meet him, drawing the coven's attention to him and away from his altar. The eco-terrorist reached down to grab hold of his collar with one hand while he reached for his belt with the other. Alain tensed, preparing to go and help his friend should Gavin do him any further harm.

No, we must finish the spell in English, otherwise it will not be tied to the present, the dog sent.

There are only four of us left; it will not be strong enough, said Master Barwick.

We can only do what we can. I will count us in because a light will be too obvious now. Ready? Three, two, one.

As Gavin led Trouble to the tree by the stone, Tabitha began directing the witches into position. One of the guards escorted each of the woman to their assigned area.

Alain turned his full attention to the spell as he needed to finish before the other coven came too close. Because he had to speak in modern English he had written the words out phonetically to ensure he didn't make any mistakes.

Fire hot, fire bright,
I cast this spell to the candle's light
Threads of flame, fed on briar,
Weave a protection cloak made of earth's fire

As he stopped to burn the hawthorn, he heard the crunch of leaves nearby. If he burned the twig anyone close by would smell it, but if he did not the spell would not be complete. He had no option—he set the hawthorn in the correct place, finished the incantation and snuffed the candle. He took a moment to send his own silent prayer to the goddess. *Goddess, please look favourably on our work and strengthen the casting.*

Opening his eyes, he waited for a sign that he'd been spotted, but nothing happened. As his eyes adjusted, he caught sight of a member of the coven about five paces to the right of him setting up her altar. She seemed oblivious to everything else around her. Luckily for Alain, the man who guarded her directed his attention towards Gavin and Tabitha.

Alain swivelled his head for a better view of the clearing around the Rufus Stone. Gavin stood by the marker, the dog beside him held in place by the make-shift lead the eco-terrorist had fashioned from his belt.

On the other side of the stone stood one of the muscle men, and beside him, Tabitha directed her witches. Across from him he caught sight of Izzy setting up her altar near Trouble's workings. In the darkness, he could not make out the others from the coven, nor those from his own group.

As he waited, his legs began to cramp. Taking a deep breath, he tried to relax. How long would it be before they finished? He hoped it was not long, because he his legs were beginning to cramp.

'Are we ready?' Gavin asked, clearly no longer worried about keeping up the pretence that Tabitha was in charge. 'All right, begin your cast.'

As the woman in front of him began incanting her spell Alain's stomach

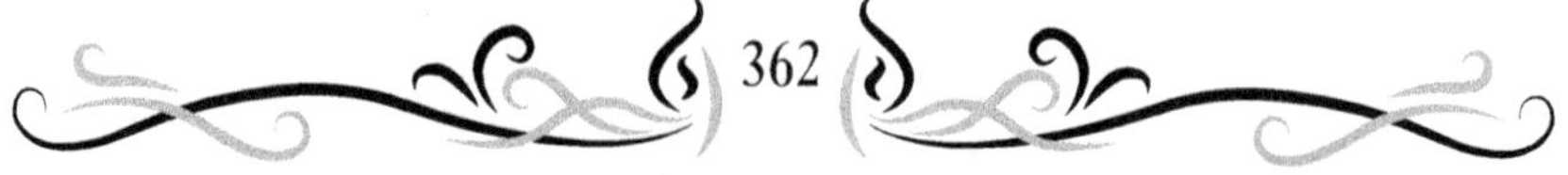

sank. Without a fifth practitioner, their own casting would not be likely to counter the coven's spell. He stifled a groan as his muscle cramped again, brushing a branch with his arm, and the guard turned towards the noise. As he tensed to run, the air around him changed. It became thick and heavy, like a blanket had fallen over the area.

The witch in front of him stopped mid-cast. The guard turned and nudged her with his gun. 'Keep going.' The poor women trembled and almost dropped the vial she held. Taking a deep breath, she carried on.

After finishing her spell, she stood and looked around as if waiting for the others to complete their tasks. Soon, all five witches stood and looked towards Gavin.

'Shall I release it now?' He turned to Tabitha, holding a vial aloft.

Tabitha stepped from the shadows. 'There is no point; something is blocking us. Our spell has fizzled like a flame with no air.'

'Did you all cast?' Gavin glared at the witches, and they in turn would not meet his gaze.

'Check the altars,' he ordered his men.

'Over here. This one has two altars.' A guard held Izzy by the arm and hauled her into the centre of the clearing.

'Traitor,' Tabitha spat at the girl.

Izzy raised her head, as if daring Tabitha to do her worst.

Two altars? Had Izzy picked up Trouble's spell and finished the cast using his altar? Alain smiled. By casting both spells she had kept her actions in balance, and by doing theirs first she'd ensured their success rather than Tabitha's.

She had helped them and he could not let anything happen to her. Preparing himself to leap to her defence, he made to move as a hand clamped down on his arm.

'Look what we have here.' Teeth gleamed in the dark as the guard grinned menacingly, pulling Alain to his feet.

Within seconds, he found himself stumbling as the man pushed him into the centre of the clearing. Everyone waited while the guards searched the entire area. Soon Jo joined Alain, along with Master Barwick and Alice. Rather than cowering in the ring of armed guards, Alice stepped forward and confronted her nemesis.

'You are too late. Your evil spell will not work here now. We have seen to that,' she said.

Tabitha raised her arm and slapped Alice hard enough for the woman's head

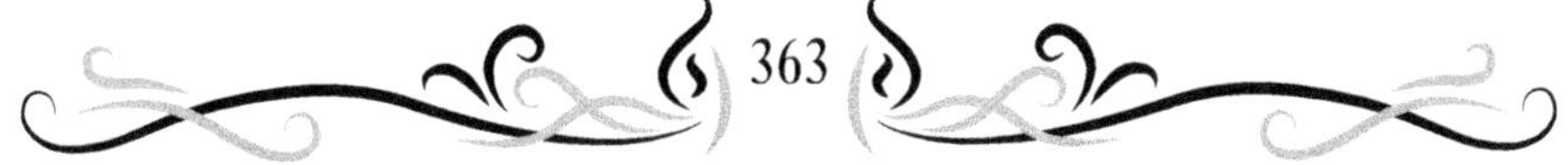

to snap back. 'How dare you,' she snarled. 'Your actions have doomed the forest—doomed it to years of overdevelopment.' Turning to Gavin, she nodded.

He stepped forward, holding the vial aloft. 'The spell might not work, but the bacteria will still spread without it. While saving others you have condemned yourselves to meet their fate.'

'You can infect us, and we may well die, but your bacteria will not infect others who come here,' Izzy boasted.

Gavin laughed. 'Your antics have merely delayed the inevitable. Tabitha and I will make more. There is another full moon in a month, but by then you will all be gone.'

Izzy opened her mouth, but no words came out. A guard shuffled uneasily beside Alain, and he turned to survey the faces of the men who held them captive. The surprise he found on them gave him an inkling of a plan.

'Are you so sure you are ready to die for your cause?' He spoke to the man behind him. 'Because if he releases that bacteria here, it will not only be us who become infected.'

The guard shoved him, but as he did he glanced at the man next to him, and then looked to his leader, the man standing beside Gavin.

Perhaps he sensed the change in his men's moods, or perhaps he'd worked out the danger himself. Whatever his motivation, the guard leader moved to confront the ecoterrorist. 'This is not what we agreed. We were to take the witches back to the car before you unleashed the bacteria.'

Confusion clouded Gavin's face, only to be replaced by a look of such cunning it sent a shiver down Gavin's spine.

'You don't think Tabitha and I would risk our own lives to set this bacteria loose, do you?'

The guard's face showed his uncertainty.

'We made an antidote which we will make available to you and your men after we leave here,' Gavin said.

'But you promised we would make the ultimate …' one of the witches started.

'Shut up, Rosalind!' Gavin glared at her and she took a step back, white-faced, fear in her eyes.

'You can't do this.' Ruth stepped forward to stand beside Jo. 'You could bully me into setting a bacteria free that would attack random people, but I cannot stand by and watch you infect my friends. That is cold-blooded murder.'

Gavin laughed a hollow laugh. 'It always was, my dear. You were just one step back from it.'

'I won't let you do this—not to us, or the forest.' Ruth stood taller as she uttered the words.

'You think you can stop me?' Gavin motioned to one of the guards, who grabbed hold of Ruth's arm.

'Let go of me.' Ruth jerked her arm out of his grasp and kicked him in the shin. The slap he delivered rang loud through the cold air. Ruth raised her hand to retaliate, but the guard would not be beaten twice. He took hold of Ruth's arm and, in a single movement, pulled it up behind her back. He marched her over to join the other captives. Ruth spat at him as he returned to his position.

'Anyone else want to join her?' No one moved, so Gavin said, 'All right, scram, the lot of you, unless you want to be infected too.'

Alain expected a flurry of activity as the other witches rushed to leave the clearing, but no one moved. Then, as if on some silent signal, all but one of them walked forward and stood beside Ruth. Rosalind alone remained.

Gavin sneered. 'All the more to act as a lesson to those who wish to harm nature. Rosalind, come here.'

Without missing a beat, the woman joined him under the tree, moving as if in a dream.

'Tabitha, if I open this vial can you call a breeze to disperse it over everyone?'

Tabitha nodded. 'I will call the wind. You wait for the count of three before releasing the contents.'

She began chanting, and a light breeze brush against Alain's cheeks. The longer Tabitha chanted, the stronger the breeze became. Gavin held his arm out in front, his thumb ready to pop the stopper of the vial. Tabitha stopped chanting.

'One …'

Out of the corner of his eye Alain caught a movement.

'... Two ...'

Trouble jumped and clamped his jaw around Gavin's wrist. The man's arm jerked involuntarily, and the bottle slipped from his hand, stopping in mid-air. It was as if everyone had frozen with it until Trouble let go and dropped to the ground, landing on all four paws. Then, in a single movement, he leapt again, picked the bottle out of the air and took off into the woods.

No one moved, then everything seemed to happen at once.

Gavin swung around, yelling, 'Someone grab that mutt.'

Trying to move out of his way, Rosalind tripped and fell to the ground.

The guards pulled out their weapons and aimed them at the captives.

Everyone around Alain dropped to the ground to avoid being shot.

Alain found himself the only one standing in the circle of guards as he tried to find out what was happening with Trouble.

'Ah, the dog owner. In spite of all evidence to the contrary, I assume the animal has had some training. Make him bring the vial back,' Gavin commanded.

Alain shook his head.

'You have five seconds. If that mutt does not bring back my property, Andy, there, will shoot you.'

While Alain was sure he did not want to die here in this faraway place, he was equally sure he couldn't save his own life at the cost of perhaps millions of others.

'Five ...'

Goodbye, Barabal. I hope you find someone else to love you as much as I do.

'Four ...'

Please take care of Barabal, Master Barwick. She can get herself into quite a bit of trouble and needs someone to keep an eye on her.

'Three ...'

It is the least I can do, young friend. I will make sure she wants for nothing.

'Two ...'

Alain closed his eyes and hoped being shot did not hurt too much, and that his death would be swift. He tensed for the final count ... but there was nothing. The tension around him eased and he opened his eyes one at a time and looked around.

Under the tree sat an obedient Trouble staring up at Gavin—his mouth empty. Alain searched for evidence of the bottle containing the bacteria, but could not see it.

'Where is my bottle, dog? Where did you put it?' Gavin's tone was friendly. Trouble stayed where he was—statue still. 'Where is it?' Gavin shouted, raising his arm to strike the animal.

'Here.'

The bushes rustled and the clearing illuminated as someone turned on strong lamps around the edges of it. A large number of soldiers in camouflage gear moved in from all sides, guns pointed at the group beside the Rufus Stone.

Once Alain's eyes adjusted, he turned his attention back to the scene under the tree, and found the balance had changed.

'Put down your weapons,' the man standing behind Gavin and Tabitha commanded. When no one moved, he said, 'Don't run. You are surrounded.

And if you did by chance manage to get away, at this precise moment the authorities are processing images we sent and should have no trouble identifying you all within the hour. Best you surrender now rather than face further charges.'

As the guards laid down their weapons and raised their hands, Rosalind scrambled to her feet and made a run for it. At the edge of the clearing, one of the soldiers tackled her to the ground and handcuffed her before leading her back to the stone.

'It was all their idea,' she whined. 'They talked me into going along with their plan.

'Oh, for goodness sake, shut up, you stupid girl,' Tabitha said.

'Do you have any idea what you are doing? Don't you want this forest safe for all humanity to enjoy? By stopping us you just signed its death warrant.' Gavin spoke passionately, like someone rallying support.

'An interesting defence,' Master Barwick said. 'He would kill humanity to save a forest for them.'

Slowly, the guards lowered themselves to kneel on the ground. Soldiers came forward, removed their guns and handcuffed their arms behind their backs before leading them away.

'I am Agent Morrison,' the man under the tree said as a group of soldiers led the guards away. 'You can all stand now.'

As they did, Alain caught a glimpse of Lee, Bebe and another man in a Macintosh coat joining the agents under the tree.

'All right, you two. Tell me which of these people are yours,' Agent Morrison said.

Not waiting for anyone to speak, Alice ran towards Lee and Bebe, and the remaining soldiers immediately raised their weapons.

Agent Morrison held up his hand, then looked to the twins, but before they could speak the man in the coat pushed past him, moving to meet Alice.

'Oh Alice, what mayhem have you caused now?' Although his words were admonishing, the tone was one of fondness. The man wrapped his arms around her, and Alice sunk in to his embrace.

A STERN-FACED SOLDIER led Alain and Lee, along with Jo, Bebe and Trouble, into a side room of The Sir Walter Tyrell pub. He waited until they'd all found a seat before taking up a position by the door. It appeared they

wouldn't be leaving anytime soon, so Alain slouched in the comfortable chair by the crackling fire and took a mug of steaming chocolate from the tray carried in by the pub's owner.

In the next room, he could hear Alice and Master Barwick talking to the men in charge, and occasionally the voice of Alice's husband could also be heard. Headlights illuminated the room as yet another military vehicle departed the car park.

'That looks like Tabitha's coven's military escort,' Alain said, peering through the window.

'Where are they taking them? Do you have any idea?' Jo asked.

'They are based in Southampton, so I guess that's where they will go,' Lee said.

'I hope Izzy is okay.' Jo wrung her hands, and added, 'And I hope they throw Gavin and Tabitha in the deepest, darkest cell.'

Alain shuddered, remembering the dungeon he'd rescued Jo's alter ego from a week or so ago. He would not send his worst enemy anywhere like that

They will spend the next few years behind bars, Trouble said from his place in front of the fire. He stretched and snuggled into the rug before continuing. *They will all be charged with malicious intent and terrorist activities for planning to release the bacteria. In this time, witchcraft is something from children's stories, so no one believes they manipulated Alabama Rot to become a deadly weapon. Although scientists will work on the contents of the vial, none will be able to replicate it.*

Thank goodness, Alain said. *What about the coven?*

The others will get a year's probation once Gavin's guard friends admit to threatening most of them.

The others continued their conversation as he and Trouble spoke, and Alain realised the Guardian's words were meant for his ears only. He returned to the conversation in time to hear Jo ask, 'So, want to tell us how we got here?'

'Of course,' Lee answered, a grin on his face. 'It all turned out to be a bit strange.'

'Stop mucking around or I will tell them,' Bebe said. Lee shrugged, so she continued, 'When we drove past the car park we saw the guards. We pulled in to find out what was going on and caught sight of their guns. Lee and I panicked and drove off.'

'Which turned out to be inspired in the end,' Lee added, earning a glare from his sister. 'Once we'd doubled back to pick up the jack and things, we decided to stop at the pub and plan our next moves.'

'Anyway, in the end we thought it best to call the police. Lee rang and

reported some suspicious activity in the car park by the Rufus Stone. He made sure to mention he thought he saw guns, as we didn't want anyone getting hurt, and I seem to remember the police here don't carry weapons,' Bebe told them.

'And the operator forwarded that call to me.'

The group turned as one to find the agent-in-charge from the clearing leaning against the doorframe, a steaming mug in his hand. He joined them by the fire, perching on the window ledge.

'Your friends here held me up earlier in the evening with their flat tyre stunt. My current intel led me to believe Gavin was up to something at The Sir Walter Tyrell. Helping Bebe and Lee fix their flat tyre meant I missed him. Like them, I stopped here to regroup. I was just enjoying a coffee when I received their call.'

'You were watching Gavin? Did you know what he was up to?' Jo asked.

'No. We picked up his trail when he entered the country. We knew he'd been in contact with some of his old friends and believed he was putting together a team.'

'But you didn't know exactly what for?' Jo was sceptical.

'No, we didn't. Bebe and Lee told me a fantastical story this evening, which I only half-believed until I watched what went on in the forest tonight. In fact, I am still getting my head around it. Fortunately, they mentioned armed men in the car park, which allowed me to call in my team and the rest, as they say, is history.'

'See? I told you—inspired. I am just not sure by what,' Lee said, grinning.

'Thank the goddess,' Alain murmured.

'I am not sure how much of what I witnessed tonight will be believed by those higher up, and even less will be able to be used to prosecute the accused. But with that vial of bacteria there is enough evidence to put the two of them away for a very long time.'

'Wait until you uncover what is at Tabitha's house,' Bebe said, but was silenced by Lee's punch to her arm as the agent turned a questioning gaze her way.

'What about my friend Izzy, and the other coven members?' Jo deflected the man's attention with her question.

'That will depend entirely on their level of involvement,' Agent Morrison said. 'None of them will get away scot-free, I fear.'

'Oh.' Jo's shoulder's slumped.

'What about us?' Alain asked.

'For you, home to bed for now. Donald will drive you all. Alice and Barnaby will give us the rest of the story tonight, but your statements can wait a few days. Please don't be going anywhere until we have spoken with you again.'

Alain's heart sank. Once Tabitha and Gavin had been taken into custody, and they were relaxing at the pub, his reason for being in 2017 was gone. His thoughts automatically turned to home. He would be sad to leave his new friends, but he couldn't wait to return to Stanislaus and Barabal, and his boring, uncomplicated life.

Trouble, can't we just leave?

Can you imagine what strife the others would be in if we just disappeared off the face of the earth? Trouble asked. *Besides, before we go I require clearance from the Council that our work here is done.*

'Are you guys ready to head home?'

Donald, Alice's husband, stood in the doorway, jiggling car keys in his hand.

'Yes,' Alain said wearily, along with the others. So much it hurts, he added to himself.

16

GOODBYES

'WHAT DID YOU think you were doing?'

Isolde was released with the other coven witches, much to her surprise. Especially given the fact it was she who'd directed Tabitha's attention to the spell to increase the bacteria's growth in the first place.

Tabitha had kept her role in proceedings secret. She had assured the authorities she and Gavin alone had developed the Alabama Rot bacteria—both the animal and human forms. She admitted to coercing the coven into helping them spread it, but denied any of them had a hand in developing it.

That, combined with the fact they had been threatened with violence should they not turn up and cast their spells, led the crown prosecution to charge them with minor offences, giving them all a year's probation.

She had not been as surprised by her summons back home to face charges for her actions.

As beings without bodies, the Council could choose any form and any location to project when she answered the charges laid against her. It told her much that they chose a courtroom and appeared as three judges.

'I repeat, what did you think you were doing?

Holding her head high, Isolde said, 'Saving humanity, just as you tasked me.'

'Your mission was to assist Tabitha in defending the New Forest.' The judges spoke as one, which threw her off for a moment.

'Surely the idea behind saving the forest was to ultimately save the planet and humanity,' Isolde said.

'That is not your call to make. As a second-level operative your role is to follow orders, not bend policy to your will.' The middle judge peered at her from the raised dais, his finger wagging as if telling off a naughty child.

Tilting her chin defiantly, Isolde stared him down. 'Are we truly in the business of correcting the world at any cost? I saved millions of lives by stopping Tabitha.'

'You have no idea whether or not you saved anyone.' The head judge told her.

'Tabitha intended to release a new bacteria into the world to kill as many people as possible. Is there any real justification for that—ever?'

The three judges looked down at her in silence, each of them almost statue still. Micro movements of their faces were the only evidence they mind-spoke, discussing her case in front of her. None of their expressions gave anything away.

Minutes ticked by, and she tried not to shuffle from foot to foot as she waited. She did not spend the time idly though. Her own mind was busy as she considered her options should they tell her they countenanced the sacrifice of so many to their cause. Her stomach sank as she realised she would be forced to leave. Mass killings was not what she had signed up for.

'We are sympathetic to your plight.' The female judge on her left finally broke the silence. 'We could not foresee the one we chose to manipulate would fall under another's influence, one that would lead her to extremeness and endanger so many lives.'

'How did you miss such a critical fact?' Isolde pushed. If the Council allowed this detail to slip through the cracks, would they miss more important ones?

Another discussion took place before the other female judge, the one to her right, answered, 'It is not your place to question us.'

'No, we placed her in a precarious position; she has a right to know.' The comment came from the head of the Council sitting in the middle. 'Our major offensive took more resources than we anticipated, meaning we were unable to offer support to some of the satellite activities intended to stretch the Time Guardians.'

The judge on the right continued, 'The assassination of a prime minster, and the installation of a replacement who would make some real inroads on climate change was critical to our plans, all our attention was directed to that mission. By the time we got round to you we were too late to change

anything—your plan was already set in motion.'

'Still, you didn't send help then either? I requested backup more than once.' Isolde attempted to keep the anger out of her voice, but the frowns on the judges' faces told her she had not succeeded.

'You only asked when it was too late for us to alter your course of action,' the head judge said. 'I could turn this around and ask why did you not call us in sooner?'

Isolde paused before answering. There was only one reason—Jo. She could not bear the way Jo looked at her when she knew of her involvement in Tabitha's plans. But the Council would not accept that as an excuse, so she said nothing.

The left-hand judge smiled at her sympathetically. 'If only you'd called us in earlier, we may have found a way to help you without having to work with Time Guardians.'

'And that is why our decision is that you should lose your current independent operating status,' the right-hand woman seemed pleased to be able to pass on this verdict.

The chief judge frowned at his co-judge, and she blushed. He turned his gaze back to Isolde. 'Our verdict is that you acted with the best intentions using your current level of abilities and training. We take responsibility for our failures in planning, but you must also take responsibility for allowing emotions to cloud your judgement. Because of this, you will be accompanied on your next assignment by a senior operative who will assess your work in the field.'

Isolde knew she should ask if she was being demoted, but she wasn't sure she cared. Her commitment to the cause was waning. These last weeks had shown her she and Jo could not be together in any life so long as they fought on different sides in the fight to improve the world.

She thought back to the time she'd first met Jo, before she knew her to be Jo or John. If she had stayed around, they might have had a chance at happiness then.

The judges all leaned forward in their seats as if expecting something. Of course, they wanted her to respond. She shook her head to clear her thoughts, then made a quick decision. For the moment she had no idea where her future lay, so she needed to buy some time while she considered her options.

'I thank you for your leniency.' She heard herself say as she sought the words she needed for her next move. 'Perhaps I need a break from assignments to reassess where I am in my life.'

Isolde took a deep breath before continuing. 'I heard it is possible to be returned to our original body at a point in time before we chose to join the World Fixers. We are given the option of reaffirming our commitment and returning here, or living our original lives until their natural end. Is that true?'

She raised her eyes to meet those of the main judge and found him shaking his head. 'Yes it is. I can see you are in distress and would be a prime candidate for such a journey under normal circumstances. However, there are so many critical missions in play at the moment we cannot afford to let you go. Perhaps after you complete your next assignment we might review that decision.'

'But if I am to accompany another agent, could you not perhaps send them alone?' Isolde pled her case.

Again the judges conferred before responding.

'In theory, yes. But our seers calculate minimal chances of success if you are not part of the team. Perhaps if I explain the task you will understand why your presence is critical.'

Isolde shrugged. 'All right.'

'The Time Guardians are sending Sigma to a particular event to ensure the flow of time proceeds. It is a critical time in human development because we cannot foresee any future beyond this event.'

'What do you want me to do about that?' Isolde asked, not sure she could face fighting against the Time Guardian she had just worked with; she respected him too much.

'Actually, we do not want you to do anything, as such,' the woman on the left said. 'We want the two of you to accompany the Guardian Sigma to ensure his actions benefit both the human race and the Earth.'

'How will I know whether or not his actions are within our guidelines if you can't direct me towards an end goal?' Isolde said. She had never heard of a mission without a specific action required to improve the future. Then again, a joint team was something completely new as well.

'We hope that, as your mission progresses, the future will become clearer, and we will send your instructions. In the interim, you are to use your common sense,' the head judge said.

'If this is so pivotal, why are you sending a screw-up like me?' Isolde said the words without thinking, but once they were out she could not take them back.

'Because you screwed up with Sigma,' the head judge shot back. 'You built a connection. No one else here has any sort of rapport with a Guardian, so we are forced to send you.'

'Oh, I understand.' Isolde did not, but if she had to get through this to earn a chance to be returned to her original life to see if she could fix her future then so be it.

'Never fear though; we are sending one of our most decorated agents with you to ensure nothing goes wrong.' The sneer on the right-hand judge's face highlighted that after her time in Burley she had made an enemy on the Council, one who would not easily forgive her transgressions.

The three judges stood, and Isolde bowed as they left. Standing alone in the now stark white room, she sighed. She had not known what to expect when she'd entered the court, and in the end it was not too bad. One more mission and she might earn a chance to find out what she wanted from life. It was not the worst outcome.

As she turned to leave, she saw a figure in the back of the room, the grin on his face telling her he had watched the whole proceedings. As her eyes met his, she sucked air in through her teeth, feeling as if she had been punched in the gut. 'Jason, so good to see you.' There was no way she would show him the effect he had on her.

'Isolde, it seems I am to take over your training once again. I told them not to send you out on your own—that you weren't ready—especially after that debacle in Athens.'

She was not having this. If they were to work together one more time, there at least needed to be honesty between them. 'The reports may not agree, but you and I both know exactly what happened last time we worked together. Beware, Jason, I am older and wiser now, and will not take the fall for your incompetence again.'

Sweeping past him, she left the room, not caring whether or not he followed.

'JO, YOU KNOW I can't stay. My new mission starts almost immediately,' Izzy said, her words creating mist in the cool morning air.

'But what about your probation? If you abscond, you won't be able to come back without facing additional charges.' Jo's face crumpled and tears welled in her eyes as Izzy hugged her, as if she realised this was their final goodbye.

Alain looked down at his feet, trying to give the two of them some privacy.

'Will you be okay?'

'Of course, but I can't come back here. They won't let me—ever.' Even to Alain's ears, Izzy sounded uncertain.

'I love you,' Jo whispered.

'I love you too, now and through time itself,' Izzy said.

Are you ready? Trouble said, giving Alain something to do other than try not to listen to Izzy and Jo.

He stomped his feet to restore circulation in the cool winter air, and glanced around the clearing. The forest was a study of reds and browns hidden in a swirling mist. Although they had only arrived here a little over a week ago, the area felt more alive, and a hint of magic tinged the air.

'Here we all are then,' Master Barwick said as he joined them, Alice in tow.

Even after such a short time, Master Barwick looked odd back in his own clothes, and Alain thought he must too. They certainly itched more than he remembered.

'Alice, thank you so much for putting up with us,' Master Barwick said as he clumsily hugged their hostess.

'No, it is I who must thank you for everything you've done.' Alice wiped a tear from her eye.

'I hope you aren't in too much strife with Donald,' Master Barwick said. 'I didn't get much of a chance to speak with him to explain you were just helping us out.'

An early phone call the morning after the casting had called Donald back to work. Knowing the couple needed time alone, the others went out for the day, and by the time they returned he was gone.

'I told you, he was fine. He would have loved to stay and meet you all properly ... but ... well, he'll be back soon enough.' Alice smiled at them all.

Alain found tears welling in his own eyes as he hugged Alice and Jo goodbye, knowing that even though he'd only met them a few days ago, he would miss them. They were all reincarnations of people back home, but their own unique personalities had wormed their way into his heart—especially Bebe's.

They had said their farewells this morning, before she'd left for the hospital to meet with Ruth and her department heads. When Ruth had called the day before and asked Bebe to come to the hospital to talk about a volunteer position, and perhaps some part-time work, Bebe had been beside herself, almost skipping back into the room to tell them her news.

'When I apologised for drugging her, she just poo-pooed me. She said we all did things we were not proud of, and we need to put the past behind us and move on.'

'It was good of her to call, especially as the hospital board placed her on probation after the hearing over her involvement with Tabitha,' Alice had said.

'I can't wait to tell Mum and Dad. They will be here in a little over a week,

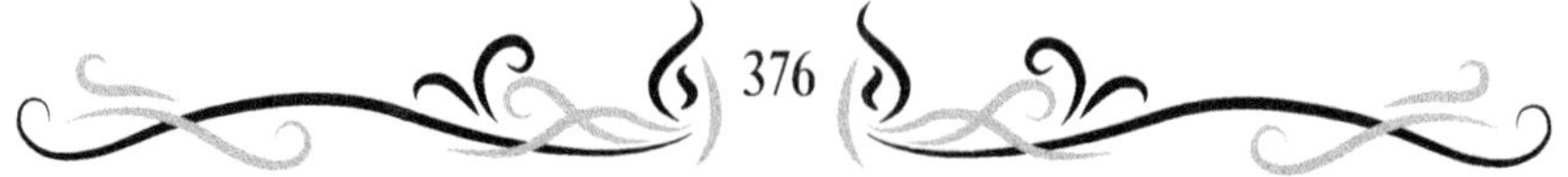

but I might just text them the news.'

With her future falling into place, Alain had thought his departure would be far down her list of priorities, but she'd proved him wrong when she'd cornered him in his room earlier that day. It was a bitter-sweet farewell. They clearly felt something more than friendship toward each other, but Alain's heart belonged to Barabal and Bebe would be concentrating on her studies for the next few years. Still, there would forever be a Bebe sized gap in his heart.

Are you ready? Trouble asked him again.

Almost.

He sighed as he remembered he still had to say his farewells to Lee.

It was almost as if his thoughts called the other boy over. They said their goodbyes as boys do, and Lee diffused the emotional scene by changing the focus.

'So, how do you do this, Trouble?'

I take everyone into the water and create a portal back to medieval England.

'Cool.'

Then I will be coming back. My new assignment requires me to leave from here.

Lee smiled wryly. 'It looks like everyone has something to do. Bebe is going to be working at the hospital with Ruth instead of doing a tour around Southern England with me. Jo is off to visit her grandparents. Alain is heading home and even Izzy says she has another mission. My parents don't arrive for Christmas for another week or so—what am I going to do with myself?'

'I am sure you will find some mischief to get into,' Alain joked.

'I don't find it; it finds me.' Lee laughed. 'Problem is, after all this excitement I am looking at the world a little differently, and I'm wondering if I am cut out to be a soldier. Too much thinking like that does my head in, and I need to find something more constructive to do with my time.'

Alain laughed, but stopped abruptly as his body tingled all over. Trouble tilted his head to the side and appeared to go into a trance, which, in his dog form, looked odd. He then shook himself all over, and became dog-like again.

Can you meet me back here in an hour or so? We need to talk about something, Trouble said to Lee.

'Sure. Want to tell me what we need to talk about?'

Not now. I'll brief you when you return.

Lee shrugged and opened his mouth to speak, but closed it as the others joined them.

'It is time,' Master Barwick said, and Trouble nodded.

There was another round of farewells before Trouble led Alain and Master

Barwick over to the stream.

'Are you sure this is the only way?' Alain said, suddenly reluctant to step into the freezing water.

'Unfortunately, yes.'

His master's response did nothing to calm the butterflies in his stomach.

'I bet Izzy has another way to travel,' he muttered under his breath as icy fingers of water clawed their way up his leg. He stumbled and gasped as he submerged his body in the swirling icy stream. Everything went black, then a bright light blinded him. Opening his eyes, he found himself sitting under a gas lamp on the banks of the Thames. Beside him, Master Barwick slowly rose to his feet.

We are later than I planned. I believe it is the evening of the day we left. You will need to explain your afternoon's absence. It's up to you whether or not you tell them the truth. Barabal and Stanislaus should be around the stables if you want to go and find them. Trouble, the dog, grinned.

'Thank you, Sigma. That was a very informative journey.' Master Barwick's voice cut through the evening air. 'These old bones are weary and I want to be back in my own rooms. Until we meet again, old friend.'

Goodbye, Barwick. It will not be long until you join us for good.

As his master departed, Alain said, 'I must thank you too. I learnt a lot ... The future was interesting, and I shall miss the people and the food—but I am pleased to be home.'

What now for you? Trouble asked Alain. *Are you off back to the New Forest to agitate for the return of the land to the Saxons?*

'No, I think I will stay here,' Alain answered. 'Master Barwick still has much to teach me and ... well, we don't know how much longer he will be here.'

And you will be better placed to use your friendship with the King to lobby for a change of ownership?

I am not sure I will. Although my heart yearns for a return to the days before the Normans arrived, my head is saying perhaps I should wait a bit before rushing to action. In the long-term, it may be better for the forest to stay as it is. Perhaps I can persuade the King to love it again so he protects it for the future.

Trouble's muzzle formed a grin. *Then all that is left to say is, make the most of your time with Barwick. Soon he will be called to a higher task, and you will be left to fill his shoes. Goodbye, my friend.*

'Alain, where have you been? Stanislaus and I were supposed leave half an hour ago, but I made everyone wait until I found you.'

Alain turned to see Barabal striding along the docks towards him.

'Oh, Barabal, I am so pleased you did.' Alain swept the girl into his arms. 'I missed you so much.'

'Put me down, silly. We only spoke this morning. Please, Alain, someone will see and they will think I am a loose woman.'

'Maybe we should do something about that then. While you are away, I will speak with the King—that is, if you want me to.'

Barabal stared at him, and his stomach started to sink when she did not answer. Then, she placed her arm through his, giving him an affectionate squeeze, and said, 'You may escort me to my mount, and I am sure I could not stop you from talking to the King even if I wanted to.'

Looking back over his shoulder as Barabal drew him away, Alain watched Trouble leap from the wharf, and the dog was soon swallowed by the churning waters of the portal before he disappeared from sight.

THE HOUSE WAS toasty warm after their morning on the common. Alice made them a pot of tea and they drank it in the kitchen by the Aga. The room seemed so empty with just the two of them, and even emptier still when Alice excused herself to go to work.

Wandering round the house somewhat at a loose end, Lee headed up to the bedroom to get his tablet. He found it on top of Alain's copy of *The Lord of the Rings*. Reaching for the device, he almost dropped it as the book came off the dresser as well. He stood there with the book hanging from his tablet cover. On the floor, he found a note Alain must have left for him on the bedside table, beside the bottle of super glue. When he grabbed his tablet it must have fallen to the floor.

I could not resist. This glue is amazing, but I could not take it back with me. I had to use it at least once. Leave the tablet alone and try the book. Your friend through time—Alain.

Laughing, Lee went to his sister's room to find her nail polish remover so he could free his tablet. Once the job was done, he returned, lay on his bed and flipped open the cover, then closed it. Placing it back on the dresser, he rolled to his side and opened the book.

He was still engrossed in *The Lord of the Rings* when the alarm on his phone went off. Reluctant to leave the story, he placed the book in his backpack,

wedged in between a water bottle and some food bars. He had no idea what Trouble had planned, but if it was a walk through the forest to check everything was back to normal, he wanted to be prepared.

After locking the door behind himself, he rushed down the street and turned the corner to be confronted with a moving van. Sliding to a stop, he narrowly missed careening into a sofa, only to lose his footing. A hand grabbed hold of him, saving him from an embarrassing fall. Once back upright, he checked everything was in working order. Someone held out his backpack, which had slipped from his shoulder as he fell.

'Thank you,' he said, looking up. The face in front of him was familiar, but different. Caught off guard, his mouth hung open. As he shut it, he whispered, 'Alain.'

The boy looked at him, frowning. 'Close. I am Allan. Do I know you?'

'Um, no, not really,' Lee stammered.

'Ah, you must be one of the guys staying with their aunt round the corner.'

'Yes, but how ...?'

'Mum was talking to a woman this morning. She said she had her niece and nephew staying, and that they were about my age. Pleased to meet you.' The boy smiled and held out his hand.

Confused, Lee shook it. 'Lee. Sorry, I am late for something.'

'Oh.' The boy's face fell and a wave of guilt washed over Lee.

'Look, perhaps we can meet properly later. I can show you around what little there is of Burley, if you like.'

'Sure, if it's no bother. But can we do it tomorrow? I am kinda busy with unloading today, and Mum'll skin me if I don't do my share.'

'Sure, catch you then,' Lee said as Allan picked up a box from the back of the truck and followed one of the removal men inside.

'Bye,' Lee said as he stepped around some furniture on the sidewalk and took off at a run, hoping he had not missed Trouble.

Arriving at the agreed spot a little late, Lee was relieved to find the dog sitting calmly waiting for him. He was not so happy to see Izzy standing by his side.

'Glad you could make it.' Izzy's smile had a sarcastic twist.

'What are you doing here?' Lee asked.

'I understand you are coming with us,' the girl said enigmatically.

'Coming with you? Where?' Lee looked at Trouble, but he sat still, almost smiling, and Lee wondered if the dog was indeed Trouble, or an actual Spoodle.

'To the future, of course!' Izzy said condescendingly, and Lee fought back

the urge to say something to wipe the smile from her face.

Trouble? He begged the dog to intervene.

Something changed before when you questioned your future as a soldier. When you queried your role in the world, the Time Guardians decided to expand your experience so you might be better equipped to decide what you want to do.

'What?'

Like Alain, you have the potential to one day become a Guardian. When you reach a certain stage in your evolution, we like to test how you do on a mission. The Council asked me to take you along on this expedition.

Izzy smirked. 'Yeah, we are finally all on the same page.'

Not quite, Izzy. Please give me a moment to explain, Trouble said. *Our next jump in time is going to be a joint mission with the Time ...* Trouble stopped and cocked his head to the side. *Um, not the time for that word I think. We are joining up with Isolde and one of her friends. We are going to work together to ensure humanity survives and thrives.*

'You want me to leap through time with you. That would be so great. But I just made plans for tomorrow, and Bebe would miss me.'

Izzy placed a hand on his arm. 'You'll be back before anyone even notices you are gone.'

She is correct. We can time your return to be within minutes of having left. And we could do with a soldier to help with this particular task.

'I am not a soldier yet,' Lee said, stalling. He was not good at making snap decisions.

'But you were a cadet at school; Bebe told me,' Izzy said.

Taking a deep breath, Lee weighed up the excitement of going through a portal against his fear of the unknown. As he tried to work through the pros and cons, the devil in his head said, *If Alain can do it, so can you.*

'All right, I'm in.' Lee gulped down his fear and he voiced his agreement.

Good, let's go then.

Trouble and Lee headed towards the stream, but Izzy did not move.

'I never understood all this jumping into freezing liquid,' she said. 'Here, let me.'

She moved her arm in a circle, her lips moving, and the air in front of her shimmered. 'Quick, I can't hold it forever.'

Trouble turned and went to stand beside Isolde. She held out her hand, and Lee took a few steps and grabbed hold of it. Taking a deep breath, he allowed her to pull him into the unknown.

EPILOGUE

'SURELY YOU UNDERSTAND why it has to be him, Alpha. He is the only one of our kind to forge a relationship with a Time Wrecker, and this mission is too delicate to leave to chance,' Beta said. Why did all his conversations with Alpha seem like a visit to a torture chamber?

'I cannot help but feel he is being rewarded for a botched mission. He almost died, which would have stranded a potential Guardian and his helper in a strange world. He was unable to eradicate the bacteria, and he worked hand in hand with a Time Wrecker.'

Beta had no answer for this. Technically it was all true, although not everything had been Sigma's fault.

'If he would just turn up as a person for his missions he would not get into these messes.'

'Oh really, Alpha, you know that is not true. Just because you do not like his methods, there is no reason to vilify him for them.'

Taking a deep breath, Beta thought of the best way to win Alpha over, or at the very least curb his antagonism towards Sigma. Until this critical mission was completed they needed to work as a team to provide the best guidance they could for their agents. Alpha thought of himself as a man of

reason, so perhaps that was the best approach?

'Barnaby Barwick is back with his apprentice in his correct time, preparing things for his imminent death when he will join our ranks. All in all, no harm was done.'

Alpha snorted at this, but said nothing, so Beta continued.

'As you well know, although the Alabama Rot is still around, they prevented the mutated version from being released, and the people who created it are in prison. The disease will not skip to humans, and they averted a mass epidemic—that's due to the people on the ground who we left largely to their own devices because of critical issues elsewhere.'

'I will concede that.' Alpha's tone was grudging. 'However, he worked with a Time Wrecker—a Time Wrecker, Beta. He will still need to be sanctioned for that.'

It had taken a while, but they had come around to the real crux of the matter. Alpha was not the only member of the Council to feel this way, so Beta needed to tread gently. 'Sigma's helpers made this alliance while he was under anaesthetic. He was not a party to it, and no one was able to contact us for direction,'

'All right. It was John—Jo who brought the Time Wrecker in. She based her judgement on emotional connections, which is not how we do things.'

'True, Alpha, and I think we should all remember that although Jo was a long way through her reincarnation cycle, she was not yet at the level where we were considering her ascension to Guardian, so she was still prone to making very human decisions.'

'Humph. What about Barwick? He is almost a Guardian; why didn't he stand against including that Isolde in their plans?'

'The fault was not his either. Without Sigma to assist him he was left with an impossible choice. Unable to talk with us, and unable to operate in the time he was in without Isolde's help, but knowing he had to do something to stop an epidemic spreading. What other option was there?'

'I guess I can appreciate his dilemma,' Alpha conceded.

'The fault is ours as well. We took our eye off them—left them without support when they needed it most. We must discuss extending trainee's powers to allow them to operate a little more independently as they progress through the levels,' Beta pressed on.

'We can discuss that at the next Council meeting. Before that, we need to agree on Jo's punishment, for there must be some sanction for collaborating

with the enemy.'

'Must there really?' Beta asked. 'It is because of their collaboration we find ourselves in the unique position of being able to launch our new mission.'

'I see why you would think that, but we cannot allow our Guardians to think they can work with Time Wreckers whenever they feel the urge.'

'You are right; that would cause chaos. Perhaps a minor sanction then—a nudge backwards on the evolutionary wheel,' Beta suggested.

'It is a shame. Her Guardian training was only one or two lifetimes away, but it is fair. After all, we do not want to lose such a promising candidate altogether. We cannot nudge her back too far though; we will need her to be ready for this new mission. Perhaps one hop back?'

'Done then?' Beta asked, and Alpha nodded his agreement.

'Right, now that is sorted, shall we go and tell Theta about her next assignment?' Beta said.

'Yes, let's. I am sure she will be thrilled to be working with her old partner again.'

'You still think this is a wise pairing?' Beta himself was not so certain.

Sigma and Theta had been Guardian trainees together. Along with himself and Alpha, the group had often worked as a team. The two trainees had fallen for each other. When they had realised they could not become Guardians and maintain their relationship, Theta had been torn, but in the end she'd listened to her mentor and ascended to Guardian without discussing it with Sigma first.

Sigma had been devastated, and it had taken a lot of convincing on Beta's behalf to have him ascend. The Council had been keeping the two apart ever since.

'Perhaps not wise, but when the Time Wreckers said they were sending two agents we needed to match that,' Alpha said. 'Theta is the only other Guardian Sigma has worked with, so it is logical to send her. Surely by now they are over their little misunderstanding.'

Beta frowned. Was it time for Alpha to step down and let a new Guardian take his place. Some Guardians stayed too long in the job, losing touch with their humanity. Alpha had been exhibiting the signs for a while now, and it was colouring the way he approached things.

'Sigma has already jumped with Lee; it will come as quite a shock to him when Theta joins them. Perhaps I should warn him first,' Beta said.

'By all means, but let us go get Theta prepared. There's no time to waste. Recent reports indicate our catalyst has disappeared, so our agent's first task

will be to find him at all costs.'

'Do we have a contact they are to meet with?'

'Not exactly. Because of the nature of the environment they will portal in to, there are few people evolved enough to assist us. I sent someone in to steal some supplies for them and alter some records to provide covers for everyone. I fear they are pretty much on their own this time, but I'm sure they will be fine.' Alpha reassured him.

Beta paused. There were so many new things in play, this was a risky mission—but there were always risks. They were sending their best agent—what could possibly go wrong?

ABOUT THIS BOOK

HOW MUCH IS Fiction and How Much is Real?

This story came to me when I was visiting family in Southampton and we spent a couple of days in the New Forest in the middle of winter 2017. The misty atmosphere and magical history captured my imagination and the book was already forming in my head. The places in the book exist, and I have to thank the lovely village of Burley for playing host to this story. It is a picturesque village and really deserves a visit.

During my time in the New Forest I noticed warnings to dog owners to keep their animals on leads to prevent further cases of Alabama Rot. It was a serious problem in the area, and I took this idea, studied it and fed it into the mix.

The other thing that struck me during that trip to England was the unrest caused by the issue of whether or not England should stay a part of the European Union. As we spoke to people on different sides of the debate we realised the country was likely set for some big changes, and this also managed to weave itself into my story.

Everything else exists only in my head, and now in this book.

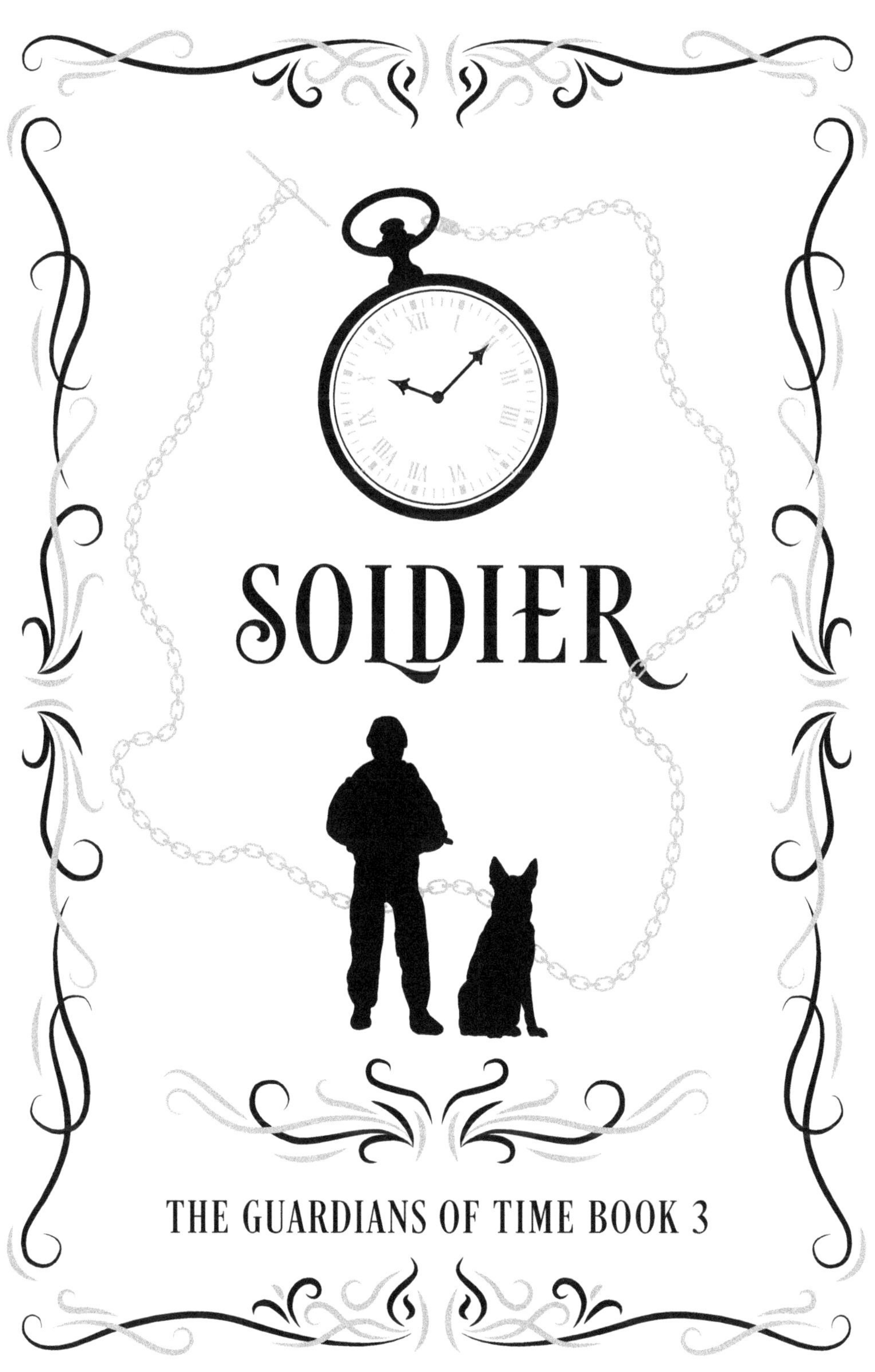
SOLDIER
THE GUARDIANS OF TIME BOOK 3

PROLOGUE: GUARDIAN CITY TO THE RIGHT OF HISTORY

BETA ENTERED THE room using a door out of respect for the inhabitants. Time Wreckers—oops, World Fixers—didn't lose their corporeal body when they ascended out of time, so just popping into the room would be rude. Alpha, however, had no such qualms. He appeared beside Beta.

'What are they doing?' Alpha whispered.

Beta moved a little further into the room before he spoke. 'I don't know. Why don't we ask them?' He raised his voice a little before he added, 'Good Morning, Gerald, Cynthia. Welcome to Guardian City.'

The man and the woman seated at the conference table both raised their heads almost as one. Beta noted that they might not have given up their bodies, but they had used their magical powers to smooth away any signs of ageing.

For the benefit of their guests, he had taken on the form of the man he was when he joined the Time Guardians. Their guests would see a middle-aged man with a full beard and sparkling blue eyes. He tried to hide his slightly rounded figure with loose chinos and a polo shirt. Alpha, forever the showman, had ascended when he was well into his eighties, but today he was a slim, dapper twenty-year-old dressed in jeans and a T-shirt.

Cynthia flicked her auburn hair aside, revealing cat-green eyes, and she smiled. Gerald, who would not have been out of place at a sixties poetry reading, ignored them and lower ed his head back to whatever they were studying, his floppy black fringe hiding his pale thin face.

'Thank you for having us here. This is an… unusual situation, but I am sure we can work on this little project together for a short time without too much stress,' Cynthia said.

Her smile warmed what was left of Beta's heart and he responded with, 'I hope your accommodation is suitable, and I will show you our other amenities a little later. I am just waiting for coffee and tea to arrive, then we shall begin.'

While Beta played the part of the host, Alpha took a seat across from Gerald and glared at the World Fixer, emanating dislike from every pore.

'What are you doing?' Alpha demanded.

Beta bristled at his colleague's tone, but it didn't seem to bother Gerald, who responded by ignoring the question.

As Beta took a seat at a right angle to Alpha, carefully avoiding a seating arrangement that might appear confrontational, Cynthia began speaking.

'Gerald is doing what we all do every day, trying to stop the end of time.'

'How, specifically?' Beta asked.

'By studying events leading up to the last world war, trying to identify for the millionth time if we could change anything to prevent the utter devastation that followed,' Cynthia responded.

Alpha grunted his displeasure, but Beta spoke before the other being was able to say anything too insulting. 'We can't help with anything along those lines as it goes against our philosophy.'

Cynthia nodded as if this was no more than she expected. 'We understand, but the point is moot since we didn't find anything that would help. We thought a review might start us thinking of ways to support our operatives on the ground. Have you managed to make contact yet?'

'We spoke with Theta yesterday their time when she managed to slip out of the underground city for a while. Their cover is all set, and it seems they will be taking part in the search for the boy causing the blip in the time map,'

Beta said before waving at a screen, which flickered a little before showing their timeline monitoring room. About thirty operatives sat around a screen watching coloured lines.

'What are they searching for?' Cynthia asked.

'A red blip.' Beta answered. 'When something deviates from history, a red blip appears and we send someone to investigate. If further action is required, we send down a team.'

'BETA!' Alpha's voice rumbled. He had stopped glaring at Gerald for long enough to listen to what was being said.

'It is not like I've given away any secrets, Alpha,' Beta said, attempting to hide his exasperation. 'Cynthia already knows we monitor history and the timeline, just as they do. I haven't revealed how the system was built, or how it actually identifies deviations.'

Alpha frowned, and Beta knew he was ready to begin a full-blown battle in front of their guests. He had not wanted the World Fixers anywhere near their home in the first place, and he was not even mollified by the fact a Guardian team was at this very moment working at their base.

Not for the first time Beta wondered whether Alpha had been at this game for too long and had lost his perspective. After all, they were all working towards the same goal here. Perhaps it was time for Alpha to retire. That was not a problem for the present though.

Beta turned to Cynthia. Hoping to change the subject, he asked, 'Have you made contact with your chief operative?'

She shook her head. 'He contacted us before entering the city, but nothing since then. I hope he managed to make it to the rendezvous point. At least Isolde and Sigma were travelling together. And… ah… who is this other person with them?'

Beta shrugged, not sure how to answer. He had argued against the boy being sent along, but he had been overruled. 'You mean Lee. We've been watching him for many lifetimes. Under normal circumstances we would not send someone like him on such a perilous mission. However, our analysts ran multiple scenarios, and it seems our best chances of saving history and time occur when he is included in the team.'

'Why is that?' Cynthia leaned forward and placed her chin on her hand.

Again, Beta was not sure what to say or, more to the point, what he should say. 'There is a team of future Time Guardians who appear together in many historical periods, and we think… well, we're guessing… that his friends

might be close by… and that they can—'

Gerald glanced up from the tablet he had been intently studying, and asked, 'Can do what? Save the world?' The contempt in his voice set Beta's teeth on edge.

'Help with whatever needs to be done when we find out what that is.' Alpha almost snarled his answer.

'Gerald, did you find anything?' Cynthia asked, perhaps to divert her partner's attention.

'No, I just reached the beginning of the war, and I can't find anyone or anything that might influence a change. I told you it would be a waste of time.' Gerald did not even lift his gaze from the screen as he answered.

Ignoring her colleague's rudeness, Cynthia swung around on her chair. 'Our system runs through history and identifies points where we might be able to intervene to alter small events to save the world from what happened.'

Alpha ignored Cynthia, but Beta was interested in this insight into how their oldest foes operated.

'Gerald has been running through time to see if he can identify anything, but clearly he was not able to. Perhaps you'd like to watch the rest with us.'

She nodded at Gerald and he scowled back.

'It might help us all to revisit what happened,' she insisted.

'Fine.' His fingers tapped on the tablet, and in the next moment an image flashed on the main screen. He tapped once and the image began moving as the distinctive plume of a bomb mushrooming up came into focus.

'Television footage of the New York bomb,' Cynthia explained, although she didn't need to, as Beta had lived through the war itself.

He still remembered watching in horror as the event was played live on the news. The commentators likened it to when planes crashed into the Twin Towers in the early twenty-first century. In hindsight this image was much more sinister; it was this bomb that had tumbled the house of cards. Its effects rippled out around the rest of the world, ending civilisations on many continents.

Beta watched as the screen flicked through more news coverage of people retreating from major cities. Many were caught by foreign missiles directed at motorways, and still more were caught in the streets as bombs fell. There were more nuclear attacks, mostly directed towards Asia and America. So many it would take years for the fallout to clear from the atmosphere.

The screen went blank. At this point most technology stopped working and news stories stopped being transmitted. Magic all but disappeared, so

time travel to the era was not possible. Although the strongest Guardians had tried, they simply couldn't open the portal on the other side. Even now they didn't know if enough local magical energy could be harnessed for their agents' return.

'History shows that even before the bombs began falling, many people in the United Kingdom retreated to underground towns. In more rural areas many realised what was coming and set themselves up to ride out the storm,' Cynthia said.

'Yes, we modelled the scenarios too. In addition to the people in the underground city of Portsdown, there are likely survivors dotted around the area we sent our team into.' Beta was pleased to finally be working with someone who shared his excitement about the opportunities this mission provided.

'Mm, even so, we have no idea what our operatives are likely to find in twenty-second century Hampshire.' Cynthia drummed her fingers on the table, as if trying to decide what to do next. 'Well, there's not much we can do here today. I suggest we all get some rest and meet back here tomorrow.'

Alpha blanched as the World Fixer effectively dismissed them, and Gerald smirked at his reaction.

'I'm happy with that. We weren't getting anything done anyway,' Gerald said as he packed up his things.

'I'll call someone to show you to your quarters,' Beta responded smoothly, a little disappointed Cynthia had ended the meeting so abruptly. Was Alpha right, had they only come here because they believed they could learn something to their advantage from the Time Guardians? He mentally shook his head. No, he would not fall into that trap.

'That would be lovely,' Cynthia said as Alpha blinked out of the room without a by-your-leave.

'I will send someone in,' Beta said as he left by more traditional means.

1

WHEN AM I?

LEE STEPPED INTO the void. Izzy followed, pushed him in the small of the back, and he stumbled forward on uncertain feet. Not only was it dark, but the air around him was wet and clammy. No, it was heavier than clammy—it was like what he imagined walking through mercury would feel like. He quickly pushed that thought from his mind as claustrophobia began to press on him.

Moments later the tension under his foot changed and he pushed himself forward, relieved to finally be able to gulp down some fresh air. Stumbling forward, he was only prevented from tumbling down the slope by Izzy grabbing hold of his shirt.

Leaning over, hands on knees, he took in lungfuls of fresh air until his body was reassured its supply was not going to be cut off again. Eventually he stood and surveyed his surroundings while he waited for his heart rate to return to normal.

The first thing that hit him was the eerie silence. Few places he had ever visited were this silent. Even in the Australian bush there were always sounds: animals moving, water flowing, or leaves moving in the breeze. Here there was nothing.

In the pre-dawn darkness, he could just make out the sun beginning to peek over the horizon as the moon still shimmered on the water. As his eyes adjusted, he could make out deserted buildings on the edge of a lake, or was it the ocean?

'Where are we?' he asked.

'Quick, insidc. It's not safc out hcrc.'

He glanced around. 'Where's Trouble?'

'I said inside. Come on.' Once again Izzy pushed him in the small of his back, urging him towards a cave entrance to their left. 'I'll tell you everything once we're safe.'

He hoisted his backpack more firmly onto his shoulder and did as Izzy asked, if only to avoid another sharp dig in his back. When he agreed to join her and Trouble on a journey to the future, he hadn't thought to ask where and when they were going. Now he was regretting that.

As his eyes adjusted to the darkness of the cave, he thought he caught sight of a faint glimmer of light ahead.

'That way?' he asked.

'I guess so,' she said, and his stomach knotted as he heard a note of uncertainty in her voice.

Where *was* Trouble? He would feel a little less nervous if the Time Guardian was with them. He looked around for a cute spoodle, Trouble's current form. He found nothing, not even a place where Trouble might be hiding.

The sound of voices drifted out, and Izzy put a restraining hand on his arm, pulling him back a little. He followed her gaze downwards. An enormous German Shepard stared up at him.

Turning back to Izzy, she placed a finger to her lips, urging him to be silent.

Let's find out what's going on before we announce our presence, she spoke into his mind.

Yes, we don't want to upset any plans by blundering in, another voice added.

Trouble? Lee asked. He had only just got his mind around the fact the curly haired spoodle was a Time Guardian, and it still threw him off when the dog spoke. *Where are you?* His eyes dropped to the dog at his feet. *Look, if you're worried about the big dog, Izzy and I will protect you.*

The dog snorted and raised his head to stare at Lee, almost as if he too understood mindspeak.

I am the big dog. Trouble's tone was amused as he made the declaration.

Time Guardian Sigma likes to take an animal form suited to the time and situation he is in. He obviously thinks this task requires him to change into this brute, Izzy explained as she bent down to ruffle the dog's fur.

Lee felt like he had lost a friend. The animal in front of him did not project the same warm, reassuring presence as the cuddly spoodle.

I can't be called Trouble while we're here. It doesn't suit my new body, the Time Guardian said, rolling over so Izzy could rub his tummy, his right back leg shuddering as she found the right spot.

How about Brutus? Izzy offered, not quite suppressing a grin.

The dog raised his eyebrows in disdain and turned pleading eyes to Lee, whose mind went blank. *Not Brutus, that's too… um, brutish.* He frowned, thinking, then he remembered the large stuffed teddy bear he spent many an hour wrestling as a child—Big Bruno Bear. Just the right mix of scary to soft. *How about Bruno?*

Bruno…. Mmm…. The Time Guardian considered the name and the dog nodded once. Bruno he would be. *Now we have dealt with the essential things, my colleague, Theta, is inside talking to someone. I don't think they're from the city, but I don't recognise the voice.*

Both Izzy and Lee listened for a moment.

'I brought outdoor gear for your Sigma as well as for Isolde. Though if they don't get here soon, there won't be any time for them to change before the others arrive. I've no idea how we will explain their lack of military clothing when they do turn up.'

Lee would describe the male's voice as posh English with an underlying whine. As the unidentified male spoke, Izzy's lips curled in distaste.

That's Jason. Her tone was bitter. *My new minder, and one of the most incompetent fools I have ever had the displeasure to work with,* she added.

Well, this is going to be fun, Lee thought as Theta's voice drifted down the cave entrance. 'As I told you earlier, Sigma won't be needing a uniform. What are we going to do with it now? It will look odd having an extra set of clothes and travel gear.'

Before Jason could answer, Izzy took step forward as she said, 'Actually, we have one extra with us, so that won't be a problem.'

Lee and Bruno joined her, and the three of them walked into the cavern together: the lanky fair-haired boy with the huge dog beside him, and the diminutive dark-haired girl on the far side.

'Isolde, nice of you to join us.' The owner of the whiney voice sent Izzy a smarmy smile as he spoke.

He was just as Lee imagined. Built like a rugby player, he was good looking in the blond, weak-chinned English aristocratic style. If Lee had been a dog

his hackles would have risen, as Jason oozed entitlement and condescension from every pore.

'Won't you introduce us to your friend.' Jason's tone suggested this was not a request.

'The name is Izzy, and this is Lee and Bruno. Guys, this is Jason.' Izzy forced the introductions through gritted teeth, not even trying to hide her distaste of Jason and the fact that he could order her about.

'Lovely Isolde, and this is Theta, or Thea as she has been asked to be called on this mission. We are just waiting for the other Time Guardians to turn up. I have a uniform for you, don't know what we'll do about your one extra though.'

Izzy stiffened and Theta—Thea—sighed. 'How many times must I tell you— ' they both said together then stopped and glared at each other. It was as if some silent message passed between them, but Lee did not feel the tell-tale tingling of mindspeak.

Whatever happened between them, they both turned their backs on Jason, and Izzy held out her hand. 'I'm Izzy,'

Thea shook the offered hand tentatively. 'Thea. Do you two want to take your uniforms and packs and get changed? You can put your current clothes inside, along with anything else you want to take with you.' She pointed at Lee's backpack.

Lee held up the all-black uniform Isolde passed to him and frowned. How would he ever fit into that?

'The fabric is self-adjusting. There are also boots in the pack,' Thea told them. 'And please hurry, as the Captain leading this expedition should be here any minute.'

Lee glanced down at Bruno. 'Don't worry, Lee. He and I are old friends. We'll be fine together,' Thea assured him.

'He's just a dog. He doesn't need a babysitter,' Jason said, attempting to regain control of the situation.

As you dress, I'll bring you up to speed. Thea's voice entered his head, causing Lee to misstep. *I've managed to assign us to a troop on a special mission to find a citizen who's headed out into the wasteland. The critical changes in time appear to be clustered around the boy, so our first task is to find him.*

Should be piece of cake if you follow my lead, Jason added.

Or perhaps we should follow the Captain of this troop's lead so we don't stand out too much, Thea said, not bothering to hide the annoyance in her voice.

Best to assess the lay of the land, as you always taught me, Jason, Izzy added, attempting to smooth things between the two.

Right, yes, of course, Jason blustered.

Our team was supposed to consist of the Captain, a medic, two grunts, and a dog handler-tracker. I altered the records so that our names are assigned. The Captain, Kiandra, and Corporal Rodgers, our medic, are still to arrive, Thea said.

Who is doing what? Izzy asked before Lee was able.

Thea answered, *Jason and I are enlisted soldiers. The Captain has met us in the city and sent us here to start preparations. Izzy, you were meant to be the tracker with dog handling skills, but I suggest you tell the Captain Lee and his dog have been assigned to you to train. Sigma, I'm assuming you are able to access all the dog's… um… faculties?*

Yes, Bruno said, his tone abrupt and business-like.

'You mean Sigma is the dog?' Jason gasped.

'Bruno,' they all said together.

'So the dog is called Bruno, and who are each of you?' A new voice entered the conversation.

AS THE OTHERS greeted the Captain and her companion in the room next door, Lee undressed and picked up his suit. The texture was a cross between rubber and cotton, and rather unpleasant to touch. Holding it up, he shook his head. He was never going to be able to fit into it.

He opened the front zip and began pulling it over each of his legs in turn, and audibly gasped as the suit expanded, then contracted around his body. As it settled into shape, it formed what felt like a hard shell on the outside while still feeling soft on the inside.

After finishing the job, he pulled the zip up and did a few squats before twirling his arms. 'Cool', he said as the suit moved with him almost like a second skin.

'Are you done yet, Lee?' Izzy called.

Realising he was taking longer than expected, he squished his clothes and trainers into the bottom of his new backpack, moving the packs of freezedried rations to make room for them. Pulling some food bars and a book from his own bag, he added them to the load, making sure they were out of sight should anyone else look inside.

He hid his own bag behind a rock, then picked up his boots and the army

backpack and walked barefoot back into the cavern. Everyone was crowded round an athletic woman whose height was accentuated by the mass of black braids wound around her head under her army issue cap. Beside her stood a rather stocky man with the stoic appearance of a career soldier found in armies the world over.

Dropping his bag to the ground, Lee watched the water bottle in the side pocket slip out. As he bent to tighten the strap, he heard a strange female voice say, 'So this is the dog handler?'

Lee raised his eyes to find Captain Kiandra giving him the once over.

'Yes, ma'am,' Izzy said.

The woman raised an eyebrow, and Lee's military training took over. Standing to attention he said, 'Yes, sir.'

The woman smiled. 'Better. I am Captain Kiandra, and I am in charge of this little foray into the outside. Although we will be a little less formal on this mission, I need you to appreciate that the chain of command still applies. That means when I say jump, you jump.'

Lee "Yes, sired" along with the others.

'When I am not around, you will listen to Sergeant Thea, my second.'

Biting back as smile as he watched it dawn on Jason that he was just a foot soldier on this mission, Lee said, 'Yes, Sir.' again.

'This gentleman, and I use that term loosely, is our medic, Corporal Rodgers. He may not look like much, but let me assure you, if we're forced into a fight you'll be pleased he's with us. There's very little he can't patch up on the run.'

The grim-faced man's expression did not alter as the Captain spoke, and Lee sneaked a few glances at him, trying to get the measure of the man. He gave very little away.

'Right, make sure your packs contain all the necessary personal items. Everything else we need is there.' She nodded towards the crate on a trolley beside her. 'Corporal Rodgers, if you would make sure they're all kitted out while I contact base and tell them we're heading out.'

Lee joined the team, noticing Izzy had managed to make it into her black uniform and her boots. As they gathered around the crate, the change in lighting highlighted purple piping on the seams of Thea's suit. The Captain's piping was silver, and the Corporal's red. The military was so predictable; rank must always be shown in some form or other.

Dropping to the floor as the others received their gear, Lee hauled on the "boots" from his pack. Unfortunately, there was nothing remotely boot-like about them. The thick, rough terrain soles had strange ridges down the side, and were almost shoe-like. The top, though, was similar to a thick cotton sock.

As he put his foot inside, he frowned. The fabric stretched, but the sole was going to be too short by at least the length of his toes. He wriggled his toes, and found he was right, they hung over the edge. To his amazement, the boot sole flexed by itself and adjusted to his size before the top section hardened around his foot and ankle. His eyes widened as he stared at the second boot, which now looked nothing like the one on his foot.

A soft wet nose touched his face, then Bruno sat beside him. *A while ago the military found it was easier to produce clothing that adjusted to fit the person rather than producing different sizes. The suit is a special weave that can expand or contract as required, and will keep you warm in the cold and cool in the sun. The boots have some sort of nano technology built in allowing them to adjust as needed.*

Lee found it hard to say anything. *So this is how Alain felt coming to our time?*

A few weeks ago, Bruno had introduced him to Alain, a time traveller from medieval Britain who had joined him to solve a mystery in the New Forest in 2017. He and Alain become firm friends when Lee took it upon himself to help the other boy adjust to life in modern times. In fact, it was Alain who suggest he read the book he now carried in his pack.

I would imagine so, Bruno said.

Lee put on his other boot and stood.

Could you please make sure you bring some decent food for me? I can't bear that freeze dried stuff. Hurry now, or you'll miss the briefing.

Lee sighed as Corporal Rodgers said, 'Righto boy, here's your equipment jacket. Check your blaster's charged when we're outside. Sleeping roll—oh, you have one already. All right, take the helmet, sunglasses, gloves. Oh yes, and this.' He handed Lee a smaller backpack type thing. 'This is for the dog. He's a big 'un, but you should be able to adjust it to fit.'

Lee took the contraption and almost laughed out loud. It was a backpack filled with dog biscuits and had a water bottle attached to the side. It appeared military dogs looked after themselves, because it was designed to be carried by an animal.

I'm not wearing that, Bruno informed him.

You will if you want to eat. The interruption came from Sergeant Thea, who frowned severely at Bruno. *Your unique form does not mean you don't need to blend in. Military dogs here either pull their weight or… well, let's just say that a society on the*

edge of extinction cannot afford to carry dead weight.

Society on the edge of what? Lee asked in alarm. *What is going on here?*

'Right, now you've stowed your gear, let's get the briefing over and done with. We need to move out at first light.'

Lee gazed around, a little uncertain in this strange environment. The others all had their jackets on, and their sleeping rolls were attached to their backpacks, which were all lined against the wall along with their sleek black helmets that were upside down with sunglasses and gloves inside.

Corporal Rodgers slipped in beside him. 'Your first mission outside, lad?'

Lee nodded.

'You can put your jacket on and sort the dog while you listen. If you miss anything, we can pick it up later.'

'Thank you,' Lee said, grateful for the help.

Rodgers clapped him on the shoulder. 'We all had a first time outside. It's a little scary, but you'll be all right.'

As Lee shrugged into the jacket, he asked, *Bruno*, w*here have you brought me?*

The future, just as I said.

Lee grunted his frustration, realised Corporal Rodgers was watching him, and feigned trouble with a zipper to cover his outburst. In the jacket pockets, he found some sort of gun, a couple of different types of knives, something that looked like string but felt like plastic, a spray bottle of some kind, a lighter, and an extra water bottle. Everything the outdoor soldier might need.

What sort of a future and what are we doing here? he asked Bruno as he put everything back where he found it.

Shh, the Captain is starting, and I want to hear what she has to say.

'THE INFORMATION IN your mission notification stated a member of Citizens for Change managed to make it outside using the very exit we came through.' Captain Kiandra turned and gestured to the wall behind.

Lee couldn't see a door, and was impressed with whatever technology was hiding it from view.

'No one knows how they knew about this place. That isn't our worry though, so we'll leave it to the interior guards.'

Citizens for Change? Lee looked down at Bruno.

Shh, I'll update you later.

'The interior guards are also compiling details about the escapee and will send them through when we next make contact. All we currently know is that it is a young male, and that he left the city early yesterday morning,' the Captain continued.

In frustration Lee busied himself sorting Bruno's pack, much to the Guardians' disgust. He couldn't do anything about it though, not if he wanted to hear what the Captain was saying.

'A platoon chased him down the old motorway for some time before losing him in the car forest.'

Lee stopped himself asking what on earth a car forest was, realising he wouldn't prise anything out of Bruno until the Captain finished speaking.

'One of the soldiers believed he winged the boy with a blaster shot, so he's unlikely to be too far from here. Yes, Rodgers?' The Captain paused to let the Corporal speak.

'If he's injured, sir, isn't this a wasted effort? The zombies will—'

'RODGERS!'

'Sorry, sir, but surely some of the Fallout Affected will… well, you know what they do to our kind. Or the scavengers will have picked him over for his belongings and left him to die.'

Lee was not sure he had heard correctly and had to stop himself from speaking out loud. *Fallout Affected! Bleeding hell, Bruno, what have you dragged me into?*

The dog shuffled uneasily as Lee tightened the straps of his backpack.

Too tight, need to breathe.

Taking pity on the dog in spite of his growing anger, Lee loosened the contraption and sat on the ground down beside Bruno.

'You might be right, Rodgers, but our orders are to make certain he is no longer a threat. I don't need to remind you all of the consequences should he tell any outsiders how he escaped. Or, even worse, what will happen if he manages to get back inside without being detected and starts talking about what he's seen,' Captain Kiandra responded.

Lee's stomach churned and he worried he might lose his last meal in front of everyone. *Bruno, I want you to tell me what I've walked into here.*

Calm down, Lee. We're in no immediate danger.

Then why are we here? Something must be going on. Time Guardians don't just drop into somewhere if things are going well… and there are two of you here, so it's likely to be something beyond bad, Lee insisted.

Well—

Lee ignored Bruno and carried on. *And it must be even worse, because you're working with Izzy, and she's a Time Wrecker. Aren't you guys like sworn enemies?*

I wouldn't—

And there are two of them, because that prat Jason is with her! Lee was winding himself up into a rant now.

Lee!

Bruno's voice did nothing to slow his outburst. *This is big, isn't it? What is big enough for a Time Guardian/Time Wrecker Collaboration?*

We are World Fixers, Izzy's voice interrupted. *And we're here to ensure time continues. Now can you shut up so we can listen? We might need to know some of this if we are to survive the next few days.*

How did you—I thought I was just talking to Bruno. Lee coloured.

Neither of you bothered to shield your conversation, so we all heard. Well, maybe not the Captain and Corporal as I doubt anyone from this world has magical abilities, Izzy answered. *Now, shhh!*

Lee shut up just in time to hear the last of the safety briefing. 'For those of you who haven't been above ground before, please ensure you wear your helmet at all times, and your gloves. Although we live with simulated sunlight, we filter out the more harmful rays. If your face or hands are exposed for any reason, there is sunblock in your jackets, I strongly suggest you use it.'

Lee half heard the rest of Captain Kiandra's safety tips, but he took very little in. The very fact that Izzy was worried about her survival raised his anxiety levels, and his foot started tapping of its own accord, as it tended to when he was stressed.

His head was spinning as he tried to put together the fact that he was now in a world where people lived underground and nuclear fallout was a real issue.

He focussed back on the Captain. She was showing them how the inside of their helmets came down to create a mask over their faces, and then tucked into the top of their uniform. 'This is standard issue external patrol gear and is designed to filter radiation. You have your safety strip, which will monitor total exposure and give you a warning when you're getting close to overexposure levels.'

Lee glanced down at his jacket to find his monitor, and was relieved to see it showed no radiation exposure.

Captain Kiandra continued, 'There are water filtration tablets in your packs. Do not, I repeat do not, drink the local water without waiting ten minutes for the tablets to work. And also in your packs are ten days' worth

of prescribed anti-radiation measures: take them daily.'

As the Captain wound up with, 'In line with patrol guidelines, this is a five day out, five day return mission to ensure our exposure to the lethal atmosphere is limited,' a worrying thought suddenly hit Lee.

Izzy, we were outside when we arrived. Will we get sick?

Not if you take the tablets. They probably contain potassium iodine and something to help your white blood cells regenerate. That should combat any radiation in the atmosphere for the short time we were outside.

Lee raised an eyebrow. *Are you sure?*

Not completely, I know very little about this time period. But I did try to get you inside when you insisted on fluffing.

Lee stared at Izzy, trying to assess whether she would actually tell him if his insides were already melting. He wanted to take his tablet right now! Was there time?

No use worrying. What he needed was more information. He hated being in new situations, especially ones he hadn't been able to investigate thoroughly in advance. If only Trouble—Bruno—had warned him he would face nuclear fallout, he could have at least been prepared. Oh no, *Bruno.*

Bruno, won't you need protection?

The German Shepard turned to look at him. *Dogs are expendable here, so they don't protect them in the same way they do humans. I should be all right, though. I can't actually die and, unless the radiation levels are extremely high, we should be gone before the body I am wearing dies.*

'Right, sun should be rising soon. Cover up and let's get going,' Captain Kiandra ordered.

Everyone stood as one and began pulling on their outdoor gear. Sunglasses first, followed by helmet. The face covering was then pulled down and tucked into the collar of the uniform. Lee adjusted his hood and breathed; it wasn't too bad.

Captain Kiandra checked everyone before donning her own gear. 'Just breathe normally. Nanites in the material will filter out any alien particles,' she advised.

The thought alone caused Lee to begin to hyperventilate. Breathe, he told himself, and slowly calmed down. He pulled on his gloves and slung his pack over his back.

'Lights off,' the Captain said, and the cavern plunged into darkness.

A torch built in to Lee's helmet turned on automatically. He and Bruno

headed out after the others, with Izzy walking in behind them. The Captain stopped in the entranceway. The sun was not quite yet up and she seemed reluctant to leave the safety of the cave until it was.

She is not used to working outside in the dark, but the locals are. She will wait until our high-tech gear tips the advantage our way, Thea told them.

Finally, they stepped into the sunlight. In the distance Lee could see a town partially submerged by a rising sea. It had the appearance of a city abandoned for centuries; some of the buildings were crumbling into piles of rubble, while others stood intact and seemingly abandoned. It reminded him of a post-apocalyptic movie set.

Almost immediately below them, he got his first glimpse of the motorway forest. The A3 he travelled along to his Aunt's place only a few weeks ago in his time was covered with a forest of green entwining hundreds of abandoned vehicles. There was no tarmac to be seen.

That wreckage is Portsmouth, he said in amazement.

Yes, Bruno confirmed.

How long ago did the nuclear war happen? Lee asked.

About eighteen years.

Lee froze, hardly able to believe that in less than twenty years such a heavily populated area could be reduced to almost nothing.

'Roll Out!' Captain Kiandra ordered, and his legs obeyed without thinking.

2

A NEW WORLD ORDER

THE CAPTAIN TOOK the lead down the slopes of the Portsdown Hill towards the A3. 'Just until we reach the spot the patrol last saw the escapee. Then we'll let the dog take over,' she informed them.

All right, Bruno, spill, Lee said as he and the dog hung back behind the others.

Give me a minute to shield our conversation, the dog answered.

Lee tried to wait patiently. *Bruno?*

Sorry, the magic here is weak, but we are good to go. As you have already guessed, we are just outside Portsmouth—

What year? Lee interrupted.

That's not important, because after the last world war they started counting again. It is the year NW19.

NW? Lee could not immediately think of what those initials might mean.

New World Order, Bruno provided.

Lee laughed. *Sounds like something out of 1984 or Star Wars.*

I guess in some places the world is a little like that.

'What are you two doing?'

Lee looked up to find Izzy had joined them.

'Bruno is getting me up to speed on the mission. From what I've heard

and seen so far, there's a lot I need to learn.' He swept his hand around, indicating the scenery.

'I think I'll stay and listen, if I may?' she asked Bruno, and the dog nodded, indicating he would include her.

'Good. I would hate for you only to hear the Time Guardian's side of the mission. After all, we're supposed to be working together.'

Bruno waited for Izzy to stop talking before continuing. *So, a brief history lesson up to NW0. Not long after your time, a pandemic swept the world, during which the United Kingdom finally ceded from the European Union. For a couple of years, things carried on as normal until a second pandemic hit. Countries around the world ping-ponged from lockdowns to periods of relative freedom while scientists rushed to find a cure, or at least a vaccine.*

It was chaos, Izzy continued. *Everyone thought a vaccine would be produced in a year like during the last pandemic, but this time it was different. As the number of deaths grew daily, countries locked their borders, airlines stop flying, and each government focussed only on protecting their own people.*

So all this devastation happened because of a pandemic? Lee asked.

Izzy laughed. *No, that was just the beginning of the end.*

Bruno took over the lesson. *During the end of the pandemic, an ultra-Conservative leader was elected Prime Minster in the United Kingdom and began isolating what he began to call Great Briton from the rest of Europe. Tempers flared and things escalated; war appeared inevitable.*

Hold on, Lee said. *Surely the United Nations intervened to stop it.*

Normally they would have, but they had their hands full trying to stop a war between superpowers after the United States had accused China of causing both pandemics. When mass riots broke out in the US after a presidential election, China saw an opportunity to hit back, Bruno said.

That doesn't sound too much different to now, Lee interrupted. *I don't see how it caused this.*

What… what are we calling you this time, Sigma? Was it Bruno? Izzy chuckled. *What Bruno hasn't told you is that during the pandemics the world became a cleaner space. Fewer emissions, rivers clearing up, people returning to producing their own food. After the first pandemic ran its course, many governments latched on to the social changes. Some countries didn't want to open their borders and they moved towards a more sustainable way of life. The rest of the world called them crackpots.*

Still not seeing how this had an impact. Lee wondered why were they bothering with this history lesson? All he wanted to find out was why the world went to war.

Patience, Lee, Bruno counselled. *Just a little more. Carry on, Isolde.*

Izzy wrinkled her nose at the use of her full name and Lee could have sworn Bruno smiled.

Izzy picked up the story, *Global warming was soon back at disaster levels, and, with escalating political divisions, no one was interested in a global solution. Eventually, some countries found they didn't have enough food or water to sustain their population. Those countries that were better off either didn't have enough to share, or relationships had deteriorated so much they didn't want to help anyone else out. In the end the world went to war over food.*

You're kidding me. Lee could not imagine a world where countries were so insular.

Unfortunately, she isn't. For all of humankind's technological advancements, it was the struggle for basic human needs that let them down, Bruno confirmed.

Lee frowned, unable to understand how a lack of food would lead to a nuclear war. Surely such actions would only make food shortages worse. *I'm finding it difficult to make the leap here, guys.*

Izzy sighed. *In a world where countries are focussed inwards, it doesn't take much to set things off. When the United States hijacked a food shipment from New Zealand destined for China, it was the straw that broke the camel's back.*

Okay, I get it. *So, what's left now?* Lee asked

Bear in mind our last solid update was in the first few weeks of the apocalypse, so it may not be so accurate now. China, Asia, and America were decimated in those first few weeks, Bruno said. *There are pockets of survivors in the United States, and in the wilds of Canada and Alaska—mostly living way off-grid.*

Izzy took over. *South America and Africa managed to keep to themselves during the war but were worst hit with nuclear fallout. They didn't have the resources to cope with the ensuing medical emergencies. I believe if anyone is still alive, they will have reverted back to tribalism.*

What about my home? And Europe? Lee asked.

Australia and New Zealand had isolated themselves somewhat before the war. They fared the best out of all of this, but their societies quickly moved away from technology and are now most likely agricultural—think nineteenth-century rural, Bruno said.

Nice the whole world didn't go to hell in a handbasket. Lee's comment was laced with sarcasm.

Izzy carried on. *Europe fared much the same as the United States, or actually, perhaps a little worse. Once the nuclear bombs began falling and the world order crumbled, many old hurts between countries flared up, and they continued fighting for years using traditional weaponry. Our last reports described a continent controlled by military units*

and living in a continuous state of war.

What about here? Lee asked.

With England already isolated from Europe, after the first few bombs decimated London, Manchester, and Edinburgh, they were left alone. Infighting in Europe meant everyone was kept too busy to invade, said Bruno

From what scientists tell us, Izzy said, *a few small communities will have survived on the surface. The bulk of people likely still live underground and intend to stay there until the world and the atmosphere settle.*

How many of these underground cities are there? Lee asked.

We believe about a hundred dotted around. They are all completely self-sufficient, with a governing council whose leader holds a seat on the National Council, which operates much like the House of Lords in your time, Bruno answered.

And the other communities—Lee started.

Would be pretty much lawless, I think, Izzy finished.

They walked in silence for a while as Lee digested the fate of the human race. The thought that this was what they were reduced to made him sick. As they recached the flattish terrain of the old motorway, Lee voiced the something that had been niggling in the back of his head for a while. 'Couldn't you guys have prevented this?'

'Them or us?' asked Izzy.

'Both. Either.'

The Time Guardian's job is to ensure time flows as it always has, Bruno said, *and this was how the human race chose to evolve.*

'We tried to change things, tried to make people more aware of their impact on other people and on the world they lived in, but we were thwarted as often as we were successful.' Izzy's tone was accusatory, and Bruno hung his head.

The Time Guardians and World Fixers both wove in and out of time, doing their best to help humanity, but they were often at odds with each other. It was unusual for them to work together. That thought made Lee stop and think—what was so bad their two Councils would allow them to be here now?

Bruno, Izzy, what are you here to do? I mean, what are you here to make sure happens?

Nothing, Bruno answered. *I am not here to ensure anything happens.*

Okay, then what are you guys planning to do that Bruno must stop? he asked Izzy.

You have this wrong, Lee. None of us are here to do anything in particular, Izzy said.

Lee looked from one to the other in confusion. *Then why are we all here?*

To prevent time from ending, Izzy and Bruno said together.

VIVIENNE LEE FRASER

'WHAT?' LEE STUMBLED over some overgrown car part.

As far as the Guardians are concerned, they cannot plot human history past the next few days, Bruno said.

Nor can my Council, Izzy admitted.

Lee could not believe what he was hearing. *But surely you have both sent someone here to find out what happens.*

It's not that easy. Bruno's head hung down as he trotted alongside Lee. *We need a certain amount of magic to do what we do. Unfortunately, World War Three dispelled the little magic left in the world—until now.*

So we have been sent here to find out what we can. The hope is that our teams will work together to ensure there is a future for us to fight over, Izzy finished.

Lee frowned and he rubbed his thumb over his middle finger, an outward sign of the worry building inside. In fact, it was more than worry. His anxiety levels were shooting off the charts.

Bruno had promised to take him back to his time before anyone would miss him. Now he was saying there was very little magic here for him to work with, and he had no idea what would happen over the next few days.

Will I be able to go home? The thought entered Lee's head and came straight out of his mouth.

We have all agreed that you are the first priority to be returned, Izzy said.

Jason agreed to that? He hoped the joke would cover the turmoil within.

Izzy grinned. *No, but he was the only one who didn't agree, so he was outvoted.*

Changing the subject so as not to dwell on what was really worrying him, Lee asked, *How much factual information do you have about NW time?*

Umm, let me see. Theta arrived here three days ago, and what little intel she gathered I have shared with you, Bruno said.

Which is not much, Lee said wryly.

Not much more than we knew already, I agree. She did have to arrange our covers and for us to be assigned to this expedition. It was a busy few days for her.

Another thought occurred to Lee. *From what you have said, the whole world is in disarray, so how can something happening in this small corner of England cause time to stop?*

We have no idea. All we know is that it does. Bruno's tone was sharp in Lee's head, and he realised the Guardian must be as frustrated over the lack of information as he was.

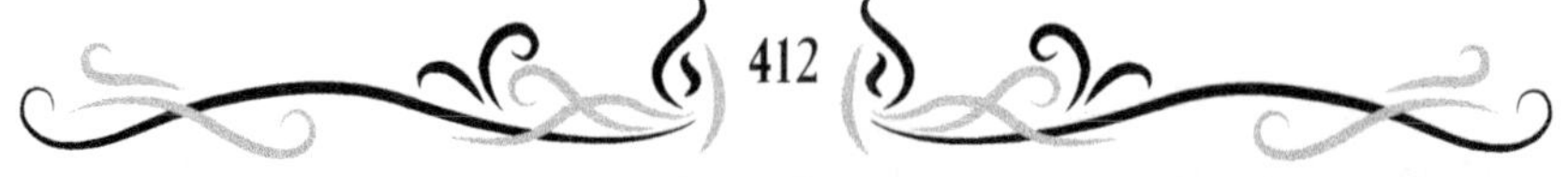

NW time has always been a blur, and no one could travel here. Then a week ago a blip showed up on both time radars. It was so unusual our Councils got together to discuss what it meant and… well, here we are, Izzy said.

So what has changed? Why now? Lee's finger was still rubbing, and he took a couple of deep breaths in an attempt to calm himself down.

From what our people can make out, the boy leaving Portsdown triggered something, Izzy said.

So, are we supposed to help find him and bring him back? Or help him stay free? Lee stopped, almost banging into Izzy who had come to a halt.

We're not sure, Bruno said as he came to a stop beside him. *We're playing it pretty much by ear. The Councils have people watching the time stream to advise us when they can. They hope that while we're here, a little more will be revealed and we can come up with a proper plan.*

Captain Kiandra was talking over top of Bruno, and Lee strained to hear her.

'… this is where the patrol last saw the escaped citizen.' She reached into her pack and pulled out a strip of fabric. 'The earlier patrol picked this up. It belonged to the boy. Bring up that dog and let him have a sniff.'

Bruno followed Lee to where the Captain stood. Lee took the garment and held it out for Bruno to plant his nose in.

Can you really do this tracking thing? Lee asked the dog once Bruno had removed his nose.

I could distinguish scents when I was Trouble, so I believe I can do this. I think all I have to do is match a scent to this one. How hard can that be?

Lee grimaced and stood to find the Captain staring at him as if she expected something else. Lee looked around and realised she was waiting on him. He took the fabric away and said with as much command as he could muster, 'Find, boy.'

Bruno stuck his muzzle in the air and sniffed, then began wandering around the abandoned vehicles, nose to the ground.

'This may take a while,' Lee informed them with more confidence than he felt.

'Break time,' the Captain said, and they all dropped their packs to the ground. Some opened their water bottles, loosened the front of their masks, and took sips through the straw.

It was Lee's first chance for a good look around. It was eerily quiet on the motorway, and he felt more like he was on a movie set than in the real world in the future. His shoulders tensed and the hair on the back of his

neck stood on end. He turned around slowly. Something moved. Someone was watching them.

Bruno paused and sniffed the air again. 'I feel it too, boy,' Lee said.

Two, over in the trees. They smell of fear, and… something else… like death, Bruno sent.

'Captain, I think we have company,' Lee said, jerking his head towards the bushes Bruno had indicated.

'Yes, soldier. We picked them up on our descent. They're probably FAs and won't trouble us too much.' After a moment she added, 'Fallout Affected… people whose bodies have some form of radiation sickness. They'll be weakened by whatever disease they have and won't attack an armed troop.'

'Why would they be out here so far away from other people?' Lee asked.

'You really are a newbie.' Rodgers leaned around the Captain to answer Lee. 'Out here they're treated like pariahs. They're a reminder of what will happen to everyone outside… eventually.'

'Don't they have drugs for treatment?' Lee asked, remembering the briefing this morning.

'Not out here, I wouldn't imagine. Not anymore.' Rodgers returned to sipping his water.

'Europe attacked Portsmouth with conventional warheads, decimating the military infrastructure. Luckily, most civilian leaders were already underground. A few people survived the attack, but they were not organised, so I doubt anyone thought to gather and distribute medication,' the Captain explained, then frowned at him. 'Didn't you learn all of this in school? I thought local history was a mandatory subject.'

'Pardon, Captain, but our dog trainer is a recent transfer from a London community. He won't have been taught our local history,' Thea interrupted.

'Of course, I forgot. It must be quite different in the old capitol.'

'Yes.' Lee confirmed, mostly because some sort of an answer was expected.

You need to be smarter. Ask less questions of the locals, otherwise we will all be found out.

The voice in his head was new, and he started when he realised it was coming from Thea.

Bruno, keep him in line. This is not a mission for newbies. I don't understand why the Council let you bring him, Thea added.

They insisted I ask him along. Apparently, his presence is essential to our success.

'Soldier, what is that dog doing lolling around? Get him moving. I want to be well on the way to catching up with this boy before midday.'

Lee shook his head to clear his thoughts before searching out Bruno. He

found the dog lying on the ground, his head resting on outstretched paws.

I was waiting for you to all finish. I have the scent. Almost before Bruno had finished speaking, figures emerged from the forest, from behind cars, and seemingly from out of the vegetation covering the road. They were armed and none too friendly looking as they circled the small troop.

LEE FROZE, HIS hand on his blaster. Captain Kiandra put out a hand and said, 'Stand down.'

Lee relaxed a little, but he didn't remove his hand, as the people surrounding wore quasi-military clothing and carried their weapons like soldiers. Nothing in their faces indicated their intentions were friendly.

Captain Kiandra took a step forward, as did one of their people.

'I am Captain Kiandra of the Portsdown Regiment. We are in neutral territory.'

'Your information is out of date. The City of Portsmouth and the Portsmouth Militia now claim the A3 as our territory. We notified your commanders over a month ago and warned them not to use the motorway.' The other woman's voice was brittle in its attempt to sound commanding. 'You will come with us.'

'We must have been given old maps. If you can show us the new boundary, we will keep to our side of it until we are out of your territory.' Captain Kiandra made as if to leave.

'Halt.' The Portsmouth Militia cocked their rifles.

'You are the second group in as many days to violate our boundaries. You must be made an example of. You have a choice— come with us, or make a stand.'

The leader of the militia stood with a hand on her weapon. She was only young, and Lee had met her type before. Promoted quickly, she likely substituted aggression for leadership.

'Can't we—' Captain Kiandra started.

'Corporal, over there. The zombie kids we were chasing.' One of the militia closest to Lee pointed to the bushes where he and Bruno had detected movement moments before.

The Corporal froze, undecided on which target would bring her the most kudos. Lee had no such qualms. He feigned a trip and fell into the person who had noticed the kids. Bruno, taking his lead, started barking and leaping at two armed men beside him.

As Lee regained his feet, he looked towards the bushes and shouted,

"Run!" His team took it as if he was speaking to them and started off down the road-jungle, slipping in between the cars and heading towards Southampton.

Movement in the bushes told Lee the children also took the warning. Ducking behind the closest vehicle, he jumped as a bullet clipped the metal beside his head—too close for comfort. Bruno scooted to a halt beside him.

Dropping to his knees, Lee stared around the side of the car. The militia had split into two groups. The first was heading after the children, and the rest were making their way in his direction.

Which way is the escapee? he asked Bruno.

The dog nodded towards their left.

Of course, towards Portsmouth.

No, I think whoever is carrying the boy headed off more towards Southampton, Bruno said.

'Come on, you two,' Thea yelled from about a hundred meters ahead, and Lee realised if they didn't move soon, they would be stranded without support.

Theta, go more right. I have a trail heading that way. We'll meet up with you later, Bruno sent.

What did you do that for? Lee was aghast. *You just sent away our cover.*

Come, this way. Bruno padded away from him, weaving in-between automotive debris following a scent only he could smell. Keeping to a crouch, Lee had no option but to follow, making sure he kept something in between him and his pursuers at all times.

When one of the Portsmouth militia yelled out, "Over by the roadside," Lee froze, then realised they had seen the others leaving the cover of the motorway. He used the diversion to pop his head above the Mini he hid behind.

Lee dropped back to the ground. A boy about his own age was standing on the other side watching the rest of Lee's team run across open ground. His heart pounded and his hands shook, and he tried to control his breathing, hoping all the while the militia man hadn't heard him.

He's gone, Bruno said. *Follow me.* A German Shepard head peeked around the side of a rolled BMW near the edge of the road. Lee crawled over to him.

Let's wait here until the militia are far enough ahead they won't look back, Bruno instructed.

Lee sunk to the ground and leaned against the car. Bruno stayed standing beside him, occasionally sniffing the air or cocking his head to the side to listen.

What just happened? Lee asked.

From what I can gather, the Portsdown and Portsmouth communities have been in consultation often enough to agree, or at least communicate, localised boundaries.

That means there are groups of people out here organising, Lee said, turning this new information over in his head, then added, *And, if I'm supposed to be on loan from London, then it sounds like the underground cities still have a structure that governs them all.*

Yes. Where are you going with this? Bruno asked.

Lee chewed the information over, trying to put the kernel of fear in his mind into words. *Local militias and a single large government—*

Ah, and if that government sees itself as the natural successor to the pre-war government…. Bruno stared at Lee. *I see where you're going with this. The local situation might be more unstable than we first thought.*

Lee listened to the sounds around him. *Is he gone?*

Yes, let's go. I will feel better when we catch up with the others, and I want to talk to Thea about this new development.

They made their way through the edge of the cars on the motorway, using a few vehicles that had tumbled down the embankment as cover to make their way towards a copse of trees. The militia was still ahead of them searching for the others, but so far hadn't thought to look behind.

Every now and then Bruno sniffed the ground or put his nose to the air, occasionally correcting their path. Lee concentrated on staying out of sight until a hand grabbed the back of his suit and he lost his footing. Suppressing a yelp, he turned to find himself face-to-face with Captain Kiandra.

'Phew, I thought you were the militia,' he whispered.

Captain Kiandra loomed in closer until their noses were almost touching, 'You might wish I was one of them by the time I've finished with you.'

Lee gulped.

'What the hell did you think you were doing back there?' she asked, her voice a low rumble.

'Sa… s… saving the children in the bushes,' Lee said as Bruno growled a warning from beside him.

'My job is to think and decide how we act. Your job is to wait for orders and to obey those orders. ARE. WE. CLEAR?'

'Yes, sir,' Lee said.

'One more stupid act like that and I will shoot you myself. You could have put us all in jeopardy.' Having delivered her threat, Captain Kiandra appeared to have run out of steam. 'Come on. We've lost the militia, and the others are over this way.'

The scent is this way, Bruno said.

'Um ....' Lee's nerves seemed to have eaten his voice.

'What now, Private?'

'The scent leads that way.' Lee pointed in the opposite direction.

The Captain sighed. 'Wait here while I retrieve the others. And Private... try not to get yourself or anyone else killed while I'm away.'

Very funny! 'Yes, sir.'

AS THE SUN sunk low in the sky, Captain Kiandra called a stop by yet another copse of trees. 'We need somewhere defensible to spend the night and I think this will do fine.'

Sergeant Rodgers pulled out the tent and arranged it in the middle of the small clearing with the opening facing the only track in. After making sure the bottom was secure, he pressed a button and it inflated. Sergeant Thea pulled an air filtration unit from her pack and set it into the vent.

Once inside, they removed their outer layer of clothing and laid their sleeping rolls across the tent. Finally, they placed their packs at the head of their beds away from the door, to provide additional protection.

It was all relatively comfortable. Lee had been on worse camping trips in his life, even if he had been forced to the outer edge of the group as a sign of the troop's displeasure. At least he'd get a good night's sleep with Bruno on one side and the tent wall on the other.

The dinner rations were cold and hardly filled the hole in Lee's stomach. He ate the tasteless food seated on his bedroll, took his radiation tablets, then lay down with his hands behind his head.

The others were in a group talking with their backs to him. Fine, if they didn't want to include him, he was good with that, really. He took his copy of *Lord of the Rings* from his pack and opened it to the first page. Reading and fantasy weren't his things, but if Alain said it was good, he was prepared to give it a go.

He had just started reading about the main character's elevenety-first birthday when Bruno stretched out beside him, his head resting on his paws.

Not eating? Lee asked, staring at the still full bowl of dog biscuits he had put out for the Guardian.

I am not eating that! Bruno said, disdain lacing his voice.

Lee chuckled. *You needn't think our rations were any better. In fact, I'd go as far*

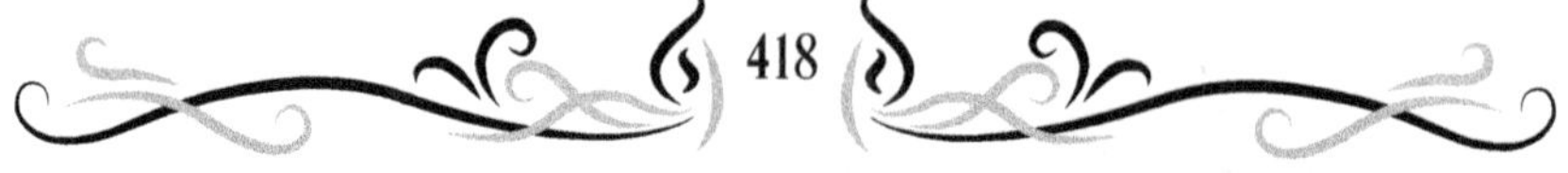

as to say your food looks more appetising.

The dog sighed a doggy sigh, humphed, then stood and chewed a couple of biscuits. Lee poured some water into another bowl so Bruno could have a drink as he ate the dried offering. The bedroll moved as Izzy joined them.

'What was that all about today, Lee?' she asked, making herself comfortable. 'You know, with the militia.'

'It wasn't them. It was the kids,' he said. 'They called them zombies. I knew something horrible was going to happen to them, and it wasn't their fault they have radiation sickness.'

'Surely you could've come up with something better than "run".' Izzy smiled to soften her words.

'It was a sort of spur of the moment thing.' Lee grinned.

Izzy smiled back. 'Well… I sort of get it, but next time maybe just give a heads-up first.'

Glancing at the others, Lee asked, 'Are they very upset with me?'

'They'll get over it,' Izzy said before reaching over and ruffling the dog's fur. *Bruno, do you actually have any idea where we're going?*

I smelt the boy exactly where Captain Kiandra said I would. Other scents around him indicate someone picked him up, and they were heading in this direction, towards Southampton.

Are you sure he's still with them? Lee asked.

When they rest they put him down, and his scent is mingled with theirs, Bruno confirmed.

Well, at least we're going in the right direction, Izzy said. *Have you or Thea heard from the Time Guardians?*

No, nothing, Bruno said as he wormed his way in between the two of them.

Izzy moved a little to make room for him. *Everything's silent from our lot too. Have you tried contacting them?*

No. Theta is in charge of this mission, so I'm leaving that up to her. I'm concentrating on what needs to be done by Bruno the dog, and of course making sure Lee is safe.

Izzy returned to the others and Lee slipped into his bedroll. Knowing Izzy was on his side gave him a warm glow inside—which disappeared soon after Jason took the spot beside him and hissed, 'You're a liability. You shouldn't be on this mission. You're gonna get us all killed.'

Izzy turned and said, 'Shut up, Jason. If anybody is going to put our lives in danger, it will be you and that big mouth of yours.'

Stunned into silence, Jason made as if to say something meaningful, then

sniggered. 'Well, Izzy, if you want to blame everything on me— go right ahead, it's par for the course for you.'

What's going on with them? Lee wondered. He got the impression the two knew each other well, and not in a good way. Bruno sat up and, when Jason tried to move him away, a low, rumbling growl came from deep in his belly, and he bared his teeth. Unsure of what to make of the dog, Jason shuffled away and started getting ready for bed

The tent was soon quietened down. Corporal Rodgers turned out the lamp, plunging them into darkness, before taking a seat by the clear doorway.

Lee barely slept that night. His mind was working overtime—mostly questioning why he hadn't stayed in England for the Christmas holidays before returning to Australia to start officer's training in February. Why had he chosen now to do something on the spur of the moment?

It was almost a relief when he felt a cold nose on his face sometime in the early hours of the morning.

Pleased you could join us. Thea's voice invaded his thoughts as her body moved in the bedroll beside him. She must be returning from guard duty, Lee thought.

Lay off him, Bruno said. *He's had enough of a whipping for one day.*

Sorry, we haven't much time before the others wake, and I want to make sure we're all up to speed before I update Jason and Isolde, Thea said

You've spoke to the Guardians? Bruno asked.

Yes. Alpha contacted me while I was on watch. They have nothing new to report. She chuckled, which sounded odd in Lee's head. *I don't think he's enjoying working with the World Fixers. He seems to have taken a particular dislike to one of them, some chap called Gerald.*

Bruno laughed along with her. *He was never one of the most flexible members of the Guardian Council.*

Anyway, all he said was that they're still working on some guidelines for us. The time blip hasn't altered, so, at best, we're not making things worse.

The lack of control over what we are doing must grate on him, Bruno said, and the two laughed again.

Hold on. They said we're not making things worse, but that means we're not making them better either, Lee interrupted.

The current line of thought is that we won't see any change until we catch up with the boy who escaped, Thea said.

They didn't report on anything from the World Fixers? Lee asked.

I suspect their update will come via Jason or Isolde. It appears working together still means having information silos, Thea answered, then added, *I'm not sure that Jason is up to much. He's a little bit…*

… *flaky?* Lee offered.

Yes. I don't believe he takes any of this seriously, and he spends his time winding up Isolde.

The others are stirring, Bruno warned as he rose to his feet and stretched, ready to start the day.

Captain Kiandra ordered them to eat a quick breakfast. She wanted to be on the road early. While they packed up camp, Jason and Izzy argued in hushed voices, Izzy's face growing more flushed as the conversation dragged on.

Lee was strapping on Bruno's pack when Izzy sidled over. Glancing around to make sure Jason was distracted, she whispered, 'We have nothing new to report. Jason wanted to make out we had something concrete we were keeping from you. The prat!'

Lee said, 'We don't have anything either.'

'I know Thea told us. Her being so open is why I shared our update with you.'

Thank you, Bruno said.

As he continued rolling up his bedroll, Lee mused out loud, 'Can't you guys just get along?'

Izzy paused, and asked in a low voice, 'Do you mean me and Jason? Or the World Fixers and the Guardians?'

'Yes,' responded Lee.

3

A SOLDIER'S LIFE FOR ME

THEY FINISHED DISMANTLING the camp and packed up before Captain Kiandra led them out of the copse. Dew still clung to the grass and the early morning sun, causing a mist to rise across the field.

'Righto, Private. You and the dog pick up the trail while I see if I can contact base,' the Captain said the minute they left the shelter of the trees. As she spoke she pulled some sort of communication device from her jacket and typed in a message.

'Are you waiting for something, Private?' she barked, finding Lee still standing in front of her.

'No, sir,' Lee responded, turning on his heel. 'Come on, Bruno. Let's find that scent again.'

I'll be lucky to catch the scent with all this moisture on the ground, Bruno grumbled, but he obediently stuck his nose into the grass and rooted around where he had last smelt their quarry. He shuffled forward a bit and swivelled his head this way and that before turning to Lee. *I can't smell much at the moment, but I am pretty sure they're still heading towards Southampton. If we take it slow, I am sure I will pick the trail up again soon.*

Lee was about to inform the others when Captain Kiandra joined the group.

'Good news. They sent through background on the boy we're tracking and, even better, a recent image,' she said.

'That's a bit of luck,' said Rodgers and he took the device. 'We're almost out of comms range.'

The Captain frowned. 'Luck had nothing to do with it. Patrols always check in before losing contact, and command tracks our progress, so they would have been aware this was the last chance for an update.'

Lee was beginning to get the impression from the way Captain Kiandra spoke to her corporal that, although she respected Rodgers as a soldier, she didn't much like him as a person.

Rodgers handed the device to Thea and Jason, who passed it on to Izzy. As she looked at the screen, Izzy's face froze, and her gazed flicked across to Lee. Taking this as an invitation, he glanced over her shoulder at the screen and the reason for her reaction hit him like a slap. The screen displayed an image of Alain, only it wasn't quite Alain. Izzy scrolled upwards to the description of the subject.

What's happening? Bruno asked.

Alain's on the screen. Well, not exactly Alain, but a boy called Allan who's an apprentice gardener from Portsdown. Only, it might as well be Alain from the looks of him.

Lee read the physical details of their quarry with his fists clenched and his stomach knotted. They could be describing Alain. Suddenly his concerns about being in a post-apocalyptic wasteland seemed unimportant—they were hunting his friend as if he were some sort of criminal.

Now I understand why your presence on this mission was so critical, Bruno said.

What? Lee shook his head, trying to clear it. *What do you mean?*

You and Alain are friends in many lifetimes. Perhaps you're destined to always find each other and renew that connection.

Lee was stunned. *You mean you're more likely to find this Allan because I am with you?*

Bruno sat up and stared at Lee, who could see his helmeted reflection in the dog's liquid brown eyes. *Yes, probably.*

Lee did not respond. He wasn't sure how he felt about being used as bait. He hadn't even met this boy but, if he was a reincarnation of Alain, he wasn't sure either person was capable of doing anything to warrant a group of soldiers tracking him down.

'Private. PRIVATE! Are we ready to go?' Captain Kiandra jolted Lee from his thoughts as she took the communicator from him.

'Sorry?' He shook his head. 'What? Oh, yes, Bruno has the scent. This way.'

'Right, you heard him. Let's go.' The Captain's voice rang clear in the morning air.

Izzy joined Lee and Bruno as the rest of the troop fell in behind. 'Are you okay?' she asked.

Lee wasn't sure how to answer. On the one hand, he'd never met Allan, but his stomach and head were certainly reacting as if he was a friend.

'He isn't Alain,' he said, his voice low so only Izzy could hear.

'From experience I can tell you that is both true, and it isn't. Reincarnations often hold the essence of previous lives.'

'Thanks, that helped a lot,' Lee groaned.

Izzy laughed. 'It helps if you remember we're soldiers and we're here to do a job. All we need to do is follow orders.'

'If I do that, what do I do with all these conflicting emotions I'm feeling?'

Ask Sergeant Thea. She'll tell you to push the emotions down as far as you can and forget about them—all that matters is the job, Bruno said.

'What about you, Izzy? What do you say?' Lee asked.

'Is there a problem, Private?' Captain Kiandra called from behind.

'No, sir,' Izzy answered.

'It's a little difficult to track in the wet,' Lee said.

'Make sure you don't lose the trail,' the Captain commanded.

'I won't, sir,' Lee said, but his heart wasn't in it.

Following orders was easy when you had no stake in the outcome. Lee had never been in a situation where he had to put his personal convictions aside and do as he was told. How had his father managed it in his military career? It wasn't something he talked about, but Lee knew his dad lived by a strong moral code. Had he ever been ordered to do something contrary to that?

Lee wished he could ask his father's advice. With that thought a wave of homesickness washed over him. He wanted to see his sister, Bee, and his mother. To walk along a Sydney beach with them, the wind in his hair and salt water running over his feet—to behave like nothing had changed.

He gave himself a mental shake. 'Get a grip,' he said under his breath.

'What?' Izzy asked.

'Nothing. Just talking to myself.'

She shrugged.

His family wouldn't always be with him. Whether he was in an apocalyptic world sometime in the future, or in the middle of a war zone in his time,

this was his problem to solve. He would gather more information, but in the meantime he would follow Izzy's advice and concentrate on the task at hand.

THE TRAIL BRUNO followed led them away from roads and across overgrown fields full of rocks and potholes. Lee concentrated on doing his job and not twisting his ankle, pushing thoughts of their end goal from his mind every time they threatened to surface.

Around midday they stopped briefly for a mouthful of water and to chew on a bar of dried fruit and nuts. Picking up his pack to head back out, Lee turned to Bruno.

Are you sure we're still heading the right way? he asked. *If Alain, sorry Allan, is being carried, we should be moving faster than the people who found him. Surely we should've caught them up by now?*

You will remember I said "they" picked him up. Bruno stood before continuing. *Those carrying him are fit and healthy, and probably used to carrying extra weights. Also, they're likely local so aren't stopping to check the way every few minutes. At best we're keeping pace with them. At worst they might actually be pulling ahead.*

Before Lee could respond, Izzy joined them, saying, 'The tracks aren't getting any fresher.'

Lee's eyes widened. 'You can actually track? I thought that was a ruse to give you a place in the troop,' he said quietly.

Izzy glared at him.

'Oh, right, I need to be able to tell the Captain how I know why we haven't caught the boy up.' Lee sighed. 'I guess I should go and let everyone in on the bad news.'

Ever since the incident the day before, Lee had been keeping his distance from the Captain. Putting his fears aside, he wandered over to where she was talking with Sergeant Thea.

'Yes?' Captain Kiandra paused as Lee approached.

'I wanted to report, Captain. We're still going the right way. Izzy—Private Isolde—says whatever tracks she finds are not getting any fresher.'

'Can you tell me how many we are tracking?'

'We think perhaps two, and of course the escapee,' Lee answered.

'So, we're about keeping pace with Allan and whoever he's with?'

'That is what we believe,' Lee confirmed.

The Captain stood and said, 'Right, gather round, everyone.'

Relieved to have the Captain's focus off him, Lee shuffled to the back of the group behind Rodgers and Jason, who had become quite pally.

'We're not gaining on our prey, so we need to up our pace to double time,' Captain Kiandra informed them.

Jason groaned, earning a glare from the Captain. Rodgers chuckled beside him and said quietly, 'Careful, boy, she's the type that'll make us go even quicker if she thinks we're bucking her command.'

I can't track as well if we go too fast, Bruno said.

Lee stared down at the dog. *Is that for real, or are you merely trying to make things easier on us?*

I'm new to this tracking thing. I can't guarantee I can keep us heading in the right direction if we speed up too much.

Lee sighed. 'Excuse me, Captain. We might lose the scent if we go too fast. Bruno and I are still only in training.'

Captain Kiandra humphed and drummed her fingers on her thigh. Everyone watched, waiting for her decision. 'Right, we move at a slow jog. Tell me immediately if we lose the scent, Private. I don't want to backtrack too often, or we'll lose even more time. I want this guy back in our custody before he wakes up or ends up somewhere we can't access him. Move out.'

The last comment caused Lee to frown. Where on earth would this boy go that they couldn't get to him? Lee started walking, Bruno and Izzy at his side, and the others falling into formation behind. An hour or so later, when they were approaching the outskirts of Southampton, the group stopped for a rest break.

'If he's in there, he'll be lost to us,' Corporal Rodgers said. 'I can't see those militia types letting us anywhere near him.' Rodger's lips curled back in a sneer. 'Not that we'd want to get too close to any of those radiation-drenched ba—'

'CORPORAL!' Captain Kiandra interrupted.

Although his glare was mutinous, Corporal Rodgers closed his mouth. The fingers began drumming against Captain Kiandra's leg again, then stopped abruptly. She turned to her team. 'He may well be in there, but we can cross that bridge if we come to it. We keep going until we lose the scent or reach their borders.'

'But—'

'Corporal Rodgers, I don't believe the Southampton Militia would pick

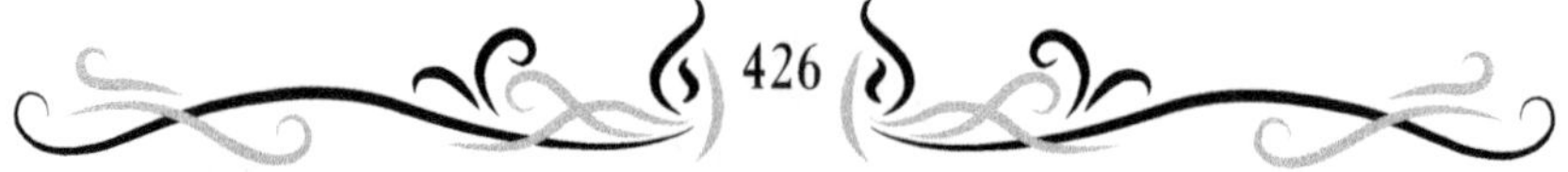

someone up so close to Portsmouth. Firstly, because their relations with Portsmouth are volatile at best. Secondly, why would they drag one of ours so far? I cannot think of a single reason.'

'With all due respect, sir, I believe those militia mongrels would do just about anything to find out more about our city.'

Captain Kiandra started to speak, then shook her head. 'We can't say for certain he's with the militia—Portsmouth or Southampton.'

'Well, if the militia don't have him, then likely the zombies do. If that is the case, he's dead meat and we are wasting our time,' Corporal Rodgers grumbled.

Captain Kiandra adjusted her pack as she glared at Rodgers. 'We in the Portsdown Regiment act on facts. While there is evidence that the fallout impaired will eat raw animals, there is absolutely no indication they eat human flesh. We also have no reason to believe they picked up the escapee. So, I'd appreciate it if you kept your opinions to yourself.'

Not hearing the message to leave well enough alone, Corporal Rodgers spoke again. 'I'm just preparing us for the worst.'

Captain Kiandra's chin rose as she ignored this last remark and ordered them to move on.

The sun had started its descent when the company caught their first glimpse of Southampton. Many buildings still stood, but they were more overgrown than derelict.

'How come Southampton did better in the war than Portsmouth?' Lee asked Izzy.

'Because the naval base at Portsmouth was bombed early on to prevent the navy from entering the conflict. Being a commercial port, Southampton was mostly left alone.'

About a kilometre out from the city limits, Bruno paused and sniffed the air before dropping his muzzle to the ground and snuffling around.

Please don't tell me they went into the city, Lee said. On the one hand, he didn't want to confront another militia group. On the other, Allan being out of reach would solve his ethical dilemma. On yet another, he was interested to meet this version of Alain.

Bruno walked around in circles, trying to find the scent. Fortunately, instead of wandering closer to the city, he was walking away from it. He finally stopped and stared up at Lee.

Whoever's got the boy went this way, around the outskirts. I think we can speed up

for a while if we follow those perimeter markers, the dog said.

Izzy and Lee crouched and found the old roadside markers Bruno was referring to. Most were overgrown, but there were enough of them to show a route around the city.

'I don't think these guys wanted to encounter the Southampton Militia any more than we do,' Izzy observed.

Lee made a great show of searching for and finding markers while Izzy went back to report to the Captain. The group caught Lee up, and he pointed out the way around Southampton.

'Righto, it looks like we have a solid trail to follow that doesn't rely on scenting. Jason, I want you and Rodgers to take point—double time. Sergeant Thea and I will take the rear. I want you trackers safe in the middle,' the Captain ordered.

They formed up, and before anyone moved, the Captain leaned forward and added, 'We will stop and check our course every fifteen minutes. I don't want to lose that scent.'

Lee would have loved to have taken a look at the city as they ran. Unfortunately, although close to Southampton, the area was clear enough for anyone approaching to stand out like a sore thumb. Their side of the markers was completely overgrown.

We haven't seen any locals, Lee said as they ran. *Don't you find that strange?*

There's a group following us to make sure we don't stray too close to perimeter, Bruno informed him.

Lee dropped back a little to tell Captain Kiandra the news.

'Already on it, Private,' the Captain said. 'But good to know you're keeping your eyes open.'

Lee blushed at the praise as he returned to his position.

Soon they veered away from the city, and Lee tensed again. How easy it would have been if Allan was with the militia and out of their reach. Now he faced a restless night wrestling with his conscience.

BY THE TIME they started raising the tent that night, they were well on the other side of Southampton and heading into the New Forest. Once again the Captain directed them to a copse of trees with a place to raise the tent in an easily defensible position.

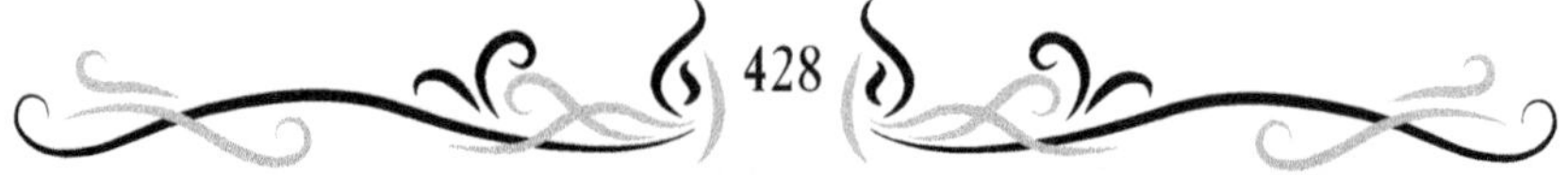

'We're out of militia-controlled territory, so we need to set an armed two-person watch tonight. We're on a four-hour rotation. Private Jason, Corporal Rodgers, take first watch—'

'But sir—' Jason started.

'Sergeant Thea and I will relieve you.' Captain Kiandra glared at Jason, daring him to say another word.

'We did it last night. How come the other two get to sleep in?' Rodgers argued, backing his new mate.

'Because we need them fresh and on their game in the morning.' Captain Kiandra's tone was firm but impatient.

'I don't know why we're doing this anyway,' Rodgers grumbled as they made camp. 'He's most likely with the zombies, and if he's not dead yet he soon will be. If they don't eat him, they're bound to pass on some filthy disease. We should just head home now.'

'Rodgers, for the last time!'

'I'm only saying, Captain, it's been years since anyone patrolled out this far. Even the militias don't come here. Everyone who was living in this area before the war is probably one of the zombie crew now.'

Captain Kiandra stood, hands on hips. 'The next person to use the z-word will be on latrine duty.'

'But we've been digging our own,' Rodgers complained, not knowing when to give up.

'For now....' The Captain turned away.

Thea moved closer to Bruno and Lee, pretending to ensure they were correctly setting up the tent for inflation.

'Captain Kiandra's older sister was on a patrol in the early days after the war. The wind changed direction and a radiation storm caught her troop. She's been ill ever since,' she told them.

'Well, that explains her dislike of the word zombie,' Lee said.

'In Portsdown there is a lot of mistrust and disinformation about what has gone on above ground,' Thea continued. 'Many people think like the Corporal because they know no better. Others think that way because it helps them deal with the guilt of leaving people outside to die.'

Captain Kiandra interrupted their conversation. 'Right, it's late and I don't like us being out here in the dark. Let's inflate and get inside.' Something moved in the undergrowth as if to emphasise her point.

Tonight the group included Lee in their conversations. Although he sat

with them, he didn't say much. Too many thoughts raced each other through his head for him to take part in the banter.

After they had eaten, Rodgers and Jason had suited up and were sitting just outside the door when Lee plucked up the courage to ask the question nagging at him all day.

'Captain?'

'Yes, Private.'

'What will happen to Allan—I mean, what happens to returned escapees in Portsdown? We lock them up in London… but what happens to them here?'

'That depends.'

'On what?' Lee pressed.

'On how long they've been away. On their reasons for leaving. And....'

There was a long silence.

'And?' Lee prompted.

'Well, I guess on how much their parents are able to influence the Representative Council.'

Lee considered this information for a moment. 'Will Allan's parents be able to influence the council?'

'I think it unlikely,' Captain Kiandra admitted. 'His father is a high school teacher and his mother is a microbiologist. While their skills are useful, they're not influential enough to change the outcome for their son.'

'And that would be?' Lee asked.

'Once we have found out all we need from him, I'm afraid... we only bring them in, Private. What happens after that is someone else's responsibility.'

'Just following orders,' Lee said, his tone a little sharp.

'Go to sleep, Private. Tomorrow will be another long day.'

Lee shuffled over to his bedroll and slipped inside, snuggling around the warmth of the dog beside him.

Bruno, we're not really taking him back, are we? We're not going to give Allan to them to be interrogated, and goodness knows what else?

We don't know what we're meant to do yet, Bruno responded.

But if those are our orders, will you do it?

There was silence in his head, and the dog shifted his weight beside him.

I hope not to be put in that position but, yes, if that is what the Guardians decide is for the best, then I will do it. I believe the Guardians only ask us to do what is best for the future of the world.

What about Allan's best interests? Lee asked.

We don't know enough about what is going on to go against orders, so we need to trust the Time Guardians. Now, I need to get some sleep.

It was like Bruno had erected a wall between their minds, signalling an end to the conversation.

'You might have to do what they say, but I'm not a Guardian,' Lee muttered under his breath. 'I can do what I like.'

'Go to sleep, Private! And that's an order.' Captain Kiandra's voice cut through the darkness.

Lee rolled away from Bruno, as if to make a point, although he wasn't quite sure what that point was. Would he actually disobey an order? It went against everything he believed in. Then again, so did betraying a friend.

He might never have met Allan, but his gut told him Allan and Alain were one and the same person. He had never let a friend down in his life. Could he start now? Still, what if supporting his friend brought about the end of time?

Was Allan's escaping from Portsdown really that bad? It was not like he had killed anyone. However, a single person could spread sedition and bring down a whole regime, and that would be wrong. Then again, if the government was corrupt....

Now he had arrived at the heart of the matter. He was joining the Australian Army because it protected his home and answered to a democratically elected government. He might not have agreed with everything they asked the military to do, but he knew the majority of Australians voted for them to protect their interests.

The Time Guardians were selected, not elected. He hadn't chosen to join their cause. He knew nothing about how the Portsdown representatives got to sit on their council, or anything about how the local militias governed themselves. So, where did that leave him?

He chewed the inside of his cheek. Normally, if he did not have enough information to make a decision, he would do some research on the internet. He needed to find out more and there was no internet here, so he would watch and learn.

Just like that his stomach stopped churning, his eyelids dropped, and his mind stopped whirring. Until he had more information, he couldn't do anything. So he would gather intel, especially about the people who lived outside Portsdown, then he would be in a better position to choose a side.

He stretched, rolled back into Bruno's warmth, and was asleep moments later.

4

AN UNEXPECTED GUEST

BASIA LAID DOWN the ax before dropping the split wood into the wicker basket. Wiping the sweat from her brow with a sleeve, she then hefted the basket onto her hip and headed inside.

The logs made a satisfying clunk as she dropped them into the wood chest sitting by the old Aga that served as oven, heater, and water heater for the whole house. Popping the basket back in the pantry, she took the opportunity to pour herself a large glass of water from the pottery purifier. Refreshed, she returned to the kitchen.

'What now, Mum?'

'Our meat supplies are dwindling, so we'll have to use some of the root vegetables from the cellar to make dinner go a little further. If you could bring me some, then collect the eggs, I'll go milk the cows.'

Basia bit back a protest. Life was busy enough, but when her brother and father went on hunting trips, it was busier still because she and her mother covered the work of four people. Even so, her mother knew she hated going into the cellar and usually took on those tasks herself. She must be tired to have forgotten.

A lantern hung on a hook beside the stairs. Basia lit it and let the flame settle before opening the door. Waiting for the stale smell of animals and dirt to hit her, she took a deep breath and descended into the darkness.

The cellar was spacious. Its three rooms spanned two-thirds of the house above and half the barn. The door on the far wall led to the bedroom her family had slept in during the years after the war. Now it was a dumping ground for everything broken or useless—things that might one day be stripped down for parts, or might work if they fixed the old generator.

In the corner opposite sat an ancient air filtration system—a useless piece of junk now that the generator was broken. Beside it was the door leading to the underground barn. Although this section was closed off now, the stalls where the ancestors of their animals had weathered the aftermath of the war still stunk out the lower level.

Tucked underneath the steps were the wooden storage bins containing root vegetables, and beside them were the shelves holding muslin-covered blocks of cheese and pats of butter. Then, next door, jars of pickles and preserves stood in a row—although at the moment it would be more correct to describe them as jars waiting for pickles and preserves. Soon they would begin the process of stripping down the garden and preserving produce for the winter.

Ensuring they had enough to eat was a continuous grind. How she longed for the times she read about in books when you took money to a shop and simply bought what you needed.

She held out her apron before grabbing some carrots and potatoes, then almost lost the lot when she was distracted by the sound of scrabbling in the corner. It won't come near the light, she told herself, but still, she rushed back up the stairs.

Even though she spent the first four years of her life living in these rooms, she always heaved a sigh of relief when she returned to the warmth of the kitchen. Perhaps it was because she was leaving the ever-present rat population behind.

After returning the lamp to its hook, she dropped the vegetables on the table. Picking up a bowl, she used the hand pump over the sink to half fill it. As she grabbed the handle, her mother said, 'Don't use too much. It takes time to collect the water and then filter it, and with the others away….'

Every moment in her life contained a constant reminder of the war. Water had to be filtrated and tested for general use, then filtrated a second time for human consumption. The soil had to be turned over every year and tested before planting. Animals and humans were tested regularly for radiation exposure. Every night she took a cocktail of pills to combat radiation particles

that might have entered her system in spite of all the other measures taken.

While she peeled and chopped the vegetables, she imagined herself living in an easier time: a time when everything didn't have to be done by hand, and people did things other than work all day. So caught up was she in her daydream, she didn't even realise her mother had left until she come back into the room carrying two pails of milk.

'Basia. *Basia.*'

'What? Sorry.'

'Can you get the cellar door for me?'

'Sure.' She opened the door for her mother and kept it open to provide a little light as she navigated the stairs. When her mother returned, Basia went back to her work as her mother checked the bread cooking in the Aga. Deciding they were done, she removed the two loaves, releasing the aroma of fresh baked bread.

'Mum, did you know Johan said the boys from over at the Simpson farm went into Southampton to see if they could find some solar panels? They think they may be able to generate enough electricity to at least light the farm, and maybe run a few small appliances.'

'Mm, what…? Yes, your father told me.'

'Do you think we could do something like that?' Basia asked.

Her mother paused, glancing up from checking the bread. From the look on her face, Basia prepared for yet another lecture on the evils of everything that made life easier in the past. Instead, her mother sighed, and her face softened.

'Basia, I know this isn't much of a life for you. You're young, and you want more than working on the farm to look forward to. I wish I could offer more, but this is all we have. Perhaps once you complete your training, we might be able to find a place for you in a settlement. That will be a little more exciting than this.'

Basia wanted to say, 'But that is years away, I want something to happen now.' She didn't, though, because without medical training, life off the farm would be no easier. Her mother had begun training her to do more than just assist with the trickle of patients who made their way to the farm for help. She had dusted off her old nursing books and began teaching Basia medicine.

In the end she said, 'I guess they still need to figure out how to get the panels working, and also fix the appliances. Dad said he might look out some of his old technical manuals for them.'

'Yes, we could do with someone who knows how to fix these things in

our little community. But I guess people like that prefer larger settlements where there is a small supply of electricity and a heap of salvaged appliances and parts.' Pushing a stray strand of hair from her eyes, her mother turned back to the bread.

'I thought this house to be so grand when your father first brought me here,' her mother sighed. 'The local stone pillars out front made it appear so imposing. Such a shame they didn't survive the war. Still, enough was left to make a lower level for the house and a sturdy barn. We should not complain.'

Basia smiled. She liked it when her mother talked of the nice bits of the past—of times before the war, or when she was little. She had been told that when the family emerged from the basement after five years of living underground, the top story was gone—destroyed in the aftermath of the fighting. Her father repaired the bottom level, making it secure enough for them to live in before tackling the barn. He and her brother Johan finished adding a wooden second story the year before last, giving them all their own rooms for sleeping.

'It was a real English manor. Many generations of your family lived here,' her mother continued, reminiscing. 'When your father brought me from Southampton for the first time, I could not believe a man from such a background, an architect in a fancy firm, had fallen in love with me, a Polish immigrant training to be a nurse.'

Basia paused to listen. This was special, the story of how her parents had overcome his parent's objections to their marriage.

'Your father was an architect for such a short time. First his parents died, then war threatened. We moved back here, and I worked for the local doctor. Johan was a baby when your father began building the shelter downstairs, a small underground life for us. We stocked it with everything we needed, and when it was time to go below, I took Johan downstairs while your father brought down the sheep, chickens, and cows. Now that was fun to behold.'

Her mother chuckled at the memory of her husband coaxing the reluctant animals below ground.

Basia added the familiar next line. 'And he wouldn't have been able to do it without the dogs.'

'Yes, Whip and Sheba were most helpful. They left their puppy with Johan and went to herd the sheep.'

Basia took the vegetables over to her mother, who stirred them through the thick stew.

'Did you collect the eggs?' she asked, as if just remembering.

'Not yet. I'll go now.' Basia was reluctant to break the storytelling spell, but the chickens needed to be locked up tight before darkness fell.

As she rounded the side of the house, two great lolloping dogs bowled into her, almost causing her to lose her footing.

'Jasmine and Baby, you're back.'

Baby rolled over for a tummy rub, while his mother stood quietly by. Looking into the dog's intelligent brown eyes, Basia paused. Something was wrong.

She lifted her head and raised a hand to shade her eyes. In the distance two figures appeared, silhouetted against the grey-blue sky, one tall and one slightly stooped under an indiscriminate load. Her mouth watered—there would be venison for the winter. Deer were elusive, but they occasionally appeared in the deepest reaches of the forest where fallout had not penetrated.

No, Juniper would not act like this over a deer. As they drew closer, she realised it was not an animal they carried, but a human.

FORGETTING ALL ABOUT the chickens, Basia sped back to the house. As she left the garden, her father called, 'Basia, tell your mother we have a badly injured boy, so she'll need to set up a bed.'

Flinging open the door, she gulped in some air before stuttering, 'Dad and Johan have a boy. He's injured… quite bad…. We need—'

'I've got this. Catch your breath, then go fetch what we need for a bed,' her mother said as Basia dropped into a chair.

Things moved quickly after that. Johan and her father took the boy into the front room and laid him out on the divan her mother used for patients. Basia put some water on the stove and went to fetch blankets while Johan left to lock up the rest of the animals.

'Thank you. Just put the bedding on the chair,' her mother said when Basia entered the living room. 'Then go and finish getting dinner ready. Your father and brother haven't eaten a proper meal in days.'

Hovering in the doorway, Basia attempted to catch a glimpse of their guest, but her mother and father presented a rather solid wall.

'Basia, dinner,' her father said without looking behind in a tone she knew not to disobey.

Johan was placing a basket of eggs on the bench and she crossed the kitchen to shut the door behind him. A flurry of dog fur flashed past her, almost knocking her over for the second time that day. Once the animals were safely inside, she closed up, turned the key, and dropped the stout wooden bar. Moving the rifle from where her father left it leaning against a chair to its position beside the door, she turned back into the room.

'Can you do the shutters in here while I close the others?' Johan asked, and she nodded.

This dusk ritual happened every evening: securing the property and animals from marauders and goodness knows what else roamed in the dark. No one stayed out in the open once the sun went down unless they carried weapons and were able to defend themselves.

Basia hustled the dogs to their beds in the washroom and gave them each some dried meat before filling their drinking bowl. Having seen to the animals, she closed the shutters and lit the lamps.

With everything secure, she checked on the stew. It simmered nicely, its rich aroma filling the room and causing her stomach to rumble. Cutting thick slices of bread, she piled them on a plate before fetching a round of cheese and some butter from the pantry. As she worked, the murmur of her parents' voices drifted through from the other room, but they were speaking too low for her to make out actual words.

'If they want you to know, they will tell you,' Johan said from behind, making her jump.

'Not everyone is prepared to wait until information is handed to them on a—'

She stopped suddenly, realising her brother was so calm because he knew something. If she antagonised him, he would not be interested in sharing it with her.

'Clean up, Johan. Dinner is almost ready.'

Frowning at her, Johan paused, then shook his head as if the reason for her abrupt change of heart was beyond him. Good. If he was off balance, he might let something slip.

He took his and his father's travel packs into the washroom, returning in a fresh set of clothes, his hair wet and sticking to his head. Basia ran the radiation detector over him, looked at the reading, and smiled. 'You're all good.'

Ladling out two bowls of stew, Basia placed them on the table, and waited for Johan to sit before beginning to eat herself.

'I hope you brought home more than that boy from your hunting trip,' she started. 'We're running short on meat.'

'I can tell,' Johan smiled, raising his fork to display the carrot on the end.

'So?'

'So what?' Johan smirked, enjoying needling her.

Basia bit back her frustration. 'Did you bring back any meat?'

Johan laughed. 'A couple of rabbits—they've been gutted and cleaned. We saw some wild beef, but their radiation levels were too high for us to be interested.'

'Well, it will be dried pulses and root veggies all winter then.'

Johan did not take the bait. 'We're planning to go out for a couple of days again tomorrow and return via the fishing hole.'

'And what about the stranger? Would you leave us alone with him?'

Johan shrugged. 'He was barely breathing when I put him on the bed. He'll be lucky to survive the night. I don't know why father insisted we bring him home.'

Basia punched her brother on the arm. 'He couldn't just leave him out there. That's not who we are.'

'You're right. We are people who look out for others.' Johan and Basia turned to find their father standing in the doorway. 'Is there any of that for me?'

'Yes, I'll dish you some. Should I get some for Mum too?' Basia asked.

Her father shook his head. 'No, your mother will be a little while longer yet. Can you make some tea if that water is boiled?'

Basia moved to serve her father's meal while he went to clean and change. By the time she placed his bowl and a steaming cup of tea on the table, Johan had checked him for radiation and he was ready to tuck into dinner.

'So, who is he?' Basia asked, unable to contain her excitement. Nothing this interesting ever happened in their quiet, boring life.

'An injured boy we found on the old motorway. He's been unconscious the entire time, so all we know is that he is badly hurt.'

'Isn't it dangerous bringing him here?' Basia said. 'I mean, the community doesn't like strangers.'

'If we're lucky we won't need to tell them anything. If he comes to, we can find out where he is from and send word to his family, and if he doesn't, well….'

As her father finished talking, his wife entered the room, poured some water from the kettle into a bowl, then left. They finished their meal in silence, then Basia and Johan cleaned up while their father went into the

pantry to joint the rabbits.

'No use putting them up for winter, Basia,' he said when he returned. 'They can go into the stewpot tomorrow.'

Basia nodded, not looking forward to a winter with little or no meat. Sometimes when a cow was no longer good for milk they would butcher it for food and to provide something to barter with. Unfortunately, all their cows were currently strong and healthy.

Johan reboiled the kettle, and Basia pulled down the jar of dried chamomile, ready to make more tea. Her father joined them at the table just as her mother came through the door from the living room.

'How is he?' her father asked.

'The wound in his side is nasty, Simon, but it seems to have missed everything vital. I've given him antibiotics for his infection. He is young, well fed, and strong, so there's a good chance he will recover,' her mother informed them as she dished some stew into a bowl.

'So, no radiation disease?' Basia asked, and her mother shook her head.

'Unusual for a person living away from a community.' Basia fished for information.

'He has a community…,' her father said.

Basia caught the look between her mother and father—it was her mother's "not in front of the children" look.

'And …,' Basia encouraged, hoping for once her father would ignore her mother.

'Where he's from isn't something we need to worry about at the moment. What is important is that I need someone to watch him tonight. Someone to give him a second lot of antibiotics, and to keep his temperature down.'

'I guess that will be me,' Basia said with little enthusiasm. The part of being a trainee medic she hated the most was sitting with patients through the night. She was a person who really needed her sleep to be able to function the next day.

'Are you sure that's a good idea, Tanya?' her father asked.

'Given the sedative he took, he's unlikely to wake,' her mother said.

Basia's eyes widened. 'Is there a chance he might be dangerous? Why ever did you bring him home, Dad?'

'He's unconscious. And if he wasn't, even you could best him in his current condition.' Johan laughed.

'He doesn't pose a physical threat,' Tanya said as she stood to rinse her plate in the sink. 'Simon, could you please help me with some bedding for Basia?'

As their parents left the room, Basia leaned towards Johan and whispered, 'He's from the underground city, isn't he?'

Johan froze, his cup halfway to the table.

'Basia, what do you know about the city?' His tone was wary.

'I know there is one.'

'Basia, please keep this to yourself.' Johan's eyes pleaded. 'If anyone finds out who he is, we will be in a lot of trouble.'

'Then why did Father bring him here?'

'You said it yourself: Dad couldn't leave a wounded human to die, no matter where he comes from.'

ANY FURTHER CONVERSATION was cut short by their parents' return. The family began to ready themselves for bed, and Basia did not get another chance to talk alone with Johan. In fact, it was almost as though he was avoiding her.

While she was in the pantry, she heard his footsteps on the stairs and then his bedroom door close. 'You don't get away that easily,' she said under her breath as she wrapped the cheese. 'Tomorrow is another day.'

By the time she returned to the kitchen her parents had cleared everything else away and moved the dogs' beds in front of the Aga.

'The painkillers and antibiotics should last him through the night. Call me if you need anything else,' her mother said before disappearing up the stairs.

Basia wandered into the living room and went around the furniture to get her first look at her patient.

The pale face framed by a blanket and a shock of wavy black hair was handsome enough to have come from one of the books she read. He appeared well fed and relatively healthy, as her mother had said. This meant the chances of him living as an outcast were slim, making it more likely he came from the underground city near Portsmouth—the one she heard so much about but must never speak of.

Reaching out her hand, she felt he was a little warm. She turned and removed the thermometer from the table and placed it on his forehead. His temperature was up a little, but nothing to be alarmed about yet.

Placing the thermometer back within easy reach, she picked up her comforter and a book from the coffee table. Taking them to the chair on the

other side of the fire from the boy, she curled up under the blanket and opened her book. *North and South* by Elizabeth Gaskell had always been one of her favourites. In fact, she enjoyed most of the books her parents called the classics. The England they told of was very different to the one she lived in, but she felt an affinity with the female heroines.

Although they wore beautiful gowns and attended parties and balls, like her their options for the future were narrow. If they were strong enough willed to want to be independent, they must choose a husband who would allow them to do what they wanted.

Sighing, she looked over at the patient—he was the most exciting thing to happen in her entire life, and she would probably still be saying that ten years from now.

She smiled, imagining herself as Margaret Hale to his Mr Thornton. He could whisk her off her feet and take her home to be waited on hand and foot for the rest of her life. Well, at least she might have a stab at a life somewhere where women were not held back because of their ability to breed.

This was just as big a fantasy as *North and South*, and never likely to happen. Her eyelids began to droop closed. Sleepily, she rolled over to check the alarm clock would wake her in time for her next check. Snuggling under the covers, she dozed to visions of balls and of dashing young men who wanted nothing more than to take her away from her life of drudgery.

SIMON FLOPPED BACK on the bed and sighed. No words could describe the pleasure of sleeping in his own bed again after four nights alternating between keeping watch and sleeping on the ground.

'I'm getting too old for these long hunting trips,' he said.

'You're fitter than most men your age—even half your age.'

He smiled at his wife as she hung her shirt in the wardrobe. 'Although I appreciate the sentiment, you are more than little biased.'

Tanya paused halfway through hanging her trousers, as if waiting for him to continue.

'The reality is I'm not as young as I once was, and this life is hard on us all. I don't know how much longer we can go on without extra help on the farm,' he said.

His wife looked over her shoulder with the piercing gaze she used when

trying to search for the meaning beyond his words. He often felt like she was attempting to pluck the very thoughts from his mind.

'Ah, so your intention was to supplement our labour force when you picked up the stray downstairs.'

Simon chuckled. 'Perhaps not consciously,' he said. 'But it certainly wouldn't hurt to have another pair of young hands around and put into practice that idea of adopting a couple of children without parents from the settlement. We could even go as far as Southampton if needs be.'

'You think they will want to live on a farm?' Tanya's eyebrows rose skeptically.

'I'm sure we could find one or two, and we have the spare room for them. Perhaps even a few older children ready to leave home might be interested in fixing up the old house on the other side of the pond.'

'And in the meantime, it might bring potential partners for our children right to our doorstep?' Tanya chuckled as she closed the wardrobe.

Simon sat back up. 'You make it sound like I brought back a husband for Basia.'

Tanya raised an eyebrow.

'It's still not safe out there, is it so wrong of me to prefer opening our doors and offering them an alternative to leaving home?'

Tanya sighed. 'You can't protect them from the big bad world forever.'

'I know, and I also know there is a chance they may leave anyway, in which case we would still need new people to help work the farm.'

Again that eyebrow rose. 'And you had to start with that particular boy?'

'He was injured,' Simon said, defending his actions.

His wife's hands moved to her hips and his stomach sank. The look on her face was another familiar one. It said, 'What were you thinking?', and he braced himself.

'Simon, that boy's from Portsdown. You took a huge risk bringing him here.'

'Perhaps not so big. No one's patrolled this far out for at least ten years,' he said.

'Even so, the town elders won't let him stay—not when they find out where he's from.'

Simon shrugged. 'Perhaps they never need to know.'

'Huh. You really think they will just let a stranger slip into our midst without questioning his origins?'

His wife was right, but he did not want to admit it. 'No, I'm saying he might move on before anyone finds out he is here.'

Tanya's stance relaxed, but Simon didn't let his guard down quite yet. 'Putting aside how I feel about people from Portsdown, you have no idea if this boy will want to stay with us or go on his way. Basia already hankers for an easier way of life. What if he offers to take her back with him?'

'I don't think—'

'And Johan is also restless, he may consider leaving with them.'

When he had decided to bring the boy back with them, Simon's one thought had been not leaving him there to die. Everything else he rationalised away on the trek home.

'I'm sorry, Tanya. I didn't think beyond saving him. I have been trying to focus on the positives to justify my actions.'

Her face giving nothing away as she walked around the bed and slipped between the covers. 'Well, I guess we can cross those bridges as we come to them. Now, this weary old lady needs her sleep… and so do you.'

Simon grinned at her. 'Maybe I'm not so tired after all….'

THE HAIRS ON the back of Allan's neck stood on end. Someone was watching him. His fight or flight instinct suggested he open his eyes and at least find the cause, but in truth he didn't have the strength. He was so tired even his earlobes ached. Far away voices murmured. He moved a little, thinking he should sit up. Pain wracked his body and he started to drift back into oblivion.

No! He fought the exhaustion threatening to overwhelm him, pushing the pain to the recesses of his mind. If he couldn't open his eyes, he could listen and try to figure out where he was—in Portsmouth, or back in Portsdown, or somewhere else entirely?

At least back in the underground city he would get decent medical treatment for his wounds before they interrogated him. If the Portsmouth militia had him, then who knew what his fate would be. They'd probably torture him for information about Portsdown.

Perhaps the radiation affected had found him? He had been so sure the rumours of their turning to cannibalism were fantasy, but he could be mistaken.

Was it wrong to hope he might have been found by the people he was looking to find? The people who had found a way to live a new life after the holocaust? Documents in the secret archives indicated radiation should have

dispersed to livable levels years ago. Then again, when they had been written, no one had lived through a nuclear war of the scale the world had experienced. Perhaps the existence of people living above ground was nothing more than a pipe dream.

Pain threatened to overwhelm him again. He rolled to get more comfortable and the covers slipped. When the wave had passed, he snuggled back into the warmth, his mind drifting back to the events that led him here.

For a moment he wondered if he had done the right thing leaving Portsdown. Food was plentiful, education was free to all, and he and his parents had lived in a comfortable apartment.

No, that was his fear talking. He needed to remember his reasons for wanting to leave—to choose the life he wanted to live.

All his life he dreamed of being a teacher like his father. When he turned eighteen, he found the Representative Council had other ideas. They informed him Portsdown needed soldiers more than they needed teachers. They needed farmers more than teachers. They needed carpenters more than they needed teachers. They invited him to choose from a range of jobs they said the community required to survive, and not one of those had anything to do with teaching. In fact, not one of those jobs required him to undertake any further study.

Swallowing his disappointment, he took the list home to discuss his options with his parents, certain he could find a way to work for the good of the community in a fulfilling job. On the way he bumped into a school friend Daniel, whose father was head of the hospital laboratory where Allan's mother worked. They had gone through school together, and Allan had spent many a lunch break helping Daniel keep up in class.

Preparing to commiserate with the shortlist of options they had to choose their future careers from, Allan drew back in surprise when he found Daniel's list looked very different to his. His list contained vacancies in university courses leading to professional careers.

Allan had been aware his whole life that there were those in charge and those who weren't, but until that moment, he had not fully understood how determined those in charge were about keeping power for themselves. Daniel's acceptance of the different futures available to them made this all the harder to take. He remembered the rest of the conversation well.

'We can still be friends,' Daniel had said. 'I mean, I might need some help with my courses and you can learn as I do.'

'And would I eventually be able to be accepted into university?' Allan asked.

'Well, of course not. If you're not admitted directly from school, you can't ever attend.' Daniel's brow furrowed, as if Allan's anger confused him.

'And would you have me as best man at your wedding?'

'But Carmel and I are not engaged,' Daniel said, bemused. 'Besides, when we do tie the knot, it will be a stuffy society affair. You would hate it.'

There was so much Allan wanted to say, but in the end he brushed past Daniel and muttered, 'See you round.'

That night he complained to his parents, hoping for some sympathy, but instead he got a lecture about how many babies had not survived the war, and he should be thankful for whatever life offered him. Allan's frustration grew. It wasn't that he believed any job to be more or less important than another, it was the way people's choices were limited by who they were, not by what they could do.

As his distrust of the ruling elite grew, he pulled further and further away from his parents. They would be forever grateful to Daniel's father for wangling a precious place in the city for his favourite assistant. They would never question the gift they had been given, or the treatment of their offspring.

In the end he chose a career in horticulture. Not because he had any affinity for growing things, but more because it came with a small room of his own close to the underground farms.

While Allan learnt about hydroponics and growing food under artificial light, he also learned more about why the people in charge of the underground community kept such tight control of their citizens. It was a question of balance, they explained to him. The city needed a certain number of labourers to run the basic services and provide amenities for the ruling elite.

His new friends thought moving above ground was the answer to their problems, except the people leaving threatened the balance, so it was prohibited. Besides, no one could say what it was like above ground, not really. Others escaped trying to find out, but no one ever returned. When one of their number found a back door to the city, Allan volunteered to go above ground and report back on the state of the world.

Getting to the entrance had been easy, as had opening the secret door. As he slipped into the cave on the other side, he sensed someone watching him. He turned to check if he was being followed, but there was no one there. He should have listened to his gut. Making his way down the incline towards and old motorway, he paused, and someone yelled, 'Halt.'

He responded by breaking into a run and was almost at the road when a cry rang out, 'Halt, go no further. In the name of the Portsdown Regiment, you are under arrest for unauthorised activity.'

At those words he ran faster, weaving through vehicles abandoned before he was born. Unauthorised activity was a euphemism for sedition and mutiny, and it was likely his life was already forfeit. He decided being killed outright while running for freedom was better than being made an example of in front of the entire community.

Pain shot through his side and he slipped, losing his footing. Using an abandoned vehicle to pull himself to his feet, he carried on moving, looking for somewhere to hide. He slipped under a nearby car and listened until the sun began to set and the soldiers finally gave up their search. As they departed, he overheard them calling for reinforcements.

Although the wound hurt like hell, he managed to struggle out from under the car. Leaning against it, he enjoyed the feeling of the setting sun on his face before he fell to the ground. As he fell in and out of consciousness, he was aware of someone picking him up and carrying him for what seemed like an age. Then all he knew was darkness and the warmth of a fire.

Icy drafts of air crept up his back. He pulled the blankets back over his shoulders and gasped at the pain in his side. That at least he hadn't imagined. He tried to will his eyes open so he could find out where he was, but they still wouldn't obey. He drifted again, back into dreams of sun on his face and the blue sky above.

5

TIME FOR A PLAN

BASIA WAS RUDELY awoken by the sound of footsteps thundering down the stairs. She was rubbing the sleep out of her eyes when Johan rushed into the room.

'Wake up, sleepyhead and let me out the door.'

'Mmm... why?' She tried to grasp what he was saying, but her brain still was not functioning.

'Just let me out and lock up after.'

'What's the rush?' Basia asked.

'Some men from the town are heading this way. You'd best go make sure Dad is coming down too.'

'What...?' A horrified thought struck her. 'They must have travelled in the dark.... I mean, the sun's not even up.'

Johan tugged at her blanket and it fell to the floor. 'Come on, get a move on or they'll be here already.'

Exposed to the cold morning air, Basia's skin goose bumped as she swung her legs around, then slipped and almost fell as her feet found the comforter Johan had discarded. Reaching down, she plucked it up and tucked it securely round her shoulders as she walked to where her brother was waiting impatiently.

She glanced over at the boy, pleased to see the noise had not woken him.

Johan grabbed the gun that stood beside the door and tapped his foot, waiting for her to pull herself together.

'Patience. You know I'm not a morning person like you,' she hissed.

'All right, I'll just tell the men outside to come back later when you are ready for them, shall I?'

She stuck her tongue out as he slipped past her through the opening. The key snicked in the lock and she turned to head upstairs. Knocking quietly on her parent's door, she said, 'Father. Father. Johan needs you. Men from the town are coming.'

Heavy footsteps sounded from the other side of the wood, and there was a creak before her mother's head appeared through the crack. 'I heard Johan go down. Your father's sound asleep. Can he not handle it?'

Basia shrugged. 'He sent me up to make sure Father was coming, so—.'

'It's all right. I'm awake,' came the sleepy voice from inside.

'We'll be down in a minute. Can you make sure the boy's okay for me… and start the breakfast.' Her mother closed the door before Basia's lips formed her assent.

She was stoking the fire into life when she heard her parents descend into the living room. She finished placing a couple of logs on the glowing embers in the Aga before rushing to meet her mother by the door.

'Make sure you lock it behind us,' her mother said. 'I don't want anybody slipping past and getting inside until we are sure of their intentions.'

Her father joined them, rifle cocked over his arm. As they left the warmth of the living room, her mother shivered and Basia glimpsed her brother leaning against the veranda post, his own weapon held casually across his body. He appeared relaxed, but the set of his jaw told Basia he was anything but.

She turned the key a second time, then quickly nipped in behind the sofa their guest slept on, opening the shutters a crack so she could watch the action. Her father had joined Johan, while her mother took up a position in front of the door. At the edge of her vision, Basia could just make out a group of men coming into view. It took an age before they were anywhere near close enough to speak.

'Good morning to you, Simon, Johan… and to you too, Tanya.'

Her mother frowned at the implied insult of being acknowledged after her son, but before she could respond with something cutting, Basia's father spoke.

'Councillor Johnson. What can I do for you this morning?'

'No need for all these weapons, Simon. This is just a neighbourly visit. We aren't armed.'

From her vantage point, Basia saw six of the men carried pistols in their holsters. And even if she could not see the others' guns, no one would be foolish enough to come this far from the settlement without some form of protection—especially not at this early hour.

'If this is a friendly visit, then why are there so many of you?' her father countered.

'Simon, why not invite us inside out of the cold and we can talk over a nice cup of tea.' Councillor Johnson took a step forward, but something in her father's face must have caused him to pause.

'I'm fine where we are,' her father answered. 'At least until I know why so many of you have turned up on my property unannounced, uninvited, and just as dawn breaks.'

'I think you know why,' Councillor Johnson said, all pretense of friendliness gone. 'One of our patrols saw you and your son carrying a body, a human body, yesterday. A rather unusual thing to be doing, don't you think? We have come to investigate.'

'Johan and I found an injured boy while on our way back from patrol. I assume you mean him? We brought him back for Tanya to tend to. I see nothing in our actions that would warrant you and your mob turning up on my doorstep like this.' Her father's voice was calm, but Basia could hear the underlying anger.

'Come now, we were the ones who asked you to patrol near Portsmouth. We know you were close to the underground city. You can't blame us for wanting to check the origins of your guest,' the councillor pressed.

Tanya took a step towards her husband, although she didn't take her eyes off the men for one moment. 'What do you mean you were patrolling near Portsdown, Simon? You told me you were on a hunting trip.'

'It *was* a hunting trip, but the council asked us to have a look at what was going on around Portsdown while we were out,' her father said without taking his eyes off the men in front of him.

'I'll get right to the point,' Councillor Johnson interrupted. 'Is that boy a runaway from the underground city?'

'I knew it,' Basia muttered. 'I knew there was an underground city close by, and that he was from there'

It seemed her mother was not interested in answering the councillor's question. 'What were you thinking, Simon? Our family relies on you and

Johan, and you risked yourselves by—.'

'To be fair, Mrs Pettigrew...'

Her mother swung around and glared at the man who had dared speak while she was. 'My name is Tanya!'

'All right, Tanya, your husband has allowed your son to patrol and scout for us for the last year, so you can hardly call foul now.'

The fury on her mother's face caused Councillor Johnson to take a step back. Even Basia could feel the waves of anger rolling off her, and she tensed, waiting for the explosion.

To her surprise, her mother pursed her lips and gave her husband a look that said, 'You and I will talk about this later.'

Oblivious to the tension, Councillor Johnson continued. 'There is a high likelihood this boy originates from the city. If by a slim chance he doesn't, you still haven't declared the presence of a new person in the settlement as our rules of association decree.'

Her father ran a hand through his hair, a sure sign he was stressed. 'Goodness, Charlie, give a man a chance to breathe. The boy is not from the city and I am not hiding anything.'

Councillor Johnson moved as if to interrupt, but her father held up his hand. 'I brought the boy straight here because he was barely alive and he needed immediate medical care. We only got home at dusk, I planned to come into Lyndhurst to declare.'

The Councillor frowned and took a step back. After a quizzical glance at her family, he turned to talk to the others. The conversation went on for quite some time, and Basia crossed her fingers, hoping her father had convinced the men to leave them be.

Councillor Johnson finally emerged from the group and said, 'We were perhaps a little premature in our actions, but given what happened last time an escapee found their way here, can you blame us?'

'We all know of the farmstead that was burned to the ground as a rebuke for harbouring the escapee—but that was over ten years ago. We haven't seen one of their patrols around here since,' her father pointed out.

The Councillor smiled a smile that did not reach his eyes. 'Listen, why don't you invite us in for that cup of tea and we can sort all this out like civilised men.'

Basia gasped and cast a worried glance around the room. She should have trusted her father though; he was a wily campaigner.

'I see no reason why all seven of you should traipse around my home first thing in the morning when my daughter's not even up,' he said.

Councillor Johnson laughed. 'I can see her peeking through the shutters.'

Basia ducked back behind the curtain.

Her father didn't falter. 'Give me fifteen minutes to ensure she is suitably attired to receive males into the house, and then one or two of you can come in, meet the boy, and put all your fears to rest.'

Councillor Johnson checked with the others, then nodded. 'That's a reasonable request. I will check out your guest, but don't keep me waiting too long, or we will think you are still hiding something.'

BASIA CLOSED THE shutter and went to open the door to admit her family. This time when she locked it, she dropped the bar back down. She did not trust any of the men outside, especially Councillor Johnson, who was known for saying one thing and doing the opposite.

'Into the kitchen. We haven't much time to save ourselves from the wrath of the Council.' Her mother's tone was brisk as she bustled them though the living room.

Johan frowned. 'Don't you want to talk about—'

'Time enough later for that, after we have dealt with the men outside,' her mother said.

Basia's father and brother exchanged a look, worried the longer Tanya had to stew over things, the worse the eventual outcome would be for them. When they were all in the other room, her mother began barking orders.

'Johan, go get a pair of your shorts and a T-shirt.' A relieved Johan immediately departed. 'Basia, stoke up the fire until it is raging. Simon, come and help me get that boy out of the rest of his clothes—one look at them and they'll know exactly where he came from. We'll burn them before we let anyone in.'

'Won't they be suspicious about that?' her dad asked.

'Of course, but we can tell them they were so covered in blood and crawling with lice we had no option but to burn them. Charlie Johnson is so fastidious he won't even blink an eye.' Her mother's lips curled disdainfully when she spoke about the Councillor.

Her father chuckled as he moved to help his wife.

When her mother returned moments later with a bundle of clothing, Basia shoved it into the fire. It started to burn… slowly.

'Pass me a log,' her mother said. 'I'll put it in front to hide the evidence.'

Basia complied, and then said, 'I'll put on the porridge for breakfast, and the kettle for tea. That can be our excuse for the fire being so hot.'

'Okay.' Her mother rubbed her forehead. 'Actually, I'll get things started. You go on up and get dressed.'

Basia moved swiftly to do as her mother asked, not wanting to test her mother's temper under the current circumstances. By the time Basia returned, the boy was dressed in a pair of Johan's cotton shorts and a T-shirt and her mother was pulling the blanket up to cover his chest. He appeared more pale and grey than he had been, and the sheen of sweat on his brow highlighted the cost of moving him.

Seeing she wasn't needed in the lounge, Basia went through to the kitchen to finish preparing breakfast while her father went to let the Councillor in. Basia kept herself quiet so she could hear what was going on in the other room.

'Well, Simon, you're right, it looks like this boy could be from anywhere. Perhaps his clothes might be of some help?'

'If only I'd realised you would want to see them—I burned them last night,' her mother's voice answered. 'His top was so caked in blood it was unwearable, and his trousers were so riddled with lice I got rid of them too.'

Oh no, his boots, Basia thought. *Where did Mother put them? There, by the pantry.* She tiptoed over and grabbed the tell-tale items along with another log of wood. Opening the door to the range, she pushed them in, placing the log in front so they couldn't be seen. She hoped it was enough, although a strange odour began to fill the room. Leaning over the sink, she opened the shutters. before pushing up the sash window to let in some air.

No, she could still smell it. Frantically glancing around the room, she remembered the rabbits in the pantry. She rushed over, opened the door, and retrieved the skins. Laying them out on the bench furthest from the food, she just had time to get back to stirring the porridge as her parents came through with the Councillor.

'Basia, what's that smell?' Her mother's nose wrinkled. Spying the rabbits, she raised an eyebrow as she said, 'Take those back into the pantry. We can cure them later. We can't have out guest putting up with that horrid smell.'

Basia moved quickly to do as she was bid, bringing back a citrus pomander they used to scent rooms after any particularly smelly work.

Her mother leaned over to check the porridge, and when Basia returned to take over from her, she whispered, 'What was that about?'

'Boots,' Basia replied, her lips brushing her mother's hair as she answered.

'That wound. I haven't seen anything like it before. Could it have been made by a laser blaster?' Councillor Johnson's voice boomed.

Her mother turned and walked to the cupboards and began gathering mugs for tea as she answered. 'To be honest, I'm not sure what made it. I have to say I was thinking it was more like someone had tried to cauterise an injury.' She placed the mugs on the table and said, 'I didn't find a bullet, so I thought maybe a stab wound. I hadn't considered a blaster.'

'Mmm, he might have come across one of the city militia. They have some blasters… or if he travelled with someone, they may have tried to help him then given him up for dead.' the Councillor mused.

Basia smiled. The pompous prat was taking the bait.

Her father now spoke. 'Perhaps we can sit down. We don't want to wake the boy.'

'Hasn't he said a word the whole time?' The Councillor's voice was moving closer, so Basia stared intently at the porridge, covering the stove door with her body.

'Not a single thing,' her father confirmed.

'Good morning, Basia.'

Basia had hoped he would ignore her, but no such luck. His over familiar attention always set her teeth on edge. Still, she could not afford to be rude, given the current circumstances.

She half turned to find the ruddy-faced man standing a little too close to be polite. His smile was almost a leer, and she forced herself not to shudder in response. She could not believe some women in their small community thought this tall, fair-haired widower was a catch. All she saw was a man of around her father's age, running to fat and full of his own importance.

'Morning,' Basia mumbled, turning her eyes forward and watching the spoon as she stirred the porridge, hoping she had satisfied the requirements of politeness.

'My, young lady, you've grown since I saw you last.' Basia's stomach heaved. 'Simon, perhaps the time has come for us to find somebody who will take on your daughter.'

Basia froze, unsure how to respond, but her father came to her rescue. 'She is still young. There's plenty of time. Besides, she's studying with Tanya.

Our community needs more than one person with medical knowledge if we are to thrive.'

'I'm sure we can find a boy to take her place when the time comes for her to marry. I mean, the females of the species hold a special place. Our future survival relies on them.' The Councillor had not moved, and Basia was holding herself very still so she did not brush against him.

'Come, take a seat, Charlie,' her father said as the sound of wood scraping across the flagstone floor filled the room.

Councillor Johnson paused, and it seemed as if he wanted to say something else. Slowly, perhaps reluctantly, he pulled away from Basia and sat down in the chair her father offered.

'Don't leave it too long to match your girl or all the strong men will be gone,' the councillor insisted. 'You want to find her someone who can look after her, don't you?'

'I can look after myself,' Basia whispered furiously.

'And we don't want the Council to have to make that decision for you,' Councillor Johnson continued, his voice hiding Basia's comment.

Her mother's laugh was brittle. 'Come, we are not barbarians. We don't arrange our children's mates.'

'Perhaps it is—'

'Anyway, Charlie, we're here to discuss the boy, not Basia. If you are happy, he can stay here until he is ready to travel. We will bring him into town in a couple of days to answer all your questions.'

'I am not sure.... There is still a risk, you know... um.... and what if a patrol comes searching for him?'

'A small risk, Charlie. It's been an age since soldiers came out here. Besides, do you think I would place my family in that sort of danger?' her father asked.

'If it would make you feel better, we have a spare room. One of your men could stay here until he is well,' her mother added.

'Umm, it could be days. We have businesses and family to consider....'

'So, it's decided. He'll stay here until he's well enough to be moved.' Her father's tone was decisive.

Smiling to herself, Basia had to admire the way her parents had handled the Councillor.

Not to be outdone, the Councillor said, 'And perhaps you can bring your lovely daughter into town when you bring him in—give her a chance to look over our fine male population.'

Basia shuddered and whispered, 'Over my dead body.'

'We shall see.' Fortunately, her mother was noncommittal. 'Now, if you're happy, perhaps I can escort you out. I am sure we all have much to do and we can't stand around here gossiping all day.'

'Well, yes.' The Councillor sounded like he would like nothing more than to while away his day in the kitchen.

Her parents bustled their guest out before he could find an excuse to stay. As the kitchen emptied, Johan appeared as if from nowhere. 'That old creep. He was leering at you the whole time.'

'Eww, I don't want to know,' Basia said, placing her brother's breakfast on the table and wishing they could forget the whole terrifying morning.

Grabbing a bowl, she sat down beside Johan, trying to ignore the voices in the other room.

'What are you doing today?' she asked conversationally after they had eaten in silence for some moments.

'Father asked me to hunt close to home. I think he wants me to keep an eye out for any unusual activity. What about you?'

'Mother is going to the Watson place. Ma Watson hasn't been well. So, I guess I will be on patient watch here,' Basia said, picking at the food in her bowl.

'I think Dad is staying close to home too, so at least you won't have to lock up and stay inside.'

You mean at least I won't be treated like a child, Basia thought, but said, 'I'm perfectly capable of looking after myself. I'm a better shot than you, and almost as good a fighter as Mum.'

Johan snorted as Basia "accidentally" kicked him on the shin as she placed a fresh pot of tea on the table. The relaxed air was sucked from the room as her parents returned, and she and Johan stared into their tea as they waited for their mother's explosion.

THEIR PARENTS ATE in silence and Basia could feel Johan's tension as he sipped his tea. Their mother still said nothing. Johan left the table to get his hunting gear, and Basia took the leftovers into the pantry. Taking her time putting things away, she eavesdropped on the conversation in the room next door.

'I want an explanation before I leave, Simon. I want you to tell me why you risked our family's wellbeing for … for …'

'... for our neighbours,' her father finished. 'For the people we trade with, who provided the horse you ride to visit patients, and who provide many of the things we need to survive.'

'I appreciate you and Johan have a valuable skill they don't, and that it makes more sense for the farmers to range around keeping our protectorate clear. We've discussed that, and we agreed it was right for us to contribute in that way. What we didn't talk about was going up to Portsmouth, and we didn't talk about Johan going out on patrol by himself.'

'Hardly by himself. The scouts go out in groups of four, and he was put with experienced men,' her father said, defending himself.

There was a long silence. Basia took the opportunity to nip through the kitchen to the lounge to tidy up from the night before. As the silence in the room next door drew out, she cuddled the comforter to her chest and slumped in an armchair. She hated it when her parents fought.

Finally, her father broke the silence. 'Portsmouth was spur of the moment. We ranged close to Lyndhurst on our outward leg, and the guards at the gate were talking of trouble between the city militias. Charlie joined us and asked if we would investigate while we were out. We agreed to go as far as the boundaries of Portsmouth Town.'

Silence again.

'There was no time to tell you, Tanya. I thought we were doing the right thing.'

Still nothing from her mother. Mum must be really angry. Basia wondered why her father hadn't sent someone back to tell them where they were going. Apparently, her mother was thinking exactly the same thing, as she asked her father the very question on Basia's mind.

'I asked Charlie to, and he said he would. But you know Charlie Johnson. He says one thing to your face while knowing he'll do no such thing.'

'What would I have done if you had got caught up in some inter-town war and not come home?' Basia's heart almost broke at the sound of fear and hurt in her mother's voice.

'I'm sorry, Tanya, I truly am. I thought you knew where we were.'

There was another long pause.

'And Johan—why on earth would you let him join the scouts?'

The words her mother uttered were so quiet Basia was not sure she heard them correctly.

'He's getting restless, Tanya, and wanting to break away on his own. He's all but a man now, and he needs to set his own path,' her father said.

'He didn't say anything to me.' Her mother's voice was weary.

'Of course not. You're his mother and he didn't want to hurt you. But there comes a time when all young men, even those with a gentle nature, need to prove themselves. He wanted to move to the township, and I struck an agreement with him. I would allow him to go out on patrol with one of the groups once a month. They teamed him up with Paul and a couple of the older men.'

'Paul? The son of the woman who runs the cooperative store?'

Basia thought her mother's voice sounded lighter and she relaxed a little.

Her father sounded a little less defensive when he answered. 'Yes, him. He was in the same boat, except he was looking to move to Southampton if they'd have him. This way they both got a touch of independence, and a chance to stretch their wings before flying the coop.'

'Okay, but I still don't understand why you didn't tell me. I would never have told Johan I knew.'

How can this be all right? Basia thought, feeling betrayed by her mother's acceptance. *I'm not allowed to go anywhere without an escort, so how come Johan gets to do what he wants?*

'I … I don't know what to say, Tanya. It seemed like the right thing to do at the time. I thought after a while he would tell you himself…. On reflection I can see how we have hurt you.'

The conversation was now too personal. Basia bundled her bedding together and headed upstairs. By the time she returned to finish her chores, her father was sitting at the table having another cup of tea. In the distance she could hear the hooves of her mother's horse as she departed.

She grabbed a clean cup and sat down just as the legs to her father's chair scraped across the floor, and he said, 'Well, I guess the jobs your mother left for me to do won't get done while I sit here drinking tea.'

'Dad?'

'Yes?'

'That boy. He's from the underground city, isn't he?' Basia blurted out before she lost her nerve.

Her father sighed and ran his fingers through his hair. 'Yes, Basia, I believe he is.'

'The one near Portsmouth?'

Her father raised his eyebrows and Basia added, 'I've known about it for a while. We all do, us younger ones, even though you older people don't want to talk about it.'

Her father's response to that revelation was not at all what Basia expected.

'We're not keeping secrets from you,' he said. 'We all have our own reasons for not wanting to talk about the city or the people who live in it.'

'Why don't you talk about it?' Basia pressed her father, unable to let this rare openness pass.

Her father sighed and leaned forward, arms resting on the back of the chair. 'For me it is because of your mother.... It was a death sentence, not to be let into the city. Our government abandoned us to the ravages of war, while choosing to save others. It was not an easy time.'

Basia tried to imagine what it would be like to be locked out of your one chance of survival in a nuclear war. 'Why? Why would they keep some people out and take others? Wouldn't you want to try and save everyone?' she eventually asked.

'In the time they had, it wasn't possible to create sustainable communities for the entire population of England, so the government made choices. And they chose the people they wanted to populate their new world with and some of us weren't considered to have the right... um... skills,' he told her.

His answer confused Basia. 'But you were an architect and a farmer. Wouldn't they need you to build a new world?'

'Yes.'

'And Mother's a nurse—'

'And a Polish immigrant,' her father interrupted. 'When the whole world is in crisis, no one trusts people born elsewhere. They wonder where their loyalties truly lie.'

'So, you could've gone, but Mum couldn't.'

Her father nodded. 'Your mother... and Johan. I couldn't leave them behind, so I decided that instead I would make our home our sanctuary, and I would ensure our family survived.'

Basia was quiet for a moment, chewing over this new information. She finished the last of her tea before saying, 'I always think of the underground city as being just like life in the books that I read. Holidays and parties, going to school with other people my age—'

'We have no way of knowing how people live in the city, Basia.'

'Still, I like to dream of a place where things are easier than they are here.

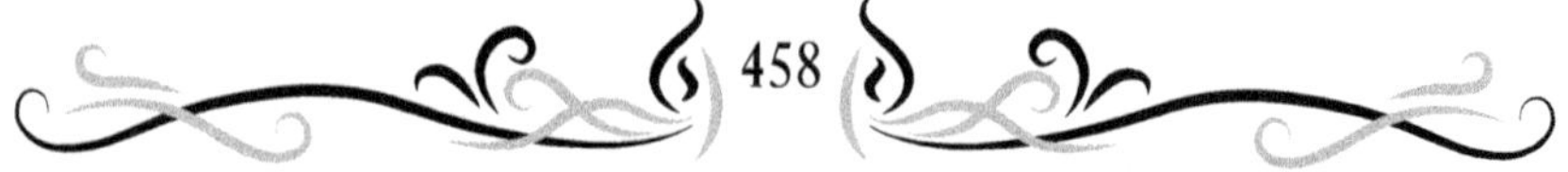

Where I don't have to wait until I am older to be valued as more than just as a potential incubator for babies.'

'We all like to dream, Basia, but as I said, there is one thing I am certain of—each community and country throughout time has good points and bad points. I'm sure some things in Portsdown aren't as agreeable as they are out here, and vice-versa.'

Basia was not yet ready to give up her escape from her daily drudgery. 'But I can still dream, can't I?'

Her father smiled as he straightened up. 'I wouldn't take that away from you, not for anything. Come on now, we've got jobs to do and we may as well get them done while the sedative your mother gave the boy is still working.'

BASIA SPENT THE rest of the morning doing the things she normally did: cleaning the house, preparing dinner, then checking the garden and pulling a few weeds. After lunch she sat down in the kitchen to study her medical books and complete the worksheets her mother had set. As she was about to break for afternoon tea, a groan from the lounge interrupted her thoughts. Walking in, she found herself confronted with a pair of intense green eyes.

'You're awake,' Basia said, stating the obvious.

'You're real,' the boy shot back.

Basia laughed and was rewarded with a smile that crinkled his eyes. 'Would you like some water? Or maybe some soup? I have some on the stove.'

'Water would be wonderful, thank you.'

Basia propped the boy into a sitting position, leaning him back against the pillows to catch his breath while she went next door for water. Supporting his head, she allowed him to take a few small sips, and stopping when he winched in pain.

'Just go slowly,' she said. 'Too much water and you might throw it right back up.'

'I'm all right now,' he said.

She placed the glass on the table within easy reach, then settled him back into a more restful position. Pushing all the questions she had for him down, she put on her best nurse face and said, 'I'll come back soon and give you some broth.'

'Wait,' he said. 'Please, I need to know where I am. Your mother…. She is your mother, isn't she? She wouldn't tell me much. She said I should concentrate on getting well and worry about everything else later.'

Basia frowned and drew her bottom lip between her teeth and considered what her mother would expect her to do. She would say not to agitate the patient, but would he be more agitated by her answering his questions, or by her staying silent?

'I'm not sure. Perhaps you should rest and wait till Father comes in for a break, or Mum returns,' Basia finally said.

'Please.' His eyes and his voice both pleaded with her to make her own decisions.

She closed her eyes and took a deep breath. Why shouldn't she answer his questions? If it was good enough for Johan to have some independence, it was good enough for her to make decisions too.

'All right.' Taking a seat, she smoothed her cotton print skirt over her knees and placed her hands in her lap. 'All right, ask away.'

'Firstly, where am I?'

Laughing out loud, she relaxed a little. 'That's an easy one—you're on my family's farm, about five miles outside of Lyndhurst, in the New Forest.'

The boy frowned, almost as if he was trying to comprehend what she was saying.

'You do know where the New Forest is, don't you?' she asked. 'Lyndhurst is not far from the old city of Southampton, now called The Southampton Protectorate.' The boy's expression didn't alter. 'You've seen a map of Southern England, haven't you?'

The boy shook his head. 'The only maps we had at school were maps of the old world, pre-war, and of all the underground towns.'

It was Basia's turn to draw her brows together, wondering what they taught in underground. How could she explain where they were in a way he would understand? She had an idea. 'So, you can visualise where your community is and where the Portsmouth Protectorate is?'

He nodded. She rose walked to the bookcase built into the wall between the kitchen door and the staircase. Pulling down the atlas, she flicked to the pages showing Hampshire. She pointed. 'This is Portsmouth, this is Southampton, and here is Lyndhurst, which is near where we are now.'

The boy's eyes widened in surprise. 'How did I get this far from where I was shot? I had only made it to the outskirts of Portsmouth.'

Returning the atlas to its home, Basia sat down again before answering. 'My father and brother found you and brought you home for Mother to tend to your wounds. She's a nurse.'

The boy smiled tentatively. 'She's done a great job. I was sure I would die. I managed to crawl away from the soldiers and hide. When they gave up and left, I tried to crawl away, but I fainted, and that is the last thing I remember.'

'Why were you running away?' Basia asked, then clasped her hand over her mouth. Her mother wouldn't like her tiring the boy with questions.

'It's okay. I wanted to find out if people were living out here, or if they had all died from radiation poisoning.'

Basia leaned forward, her elbows on her knees, and peered suspiciously at their guest. 'Of course there are people living out here. We do have to take some precautions, though. Some people still become sick from radiation when a nasty pocket of air comes through, or they eat food from contaminated sources. But we're not barbarians. We have medicines and very few die from the sickness anymore; well, at least in our community, they don't.'

The boy half rolled so he could see her better, his eyes bright with interest. 'What do you live on? I mean, do you grow your own food. Is the soil okay? What about meat sources? Do you have your own currency, or do you barter?'

'Whoa, slow down. Our protectorate has a number of farms, and yes, we grow our own food and keep animals. When we have surplus, we barter for other things we need with Lyndhurst, and sometimes with Southampton. When you're more mobile we can show you around and you can find out more for yourself. That reminds me—are you hungry? Would you like some broth now?'

As if on cue, the sound of a stomach rumbling filled the room. The boy looked down at the sound, and they both laughed. 'I'll take that as a yes,' she said.

Nipping to the kitchen, she half filled a bowl with broth from the pot of soup on the stove and returned to the lounge. She helped the boy to sit up.

'Would you like me to feed you, or are you able to do it yourself.'

'I should be fine.' He took the bowl she offered, but his hand shook so much he almost spilled the lot.

Deftly, she took the plate, perched on the edge of the bed, and fed him small sips from a spoon. He managed to get halfway through before he said, 'Thank you, that's enough.'

Leaving him propped up a little, she said, 'You should get some rest now. I'll come back and check on you later.'

The boy's eyes were already drooping closed, but at the sound of her voice he forced them open. 'I'm Allan, by the way.'

'And I am Basia,' she said, but Allan was already snoring gently.

VIVIENNE LEE FRASER

JOHAN SURVEYED THE clearing in front of him, thanking his lucky stars he had heard the group before he stumbled into their midst. It was only due to his and Baby's hunting skills that they hadn't heard him approach.

From his vantage point, he observed the group. They were covered from head to toe in black. The material of their suits appeared similar to clothing on the boy Johan and his father had rescued. The way they interacted told him they were trained soldiers, and well-armed ones at that. His father had been wrong; a patrol had come searching for the Portsdown escapee.

Crouching in the cover of the bush, he calmed his heart and signalled for Baby to wait before he tried to hear what they were saying.

'What do you mean the dog lost the scent?' the one farthest away asked, a woman from the pitch of the voice.

'He can't find it. It is as if someone has broken the trail and we can't find the next bit,' the lanky soldier standing beside the largest dog he had ever seen explained.

Without moving, Johan tried to pinpoint where they were, and he smiled. Yesterday, about half an hour from home, his father had suddenly worried what might happen if someone decided to track them.

They had stopped in a clearing, then carefully backtracked out about a hundred metres. His father gutted a couple of rabbits, fed the innards to the dogs, then he and Johan smeared some gore on their boots and the dog's paws. Father then sent the dogs home one way, and they left in the opposite direction, avoiding the clearing all together.

'Go back and check if the dog can pick anything else up,' the first voice commanded.

Two soldiers and the dog peeled off and retraced their steps, returning a few minutes later.

The smaller of the two soldiers reported, her clear voice carrying all the way to Johan. 'Still nothing. There are other tracks, but they are all intermingled. Some are from hunters, we think, and others from animals. Everything is mixed up, but we identified at least two distinct trails—we're not sure if either of them are the one we want though.'

The soldier giving orders cursed, then said, 'So, we have nothing?'

'Not quite,' the lanky soldier said. 'I asked Bruno to see if he can scent humans. He indicated there are traces that way.' The soldier pointed in Johan's general direction. 'But the scent is strongest there.'

Johan's stomach clenched because the soldier indicated the way he and his father had gone. It also happened to be the direction of the Watson farm where his mother was today. Neither option boded well for their family.

The best thing would be if they went the other way. If they didn't though, maybe if he timed it right, he could run into them and send them off in the wrong direction. Luck was not with him today. The woman in charge chose to head directly towards the Wilson's place.

The soldiers moved out in formation, with the trackers in front, two soldiers in the middle, and two dropping behind to make sure they weren't ambushed.

'Damn,' Johan muttered. The path that was too narrow and overgrown for him to get ahead and force a chance meeting. And he would not be able to follow them without being seen.

Waiting until they were out of sight, he told Baby, 'Home.' The dog obediently trotted off. Johan skirted the clearing and sped to a jog, taking the long way to the Wilson farm, hoping to reach it before the soldiers did.

6

MEETING THE LOCALS

BRUNO AND IZZY took the lead. Lee wandered after them, marvelling at how different this place was to the New Forest in his own time. The area appeared greener, more wild somehow, in spite of the war it had lived through.

Do you feel that? Izzy asked.

What? Lee looked around to see what she was talking about.

Izzy nudged him with her elbow. *Not you, Lee. I was talking to Bruno.*

You mean that tingling? Bruno asked. *I think magic is starting to regenerate here. Perhaps enough for us to be able to speak with our handlers tonight.*

As he half listened to the others, Lee allowed his senses to expand as much as they were able within the constraints of his suit. The dappled sun warmed his skin even through the protective layers, but he longed to take off the mask, if only to feel the sun and the breeze on his face.

What was that? His skin tingled with tiny electrical pinpricks.

I felt you reaching, Lee. You almost had it. The joy in Izzy's voice was infectious.

Is this what Alain felt when he did magic? he asked the girl.

Yes. If we find more pockets of magic, I might be able to teach you a few simple spells, Bruno said.

'Izzy, we have work to do tonight. I trust you can pull yourself away from your new friends for long enough to see to your duties.'

At the unwelcome intrusion of Jason's whiney voice, Lee's hackles rose and Bruno bared his teeth. Izzy placed her hand on the dog's shoulder to calm him. No matter how irritating Jason was, she clearly did not want any trouble.

'Oh, look, you have protectors.' Jason's supercilious smile grated.

For a moment Lee pondered how liberating it would be to tell Bruno to attack. He bit back the urge, and merely moved closer to Izzy in support, his clenched fist the only indication of his anger.

'I always do my duty, Jason.' Izzy's tone was icy. 'Now, go away.'

Jason's smile froze in place, and he glared at them. 'How dare you give *me* orders.'

'Private Jason, the Captain would like a word—something about not distracting our tracking team.' Thea's timely interruption prevented Izzy from cutting Jason down to size.

Jason didn't move. In fact, he looked about to object to being ordered about by anyone. Izzy tensed beside Lee.

'Now, Private,' Sergeant Thea commanded.

Jason actually huffed as he turned on his heel and headed back towards the Captain. Izzy relaxed, and Lee released his fingers from their fist.

'Must you aggravate him?' Sergeant Thea asked the trio.

'Must he continuously annoy us?' Izzy responded.

'He is like a child who must always be appeased. On the other hand, you are all adults and should be able to take the high ground,' Thea told them.

'You sound like my mother,' Lee said.

'Only because you are behaving like children,' the Sergeant fired back.

Lee had another retort lined up but laughed, suddenly seeing the absurdity of the situation. 'Fair point. We'll try to behave better.'

Sergeant Thea didn't smile often, but when she did it lit up her whole face and her blue eyes twinkled. 'Thank you, Lee. I am sure it will make life easier for all of us.'

Lee thought he would take advantage of her goodwill. 'Sergeant, may I ask a question?'

'Go ahead, Private.'

'Has anyone said why Allan ran away from Portsdown?' he asked.

Thea didn't answer immediately. She stared at Bruno for a long while before pulling her attention back to Lee.

'Our briefing was a little sketchy. We believe Allan ran away to find out if people were doing more than surviving above ground, and report what he found upon his return.'

'And is that really possible? Thriving above ground? I mean, our radiation tags indicate very little exposure these last two days. And the Portsmouth Militia looked quite healthy,' Lee pointed out.

Thea checked behind to ensure Captain Kiandra could not overhear their conversation before saying, 'The truth is, we don't know. I can feel a little magic now, so the earth is healing. Two city-based communities are active in the area, but the Captain tells me the actual townships and farms are comparatively small in number.'

'Perhaps they would welcome some new blood,' Lee suggested.

'They spend a lot of resources protecting themselves from marauders. Life is very hand-to-mouth, and most people no longer live to a ripe old age. Who would choose that life?' Thea responded.

'Doesn't sound like much of an existence,' Izzy commented.

'Compared to what I saw underground, it probably isn't,' Thea agreed.

But should they be given the choice to try living out here if they wish? I guess that that is the question, Bruno added.

Thea considered Bruno's answer for a moment, then shook her head. 'In this instance that point is moot. Our role is not to interfere, but to work with the local people—'

'You say that, Thea, but in this instance both our roles are the same: to find out why time ends and prevent it. Can you honestly say that taking this boy back to the city will achieve that?' Izzy asked.

'Can you be certain it won't?' Thea countered.

No one can be certain. All we can do is wait, watch, report back to our handlers, and hope they will provide us with useful guidance, Bruno said, playing the peacemaker.

'What does Captain Kiandra say?' Lee asked Thea. 'You and she are quite chummy I imagine she's said something.'

Thea's eyes widened in surprise. 'An interesting question, Lee.'

Don't look so surprised. He was sent along for a reason. Was Bruno smirking? He certainly looked like he was to Lee.

Ignoring Bruno, Thea continued. 'Kiandra believes the balance of life in the city must be maintained at all costs. When the needs of the few were put before the needs of the many, the world went to war. That has scared her, and many others.'

As I am sure it has done to many survivors, Bruno said.

'She is a strong believer in sticking together and following their leaders. She joined the guard to help maintain law and order, and to help prevent another war, so I guess she supports bringing Allan back to face the music, although she hasn't specifically said that,' Thea concluded.

'Would another war be on such a grand scale?' Lee asked. 'Surely all the weapons of mass destruction are gone?'

Theta laughed out loud. 'What makes you say that?'

'Well, I just assumed....'

From what we understand, the world was decimated by only a small proportion of the weapons that had been stockpiled over the years, Bruno said.

'History shows the underground cities in the old United Kingdom were built around or close to stockpiles of weapons.' Izzy said.

'So... they didn't use them all, but they didn't think to dispose of them either when they witnessed the devastation they caused?' Lee was incredulous. Was humanity destined to repeat its mistakes?

'We do not believe so,' Thea said. 'Part of my mission was to find out what weapons were in and around Portsdown. Unfortunately, a number of the more heavily guarded areas were off limits to me. Given more time I might have found a way in....'

The group fell silent, and Lee was left to his own thoughts. He didn't like where his head was going. Not only was he in a post-apocalyptic future, but the locals still had enough firepower to annihilate what was left of the world.

Moments later the trees began to thin, and Izzy halted them until the others caught them up. As Captain Kiandra led them out behind the back of a house, they were greeted by a horse's knicker. It eyeballed them, then calmly went back to munching grass.

'We'll go round the front,' the Captain said.

'Perhaps we should take off our masks before we do. I mean, we look a bit intimidating like this,' Lee suggested.

'Are you mad?' Rodgers spluttered. 'You want to expose us to radiation just so we don't scare the locals? No way am I doing that—you're on your own, boy.'

Unfortunately, the others agreed, and they emerged into the clearing in front of the house as an imposing group of soldiers armed and with their faces covered. Lee hung back a little, thinking there was no way this encounter was going to go well.

VIVIENNE LEE FRASER

THE TWO TALL, well-muscled young men on the veranda froze mid conversation when they spotted the intruders. They spoke quietly before walking down the stairs towards the group, their weapons casually hung across their bodies. The glint in their eyes told Lee it wouldn't take much for them to use those guns.

The men stopped about ten paces away and glared at them, waiting for someone to speak. Captain Kiandra moved forward. 'Good day, we are from Portsdown and we—'

The door to the house creaked open, causing Captain Kiandra to pause. An elderly woman walked out, leaning heavily on a stick. Behind her followed a tall blonde woman carrying a rifle, looking as though she knew how to use it.

The younger woman remained on the veranda while the older one made her way forward until she stood by the men. Out of the corner of his eye, Lee saw two other men emerge from nowhere. They stood by the house with guns cocked and ready to fire.

As the woman stepped forward to speak to them, Captain Kiandra took a step back, raising a cackle from the other woman, who said, 'I'm suffering from old-age, not the plague—and not radiation sickness.'

Captain Kiandra straightened her back. 'Old people live underground too.'

'Well, we have nothing like you guys out here.' Pleasantries over, the woman's voice turned cold. 'Why are you wandering across my property as if you own it?'

'We mean no offence. We were not aware anyone owned this land—' Captain Kiandra started.

'You know now, so you can be on your way.' As the woman spoke, the boys beside her moved their guns, ready to fire at her command.

Captain Kiandra tried again. 'I apologise. It has been a long time since someone from Portsdown has been out here—'

'I'm old enough to remember the last time your lot came around this way hunting down strays. You are not welcome here. I want you gone from my property.' The woman held a hand out, inviting them to leave.

'We are not here to harm you. We simply want some information, then we'll be gone.' The Captain's tone was neutral, but it did not soften the look on the older woman's face.

'About one of your own?'

Captain Kiandra nodded.

'A runaway?'

Captain Kiandra nodded again. 'He didn't request permission to leave they city.'

The old woman's face hardened almost imperceptibly as she asked, 'Is he over eighteen?'

'He is.'

Shrugging, the woman smiled, and Lee could see gaps where her teeth had once been. 'Seems to me since he's over eighteen, he should be allowed to come and go as he pleases. Makes no difference to me though. I have no information for you.'

Lee made ready as if to leave, but Captain Kiandra had other ideas. 'He broke the laws of our community. Would you harbour a law breaker?'

Again the woman laughed. 'Not all laws are equal. Did he harm anyone, or steal from your people?'

'No, but—'

The woman folded her arms across her chest. 'Then as far as I can see, his actions won't impact anyone else.'

Captain Kiandra started to speak, but the woman held up a hand. 'We can debate the morality of his crimes all you like, but it will make no difference. As I said, I haven't heard anything, and I can't tell you what I don't know. Now be gone.'

Thea moved alongside the Captain, and Lee heard her say, 'Do you know the saying "there's more than one way to skin a cat"? Perhaps if we camped close by tonight, we might be able to root around and find out if there's anything they're not telling us.'

The Captain nodded slowly, then said, 'It's getting late. Would you mind if we slept in your barn tonight?'

'I would,' the woman answered almost before Captain Kiandra had finished speaking.

Lee smiled at the abrupt answer, finding himself warming to the elderly head of the family. Captain Kiandra obviously did not feel the same as she attempted to negotiate for them to at least make camp at the edge of the woods.

As the conversation drew out, Lee caught sight of a skinny boy clambering over a tractor in the barn to the right of the house. The boy jumped down, picked up a wrench, then clambered back up, making eye contact with Lee

as he did. It gave Lee an idea.

He stepped forward and said, 'What if I work on your tractor? I used to tinker with engines, so I might be able to get it going. Would you let us stay then?'

The woman's grey eyes swivelled towards him, assessing him and his offer. At the same time, Captain Kiandra hissed, 'Private, what do you think you're doing?'

'I thought you wanted to stay the night,' Lee whispered he as rolled up his mask to reveal his face, then took it off all together.

The woman smiled, and this time it even reached her eyes. 'The tractor is dead. I doubt anything but a miracle can save it.'

Lee grinned at her. 'I love a challenge.'

She chuckled. 'All right, young man. It's a deal. And if you actually manage to get it running, I'll throw in a homemade meal.'

'Done,' Lee said, then realised his mistake and glanced sheepishly at his Captain.

'We accept,' Captain Kiandra confirmed. Turning on her heel, she glared at Lee before saying to the others, 'Right, let's set up camp.'

They started moving as one towards the barn.

'Wait, nobody enters my buildings without being checked first. I don't want any of you getting sick and dying on me. Someone might assume it was something we did.'

Lee waited by with the others while one of the boys pulled something from his pocket and ran it over Captain Kiandra. Lee realised the device checked radiation levels.

Once they were all deemed safe, the old woman said, 'Make yourself at home, but stay in the barn. The privy is round the back, but tell one of the boys if you need to use it—we don't want one of them shooting you for an intruder.' She turned to Lee. 'Knock yourself out with the tractor.'

Having dismissed them, she made her way slowly back to the blonde woman on the deck. As Lee headed to the barn, he watched as the two women talked for a moment before the younger one handed over a bottle, hugged their host, and departed round the side of the house. He turned to enter the barn only to find Captain Kiandra had also watched the exchange.

'I wonder what that was about?' Lee said.

'I would be wondering more about what your punishment might be for acting without orders.' The Captain's voice was cold.

'But I was only trying to help,' Lee said, defending himself.

'You are a soldier. You take orders. When you act on your own initiative, you put us all at risk. One of these days you might get us all killed. I will be taking a note of this, and you will face disciplinary action when we return.' The Captain stalked away, leaving a speechless Lee staring after her.

Shrugging, Lee muttered, 'If I return,' before following her into the barn.

'LEE, WHAT ON earth possessed you to take your mask off?' Izzy asked as he entered the barn, and he imagined her face screwed up with worry. 'Put it back on,' she ordered. 'The air purifier will soon be running, then you can remove it safely and play hero with the locals.'

'Come on, Izzy. Didn't you take notice of the radiation levels on their monitors? They hardly registered anything, not even in the air when they moved it away from us.'

Lee stepped to move past her, but she blocked his way.

'Why did they want to check us if the levels are as low as you say?' she said, challenging him.

Lee thought for a moment before answering. 'It could be habit, but I think that although these people do all right for themselves, they don't have enough resources to take care of the long-term sick.'

Izzy's head dropped to the side. 'Mm.... That's definitely possible. These people seem remarkably healthy, as did the Portsmouth Militia, for people living in radiation saturated air.'

Smiling triumphantly, Lee said, 'I don't think we need to cover up so much. With care, people are actually living a normal life out here.'

Izzy rubbed her chin with her forefinger, and Lee could almost hear the cogs whirring inside her head. 'Mm, you may be right,' she said. 'Perhaps it's time people from the underground city took a closer look at how people are living outside of its walls.'

A movement behind Izzy caught Lee's eye. Glancing over the girl's shoulder, he saw that the boy who had previously been crawling over the tractor had stopped his tinkering and was staring intently at them.

'Good afternoon,' Lee said, and the boy's eyes rounded with curiosity—but he said nothing.

Lee shrugged off his pack and handed it to Izzy, who left to go help set up with the others. Lee wandered over to the tractor with Bruno padding alongside.

'Nice John Deere you've got,' he said conversationally.

The boy's mouth dropped open before he managed to stammer out, 'You… you know about tractors?'

Lee laughed and pointed to something on the side of the vehicle. 'I can read,' he said. 'What's wrong with her?'

The boy shrugged. 'I'm not quite sure. I turn her on and nothing happens.'

'Did you check the spark plugs?' Lee asked.

The boy snorted. 'First thing I tried,' he said. 'We had a man with the sickness stay a while a few months back. He used to be a mechanic and he showed me a thing or two before he passed.' The boy stopped talking, and looked a little lost.

'And?' Lee asked.

The boy's face was blank.

'How were the spark plugs?' Lee prompted.

'Oh…. They're shot, but we ain't got no more here. When one of the bigger boys goes scavenging on the motorway... well.... Gram won't let any of them leave while you're here, so it's no use wondering about that.' The boy's brows drew into a frown as he spoke.

'Still—'

'But you'll be gone tomorrow, so we might be able to get her running then if Gram will let one of the boys go.' He turned a gap-toothed smile towards Lee.

'How long since the old girl started?' Lee said.

'A month or more. She's a good runner, just needs a few parts.'

'Well, if we can't get any new spark plugs, perhaps we can take the plugs out and give them a good clean,' Lee offered. 'My grandad taught me there is always something to do to make a machine run a little more smoothly.'

The boy grinned and deftly removed the spark plugs, handing them to Lee so he could climb down.

'We can clean them in the workroom.' He pointed to a door behind the tractor.

For the next hour the two worked in silence doing what they could to revive the clearly very old spark plugs. As they worked, Lee's mind drifted back to the days he spent with his grandfather in his garage at home, helping him restore classic cars.

With the army regularly sending his father away, the older man had taken Lee under his wing, rescuing him from a house dominated by women. Those times they spent pottering with engines were some of the happiest Lee could

remember, and his heart had nearly broke in two when his grandfather died earlier that year.

Shaking his head, Lee dispelled any lingering sadness and decided to befriend the boy. 'I'm Lee,' he said.

'I heard the girl say your name already.'

'And you are?' Lee prompted.

'Colin,' he said.

Lee hid a grimace. This was going to be hard work.

'Where do you find fuel for the tractor?' Lee asked, spying a number of gerry cans around the room.

'Same place we hunt for parts—abandoned cars on the motorway.'

Lee was surprised. 'Not from pumps in Southampton?'

Colin shrugged. 'Sometimes, when we have things to trade with them. Siphoning diesel from car tanks is cheaper.'

'What do you do when the tractor is broken?'

'Some neighbours have horses. They loan them to us, just like they use our tractor when it goes.'

Interesting, Lee thought. *This area has a good support network.*

'Are there many other farms around?' he asked, wondering just how big their local community was.

Colin frowned. 'Gram wouldn't like it if I told strangers too much about the people round here.'

It was a statement of fact, and Colin would not budge from his position, no matter what questions Lee asked. The sun was setting when Lee and Colin had the spark plugs back in their original positions.

'Give her a go,' Lee said.

Colin turned the key and the tractor spluttered.

Lee jiggled the plugs and tightened some connections. 'Try it again.' He held his breath and crossed his fingers. The tractor finally chugged into life.

The grin on Colin's face was enough reward for Lee, but the pot of stew he bought out to them later was most welcome. Sitting down beside Lee, the young boy joined in their conversation, though the rest of the family continued to keep their distance. And Colin didn't appear to mind that Lee, Izzy, and Bruno were the only ones eating Gram's thank you meal.

'What's wrong with the food?' Lee had asked the others.

'It will be radiation riddled—the ingredients were grown out here.' Rodgers grimaced as he spoke.

Asking Colin for a radiation detector, Lee swept it over their plates and the pot, and the dial didn't move. Still, they carried on eating their own dried rations, although Thea was looking longingly at their hot meal.

It's delicious. Why don't you try some? Bruno asked her.

I want to, but I also don't want to break my cover. A Sergeant with my supposed experience wouldn't make that leap. Thea's voice in Lee's head sounded disappointed.

Suit yourself. Bruno licked his bowl clean, then ran his tongue around his muzzle to mop up every last bit.

That night Lee had a full belly and the best sleep he'd had since arriving in this weird and warped version of the world.

7

A DECISION IS MADE

BASIA WAS SO engrossed in her studies, chin leaning on her hands while she read the text in front of her, she jumped when the door hit the kitchen wall with a loud bang. Her mother entered, followed moments later by her father, who let Jasmine and Baby in by the stove and shut the door.

'Where's the fire?' she asked as she closed her books. Frowning at Baby, she thought, *Hadn't he been out with Johan?*

'Fire would be preferable to the situation we find ourselves in,' her mother said as her father went into the washroom to clean the mud from his hands.

'What's going on? Did something happen at the Wilson's place?' Basia stood to move the kettle over onto the hob to boil. Unused to seeing her mother so flustered, she felt the need to do something.

'Wait until your father is finished, and I'll explain everything to you both. How's the boy?'

Shaking her head at the swift change in direction, Basia focused and reported, 'He woke for a little while. He was coherent and it looks like his temperature has dropped almost to normal. I gave him some broth and he's been sleeping for the last hour. He was restless a few moments ago, so he'll probably wake up again soon.'

'Excellent. I'll just go and—'

The door was flung open again, and Johan rushed in. 'I found soldiers from the underground city in the forest,' he blurted out, then he spotted his mother. 'But you already know that, don't you, because you met them at the Wilson's place?'

'What's that you're saying?' Her father emerged from the washroom, drying his hands on a towel. He closed the door for a second time as he said, 'There are soldiers from the underground city? Here?'

'Stop panicking. We are okay for the moment. Ma Wilson's let them stay in her barn overnight.' Tanya turned to Basia. 'Do you think the boy would be ready to travel into town tomorrow? I am thinking we might all be a little safer if he moves to Lyndhurst.'

'Hold on a minute,' Simon said. 'Let's not panic. Firstly, the Council won't want to come under fire for harbouring a citizen of the underground city. And we've no chance of convincing them now that he's from somewhere else.'

Her mother's hands planted themselves firmly on her hips, which was never a good sign. 'You want him to stay here and put us all at risk, Simon?'

'Both of you, please calm down,' Johan said. 'This arguing isn't helping anyone. Mum, after you left the Wilson's and the soldiers were setting up in the barn, Ma Wilson sent one of her boys into town to inform the Council. It won't be long until they put two and two together.'

'Then we need to get the boy to Lyndhurst quickly,' her mother said. 'We need to tell them that as soon as we realised who the boy was, we brought him straight in. If we don't, we risk being kicked out of the protectorate. Lord knows we won't survive for long without being part of their community.'

'But they'll decide to send him back with the soldiers to save their own necks,' Basia said. 'I can't imagine his treatment will be fair when he gets there.'

Her mother placed a hand on her shoulder. 'We don't know what will happen to him when he returns home. On the other hand, your father and I experienced firsthand what happens to people who harbour escapees from the underground city.'

'Are they killed?' Basia asked, not actually believing they would be.

'No, worse than that,' her father said. 'Their homes are burned, their livestock butchered, and their crops spoiled. They're forced to rely on others to survive—if anybody will agree to care for them after the pillaging soldiers depart.'

Basia's mouth formed an "o" as she realised the full extent of the risk her father had taken by bringing the young boy back here in the first place. 'So,

it's Allan or us,' she said.

'I'm afraid so,' her mother answered.

'You must give me to them. You can't put your own lives at risk,' a voice said from the other room. It still sounded thin and frail, but full of determination.

Her mother left Basia's side and moved to the doorway, where she could still see her family, but could also talk with the boy.

'Tell me the truth, young man. What did you do in the city that they sent out soldiers to hunt you down?'

Her mother was using her "don't mess with me voice", and Allan acknowledged that by giving her a direct answer. 'I swear, all I did was leave. Even so, you must hand me over to them.'

'That is not our way. If the Council agrees, we may be able to offer you sanctuary. Young, strong people are needed if our community is to survive, and they may take that into account.'

'But the soldiers will simply return to Portsdown and bring back a larger force to take me home. The backlash would devastate your whole community,' Allan said.

'That is if the soldiers ever get back.' A fierce look of determination set itself on her mother's face as she crossed her arms over her chest.

Her father tensed. 'What exactly do you mean by that, Tanya?'

Shrugging, her mother said, 'If the soldiers never return to Portsdown, what are the chances the city will send anyone else out this far to search for them? They'll likely assume it's wild and dangerous out here and let it go.'

If Basia had been surprised by her father putting them at risk in the first place, she was shocked by what her mother was suggesting. 'You mean the Council might—'

'I'm not saying anything… yet,' her mother said. 'Although many of us would not bat an eye at doing harm to soldiers from the city.'

'We can't do anything more tonight, so let's take a step back and sleep on this,' her father said. 'Perhaps we can approach it with clearer heads in the morning. Kids, go lock up.'

Basia held her breath until her mother nodded her agreement. 'Yes, it would be too dangerous to leave tonight. Come on, you two.' She gestured to Basia and Johan. 'Evening chore time.'

Heaving a sigh of relief, Basia left the room before her mother changed her mind.

THE OTHERS HAD gone to bed. Allan was dozing. Basia curled up in a chair by the fire, the book in her lap sitting unopened. Now that she was alone, she had time to consider the events of the afternoon and their dinnertime conversation—or the lack of it.

With four people living in the house together with few visitors, you would think a meal eaten in silence would be a common occurrence, but it wasn't.

The lack of banter unnerved Basia, perhaps more than anything else that had occurred in the past couple of days. In fact, she was still unsettled, even though her father had decided they wouldn't make a decision about what to do until the morning.

'You must convince them to let me go my own way tomorrow,' the boy's voice said, interrupting her thoughts.

Basia looked up and found Allan regarding her with those cool green eyes. He wriggled a bit and used his elbows to prop himself up a little. The pain on his face as he moved himself into a more comfortable position told her he was still not ready to do things by himself. Still, she liked that he had tried.

'Basia? Did you hear what I said?'

'What? Yes. Sorry.' Basia took a breath to centre herself. 'They'll do what they will do, and I'm afraid nothing I say will change their minds. In fact, I'm the last person they're likely to listen to.'

Allan's jaw tensed, giving a stubborn set to his face. 'The soldiers from my home are worried about what I will do. They won't just let me go my own way, and they won't show mercy to anyone who has helped me.'

'Surely they would let you stay here…. Hold on. Are you sure you didn't do something awful?'

'You mean, like kill someone?' he asked, a smile playing around the edges of his mouth.

Basia felt a blush rising. 'No, well, yes…. Something they could not let you get away with.'

He drew a cross over his heart with his index finger. 'I promise you, I didn't hurt anyone, or steal anything. I merely left the city boundaries.'

'Phew.' Basia was strangely relieved. 'In that case, the soldiers might let you stay here with us.'

He gave her words serious consideration before answering. 'You're right, they might be convinced to leave me if I swore never to return—if that was my intention.'

Basia's hopes of a peaceful resolution were not looking good, and she

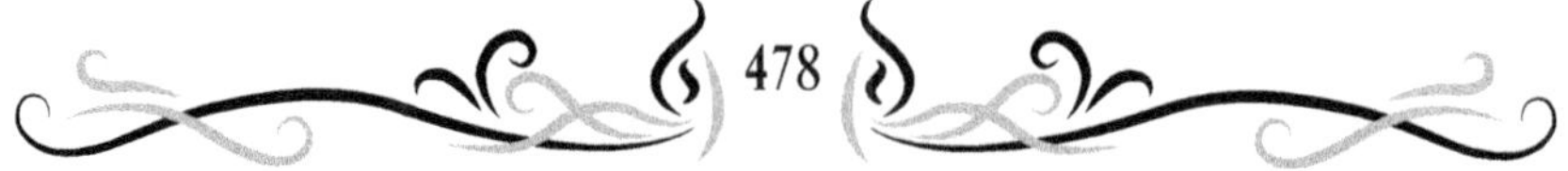

wanted to know why. 'What do you mean?'

Allan closed his eyes. 'I came out here to find out what it was like outside so I could return home and tell everyone whether or not it was safe to live above ground.'

Frowning, Basia asked, 'Why would you want to do that? Surely your people can come and go as they please?'

The boy's laugh was hollow. 'Where I come from, we can choose very little for ourselves. Unless of course your parents have money or power.'

'So you can't leave Portsdown? Ever?'

Again that hollow laugh, and it chilled Basia to the core. She leaned in closer to the fire, stirring the embers with the poker while she waited for Allan to answer.

'That's the funny thing about the underground community: it needs a certain number of people to maintain itself. Too many and resources are stretched. Too few people, and there aren't enough hands to produce everything the community needs.'

Basia drew her bottom lip between her teeth, then asked, 'How do they maintain the balance? You must practice some form of population control… am I right?'

'Yes, you are. When someone dies, a token is created, and people who want children participate in a draw to win it.'

Basia shrugged. 'Sounds fair. A life for a life.'

'It would be if it were as simple as putting your name in the draw, but there are rules.'

'Of course. All societies agree on rules to ensure fairness.'

'Oh, nothing is fair about these rules, I assure you.' Allan rolled over and reached for the cup of water on the table. Basia forced herself to watch him strain, not wanting to help unless he asked for it. He took a sip from the cup, placed it back on the table, then relaxed before he continued.

'Only married women can apply for the lottery, and they must be able to pay the application fee—which is about six month's wages for the average worker.'

'That's a little discriminatory, but not drastic,' Basia said when she had worked through the implications. Men could not apply, nor could same sex couples, and some people would have to save for years to get the application money.

'The worst part is, you can apply more than once.'

It took a moment, but then the penny dropped. 'So people with money apply more than once and stack the odds in their favour?' she asked.

'Exactly.'

They were silent for a while as Basia considered everything he had said about the city she had always believed to offer a perfect alternative to their way of life. Finally she asked, 'If you return and tell people they can come up here and live, wouldn't you be helping out the city by reducing mouths to feed, and increasing the number of people allowed to become pregnant?'

Allan smiled a sad smile that told Basia she had not fully understood the problem.

'Unfortunately, I believe the number of people who would want to take their chances above ground is high, and they're mostly from lower orders—the people who work at keeping those with money comfortable.'

Basia mulled over his words, comparing his reality to her fantasy of what life in the underground world was like. Between them, Allan and her father had dispelled any idea of a better, easier world she could escape to. That ease of living came at a price, and she for one would not be able to live with it—not that she would ever really get the chance.

'Okay, the soldiers want to make sure you don't tell people they can leave Portsdown. That, in turn, will maintain the status quo for an elite group of people?'

'Exactly, although the soldiers might not be aware of the true reason for their mission. I hope if they did, they might be inclined to support me—but I doubt I'm best placed to convince them of the error of their ways.'

It was Basia's turn to chuckle. She held up the book in her lap, *Middlemarch*, so he could see the cover. 'Have you read any of the old classics?' she asked.

He half shrugged. 'A bit of *David Copperfield*, and some of *Great Expectations* when I was at school—English wasn't my favourite subject. I was more a maths and science kind of guy. I don't see the relevance of an old book though.'

Basia smiled. 'In nineteenth-century England, the upper-class elite made the rules and the bulk of the people, the workers, kept society going, maintaining the status and power of those in charge. What you are describing to me is exactly what used to happen then.'

'Is it any different out here?' Allan asked.

'We are much more like the American frontier. Our community, and I believe many others, are run by white men who believe their superiority gives them the right to be in charge, which derives from their certainty that they are best placed to physically defend us.'

'White men?' Allan raised an eyebrow.

'Yes. We're in the English countryside. The few people who had enough resources to survive out here during and after the war were farmers and

landowners who were predominantly white middle-class males. The mix in the protectorates is a little different— though men are still in charge. Only the skin colour changes.'

'What about women?' Allan asked.

'Older woman born pre-war are an independent lot. Most of the businesses in Lyndhurst are owned and run by them. A couple even sit on the Council,' she told him.

'I sense you're holding something back.'

This was a sore point for Basia, and she tried not to let her voice sound too bitter when she replied. 'Younger women are a rarity, and because mankind relies on us to reproduce, everyone else thinks they should be able to decide what is best for us.'

'That sounds bleak.'

'Fortunately, my father is different. He trained me to fight and defend myself, and I'm studying to be a healer. The rest of our community may value me as a brood mare, but I am lucky my family values me for being me.' Basia gnawed her lip. 'Even so, I probably have less control over my life than you.' As she finished speaking, Basia relaxed back in her chair, feeling a little less satisfied with her lot in life now her fantasy of escaping to the underground city was gone.

'I am sure your parents will do their best to ensure you choose your own future,' Allan said.

'They will try to give me a say, but in the end, it may come down to politics.'

'Doesn't it always,' Allan said.

They fell into silence.

'Did yours not stick up for you?' Basia asked a little later.

'I don't think they would have, but to be honest, I never gave them the chance,' Allan admitted. 'We were never close.'

The room fell silent again. The only sound was the crackling of the fire. Allan took another sip of water before asking, 'What about the militia-controlled territories?'

'How do you mean?'

'I came across the Portsmouth Militia on the way here, although they didn't see me as they chased my pursuers from their territory. Perhaps your future lies in one of the old cities.'

'Life in the towns is pretty hand-to-mouth,' Basia said. 'They farm what they can, but most of the people spend their time defending themselves

against marauders.'

'I see. Perhaps not the best option for you.'

'There are so many small groups in England now. Maybe what we need is someone to inspire us to join up and do something better,' Basia sighed. 'I don't know where that came from.'

Allan chuckled, and this time the laugh was genuine. 'Perhaps from your books…. Still, you're right. There are so many little groups dotted around spending all their resources on surviving, when what they actually need is someone to show them a better way forward together.'

Each sunk back into their own thoughts until Allan tried to sit up and winched in pain. 'Nice though this dreaming of a great future is, if your parents won't listen to reason, I'm just going to make the decision for them.'

He tried to swing his legs around to stand, but his brow knitted in pain and drops of sweat stood out on his forehead. Basia shook her head as he struggled.

Finally he stopped and stared at her. 'I could do with a little help.'

'You're kidding me, right? If you can't get out of bed without my help, how do you think you would survive out there? Let alone get back home.'

'But—'

'Not to mention it's nighttime,' she added. 'There are all sorts out there: bandits, fallout victims, people ejected from other communities for their crimes. The night belongs to the desperate. You won't last five minutes before you're stripped bare and left to fend for yourself without food or weapons, and probably clothing as well.'

'Wow, sugarcoat it, why don't you?' he said, flopping back on the bed. 'I guess we're back to trying to convince your parents of the right thing to do.'

Basia moved to help make the boy more comfortable again. 'Good luck with that. I've been trying my whole life and never changed their minds a single time.'

Once Allan was settled, she curled back up in the chair and opened her book as he dozed off. This time she concentrated on the words, trying to block out the bleak images of her world their conversation had raised to the surface. It didn't work. Her mind was too active to lose itself in fantasy. Something had shifted inside of her, jerking her out of her complacency.

She knew now there was no ideal world to escape to, no magic wand to give her a better life. If she didn't like the life she had, it was up to her to do something to change it. And she decided she would start with ensuring the soldiers didn't take Allan back to Portsdown. She would help him return on his own terms.

8

A CHANGE IN TIME

BETA TOOK A deep breath and willed himself into physical form. Clasping his hands behind his back, he made to enter the conference room, then paused. This was his third meeting with Alpha and the two representatives from the Time Fixers. Rather than bringing their actions more in line, each meeting escalated tensions between the two groups.

Actually, that wasn't quite true. He and Cynthia had been working together to find a way to use both parties' unique set of skills to help their teams on the ground save humanity.

In stark contrast, Alpha seemed intent on aggravating Gerald, and the other Time Fixer acted like he just didn't care. They squabbled incessantly, which often resulted in Alpha storming off and Gerald retreating into himself.

Earlier today he suggested he meet alone with Cynthia. Of course, Alpha overheard and said, 'I think not, Beta. We will make more progress if we work together.'

Beta responded, 'Maybe that would be true if you did something other than stir up Gerald.'

'I wouldn't need to prod and poke at him if he actually contributed something,' Alpha said and nodded towards Gerald.

Gerald leaned laconically back in his chair. 'I would make an effort if I thought we could do something, anything, to change the course of time.'

Alpha had picked up his tablet and winked out of the room.

Oh well, best he get on with it. He pushed the door open and, plastering a grin on his face, he entered the room.

'Good afternoon, everyone,' he said. 'Are we all ready to see how we can help our friends on the ground?'

Cynthia smiled and he momentarily allowed himself a small sliver of hope that things would be different this session. It lasted until he turned to Alpha and Gerald. They sat on opposite sides of the conference table, locked in a staring contest.

Stifling a sigh, Beta took the seat beside Alpha and placed on the table the papers that a monitor handed him on the way in. They contained detailed reports from the monitoring stations both here and at the Time Fixer's headquarters—carefully approved reports.

A furrow formed between his brows as he scanned the summary sheet. They were no further forward than they had been this time yesterday. He raised his eyes and caught Cynthia watching him.

'This isn't good,' he said to her.

'No, it isn't. I am uncomfortable having a team on the ground when I can't provide them with directions,' Cynthia said.

His brow furrowed. 'We only sent them because we had expected to see changes in the timeline which would have helped us direct them.'

'It is disheartening. Our people are having no impact at all,' Cynthia said.

Beta's fingers drummed on the table as he considered his next words. *I had forgotten some of the satisfying things about having an actual body,* he thought. 'At best, this tells us we haven't made anything worse….'

'Which is saying very little at all,' Alpha said, not taking his eyes off Gerald for even a second.

'It shows you're not mucking anything up.' Gerald smiled at Alpha.

'Should we be doing something different? Change it up a little…,' Beta trailed off as Alpha directed his scowl at him.

'It would be a stretch to say we are winning this battle at the moment, but we are making progress, even if the teams monitoring cannot see it,' Cynthia said.

'How so?' Beta asked.

Cynthia leaned forward, resting her arms on the table. 'People from our

organisations are on the ground for the first time ever. We are getting occasional reports, which add to our pool of information on the period. In time, we will be able to stitch these pieces together to give us a more complete picture if we get another chance at fixing things.'

The Time Fixer paused. When no one else said anything, she spoke again. 'Plus, our team at Time Fixer headquarters have been relaying to us occasional thoughts from our operatives registered on our recording equipment over the past couple of hours.'

Alpha frowned. 'I don't remember reading anything about a change in the documents.'

'No,' Cynthia confirmed. 'Our information is reviewed before being included in the reports we share. I was just told the good news now, and it will no doubt be in the next release. I simply wanted to give us a little hope in advance.'

'Interesting,' Beta mused. For a moment he considered not saying anything else, but he felt Cynthia's leap of faith deserved an equal move from him. 'Just before I came in, our monitors told me they can now track our people on the ground—they are in the New Forest area of Hampshire. The monitors suggest this shows a regeneration of magic in parts of Southern England.'

Alpha swivelled in his chair, again turning his glare on Beta. 'Should we be sharing that if it hasn't been approved?'

'In the light of Cynthia's revelation, I thought it only fair.'

Alpha continued to glare at him. Beta decided to ignore his colleague. 'All indications are that we should be able to contact our operatives and provide more direct support from here on in.'

Cynthia smiled. 'Perhaps we should each try to contact our teams tonight and regroup tomorrow to share what we find.'

'I think that's a brilliant idea. What do you say, Alpha?' His colleague mumbled something Beta took to be agreement.

'I feel we've turned a corner. Now more than ever I believe our people will change the future for the good of all humanity,' Cynthia said.

Alpha humphed, turning in his seat with his back towards her. Gerald's eyes followed him as the Time Fixer leaned back in his chair, folded his arms, and chewed his lip as if he was thinking.

Beta smiled at Cynthia, hoping to transmit his support, but she was too busy trying to attract Gerald's attention to take notice.

Clearly there was nothing more to be done here. He stood, gathered his papers, and said, 'See you tomorrow,' as he left the room.

He decided to return to his quarters via the flow of history, which ran through the centre of the city and appeared as an infinite number of strands of light energy. Like so many others, when he first joined the Guardians, he had been awed by history, and honoured to be chosen to protect it. Back then he had not realised how restrictive the Time Guardian's approach to protecting the timeline was. Nor had he understood how dogmatic they would be.

Then he began mentoring Sigma. The issues he raised started Beta thinking, and he began questioning the Guardians and what they were doing. Since then, he found the eternity he had chosen increasingly frustrating.

Recently he had wondered if Alpha was losing touch with his humanity and should perhaps stand down from the Council. Over the last few days, Beta's thoughts ran more along the lines that perhaps it was he who should be reconsidering his own future.

ONCE ALPHA BLINKED out of existence without even a goodbye, Cynthia finally managed to attract Gerald's attention. It infuriated her that he only responded because he could no longer play his mind games with Alpha.

'Really, Gerald, we are not in the war with these people. If we don't work with them, we risk all humanity ending here.' She could not keep her exasperation in check.

'Come on, Cynthia, there's nothing to say we can't have a little fun while trying to save the world.'

'You're such a child. We're the first ones to get a chance to fix this mess, and I won't let you screw it up.'

Gerald laughed. 'Whatever we do, history will continue to run up until the point that it doesn't, and time will carry on whether or not humans populate the earth. Whatever happens on the ground, Time Fixers still be able to move backwards and forwards through the time periods populated by humans, trying to save people from themselves, and trying to prevent this event from continuing. So chill out. Take a moment to enjoy this experience.'

Cynthia's jaw dropped. She couldn't believe what she was hearing. Gerald stood and picked up the reports and flicked through them. 'Have you ever considered that nothing we changed over the years, or the Time Guardians changed, for that matter, has altered the end of humanity?'

'If you believe our work is futile, what are you even doing here?' Cynthia's

tone was icy as she posed the question.

'I made a commitment and I am in this till the end. Besides, what else can we do? I'm going to live forever, and that is a lot of time to fill.' Gerald smirked.

Disgusted, Cynthia said, 'If you are weary of all this, then why don't you will yourself out of existence—you don't need to put yourself out trying to save the human race.'

'But this game we are playing with the Time Guardians has given me a whole new purpose, and hours of amusement.'

Cynthia glared at Gerald, not sure whether he was having her on, or whether he was truly this self-centered. She half stood, then sat again, not quite sure what to do next. Her shoulders slumped with defeat.

'Are you ready to go?' Gerald asked, unaware of her internal conflict.

Shrugging, she decided he was not her problem to deal with. She had a job to do, and she would do it regardless of whether or not Gerald was engaged and effective. She owed it to Izzy.

'Jason is your man. Do you want to contact him this evening, or shall I?'

'Knock yourself out,' Gerald said. 'He's all yours. You might find him a little tedious, though. Perhaps you will have better luck getting him to listen to your directions than I've had.'

Again Cynthia didn't know whether Gerald was serious, but she took him at face value, if only to end this conversation as quickly as possible. Closing her eyes, she reached out and felt for the magic. It was easy to link with Gerald, but it took some time to find a sense of Jason. Eventually she found his personal signature.

Jason?

No response.

Jason? Isolde? Are either of you in a position to report?

A slight tingling tickled at the edge of her senses. She drew a bit more power to herself and concentrated.

Cynthia, is that you?

The voice was weak, but she could hear it.

Isolde—can you report? Or can you ask Jason to?

Jason has just arrived to relieve me from guard duty. We can't gather enough magic for both of us to speak. I will talk and relay messages, Isolde sent.

Cynthia looked up and Gerald nodded. 'We're likely to get more from her than we ever would from him.'

The two of them listened while Isolde went through the events of the last

few days up to their arrival in the New Forest. *We think we're close to finding the boy who escaped, but….* Isolde stopped.

What? Cynthia asked.

Can you provide clearer instructions on how we should proceed once we catch up to him?

Cynthia shook her head, then remembered Isolde could not see her response. *With no significant changes showing up on our equipment, your only option is to continue to work with the guard troop.*

There was silence. It lasted so long, Cynthia was beginning to wonder if the link had disappeared. *Isolde?* she asked.

Sorry, I was thinking. There was another short silence before Isolde spoke again. *Some of us are worried that if we take the boy back as we are expected to do, they will end his life. I am not comfortable with that. How can sending a person to their death be the best way forward for humanity?*

Cynthia considered this for a moment, then said, *Isolde, we all understand that sometimes the sacrifice of one is needed for the many to survive.*

Isolde was silent again. *Isolde? Izzy?*

Wait a moment. Jason is saying something. He says to tell you he is good whatever you decide.

Gerald smirked. 'What a surprise. That guy has never had a unique thought in his head—ever.'

So, you have nothing more for us? Nothing at all?

I don't know what you want me to say, Cynthia said.

All right.

Wanting to give her something, Cynthia said, *The only consolation I can give you is that the blip alerting us to the possibility of change is still showing. We know you're in the right place and in the right time, and that's all we know.*

Okay, Isolde said. *We will try and contact you this time tomorrow.*

The girl's presence blinked away, but Cynthia kept her eyes closed for a moment, not wanting to open them and face the inadequacy of their support of the team on the ground.

'And you still see value in doing this?' Her eyes flew opened to find Gerald leaning on the table, a smirk on his face.

Cynthia fought the urge to slap him. Rising in a single movement, she gathered her papers and left the room before she said something they would both regret.

THE GUARDIANS OF TIME: SOLDIER

'REALLY, ALPHA, MUST you bait him so?' Beta asked as his colleague joined him by the flow of history.

Then he mentally kicked himself. Why did he bother? Alpha simply didn't care whether or not they got on with the Time Fixers. He thought trying to work with them was beneath his dignity.

'You must agree he is incredibly irritating,' Alpha said. 'I am sure that was why they chose him.'

Beta sighed, unable to deny Gerald rubbed him up the wrong way too. He was also aware of how annoying Alpha was being, which prevented him revealing this fact—so he said nothing and changed the subject. 'Have you tried reaching out to Theta?'

'Not yet. I assume you talked with Sigma already?'

'No, although there is something pulling at the edge of my consciousness. It could be him trying to activate our link, or it could be the boy he took with him. Lee is quite strong, and he hasn't learnt to dampen his psychic thoughts yet.'

'It might be one of our other prospective Guardians too. That boy Alain—Allan—was close to becoming a Guardian before the war erupted. It was a shame he died so suddenly. In this incarnation he might actually be ready to make the move. Perhaps we should talk to the Council about recruiting him before time ends. What do you think?'

Bringing a new person into the ranks of the Guardians was the last thing on Beta's mind. He really just wanted to go home, power down, and be by himself. The frustrations of working with Alpha and Gerald these last three days had worn him out.

Ever the diplomat, though, he said, 'I think that is a discussion for another time. Do you want to try and contact Theta, or shall I try for Sigma?'

Alpha closed his eyes, and the air around Beta began to tingle.

Alpha, is that you? a female voice said in his head.

It is. Beta is with me. Is Sigma around?

Yes, we're both here, she said before launching into her update.

We are currently staying on a farm, she informed them as she finished up.

So, you are finally in contact with the locals? Beta asked.

I wouldn't quite put it that way. They allowed us to camp the night in a barn in exchange for Lee fixing their tractor.

And how is Lee doing? Beta had been concerned about the Council's decision to send an untrained boy on this mission. Especially as their ability to maintain contact was severely limited, not to mention the worry that they might not be able to portal him to safety should anything happen.

Funny you should ask that, Theta said. *He has raised some interesting issues these last couple of days. He is concerned about taking Allan back to the underground city. He believes they will terminate his life.*

Your orders are to support the soldiers on the ground, Alpha said.

I understand that, sir, but things are very different here than we imagined. The world has started to regenerate, and there appear to be communities living quite happily above ground. From what I can make out, the stringent rules required to maintain life in Portsdown are no longer essential for the survival of the human race. It all leads me to wonder if we are doing the right thing.

Alpha's energy became more red tinged as Theta continued speaking. *It is not your job to wonder. You have your orders and you will continue to follow them.*

The silence after Alpha's remark was heavy, and Beta felt compelled to add, *I think what Alpha is trying to say is, nothing in the timeline or in history has changed–*

No change at all? Theta's voice sounded dismayed.

I am sorry, Theta, but your presence so far has not done anything to change the future, Beta said.

There was a longer silence this time, long enough for Beta to wonder if they had ended the conversation.

Theta? Alpha asked.

I'm still here. Please wait a moment. Sigma asked me to tell you that a couple of our team are unwilling to return the runaway to Portsdown. They won't hinder the mission, but nor will they actively assist either, Thea said.

Alpha sighed, then sent, *The Council says–*

Which leads us to the end of humanity, which is what I thought we were all sent here to prevent, Sigma interrupted.

The appearance of Beta's protege had an immediate effect on Alpha. His energy changed from red tinged to bright red.

You must not interfere, Alpha barked.

They know they cannot take direct action and are not asking for you to agree to that. I guess in the light of no new direction from you, we would all like some leeway to react to what we find, and be allowed to follow our instincts.

Sigma's proposal sounded reasonable, but the tension in the air around him signalled Alpha's disagreement.

How would you behave differently if I were to say go ahead, follow your instincts? Beta asked, hoping to diffuse the situation before Alpha exploded.

We have not discussed this, Theta said, sounding a little flustered. *An example might be for Sigma as Bruno to run off, meaning we can no longer track scents. The team would then need to return to Portsdown to arrange a new tracking team.*

Beta had hoped that by Theta showing some support for Sigma's suggestion, Alpha might be more amenable to the change. However, he had severely underestimated the Guardian's dislike of Beta's protege.

I find no reason to change what you are doing, Alpha said. *Proceed as is, and report back tomorrow night.*

Alpha cut the conversation short before Beta could say anything. 'That was a bit abrupt, don't you think?' he said. 'They raised a fair point. If they don't change anything, then their mission might be a failure.'

'It's the Council's agreed course of action. We can't change that without going back to them. And I, for one, am not prepared to take such a step at the moment. Are you?'

Not when you obviously won't support me, Beta thought. He tried a different approach. 'Sigma and Theta have more current information, and Theta is a seasoned operative, so perhaps we should take their concerns to the Council.'

Alpha said nothing, and the crimson hue of his energy told Beta any further discussion would be futile.

'Just think about it,' he said before turning and heading towards his quarters.

'See you tomorrow,' Alpha said as he departed.

As he moved through the other light beings, Beta pondered the events of the day. More and more he was becoming convinced the Time Guardians must change the way they approached history. They could not change things directly or history itself would redress the balance, but perhaps they could review how they chose who to support in any given situation. Or at the very least, give more control to operatives on the ground to adjust their approach as events unfolded.

Perhaps this minor tweak to procedure might help deal with the problem they always had with preventing the end of human history. This was their first opportunity–perhaps their only opportunity–to save humanity at the point of extinction, and they were not rising to the challenge.

He sighed as he reached his dwelling. He was only one voice on the ten-person Council. What could he do? Still, there was another day tomorrow.

9

THE LOCAL PROBLEM

LEE OPENED THE barn door, blinked, and squeezed his eyes shut in the glare of the morning sun. Without his protective helmet, it was almost blinding. He stretched long and loud before opening his eyes and freezing, arms still above his head.

'Um, Captain Kiandra, you might want to come here,' he said, slowly lowering his arms by his sides. 'We have a bit of a situation.'

'A bit of an understatement, Private,' the Captain said under her breath as she joined him in the doorway.

Lee smiled warily as he surveyed the thirty or so men surrounding the barn, weapons raised and pointed directly at them.

'I don't think they're friendly,' Lee observed dryly.

'You don't say?' she responded. Turning to him, she added, 'Private, I'm giving you fair warning. This is not the time for one of your inspired off-reservation ideas.'

'As if,' Lee said under his breath, then added, 'Understood, Captain,' for his boss' benefit.

The group had joined them in the doorway and Thea asked, 'What do you want us to do, sir?'

'I'm not sure yet, Sergeant. Where was our warning? Who was on guard duty?'

Lee looked around and spotted Jason standing at the back of the group surrounding them with his hands behind his back.

Captain Kiandra's gaze found him around the same time. 'I might have known,' she said. 'How that boy ever made it through basic training, I will never understand.'

'Indeed,' Corporal Rodgers said. 'He must be supported by some powerful sponsors.'

'I don't see much point in fighting,' the Captain said. 'By the time we draw our weapons, we would most likely be dead. Let's see what negotiating will do.'

As the Captain stepped forward, Lee felt movement beside him and he glanced down to find a worried face staring back.

'It wasn't me,' Colin whispered. 'Gram said we needed to tell the town Council you were here, otherwise we'd be in trouble. We didn't know they'd do this.'

Lee ruffled the boy's hair. 'Don't worry, Colin, it'll all sort itself out. Just in case, you'd best hurry back inside. I don't want you caught in any crossfire.'

He turned his attention back to the Captain as she slowly walked forward, hands in front and palms facing outwards to show she would not do anything stupid—like make a move for her blaster. The rest of them remained where they were, hands visible so the townsmen could see they were no threat either.

Lee noted that, unlike his troop with it its mix of gender and race, the group in front of him was all white and all men. He briefly wondered where the women were.

Bruno shuffled forward to sit in front of Lee before laying down to make himself less conspicuous. *I guess we should have seen this coming,* he said.

If Jason had only warned us, we would not be in this position, Thea commented. *Why would the Time Fixers send someone so clearly incompetent on this mission?*

Rodgers couldn't have been more right if he tried, Izzy said. *Jason's family have been supporters of the World Fixers since time began. Most of them are pretty decent operatives, but I guess every family has one exception.*

'Good morning,' Captain Kiandra was saying, and they turned their attention to her. 'There's no need for guns. We are not here to harm any of you.'

One of the men stepped forward. He was perhaps in his thirties, lean and weather-beaten. His face was all hard lines, displaying no obvious signs of welcome.

'Places around here are still suffering from your kind's last visit. We're not taking any chances with you. One of my men will remove your weapons. Then we'll be taking you to town with us to talk with the Protectorate's representatives.'

Captain Kiandra paused for a moment as if she was considering this as a request rather than an order. 'I can agree to that,' she said. Turning back towards the barn, she spoke to her team. 'Come forward, slowly.'

Two men broke away from the main group and entered the building, probably to collect their gear, while a third removed blasters from those who had thought to grab them. Lee was pleased they didn't search for any handheld weapons—they all had at least one knife about their person. At least he could still defend himself should it come to a fight.

When the man in charge was certain all their gear was rounded up, he said, 'Right, let's head into town.'

'Can we at least put on our anti-radiation gear?' the Captain asked.

Everyone except for the soldiers laughed. 'This is one of the most radiation free areas in the Southern Zones. You'll be fine for the little walk we'll be taking.'

The Captain didn't look convinced, but with the number of guns pointed at her and her troops, she didn't have much choice. 'Fall in,' she commanded.

Thea joined the Captain, and Lee and Izzy dropped in behind them, with Rodgers bringing up the rear. As they walked forward, Jason was pushed into line beside the Corporal, still bound. Bruno padded up beside Lee, but the leader of the local guard halted the group.

'The dog can stay here. Ma Wilson and her boys will look after him.'

'He comes with me,' Lee insisted, not willing to leave his friend behind.

Izzy placed a hand on his arm and sent, *He'll be fine here, and it won't hurt to have someone on the outside.*

Lee was about to object when Bruno said, *Don't worry. I'll slip away and follow behind.*

The walk into town was taken at double time. Lee was pleased he had spent the last three days walking so he didn't embarrass himself by dropping back too far. Throughout the journey Captain Kiandra attempted to engage the guard captain in conversation. He either ignored her or told her to shut up.

She's trying to force him to identify with us as guards like him, as people following orders, Izzy said.

It isn't working. In fact, Lee would say she was actually annoying the guard leader, causing him to push on faster, almost as if he wanted to be rid of his troublesome charges.

The sun had barely warmed the earth when he spotted a series of dilapidated buildings on the edge of the settlement. The group joined a road crisscrossed with a barrier at the entrance of Lyndhurst proper.

Two guards appeared as they drew closer. One raised the barrier to allow the group through while the other had a brief word with the man who had led them.

Lyndhurst, Izzy said. as they walked along the road. *This was the old High Street.* The bottom level of the buildings had obviously once been shops. Wooden barricades covered the windows on the left-hand side. On the right, everything had been collapsed so the area beyond could be seen from the top floors on the left. The debris also made it difficult for anyone to rush in and attack. Lee admired the ingenuity.

In behind there is roughly a triangle of suburbia, Izzy continued, pointing towards the boarded-up shops. *It looks like they are set up to defend that area as the centre of their community.*

Even though it was still early, he expected to see more people. It was surreal walking through what had once been a thriving town and not seeing a sole person.

As they reached a lane on left, the guard leader caught them up. 'Down here,' he said, then proceeded to lead them through an old carpark, past a building with a dilapidated sign proclaiming it as "The New Forrest Heritage Centre", to a small building on the right.

'You lot you can wait inside.' The leader gestured towards the open door.

'No way! That's an old public toilet,' Izzy said, taking a step back.

Lee wasn't particularly keen either, but the guards did not give them a choice. The old building had been repurposed as cells. It was relatively clean, even though it still retained the distinct whiff of public toilets the world over. They had left a stall intact at the back, which meant they could at least use the bathroom in private. The rest of the room contained bunk beds behind some pretty hefty iron bars.

'I thought you said we were going to meet with your Council,' Captain Kiandra said as the metal door was closed behind them.

'You will,' the guard leader said. 'When they're ready to see you.'

Left alone in the rather bleak building, Captain Kiandra told them, 'You might as well make yourselves comfortable. No telling how long we might be here before we get a chance to speak to the people in charge about being released.'

'You seem certain they will let us go,' Izzy said, skepticism lacing her words.

'Of course I am. With their limited manpower, small communities like this would struggle to stand up to Portsdown,' the Captain said as she lay down on a bunk.

'They looked well armed to me, and they had enough men to come get us and leave the town well defended,' Izzy insisted.

'You are obviously new to interactions with the locals,' Corporal Rodgers said. 'They like to show their power, but our forces are superior, and they always roll over in the end.'

Izzy shook her head. 'I am not getting the feeling these are people prepared to give way to anyone. They are a disciplined unit who are annoyed at our wandering over their lands.'

Lee had to say he agreed with Izzy, but Corporal Rodgers had other ideas. 'They're the dregs, the leftovers. They can never defeat us.' He took the lower bunk beside the Captain, ready to make the most of the downtime provided.

'I think you're wrong,' Izzy mumbled, moving to the bars and peering out.

Lee also moved to the bars and peeked through the door. A couple of guards stood about outside, but the street was clear.

Bruno? he sent.

No reply. Sighing, he took a bunk opposite the Captain and Rodgers. Theta joined him, easily swinging herself up top and rolling over to look out the slit window across the way. Izzy kept her vigil by the door.

Bruno? Lee tried again, his stomach sinking as he was met with silence.

BRUNO PADDED THROUGH the undergrowth, staying a little way behind the last of the Lyndhurst guardsmen. It was difficult to remain close enough so their scent was still fresh, but far enough away that they would find it difficult to pick him out of the surrounding greenery.

He had gone some way when he began to suspect he himself was being followed. Slowing down a little, he cocked an ear, but couldn't quite make out where the footsteps were coming from. Sniffing, he recognised the smell and he waited until its owner drew a little closer before revealing he knew of their existence.

Timing it just right so he barred the pathway as a figure emerged around the bend, Bruno bared his teeth and growled menacingly at Colin. The boy stepped around him and carried on towards Lyndhurst. Frustrated he couldn't make the boy understand the danger he was in if he continued, Bruno trotted after him, wondering what else he might do to send the boy home.

He caught Colin up and tried leaning into the boy's legs in an attempt to

use his weight to turn him around. When that didn't work, he gripped at the boy's clothes, only to find himself swatted on the nose. It seemed Colin was determined to follow the others to their final destination.

In light of such stubbornness, Bruno wondered if Colin was actually meant to be going to Lyndhurst. If that were the case, stopping him would be interfering directly with history. Dropping behind, he allowed the boy to take the lead as he clearly knew where he was going.

When they reach the edge of the forest, Bruno's skin stopped tingling and he realised the magic around him was thinning out; it appeared regeneration had not yet reached the Lyndhurst settlement.

Plonking himself down, he surveyed the open road. The rear guard were still filing through the barricade, but he couldn't find Lee and the others. Not wanting to be seen, he slunk behind a bush. Colin joined him.

'Ah, smart dog,' the boy said. 'Best to wait until they're inside the settlement before we approach.' He dropped to the ground and sat cross-legged beside the dog.

Their spot under the shady tree was pleasant and Bruno relaxed a little, leaning into his companion. Comfortable for the moment, Bruno decided to make the most of his enforced break.

Beta, he sent. *Where are you?*

Nothing came back.

Beta. Beta, I need to talk with you.

Still nothing. No, there was a faint buzzing. Bruno expanded his senses and drew a little more magic to himself.

Sigma, is that you?

Beta? Yes, thank goodness, Bruno sent, then tuned his thoughts until the voice of his mentor came in loud and clear.

I'm here, Sigma. What is it? You're not due to report again until this evening. Has something happened? The urgency in his mentor's voice highlighted his concern

Calm down, Beta. I'm not sure it is anything to worry about—yet. Some local guards escorted the others from the New Forest a little while ago. I will be joining them soon. Magic is weaker around here, so I'll keep you posted when I can.

This is not good, Beta said. *No, not good at all. We were waiting for something different to happen, but not something like this.*

Bruno resisted the urge to say, 'I'm still here.' One of the downsides of taking animal form was that others often disregarded him. *I wouldn't be too worried. The original team on this mission may have been taken into Lyndhurst—*

Sigma, I thought about things after we spoke last night. It is possible Lee offering to fix the tractor, which in turn allowed your troop to stay at the farm, may have already altered the timeline. Beta could barely keep the excitement from his voice.

Bruno didn't answer immediately. Had Lee actually changed history? Could this be the real reason he was with them? He shook his head, and Colin rubbed the fur round the ruff of his neck as if he needed calming. The action helped him focus his thoughts.

It is possible, Beta, and we should definitely discuss the potential ramifications… some other time. For now, I must focus on going after the others.

Oh, right… of course. Perhaps I will head to the monitoring station and keep an eye on what's happening, Beta said.

Of course, you must go help them. Just call me tonight as agreed, no matter what! Updates are critical at this point.

Understood, Bruno said and opened his eyes to find Colin staring down at him, his mouth hanging open.

'Was that you talking? Who's Beta?'

Bruno shook himself and stood. Had he been speaking out loud? No, he was a dog, and dogs can't speak. He had been worried about the magic, so he hadn't shielded his thoughts. *Can you understand me?* he asked.

Colin shook his head as if trying to clear his ears.

Bruno drew and a bit more magic and tried again. *Can you hear me, Colin?*

The boy's eyes widened in surprise and he stuttered, 'Y… you can talk. But you're a dog.'

I'm a special sort of dog, and I can only speak to special people.

Colin giggled. 'It's like you're whispering in my ear, but you're really talking to me. This is so cool. Wait until I tell my brothers I met a talking dog.'

No, stop, you can't tell anyone I talk to you, Bruno said.

Colin considered the dog for a moment. 'Okay. But only if you tell me what you're doing.'

If Bruno had been anything but a dog, he probably would have sighed, but instead he flopped to the ground and rested his head on his paws. *Well, obviously I'm following my friends to make sure they're going to be okay.*

Colin laughed. 'I'm going to help Lee and his friend escape.'

You can't. I mean, you're just a boy. What are you going to be able to do against a group of armed men? Bruno laughed

'More than a dog can do,' Colin said disdainfully.

Bruno thought about this for a moment before letting out a sharp bark.

I think you may be right. So, do you have a plan?

'Sort of. I'm good at distracting people. I thought if I annoyed the guards, Lee and Izzy might be able to escape.'

Only Lee and Izzy?

'The others weren't too nice to me, but I guess if they got away too, that'd be okay.'

Bruno bared his teeth in a grin and rose to his feet. *Come on. Let's go see what havoc a boy and a dog can cause.*

STANDING IN THE stuffy room at the back of his troop, Lee shuffled uneasily from one foot to another. The Council had summoned them over an hour ago, then made them wait until they had attended to everything else on their agenda. Now it was their turn to stand in front of the sixteen men and four women who represented the Lyndhurst Protectorate.

A rather pompous looking middle-aged man, whose stomach almost popped out of his clothing, called them forward. Although he was nominally in charge, Lee noticed that the woman sitting on his right actually ran things. Dressed in brown, with an angular face and piercing eyes, she appeared more predator than person. Her sharp eyes narrowed as they focussed on the confident figure of their Captain as she introduced them.

'I am Captain Kiandra from the Underground City of Portsdown. The motley crew behind me are my troop. Our current assignment is to return a runaway boy to our city elders for judgement. We respectfully request your help to apprehend him.'

The pompous man continued to smile inanely while the hawk-like woman sat forward in her seat and pinned the captain with her gaze.

Lee's stomach did a flip. *This isn't going to go well,* he sent to Izzy.

Shush, she said. *I want to listen.*

'You ask for our help, yet you sneak into our community bearing arms, and only come before us once you have been found out,' the woman said.

Although it was difficult to see from behind, Lee thought Captain Kiandra's cheeks reddened under the scrutiny. He couldn't tell whether it was from embarrassment, or anger at being challenged.

'We had no way of knowing the region had formally organised itself, otherwise we would have come here first. But, as I told your men, we are not

here to hurt anyone. When we find the boy we are looking for, we will leave you in peace.'

The bird-like women scowled at the Captain. 'You want us to help you return one of your own because he has broken your laws, yet you walk around our protectorate without paying any heed to ours.'

The pompous man shifted in his seat as if he wanted to say something, but the bird-like woman held up her hand, cutting him off before he could get a word out, saying, 'No, Charlie, this is important. If we are to exist this close to the underground city and stay independent, we need to set some ground rules. We can't just roll over and die every time they send a few soldiers our way.'

'I apologise if we offended you,' Captain Kiandra said, but the hesitation in her voice was obvious even to Lee. 'We will, of course, update our command upon our return and ensure any future soldiers who come into your area contact you first.'

'That's a start,' the woman conceded. 'If we were to help you, what would this look like?'

'We would want access to any new people who entered your community in the last week. If we don't find the boy amongst them, then we would want to question anyone who has been out and about during the last few days.' The Captain was back in command, her voice more certain.

'And were you told to bring him back even if he doesn't want to go with you?' the woman asked.

'Yes.' The Captain's answer was crisp and direct. Lee thought she should have been a bit more wary. He sensed a trap.

'Were you told to bring him back at any cost?' the bird woman pressed.

Captain Kiandra chewed on her lip, suddenly seeing where this was going. Standing a little more erect, as if she intended to confront this assault head on, she said, 'Yes, that is exactly what I was told.'

'And would that mean forcing us to bend to your will if we did not agree with you?' The woman leaned forward so she could better peer at the Captain.

Captain Kiandra didn't flinch this time. 'That would only ever be as a last resort—for instance, if some of your people attacked us in an effort to prevent us from carrying out our orders.'

'Well, I guess that says it all,' the pompous man said as he leaned back in his chair, indicating the discussion was over.

'No! No, it doesn't,' Captain Kiandra insisted. 'I cannot imagine a situation

where your people would attack us—can you?'

'Yes,' one of the other men said. Lee turned to meet the gaze of an elderly man on the far left. 'By our laws, anyone eighteen or over has the right to decide to leave the community and make their own life elsewhere. Many of us would see handing this boy over to be breaking one of our own laws to meet one of yours. Not many here would be prepared to do that—well, for you and your kind anyway.'

Sergeant Kiandra assessed the man before allowing her gaze to wander over the faces of the rest of the Council. From his own position, Lee saw the same thing she did: a group of people hostile to their mission. No, not to their mission. They were hostile towards *them*.

The Councillor's demeanour threw the Captain and she was momentarily speechless. On the way here, she had given the impression that soldiers from Portsdown were treated with deference, or at least kept at a wary distance by above ground dwellers. First they had been challenged by the Portsmouth Militia, and now it appeared the Lyndhurst Protectorate would not help them.

Much had clearly changed since soldiers from Portsdown had last been here. For all their sakes, Lee hoped Captain Kiandra would take this into account when she answered.

'Well… it wouldn't be optimal to attack your people for sticking to their beliefs… but we were given a mission... and… we can't return home until that mission is completed. So all I can do is hope that your people do not force us into that position.'

Lee's stomach sank. This was not going to go down well.

The bird-like lady leaned forward again, clasping her hands on the table in front of her. 'Last time your people came out here with a troop the size of yours, we were a people beaten. We were barely surviving in the harsh post-war environment, and you were all well armed and well trained. In the last ten years, we have grown. As you can see, we are no longer at your mercy. We have much to protect, and much to defend, with the people and resources to do it.'

'Does that mean you will not help us?' Captain Kiandra asked, clearly a little bemused by how these people were reacting.

The pompous man answered, almost as though making a proclamation. 'We are not so inclined to be of assistance at this time. Our guards will escort you to our boundaries and you may leave.'

Captain Kiandra took a deep breath. 'I am sorry, but we cannot do that

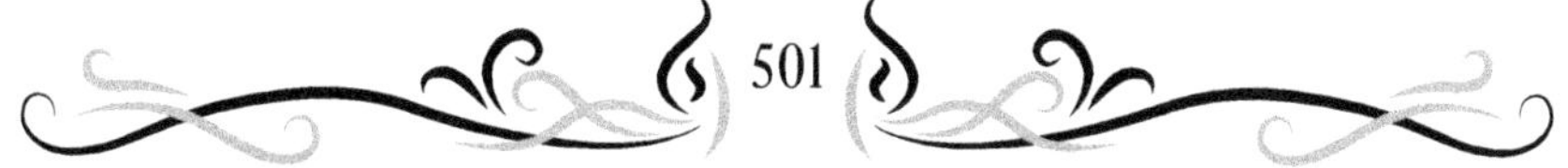

because it would be going against orders. We tracked the boy to your lands, and we need to check whether or not he is here.'

The woman turned in her seat and considered the Chairman. 'To avoid a confrontation, I believe we should let these people go back to the cell and give them time to consider whether or not they might want to proceed a little differently with their mission. Perhaps find a compromise solution to how the boy is dealt with if he is found on our lands.'

'Whoa, hold on a moment,' Rodgers said, stepping forward. 'We are soldiers of the Portsdown Army, who are part of the largest fighting force in the country. We will not be locked up again like common criminals. You will let us go so we can complete our mission.'

Whirling round, Captain Kiandra glared at her Corporal, but before she had a chance to speak, the chairman of the Council rose to his feet. 'We don't take kindly to threats—'

'I'm sure Corporal Rodgers didn't mean to threaten you—'

'Yes, I did. You can't let these… these above grounders treat us like this. We represent the ruling authority in England. They have no—'

'Shut up, Corporal. That is an order.' The commanding tone of Captain Kiandra's voice silenced everyone in the room.

Sergeant Thea shuffled closer to Corporal Rodgers and gripped his arm tightly in warning. Once she was sure Rodgers wasn't going to say anything else, Captain Kiandra turned back towards the Council.

'In light of recent events, I think we will take up your kind offer to return to our quarters and discuss the situation amongst ourselves.' She turned on her heel and led her troop out of the chambers, gripping Sergeant Rodgers firmly by the other arm as she did.

'Well, I thought that went well,' Jason said once they were alone in the cell, a bright smile plastered across his face.

'Went well! Are you serious?' Sergeant Thea asked incredulously. 'Corporal Rodgers all but invited them to take us out back and shoot us.'

Jason looked at the Sergeant, a picture of puzzlement. 'What do you mean?'

'He basically told them if they don't do what we want, we'll return to Portsdown bringing the might of all the underground cities down on their heads,' Thea said patiently, using the tone people use when explaining complex issues to children.

'Yes, I know. I was there. And I say good on him too. They can't go around treating us like common criminals.' Jason clapped Rodgers on the back.

'You idiot,' Izzy said. 'He gave them incentive to see we never return home.'

They all waited a moment for Jason to figure it out. His mouth formed an "o" and he backed away from Rodgers as if he had a contagious disease.

'And for that, Corporal, you are not only on report, but I am demoting you back to the rank of Private for the rest of this mission,' Captain Kiandra growled.

'But—'

The Captain crossed the room and towered over the Corporal. 'And if you carry on speaking out of turn, I may decide to turn you over to these people as a sacrificial lamb.'

'Go ahead, do your worst. When we are back home, I will denounce you as a traitor for negotiating with these barbarians,' Rodgers said with a sneer, turning his back on the Captain.

'If we make it back, do what you will,' Captain Kiandra said, her eyes as black and hard as obsidian.

Izzy, would you be able to portal us out of here if we needed to leave in a hurry? Lee asked.

Not from here, perhaps if we could make it to the New Forest….

Lee's stomach plummeted and he felt sick. Walking over to his bunk, he sat down and rested his arms on his knees.

Bruno, are you there?

Nothing. He tried again.

Bruno, we need you!

10

HISTORY IN PERIL

AFTER HIS CONVERSATION with Sigma, Beta felt strangely reluctant to move. He knew he should head to the monitoring room, but part of him did not want to go to all that effort only to find out nothing had altered.

He could advise Alpha of the change in the ground team's situation. Perhaps he should, given Theta was potentially in danger. Not that they could do anything to help. If the team on the ground could not gather enough magic to portal out, there was no use sending more operatives to rescue them. Besides, he couldn't face another moment with the other Guardian without recharging his energy.

Before he raised any alarms, he should find out whether the team was still in the same timeline, or whether there had indeed been a shift—it was really better if he spoke to the Monitors first.

As he finished the thought, the light around him brightened, indicating someone wished to join him.

'Come,' he said.

A moment later the Chief Monitor herself joined him, almost as if he had summoned her.

'Sorry to bother you, Beta. I thought you would want to know that about

half an hour ago, we identified a change in the timeline.'

'I rather thought you might have,' Beta said wryly before asking, 'For better or worse?'

'Difficult to tell,' she said. 'The original blip is still orange, and it is still in exactly the same place on the timeline….'

'If it hasn't changed, what is different?' Too tired to deal with this, Beta's tone was terse.

'The timeline itself, it appears to be.... I can't describe it… but it looks like it's quivering.'

'Quivering?'

'Yes. It begins to move like it does before it changes, then it snaps back in place. Moments later it starts to move again. We watched it for some time, but it does not appear to be able to keep to the current timeline, or move to the altered one.'

'Have you informed the Council? Or Alpha?'

'Well... I rather thought you might like to do that,' she said. 'Or maybe we don't need to tell anyone. I mean, we can't really say what is happening, can we?'

Beta sighed. 'You tell me.'

The Monitor coloured. 'It's just…. Well, you know how Alpha likes to deal in absolutes, and I can't say definitively what is happening here.'

'Humph,' Beta said, secretly pleased others also found Alpha difficult to deal with, but not wanting to face the Council of Ten with such flimsy information. Sighing, he added, 'All right, I'll deal with it. What exactly should I say to them though?'

Frowning, the Monitor did not immediately answer.

'Hm.' Beta cleared his throat. 'Chief Monitor?'

'Sorry, but there is no simple answer. At best guess, I would say something going on in Hampshire has the potential to change history.'

Hope wormed its way into Beta's heart, although he resisted letting it all the way in. It was still too soon to believe they had changed the future of mankind. 'Thank you. That is exactly what I will tell them.'

The Monitor beat a hasty retreat before Beta could change his mind. No sooner had she left then there was a tingling indicating someone else was trying to contact him. He opened his awareness and barked, 'Yes.'

'Did someone get up on the wrong side of the bed? Do you even sleep in a bed? No, forget I asked—'

Beta felt even less able to deal with Time Fixer business than tacking Alpha.

'Cynthia, I am kind of busy. Did you need me for something in particular?'

'No need to be so touchy.' Her tone switched from friendly to tart.

This was the first time the Time Fixer had contacted him outside of their conferences, and certainly the first time she had spoken mind to mind. Perhaps she had news from their side.

'I'm sorry. I'm still half asleep. Please excuse my abruptness. I'm sure you wouldn't have bothered me unless it was important.'

'I wanted to inform you that we've had a change in the last half an hour—an interesting one.'

'Us too. I was just talking to our Chief Monitor and the timeline is a little off… unusually off….'

'Mm… that is interesting. Our Head Timeline Specialist has reported a change too.' Cynthia's voice was excited.

The significance of the changes happening began to dawn on Beta. 'What are you seeing?' he asked, unable to keep the hope out of his voice.

'The future has split into three paths.' Cynthia's excitement was slow to seep through his fug of lethargy.

Beta changed into solid form and began pacing. Sometimes a being simply needed a body to be able to deal with life. 'I… I don't know what to say to that. Is this a good thing?'

'Maybe, maybe not. Normally when history splits, one line is clearer than the others. This time all three lines are weak. The only positive thing is that one of them extends beyond the last known end of the world.'

'Am I sensing a "but"?' Beta's stomach began to churn.

'One of the lines stops where we expect it to and—'

'Don't tell me—the third stops earlier?' Beta knew it was too good to be true.

Cynthia's silence confirmed his worst fears.

'I guess we had better meet. I'll call Alpha and we'll join you soon.'

11

ESCAPE

BRUNO, BRUNO, CAN you hear me? Lee's voice sounded panicked.

No need to shout. I'm close by. Bruno tried to calm him down.

I've been calling you for ages, Lee said, desperation tinging each of his words.

Sorry, but there is not much magic in Lyndhurst, Bruno said calmly.

You've got to get us out of here as soon as possible, please. Corporal Rodgers has stirred up the Council and they're probably deciding whether or not to kill us as we speak.

I can't just wander in and take you away, Bruno responded. *Firstly, Captain Kiandra would have to want to leave.*

What? Why?

It was unusual for Lee to be this flustered. Things must be worse than he thought.

That pesky little rule about not being able to act on our own. We can only support a person living in this time, Bruno said. *If we don't follow the rules, history or time will balance everything out and we might end up with worse problems.*

Oh. I forgot about that. Lee's voice sounded sheepish.

If we can get past that little glitch, have you any ideas how we might physically be able to break you out? Bruno asked.

Well, I thought you might magically open the lock or—

Magic isn't the answer to everything, you know, Bruno admonished. *Is it digital?*

Is what digital?

Bruno sighed and slumped, dropping his head on his paws. *The lock.*

Oh…. No, it's an old style mechanical one.

Bruno said, *Give me a minute. Don't go anywhere.*

He chuckled at his joke, but Lee did not join in. Crouching beside the small figure of Colin, Bruno surveyed the area. There was an office building to his left, and a smaller structure to the right of it.

'That's the Council Chambers,' Colin said. 'The smaller building beside it is the prison. Your friends are probably being held in there.'

It looks like a public toilet, Bruno said.

'You're funny. A toilet for everyone to use? Why wouldn't they just go in the bushes?' Colin laughed.

For privacy—oh, never mind. Bruno had more important things to worry about than providing a potted history of toilets.

He surveyed the area, trying to think how he might get the others out of their cell. The street itself was deserted. It was the two men standing guard outside who were the problem. They seemed quite relaxed, but their guns were propped against the building within easy reach.

As he watched, the blonde-haired woman who had been at the farm yesterday walked down the road and entered the council building. She was the first person he had seen on the street since they had been here, so it was likely foot traffic would not be a problem.

So, your plan is to wait until the prisoners are being moved and cause a distraction? Bruno asked. And Colin nodded.

What if they don't move them today? he prompted the boy, needing Colin to come up with a plan.

Colin's brow puckered into a frown. 'I hadn't thought of that. Gram would be mighty angry if I didn't get home for dinner, so….'

Although he was aware this was on the edge of permissible interactions with locals, Bruno said, 'So, you might have to consider breaking them—'

'Breaking them out of jail is a good idea. You could help me do that.' Colin's face broke into a grin.

If that is what you want. Has anyone ever broken out?

Colin snorted. 'No. Most people aren't in there for long enough to try. Sometimes someone gets drunk, or some of the boys fight, so mostly people are only there for a few hours until they cool off. Except when it's something

more. Then they are only held until….'

Bruno waited for Colin to finish, but when it became obvious he had said all he was going to, the Guardian asked, *Until what?*

'Punishment is administered,' Colin mumbled.

What sort of punishments are we talking about?

'For stealing you lose a hand, for anything worse banishment, or... you know....'

Bruno could well imagine. Justice in subsistence communities was often harsh. When people could barely look after themselves, they had little time and resources for rehabilitation and lengthy prison terms.

Interesting though this was, Bruno's brain needed to come up with a plan. Lyndhurst was pretty well set up to keep people out, but he hoped they didn't worry too much about keeping the locals in.

'Colin, are there any empty buildings down the end of the street? One close enough to the edge of town for someone to get to the forest without being seen by the guards at the gate?'

Smiling, Colin said, 'My friends and I play in an old shop down that way. It has a lane down the side where you can cut across the road and into the old town. From there you can slip into the forest without being seen—if you time it right, that is. Usually, the guards walk through town every hour to change posts.'

Excellent. And do you think you could distract those guards outside the jail long enough for me to get inside and talk to my friends?

'Of course I can. Gram says I'm good at being a nuisance.' The boy grinned from ear to ear.

A sudden twinge of guilt tugged at Bruno's conscience. He had led Colin into this plan, and he didn't like placing the boy in danger. Having second thoughts, he said, *This could be dangerous, Colin. You might get hurt. If you want to back out, it would be all right.*

'Pah, I'm not scared. Let's go.'

Shaking his head, Bruno stood to move, then paused as the sound of horse's hooves and the wheels of a cart filled the alley. Moments later a tall, lean man slowed his horse to a stop outside the Council building's door. He was joined moments later by a short titian-haired girl and a tall lanky boy, and a rather large shaggy dog.

The dog sniffed the air. Turning her head, she looked directly to their hiding spot while her owners conversed in muted tones. The door to the Council building opened, and the blonde-haired woman came out. She helped a young man out of the back of the cart while the man tied the horse's lead rein to a bollard. The group went inside.

Colin, do you know who those people are?

'Of course. Everyone round here does. The man is Simon Pettigrew. The woman is his wife, Tanya. The others are his children. The boy in the cart is not from the Protectorate. I have never seen him before.'

I think I know who he is, Bruno said.

'You don't mean....'

Yes, I think he's the one the soldiers are looking for.

With the arrival of Simon and his family, the guards outside the jail stood to attention, their guns back in their hands.

I think we might need to wait until the street is clear again before we move.

'I wonder why they're taking the boy in to see the Council?' Colin asked.

I don't know, but it won't be anything likely to assist us in getting our friends out.

Bruno slumped back to the ground, wondering if the arrival of the boy they were searching for was history's way of paying him back for overstretching his authority. Another thought occurred to him: perhaps this was a sign he should be thinking on a broader scale.

HIDING AT THE back of the room, Basia attempted to avoid the unwelcome attention of Councillor Johnson, who kept trying to catch her eye. When she had complained about coming into Lyndhurst today, it was this exact situation she had wished to avoid.

Her mother had overruled her, saying it was important the whole family come to present a united front to show they all supported a decision not to give Allan over to the soldiers.

When Basia went to raise further objections, her mother offered to take her to the recycle stores to look for some new books after this was over. The lure of something new to read was too much, and she backed down.

Feeling uncomfortable, she took the extra chair beside Allan under the guise of checking he was all right. Out of the Councillor's direct line of sight, she immediately relaxed.

Her charge's jaw was tense and he looked a little grey. Clearly the journey into town, even resting in the back of the cart, had taken a lot out of him. She hoped he would be well enough to speak in support of her father's plan when it was his turn to talk.

Their continued acceptance by the community relied on him confirming

he had been injured during his escape from Portsdown. He also needed to confirm he had managed to steal some clothes, then when he tried to leave the area, he collapsed. Finally, he needed to testify that he had been unconscious until he woke up this early morning. Her father had tried to persuade him to request sanctuary in Lyndhurst.

Allan refused, saying, 'Please, just hand me over to the soldiers. It will be far better for everyone. Besides, I must return home and tell people what I found out here. Going back with the soldiers will achieve that.'

'You can't believe they will let you do that, can you?' Johan had asked.

'I am sure I will have to serve a sentence for escaping, but once I am out—'

'They shot you. You can't believe they will ever release you,' her father said.

'Even so, it would be safer for everyone if you handed me over to them.'

In a firm no-nonsense tone, her mother had explained in no uncertain terms why that was not going to happen. 'We are not handing you over to Portsdown.'

'I'm *from* there,' Allan countered.

'But you were trying to escape, so that makes you different. Anyway, we're not debating this. If you want to return when you are well, that is your choice. Until then, while you're my patient, please let me negotiate some time for you to heal properly.'

It was her mother's way to end discussions, and Basia shook her head, warning Allan that saying anything now would not change her mother's mind.

A sharp laugh brought Basia from her reverie, and she leaned around to get a better look at what was going on.

'Any other day I would hand him over to the soldiers to keep the peace without batting an eyelid. But it seems like it's your lucky day,' Monica, the owner of the recycle shop, said.

'So what's different about today?' Basia's father asked.

'Less than an hour ago, a soldier from Portsdown threatened our very town with the might of all the underground cities if we did not allow them to do what they wanted on our lands,' Monica said.

Basia gasped at the implication, but the look on her face was nothing compared to the shock on her mother's.

'Monica, there are rumours that the cities still have missiles. We can't risk the whole community for the sake of one boy, much though I might want us to,' her mother said, turning and smiling regretfully at Allan.

'That is certainly something we must take into consideration,' Monica

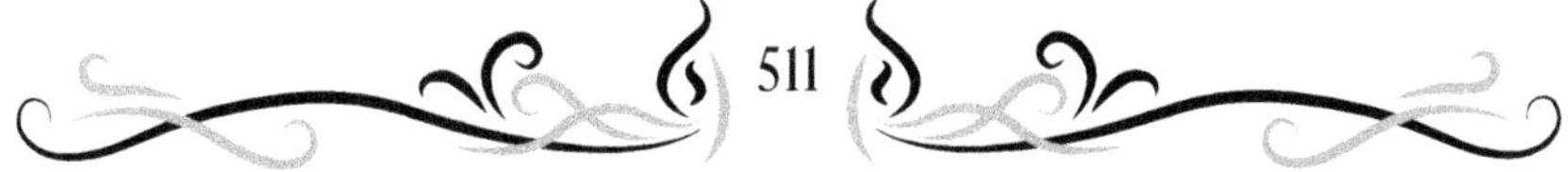

said. 'But we must also take into account that the numbers of people outside of the underground communities is growing. Perhaps it is about time we asserted our right to be here, and to be self-governing. If we don't take a stand now, they will forever be treating us like cast-offs and challenging our right to govern ourselves.'

'Hold on, Monica. Not all of us want to take on the underground armies. We should take a vote on this,' Councillor Johnston, the supposed head of the Council blustered, and a few of the other men nodded.

Monica turned in her seat. 'As Chairperson, of course it is your right to call for a vote. However, our constitution states we must invite all members of our community for a full vote when we are considering committing them to armed conflict.'

Bemused, Councillor Johnson said, 'We're only voting on whether to hand the boy over.'

'But are we? The soldiers told us if we decide not to help them, then they will bring down the full force of their military might on us,' Monica said. 'That means we are actually considering whether or not to enter an armed conflict with Portsdown.'

'Then let's call everyone in and take a vote,' Councillor Johnson said.

'All right. I think we should be able to get everyone here by tomorrow afternoon,' Monica calmly answered, which flustered the chairman even more.

'We would have to wait that long?' he asked.

'Perhaps longer if we don't get runners out now,' Monica said.

'And what do we do with the soldiers in the meantime?' Councillor Johnson sounded completely lost, and Basia had to smile.

'Totally up to you. We could let them go? Which means they could wander our lands doing what they will. Or leave them where they are, though they might not be too happy when we finally set them free, whether we give the boy to them or not.'

Basia bit back a smile, enjoying Councillor Johnson's discomfort. He had been outmaneuvered by Monica, and he didn't seem to realise it.

'Or you could decide we need a little more time to discuss the best way to handle this for the good of our community,' Monica suggested.

Councillor Johnson and the others nodded their agreement, and the deputy head turned back to her father.

'Simon, why don't you let the Council talk about this in private. Perhaps you and your family could go to the eating house and have some lunch while we do.'

'I'm afraid Allan is not well, and he wouldn't be up to that,' Basia's mother said.

'How about I have a guard take him over to the single men's quarters. They can find him a bed and he can rest while we sort matters out,' Monica allowed.

'I can decide for myself.' Allan's voice sounded thin and shaky in the cavernous hall. 'Rather than going through all this palaver, you should give me over to the soldiers.'

Monica glared at him. 'Your wishes are noted young man, but we must consider the bigger picture. If we hand you over, we are tacitly agreeing to remain subjugated to people who told us we were not good enough to be a part of their community. We will not hold you here against your will, but we ask that you work with us towards a solution that is in all our best interests.'

Allan's jaw set, and Basia placed a hand on his arm. 'You need to pick your battles. This one is lost. Don't waste your energy,' she whispered.

'But—'

'Shall we meet here at about two?' Monica suggested. 'That gives us ample time for a discussion, and you can still be back at your place before night fall.'

'Sounds fine,' said her father. 'Johan, go see to the horse and cart. Tanya and Basia, perhaps you could go and do your shopping and we will meet you at the eating house after we see Allan settled.'

As Basia helped Allan to his feet, she said, 'Trust me. I won't let them hold you here if you don't want to stay.'

'It's not that I don't want to stay.... I mean, I think I could quite enjoy sticking around.' His eyes crinkled with a smile and she felt a blush rising. 'It's just I made a commitment. I can't let all those people down. They deserve to know they might have a good life up here.'

'I understand, and we will find a way to get you home,' she promised as they followed her father.

Out of the corner of her eye, she caught Councillor Johnson watching her. She quickly turned away and shuddered.

'What's up?' her mother asked.

'Nothing,' Basia mumbled.

Turning to glance behind Basia, her mother found the cause of her unease. 'Oh, I see. We must do something to squash the Councillor's ambitions once this is over.'

VIVIENNE LEE FRASER

CROUCHING BEHIND SOME bushes, Bruno was still waiting for an opportunity to break the others out of jail when Simon and his family emerged from the Council building. He was close enough to confirm the boy Simon helped into the cart was indeed Allan, the escapee they were looking for.

The group began walking and Bruno stood to follow. *Colin, wait here and keep an eye on the jail. I'll be back in a minute,* Bruno sent as he left.

Keeping the family in sight, he slunk behind bushes and fences until the group split. The two women went one way, and the two males led the cart along a residential street. Deciding to stick with Allan, Bruno found fewer places to hide as they meandered through the township.

He thought he was going to lose them when they turned a corner and the lack of cover meant he had to duck back. When the street was quiet, he peeked his head around to find the cart was stopped outside the two-story building taking up most of short road. Simon was helping Allan out of the cart. As they headed inside, the large golden retriever following behind turned and stared straight at Bruno and bared her teeth.

Bruno slunk behind a single rosebush in the garden opposite and peered through the branches. What seemed like an age later, but was probably only moments, Simon and his son reappeared. They spoke briefly before the son headed in one direction leading the horse and cart, and the father returned the way they had come.

The Guardian waited until they were both out of sight before crossing the road and nudging open the door they had come through. Laughter drifted from one of the rooms to the right. The noise made by the men sitting inside masked the sound of the door shutting behind him.

Down from the dining room the men occupied was a dark corridor. On his left was a closed door. In front of him was a set of stairs. The faint smell of dog drifting down told Bruno which way to go. Keeping to the shadows, he crept up the stairs and found himself in a large dormitory. At the far end of the room, a figure lay curled up on a bed, snoring gently.

Bruno approached, and a dog growled low and slow, rising to her feet from where she had taken a position under the bed. He stopped, wondering how to let the animal know he was a friend. For the first time in a long time, he wished he had taken human form; he didn't have time to establish a pecking order with this animal.

Keeping his head down, in what he hoped was a submissive stance, he moved forward again. This time the growl was louder and more menacing. The figure

on the bed stirred and rolled. He saw Bruno, and leaned over to pat the dog. He said, 'It's okay, Jasmine. It's just another dog, and he seems friendly enough.'

Jasmine growled her disagreement.

It was now or never. Either history was with him and this would work, or it wasn't and he had lost nothing. Gathering what little magic he could find, he said, *I am a friend and I have come to help you.*

'Who's there? Is this your dog?' Allan asked, glancing around the room.

Jasmine took another step forward and growled again.

Must we go through this…. I'm no threat.

Allan's gaze returned to the dog. His eyes widened. 'Is that you talking? No, you can't be. Must be the painkillers addling my head.'

The golden retriever whined and moved back towards Allan. Bruno couldn't tell whcther it was because she heard the distress in the boy's voice, or because she sensed something odd was going on.

I am a dog, and yes, I am talking. I came to help you get out of here, if you want to leave, that is?

'That depends,' Allan answered. 'Where will we go after we leave here?'

Bruno could not believe he was having to talk this boy into accepting his help. *Wherever you want to,* Bruno said.

'If I say I want to go back to Portsdown, will you take me?'

Why would you want to go back after they shot you, then sent soldiers to hunt you down?

'Because I made a promise to return and tell people what it is truly like out here. I believe they deserve to know there is life again on the surface.'

Bruno frowned at the boy. *Very commendable. Still, it would not be my first choice of destinations. But if you want to return and you want my help to get there, then I guess we'll do just that.*

Allan stared at him, then shook his head. 'This is all very odd. How do I know this is for real? I mean, I could tell you to do something, but then you might just be a very well trained dog.'

We don't have time for this…. Look, why don't you think of something for me to do.

'Ah, like a telepathy sort of thing. Is that what we're doing?'

Yes, you could say that. It's actually more like magic, but who's to say what magic really is.

'Now I know I'm going crazy, talking philosophy with a dog.' Allan lay back down on the bed.

Look, there isn't much time, and I have quite a bit to organise if we are going to do this. Are you in or not?

'Roll on your back,' Allan said.

Are you kidding me? You want me to roll on my back with a killer dog in the room? Bruno looked at Allan's guard dog and she glared back as if she understood every word of the exchange.

'Jasmine, sit,' Allan said. The dog obeyed and relaxed a little.

'Okay, that was probably a bit much to ask. Jump up on the bed beside me and lie down,' Allan instructed Bruno.

Bruno did as he was asked. *Are you happy now?*

Allan's eyes widened in surprise. 'Who *are* you?'

I am a Guardian, a special being sent to help those in need, and I'm here to help you, if you want me to. Bruno jumped down from the bed. *But I need to know right now if you will work with me.*

'I guess. You're the only one who is listening to what *I* want. Worst case scenario, I have gone nuts and I'm agreeing to escape with a talking dog. Best case, this is for real and I actually get to go home,' Allan said wearily, lying back on the bed.

Can you walk?

Allan didn't move a muscle as he answered. 'What? Yes, but not very far.'

Okay, this might take a little longer than I expected. I need you to wait here while I organise a couple of other things.

Without waiting for an answer, Bruno turned around and left the room, already moving on to the next part of his plan. Jasmine's low growl followed him out and he wondered what he was going to do about that dog when it came time to move Allan.

His tail held high, he trotted down the road. He had chosen his side and he somehow felt lighter and more purposeful. Now all he needed to do was to try and persuade the others to join him.

RIGHTO, COLIN. DO you have any objections to helping the boy the soldiers were hunting to escape? Bruno asked when he arrived back at the hiding spot.

'Boy? The one the soldiers are looking for? Won't Lee and Izzy hurt him? I am not sure I'm good with that,' Colin said.

Lee and Izzy want to get him away from the other soldiers, Bruno told him.

Colin looked doubtful, and Bruno wondered if he had overreached again.

He wants to come with us too, I promise, Bruno said.

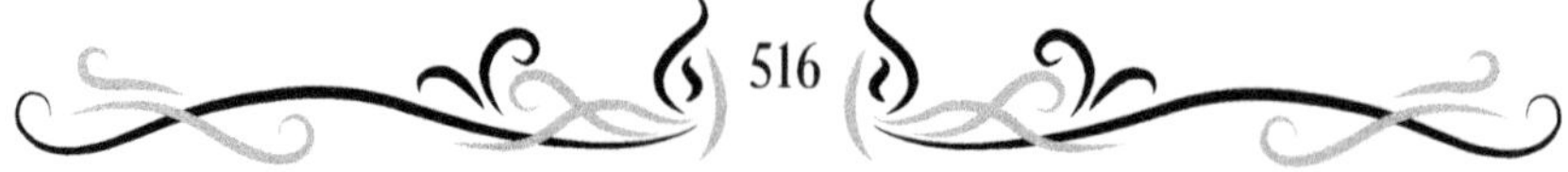

Frowning, Colin pulled his bottom lip between his teeth. Bruno saw his escape plan slipping away.

How about we make a deal? If at any time you find he changes his mind, I will return him to Simon and his family, Bruno offered.

The boy shrugged. 'You absolutely promise?'

I do.

Bruno expected the boy to put up more of a fight, but he had forgotten how suggestible children were.

'Okay. There could be a bit of a problem though,' Colin said as he unwound himself from his hiding place. 'A little while ago, some guards arrived and took some of the soldiers back to the Council rooms—the dark-skinned lady, the tall lady with red hair, and the short grumpy man.'

Bruno took that to mean Captain Kiandra, Sergeant Thea, and Corporal Rodgers. He cocked his head to the side and considered his options. His plan still might work. Theta was a strong enough operative she would be able to ditch the others and catch them up if she chose, which he doubted she would. And now that he was supporting Colin and Allan, he no longer really needed Captain Kiandra.

I don't think the others would come with us if they were here. Let's go and rescue the ones we can for now, Bruno said.

The boy nodded before sauntering over to the guards with Bruno padding beside him.

'Good afternoon,' Colin said in an extremely polite voice. 'My tractor broke again and I wanted to please talk to the soldier who helped me fix it.'

'Sorry son, orders are not to let anyone in, no matter who they are,' the guard closest to them said before turning back to the conversation he'd been having.

'That can't mean me. I'm just a boy. I only want to…'

Bruno didn't hear the rest of the sentence because he had slipped inside. Sitting down in front of the bars, he surveyed the room. Lee and Izzy were resting on the bottom bunks. Jason was lying on the one above the girl, one leg swinging over the side.

'How long do you think it's been?' Jason asked.

'About two minutes more than when you asked last time,' Izzy responded, not attempting to conceal the disdain in her voice. 'And quit swinging that leg in front of my face,' she added, taking a swipe at it.

'I'm not hurting you, and you should show more respect for your superior.' Jason grinned, clearly enjoying needling Izzy.

'Superior. What a laugh!' the girl spat.

'Could you two quit it? You're giving me a headache.' Lee raised his voice to be heard over the bickering.

Before a full-scale argument erupted, potentially bringing in the guards, Bruno sent, *Time to go, guys.*

Lee swung himself off the bed and moved to the bars before whispering, 'Man, am I pleased to see you.'

Jason pulled his leg up, leaned over the edge of his bunk and stared at Bruno. 'What do you mean "go"? The others are still with the Town Council. We must stay together—after all, we're supposed to be assisting with the Captain's mission.'

Theta—sorry, Thea—can catch us up if she wishes to, Bruno said. *But we have to go now. We may not get another opportunity to escape.*

'*We* are not going anywhere,' Jason said, his superior tones almost sounding commanding. 'If we are not supporting the Captain and Corporal Rodgers, we're acting alone, which is a big no-no.' His jaw set in a stubborn line, which on anyone else would make them appear stern, but it turned Jason into a petulant child.

There's no time to explain the details, Bruno said, *but we're not acting alone. Someone was already coming to rescue you, and I am helping them out.*

'And what then? Our assignment is to help the Captain return the escapee to Portsdown.'

I'm suggesting we help someone else from this time period—the key player in all of this, Bruno said. *Now let's get going.*

'Have you spoken to someone in charge? Are these new orders?' Jason said at the same time Lee asked, 'Have you spoken to Allan?'

Bruno chose to ignore Jason and answer Lee. *I spoke with him, and he wants to leave here too. I have agreed we will help him go back to Portsdown to complete his mission.*

'Are you sure that's a good idea?' Izzy asked. 'I mean, what will that do to the timeline?'

Bruno swallowed his own guilt at going against his mentor's wishes and said, *My latest news was the timeline might already have changed. But that is not why I am doing this. In my gut, it feels wrong to be supporting strangers when one of our own needs our help.*

Izzy nodded. 'I know what you mean.'

Lee grinned, 'I'm in.'

'No,' Jason said stubbornly. 'We are staying here until the others return.'

'Speak for yourself,' Izzy said, joining Lee by the bars.

Are you ready to go? Bruno asked.

'Yes, but how are you going to do this?' Lee asked.

As you suggested, I'm going to magic the lock.

'Isolde….'

'No, Jason, I'm going with Bruno and Lee.' Izzy placed her hands on her hips and glared Jason into silence.

Bruno quickly explained the escape plan, then blocked out the room around himself and drew every piece of magic from the air. He concentrated on moving the lock mechanisms, and after a few moments it clicked and the door released. Lee pushed it open.

Last chance Jason, Bruno said.

'I'm staying.' He crossed his arms and rolled away, turning his back to them.

'Have it your own way,' Izzy said, shutting the gate.

Bruno made sure Izzy and Lee were out of sight by the door before he stepped outside and moved back into position beside Colin. The boy was still trying to argue his way in, but when Bruno joined him, he said, 'Well, if that is the way you're going to be, I guess—'

Bruno jumped up, placed his front paws on the shoulder of the guard closest to him, and began licking his face.

'What the…!'

'Bruno, get down.' Colin made a half-hearted attempt to pull the dog off. The other guard joined him, yelling at Bruno to let go.

'Hey, leave my dog alone!' Colin began swinging punches at the second guard, who defended himself against the boy's ineffectual blows.

From the corner of his eye in the midst of the melee, Bruno caught Lee and Izzy running to the closest building. Once they had ducked in behind it, he dropped down and sat calmly beside Colin, who had a wide grin plastered across his face.

'Sorry about that, boys,' Colin said. 'He forgets he's so big and scary. He's a big softie, really.'

'Be off with you. You've caused enough problems,' said one of the guards, wiping Bruno's saliva off his face.

Dismissed, Colin and Bruno headed back the way they had come.

'That was fun,' Colin said, laughing as he walked. 'What's next?'

Can you show me where the stables are? We need to borrow a horse and cart.

12

GETTING AWAY

THE IDEA WAS to borrow a horse and cart from the stables to transport Allan back to Portsdown. Everything else had gone to plan, so Bruno had no reason to think this phase would go any differently. As they entered the building, everything fell apart.

Sneaking in through a back door, they found a girl and boy talking heatedly by the only cart in sight.

'What are we going to do?' Colin looked down, waiting for him to take the lead.

Aren't they the kids from before? Bruno asked.

'Yep. Johan and his sister Basia.'

All right, I guess we'll wait until they're gone.

Bruno searched for a hiding place. The room fell silent. Bruno glanced up to find brother and sister had stopped talking and were staring at them.

'Hi, Colin,' the girl said. 'Who are you talking to?'

'My dog. This is Bruno.'

The girl laughed. 'Don't be silly, Colin. I haven't got time for games today. There is someone else here. I heard them speaking.'

'But it was him I was talking to,' Colin insisted, folding his arms across

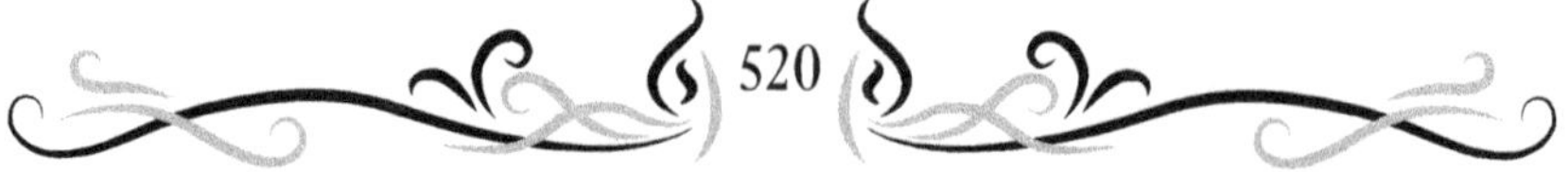

his chest.

'It can't be. We heard someone answer you,' Johan said. 'He suggested you hide until we leave.'

I should have shielded my speech, Bruno thought as the girl, Basia, searched the stalls for another person. I am getting sloppy.

Hi, my name is Bruno.

Johan's eyes widened. 'Either my mind is playing tricks on me, or that dog *is* talking.'

Colin perched on a hay bale, and Bruno flopped to the ground, resting his head on his front paws while they waited for Basia to finish.

'Basia, I think the dog really can talk. He just introduced himself.'

'Dogs don't talk, Johan.'

'Our dogs don't, but maybe dogs from the underground city do. The cities are more scientifically advanced now than in the pre-war world, so who's to say enhanced dogs aren't commonplace.'

I am not an enhanced animal, Bruno protested. *I use the magic around us to communicate.*

Basia spluttered. 'Now I know you're kidding. Magic is for fairytales.'

Bruno sat up and tried to look as commanding as he could. *You're wrong. Magic is merely another form of science. But I have not got the time to debate this. I'm a Guardian, a Time Guardian in fact, and I'm here to help Allan.*

'Skipping over the magic and Time Guardian thing—which are too weird to contemplate—if you're here to help Allan, how do you propose to do that?' Basia asked, staring intently at Bruno, almost like she was boring inside his head in an attempt to read his intentions.

What do you think would help him? Bruno countered.

The brother and sister looked at each other, and finally Johan nodded.

Basia said, 'When Mother and Father were called away from lunch, we came here to think about what we could do to help him. We think the Council will hand Allan over to the soldiers.'

'It is their only option if they want to protect the community,' Johan added.

'And Allan wants to go home so he can tell everyone what it is like out here now.'

Won't the soldiers take him back? Bruno asked, wanting to check they were all on the same page.

'Of course, but we believe when they get there, the best case scenario is that he will be locked up for the rest of his life. Worst case…. Well, I don't even want to think what that might look like,' Basia said.

'So, Basia thought we should take him home ourselves,' Johan finished up.

Bruno cocked his head to the side and contemplated Johan and Basia. Up close, he had the familiar feeling he got when meeting with souls he had encountered before, and these two were very familiar. He had first met them as Barabal and John, and they had a history of resolving historical anomalies with him. Was this the universe trying to tell him something? Were they destined to save humanity together?

They obviously had no idea who he was, so he would have to tread carefully if he was to ensure they worked together.

Sounds like you have a plan, Bruno encouraged.

'Sort of, but there are only two of us, and Basia hasn't much experience outside of the community. And we only have this for protection.' Johan patted the revolver at his side. 'We can't take father's rifle—

'We—'

'No, Basia. He and Mum will need it to protect themselves on the way home.'

'We can take Jasmine with us. She can be pretty fierce,' Basia added.

Bruno was about to object to their taking the dog guarding Allan with them as the animal clearly did not like him, but Johan and Basia continued talking as if he and Colin were not there.

'Yes, but Allan's injured. He won't be able to walk far,' Johan pointed out.

'We can take the cart. I am sure Mum and Dad won't miss it for a few days,' Basia said, then laughed. 'And when we return, having taken the horse and cart will be the least of our worries.'

Finally, they fell silent. Basia stared at Johan, and eventually he nodded.

Well, it seems we are in agreement, Bruno said. *We take the horse and cart, pick up Allan, then meet up with a couple of my friends who also want to help Allan go back to the city.*

'Sorry?' Johan turned to look at Bruno. 'You're coming with us? And what other people?'

Bruno drew himself up even taller and said authoritatively, *Of course I am coming with you. I pledged my assistance to Allan, along with two friends who are waiting to join us. They are able to provide additional protection.*

Johan's eyes narrowed as he contemplated Bruno.

'He's a good guy,' Colin piped in. 'So are his friends. I can vouch for them.'

With his lips curling into a smile at Colin's words, Johan said, 'All right, I guess you can come along.'

'So, we're going to do this?' Basia asked.

Johan nodded. 'Mum and Dad are with the Council and some of the

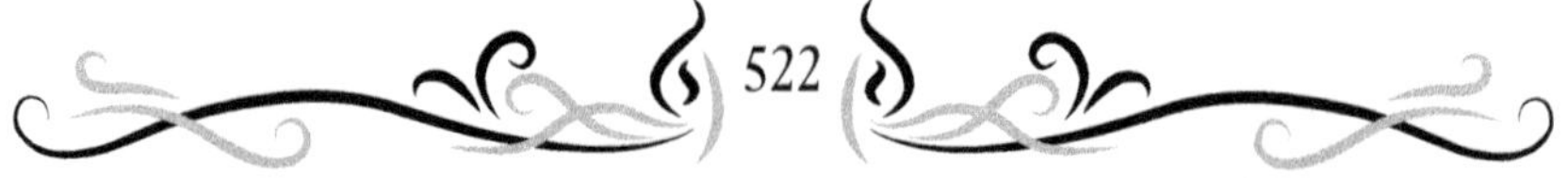

soldiers now,' he said. 'We need to act fast if we're going to put some distance between us and them before they realise we're gone.'

Bruno didn't need to be told twice. *Right, here's the plan. You two hitch up the horse and head to the single men's quarters. I'll help Allan down the stairs and meet you at the bottom.*

He turned to Colin. *Can you go and find Lee and Izzy and meet us round the bend from the barricades? And if you can find some sort of weapons for them to bring, that would be great.*

'There is a small armoury as you go into the men's quarters,' Johan said. 'I guess we can borrow an extra couple of rifles from inside. We have to bring them back though—arms are precious out here.'

Right. Everybody has their job, Bruno said.

'Wait a minute,' Basia interrupted. 'They're not just going to let us take Allan out of here. We'll need to hide him—unless you want to fight your way out, that is?'

'You can take some hay and some of the old sacks from over there. Make a nest for him to hide in,' Colin said, blushing as he earned a smile from Basia.

'Perfect,' she said. 'Let's get moving.'

BRUNO WAS PATTING himself on the back as he made his way to the building where Allan was. He wasn't usually this positive about his plans. Then again, this was the first time in a while he had been able to operate without constant scrutiny and direction from Beta.

Being in a magically barren time meant it would be difficult for the Guardians to monitor his every move. That meant he was able to rely on his own intuition, and it was liberating. Then his bubble burst.

After this was over, he was going to have to answer to the Time Guardian Council, just as Basia and Johan would answer to their parents. It was likely they would not be happy with his decision to support Allan in his quest to return to Portsdown. Leaving Thea behind would not go down well either.

He pushed his concerns aside. He would worry about all that later. For now, he believed the course they were on was their best chance for saving humanity. Not least because what they were doing before had not changed anything. Mostly, though, it was because Allan was the person at the centre of the anomaly, so he was the most likely catalyst for changing the fate of the world.

The Council may not see that now, but once he explained it after they saved the timelines, he was sure they would understand. And if they did not save humanity, then they would all be stranded here or worse, and facing the Council would be the least of their worries.

There was nobody on the street outside the building when he arrived. Bruno nosed open the door and darted up the stairs. Fortunately, no one was around up here either; no one except for Jasmine. Allan was asleep in the same bed with the dog stoically guarding him.

Bruno approached and the dog growled her warning. As Bruno moved closer, the noise grew louder.

Please be quiet, Bruno sent. *I don't want anyone to know I'm here.*

His efforts were in vain. Jasmine stood and began barking, ready to defend her charge at all costs. Fortunately, the noise woke Allan, and he leaned over to pat the dog.

'What is it, girl?'

Allan, time to go, Bruno said.

The boy's hand withdrew and he rubbed the sleep out of his eyes.

Please, if you want to leave Lyndhurst, we must go now, Bruno said, a little louder this time.

Finally, Allan got the message and levered himself off the bed. As he sat on the edge, he winched and turned a pasty white colour.

Bruno's dog eyebrows drew together and he put his head to the side as he considered the boy, wondering if he had overestimated his capacity to walk unaided. *Are you going to be able to make it downstairs by yourself?*

Allan stood, swayed, then righted himself before surveying his path to the door.

'I can lean on each of the bed ends until I make it to the door. Did you happen to notice if there was a handrail on the stairs?' Allan asked as Jasmine nudged his leg, as if she were directing him back to bed.

The boy ran his fingers through the fur on her head and said, 'It's all right, girl, just a little change of plan. You stay here and wait for Simon and Tanya.'

Bruno was sure Jasmine understood Allan's words, but, instead of obeying, she walked beside him as he shuffled his way to the door. It was as if she were helping him stay upright.

Bruno wandered ahead and checked the stairs. *We're in luck,* he sent. *There is a rail. Hold on. Wait by the door a moment. There are a couple of people in the dining room.*

Bruno dropped to the floor, hoping to make himself smaller so the men

downstairs couldn't see him. He heard Allan close the door, and he turned his head to see the boy lean against the wall and take a breath. Jasmine stood beside him, and Bruno could sense her concern.

Through the glass in the front door, the outline of a horse appeared. Dampening his impatience, he humphed, dropped to the floor, and waited for the men to leave. When the two men headed down the corridor beside the stairs, he allowed himself a sigh of relief.

The front door opened and Basia popped her head in. Seeing the way was clear, she ran upstairs to help Allan down. Johan followed behind and tried the door opposite the dining room.

'Damnation. It's locked. It isn't usually,' he said as he tried the handle.

Bruno descended the stairs, sat down, and studied the lock. Relieved to find it was a simple padlock, he worked his magic and it fell open. Johan stared at him, amazement written on his face.

Bruno couldn't resist saying, *See, I told you magic was real.*

Shaking his head, Johan entered the room, returning with two rifles and a box of ammunition.

As he resecured the door, he said, 'I reckon we've only got about an hour before people start looking for us, and we want to be well on our way by then. We need to move faster.'

I couldn't have said it better myself, Bruno thought.

They exited to find Basia had helped Allan into the back of the cart and was arranging hay-filled sacks to make a comfortable bed and to hide him from view. Johan helped, and soon the escapee was hidden so well he could not be seen unless someone was looking down into the back.

'Jasmine, go.' Johan pointed back inside. The dog ignored him and jumped up into the cart, arranging herself so she was beside Allan.

Johan sighed. 'Well, I guess you're coming too.'

Bruno was congratulating himself for a plan well executed when he saw a rather rotund, flush-looking man rushing up the street heading towards them. Praying he would pass them by, he was out of luck. The man saw Basia and made a beeline towards them. Bruno slunk behind the cart, keeping out of sight.

'What a happy coincidence I should bump into you alone.' The man smiled at Basia.

'She's not alone,' Johan said. 'I'm with her. Is there something I can help you with?' The boy insinuated himself between the man and his sister.

The man glanced around, a little flustered, then moved to the side so Basia

was in his sights again. 'I didn't realise you were doing quite so much stocking up while you were in town,' he said, moving towards the cart and avoiding Johan.

Bruno held his breath. Any close scrutiny would reveal Allan hiding in the back. As the man drew closer, Jasmine stood, placed her paws on the edge of the cart, and growled.

Taking a step back, the man blustered, 'Great guard dog you have there.' He frowned. 'I thought the animal was guarding the boy from Portsdown.'

'Basia and I are heading home. Dad asked us to take Jasmine with us,' Johan said, trying to draw the man's attention.

'We only came to pick her up and say goodbye to Allan,' Basia added. Although her voice was calm, Bruno sensed the girl's unease around the man, and his hackles rose.

'Well, my dear, I shall be sorry to see you go. I had hoped we might spend some more time together. Perhaps get to know each other a little better.' The man's voice was oily and ingratiating.

From his hiding place under the cart, Bruno could tell Basia was holding herself very still and very stiff, as if she were willing herself not to show how uncomfortable this man made her.

Her voice carried no trace of her unease as she said, 'I'm afraid not this time, Councillor. We must be on our way as soon as possible.'

'Um, well....' The man made no move to leave. 'Hmm, I think I might invite your parents over for a meal soon. You too, Basia. Time we put our relationship on a more formal footing.'

Over my dead body, Bruno heard Basia think.

As if e knew his sister would not be able to respond to this without giving something away, Johan said, 'We need to be heading home, and shouldn't you be at a Council meeting? Surely they must be waiting for you.'

'Um, well, yes, I was on my way there. See you soon, my dear.' The Councillor's voice was even more oily, if that was even possible, and Bruno felt nothing but sympathy for Basia. He fervently hoped for her sake this man was not going to play a big part in her future.

As the man walked off with a new spring in his step, Johan secured everything and started the horse moving. 'If he tells Mum and Dad he saw us, we have even less time than I thought.'

Bruno prepared to jump up onto the cart as it passed him, but Jasmine's growl assured him he would not be welcome. Running along behind, he soon caught up with Johan and Basia as they joined the Old Southampton Road.

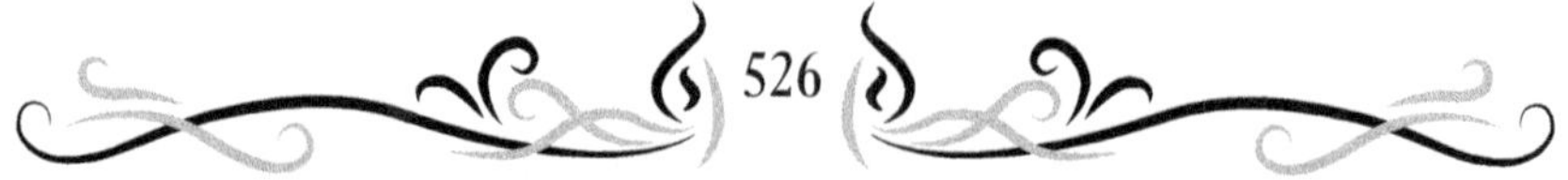

THE GUARDIANS OF TIME: SOLDIER

THE DILAPIDATED BUILDINGS cast a long shadow over the high street as they walked towards the outskirts of town. Basia stayed ahead of the cart, steering a course that kept them away from anyone who might take note of their passing. She need not have worried. The streets were almost empty and the people they did pass were too busy with their own thoughts to take much notice of the group. Even so, it was a very long ten minutes to the barriers. At any moment she expected someone to call for them to halt.

Also disconcerting was listening to Johan muttering under his breath. 'I've taken arms from the armoury, and Mum and Dad's horse and cart. My future is down the toilet.'

Dropping back to walk beside him, Basia said, '*We* are doing this, brother; *we* both bear responsibility.'

'But I am the oldest, and the male. You know what they're like. They'll blame me regardless of your role.' Johan's head dropped.

Basia hated seeing him like this. Her brother had always followed the rules, and this must be eating him up. 'You can still change your mind once we are through the gate,' she said. 'The dog said he has friends who will help. I will be all right without you and Jasmine once we find them.'

There was only one thing Johan took more seriously than following the rules, and that was doing what he believed to be the right thing. As she gave her brother a way out of this, Basia hoped he would choose to continue with her.

'This is what Allan wants, so I believe it is the right thing to do. We will only be gone a couple of days—three at the most,' Johan reasoned, talking himself back into coming along. 'Besides, none of you will get far without me.' He laughed and she joined him, relieved he was back on board.

Bruno snorted. *We got here without you. Please don't stay on our account.*

'I am staying for my sister, dog,' Johan said.

I told you, my name's Bruno.

'Sorry, of course you did. Anyway, it will be quicker with me along, and we will all have more chance of surviving. Besides, I'm not going to let my sister head off with a bunch of strangers.'

Suit yourself. And for what it's worth, I'm pleased you're coming, Bruno told him. *I think our chances of succeeding will increase and I believe your cool head might be needed.*

The gate across the main road was fast approaching. The bar remained firmly down as guards patiently waited for the cart.

'This is not good,' Basia whispered. 'They don't normally stop people leaving.'

'Hi, Ben,' Johan said. 'What's with the hold up?'

'Our orders are to question anything unusual, even slightly unusual... what with the soldiers in custody and all.'

'We've left like this a hundred times before. What do you think is strange about us?' Johan asked.

'The dog, Johan,' Ben said.

'Jasmine?' Basia laughed.

'No, the other one,' the other guard said.

Johan looked down at Bruno in puzzlement. 'This dog? What's odd about this mangey mutt?'

Bruno bared his teeth at Johan's comment.

Ben moved around beside Bruno. 'He was with the soldiers? We left him at Ma Wilson's place this morning. Now he's here.'

Johan's face froze. 'You're kidding me.... With the soldiers? You're sure he's the same one?' Johan's voice wavered slightly, and Basia hoped Ben would not hear.

'Yep, I was at the farm when we captured them,' Ben confirmed.

I can explain, but we need to be on our way first, Bruno interrupted.

Basia looked around, wondering why the guards did not react to the dog speaking.

I have shielded my voice so only you can hear, he told her as if he could hear her thoughts.

Trying not to react, Basia watched Johan struggling with the fact that this dog was indeed from the underground city.

'And you're sure this is the exact same dog? And that he was with the soldiers looking for the escapee?' Johan asked again.

Bruno hung his head, and Basia's stomach clenched. What would Johan do? Was the dog double-crossing them? Did it matter who the dog was with? They just needed to get Allan out of here. Everything else could be worked out later. The dog looked as though he was preparing to run. She had to do something, and now.

'Honestly, Ben, we had no idea about the dog,' Basia said. 'He isn't actually with us. He started following along a couple of minutes ago. We think he's taken a shine to Jasmine. Nothing we say puts him off.'

Really? This is what you're going with? Bruno looked pained, and Jasmine

glared at Basia. *Honestly, can all dogs understand everything?* she wondered.

Ben laughed. 'I don't think Jasmine is too interested. I've never seen her ride on the back of the cart like that before. I think she's putting as much distance between her and him as she can.'

'We can't shake him, so he must be keen.' At last Johan played along, and Bruno groaned in her head.

'Well, if you decide to breed them, it will be a nice litter of puppies. Don't forget me when they're ready to be weaned.'

Not happening, ever, Bruno sent as Ben returned to his companion and the barrier was raised.

'Do you want me to keep him here with us?' Ben asked as they walked through.

Basia stifled a grin as Bruno bared his teeth, causing Ben to back away. 'No, I'm sure he'll tire soon and head back to his friends,' she said.

Basia did not relax until she heard the barrier clip behind them. Beside her, Johan actually expelled a breath, he was so relieved to pass the first hurdle. Then the worst happened.

'Hold on, wait up,' the second guard called out.

Basia's stomach clenched so much she almost threw up. They must have caught sight of Allan in the back.

Try and stay calm, Bruno sent. *It might be nothing.*

Johan's fingers holding the lead rein were trembling. She shoved her own shaking hands into the pockets of her jeans, and sent a prayer to whatever gods might still be around to keep them safe. Johan took a calming breath, halted Nellie, and turned to face the man running towards them.

'Sorry to hold you up, guys. Ben forgot to ask if you could join the patrol tomorrow. We're a little shorthanded, what with needing to guard the prisoners.'

'I'd love to, but unfortunately, my mother's found out about my patrols, and to say she's not happy would be an understatement. So I'm going to have to beg off for a while until she calms down,' Johan said.

The man chuckled. 'Bad luck mate. I don't want you to end up on the wrong side of your mother. We'll find someone else.'

'Hey,' Johan called as the man turned to head back to the barrier. 'Put me back on the duty roster next week, though. Hopefully it will all blow over by then.'

'Okay, be seeing you.' He raised his hand in farewell.

Basia watched the guard retreat and made sure he was on the other side of the gate before she followed after the slow-moving cart.

'This is quite exciting,' she said as she caught Johan up.

'You're joking, right?' he said. 'My heart is beating so fast I think I'm going to have a heart attack.'

'So, you can go out hunting overnight with goodness knows what in the woods around you, and that's fine. We help one boy escape and suddenly you're a mess,' she teased him, trying to lighten the atmosphere.

Johan chuckled. 'What can I say, a life of crime doesn't suit me.'

As the road bent around towards Southampton, Bruno began to range ahead, searching for something. When he didn't find it, he asked them to slow down.

I thought my friends would be here by now, he said.

If it was possible for an animal to sound worried, Bruno did.

'Can you contact them like you talk to us?' she asked.

I'm trying, but there's no response, he told her.

'We can't wait for them,' Johan muttered. 'They'll be after us soon, and besides, I'm not sure I want to wait for underground soldiers.'

They're on Allan's side, I promise, Bruno said.

Basia placed a hand on Johan's arm. 'It will be fine. Colin vouched for them. I am sure they will be here in a moment and you can see for yourself.' She glared pointedly at Bruno.

I'll keep trying. I'm sure they'll be here soon. The dog did not sound confident, and she wondered briefly if their venture was doomed to failure before it had even begun.

LEE DUCKED INTO the shell of a building, pulling Izzy behind him. Pressing his back against the wall, Izzy followed suit. Colin was not quick enough to join them and they listened as he greeted the Lyndhurst patrol they had spied moments earlier.

'Say, aren't you one of Ma Wilson's strays?' a male voice asked.

'What if I am?' Colin responded in his usual cheeky tone.

The man ignored his comment. 'Have you seen anything unusual out here?'

'Apart from you guys, you mean?' Colin quipped.

'Watch it, lad, or you'll get a clip around the ear,' another one of the men said, and Lee sensed the mood change with those words. 'There are soldiers in our jail and these men are risking their lives to protect our community. The least you can do is show them some respect when they ask you a question.'

'Please don't push it,' Lee muttered under his breath, willing Colin to let it go so they could leave.

'What do ya think you'll find out here? More soldiers?' Colin laughed. 'It's just me and my mates, and some old buildings.'

'You guys know you aren't meant to be out here, don't you. We don't normally patrol this far out. Anyone could be hiding in these buildings,' the first voice said.

'Good point,' the second voice interrupted. 'What are you doing out here?'

Lee's stomach sank. Already nervous that they would miss their rendezvous, the close proximity of the guardsmen was not helping it settle down. Now their ability to successfully escape capture depended on a boy who seem intent on baiting their captors.

'Nothing much,' Colin said. 'Looking for an escaped dog. I was supposed to be taking care of him, but he ran away.'

Lad's smarter than I thought, Izzy sent.

'Well, don't let us hold you up,' the first guard said.

Frustrated at not being able to see what was going on, Lee listened. Some rocks fell nearby, and he suspected Colin was heading away. A few minutes later, the second guard said, 'Okay, lads, let's finish sweeping the area. I want to be back in time for dinner.'

About five minutes later, Izzy whispered, 'I think they're gone.' Moments after that Colin's head appeared through a crack in the crumbling wall opposite.

'Couldn't you have been a little more polite?' Lee admonished. 'What if they had captured us—again?'

'You're kidding. If I didn't be me, they would have been suspicious.' Colin appeared unfazed by the criticism.

'He's got a point,' Izzy told him.

Before Lee could think of a suitable response, Bruno's voice broke into his mind. *Lee, Izzy, where are you?*

On our way, Lee sent.

About ten minutes later, the group broke through the undergrowth and onto a road. Bruno let out a bark of greeting.

'Got you here,' Colin said, a smirk plastered on his face.

As they approached the people Bruno was travelling with, the girl placed her hands on her hips in a gesture so familiar Lee could not help but feel homesick. Even the tone of her voice when she said, 'Okay, Bruno, time to convince us these guys are on our side,' reminded him of his sister.

'Yes, Bruno. How come the very soldiers Allan was running from now want to help him get back on his own terms? How do we know it isn't some sort of trick?' the boy asked.

He also seemed familiar, but Lee could not immediately place him. Then Izzy went googly-eyed, and he thought, *Jo, he is Jo—different body, same soul.*

You said we were running out of time. We can't stand around here while we sort this out. We need to go, Bruno said.

When no one moved, he continued, *Thanks for all your help, Colin. We couldn't have done this without you.*

'That is why I'm coming with you,' the boy said, his tone resigned.

'I'm not sure that's the best idea,' the Bebe-like girl said. 'Ma Wilson will miss you, and she'll skin us alive for letting you come along. If you leave now, you'll be home in time for dinner.'

Colin folded his arms, not budging. Izzy turned to Lee and nodded encouragingly.

What do you want me to do? he asked, careful to direct his thought to Izzy only, as Colin could clearly hear mindspeak.

Talk him into going home, she said.

He didn't know what to say. He hadn't much experience dealing with kids. Finally, he came up with, 'Colin, what we are doing is dangerous. People could get hurt, and maybe even killed.'

Great, Lee. Give him a gold-plated invite, why don't you, Izzy said.

He shook his head. What was she talking about? *What?*

'I'm not a baby, you know,' Colin said.

The stubborn set to his jaw told Lee Izzy was right: he had totally gotten this wrong. He changed tactics. What he needed was something for Colin to do that they could not.

'You're right. We do need your help. We just didn't want to ask. If you're not too scared….' Lee threw out the line and waited.

'I'm not scared of anything,' boasted Colin.

Now to gently reel him in. 'Then you're just the man I need,' Lee said. 'Colin, we need to delay anyone who might follow us to give us a chance to get a bit further ahead.'

Colin nodded his head. 'Of course. You don't want them catching you up before you reach the city.'

Lee smiled. 'Right.'

'And I can help you with that?' the boy asked, eyes round with excitement.

'I have an idea,' Lee said, trying to build the suspense. 'I was wondering if, when they realise Izzy and I escaped, you can do a big song and dance about looking for your dog Bruno. It might distract or annoy them. Do you think you're up for that?'

'Just ask Bruno. I'm good at this sort of thing,' Colin said.

'You might be late home for dinner,' Izzy told him.

'I don't mind,' Colin insisted. 'But will you be okay without me? You don't know much about life around here. Perhaps I really should come along.'

'They've got me with them,' Jo-boy said. 'I think I can do almost as well as you can. Besides, I want to ask you a special favour. When things quieten down, would you tell our parents Basia and I are fine and will be back as soon as we can? I want them to understand we will only be away a few days.'

Colin stood tall and said with a voice bursting with pride, 'I can do that. You can trust me.'

'Excellent. Can you sneak back in without being seen?' Lee asked.

'There's no one better at sneaking around than me,' Colin said as he happily trotted off. 'I'll see you all later.'

'I believe he thinks he is going to come back and catch us up,' Bebe-girl said.

'That is why I thought about the message for Mum and Dad. They won't let him skip off that easily,' Jo-boy laughed.

Once Colin had disappeared into the trees, Bruno said, *Come on, let's move. They'll be after us sooner than we think.*

'Before we do, you owe us an explanation,' the boy who looked like Jo said, glaring pointedly at him and Izzy.

'We can walk while we talk,' Lee offered, sensing Bruno's impatience. 'If you don't like what we say, we can part ways.' As he said the words, he hoped they were not prophetic.

The other boy thought for a moment, nodded curtly, and said, 'You're right, we can. Let's go.'

He clicked as tongue and the horse began moving. Lee walked beside the Bebe look-alike and Izzy slotted in between her and the other boy. Although he didn't know their new companions, something about this felt right.

Let me finish the introductions, Bruno said. *Lee and Izzy, this is Johan and Basia. Their family looked after Allan, and they are going to help us take him back to Portsdown.*

'I thought it was *you* helping *us*,' said Johan.

Yes, indeed. That is what we are doing, said Bruno.

'Where is Allan?' Lee asked.

'Hiding in the cart,' Izzy snorted, not taking her eyes off Johan.

You only left Jo a few days ago, Lee said.

He is Jo, you moron, Izzy sneered.

'While it is nice to have names, it doesn't shed any light on why we should trust these guys,' Johan pressed.

'We've had a change of heart,' Lee explained. 'We don't like what's going to happen to Allan when he is returned to the underground city, so we decided to help sneak him back in.'

Johan snorted. 'Really? You expect us to believe that?'

'Why wouldn't you?' Lee asked.

'Isn't it obvious? You're soldiers. Soldiers follow orders. They don't change their minds mid mission,' Johan snorted.

'What he said. So, what's the real story?' Basia asked. 'Why are you here?'

'I hate this bit,' Izzy said. 'Either we lie and try make up something relatively believable, or we tell them the truth and they never believe us anyway.'

'Why don't you try the truth? We're not complete yokels,' Basia said.

'What do you know about things that are beyond your wider world?' Lee asked, thinking his own sister would never believe the truth of what was going on.

'Are you going to start talking about things like magic?' Johan said. 'Because I watched Bruno use it to open a lock today with his mind, and I'm a believer. So, you tell me other strange things are going on—I'm listening.'

Long story short, we were sent here to stop something bad from happening. We became soldiers to do that, Bruno started.

'Soon we began to believe getting Allan back to where he belongs in one piece might be the best way to achieve that,' Izzy finished.

'See, no changing of side involved. We simply redefined our mission,' Lee added.

'You actually expect us to believe that?' Basia asked.

Bruno sighed, *I'm running out of energy, and part of me doesn't care what you believe. Trust us. Don't trust us. It is up to you. Either way, we all want to help this boy reach Portsdown. The only real question is: are we going to work together to do it?*

'I thought we agreed you were helping us,' Basia laughed and Lee joined in.

He felt comfortable with this girl who was his sister, but not his sister. He wondered if Basia and Johan also sensed some sort of bond. His question was answered when Basia spoke again.

'It sounds odd, but I think we're meant to do this together,' she said to her brother.

'I don't think it is odd at all,' he said. 'I feel the same way, though I can't for the life of me say why.' He paused, then added. 'I am travelling with you, but let me make it clear: I don't actually trust any of you. Double-cross us or put my sister in danger, and I'll shoot you without a second thought.'

Johan's statement hung heavy about them until Izzy said, 'So, we're all good then?'

They laughed.

Izzy placed her hand on Johan's arm. 'You're doing the right thing helping us take Allan home. What you're finding difficult to reconcile is that you are doing something wrong to achieve that.'

Johan looked down at Izzy with wonder in his eyes. 'How did you know that? Do you have some form of telepathy as well as the ability to mindspeak?'

Izzy laughed. 'Let's just say I'm close to someone very like you.'

13

A SUCCESSFUL ESCAPE

SILENCE FELL FOR a while as they pushed hard to put as much distance between them and Lyndhurst as they could. As they drew further away from the settlement, Lee noticed the lack of vehicles on the road.

'When we came out of Portsdown Hill, old cars and trucks littered the motorway. What happened here?' he asked.

'Trade happened,' Basia said. 'Over the years we've built up a bit of a commercial relationship with the Southampton Protectorate. With carts moving backwards and forwards all the time, it made sense to spend time clearing the road. It made trips quicker, and trade became more frequent.'

There was only one cart the stables, Bruno said.

'When a market is arranged, carts and tractors with trailers make the trip into Southampton and return with what we need: food for the city and items that are hard to come by for us—machinery parts, clothing, books and things.'

'And you should be pleased we went to all that effort,' Johan said. 'It means we've got a straight through trip to the edge of Southampton, and we should be close to Portsdown Hill by early tomorrow afternoon.'

'Where are we stopping tonight?' Basia asked.

'There is a safe house along this road. Our patrols use it all the time. We should reach it just before sundown,' Johan said.

'Are you sure stopping at a safe house is such a good idea?' Lee asked.

'Why wouldn't it be?' Basia's tone was defensive.

'For starters, that is the first place people following us are going to look,' Lee said.

'We need to stop somewhere,' Basia insisted. 'The night is owned by the homeless and those who have nothing left to lose. Only those who are desperate themselves would be out with them. Besides, we will travel better if Allan is rested.'

Johan chewed his lip. 'It does make sense to keep going. If the guard expect us to stop overnight, they won't be in such a hurry to catch us up.'

Izzy looked up at him. 'What do you do when you're on overnight hunting trips or patrols and there is no shelter nearby?'

Johan frowned. 'How do you know we even do that? Do you guys in the city spy on us?'

Izzy winked. 'You wish! Anyway, we're not actually from the city, remember.'

Johan's gaze didn't waiver.

'All right, I overheard some of the guards talking on the way into town about the best places to hunt when they are out on patrol. Some of them are too far away to be reached in a single day,' Izzy admitted.

He grinned down at her. 'We stick to open spaces and keep moving, weapons drawn. When we sleep, we do so in the open, or in an easily defensible position, taking turns to keep watch.'

'So, we can keep moving all night if we need to?' Lee said.

'Yes,' Johan admitted. 'Although we will need to rest and water the horse at some stage.'

So, if you led us through the night, how would we do this? Bruno had moved up beside them and looked up at Johan, tongue lolling out of his mouth.

Johan nudged Izzy. 'That dog of yours—is he just for show or can he help defend us?'

I'm not their dog, Bruno said, pulling in his tongue and trying to look less doglike. *Still, I am more than capable of using all the skills this body possesses—including the attack functions.*

Johann looked each of them over as if assessing their capabilities. 'It might be doable,' he said, 'but I'm taking a big leap of faith. I put a couple of spare rifles in the back you can have, if indeed you are able to handle one.'

'Why would you think we wouldn't be able to?' Izzy asked.

Johan's head tilted to the side as if he was assessing her as he responded. 'Because you told me you aren't soldiers. And if you're not soldiers, it is possible you have never shot a rifle before.'

'We needed some skills to pass as soldiers,' Izzy said. 'I've had some military training, and I'm pretty sure Lee has had a bit more.'

'I can hit what I aim at,' Lee confirmed. 'Without blowing off my foot,' he muttered under his breath and was rewarded with a chuckle from Basia.

'We also have knives if the fighting gets up close and personal,' Izzy said.

Johan raised his eyebrows. 'Once again—'

'Yes, I can use them. Knife fighting is a speciality of mine.' Izzy grinned.

'I can hold my own,' Lee added, hating to be outdone by Izzy.

They walked on a little longer, allowing Johan time to think. Finally, he said, 'Okay, here's the plan. We carry on along this road until sunset and perhaps a little beyond. Then we look for somewhere with running water and a defensible area where we can rest for a couple of hours.'

All right, Bruno said.

'Once the horse is good to go, we keep on until we hit the old M25. We don't start along there until daybreak because we're going to need light.'

'Why?' Lee asked.

'There are too many places along the road for the night people to set up an ambush,' Johan told them.

Remembering their experience leaving Portsdown, Lee agreed he would rather navigate the car graveyard in full light, and he was pleased Johan had thought of it.

'What about Allan?' Lee asked, worrying about a boy he had yet to set eyes on.

Johan said, 'We might be able to keep the cart for a while, but on the motorway it will be a hinderance. We will put Allan on horseback when we reach the M25.' Johan turned to Basia. 'Will he be able to ride, do you think?'

'He can ride with me and I will support him.'

This is odd, Lee sent to Izzy. *It's like being with Bebe and Jo but different.*

You get used to being with different incarnations of the same people, Izzy said. *Besides, do you think they would have trusted us so easily without our past selves knowing each other?*

Lee looked down at Bruno. *Is this plan going to work? Is this going to make a difference? Or are we putting ourselves in harm's way only to make things worse?*

We won't find out the outcome of today's activities unless I contact Beta tonight, which I don't want to do because he will expect an explanation of all this.

But surely you and Izzy have some idea… a gut feeling? Lee pressed.

Bruno glanced up. *I could tell you it will all be okay and nothing we did will make*

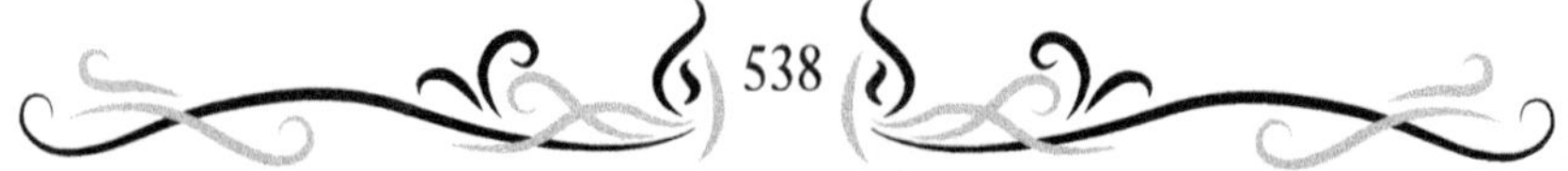

the world end any sooner. Would you prefer me to lie like that?

Maybe…. They walked a little further in silence before Lee said, *Bruno, are we ever getting out of here?*

The dog paused for a moment, then started walking again. *There are pockets of magic all around. I believe I could open a portal to return you home if things turn hairy.*

Lee was surprised at the wording. *Just me?*

You are our first priority, was all Bruno said.

'The sun will be going down soon, so we may as well form up,' Johan said, walking round the back of the cart to retrieve the rifles.

'Allan's still asleep,' he said when he returned.

Basia nodded. 'He was in a lot of pain after going down the stairs. I gave him a strong painkiller to knock him out for a while.'

'I hope it wears off before we need to put him on the horse,' Johan said, a furrow creasing his brow.

Basia laughed. 'He'll be awake well before then.'

'Where do you want us positioned?' Lee asked as he took a rifle offered to him and checked it was loaded. Johan handed him a couple of spare cartridges, which he placed in an easily accessible pocket.

'Basia, you lead the horse. If anyone attacks us, it is your job to keep her calm and stop her from bolting.'

'Yes, sir.' Basia smirked.

Ignoring his sister, the older boy continued. 'Jasmine can stay on top of the cart and defend Allan. She's been doing that anyway, and can be quite fierce when she's protecting someone.'

I know, Bruno sent.

'Ah, yes, Bruno. Can you track?'

The dog nodded.

'Excellent. You can walk ahead and warn us if anything comes from the front. Izzy, Lee and I will work the back and the sides in rotation, keeping a look out for anything that might attack us. Out here we shoot first, ask questions later,' Johan finished off.

'What about radiation? Isn't it stronger at night, so we're more at risk, aren't we?' Izzy asked.

'The winds are blowing the wrong way to bring radiation over at the moment. We are safe to be out for the next few days,' Basia assured her.

'Any more questions?' Johan asked. 'No? Let's pick up the pace. We have a lot of ground to cover if we want to be at the M25 by tomorrow morning.'

THE SUN WAS just beginning to set when Bruno felt the tingling. He opened his mind just a little, enough to sense who was trying to contact him.

Sigma? Bruno? I know you can hear me. Tell me where you are.

I can't, Thea. Before I give away our location you need to tell me where you stand.

Here we go again, Bruno. My allegiances lie where they always have—with the Council. They gave us a mission and I will follow it through to the end. Tell us where you are and let us come and collect you.

No. Although Bruno had suspected this would be the likely outcome of leaving Thea behind, he had hoped this time would be different. It never was. Now he felt the same loss he had when he realised the love of his life had chosen the Time Guardians over him. She would always choose them, but in his heart he still waited for the day when she would put him first.

This is such a waste of time, Bruno. Even though there is very little magic here, it's only a matter of time before the monitors figure out where you are and tell me.

Of course, but by the time they do, we will be so far ahead of you, you will not be able to catch us. Are you still locked up?

Oh Bruno, you still care.

I do, and that is the problem, Bruno thought, but said nothing.

When he didn't respond, Thea said, *The Council kept us with them all afternoon. They went to take food in to you guys about half an hour ago and found out you had escaped. Jason is being interrogated.*

Well, at least something good has come from this, Bruno chuckled, and Thea laughed with him.

He's swearing blind you let the others out. The guards think he is winding them up.

I bet that's going down well. Bruno enjoyed the thought of what they were putting the Time Fixer through.

No, and he's too stupid to see they think he is disrespecting them. Thea's tone was disdainful. *Did you truly not see this would happen when you encouraged the others to go along with you?*

Sighing, not believing he had to explain this, Bruno said, *I didn't incite them into rebellion. They could both see what we were doing was wrong—and I think you can too.*

That is not the point, Bruno. The Council gave us a job to do. We have to trust they know what is best, she said.

The mission is wrong, Bruno told her. *Alpha is wrong to force us to go through with it.*

Not our call to make, Bruno.

This was an argument they had had many times before.

After a long silence, Theta said, *I assume you realise you might be making things worse?*

Yes, Bruno admitted, *but I don't believe we are.*

But you cannot say for certain….

This was another variation on the same old argument, and it always led nowhere. Bruno changed the subject. *What have the Lyndhurst Protectorate decided about the boy?*

Nothing yet. The guards left a few moments ago to collect him. I think they're going to let him make his own decision…. That is certainly what Simon and Tanya are pushing for now.... Bruno? You didn't do what I think you have?

Bruno didn't feel the need to answer that question, and Thea didn't speak for a few minutes, then said, *Something is happening, I've got to go. Don't do anything else stupid. We should be able to catch you up in a day or so.*

Not if I can help it, Bruno thought as Thea winked out of his head.

AFTER AN UNEVENTFUL night, the group wearily walked towards the outskirts of Southampton. Johan led them along Hunters Hill, where they picked up the old A836 to follow all the way to the M25. Izzy, having spent a lot of her life in and around the New Forest, was proving useful as a guide, and Johan appeared confident in leading them along the route they plotted together. Lee relaxed back into doing as he was told.

'Strictly, this is militia-controlled territory,' Johan said, 'but I'm sure they won't mind us being here so long as we stick to the far side of the road.'

'Why take the risk if we could go a different way?' Basia asked.

'Because it is quicker and safer,' Johan told her.

Lee simply didn't care. They had rested for a couple of hours last night, but when the horse was ready, Johan had roused them.

'You wanted to do this,' he said when they complained and begged an extra hour.

'Allan rests better when the cart isn't moving, and we want him at his best when we have to put him on the horse,' Basia countered.

Bruno, can you find out from Thea if anyone is tracking us yet? Lee asked. *We might be able to rest a little longer if they are not close by.*

When I spoke to her at sundown, they had only just learned of our escape.

Can you talk to her again? Lee asked.

It is best not to. The more I contact her, the more likely it is we can be traced.

'Johan's right,' Allan said from his bed in the cart. 'The longer we stay here, the more likely it is we will get caught up.'

'It's all right for him,' Lee grumbled. 'He can go back to sleep.'

Not that he begrudged Allan his rest. The boy's appearance had shocked him. He was wan and pale, and his skin tone could only be described as grey. He needed all the rest he could get. Lee's grumbles were all for his own benefit. The only decent night's sleep he had had since arriving was the night in Ma Wilson's barn.

For the next couple of hours, Lee concentrated on placing one foot after the other. Every now and then he scanned the woods around them for signs anyone was following or preparing to attack them.

He and Johan had not long taken the rear guard when Bruno barked a warning from up front. The cart stopped moving and adrenaline kicked in, wiping away any thoughts of sleep. He scanned the area around him, but seeing nothing amiss, he looked to Johan.

'Stay back here. Izzy come with me and we'll go find out what is happening. Jasmine, guard,' Johan said as he walked past the cart. The dog rose, instantly alert.

It was an age before Izzy returned to tell him what was happening up ahead.

'Bruno ran into some of the Southampton militia out on patrol. They were about to send us packing until Johan appeared. Apparently, he's been on some scouting missions with one of their leaders. Now they're taking us on a shortcut along Spicers Hill. Their barracks is at a Tesco's superstore along the way.'

Lee perked up. 'I'm all for that. Anything that involves less walking,' he said.

'Even better, from the barracks they're going to take us to the M25. They'll store Johan's cart there while we drop Allan off. Couldn't have turned out better if we had planned it.'

Lee was impressed. 'They like Johan that much that they'll do all that for us?'

'No, silly. When they found out we are running from soldiers from the underground city, they were more than happy to help. Their leader said something along the lines of, "Anything to stick it to those bastards".'

'Weren't they concerned *we* are soldiers from Portsdown?'

'Johan convinced them we only dressed like this to help Allan escape.' Izzy smiled.

'Man, they must hate people from Portsdown,' Lee said as the cart began

moving again.

'Of course they do.' Izzy said. 'The people out here are the ones the world left to die when the bombs dropped—the people they sacrificed for their own well-being.'

'I guess that would make you angry,' Lee admitted, thinking he would not be too happy at being told he was not good enough to be included in the elite club.

Izzy carried on. 'Through their own tenacity, these people survived, built their own societies, and have started trading with each other. Now that they are stronger, they're only too happy to deal some payback to those who sentenced them to death.'

'Well, when you put it that way, it sounds almost reasonable.' Lee laughed.

Even though the route was shorter, it still involved quite a bit of walking. Tired as he was, Lee was fascinated as they walked the outskirts of Southampton, through suburbs that he had driven in during another time only a week ago.

If he had been designing a set for a post-apocalyptic film, this would be what it would look like. Crumbling buildings, overgrown with vegetation and the air made heavy by the eerie silence. In eighteen short years, nature had reclaimed much of what man had taken.

'It must be a nightmare policing all this,' Lee commented, gesturing to the urban forest.

'I suspect they focus on stopping people from getting into the main residential areas, and leave all of this alone, much like Lyndhurst. And, as Johan said, any who slip through the gaps are pretty much shot on sight,' Izzy told him.

Lee blanched. 'That sounds barbaric.'

'It is, rather, but small settlements have been controlling large areas in this way throughout history.' Izzy's tone was matter-of-fact.

Lee had never been so pleased to see a supermarket in all his life when the cart finally rolled into the Tesco's carpark. Although not exactly invited inside and welcomed with open arms, they were led to some park benches outside the building, and were brought hot tea and porridge.

'This is luxury,' Lee groaned as he took a sip of real English Breakfast tea.

'Yep, almost like a home away from home,' Izzy laughed, but Lee could tell she was also enjoying the break and the little piece of normalcy.

The sun was fully up when a cart pulled up in front of them.

'Hop in,' the driver ordered.

Lee hauled his weary body up on to the tray in the back, then leaned down to help Izzy.

'I can do it myself,' she said.

'I know you can, but I thought it would be a nice gesture,' Lee said, trying not to feel hurt.

A puzzled look crossed Izzy's face, but she reached up and grabbed his hand. Once they were seated, Johan and a militia man lifted Allan up. He was made comfortable before Johan, Basia, and the two dogs joined them, Bruno making sure there was plenty of space between him and Jasmine. Another militia man tied Nellie to the back of the cart, and they were off.

Lee wouldn't say it was the most enjoyable ride he had been on, but it was a thousand times better than walking. They also had a chance to close their eyes for a few minutes and doze. All too soon, though, the wagon rolled to a stop and they were told they had arrived.

Lee and Izzy surveyed their surroundings. They were on one side of a barbwire barrier across an intersection by a roundabout. It took him a moment to work out they were on a slip road for the M25.

'Portsmouth's that way.' Their driver pointed.

'Thanks,' Lee said. 'We appreciate the help, and the break from walking.'

'No problem. If you come back this way, ask for Patrick. The militia is always happy to take on deserters from the city.'

'I'm not a—' Lee started.

'You guys never are.' Patrick smiled. 'But you make good militiamen anyway.'

Shaking his head, Lee joined the others. Allan was standing for the first time since he had met him, and Lee was shocked at how much the boy looked like Alain. A little thinner, and there was a fire in his eyes that Alain had not had, but their similarities far outweighed their differences.

Allan leaned against the cart and smiled at them as they walked over. 'I would like to thank you for helping me,' he said by way of a greeting.

'We are only doing our job… and what is right,' Izzy said.

Allan's face clouded over. 'In my experience soldiers follow their orders, no matter the right or wrongness of it.'

'Well... um ….' Izzy was saved from fumbling for an answer by the arrival of Nellie with Basia on her back.

Allan was helped back up onto the wagon, and then onto the horse in front of the girl. By the time he was in place, he was as white as a sheet.

'Are you going to be all right to ride?' Lee asked. 'I mean, is your wound hurting?'

Allan shuffled closer to Basia and wrapped his arms around her. 'It's not that. It is just....'

Izzy laughed. 'I don't think he's ever ridden a horse before. The world looks quite a bit different from up there, doesn't it?'

'I'll be fine.' Allan sat a little straighter and pursed his lips, ready to endure anything to make it back home.

'Thanks, mate,' Johan said to their driver. 'I owe you guys one. I'll remember you when the strawberries come in this next year.'

'Our pleasure,' Patrick said as he drove away.

With Johan leading the horse, Izzy and Jasmin on one side and Lee and Bruno on the other, the strange group continued their journey.

THE M25, OR the car graveyard as Lee like to call it, was exactly as he remembered: littered with abandoned vehicles that had either been stripped for parts, rusted away, or overgrown with vegetation. It was heartbreaking to see such sleek machines reduced to this.

As he walked he saw a number of things that could be salvaged from the vehicles which, if modified correctly, would improve the lives of people like Colin and his family. With the wealth of stuff for repurposing, why weren't more people harvesting it and making their lives better?

A movement caught his eye and he readied his rifle, preparing for potential danger.

'Basia, Allan, did you see anything behind that green car?' he asked.

Allan leaned forward. 'No. Wait a minute.... Wow, that is amazing.'

'What is it?' Lee asked, raising his rifle.

'A fox,' Basia said. 'Nothing amazing about that.'

'There is if this is the first one you have seen outside of a book,' Allan said, and Lee grinned at the look of wonder on the boy's face.

Relaxing, they carried on. Not long after, Allan asked, 'Lee, why are you a soldier?'

Lee's immediate reaction was to say he wasn't one, but he stopped himself. When he returned home, he would be joining the army, and he and been a military cadet ever since he started high school. So, in many ways, he was a soldier.

'I guess because my father was one,' he finally said.

Allan raised his eyebrows. 'Really?'

'Yes, and I wanted to be like him,' Lee said, defending his decision.

'What, you mean someone who follows orders?' Allan's voice was incredulous.

'Not exactly, although it can be quite comforting knowing exactly what to do and when to do it,' Lee answered, but the words sounded weak to his own ears.

'What was it about your father you wanted to be like?' Allan prompted.

'Allan, stop badgering the guy. You only met him today and you want him to tell you his life story,' Basia said.

'I think I deserve to know if I can trust him. After all, he was hunting me yesterday and now he's not,' Allan told her.

'No, it's okay, Basia. I will tell you, Allan, if you'll tell me why you want to go back to Portsdown, even though it is likely you will end up in prison.'

'Deal. At first it was because I wanted to tell everyone about the world out here. I wanted to hit back at what I believe is a corrupt system in Portsdown. Now….'

Lee waited for Allan to continue. When he didn't, he prompted him. 'And now?'

'It is difficult to put into words. I've seen a little more and had time to think. Everyone is doing their best to survive after the war. I can't help thinking that if we all worked together, pooled resources and ideas, we would all have a better chance of surviving and developing and building a better world.' Allan blushed. 'That sounds trite, doesn't it?'

Lee smiled at how much Allan sounded like Alain. 'No, I think it is commendable.'

'I'm in no position to force our communities to work together. What I can do is provide the people in Portsdown with information so they can make up their own minds,' Allan finished.

'Fair enough. And in answer to your question, what I admired about my father was how he protected people. How he always tried to help them. I wanted to do that too.' Lee looked defiantly up at Allan. 'And I thought joining the army would allow me to do that.'

Allan grinned. 'I knew there was more to you than a black uniform. Tell me, did you find what you were looking for with the army?'

Shrugging, Lee said, 'No, not really. Our mission did not allow much time for helping others, and I think I've found I'm not so great at following orders.'

Allan laughed. 'Not so surprising you're here with us then. What about you, Izzy. You don't strike me as a rule follower either.'

'Cheeky. I'll have you know I used to be just that. Before I found out that

the people who make the rules always make sure the odds are stacked in their favour. After I learnt that, I decided to look for ways to change the rules.'

'In the Portsdown Army?' Allan asked.

'We weren't actually part of the army,' Izzy laughed. 'Didn't Bruno tell you? We've been sent here to stop something bad from happening—the soldier thing was just a cover.'

'Bruno? The dog?' Allan looked incredulous.

'He's the one who helped you escape,' Basia said.

And this is all the thanks I get, Bruno added.

'I am sure Allan appreciates it,' Basia told him.

'Hold on. You can hear the dog talk too?' Allan blushed. 'I thought I was hallucinating when he spoke to me in the barracks.'

'He's for real,' Izzy said. 'And for better or worse, he's committed to escorting you home.'

'I guess the joke's on me,' Allan chuckled.

Or on me, Lee thought. The previous conversation had been too close to the bone for him. Inside his head his own war was raging. His whole life he had planned to be a soldier, and now weeks away from achieving that goal, he was having second thoughts.

'Lee, if you could not be a soldier, what would you be?' Allan asked, and again Basia poked him in the ribs.

'These guys are helping you. The least you could do is show them some respect,' she told Allan.

Watching the two of them on the horse, Lee had an epiphany. Why hadn't he seen it before? Bebe and Alain, Basia and Allan—they belonged together.

'Come on, Basia. I only want to find out what makes Lee happy.'

It should be an easy question to answer—what makes you happy—but Lee had no idea. He loved his family. He enjoyed various activities and had a few friends he hung around with, but he couldn't remember the last time he was truly happy.

Actually, that wasn't strictly true. Pottering around in his aunt's shed pulling together a letterbox bomb with Alain had made him happy. Before that, it was hard to remember a time. Maybe when he was with his grandfather. Yes, definitely working in the shed with his granddad. It hadn't just been the company. Something about working with his hands made him happy.

'Lee, are you all right?' Allan asked. 'I didn't mean to stress you out.'

Lee wondered what he was talking about. He followed Allan's gaze down

to his hands. He had twisted the rifle strap around and around his fingers and was working his worry out on the leather.

'Yes. No. Sort of. You made me realise I was so focused on the goals I set myself, I forgot to be happy.'

'Allan, can you say when you were last happy?' Basia tested her riding mate.

'Easy. When I walked out of the cave the other day and saw the sky. Not just because it was the first time I had seen it, but because it gave me hope for the future.'

'Oh,' Basia said, like the wind had been taken out of her sails.

Lee laughed, breaking the tension. 'You didn't expect that, did you?'

'No, Lee, I didn't. Izzy, how about you?'

'Mine's easy. A few days ago when I helped stop some people from hurting the planet.'

'Are you sure that made you truly happy?' Lee asked, remembering that Izzy had then said goodbye to her girlfriend, Jo, a previous incarnation of Johan.

'I was happy, just a different sort of happy. I fell in love with someone forbidden to me a long time ago. I can never be with them. But I'm happy enough.'

'Do you ever wonder what sort of life you would have lived if you stayed with your Jo?' Lee asked.

'All the time,' Izzy sighed.

Lee thought of asking the taciturn Johan what would make him happy, but he didn't think the boy would answer. Instead, he asked his sister, and was surprised by her response.

'I am not sure I will ever be truly happy,' she responded in a voice so bleak Lee 's heart almost broke.

As if everyone else was feeling it too, the conversation petered out. Allan said something only Basia could hear and wrapped his arms more tightly around her. Not long after, the group bunched up as they came to a blockage in the road. Johan led the horse through a thin gap between some overgrown cars, and Lee waited with Izzy and Bruno for their turn to go through. While he waited, Lee pondered why finding his happiness was so difficult for him, and came to the realisation it was because he had spent much of his life living up to others' expectations.

Now it was their turn to go through, and just as he emerged through the gap, a ping against the car beside him caused him to dive to the ground.

'Take cover,' Johan ordered as he pulled Allan from the horse.

Basia jumped down after. Lee was busy trying to identify where the shot

came from, but he couldn't get a clear view.

Bruno, can you see anything? he asked.

No. They're well hidden. All I can say for certain is there is more than one.

He listened, trying to work out what was going on.

Did you catch their scent? he asked the dog.

They must have approached from downwind.

Crawling for cover behind a car, Lee thought, *Great, this is where my life ends, on the M25, just as I am getting to know myself.*

Everything suddenly went quiet. Lee strained, listening for anything that would indicate what was happening.

Bruno? What's going on? Lee asked.

I think we're surrounded, so our best chance is to try and make it to the hills and regroup later. I will try and find you all.

Lee leaned forward and took a quick peek around the car, only to find himself face-to-face with the barrel of a gun.

'Drop it,' a rough voice commanded.

Lee did as he was told and raised his hands.

'And the knives.'

Reluctantly Lee complied, dropping the two knives concealed in his uniform beside the rifle.

'Now stand and walk that way.' The gun barrel indicated he should go right.

Standing, Lee realised he was not the only one being herded into a clearing between cars. All their group was banded together, even Nellie, Jasmine, and Bruno.

'I was certain we would catch you on the way back,' one of the men said, removing his helmet.

Great, Lee thought, the Portsmouth militia—again.

'Righto, move out.'

Basia refused to move. 'Allan has been injured. He can't walk very far.'

'Then I can shoot him now, or he can take his chances walking. His choice.'

The militia leader's voice was uncompromising. Basia looked mutinous, but Johan grabbed her arm and pulled her along. Lee moved beside Allan.

'Lean on me,' he said, taking some of the boy's weight.

It was a long, slow walk in the hot sun. The militia moved at their normal pace, and the weary group who had been walking most of the last twenty-four hours were expected to keep up. Supporting Allan made the journey doubly tiresome.

The passed the trail to Portsdown before moving past Cosham and into

Portsmouth proper. If Southampton had appeared worse for wear, Portsmouth had been devastated. On the way into the Old Town, few buildings had been left standing.

'The naval base was a prime target for bombs,' Izzy commented.

A little while later, the Navy Yard came into view, and Lee smiled. 'Their targeting must have been off. Most of it is still standing.'

The smile disappeared when The Old Naval Shipyard Lee had promised himself he would visit one day came into view. It had been reduced to a pile of rubble. All that history, all those ships, the remains of the Mary Rose, the Warrior, boats of all types—all gone. That more than anything else brought home the devastation his world had experienced.

The militia halted them outside a barracks building that had been reinforced with bars over the windows and a sturdy metal door. It looked more like a jail than a place to sleep.

'Guess we're back in prison,' Izzy said as their escort led them inside.

The room was filled with bunk beds in two lines down either side, with a toilet block at the end.

'At least we'll get some sleep,' Lee answered. His legs were shaking with exhaustion and he barely made it to the bed after gently lowering Allan to the bunk beside him.

He tried his best to stay awake, not wanting to be vulnerable in a strange environment. Soon, though, his eyelids grew heavy and he gave in to sleep.

14

NEW ALLIES

'HOLD THE PLANE like this and you'll get a better finish.' His grandfather placed his hands over top of his as he demonstrated. When they were done Lee ran his fingers along the smooth wood—

'LEE!'

'Wh... what?'

'They're asking to speak with you.' Was that Johan?

Lee shook the dream from his head and opened his eyes to find Johan standing over his bunk looking fresh as a daisy. It was as if the almost sixty-kilometre hike they had done in less than twenty-four hours was nothing to him.

'Why do they want to speak with me?' Lee asked, a little confused. 'Izzy's more senior, and Bruno too. I mean, he's the one really in charge.'

Johan grinned. 'Bruno is a dog, so he can't go. And the militia here are not enlightened enough to believe a girl would be in charge. So you are the only one they will speak with. Come on. Allan and I are waiting.'

Lee tried to bring the door into focus. Eventually his eyes adjusted enough to see Allan standing and waiting for him with the assistance of one of the militia.

Propping himself up on his elbows, he asked, 'Is he all right? I mean, that walk was hard on him.'

'We took turns helping, which made it a little easier. And, while you were sleeping, a doctor came and checked him out. He gave him some more painkillers, and said the wound is essentially healed. Now he just needs to build up his stamina.'

'Good to hear,' Lee said, pushing himself to his feet and letting out a groan. 'I, on the other hand, am not so lucky. A sauna and a massage wouldn't go amiss.'

Everything ached. Lee concentrated on putting one foot in front of the other as he walked behind Johan. With every step he took, a new muscle twinged, and he couldn't wait to sit down. That was, until he was led into an office and plonked into one of the three chairs facing a large mahogany desk. Suddenly sitting seemed like too much of an effort, but the look on the armed militiaman's face discouraged any protests.

He groaned as he adjusted his position to get comfortable. Johan took the chair on the far side of him, and Allan was helped into the final seat. The chair behind the desk remained empty.

Lee fixed his gaze on the devastated dockyard through the window and took some calming breaths. His mind started to wander and his eyes had just begun to close when the door behind them opened and he started awake.

He resisted the urge to turn, and waited until a middle-aged man with greying military-cut hair pulled out a chair and sat down, resting his arms on the desk in front. A lean face with hawklike blue eyes surveyed the three of them. Lee shifted uncomfortably. This meeting was reminiscent of visiting the principal's office.

'So,' the man started, leaning back in his chair. 'You must be Johan from the Lyndhurst Protectorate. And you two are the people who escaped my men after trespassing a few days ago—Allan and Lee, is it?'

It was a statement, not a question, but Lee still felt the urge to correct him. Johan placed a hand on his arm, warning him to remain quiet.

'I am Commander Dunstan. Now that we have the formalities out of the way, what are you doing back in Portsmouth?' the man continued.

This was clearly a question, and it required an answer. Lee hesitated, trying to clear his head. Fortunately, Johan had nominated himself as spokesperson. Leaning forward, he said, 'We are all returning Allan to Portsdown. We were not aware your borders now stretched so far.'

Leaning his head to the side to better pin Johan down with his sharp gaze, the man responded, 'And you didn't think to request permission to come through?'

'To be honest we didn't think we had crossed into your lands yet—we were only just coming up into Fareham.'

The Commander's gaze swung upwards and focussed on their guard. 'Is that true, Roberts? Did you capture these people outside our boundaries?'

Behind him Lee could hear the man shifting position, and he bit back a smile. Maybe they would actually get out of this unscathed.

'Yes sir… just. We spotted the two soldiers and their mutt. They were wanted for a previous infraction, so we were within our rights.' The man's tone was defensive, and Lee could not help but smile at his unease.

A look of anger crossed the man's face and then disappeared as swiftly as it had surfaced. 'I'll deal with you later,' he said to Roberts. Turning back to Johan, he said, 'My apologies for the misstep. Our quarrel is not with you, or your sister. You are both free to go, with my apologies.'

'What about Lee, Izzy, and Allan?' Johan asked.

Commander Dunstan shook his head. 'As Roberts said, they are wanted for a previous infraction.'

'Maybe Lee, but not Allan,' Johan said. 'My father and I found him on a hunting trip a little ways back from where you found us.'

Nice, Lee thought, *We are getting out of this, one by one.* He blinked suddenly, realising that perhaps Izzy, Bruno, and he weren't. They had been in Portsmouth when they had run into the militia last time, and it seemed they didn't take too kindly to trespassers. As Johan had said to them, this place was a shoot first ask questions later type of environment.

The Commander clasped his hands, staring at Allan. 'So, you're an escapee rather than a soldier?'

'Yes, sir,' Allan answered.

'Were these soldiers returning you for interrogation and trial?' He nodded at Lee.

Allan smiled, 'No, sir. I was returning willingly and they are my escort.'

Commander Dunstan's eyebrow rose as if he was surprised. 'You were going back? Why on earth would you do that? You'd be signing your own death warrant.'

Allan blanched beside Lee. 'I wasn't planning on them capturing me, but I guess it is likely once I'm back inside. It doesn't matter anyway. I must return home.'

'Because?' The man encouraged Allan to continue.

Allan looked towards Johan, who nodded for him to go ahead.

'I came to find out if people were living a normal life above ground—if people from the underground could survive up here. I must report my findings.'

Sitting forward in his chair, the man now stared intently at Allan. 'I'm curious: what do you intend to say to them?'

Allan's hands twisted in his lap. 'That it's complicated.'

'Go on,' the Commander encouraged.

Allan took a deep breath and steadied his hands. 'Well, it is obvious people can live above ground, but I'm no longer sure thousands of people leaving the city is in anyone's best interests. It might make things worse for everyone, and I'm not sure we'd be welcomed. People from Portsdown tend to be vilified in your Protectorates.'

The Commander barked out a laugh. 'You're definitely not thought of in the best light, but we have absorbed some people from your community quite successfully, as has the Southampton Protectorate.'

Lee's head drew up in surprise. 'There are others like Allan?'

The man smiled. 'Of course, although they don't feel the need to risk their lives returning to tell others what it's like out here.'

Edging slightly forward on his chair, Allan asked, 'So, would you welcome more refugees?'

'That is a very broad question, and I'm not sure I can answer it. We certainly appreciate the skills people from the city bring with them—they're mostly workers and farmers—and we can always do with more farmers.'

'There is a "but", though,' Allan said.

'We cannot support the influx of a large number of refugees, and we certainly would not welcome any of your ruling class,' Commander Dunstan said.

The tension left Allan's body. 'I suspected as much.'

'Do you still wish to return, knowing this?' the man asked.

Lee shifted in his seat and watched a range of emotions pass over Allan's face as he considered the question. It settled on determined. 'If no one returns, how will people ever know there is an alternative? And if there is no alternative, how will the Representative Council ever change the way they treat the people? So, yes, I will still return.'

'It won't be easy for you to get in,' the Commander warned. 'Over the last week, patrols have tightened up. However, we may be able to help you.'

'Help me? Why?' Allan's tone was wary.

'Let's just say we share a common goal: a change of power inside Portsdown.' The man steepled his fingers as he spoke.

'How would that help you?' Lee asked before Allan could get a word out, then blushed. This really did not have anything to do with him.

The Commander smiled. 'Well, young man, soldiers from the city patrol our protectorate like they own them. Although we speak with the military commanders and have come to an uneasy agreement on boundaries, our leaders would like to deal with Portsdown on an equal footing; we no longer want to be treated as second rate citizens. I, and others, believe this will only happen if there are changes on the Council.'

Lee nodded. This was a similar argument to the one he heard in Lyndhurst.

'So, do you want our help or not?' the Commander asked again.

There was silence while Allan considered the question. 'What would you want in return?' he eventually asked.

'That is easy: for you to talk with your group and tell them we would welcome skilled workers out here. Hopefully, it might encourage a few to leave, and maybe it will boost the resistance.'

'Sounds doable,' Allan said.

The Commander was not finished. 'The difficult bit is, I want you to set up regular communication lines, then return and tell me how we are to work together in the future.'

'That is a big ask,' Allan said. 'I am only a small cog in the resistance. How do you know I'm up to it?'

The Commander shrugged. 'I don't, but I am prepared to take the risk. And you also won't be going alone. I will send a small team in with you.'

Allan took a deep breath. 'All right, but only of Lee and Izzy can come back with me. I won't leave them behind.'

The Commander frowned. 'Lee and… um… Izzy, is it, are from the underground city and they trespassed on our lands in violation of our accords. They and the other soldier must be punished to set an example to others.'

Allan shook his head. 'Before they left the city, they didn't even know about the militia or any agreement. They were only following orders. Besides, they are only here now to help me return to the city. It doesn't seem fair to punish them for any of that.'

Lee felt warm inside at Allan's words of support, and a little bit of hope at being set free began to grow.

The Commander frowned and rubbed his temples. 'I…. Although I have some sympathy, they are soldiers—symbols of the ruling elite—an elite who sentenced many of us to die. For me to show him leniency would cause an

uproar in my own ranks, not to mention what my fellow Councillors would say.'

'You believe the world has changed in eighteen years, and you want more change, yet you won't even consider that some of the soldiers inside Portsdown might support that change. Besides, you are asking Lee here to pay for something that occurred before he was even born,' Allan argued.

You have no idea how wrong that is, Lee thought as he suppressed a smile.

'I understand, but—'

Allan did not allow the Commander to finish. 'And if we hang on to old grievances, how are we ever going to forge a new path together? How can we work with each other if we can't show tolerance and mercy?'

The Commander rubbed his brow again, 'You talk a good talk, son, and the future you outline is certainly one worth fighting for.' He took a deep breath. 'I really can't make that decision alone, but I guess it would be all right if we allowed Lee and the other soldier to accompany you back to the underground city to finish their mission. If they decide they don't want to remain there, then we can deal with their transgressions when they return.'

'I'm happy with that,' Allan said and turned to Lee.

Lee took a moment to respond. His mind was still whirling from Allan's words. For the first time since he had arrived in this crazy version of Hampshire, he felt like he was helping change the course of the world for the better.

'Lee? Lee!' Johan nudged him in the ribs.

'What? Sorry?'

'The Commander asked you a question,' Allan prompted.

'Oh, yes, I'm good with that, and I'm sure Izzy will be too.' He turned to Johan. 'What about you and Basia. Will you come too?'

'I think we will rest up before returning home, with your permission of course. Our parents will be worried about us.' Johan said. 'Although we will wait until you come back from your visit to Portsdown before leaving.'

'Please, make yourself at home in the meantime,' the Commander said.

WITH THE THREAT of imprisonment, or worse, lifted, and a decision to return to the underground city made, Lee relaxed. Perhaps now he would be allowed to go back to sleep. When the Commander spoke his next words, he knew this was not to be.

'Now, young man, do you have a plan?' Commander Dunstan asked.

'I do,' Allan said. 'I used to work in the herbarium. I'll make my way back there and leave a message for my boss, as she'll be checking in daily. Then I will go hide in the cave entrance until they come and find me.'

The Commander again steepled his fingers, and Lee realised he did this when he was thinking. 'The first bit seems fine, but hiding in the cave you left through is out of the question. It will be guarded now.'

Lee watched the changes in Allan's expression as he processed the information. He went from hopeful to defeated in a matter of seconds.

'We didn't think this through,' he finally admitted. 'We assumed I would sneak out unnoticed.'

'No, son, you didn't. Then again, you and your friends aren't soldiers. You are regular people trying to make a difference,' the Commander said.

Allan shrugged. 'Knowing that doesn't help much.'

'We might be able to find a solution if we work together,' the Commander said. 'How many people work in the herbarium and how many of them are sympathetic to your cause?'

'Rosie, my boss, she's one of the leaders of the movement. She recruited me. Her assistant, Janet, is also part of the group. The two of them are only ones who attend meetings and actively fight for change,' Allan said.

'Out of how many workers?'

'There are six of us altogether,' Allan answered the Commander.

Lee's eyes began to drop as the Commander's questions began to mount. He shuffled in his seat to find a more comfortable position, then raised his head to find the Commander watching him.

'Not much longer now, son,' he said before returning his gaze to Allan. 'Out of the other three, how many of them would turn you in if they found you in the herbarium?'

Allan thought for a minute before answering. 'I don't think any would, but I can't be certain. Everyone who works there is loyal to Rosie; they would do anything for her. Whether this would extend to their turning a blind eye to my return, I couldn't say.'

The Commander turned and gazed out the window before swivelling back around and pushing himself out of the chair. He paced around the room, paused, and turned to Allan. 'How big is the herbarium? I mean, how many people can you hide in there?'

'It is the size of a big room— about three times the size of this office. There isn't anywhere to hide. But… you could hide… I guess… about ten

people in the equipment sheds. The large machinery is hardly ever used, and a small group could stay there for days without being found.'

'But no one in the herbarium itself?' the Commander asked.

'Why is it important for someone to be there?' Lee asked.

'Allan needs to pass his message to someone high up in the movement, agree on lines of communication, then get out. His best chance of doing that is talking to this Rosie person, and the only place we know she will definitely be is the herbarium.'

Lee nodded, and Allan sat forward on his chair. 'If we arrived for the early morning start, we wouldn't need to hide. Rosie and Janet are normally the two rostered on that shift. Sunrise is the best time to pick medicinal herbs, and the three of us are the only ones trained in that speciality. Otherwise, one, maybe two people could hide without being seen for a short period.'

The Commander retook his seat. 'Right, we have a plan. We found a back entrance a few months ago. We use it when we need to enter the city unseen. If you go in at night, deliver a message to Rosie, hide in the equipment sheds for the day, then leave the following evening, this could work. Are you up for that, young man?'

'I guess,' Allan said.

'Fine, we're done here then. Roberts will see you're all kitted out for your respective journeys. You're dismissed… and good luck.'

The three boys stood. Roberts opened the door. As they were leaving, the Commander said, 'Roberts, after you've taken them to the commissary and made sure they have everything they need, go pick a small team to go with you into the city.'

'But—'

'Or do you want to stay and talk about how you left our lands to pick this group up?' Commander Dunstan's voice had taken on a threatening tone.

'No, sir.'

ROBERTS STOMPED DOWN the stairs ahead of them, and didn't speak another word until he dropped them back at the prison, when he told them to be ready to leave at three in the morning. The only sign of their changed status was his taking the guard with him when he departed.

As they dropped their new packs inside the door, Allan turned pale and

swayed. Basia rushed to his side and helped him to a bed.

'You should be resting,' she scolded, and Allan didn't object.

What happened? Bruno asked as Lee and Johan sat on a bunk, watching Basia fuss over Allan.

Izzy rifled through the packs. Looking up from her investigations, she asked, 'Are we going somewhere?'

'Yes. You, Bruno, and I are to join an escort taking Allan into the city so he can complete his mission.'

'What about Johan and me?' Basia asked, standing to face them.

From the tone of Basia's voice, Lee guessed she would not be happy with the answer, so he left Johan to respond.

'We've done our bit. We're heading home. We can wait until they return before leaving, if you want to make sure they are safe.' Johan braced himself.

Basia placed her hands on her hips. '*You* might be leaving, but I'm going with the others.'

'Basia, we are going home.' Johan's voice was low and commanding.

'No, Johan. This is my decision. I believe in what Allan is trying to do, and I want to help.'

'But—'

Izzy moved over and placed a hand on Johan's arm. 'She's old enough to know her own mind. Besides, we'll be with her.'

'Are you sure this isn't simply you wanting to see inside the underground city? I mean, you have been dreaming about it for years,' Johan asked.

Basia smiled. She had won even if Johan had not yet realised it. 'I can't deny there is a bit of curiosity involved. Mostly though, I want to help. If Allan is prepared to risk returning to the city, I want to do what I can to support him.'

'But….' Johan sighed. 'All right. I'm still staying here until you are all back safely.'

'Don't you want to come with us? I mean, for Basia's sake,' Izzy asked.

Johan shook his head. 'Sometimes too many people can place the mission at risk. Besides, if something happens someone needs to tell our parents and to be….'

Izzy nodded and squeezed Johan's arm. 'I understand.' Turning to the others, she said, 'There's a change of clothes in each of the packs. I bag first shower. I hope the water's hot!'

By the time Lee had taken the last shower in lukewarm water, food had

arrived—accompanied by another pot of real tea. Appetite satiated, Lee lay down to try and get some rest before their early morning start. He had barely settled when he felt a cold nose touch his hand.

Lee, something must have changed in the timeline. Beta has been trying to contact me for the last hour or so, the dog sent.

That is good, isn't it? I mean, we wanted this, didn't we? Should we tell the others?

We did, and no, not yet. Bruno paused, laying his head on the bed beside Lee. *The Council might be able to tell us whether we have made things better or worse. Only, I don't want to talk with them in case they tell us to stop what we're doing, or worse, tell Thea where we are.*

Lee rolled over and stared into the dog's liquid brown eyes. *Is that wise, Bruno? We need to find out what is happening. Don't we need to know if our actions have sped up the end of humanity's time on earth?*

The dog flopped to the floor. *The problem with only being able to influence people from within the current timeline is that sometimes you set things in motion, and although you can control them for a time, after a while you realise they have taken on a momentum of their own. Once that happens, your ability to influence change is lost.*

I'm not quite sure what you mean, Lee said.

Do you think there is any way you can stop Allan from returning to Portsdown?

Lee thought for a moment. *Perhaps if he knew his actions would cause the end of time….*

But that happens anyway, regardless of what Allan does, Bruno pointed out.

Then no, I think there is no way we could stop him.

Bruno's head tipped to the side. *That is why I believe we have lost our ability to control what happens from now on.*

Lee nodded. *And so, knowing whether the changes are good or bad won't alter anything.*

Bruno sat and his ears pricked. He closed his eyes, then they opened in shock. *Thea and the others are close by. They must have been let go.*

Lee's stomach clenched. *Do they know exactly where we are?*

No, just that we are here. I overheard a snippet of conversation. They may be going for a bigger force to try and extract Allan.

As the full impact of Bruno's words hit Lee, he sat bolt upright. *If they realise we are working with the Portsmouth Militia then… Well, if the Portsdown Representatives get wind of it—*

And with Portsdown maybe having nuclear warheads, Bruno added.

Lee tensed. *Why are you telling me this now?*

If Portsdown took exception to the militia interfering in their affairs, they could

potentially take it upon themselves to make sure they never interfere again. And that could be how the end of the world starts. Bruno's voice was flat as he spoke the doom laden words.

Suddenly I am not feeling so positive, Lee said.

There isn't much we can do except get some sleep and follow through with what we have started, Bruno told him.

I guess so. Lee rolled over and pulled the woollen blanket tightly around himself, no longer feeling sleepy.

15

PORTSDOWN

MOONLIGHT THREW THE forest into a series of shadows, but still Basia could barely contain her excitement— she couldn't believe she was finally going to visit the underground city. All right, so it was more creeping in through the back door rather than turning up as a fully-fledged visitor— but the thought still thrilled her.

Mindful of the danger they were in, she tamped down her feelings and concentrated on moving quietly up the hill. She was out to show everyone she was more than just the tag-along Johan believed her to be.

Not only had she made it this far, but it was doubtful whether or not Allan would be here without her medical skills. Her father trained her to fight, so no one would need to look after her if anyone attacked them. She was ready to make a difference and she would not be left behind again.

The jeans and knitted top she had changed into back at the barracks were as black as the shadows, and she made use of them by avoiding the strips of moonlight. Taking a sip from her water bottle as she moved, she placed it back in the side pocket of her pack, which was heavy with basic medical supplies.

Ahead of her, Izzy and Lee walked companionably together. Behind, one of the four Portsmouth militiamen protected their rear. Beside her walked the huge German Shepherd called Bruno, who could speak to them, but would not talk to any of the militia. She was still getting comfortable with the idea he was a sentient being, which was something being kept secret from their companions.

Roberts, the militia leader, had been keen on leaving the dog behind, saying he would be a liability once they reached the city. Lee insisted on his coming, and Allan agreed, which killed any further discussion. Allan explained later they might need Bruno's ability to facilitate talking without speaking, but Basia knew the dog's skills extended beyond mere talking—he knew things no one else did.

Johan's decision not to come disappointed her. Not only was his presence reassuring, his tracking skills were second to none and, by all accounts, he was pretty handy in a fight too. He wanted to make sure one of them was able to return home to reassure their parents they were all right. He could be pretty stubborn when he made up his mind.

The long silent uphill walk to the cave entrance left Basia exhausted again; adrenaline and fear were the only things keeping her going.

Pausing outside the cave entrance, they put on head torches. Roberts moved between them, reminding them all to keep silent as they walk through the caves. 'Voices echo and carry. Night patrols are not as regular, but we do not want to risk them finding us.'

Winding through the caverns, Basia stuck close to the others, sure that if she lost sight of them, she would be lost underground forever. A cold nose touched her hand. Bruno's gesture reassured her and calmed her nerves. Finally, they reached an internal door, and Roberts whispered for them to turn off and stow their torches.

In the gloomy half-light, the white corridors shone luminously. All her life she had dreamed of the underground city and the wonders it held, only to be disappointed by her first glimpse. She shook it off. The girl who dreamed of an easy life underground had gone. Basia was here to help change the world.

Allan led them through another maze, this time one of hallways with doors spaced at regular intervals on either side. As they walked, Basia counted up the door numbers, measuring their progress. 1-72, 1-74, 1-76. She guessed they worked like the old street address system she had seen in Lyndhurst.

Eventually they came to a stairwell. The group descended one flight, and Allan opened the door to another corridor. The label on the door opposite Basia read 0-263.

The lighting was dimmer. Allan explained that they had left the living quarters and were now traversing the industrial and agricultural level. It was still a little too early for people on the first working shift to be around, and their footsteps echoed in the empty hallways.

They stopped in front of a door numbered 0-000. Allan placed his hand on a grey panel about chest height, and the door swung open. From the look of shock on his face, Basia realised he had not expected to be granted entry.

Trailing through after the others, her eyes opened wide as she surveyed the farm. Many stories high, a domed ceiling through which she could see the night sky crowned the structure. Looking closely, she did a double take. The stars were too bright and were arranged in a pattern that had long since passed at this time of year—the sky was fake.

She dropped her gaze and studied the mass of garden beds in front of her. Fields of grains and vegetables covered the floor. Around the edges were fruit trees and berry bushes. To her left she found a section dedicated to different types of nuts. Hanging from beams across the roof were vine plants. She spotted tomatoes and grapes and some foods she could not put a name to.

The produce was lush, the plants healthy, and the garden beds well tended. What she would not give for a garden such as this at home. In the distance large sheets of opaque plastic hung, rustling as the door closed behind them.

'The fallow fields are at the back,' Allan said from close by.

She turned her head to find him watching her, an amused smile on his lips.

'This is amazing,' Basia said, not wanting to be impressed by the underground garden, but unable to stop herself.

Their eyes met, sending a warm rush through her. She felt the heat rise to her cheeks, and broke the connection.

Taking her hand, Allan said, 'If you're impressed with this, wait until you see my favourite place—the herbarium.'

LEE FOLLOWED THE others into the specialist herb growing area Allan called the herbarium. The room was smaller, and crammed full with all manner of herbs, along with other strange plants Lee was unable to identify. Allan's description had been accurate. The only place a person might hide was the space behind the sole workbench.

Like Lee, Roberts was surveying the room. 'Right, Allan. You hide yourself

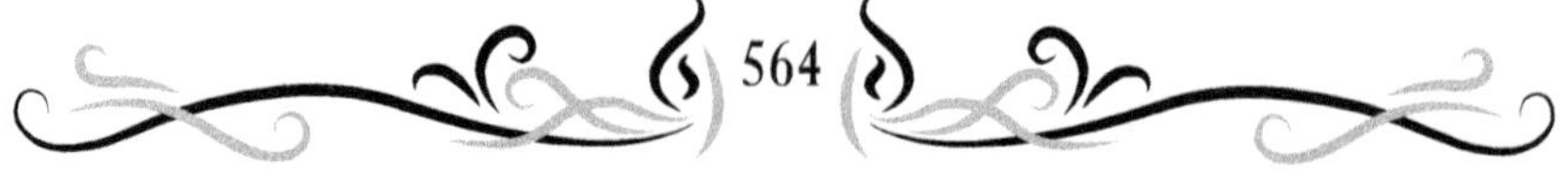

away and the rest of us will head to the equipment store,' he said, then added, 'You can join us after you've made contact and set up the lines of communication.'

Beside Allan, Basia folded her arms. 'I'm not going anywhere. I didn't come all this way to spend an entire day in the equipment shed.'

Lee also shook his head. 'Bruno and I are staying too. If anyone unexpected arrives, Allan may need support.'

'And me,' Izzy added. 'If there is fighting, Lee will need all the help he can get.'

Lee started to object, but Izzy winked at him, sending a terse, *We are in this together now.*

Roberts stared at them, shaking his head. 'I can't order you guys, so stay, go, do what you want. Remember though, I won't be sending any rescue parties for you. Allan is the only one I have been charged with bringing home safely.'

He jerked his head sideways. 'Come on, you lot, let's go hide ourselves and catch some sleep; we won't be needed again until this evening.'

As the militia departed, Lee and Izzy took up positions either side of the door, hidden enough not to be seen from outside the room.

'Give us a nod if whomever arrives is not who you expected,' Lee said. 'Although I'm sure we'll be able to figure it out by their reaction to you.'

'Where do you want me?' Basia asked.

Lee said, 'I think we are counting on you to move Allan out of the road so we can deal with any threats.'

Izzy nodded.

'Hey, I can look after myself,' Allan protested.

'Under normal circumstances, sure. But your injuries aren't completely healed, and we've had an arduous journey. Let Basia help you out,' Lee said.

I could be good at this being in charge thing, he thought, followed by, *Is being good at something really a reason to do it?* Shaking his head, he pushed all concerns about his future to the back of his mind and focussed on the situation at hand.

So great and wise leader, what do you want me to do? Lee looked down at Bruno. He had totally forgotten about the dog. Perhaps he was not such good leadership material after all.

Stay behind me and keep yourself out of sight if you can. We might need you, even if only to frighten someone.

Leaning against the door frame, Lee relaxed a little while they waited for the day shift to arrive. Allan wandered round the herbarium showing Basia

the gardens, explaining the uses of some of the more obscure plants.

'Most of these ones are medicinal,' Allan said, pointing to a group of herbs. 'If we had more time together, I could show you how to use them.'

Lee was so engrossed in their conversation he almost missed the entrance of the morning gardening crew. Only Izzy's hand signal alerted him to their presence, giving him time to ready himself for action.

'Allan, my dear boy, you made it back.' The cry came from a short, rotund woman with the wildest hair Lee had ever seen. A mass of black curls threaded with grey seemed to explode from the woman's head. She beamed as she rushed to Allan, wrapping him in a hug—quite a feat given she barely came up to the boy's chest. 'Are you okay?'

Lee became aware her companion still hung back, not saying a word. Allan had not described Janet, but Lee had no doubt the person in front of him was not her. A tall lanky man stood in the doorway, the scowl on his face sounding alarm bells in Lee's head.

Slipping in behind the man blocking his exit, Izzy's curt nod told him she was ready to act. The man's eyes were riveted on Rosie and Allan, and he appeared not to have noticed his new companions.

'I'm fine, Rosie. I promise you my wound is small, and I'm almost recovered.'

'The vid reports said you were mortally wounded,' Rosie said, worry lining her face.

'You know better than to listen to those.' Allan laughed. 'They like to blow things out of proportion to keep viewers switched on.'

'Still….'

'Rosie, this is Basia. She and her family found me and tended to my health.'

'Hello, Basia,' Rosie said. 'Are you from around old Portsmouth?'

Basia smiled tentatively at the woman. 'No, ma'am. We have a farm in the New Forest.'

Rosie bustled Allan out of the way, now more interested in Basia than him. 'You mean people are farming there? That far away? I knew it!'

'We are farmers,' Basia confirmed. 'But we don't have half the range of food you have in your gardens. Compared to this, we are mere subsistence farmers.'

The grin did not leave Rosie's face. 'But still, this is marvellous—absolutely marvellous. You have no idea how pleased I am to find the world is repairing itself, and people can actually live outside of this cave.'

Lee's eyebrows rose in surprise as Rosie actually clapped her hands in glee.

'Rosie, he's a fugitive. We have to hand them over to the authorities.' The

lanky man stepped forward as he spoke.

'Come on, Joshua, this is Allan. Yes, the soldiers are looking for him, but what has he actually done wrong? Gone for a walk outside?'

'I am happy to hand myself over—after I finish telling everyone what I found out there,' Allan reassured the man.

'I'm not a part of your fantasy group,' Joshua said and almost sneered. 'I keep telling you we're better off where we are, and always have been.'

Rosie turned, her hands outstretched as if pleading with the man. 'Joshua, there are a lot of naysayers and I know you're one of them, but humans are not made to live underground.'

'How can you say that? We have a roof over our heads and plenty to eat,' the man said.

'The air doesn't feel right, the lack of sun doesn't feel right, and the food definitely isn't right. It can't be, because we have to take a daily cocktail of multivitamins to stay healthy. It is past time we reconnected with Mother Earth,' Rosie lectured her co-worker.

Joshua's hands rose to his hips, and he took a stance blocking the doorway. 'I am aware of your beliefs, Rosie, and I wouldn't hurt you for the world. But what is important to me is not losing my position over something I don't want to be a part of. And I certainly don't want to be caught harbouring a fugitive.'

'Then go home. Forget you ever saw this. I'll record it that I did this shift alone,' Rosie pleaded.

'Too late. I'm on camera. My handprint opened the door.' Joshua took another step forward as if to grab hold of Allan.

Lee reacted, blocking the man's path, hand on the weapon at his hip. 'I'm sorry, that won't be happening. Allan will be leaving here with us. Someone will come set you free once we are gone. Then you can tell whoever you like whatever you like.'

Joshua started, then his gaze fixated on Lee's weapon. This hesitation allowed Izzy time to pull handcuffs from her pocket and snap it around a wrist. Joshua's shoulders slumped for a moment, then a blaze of defiance burned in his eyes. He turned as if to run, and almost bowled Izzy over as she grabbed the other end of the cuffs. Catching sight of Bruno beside her, he flung himself backwards, and the only thing that stopped him from falling over was Lee's grip on his upper arm.

'We can't have you going off alone,' Lee informed him. 'Izzy, could you do the honours?'

Deftly the girl pushed Joshua towards the worktable, aided by a growling Bruno. Pushing the man to the ground, she passed the handcuffs behind a table leg, then snapped it closed on Joshua's other wrist.

As she stood, she said, 'If you can promise to be on your best behaviour, I won't gag you.'

His mutinous gaze told her all she needed to know. From another pocket she pulled out a black gag and tied it in place. He struggled, but his actions were futile. Izzy had clearly done this before.

With the threat neutralised, Lee turned his attention back to Rosie and Allan, who were quietly discussing the information he had gathered, and what should be done with it.

'Rosie, we have to tell people what I have seen. Not just our group, but as many people as possible,' Allan was saying.

'I'm not sure—'

'I came back to do this, Rosie. I want to tell everybody about the outside. Force them to question what the Representative Council is doing, what they have been telling us—force a change.'

Rosie studied Allan carefully. Taking his hand, she said, 'If you are intent on doing this, the best way is to make a public declaration. And you'll need to do it soon because we can't hide you down here for long.'

Allan thought for a moment, then shook his head. 'The Council will never call a public meeting for this, and I doubt very much the vid network will allow me to speak, given everything they broadcast is pre-approved.'

'Then we'll have to do it the old-fashioned way.' Rosie's eyes glittered, with excitement.

'The old way?' Lee asked.

'Back before the war, when somebody wanted to talk about something, they set up a soapbox and made a speech. In fact, Speakers Corner in Hyde Park, London provided a specific place for such activities.'

'We could do it now. Go to the grand concourse, stand up on the dais, and tell everybody about how fantastic it is above ground,' Allan said, clearly infected with Rosie's enthusiasm.

Grinning, Rosie said, 'Perfect. It will be at its busiest now, and I'm sure we will persuade a few people there is life outside before the guards catch us.'

'We?' Allan asked.

'I'm coming with you. I wouldn't miss this for the world,' Rosie said.

And me,' Basia added.

Allan shook his head. 'No, Basia. This will be dangerous. Once I begin speaking, the guards will have no option but to lock me up. It may even mean a death sentence.'

'I'm done with others telling me what to do. I'm coming.' Basia's mouth set in a stubborn line Lee knew well from his sister.

'You may as well give up now, mate,' Lee told Allan. 'Her mind is made up.'

The boy took one look at the set of Basia's jaw and admitted defeat. Lee chuckled.

'If we're going to go, we better go now,' Rosie said.

Lee held up his hands. 'Hold on a minute. We should really tell Roberts.'

'You can update him when you join the militia in the equipment sheds,' Allan said as he made to move around him.

Lee grabbed his arm. 'We're coming too.'

Izzy and Bruno drew up beside Lee. 'We're your protection detail,' Izzy added.

Sighing, Allan said, 'Please listen to me. I don't want anyone getting hurt on my account.'

Lee and Izzy exchanged a glance before she said, 'We believe in what you are doing, and we will support you any way we can.'

'And all the while pray that humanity does not end because of it,' Lee added under his breath, earning a frown from Izzy.

'I can't talk you out of it?' Allan asked.

They shook their heads.

Allan sighed. 'Okay, let's do this.'

'What about Roberts?' Lee asked.

Allan shrugged. 'Either we'll be back in time for him to escort us back to Portsmouth, or we'll be somewhere where even he won't be able to help us.'

AS THE GROUP made their way to the grand concourse, they received some strange looks, mainly because of the huge Alsatian accompanying them. Rosie greeted everyone as if walking through the corridors with a fierce-looking dog was something she did every day, which dispelled some of the tension. Lee's stomach clenched when they passed some patrolling soldiers. Surely, they would notice the dog? None of them did.

Lee frowned and looked down at Bruno. *How come they didn't stop us?*

There is enough magic for me to do an occasional "don't see me" spell, Bruno explained.

That's a thing? he asked.

Bruno nodded, as if not only was it a thing, but it was perfectly normal for him to do it.

How come you did not use it when we fought the eco-warriors? Lee asked.

Bruno chuckled. *I did, but I can only do it for a short time.*

As the flow of people around them increased, Lee realised they were in the equivalent of rush hour traffic. Everyone stayed to the left, creating two opposing flows of human traffic.

Allan led them into an octagonal space with eight corridors spoking off at even intervals. Traffic was guided through the central area by a roundabout, which stood about knee height. For four flights above, the spoke pattern was duplicated, only the central hub was smaller and the spokes were walkways, allowing a clear view up to the ceiling between each spoke.

Allan and Rosie were making their way to the central platform, with Izzy and Basia moving in their wake. By the time Lee had managed to catch them up, Allan was standing in the middle of the dais, clearing his throat. Lee joined the others, arms outstretched, trying to make a bit of space around the roundabout to protect Allan from the crowd. Bruno slipped in between them, lying at Allan's feet, ready to jump into action should he be needed.

Allan's polite "Fellow citizens" was swallowed up by the noise. Bruno rose to his feet and used his voice to attract people's attention. Bruno barked for almost a minute before people stopped to find out what was going on. Lee gazed up to find people were also leaning over the railings of the upper levels.

'Most of you won't know me. My name is Allan Gordon, and I'm a gardener. I didn't want to be a gardener, but I was forced to do it to help humanity survive underground.'

People shuffled nervously, and some started to move away.

'Get to the point before you lose them,' Rosie said.

'But what if we didn't have to stay here? What if our lives didn't depend on everybody following the rules?' Allan carried on as if this was his plan all long.

People stopped moving, and the noise slowly died down.

'Where else would we go?' someone yelled out.

'The world is dead. We have no choice but to live here,' another responded.

'You're wrong. I just spent a few days above ground.' Allan's voice now rang out loud and clear.

There was a collective gasp and people drew back, horror on every face. It took a moment for Lee to realise they were behaving like him when he first arrived, fearful of radiation and what it might do to them. So fearful in fact, they instinctively avoided any hint of contamination even though it couldn't be passed person to person.

Ignoring this, Allan carried on speaking. 'I saw things out there you're probably not going to believe. There are communities of people living and, if not quite thriving, they're growing food, keeping livestock, and getting on with their lives.'

'Zombies and the dying,' a man yelled.

'You won't ever convince me the air is safe out there,' a woman close to Lee said.

A burly man pushed his way forward and challenged Allan. 'I bet they're riddled with radiation and die young. Probably not even able to have kids.'

'You are wrong,' Allan responded. 'There are some people with radiation sickness—' The crowd murmured, and Allan held both hands out as if to stop another tide of remarks. '—but most people are perfectly healthy. They face different challenges to us, but they live out a normal lifespan, and they're building a new world.'

'Prove it!' the man said. 'Prove you're not just telling us a story to stir up trouble.'

Allen mumbled, 'What now?'

Lee wondered if he'd lost the battle to change the tide of opinion. Then Basia placed a hand on his shoulder and pushed herself up on the dais.

'I am all the proof you need,' she said. 'I was born and grew up outside. Do I look radiation riddled to you? Do I look unhealthy? Do I look any different to any of you?'

'Her skin's a funny colour,' a young girl in front of Lee said, and at that moment he realised everyone around him, save the people with black skin, were pale and white, almost translucent.

Behind him Basia laughed. 'That is because I live outside. Sunlight changes skin colour. It would happen to you if you decided to leave here.'

'I'm not sure I want to look all dark like that,' the girl muttered, and earned a glare from the black woman beside her.

'I'm not saying our life is easy, and few of the luxuries you are used to down here are available to us. But I do see the sky every day. I feel the wind on my face, the ground beneath my feet, and each year the earth gets a little better, and life gets a little easier,' Basia finished.

Allan stepped forward. 'Basia and I wanted you to know we can choose where—'

A strange crackling noise filled the air, and everyone ducked. Lee searched the crowd and found Captain Kiandra. Beside her stood Corporal Rodgers, his blaster raised. The Captain moved to prevent the Corporal from firing again, but was too slow to stop him. Lee half turned and saw Allan crumple to the ground.

Time slowed down around Lee. 'You dirty traitor!' Rodgers yelled.

'Grab Allan and let's get out of here.' Izzy's voice galvanised him into action.

Basia was shaking, but she took one of Allan's arms, and Rosie the other. Lee and Izzy grabbed his legs. The four of them carried Allan towards the corridor opposite the soldiers, a growling Bruno clearing a path for them.

Allan was a dead weight, and he slipped from their grasp. 'Drop your packs, then it'll be easier to carry him,' Lee instructed.

They followed his order, and Lee hauled one of Allan's arms over his shoulder. Izzy took the other. They moved more quickly now, and it appeared people were parting for them, then closing in behind. Were they trying to slow the soldiers down so they could get away?

They made it to the corridor, and stopped for a moment to catch their breaths.

'What now?' Basia asked.

Lee looked at Allan's white face, and wondered how long they could carry him. Not very long, he surmised, but he was damned if he would leave him behind.

'We have no option but to keep going,' he said, hauling Allan up again. He and Izzy moved more slowly under the burden, but they were putting a little distance between themselves and their pursuers.

'Rosie, can we escape this way?' he asked.

'Not easily,' she responded. 'What we need to do is find somewhere to lay low… but….' She looked up to the camera at the junction further down the hall.

Someone shouted their names, and Lee pushed himself harder, though every muscle burned. How were they going to make it out of this alive?

Over Allan's head he caught Izzy's eye. *Any ideas?*

No. Bruno?

Lee looked around. Where was Bruno? He half turned at the sound of a bark in time to see the crowd part and Bruno dash through the gap, followed by Roberts and his men.

'What the—' Lee started.

'No time for explanations, lad. We need to find somewhere to—'

Roberts was cut short as the door opened beside them. 'Quick, in here,' a diminutive dark-skinned girl said.

Looking around to make sure no one was paying attention to them, Roberts pushed the group through the door. 'Wait here. I'll be back.'

Lee found himself in the living room of an apartment which was reassuringly familiar in this strange new future. The door closed behind them, muffling the noise of the riot. He took a step forward, stumbled over a rug, and almost dropped Allan.

'Bring him in here,' the girl said, leading them to a bedroom.

Izzy and Lee placed Allan on the bed. Basia nudged them out of the way. 'My medical supplies were in my pack. Can you bring me some hot water and towels, and perhaps some painkillers?' she asked their host.

The girl nodded solemnly. 'Give me a moment.'

'All of you, out,' Basia commanded. 'I need space to work.'

It was only when he joined the others in the living room that Lee realised Bruno was not with them. Sinking into a sofa, he dropped his head into his hands, exhausted. How had everything gotten out of hand so quickly?

They had had a plan, one that moved everyone toward change in a controlled way. Now the underground city was rioting and there was.... He paused for a moment, trying to form the thought.... There was a kind of electricity in the air. Change was coming whether they were ready for it or not.

16

THE PATH TO WAR

FOLLOWING THE PORTSMOUTH militia down the corridor, Bruno took time to glance back over his shoulder to check the progress of the riot. He padded to catch up with Roberts, determined to help the militiamen lead the chase away from his friends.

Sigma? Bruno? You're here somewhere. Answer me, dammit.

Thea, you're with Captain Kiandra? Bruno asked.

Yes, Jason and I are here. Give yourselves up. They only want Allan. I should be able to buy us enough time to take you three out of here.

Come on, Thea. You don't even know if we can gather enough magic for us to leave. Who knows what will happen to us.

Captain Kiandra and I will protect you, Thea said.

They shot him, Thea!

No, Roberts shot him, Bruno. He's gone off reservation. Our orders were to capture him and bring him in.

Bruno sighed. No matter how much he wanted to, he could not just give up. *We helped start this. We cannot just walk away.*

Bruno, do you know what you have done? History is in flux. The timeline has split into so many branches it is in total chaos. Please, stop this foolishness now, for everyone's sake.

Thea sounded scared, which worried Bruno. Thea was never scared.

I'm not sure even I could gather enough magic to portal you all out of here if all hell breaks loose, Thea added.

Bruno said nothing, thinking about his next moves as he padded after the militia, making sure the camera was able to track him heading down the left-hand corridor. The team moved a little way further down, then halted.

'Anton and Dries, you carry on,' Roberts ordered. 'Make sure the cameras catch you on the way out. Once you're out, head back to Portsmouth and let the Commander know what has happened. Henry, you come back with me. I think Allan could use your medical skills.'

Bruno sat and waited beside Roberts until his men disappeared from sight. The man took something out of his pack and pointed it at the screen. A few people trickled past them towards the riot, but Roberts made no attempt to move.

Bruno? You still there? This feels wrong. Something bad is happening.

I know, Thea. Sorry, I must go. I must make sure Lee gets out of here safely, and he won't leave Allan. I'll keep in touch.

All right. Thea's voice was resigned. *But please, can you speak with Beta? He is beside himself with worry.*

'Henry, a big group is heading this way. Big enough for us to blend in,' Roberts said as Thea left Bruno's head.

Packing his device away, Roberts and Henry removed their packs and joined the group running down the corridor towards the hub.

'Come on, guys,' the leader yelled. 'If we don't hurry, we'll miss it—our one chance to show the soldiers we're not going to take their crap anymore.'

Others shouted encouragement as people rushed ahead, pulling hoodies up as they reached the area covered by surveillance camera. Bruno made sure to stay hidden on the far side of the group. Still, he incanted a "don't see me" spell just in case.

The corridors were filling up. Roberts and Henry linked arms to form a protective zone around Bruno, and began steadily working their way through the crowd. Moments later the three of them stood before the apartment door, ready to retrieve their friends. A quick knock and they were soon pulled inside, away from the chaos of the riots.

SOON AFTER THE guards left, Lee found himself with nothing to do. 'Won't you be missed at work?' he asked Jane, the girl who had let them into her apartment.

She pointed to the scenes of riots being shown on the room's television screen. 'I don't think anyone is going to miss me for a while. More so because I was supposed to be working the representatives loop today, and I think they are going to have their hands full for some time.'

He and Izzy continued watching the screen, making themselves comfortable on the sofa. Jane took supplies in to Basia, then she and Rosie moved to the door, talking quietly and keeping an eye out for Robert's return.

Lee allowed himself to switch off until a rather regal looking woman in her fifties appeared on the screen. With her red hair pulled into a severe bun and the equally severe lines of her military uniform, she immediately drew his attention.

Jane turned the sound up. 'She is the head of the Civil Guard,' she explained.

'I repeat: everyone is to return to their quarters immediately. We are suspending all work details and declaring a curfew until those who infiltrated our city are behind bars. Anyone who does not comply with the emergency orders will be detained by the guards and questioned carefully.'

'Held without recourse to legal help,' Rosie said under her breath,

'That's just great,' Izzy said. 'We're never gonna get out of here now.'

Rosie checked the peephole in the door before saying, 'I think it will be a while before things quieten down. We need to get you out of here before they do, because once everything is clear, the house-to-house searches will start.'

'Of course they will,' Lee said, feeling despondent. It would be hard enough moving an injured Allan—why not make it even more difficult? He placed his elbows on his knees and rested his chin in the palms of his hands, getting more and more depressed as each minute passed.

He jerked to attention moments later when the door opened and Roberts entered, followed by Bruno and one of his men. Roberts opened the door to the bedroom to check on Allan. Seeing that Basia was struggling to deal with his wounds, he instructed Henry to do what he could to patch Allan up so he could be moved.

Once the door was again closed, and the militiaman said, 'We've left a trail away from here, and that should buy us a little time. We still need an escape plan though.'

He ran his hands through his hair in agitation. 'If only you had stuck to

the plan and not gone sneaking off.' He glared at Izzy and Lee.

Lee didn't want an argument, but he realised Roberts deserved an explanation. 'Allan came here to tell people about an alternative way of life. Once Rosie suggested the idea of a speech, he was going to do it whether we went with him or not. I thought it best to at least protect him.'

Roberts shrugged. 'Fair enough, but why didn't you come and get us?'

'We didn't think you would agree to let us go,' Izzy said.

Roberts paused, stroked his chin, and said, 'Fair point.'

'How did you know we were in trouble?' Lee asked.

'Luckily, the agri workers were talking about a commotion on the main concourse. We overheard them and realised only one group of people could cause that much mayhem.' Roberts grinned, taking some of the sting out of his words. 'Look, I guess Allan has done what we wanted him to do—caused unrest and set up some internal contacts—the least we can do now is get him out of here.'

Lee was glad Roberts had taken charge again. If you had told him a month ago that he would give up leadership so easily, he would have laughed. In truth, though, he was relieved to let someone else make the decisions. It wasn't that he wanted to blindly follow another person's orders. It was more that he didn't want to be responsible for the lives, or potential deaths, of the others.

Roberts walked to the bedroom door and opened it. 'How's he doing, Henry?'

Through the door, Lee caught a glimpse of Basia and Henry working on Allan, who was attached to a drip.

'A lot of blood loss, but no lasting damage. Basia managed to clean the wound. I cauterised it and patched him up. We've given him fluids, which should help. I had to knock him out completely, so he can't walk. Moving him is not optimal, but if we have to, we can make it work,' Henry informed them as Basia frowned behind him.

'Moving him could kill him,' she declared.

'If he stays here, he will definitely die,' Roberts said.

'You can't know that for certain.' Basia's chin jutted out defiantly.

'But we do, love,' Rose interrupted. 'The soldiers want him, and they'll want to make an example of him once this period of unrest is over. The best chance of saving him is to get him out of here, and Jane and I think we have a way you can do that.'

'I work in the laundries. Today I was supposed to be doing the upper floors. My trolley and uniform are in the closet. You can put your boy in the

trolly and one of you, well, the girl with you, can dress as me. There is an exit to outside near the laundries,' Jane told them.

'Jane and I contacted a few of the residents. They are on their way here and will swap clothes with you. They will draw any soldiers away from your route,' Rosie added.

'It will be dangerous for them,' Roberts said.

'They have been training for this. They know the risks and will take them happily.' Rosie sounded almost gleeful as she spoke.

Things happened fast after that. Less than twenty minutes later, the small apartment was crowded with people. Clothes had been exchanged. Allan was placed gently in the trolley, drip and all, and covered with dirty linen. Basia was ready to wheel him out. The main group was debating how to cause enough mayhem to draw the guards.

'How will she know where to go?' Lee asked as everyone gathered by the door.

Roberts handed Basia a handheld device. Pointing to the screen, he said, 'I marked the quickest way to the laundry. Just avoid these blue dots if you can. They indicate large groups of people. It also disrupts the cameras a little as you pass. Not enough to worry security, but the picture blurs or shows a bit of static until we pass by.'

The decoys left first. A couple of minutes later, Rosie stuck her head out, waited for a large group to pass, then indicated they should go.

'Look after my boy,' she ordered them as she shut the apartment door.

The corridors were crowded and noisy, and at first it was difficult to keep Basia in sight. As the crowd thinned, a new problem presented itself. With the order to return to quarters given, the army was out in full force, and they had to take quite a few detours to avoid them.

Lee's palms sweated, and he shoved his shaking hands into his pockets. Moving closer to Bruno for comfort, he wondered once again how things had fallen apart so quickly, and if he would ever see his family again.

EVERYTHING WAS GOING according to plan. Basia used the device to steer them away from soldiers and rioters alike, although they could hear confrontations happening all around them. Lee had almost started to believe they might escape unscathed when Basia halted, having just turned the corner to the laundry wing.

'What are you doing here?' a voice boomed.

Basia trembled, and Lee thought they were doomed. He waited out of sight, close enough to grab Basia and the trolley should he need to. The others ducked into doorways, out of sight.

It's all right, Lee, Bruno sent. *Soldiers love a bit of fear, and they would be surprised if she hadn't reacted that way.*

'I… I was working upstairs and I… I got sent home. I thought I would just drop the laundry off on the way. I don't want to get into trouble when it is not ready for tomorrow.'

A laugh echoed down the corridor. 'Love, no one is going to be worrying about their linens for a while yet.'

'Leave her alone, Peter. Can't you see she's scared. Come on, love. Do what you need to, then hurry home. You don't want to get caught up in all this fighting.'

'Th…thank you.'

Basia wheeled her cart forward. 'Um, my friend came with me to make sure I was all right. Can he come too?'

Basia waved Lee forward. The soldier in front of her gave him the once over before the nicer one said, 'Brave of you to escort her through this mayhem.'

Lee gave a nervous laugh as his stomach flip-flopped. 'She was determined to come. I couldn't let her go alone.'

'Good lad. Come on, Peter, we need to finish checking this section.'

The soldier moved past them and continued along the corridor. His mate followed, smirking. 'Don't stay too long. You don't want to get caught in a compromising position.' He sniggered.

Lee and Basia slowly walked forward. Behind them a radio crackled, and the first soldier responded. The second soldier's eyes bore into the small of Lee's back, right between his shoulder blades, raising the hair on the back of his neck.

In front of the door, Basia whispered, 'Oh no, they didn't give me a code for the lock.'

Bruno, there is a lock here. Can you magic it open? Lee asked.

No, the magic down here isn't strong enough for that, the Guardian sent back.

'Something wrong?' the second soldier called.

Lee thought he was going to throw up. Instead, he turned and said, 'She's scared, and forgot the code for a moment."

'Peter, go help them. We need to clear this area.'

'It is my first time being sent upstairs... then the lockdown...,' Basia said breathlessly as the guard reached over her shoulder and keyed in a number.

'Okay, unload your stuff and get out of here as quickly as possible,' he grumbled.

As Basia went inside, Lee watched the soldier return to his friend.

'What now?' Basia whispered.

'I don't... hold on....'

The first soldier put his hand to his ear, listened, then said, 'Insurgents are overrunning the green sector.' Looking down the corridor towards Lee, he yelled, 'Can I trust you both to go straight to your quarters after your friend is done?'

'Yes,' Lee answered to the soldier's retreating back.

Much to Lee's relief, he was soon joined by the rest of the team. Basia removed the drip from Allan's arm, and Lee helped her take him out of the basket. Meanwhile Henry fashioned a hammock out of the sheets.

'Wait here,' Roberts ordered. Retuning a few minutes later, he said, 'The exit is around the corner. One camera covering the door, no guards. We need to go through two at a time so we can disrupt the feed. I'll go first. Henry, you send the others through in twos at two-minute intervals after. The code is A256.'

They made it to the door without further mishap and waited just out of view of the camera. Lee's heart was pounding and his arms ached as Allan shifted in his makeshift stretcher.

He watched as Roberts keyed in the code and slipped through. The two-minute wait seemed like two hours. Then Henry was sending Basia and Bruno through.

Lee's palms were sweaty, and the sheet slipped.

'You need to carry him—fireman's lift style—otherwise we risk the cameras picking you up,' Henry said. 'Can you do that?'

Lee nodded.

He and Izzy placed Allan on the ground.

'Ready?' Henry asked.

'Yes.'

'Right, up.' Lee bent and scooped up Allan, still wrapped in the sheet hammock, staggered a bit, then righted his load. 'Go.'

Lee made it to the door as Izzy punched in the code. Then they were through and on their way up the flight of stairs behind.

After four flights Lee's knees were beginning to buckle. He was about to

drop Allan when he felt the weight over his shoulder ease slightly.

'I can take him from here.'

With a sigh of relief, Allan handed over his bundle to Henry and made his way up to the cavern above.

Roberts waited for them at the top. 'Take a rest,' he ordered.

Henry placed Allan on the floor by Bruno and Basia. Lee stumbled over and joined the rest of the team. Roberts joined them, while Henry took his place by the external door.

'There are increased patrols,' Roberts said. 'I'm just trying to decide whether to make a run for it or hide for a while. The dogs aren't out yet, so I'm leaning towards hiding.'

'I don't like the idea of that,' Izzy said. 'I'll feel much better when we are all back and secure in the Portsmouth Protectorate. Roberts, your device can sense body heat, can't it?

'It can, but it is likely they would hear us coming before it picked up their heat signatures. Besides, they have similar technology to use against us.'

I can help with that, Izzy, Bruno said. *I think I can dampen our sound enough to not be heard unless someone is right beside us.*

Izzy smiled. *I can do that too. Between us we might be able to make this viable.*

'I can get us through the forest without making a sound,' Izzy said.

'What, you do magic or something?' Roberts scoffed.

'Don't knock it until you've seen it,' Basia said. 'Magic aside, we can't wait here forever. Allan needs medical help, and soon.'

Roberts frowned. 'You guys are strange, but I *am* tasked with getting Allan back alive…. So, what exactly are you proposing?'

Izzy said, 'I need Bruno to range ahead and check for patrol. Henry, Basia, and Lee can carry Allan. Roberts, you and I will take the rear and use your monitor to check for soldiers.'

Shrugging, Roberts said, 'This is the flakiest plan I have ever heard of.' He took a deep breath. 'I don't like having to move in the light, but I guess our options are limited. All right, if we are going to go, we may as well go now.'

They took a zig-zag path back to Portsmouth, avoiding tracks and moving through the bushes where they could. They had to backtrack a few times to avoid the alarming number of soldiers saturating the area.

The sky was just beginning to darken when Izzy called for a break. They hid under forest debris to wait for yet another patrol to pass. When Lee went to pick Allan up again, his arms shook and he suppressed a groan.

'I need a rest. I can't carry him anymore,' Lee whispered.

Roberts frowned. 'We are only about ten minutes away from the crossing. Let's make it to the edge of the bushland, then we can rest until the sun goes down. I don't want to be crossing the cleared defensive section in the light.'

Lee sighed. 'I think I can make it a little further.'

'Let me help you for a while,' Basia said, taking part of the sheet.

Just when Lee thought he couldn't take any more, Roberts led them to a bush. Pulling back the boughs, he revealed a herbaceous cave. They scrambled in and Lee immediately sunk to the ground, his limbs trembling with fatigue.

Basia unwound Allan from his bindings. He was grey, and a sheen of sweat had formed on his brow, but his breathing was regular.

Henry passed his water bottle around and shared some dried beef while Izzy took first watch. Lee curled up beside Bruno and tried to get some sleep.

He did not know how long he had been out for when he heard bushes rustling nearby. His eyes flew open to find Roberts staring down at him, finger to his lips. He froze as a large number of soldiers passed so close to their hiding place their feet shook the ground and their clothing brushed against the branches, revealing twinkling stars in the dusk sky.

'We're going to do some reconnaissance,' Roberts whispered once they were again alone. 'Henry is in charge until we return.'

Izzy stood to leave with Roberts.

Izzy? Lee said in alarm.

Don't worry, Lee. We won't get caught. She grinned at him. *And if we do, you and Bruno can rescue us.*

Take Bruno with you, he said.

The Time Fixer frowned. *What about you guys?*

We are safe here for the moment. Please, take him with you, Lee pleaded.

The boy is right. With the two of us, there is a better chance of all of us returning, Bruno said, rising to follow Izzy out.

SURVEYING THE SCENE below, Bruno felt sick to his stomach. Spread out as far as the eye could see, a ring of Portsdown soldiers encircled Portsmouth. Facing them from inside the Portsmouth Protectorate's boundaries was the Portsmouth militia. Their ring consisted not just of soldiers, but of heavy artillery and mobile rocket launchers.

His first thought was, *What have we done?* His second was to test the air for magic to decide if he could build a portal. Izzy looked down at him.

There isn't enough magic. Not here, anyway. And not for all of us, she said.

Her violet-blue eyes reflected his fear and worry. Beside him, Roberts shifted position and pulled something out from one of the pockets of his trousers—night vision goggles.

'Not a single gap in the band around Portsmouth,' he noted. 'I'm not sure whether they are here to keep us from getting back, or if they are here as retaliation for our entering the city.'

'Does it matter?' Izzy asked.

'Of course. If it is option one, we can give ourselves up and everyone backs down. Option two is more difficult... and your guess is as good as mine. Portsdown enjoys threatening to use their military might to wipe us out. Maybe this time it isn't a threat.'

'Can we make it across without being seen?' Izzy asked.

'No way. We are better to return and wait this out.'

About half an hour later, they were back in their hiding spot, and had broken the bad news to the others. Allan was awake, his head resting on Robert's pack. He had refused strong painkillers, wanting to keep his head clear.

'Will they stand down if I give myself up?' he asked.

Roberts shook his head. 'I don't think it's that simple. They might, but it is unlikely. Our situation would be so much better if we could communicate with base.'

Izzy looked at Bruno and he nodded. 'We might be able to help with that.'

Roberts chuckled. 'Magic again.'

Izzy smiled with not a hint of embarrassment. 'Yes. And we may also be able to tell you what is going on in Portsdown as well.'

'Knock yourselves out,' he said as he stretched out on the ground. 'I'm going to get some shut-eye.'

'Bruno, you talk with Thea while I try and make a connection with Johan—after all, we do have a history, so it's our best bet for Portsmouth.'

Roberts chuckled. 'Now I know you're having me on. You're getting the dog to talk to our enemies.'

Basia glared at Izzy. 'What do you mean you and Johan have a past?'

Lee placed his hand over Basia's. 'I'll explain later, but for now we need to let these guys work.'

17

THE DRUMS OF WAR

IZZY CLOSED HER eyes and concentrated on the pin pricks of magic on her skin. In her mind she pictured her one true love, Josephine—remembering her brown hair always neatly held back in a bun, her warm brown eyes, and the dimple in her left cheek when she smiled.

Love filled her heart as she allowed it to open just for this moment. Using that connection, she reached out for Johan.

Johan, can you hear me?

Mmm, what? Who? a sleepy voice answered.

Johan, it's me, Izzy.

She felt a jolt, like electricity, followed by confusion. Izzy hated using this type of mind link to communicate because emotions as well as words were exchanged. Trying to shield herself as much as possible from Johan's feelings, she spoke again.

Johan, we are trapped outside the perimeter, and we need to know what is going on before we decide what to do.

Fear and worry worked itself through the bond. *Basia? Is she all right?*

Yes, she's fine. She's with me now, Izzy said.

Relief almost overwhelmed her. *Good. I don't know what I would do if anything*

happened to her.... How would I explain it to—

Johan, do you know what's happening?

Yes, a little bit. Mum and Dad arrived with a contingent of the Lyndhurst Guard early this morning, along with some of the Southampton militia.

What? Why are they all there? Izzy was not sure if the fear building in her stomach was her own, or was a result of her connection with Johan.

After the meeting at Lyndhurst, everyone was worried there would be a retaliation from Portsdown, and none of us can face it alone, Johan told her. *I was with Dad and the Commander trying to sort out accommodation when the call came through about your activities.*

What call? It was Izzy's turn to be confused.

From Portsdown, threatening war if Allan and all of the Portsmouth spies were not handed over for trial.

Izzy's heart sank. *Oh dear, that is not good at all. What did the Commander say?*

A Militia Council was called. Mum and Dad are in there, along with Representatives from Southampton. I believe, from rumours flying around, they are also looping in Protectorates as far away as Guildford and Chichester.

Still not sounding good. Izzy knew now the churning in her stomach was all her own.

It isn't. They are talking about taking a final stand against Portsdown, saying they will never give in to the cities again.

Oh, no. Can anyone talk sense into them, Johan? They can't really mean to go to war.

Johan's voice was firm when he responded. *They won't back down and hand you over, if that is what you are worried about. My father is trying to convince them to consider peace talks to agree on an accord between our communities.*

How likely is that to happen? Izzy asked.

He has a little support, but your guess is as good as mine, Izzy.

The connection was growing fuzzy and she was just about to break it when a flow of worry overwhelmed her.

Izzy, bring Basia home... please.

I will do the best I can, she said. *It would be easier if there weren't so many soldiers between here and you.*

I will see what I can do about that, Johan said.

Izzy smiled and broke the link that was both so familiar and very foreign.

When she opened her eyes, she found three faces turned towards her, a triple mask of expectation. Henry and Roberts snored gently and Bruno was curled up by Allan, clearly not yet finished with whoever he was talking to.

IT TOOK A while for Bruno to gather enough magic to make a connection, then it took a few attempts to actually reach Thea. At first, he thought she was blocking him, then he remembered magical energy was limited underground, so he put a little more force behind his call.

Sigma?

Yes, it's me, Thea. I was just touching base to find out what was happening underground since Allan dropped his bombshell.

First, tell me, are you all safe?

Bruno was touched by her concern. *Yes. I won't tell you where we are, I don't want to compromise your position, but we are all right.*

Good. Now what is it you need?

Did you know Portsdown is holding Portsmouth to ransom for our return? Bruno asked.

Yes. Our regiment has been assigned to guard the Representative Council, and they have been in nonstop meetings since I spoke with you last.

Bruno felt a wave of relief that Thea was so close to the action. *Are they going to declare war?*

I believe they have given the Portsdown Protectorate twenty-four hours to produce you. Time runs out at two o'clock tomorrow afternoon.

They might find that difficult, Bruno chuckled. *They have no idea where we are.*

That is interesting, and exactly what they are saying. I will see if I can make it known they are telling the truth. It might buy us some time to sort this out.

Thea, how serious are they about going to war? Bruno asked.

They are divided. Most want to wipe Portsmouth off the face of the earth, but a small group want to work with the Protectorates to find a solution to end all these small attacks, Thea informed him.

What's stopping them from acting, then?

Thea laughed. *The little matter of a full-scale riot, which is taking longer to control because representatives sent the bulk of the army to encircle Portsmouth.*

Is there anything we can do to stop a full-scale war? Would turning ourselves in help?

Thea said something Bruno was unable to make out as the connection slipped. Reaching out a little further, Bruno gathered more magic and tried again.

What was that, Thea?

Oh, you're back. I said, it would help, if we could find a safe way for you to do it,

maybe as part of peace talks.

That sounds ambitious. Bruno was skeptical. *Are you able to influence anyone to that end?*

I've managed to get myself attached to one of the more moderate Representatives, Thea told him.

Representatives? I guess you're using that term loosely, Bruno said.

Actually, no. He's one of the few original elected members and he will not retire until they stop passing seats down to their children and actually hold elections.

Bruno laughed. *That sounds novel.*

You'd be surprised. There are three or four Council members who agree with him, including two who inherited their seats. They believe agreeing to hold elections in Portsdown followed by peace talks with the Protectorates is the only way humanity will survive in this part of England.

Oh, Bruno said, wondering how such a small group could make a difference.

They are concerned putting down the riots with force will not extinguish the movement for change. Thea's tone was worried. *They see the big picture and believe Portsdown cannot withstand sustained attacks from within and without.*

Combine this with the Protectorates wanting to flex their muscles…, Bruno added

Look, Bruno, we are where we are. All we can do now is work with the moderates in both camps to prevent war. I will work on Tobias. Can you do the same on your side? Thea asked.

Um….

Bruno, just for once can we work together? Exasperation filled Bruno's head.

Thea, it's not that I don't want to help, it's more I don't know how much help I can be from where we are. But I will try. And I will talk to the group about giving ourselves up in return for peace talks happening.

Did you contact Beta yet? Thea asked out of nowhere.

If Bruno could have blushed, he would have. *No, I thought it best to leave him out of this. I don't want him to get into trouble for something that I decided to do on my own.*

If you need any help once we sort this out—

Thanks for the offer, but I know you didn't want any part of this, so I won't drag you into it, Bruno said.

Now that I've seen more of Portsdown, I think perhaps we should have done things differently from the outset. Portsdown was set up by good people trying their best to save humanity, but the ruling elite has become corrupt and will do anything to protect their position. If Allan had been returned to them, it would only have bolstered their iron control of the Representative Council.

A small flicker of hope began to grow in Bruno's heart. *You mean you actually think I did the right thing?*

Don't be ridiculous. You disobeyed orders, Thea said, dashing Bruno's sliver of hope. *You should never have gone against the Council; that isn't our role.*

There she was, the same old Thea seeing everything in black-and-white. He changed the subject. *And Jason? Is he all right?*

He is with Rodgers. They are assigned to policing the riots. I think Captain Kiandra had had enough of the two of them and was more than happy to loan them to another regiment.

Bruno gasped. *I thought Corporal Rodgers would be behind bars after shooting Allan.*

Although Captain Kiandra demoted Rodgers to Private for his behaviour on our mission, he is now being hailed a hero and was promoted to Captain for his actions. Jason has become his lapdog and seems to relish the opportunity to enforce the anti-riot emergency acts. When we leave, I am not sure he will want to come with us.

However much he is enjoying himself, at some stage he will have to escape and find Izzy. Jason is not strong enough to magically portal out of here by himself, Bruno said.

If I had my way, I'd leave him behind, but I have promised to return him to his people if he can't find his partner.

There was little left to say, or perhaps there was so much but now wasn't the time—there was never a time to say all the unsaid words. Bruno sighed. *I had best go. Good luck with trying to sort things out from your end.* Bruno cut communications.

He lay with his head resting on his paws for a while, enjoying the peace and quiet. Although he hated to admit it, his conversation with Thea had struck a chord. He no longer had confidence in the Time Guardian Council, and at some stage he would need to decide whether or not he had a future with them. He stretched. But not now—now he had to stop a war, then he had to find enough magic to return everyone home. When that was done, there would be time to worry about the future.

THE TREE HIDE was quiet when Bruno opened his eyes to look around. Izzy smiled at him as she met his gaze.

I told them all to get some sleep, and that you might be a while.

Izzy, I am wondering if we should contact someone at headquarters before we decide our next move.

If you contact Beta, you are braver than me. I have not contacted Cynthia since we left

Lyndhurst.

Bruno bared his teeth, which seemed to be what dogs did when they wanted to smile. *I don't want to do it, but perhaps we should find out what is going on up there before we decide anything.*

Allan stirred beside him, snuggling into the warmth of his body. Lee snorted and rolled over. Bruno envied them their rest.

Okay. The sooner you do this, the sooner you can sleep. Izzy's tone was sympathetic, and he appreciated the support.

Reaching out with his senses, Bruno found a pocket of magic and drew it to himself. He searched for more and added it to his store. This would be a long conversation and he wanted to make sure he had enough magic to see it through.

Finally, he could put it off no longer. He called to his friend and mentor.

Beta.

Sigma, is that you? Finally! I've been trying to get hold of you for days.

Already on the defensive, Bruno humphed. *I only spoke to you two days ago. I don't know what all the fuss is about.*

Not long after we last talked, total chaos broke loose here. Alarms went off, and the World Fixers… what a stupid name that is… had something similar going on over there. I don't know what you are doing, but you have to stop it—now!

Bruno took a deep breath before answering. *Beta, we can only suggest things, and once I decided to help Colin break Lee and Izzy out of jail, things sort of snowballed into helping Basia and Johan free Allan. I'm afraid things took on a bit of a life of their own.*

We can go into the rights and wrongs of things after this is over. What we need you to do now is convince Allan to lay low for a while. Keep him quiet so he doesn't fan the flames of rebellion any further, Beta instructed.

I don't think he is going to be a problem for a while. He has been injured and can barely sit up, let alone stand to make any more speeches, Bruno said.

At least that is one less thing to worry about.

Beta!

I hate to be the harbinger of doom, Bruno, but it is chaos here. The timeline is split and monitors from the Time Guardians and Time Fixers are in agreement—war is imminent, and that war is likely to cause the end of mankind on earth.

We may be on the brink of war, Bruno agreed, *but I fail to see how that would result in humanity being exterminated.*

And that is why you should be listening to us and not branching out on your own, Beta admonished. *We have access to more information than you do.*

The rebuke churned Bruno's stomach. He was already afraid their actions

had accelerated the very thing they had been sent to prevent.

Okay, I'll bite, Beta. How do they see this playing out?

The academics believe the world is in such a precarious balance that another couple of nuclear explosions will see the onset of nuclear storms even more violent than the ones after World War Three. It will push the environment over the edge and the earth will become a barren wasteland. It will only be a matter of time before all life dies out.

You can't seriously believe that? Bruno asked, his heart thumping, not wanting to believe what he was hearing.

It fits in with what we are seeing here, Beta said.

Bruno rested his head on his paws, feeling sick to the stomach. *We have to fix this, Beta. We have a plan.*

No, don't do anything. Find a pocket of magic and return everyone home, Beta instructed.

Thea says the only way to prevent this war and save the world is for us to turn ourselves over to Portsdown, Bruno said.

Sigma, you could die in the nuclear explosion. And if you don't, then any magic in the area will be extinguished. None of you will be able to return home. If you leave now, you will have a front row seat to the future, and if you don't, you will be a footnote in history.

Bruno wanted to argue that of course they would stay and fix this, but he knew this was a major decision and he believed that each member of his team should make up their own minds.

I will ask the others and let you know what they say, he finally said.

Well, that is better than nothing, I guess.

Beta, what about Thea and Jason?

They are safe enough underground for the moment. She has asked to be allowed to stay until the point war is declared.

Bruno felt a small glow inside. Thea was staying to help.

Jason has gone off reservation. He told his handler if it was good enough for you to do whatever you wanted, then it was good enough for him, Beta said.

Bruno chuckled. That guy was a moron.

Bruno?

All right, give us until the end of the twenty-four-hour deadline to fix this. If we aren't able to, I will send all those who want to go home at two o'clock tomorrow, he confirmed.

Good. And you?

I don't know, Bruno admitted.

Bruno… we have to…. Beta sighed. *Good luck.*

Thanks, I'm going to need it.

Bruno felt strangely alone after the link was severed. In the past he had relied on Beta's guidance and had followed his lead blindly. It was odd to be taking this first step alone, and in such a critical situation.

Whatever happened, whatever everyone else decided, he knew he would not leave this world to a war he had had a hand in starting. Would the others agree with him?

This time when he opened his eyes, he found Allan staring at him.

'Will you stay and try and sort this out?' the boy asked him.

Bruno started, realising he had not shielded his conversation. *You heard that?*

'Some of it,' Allan admitted.

How much?

'From when Beta said he had been trying to reach you for days.'

So pretty much the whole thing.

'I guess so. Bruno, we have to do everything we can to stop this war. I won't be able to live with myself knowing I caused this to happen.'

This is not all you, not by a long shot… but I understand, and I feel the same. Let's wake the others and see what we can do.

18

A GLIMMER OF HOPE

BRUNO'S COLD, WET tongue swept across Lee's face, waking him instantly from his doze.

'Wha—'

Basia's hand slapped down over his mouth. 'Shh,' she whispered.

Groggily looking around, he remembered where they were—in their tree cave with thousands of soldiers from Portsdown roaming nearby. He nodded, and Basia took her hand away.

'What's going on?' he asked, scanning the faces around him.

'Time to talk turkey,' Izzy said. 'Bruno and I spoke with Portsmouth, Portsdown, and… well… someone with an overview of the whole situation.' She looked pointedly at Roberts and Henry, as if waiting for them to say something. When they didn't, she continued. 'Things aren't looking good. There is a way we can help, but we must all decide whether we want to do what is asked of us.'

For a moment Lee stared at Izzy and Bruno blankly. How could things get any worse than they were now? As Izzy began to explain the situation they were in, he wished he hadn't asked.

When she had finished, leaving out a piece Lee could guess at, that humanity's survival hung in the balance, no one spoke. Lee's instinct was to say, 'Take me home now.' He didn't, though, as he was well aware some of his own actions had led them to where they were now.

Roberts laughed. 'You expect me to believe this is real?'

It was Henry who answered him. '*I* think it is. During the past few hours, strange voices have been floating in and out of my head. Maybe these people can mindspeak to each other. If they can do that, who's to say they can't talk to people further away.'

'I must be the only sane one here.' Roberts shook his head. 'But it doesn't matter. My orders are to take Allan back to Portsmouth, and I am going to do just that. The rest of you can do what you want.'

They all whispered frantic responses to this challenge, then all stopped at once as the sound of a twig snapping filled the air. While they waited for this new threat to pass, Lee peered at the faces of his travelling companions, trying to work out what each of them might decide to do.

When Bruno signalled it was all right to continue, he added, *One at a time. Allan, you go first.*

'I am going to give myself up, and I am hoping some of you will come with me, if only to help me get there,' he said.

'No, you're not,' Roberts responded. 'You are going back to Portsmouth.'

Allan's jaw set. 'I started this, and if there is even a small chance I can prevent thousands of people from dying, then I need to take it.'

'The Commander told me you are important as a symbol for change. He wants you back and I will be taking you,' Roberts argued.

'And that is the very reason he must go,' Henry said. 'With him on the loose, Portsdown will never bargain with us.'

Roberts frowned. 'You're on his side?'

'I am going to go with him to turn myself over, but only if that means there will be peace talks.' Henry confirmed his decision.

'What about the rest of you?' Roberts asked.

'Bruno told me he is going,' Izzy said. 'And if he goes, I must go too.'

'And you?' He looked at Basia, who was glaring at Allan.

Ignoring Roberts, she said to him. 'Soldiers shot you once, yet you stood up and spoke out for change, earning yourself another wound. Maybe it is time to sit back and let others place themselves in the line of fire.'

Allan took her hand. 'That is not who I am, Basia. I believe we must all fight for the changes we want, and I did that. Now things are out of control,

and I can't just walk away and leave it to others to tidy up my mess. I must take responsibility for my actions.'

A sad smile drifted across her face. 'I know who you are, and I didn't think you would do it, but I had to ask.' Raising her head, she finally answered Roberts. 'I go where Allan goes.'

'That leaves you, Lee. Please tell me someone else here has some common sense,' Roberts pleaded with him.

Lee did not answer immediately. He had come here because he felt good about what he and the others had done in the New Forest, preventing the spread of a vicious disease. He had wanted to feel like that again. Instead, they had brought humanity to the brink of extinction. It would be so easy to leave, return home, and let the Time Guardians try and fix this another time.

Unfortunately, like Allan, he found it difficult to walk away from his mistakes. And to make matters worse, he believed in what Allan was trying to do. This world needed to change if humanity was to survive, and if there was a small chance he might be able to help make that happen, he had to try.

'Sorry, Roberts. You're on your own,' he said.

Having taken his stand, Lee's stomach decided to do somersaults, and it took all his willpower not to throw up. His life was on the line here. Not just because he might die, but also because of the even bigger risk that he would be imprisoned in the underground city, unable to return to his home because of the lack of magic.

'If you believe you must do this, then I will leave you here. Alone, I can sneak through the Portsdown lines and be back in Portsmouth within the hour. While I think you are all barking mad, I will do what I can to persuade people to set up the peace talks you all believe will prevent all-out war.' Roberts rummaged in his is pack as he spoke.

Pulling out his water bottle and rations, he passed them to Lee.

'Eat what you can, drink plenty of liquids, and rest until sunrise.'

Lee took a sip of water and passed the bottle around.

Roberts gave his handheld to Henry. 'We are not far from Cosham. Do what you can to get the talks held near the Marriot Hotel on the corner of the A3. It is close enough that you can be first to arrive. Also, no one holds the land, so it is neutral, and the area around it is relatively clear, eliminating chances of a double cross.'

'Thank you,' Allan said. 'We appreciate the advice.'

'And listen to Henry. He's sensible and knows the area like the back of

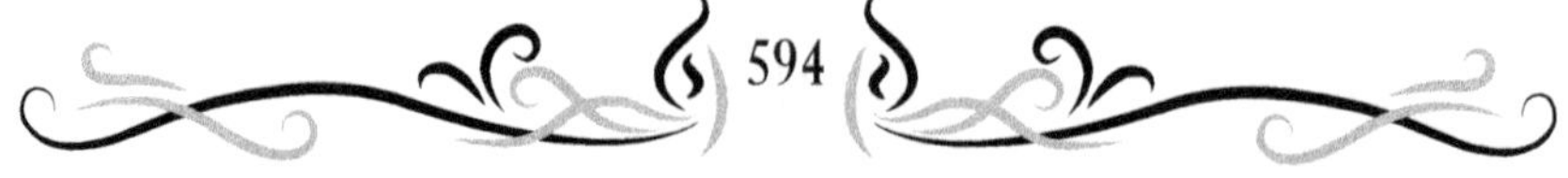

his hand. That is all I can offer. I hope it goes well for you.'

They said their goodbyes, and Roberts slipped quietly through the branches.

'Bruno and I need to make some plans. You guys get some rest,' Izzy said.

'I'll take first watch,' Henry said.

'Can I help with anything?' Lee asked.

Izzy thought for a moment. 'Can you still sense magic in the air, Lee?'

He concentrated and expanded his senses until he felt pinpricks on his skin. He smiled. 'I can.'

'I will get you to join with me while I contact Johan. You can boost my power and make it easier for me to concentrate on the conversation.'

Reaching for Lee's hand, she said, 'Okay, let's get busy.'

IZZY'S HAND WAS warm, and her grip firm. She exuded a calm that helped slow Lee's racing heart.

Johan, can you speak?

The response was immediate. *Izzy, I have been waiting for you. I have my father here too in case we need him, and we have some good news.*

Beside him Izzy relaxed. *I hope you are going to tell me you arranged some sort of peace talks.*

No, but I believe we have the next best thing. My father and the Commander have agreed to meet with two representatives from Portsdown to discuss a cease-fire.

One of the knots in Lee's stomach loosened.

There is only one problem, Johan said. *You all have to be there. They will not meet under any other circumstances.*

His stomach clenched again. He should have known it was too easy. Izzy did not respond immediately, and the silence hung heavy in Lee's head.

Johan, Lee here. How can we be sure this isn't a ploy to draw us out?

Short answer is, we don't, completely. The only reason we are considering it is because one of your troop was there with a man called Tobias.

That would be Thea, Lee said.

Correct, Johan confirmed. *She said to tell you she did her bit, now you must do yours. We took that to mean you had been working with her to bring this about.*

We have, Izzy acknowledged. *We have spoken about it and agreed we will face the consequences of our actions, but we want to choose the place.*

This time Johan was slow to answer. *We can agree to that, within reason.*

Portsdown gave us a list of sites they believe to be suitable. We are to pick one. The deal is each side will send a troop in at 09:30 to secure the area. The meeting will begin at 10:00 sharp.

Roberts suggested the old Marriott hotel in Cosham. Is that on the list?

Johan confirmed it was, and Lee began to believe this plan might just work.

Your way there should be pretty clear, as we have agreed no further troop movements, Johan informed them.

Roberts should be back with you soon, and he will update you on our position in person. I need to go now, Izzy said.

Wait! Did you say Roberts is no longer with you? Johan asked, sending panic down the link. *Damn. We agreed Basia and the Portsmouth militia would not be included in the exchange. Henry was to guide you to look after Allan, and Rodgers was to bring Basia back to Portsmouth.*

Lee was overwhelmed with Izzy's sense of fury and betrayal.

So, you are happy to sacrifice strangers to save yourselves, she spat.

Sorry, Izzy, that was not our intention. We thought the city was only interested in having their own returned, Johan said.

Apart from Allan, we no more belong to them than we do to you. I thought you understood that. Fortunately, your sister has more integrity than the lot of you put together. She and Henry decided they would give themselves up along with us if it meant stopping a war, Izzy said.

Izzy, I'm sorry. I tried to do my best, but no one would listen to me. Please, can we talk about this when you get back?

Lee sensed Johan's confusion and regret, and he was sure Izzy was able to as well.

I think it is unlikely we will be seeing each other again, Johan.

But….

Thank you for all you have done. You can leave the rest up to us now.

The connection was abruptly terminated. Lee turned to find tears streaming down Izzy's cheeks. She wiped them away furiously. 'I cannot believe Jo was happy to hand me over like that,' she said.

Lee squeezed her hand. 'It wasn't Jo, or Josephine, it was Johan, and he probably had no say in the matter.'

She smiled tremulously at him. 'Thank you for trying to make it better. My head understands that, but it doesn't lessen the wound to my heart.'

A wet nose nuzzled its way under his hand, and Lee patted the dog's head. *She will be all right.*

'I will be fine,' Izzy confirmed. 'Okay, everyone, everything is in place. Cease-fire talks are being held at Cosham and we need to be there before the others arrive at 9:30 tomorrow. Henry, can we make it there in time?'

Henry narrowed his eyes and looked at the handheld device Roberts had left for them. 'We will need to leave about 06:00 to arrive in time. That gives us time for three hours sleep before we need to leave.'

'I am not going to be able to walk very fast, so perhaps we should leave at 05:00?' Allan smiled wanly.

'You guys catch some rest. Bruno still needs to talk to Thea. I will keep him company and keep watch,' Lee said.

As the others settled down, bodies close together to preserve heat, he and Bruno moved to the outer edge of the group. The dog lay beside him, and Lee curled his hands in his warm fur.

Do you want me to help you like I helped Izzy? Lee asked.

Please. Mindspeak in a magical limited world is taking a lot out of me.

Lee drew some magic to himself, then concentrated on feeling the warmth of Bruno's body beneath his hand.

Thank you, that is perfect, Bruno told him.

Bruno, perfect timing. I was about to reach out to you. Thea's voice rushed into Lee's head. *Hello, Lee, nice of you to join us.*

Just a quick one this time, Thea. We only wanted to let you know it is on. We will be at the cease-fire negotiations, Bruno informed her.

I knew you would be. Allan is not going to do anything foolish to screw this up, is he?

We are all aware of the consequences of our previous actions. We don't want to place these talks in jeopardy, if indeed they are genuine, Bruno said.

They are genuine, Thea confirmed. *Rioters control much of the underground city, and Portsdown cannot fight a war on two fronts. Tobias will attend representing the moderates, and one of the Generals will be going with him to ensure any agreement will be supported by the Representative Council.*

Good.

See you tomorrow, Thea sent.

Today, Bruno corrected.

Thea winked away. Lee let go of his magic, and leaned back against the branches. He closed his eyes, willing sleep to come, but he was too keyed up. Opening his eyes, he found Allan watching him.

Allan propped himself up on an elbow, wincing in pain as he did, and whispered. 'I can't sleep.'

Basia rolled over and sat up. When she was comfortable, she moved to help Allan into a semi-sitting position where he was able to talk without straining too much.

'Why can't you sleep?' Allan asked as he rested against Basia.

'We may be on the verge of all-out war, and the only thing that will stop it is us turning ourselves over to the enemy,' Lee answered, and they laughed. 'It doesn't do much for my stomach… or my anxiety.'

'I mean to negotiate with them. I hope they will agree to take me, on my own,' Allan said.

Basia tensed, as if she was about to object. Then she shook her head. 'I want to tell you not to be so noble, convince you that we all had a hand in this. But you won't listen.'

Allan smiled and took her hand. 'I would listen to you, but it wouldn't change anything. I believe they will settle for me. Once I give myself up, I will probably not see the light of day again, so I need people to carry on fighting for a better world, for a united Hampshire. I want you to promise me you will do that, Basia.'

Basia caught her lip between her teeth and worried it for a moment. 'I want to make a grand declaration that I will carry on the fight. Not just for you, but because I believe in what you tried to do, but I am just me. I am not sure I can do it.'

Allan turned slightly so he could face Basia. 'I know you, Basia, and I believe you can do this. I am not sure how I can say that after such a short time together; maybe we are soul mates who keep finding each other through time.'

You have no idea how true that is, Lee thought. 'I hope they will let us *all* go, but if they don't, I will help you, Basia. Whatever it takes. I will be there for you.'

Lee, Bruno warned. *You should not make promises you can't keep.*

He ignored the Guardian. 'If we are all awake, why don't we head out. Perhaps if we move now, we can sleep a little before the others arrive.'

Basia frowned. 'Allan should rest a little more.'

'I don't think one hour more is going to make a difference to Allan either way,' Henry said. 'There are painkillers in my pack that should block out the pain but leave him able to walk. They only last for four hours, and I only have two doses.'

He reached into his pack, extracted the medicine, then passed the pills and some water to Allan. 'They are pretty quick acting, so by the time we're packed and ready to go, they should be taking effect.'

As they got ready, Basia kept glancing at Allan, almost as though she couldn't believe she was helping him walk towards capture and imprisonment. When they were ready to leave, she schooled her face into a bright smile and offered her arm to Allan. Lee's heart almost broke at the gesture.

'I don't think Allan believes he will live through this,' Lee said quietly so no one would hear him, a tear slipping down his cheek.

AFTER THEIR ESCAPE through the bush the evening before, their journey to the Marriott in Cosham was a breeze. Henry kept them within the tree line, but far enough away from the Portsdown circle of soldiers that they did not need to worry about being spotted. They made better time than expected, and reached the road in front of the hotel just after six.

There they hit a pinch point. They did not want to give themselves up until they were sure the peace talks were happening, which meant they needed to break through the ring and run across the open ground to the hotel carpark.

As they crouched in the bushes, Henry shook his head. 'I can't see a way through without being seen. Perhaps if we go further round back.'

'By then it will be light and they will spot us for sure,' Lee argued.

'If we can make it to that outcrop, the open ground is only about fifty yards across. Bruno and I could try a "don't see me spell",' Izzy said.

It would be tricky to do it for this many, for that long, Bruno said.

Henry frowned. 'What if you had a distraction? Could you do it then?'

'You're not thinking of doing anything that would result in your capture, are you?' Izzy asked in a way that clearly transmitted she would not agree to any such thing.

Grinning, Henry said, 'I'm not a martyr. No, I thought I would light a little fire to take their attention from the road. I promise to hide well so they won't catch me, and I will try and meet you in the hotel if I can make it through.'

'Perfect,' Izzy said.

Without another word, Henry passed something to Basia, then melted back into the forest. The rest of the group headed towards the cover Izzy had pointed out.

'Right, gather as much magic as you can—you too, Lee. We will need to stay physically connected as we cast the spell for this to work. Basia, can you help Allan across?'

Basia nodded, and they all readied themselves, waiting for a smoke plume to appear to tell them it was time to go. Lee's palms were sweaty. The sky was just starting to lighten. If they waited much longer, this would not work.

A shout rang out into the night, and the forest behind them became a hive of activity.

'Now,' Izzy said, and they moved from their cover.

Lee grinned. It was working. There were no yelling voices indicating they had been seen. No footsteps rushing after them. They were going to make it. Just as they reached the edge of the clearing, Basia tripped and stumbled, almost dropping Allan. Lee rushed forward to stop him from hitting the ground.

'Damn,' Izzy said. 'Spell's gone. Everyone run.'

Lee practically dragged Allan the last few metres, his heart pounding, expecting to be shot at any moment. Fortunately, Henry's fire distraction worked as planned, perhaps even better, as they made it to cover unscathed. Huddled in the shadows of an overgrown garden, scanning for sounds that would indicate they had been seen, they caught their breaths.

They waited a at least ten minutes before Izzy said, 'I think we are okay to move.'

I agree. And if we don't go now the sun will be up, and we will be easier to spot, Bruno added.

Surveying the building, Lee wondered how they would get inside to hide. A functional motel like many others in the pre-holocaust world, it appeared to still be structurally sound, although the windows were boarded up, and it looked desolate and abandoned.

The weary team made their way through the gardens. Round the back of the building, they found a loose board covering a window. Izzy and Lee prised it off while Bruno kept watch.

Lee climbed inside first, and waited while Izzy and Basia propped the board against the wall and helped Allan and Bruno through the opening. Once the girls had joined him, Lee leaned out and hauled the board up, wincing as it scraped up the crumbling brickwork, then pulled it back in place, hiding their entry point as best he could.

They made their way through a darkened corridor to what was once the lobby of the hotel. There were still a few random chairs, and the carpet, although a little mouldy in places, was not too bad.

'This is cleaner than expected—too clean to have been completely abandoned for almost twenty years,' Basia said as she made Allan comfortable on the floor.

'There may still be running water in the kitchens. I'm going to see what I can find.' She walked back the way they came, with Bruno padding behind.

The morning dawned purple-red through a gap in the wooden boards over the doors. Lee peeked through, keeping watch as Izzy took up a position at an uncovered window to the side, able to see through the foliage that had grown over the building.

Basia returned with a jug of water, two white mugs, and a bowl. She put some water in the bowl on the ground and Bruno moved over to drink from it. She handed a cup of water to Allan, and Izzy walked over to drink from the other one while Lee remained on watch. 'You'll never guess what else I found,' she said, winking as she left the room.

She came back a few minutes later with bowls of steaming liquid. 'There was still gas in one of the stoves, and I found some tinned soup. It should be okay to eat.' She grinned and Lee could not help but join her.

He was starving, and he was sure that although the food was probably well past its use by date, it wouldn't harm them. The warm tomatoey liquid filled his stomach and he almost groaned in pleasure. *What a great last meal*, he thought darkly as he returned to his post.

Over the next few hours, they changed positions, taking turns at watching. Boredom began to set in. At around nine, Basia gave Allan the last of the medication for his pain, and he dozed for a while. Lee wished he could do the same, but he was still way too keyed up.

Lee? Bruno's voice popped into his mind. *Something is happening.*

Staring through the gap between the boards, he could just make out a large group of soldiers wearing Portsdown colours enter the carpark. He smiled when he recognised Captain Kiandra and Sergeant Thea as they ordered the troop to form up about twenty metres from the doors.

Moments later a similarly sized contingent wearing mismatched military gear joined them. Roberts ordered them to stand at attention, and went over to talk with Captain Kiandra.

'I think this is the real deal,' Lee informed the others as Basia and Izzy rushed to the window and looked out. 'Roberts and Captain Kiandra are in charge of security, and I would trust both of them with my life,' he added.

What are they doing now? Bruno asked, pacing behind Lee, frustration tinging his words.

'They are pairing up and checking the area. Oh, that's unexpected. An electric car has just pulled up and they are erecting a gazebo and putting tables

and chairs inside.' Lee chuckled. 'I wonder if this is what peace negotiations looked like in medieval times? Tents set in the middle of the battlefield, and all that. All we need are brightly coloured pennants and we will be set.'

'I think you have a romanticised notion of medieval battles,' Izzy responded dryly.

'Has anyone thought about how we are going to leave when it is time?' Allan asked from behind them. 'I mean, we can hardly break through the doors, given they are boarded up.'

'Since you ask,' Lee smiled. 'These doors are boarded up from the inside and held on with nails. I think I can use my knife to quietly prise enough of them out to be able to remove a panel when we are ready to leave.'

Izzy joined him and inspected the door.

'What, don't you trust me?' Lee asked.

'It is not that—well, yes it is that, sort of. It's just this is too important to stuff up our entrance.'

'Thanks for the vote of confidence,' Lee said dryly.

'You are right though. You start working on the nails and I will keep an eye on what's going on outside.'

Lee pulled out his knife and set to work removing every second nail. It was tough, slow work, especially as he had to keep the noise down, and he wished he had started sooner.

'Something is happening,' Izzy said when he was almost done.

He stopped and joined Izzy by the window, leaning his forehead against the cool glass. Cars were pulling up outside, and the two sets of soldiers formed a corridor between them and the gazebo.

Captain Kiandra leaned down and opened the door of the first car. A broad well-muscled man exited. His military bearing told Lee he was probably the General Thea mentioned. He was followed by a slim dapper man, bent with age, who tidied his wispy white hair before following the General to the gazebo, where he took a place beside Captain Kiandra.

The door to the second car was opened by Roberts. The Commander was first to alight, and he was followed by a middle-aged man. If Basia's gasp of delight was anything to go by, this was most likely her father.

Once the formalities were completed, the delegates took their seats and Captain Kiandra and Roberts moved to order their troops to encircle the tent.

After the initial flurry of activity, nothing happened. No one spoke. No one moved.

'What are they waiting for?' Lee asked.

Bruno, if you're here, now would be a good time to show yourselves. Thea's voice entered Lee's head.

He laughed. 'Oh. They're waiting for us.'

Basia went to help Allan to his feet, while Izzy and Lee pulled at the door covering. In spite of all Lee's efforts, it wouldn't budge, no matter how hard they pulled.

'What now?' Lee asked, as the door shuddered. It shuddered again, and they moved out of the way just in time to avoid the wooden panel falling to the floor.

Wide-eyed, they were greeted by a grinning Roberts. 'Well, that could have gone better,' he said.

They all piled out, and a Portsdown soldier patted them down to make sure no weapons were taken into the pavilion. The group slowly walked over to the gathered officials. As they walked past Captain Kiandra, she actually smiled in welcome and said, 'Of course you'd be at the centre of this upheaval, Private Lee.'

Lee grinned back, but couldn't think of anything suitably cutting to say in response.

Just as they reached the gazebo, a shout rang out from where the cars were parked. Everyone turned as one to find out what was going on. Behind a wall of soldiers, Lee couldn't see a thing.

The Commander looked across at Tobias and asked, 'What is this? Some sort of double cross?'

'No, nothing like that. General Wilson, is this your doing?' the dapper man asked.

The general shook his head as the soldiers in front reached for their weapons and moved into attack formation.

Lee's eyes widened in surprise. In front of him stood Jason, brandishing a weapon and yelling something about stopping the fall of civilisation.

'Jason?' Izzy said. 'What in the—'

A shot rang out, and Lee turned to see a red stain spread across Allan's shirt moments before his friend crumpled to the ground, almost in slow motion.

'No!' Basia wailed, dropping to her knees beside him.

Lee took a step to join her, but was pushed out of the way as soldiers moved to support the delegates. Then all hell broke loose.

MORE BODIES PUSHED their way between Lee and Allan. He tried to break through, but each time he was pushed even further backwards. He turned his head, frantically searching for Izzy and Bruno. Where were they? Where they okay?

Bustled to the edge of the crowd, he was in time to see two Portsdown soldiers grab a figure by the side of the hotel. 'Corporal Rodgers,' Lee said in amazement.

Then the amazement turned to fury. He had shot his friend again. This maniac had to be stopped. He charged forwards, only to be hauled back into place by someone grabbing his arm.

'Stand down, Private,' a voice said, and he whirled around to break free only to find himself face to face with Captain Kiandra.

'But he—'

'He will be taken care of, I assure you,' the Captain said. 'But if you rush in there now, it could be you joining your friend. We are one shot away from these talks collapsing.' The Captain's voice was firm, and her grip was even firmer. 'Don't do anything to undo what might be achieved here today,' she said in a voice meant only for him.

Over the shoulder of a Portsdown soldier, Lee saw Captain Rodgers brandishing his weapon and shouting obscenities at anyone who tried to approach him. Then he began babbling about Allan bringing about an end to civilisation.

As he watched the scene unfold, his anger towards Rodgers was replaced by fury at himself. Why hadn't he been more careful? Why hadn't he realised Jason was merely a diversion, and that Rodgers would be the real danger? Jason? Where was Jason now?

He looked all around and found that while everyone else's attention was turned towards the hotel and Corporal Rodgers, Thea had grabbed Jason by the arm and was physically hauling him towards the tree line. The Time Fixer was pulling back, yelling, 'You all got to choose who you supported in this bun-fight! I chose to support Rodgers.'

'You moron,' Thea snarled, reaching for her handcuffs. She snapped one end on her wrist, and the other around Jason's. Once he was secured, she stopped pulling and stood very still. Lee saw the air behind her shimmer.

Jason, his attention still on Rodgers, obviously had no idea what was happening, because when Thea relaxed he did too, thinking he had won. As he did, Thea gave him one final tug and the two of them fell through the portal and disappeared.

As the portal snapped closed, Lee dragged his gaze back to the scene of chaos in front of him. Now both sides had their weapons pointed at each other and accusations were flying. *No,* Lee thought, *Captain. Kiandra is right. Everything has all fallen apart.*

On the ground, Basia cradled a very still Allan, tears streaming down her face. She raised her eyes and met Lee's gaze. She shook her head, and with that simple gesture Lee knew the truth. Third time was not lucky for Allan.

He stumbled and would have fallen except for the Captain's grasp. 'Stay strong,' she said. 'This is not over yet.'

Roberts stood beside Basia, making space for her father to get through. The man reached down and pulled Basia to her feet. He hugged her and said something into her ear. She struggled free of his grasp and turned to look at the soldiers around her, as if seeing them for the first time.

'No,' she shouted. 'No, don't do this. If you stop the talks now, he will have died for nothing. Don't let hatred and fear be his legacy. Show that madman he is wrong, that this is not the end of civilisation, but the beginnings of a new one.'

No one moved. Basia wrung her hands. *Come on,* Lee thought. *You can do this.* As if Basia heard his words, she turned to him. He nodded once, and she drew herself a little straighter.

'Please, we all need this cease-fire,' she pleaded. 'Finish the work you came here to do.'

'She's very compelling,' Captain Kiandra said.

'Will you support her?' Lee asked.

The Captain frowned. 'I will do what the General and Representative Tobias order me to do. Soldiers must follow orders or everything will crumble in to anarchy.' She looked pointedly over to where two soldiers were bundling Rodgers into a car.

'Will you kill us if they tell you to?' Lee asked.

'Let's hope it doesn't come to that,' the Captain said, her lips curling into a smile as she returned her gaze to the scene under the gazebo, waiting for her orders. 'But if it does, I will be sad about it. I commend what you're trying to do.'

With Rodgers removed from the scene, the carpark was eerily quiet. It

was like the hundred or so people there were held captive on a knife's edge, trapped in a moment in time. Then Basia's father glanced at his daughter before walking to the table and sitting down. 'Well, gentlemen, shall we get on with what we came here to do?' he asked.

No one moved. Lee's heart thudded in his chest. This could still go either way. Representative Tobias surveyed the scene, then retook his seat, shooting a meaningful look at the General.

General Wilson locked eyes with the Commander and no one moved. Lee's stomach clenched.

'Show some faith, Lee. No soldier truly wants to go to war. We face death every day, and we will do almost anything to avoid all-out bloodshed among our comrades.' Captain Kiandra's remark was more comforting than it had a right to be.

As if on some secret cue, the two military men turned and took their respective seats at the table. Crisis averted, soldiers began moving back into position. Roberts ordered two of his men to take Lee and Basia into the hotel. Izzy and Bruno suddenly appeared beside Lee.

Where were you? he asked, his worry making the words sound more tart than he intended.

Thea needed a little help making the portal, Bruno said.

'Where do you want us, Captain?' Izzy asked.

'Go inside with your friends. I don't think we will be needing you any more today.'

They didn't need to be told twice.

19

AFTERMATH

ALLAN'S BODY WAS laid under a sheet in one of the conference rooms off the main lobby. Basia followed the soldiers in, and stayed with Allan when they left.

Lee, Izzy, and Bruno sat in the corner where Allan had slept less than an hour ago. Exhausted and defeated, no one said anything. Lee dropped his head into his hands and let the tears flow. Izzy hugged him, and Bruno lay across his lap. When his tears ran out, they stayed like that, drawing comfort from each other.

'We brought a change of clothes and food for you. If one of you wants to come with me to the car,' Roberts said some time later.

Izzy rose to her feet and followed him outside while Allan's two escorts remained just inside the door. To protect them or to keep them in, Lee had no idea, and he was too tired and emotionally drained to care.

So, you opened a portal? Lee asked.

Bruno humphed and laid his head on his paws. Lee ran his hands through the Guardian's coat, somewhat soothed by the action. Bruno appeared to feel the same way as he relaxed against Lee.

Bruno, did we help, or did we just bring things to a head?

The Guardian did not answer immediately. When he did speak, his voice was uncertain, and this concerned Lee.

We had no history of what originally occurred here, and therefore no way of knowing if we made things better or worse, only that we created a number of options that weren't available before. We should find out more in a couple of days, but our role is over. I will be able to take you home and we can put all this behind us, Bruno said.

Lee started. Of course he would be going home soon—Thea had already portalled out. Only, he was not ready to leave. Allan had started something with his speech, and he wanted to be a part of it a while longer. Besides, he was not yet certain what he would be going back to. He glanced at the door they had taken Allan through. Could he leave Basia to do this alone? After all, he had promised her he would be there.

How do you decide when your job is done? Lee asked, buying some time to think.

Normally we leave when history is back on track, but we can't tell that here. I am guessing that when the timeline extends beyond what we could see before, we can consider our job done. What will you do when you go home? Bruno asked, as if he guessed the root of Lee's questions.

You know, I'm not sure. My life was all planned out. I knew who I was and I knew where I was going. After recent events, I'm not sure I want to be a soldier anymore. Not least because I found I am not good at blindly following orders. I don't know how my father's been able to do it all his life.

Given your career path, I think you will end up doing more of the ordering and less of the following, Bruno said with a laugh.

But everyone starts at the bottom, even if they are an officer at the bottom.

You can still change your mind—I mean, you don't have to report for duty for another two months, Bruno said.

True. So many thoughts were running through Lee's mind, it was difficult to catch hold of a single one.

He had no real reason for wanting to rush home, and lots of reasons for staying here. But he wasn't sure if he was ready to make that decision. Yet he knew Bruno was on the brink of suggesting they would need to leave sooner rather than later.

Mixed up with all the worry about his future was a longing to get back to his family. His parents would arrive in England soon, hoping to celebrate Christmas with him and his sister. Ah, Bebe, his twin. He wanted to share this adventure with her so badly.

Bruno, you said when we came here you could take me back to almost exactly the same

time that we left. Is that true no matter how long we stay? Lee asked.

Bruno shifted slightly in his lap. *It is not an exact science, but yes, I can get you back within a few hours of when we left, no matter when we leave.*

Are there any limits on that?

No limits in terms of time travel, Bruno said, *but you wouldn't want to leave it too long. I mean, a month or two is fine. After that, especially at your age, it becomes difficult to explain away the physical changes.*

Physical changes? Lee was curious.

Well... you're still growing and... your facial hair is growing in thicker. And I've noticed your physique has become a little leaner, and you're a bit sunburnt, Bruno said. *That alone will be difficult to explain away in the middle of an English winter.*

Lee laughed, earning a strange look from the Portsmouth guards. *Oh, I see what you mean. Still, if we don't go back straight away, will that cause any other problems?*

Bruno tilted his head to the side, as if to get a better look at Lee. *I guess for me it would. I'm not supposed to stay too long in one place because it might alter history. Your staying would probably do the same.*

If that's your only worry, then I think we'd be okay. I mean, we came here because history and time were going to stop, so there really isn't anything more we can alter.

Lee could almost hear Bruno's mind ticking over as he worked out how big a problem staying on a little longer would be.

Finally, the Time Guardian said, *You know, I think you're right. An extended stay shouldn't make any difference whatsoever, or if I'm wrong and it does alter something, history will right itself anyway. I take it you're seriously considering not returning for a while?*

Lee did not answer immediately. He still has some doubts, but part of him knew it was the right thing to do, given the havoc they had caused here. *Yes. I promised Basia. And… and I believe I can do something more here.*

What about home? And your family? Don't you want to see them? Bruno asked.

Of course he did, but he could wait a few more weeks.

Let me think on it and talk with Izzy. I don't see why we must rush away and if we are in agreement it will be easier to deal with our Councils.

Unless of course we've got it all wrong and the world still ends in the next couple of days, in which case this conversation is moot, Lee said.

Bruno snorted, *Well, that's a lovely thought.* The Guardian rose to his feet. *I'm going to see how Basia is doing.*

Now that he had made his decision, it was like a weight had been lifted. Lee leaned back against the wall and closed his eyes.

VIVIENNE LEE FRASER

THE ROOM WAS dark, and Bruno was pleased dogs were gifted with night vision. He found Basia sitting on an old wooden chair, head tucked into arms that leaned on the table soldiers had placed Allan's body on. He had been covered by a tarp, but Basia had reached underneath to clasp one of his hands in her own.

She didn't move as Bruno settled in beside her, placing his head on her lap.

'I suppose you all think I am mad, grieving so hard for someone I only met a few days ago.'

Not at all. I have met you and Allan in many lifetimes, and in each one you found each other and formed a bond like no other, Bruno told her.

Basia's voice was barely above a whisper when she asked, 'In any of those times, did Allan and I ever end up together?'

Yes, but it was a very long time ago. You were a lady in the English court, and he was the King's apothecary.

A smile tugged at her lips. 'What was I like then?'

Much the same as you are now. You fought against the limited role you were born into, and tried to improve the lives of others. In fact, in many of your previous lifetimes you were known as a force for change.

'I am pleased I was once so strong. I don't believe women can actually make any difference in my time. Or maybe just not this woman.'

I don't believe that is true. I think you can do anything you put your mind to.

She turned her head and gazed into his eyes. 'I made this promise to Allan, and I don't think I can keep it. I am not a leader. I don't think I can stand up in front of others and inspire them to change.'

You did inside the city.

'I was able to do that because Allan was there,' she said

You will have Lee with you, Bruno told her.

She smiled a little. 'I will, but I am not sure that will be enough.'

I believe in you, Basia.

'Wish I did. Perhaps if I had other girls my age stand up and be counted, I might have more confidence….' Her voice trailed off.

Bruno had an idea. *I believe Izzy will be returning to her original timeline after this. Your incarnation is far away, in Australia, another country on the other side of the world. Would you like me to ask her to take you with her so you can see what women are*

really capable of?

'You mean like you brought Lee here?' Basia's voice was uncertain.

Yes.

'But I promised Allan I would carry on his fight.'

As far as the people here are concerned, you would only disappear for a few hours. You can leave tonight, and Izzy will return you before everyone wakes up.

'If I did this, do you believe I would become a better leader?' Basia asked.

I can't promise that. What I can promise is that you will learn more about yourself and be better able to decide whether or not leadership is for you.

Basia let go of Allan's hand, and sat up straight. 'I can't go back to my old life, and I guess it won't hurt to learn more about myself so I can carry on Allan's work. I will go with Izzy, if she will take me.'

BACK IN THE barracks in Portsmouth, Bruno saw Lee and Izzy settled. Basia was spending some time with her parents before her father returned to the peace talks in the morning. Jumping up on a bed, Bruno settled down. It was time to report.

His stomach churned. What would he say to Beta? He had let him down by going off on his own. And by now Theta would have had a chance to convince everyone her story was the only one to be believed. Surely she would have painted him as the bad guy for not following orders and bringing the world to the brink of extinction.

He sighed. He could not put it off any longer, especially as he knew Izzy would be contacting her handler as soon as she had the energy to do so. They had made sure their stories were aligned, and they were best presented close together if their version was to be given credence.

Beta? It's Sigma ready to report.

Sigma, I have been waiting for you.

Hold on, this was not his mentor. The voice was female for a starter, and sort of familiar.

Gamma, where is Beta? Bruno asked.

I am afraid Beta was reassigned—

Because of me? He had nothing to do with anything I did here. Bruno could not live with himself if Beta had been reprimanded for something he had done.

Oh, we know that. No, Beta's work with the Time Fixers during this crisis was

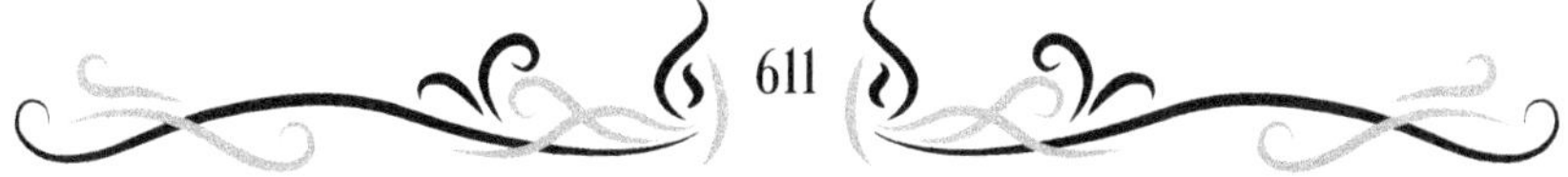

exemplary, and he was promoted to the new role of Time Guardian Ambassador. He took up his post this morning. We felt it better he move sooner rather than later, lest he be tainted any further by your actions.

Oh, that's good, I think, Bruno said, a little uncertain. With his ability to consider all sides in a conflict, Beta would make a great ambassador. Bruno only wished he had stayed around long enough to say good-bye to him.

I am to be your mentor now, and I want you to come home so we can sort out this mess you created, Gamma instructed.

I am not finished here—

The timelines remerged, history is stable, and the world will go on for a good few more years yet. There is nothing more for you to do. In fact, I would say given recent events, the sooner we extract you from the situation the better.

Bruno tried again. *I want to at least stay for Allan's funeral.*

Oh yes, Allan. You know, we offered him a chance to ascend when he was at death's door. He told us given the constraints he saw you work under, he could do more if he was reincarnated. He turned us down. Can you believe it?

Bruno bared his teeth in a smile. Yes, he could well believe it. Events over the last week had him wondering what would have happened if he had made the same decision when he was asked to ascend all those years ago.

We had news he was reincarnated straight away, Gamma continued. *Born this morning to a family in Guildford. His five-year-old brother was overjoyed at the news. We believe his brother to be a reincarnation of Lee. History must love them for their souls to endure for so long.*

Hearing the news warmed Bruno's heart. With those two in the world, and Basia leading the reformers, there was real hope for the future.

So you will come right away.

What about taking Lee home? Bruno had to ask, as it was expected he would.

He was not going to explain to this dour soul that he had agreed to let Lee stay a while longer. Beta might have been persuaded, but he was sure she would not allow it.

The Time Fixers agreed Izzy can take him home before she returns.

Well, that sorted that problem. Now all he needed to do was decide if he cared enough about being a Time Guardian to return and fight for his position.

Sigma?

All right. I will come. Just give me a couple of hours to say my good-byes and head back into the forest, he said.

Report to me immediately on your return!

The connection dropped.

Uncoiling himself from the bed, Bruno trotted over to Lee and gently snuffled by his ear. The boy reached out a hand to push him away. *This calls for something stronger*, Bruno thought as his tongue darted out and washed over Lee's face.

'Bruno. Yuck.'

Good, you're awake.

'I wasn't.'

Lee, I have been called back. I need to leave now.

'What? No! Bruno, you can't go! I thought you were staying too.'

So did I. But I have to go back and face the music. Do you still want to stay here if I am not around?

Lee screwed up his face, then rubbed his hands over it as if rubbing away the last vestiges of sleep. 'Are you heading to the forest, you know, to gather enough magic to make a portal?'

Yes, sort of.

Lee sat up and began pulling on his boots. 'I'll walk with you.'

As Lee sorted himself out, Bruno padded to the next bed. Izzy's eyes were already open, and she reached out a hand to scratch between his ears. It was disturbing how pleasant it felt.

'I heard. Don't worry, Bruno. I will take Basia with me and look after her. And I will make sure I come back in time to pick up Lee if you don't get a chance.'

Thank you, Izzy. It has been a pleasure working with you. I hope we get a chance to do so again. Perhaps I will try to join you and Basia in Winchester.

'Back at you, Bruno-Trouble-Lala.' She laughed and gave him a final pat between the ears.

The cool breeze off the ocean ruffled Bruno's coat as he and Lee walked along the docks towards where the forest met the sea. They could not go out of the protectorate boundaries as the town was still circled by Portsdown soldiers, although there were fewer of them and they were less heavily armed.

Are you sure you don't want to go home? Bruno asked.

'I will be fine. Izzy told Basia they are going to leave tonight, and she will have her back before morning. If I change my mind, she will portal me back then. Otherwise, she will send someone to check on me once a week until I am ready to leave, just as you would have done.'

Sounds like you don't need me around anymore. Bruno hated sounding so sulky, but he was surprisingly hurt by how well everyone was doing without him.

'I don't need you, Bruno, but I wish you were able to stay. I thought we were going to make sure things stayed on the right path together. Can't you come back once you have had your telling off? I understand there is enough magic for you to be able to.'

Bruno sighed. *If I did that, the Council would find out you had stayed on, whereas if I don't return, then it will be a couple of months at least before they pick up a deviation in either timeline.*

'Doesn't that also apply to Izzy?'

Her people are a little more loose about these things, so she should be able to get away with leaving you here for a little longer, Bruno said.

'Oh. So this is really good-bye?' Lee's voice wavered.

I am afraid so, Bruno said, stopping at the boundary.

'I don't know what to say. I'm going to miss you, and thanks for bringing me,' Lee said, his words charged with emotion he could not articulate.

You're thanking me for almost getting you stranded or killed in an apocalyptic future? Bruno laughed.

'Life is never dull with you around. No, seriously. I will miss you. And good luck. I hope we get a chance to meet again. If not in this life, then in another.'

Bruno was swept into a hug, one he was strangely reluctant to leave.

Sigma, it's time.

I must go, Lee. I hope it goes well for you, both here and when you return home. I know whatever you choose to do, it will be the right thing for you, and for the world.

Bruno walked across the dock and down to the shore, not able to look back, tears streaming down his face. The water swirled around his feet and he leapt in.

HER HAND COULD still feel the brush of Bruno's fur as she rolled onto her back and wiped the tears from her eyes. How had that dog managed to get under her skin? She had thought her shell strong enough to keep everyone out.

Izzy calmed her breathing and forced her sadness to the back of her mind. It would not do to speak with Cynthia when she was so emotionally charged. Just in case the Council denied her request to return to her original life so she could reconfirm her commitment to the Time Fixers, she wanted to have her thoughts and arguments marshalled.

Cynthia, hello?

Oh, Izzy, sorry, I wasn't expecting you quite so soon. Can you wait a moment?

The connection was muffled, and Izzy thought she heard her mentor saying, 'Sorry, Beta, I have to take this. Can you pop back later?'

Izzy?

Yes, I'm here, Izzy said.

I'm not sure whether to yell at you for your actions, or hug you for extending the timeline. Cynthia's voice sounded amused, so Izzy knew she was in the clear.

If I get to choose, I go for option number two.

Cynthia laughed. *Isolde, you are truly exasperating.*

There was a fondness in Cynthia's voice under all the scolding, bringing a smile to Izzy's face.

Is there even any point in getting you to report formally?

You mean, come back to headquarters? Izzy asked.

Yes.

Izzy grimaced. *I will if you ask me to, but you had sort of promised that after this mission….*

Cynthia's sigh was loud and heavy over the connection, transmitting the weight of her feelings. *They have agreed, Izzy. You can go. They have given you one month to extend your timeline from the point you decided in London to join us. You must return to London just before your death.*

It was all Izzy could do to stop herself from clapping her hands in glee.

Before then you must return Lee to his time, then you can return once you can gather enough magic to go back that far in the timeline, Cynthia instructed.

I will fulfil my promise to return Lee, Izzy confirmed, not feeling at all obliged to inform her mentor of the deal she had made with Bruno. That reminded her.

Cynthia, have you got something going with Bruno's mentor Beta?

Cheeky! Perhaps we should be following the "don't ask don't tell" rule here. Unless, of course, you want to go over some of your decisions over the last few days back here in headquarters.

Smiling, Izzy said, *Point taken.*

Off with you now. I have things to discuss with our new Ambassador. We will talk in about a month, although you can always contact me before then if you need to.

Bye, Cynthia.

Izzy was smiling as she swung her legs off the bed. Lee was coming back through the door as she pulled on her shoes.

'You ready to go?' he asked.

'Yep, I'm going home. Back to my dingy bedsit in London, to be precise.'

He wrinkled his nose. 'Couldn't you think of somewhere nicer to take Basia?'

Laughing, Izzy said, 'It's easier for boys, this time travel thing. How do you think Basia and I would do walking around London in 1913 in these?' She swept her hand down, highlighting the combat trousers and shirt she wore.

'Oh, I guess not so well,' Lee said. 'You might gather some attention.'

'And not good attention as we will be right at the peak of the suffragette movement, when women who dressed like men were often brutally attacked.'

'I will miss you,' Lee said.

Izzy's heart melted a little more at his comment. She would miss him too. Dammit, what had happened to the shell of indifference she had built around herself? Impulsively she gathered Lee into a hug. 'I have to go. Stay safe. Basia and I will be back before you know it.'

She pushed him away, and Lee's lopsided smile was the last thing she saw as she rushed from the room.

Basia was waiting at the edge of the encampment where they had agreed to meet on the opposite side of the protectorate where Bruno had already made his portal. Izzy was pleased they had prepared for the worst when making their plans on the way back from Cosham.

Basia pulled her cardigan around herself. She looked nervous.

'Are you having second thoughts?' Izzy asked.

'Yes.' She shook her head. 'No. I'm just a little… scared.'

'That is perfectly normal. We all are, our first time.'

'Will it hurt?'

Smiling, Izzy took the girl's hand and led her into the forest. 'No, but it's not pleasant. I am told it helps if you hold your breath as you walk though.'

Quickly gathering her magic, Izzy swept her hand in a circle to create the portal. Without a backwards glance, she pulled Basia close and stepped through before the girl could change her mind. As the portal closed behind her, all she could think was, *Wait for me Josephine, I'm coming home.*

BETA SETTLED INTO the 1970s style sofa and accepted the drink Cynthia held out towards him.

'How are you settling in?' she asked.

He shifted slightly as she sat down, still not used to being in a true physical form.

'It is odd, but your people have made me welcome. Perhaps more so than Gerald will be finding back at Time Guardian headquarters.'

They laughed at the shared joke.

'So, Izzy has gone?'

'I believe so. We cut contact with our people taking the opportunity of recommitment. It allows them to fully emerge themselves in their old lives.'

'And I hear from Gamma that Sigma is back at headquarters, being hailed as a hero by all accounts.' Beta smiled, happy his protege was finally getting some recognition for his work.

'Alpha must be spitting tacks,' Cynthia laughed.

'Oh, he is, and that has made this whole adventure worthwhile—that, and… dare I say, meeting you.'

Cynthia's smile turned her face radiant. 'I feel the same.'

Taking his glass from his hand, she helped him to his feet. 'Now we have a bit of time, I want to show you some of the highlights of my world.'

'You know, you don't need to convince me to stay. I am right where I want to be.'

'I know, Harold, but I can sweeten the deal for you.'

Hearing his name for the first time in hundreds of years brought a glow to Beta's heart, and where Cynthia led him next brought a blush to his cheeks. Yes, he was definitely right where he wanted to be.

ABOUT THIS BOOK

WHEN I WAS fifteen, too many years ago to remember, I wrote my first book—*After the Holocaust.* It was inspired by the movie *Logan's Run*, and was set in America. It had a readership of two, my sister and my best friend. Then it got tucked away in a box when I left home.

Fast forward a lifetime later. On a visit home I found my handwritten books. So much about this series has been about serendipity. I found this old story when I was about to write a jump to the future in the GOT series, and it sparked the idea for Soldier.

I moved everything to England, kept the main story line and Soldier was born.

SUFFRAGETTE
THE GUARDIANS OF TIME BOOK 4

PROLOGUE: TIME FIXER HEADQUARTERS JUST TO THE LEFT OF TIME

SUNLIGHT FALLS ACROSS the bed. Beta squeezes his eyes closed, trying to block it out, but finally the light forces his eyes open. Drowsily rolling away from the offending brightness, he snuggles into Cynthia's sleeping form. His lips curl into a smile. He had forgotten what a pleasure it was inhabiting a body, but over the past week, Cynthia had made it her mission to help him remember.

As if sensing his gaze, Cynthia's lids flicker open, and she smiles sleepily. 'Harold, how come you're awake so early?'

'I guess it's this new body. I was a Time Guardian for so long, and without a corporeal form, we didn't sleep. Now I'm out of the habit.' He sighs. 'Besides, I'm so used to Sigma contacting me at odd hours, I expect him to call at any moment.'

'After having been lauded by the Time Guardians and Time Fixers for preventing the end of the world, isn't he taking a well-earned sabbatical?'

'He is, and I fear it might be a long one. That last mission…. Well… let's just say he has much to think about.'

'Then he won't be calling, and you can relax.' Cynthia cups his face, leans in as if to kiss him, then pauses. 'What is it?'

'Sigma's never taken leave before, and I fear he will find some trouble to get himself into even while he's on a break.'

Chuckling, Cynthia raises herself onto an elbow, and waves of unruly red hair tumble across her shoulders. 'You know, Isolde is a real pain in the butt, but I miss dealing with her little rebellions. Funny, but I think they might actually keep me from becoming complacent.'

Beta reaches out and tucks a stray strand of hair behind Cynthia's ear as he muses, 'That's an interesting spin on a difficult situation.'

Cynthia touches his hand in thanks. 'I find myself hoping that her little jaunt back to her own time will renew her commitment to the Time Fixers.'

Beta scratches his chin, surprise stilling his hand when his fingers rake across stubble. Yes, it's definitely odd being back in a body.

'Just out of interest, what period is Isolde actually from?'

'The turn of the twentieth century,' Cynthia says, then chuckles in amusement. 'Not a great time for women, especially not independent, thinking ones like Isolde.'

'I can imagine. I assume she was part of the suffragette movement,' Beta says, rolling onto his back and linking his fingers behind his head.

'She was, until she became disillusioned,' Cynthia confirms.

'Because of the lack of progress? Or because of the violence?' Beta closes his eyes, and scenes of women being manhandled by constables play in his mind from the one time he had been in England during that period.

He rolls a little as Cynthia pushes herself up and leans against the headboard. 'Both, actually. Back then Isolde could not quite come to terms with the idea of using, shall we say, more militant tactics to change people's minds about giving women the vote. After the supposed suicide of one of her mentors, Emily Davidson, she lost heart.'

Beta opens his eyes, and his brows draw into a frown as he struggles to remember his history. At the time, the newspapers had been scathing of the suffragette who had thrown herself in front of the prince's racehorse. Years later historians theorised that Miss Davidson might not have launched herself forward but could have actually tripped.

'I thought later investigations found Miss Davidson's death was as likely to have been a tragic accident as a suicide.'

A sad smile pulls at Cynthia's lips. 'True, but that came much later. At

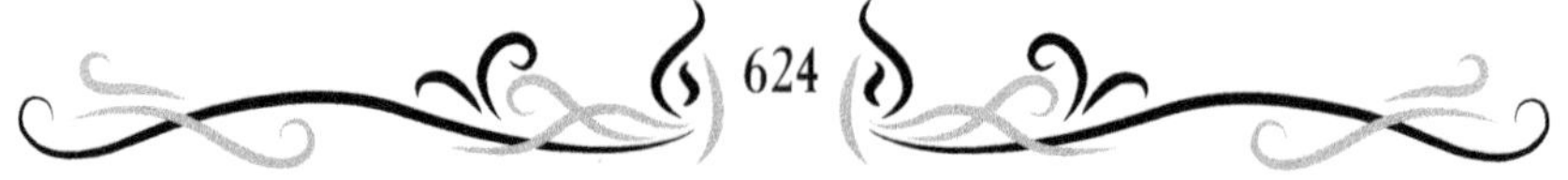

the time, Isolde was torn. Even with such a great sacrifice, the position of women in society seemed unlikely to change in her lifetime. And if they couldn't even get voting rights for women passed in Parliament, how would they ever change society's view on what really mattered to her?'

It takes a moment for Beta to catch on to what Cynthia alluded to. 'Ah, you mean changing how society thought about marriage so she and Jo could be together? I thought things were loosening up after Queen Victoria's death.'

'They were, a little. Perhaps in London among the bohemian set, they would have been able to be together and be accepted.' Cynthia's shoulders rise in a shrug. 'In the rest of the country, though, things had changed very little.' She sighs. 'Without the love and support of her soulmate, Izzy was cast adrift and was looking for some direction. It's such a tragic love story.'

Beta rolls over towards Cynthia. 'So, she became disgruntled and joined the Time Fixers?' he prompts.

'We offered her a place, and she didn't have many options at the time. She was living in London, and her only friends were in the movement.'

He places a hand on her thigh and gives a gentle rub of support. She reaches down and wraps his fingers with hers. Her grip tightens, and her green eyes shimmer with unshed tears as she says, 'She couldn't bear to return to her home in Hampshire because Jo was about to marry another.'

He gives her a moment to wipe the tears from her eyes. She sniffs and releases his hand. 'That's why Basia could not have chosen a better guide to take her back in time.'

Unable to make the connection between Izzy's love life and the girl from their last mission in a dystopian future going back in time, he asks, 'How so?'

Cynthia runs a hand through her hair, but it drops back over her face. Irritated, she reaches over and grabs a hair-tie from the bedside table. As she pulls her tresses back into a loose ponytail, she says, 'They have both lost their loves, although obviously Basia's Allan was shot, and he died. Then there's the way both of them are searching for a way to move forward and build meaningful lives in the wake of their loss.'

Silence falls heavy in the room as Beta's thoughts turn to Basia. Within the space of a week, the young woman had met the love of her life and followed him halfway across Hampshire, only to have him literally die in her arms like something out of an old movie. Suddenly a thought creeps into his head, and he sits up, turning to face Cynthia.

'I thought Izzy said something about seeing if she could make a life with

her Jo, and that was why she wanted to rejoin her timeline. Did she change her mind?'

Cynthia shakes her head. 'No. She decided to spend a little time in London with Basia first. The idea was, when Basia returns to her timeline, Izzy will go down to Winchester and see if she can pull together the threads of her life.'

'Oh, so she's a Hampshire lass. That explains why Sigma kept running into her on his missions down there.'

'She has always had a soft spot for that area, and, well, I guess she had a certain person she wanted to keep tabs on throughout her reincarnations.'

'Jo?' Beta asks.

'Jo, John, Johan, Josephine—it's all the same to her. Still, it was Josephine she lost her heart to, and Josephine she wants to be with.'

Beta's eyes widen as the full weight of Izzy's plight hits him. 'Now I understand her a little better. Her desire to shake up the world has its roots in her love for a woman she could never have.'

Cynthia nods again. Then she covers his hand with hers as if the touch gives her strength. 'Unfortunately, when she time travelled with us, she found out that even once women had the vote, it would still be a long time before love between two women would be accepted by society.' Cynthia smiles wanly and sighs. 'As I said, a sad story, but not one we can do much about.' She squeezes his hand. 'So, enough of this maudlin talk—what is on your agenda for today?'

'More meetings to sort out communication protocols for joint missions. And you?'

A grimace settles on Cynthia's face as she says, 'I have an appointment with Jason and his parents. I hope to persuade them to take him home and keep an eye on him while he undergoes retraining for a head office role.'

'You want him working in mission control?' As he speaks Beta is sure his expression mirrors Cynthia's grimace. To him, Jason is a bad egg, and the Time Fixer should be thrown in jail for what he did—fatally shooting a key player on the first ever Time Fixer/Guardian mission, a person who was instrumental in saving humankind from annihilation. And if they threw away the key, well… he'd be okay with that as well.

A finger pokes him in the ribs. 'Hey, are you listening?'

'Sorry, I was miles away.' Beta smiles and pats her hand.

'I was saying I don't really want Jason out and about at all, but at least if he's in head office, we can keep an eye on him.'

It's Beta's turn to laugh. 'I guess that's one way of looking at it, but wouldn't you prefer him out of the Time Fixers altogether?'

Cynthia snorts. 'Of course I would—'

'Hey, they won't foist him on us, will they? I mean, it's difficult enough to set up this joint unit as it is….' Noticing Cynthia's furrowed brow, he stops. They wouldn't do that… couldn't do that… could they?

'Unfortunately his family have built up a lot of influence in the Time Fixers over the years, so I really can't say. What I do know is no other team leader wants the man who killed Basia's Allan and nearly brought about the end of history on their team.'

Cynthia picks at the duvet cover with her other hand, a sure sign she is bothered about something.

Wanting to ease her burden, he quickly glances at the clock before snuggling back down in bed. He half rolls over and pulls Cynthia into his arms. 'Enough work talk. We still have some time before we're required elsewhere, don't we?'

She leans close to him and whispers, 'We most certainly do,' before covering his lips with hers.

1

WELCOME TO LONDON

BASIA'S NOSE WRINKLES with distaste as the smell of London hits her in all its decaying glory. She had been so excited about travelling back to a period in history she adores in books that she hadn't considered her imagination might be holding on to a sanitised version of reality.

The next assault to her senses is the noise. The loud, bustling background sounds of people moving in the underground city of Portsdown had been a surprise for someone growing up on a farm. Here, in early twentieth-century London, her ears are assaulted with the clamour of goodness knows how many people going about their daily business. The calls of street vendors, the din of machinery, and the sounds of moving vehicles have merged into an ear-splitting racket.

Isolde pulls her from the alleyway they appeared in and into the hustle and bustle of a main thoroughfare, giving her eyes a view of what her ears have been telling her. There are people everywhere, and the street is full of motorised buses, horse-drawn carriages, and a handful of cars. Her jaw drops at the sight of the vintage cars—only they aren't considered vintage here. Isolde yanks on her arm, pulling her out of the way of a car turning down the alley they had just left, and her jaw snaps shut.

THE GUARDIANS OF TIME: SUFFRAGETTE

Izzy drags Basia back onto the footpath. 'You're not in Kansas now, Dorothy.'

'Huh?'

'I guess that's a little before your time,' Izzy says as she leads the way through the throng of humanity crowding the street.

Basia has never seen so many people in one place before, not even when she had been in Portsdown, and they are all staring at her and Izzy.

'We have to go home and get changed,' Izzy says, scanning the street, her lips pursing as her gaze falls on a couple men who are watching them. 'We're attracting too much attention dressed like this, and with recent suffragette activity on the rise, there are some who would not think twice about attacking us for dressing in male attire.'

'You're joking, right?' Basia asks. Izzy turns and directs a frown her way. 'All right, you're serious, but surely we're not in any real danger.'

'We could be. Look, let's just go home, and I will explain there,' Izzy says, tugging urgently at her arm.

Suddenly this little trip back to London's past seems less like an adventure and more like risking her life again. This is meant to be a fact-finding mission for Basia to learn how the suffragettes led a social change movement, not a dance with death.

Okay, it's also a chance for her to recuperate and mend her heart after a life-changing week—a chance to take stock of her life and to decide where she wants to go from here. It's hard to believe that it was only a few days ago she was a farm girl. Her daily routine in a post-apocalyptic Hampshire had been boring, her days taken up with learning to be a medic, reading, and bemoaning just how boring her life was.

In a single week, she had helped a team of time travellers save the world from ending. She had promised the man she had hoped to spend the rest of her life with that she would carry on his work uniting the different factions of survivors, therefore ensuring the continuation of humankind. It's been a lot to process.

Leadership isn't a mantle she wears easily, which is why Isolde—or Izzy, as she prefers to be called—had agreed to take her back to the turn of the twentieth century. She wanted to introduce Basia to some of the people working in the women's movement so she might learn how even the most mild-mannered person might change the world.

'Harlots! Think you can replace us men, do ya?'

Basia's head whips round as if pulled by the anger in the words, and her

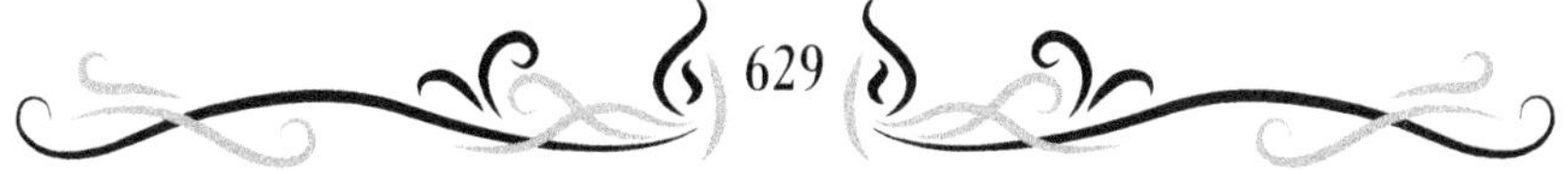

eyes focus on a group of about five boys around her age peeling away from the horse-drawn cart they're loading. As they stride towards Izzy and herself, they emanate such menace that everyone clears out of their way.

Izzy tightens her grip until Basia's fingers complain. 'Run!' she commands, and Basia has no choice but to follow.

Her feet thud against the hard, uneven stones of the London streets as they dodge through the mass of people. Some move out of their way, but many attempt to hinder them, perhaps hoping their pursuers will catch them up and teach them a lesson.

As the boys gain on them, Izzy turns down an alley, and Basia gasps in panic. It's a dead end. She stops, pulling Izzy to a halt in front of her. 'We can't go down there. We'll be trapped.'

'Come on,' Izzy urges, tugging at her hand again. When Basia doesn't move, she lets go and says, 'Your being here isn't going to work unless you trust me.'

Glancing over her shoulder, Basia sees the shadows of their pursuers as they enter the alley. Something hits her shoulder. 'Ouch.'

'We have you now,' one of their attackers brays, his voice echoing off the buildings, adding to the menace.

All right, trust Izzy it is, then. Basia takes off, following her friend as she streaks between the towering alley walls. *I hope she has a way out of this.* They're almost at the end when Izzy pulls her into an opening.

Pushing Basia in front of her, Izzy turns and slams the wooden gate closed before ramming an enormous lock across. Leaning against the brick fence, Basia's chest rises and falls at a rapid pace as she tries to catch her breath. Fists pound the wooden planks in frustration, but the bolt holds. *We made it. We're safe.*

'C'mon, youse can't stay in there forever,' a voice shouts in frustration.

Basia looks at Izzy, her eyes sharp with amusement as her mouth pulls up in a smile, and the girls burst into laughter.

'Hey, this ain't no joke. You get out here and face up to what's coming to you.'

The new command sets them off again and results in more banging of fists against wood. Drawing in great gulps of air, Basia quells her laughter, then pushes herself off the wall and turns in a circle, checking out her surroundings.

They are within a gated yard at the back of a dwelling. The brick walls on either side are taller than she could easily reach, and in front of them is a three-storeyed brick house. Directly opposite the gate that had saved them

is a stout wooden door—and it's firmly shut. They may have avoided a beating, but there's no way out.

Their only option is to hope the boys tire of waiting and leave. Hopefully that happens before the owner of the house finds them camped out in the yard.

'We're trapped,' Basia groans, giving voice to her fear.

'No we're not.' Izzy grins. 'Have a little faith.' She reaches up to dislodge a brick near the gate. Her fingers disappear and return holding a key.

'We're breaking in?' *Great, my first day in London, and I'm already a criminal.*

Izzy chuckles. 'Not exactly. This is where I live. I leave this key here for emergencies.' The wooden gates rattle as the thumping grows more vigorous. 'And I would say this is an emergency, wouldn't you?'

Izzy turns the key in the lock before letting Basia into an empty kitchen. A fire crackles in a coal range, but the room is otherwise silent. After closing and locking the door, Izzy joins her.

'This room doesn't look much different to our kitchen on the farm back home,' Basia says, allowing her amazement at the similarities to show.

'Mrs Gardiner is thinking about getting a gas oven, but it will be a while before we get any running water inside round this area,' Izzy responds as she pushes Basia into a dark, narrow corridor.

The inside of the house smells of boiled cabbage and something else… something greasy. Basia wrinkles her nose in distaste. She can't see where she's going and takes tentative steps along the carpeted floor.

Izzy pushes past her impatiently, leading them up three flights of narrow stairs. It's all so odd and unfamiliar, and it has Basia questioning her decision to leave her own time to come to this dismal place.

I should go back.

As soon as the words enter her head, her stomach knots.

No I shouldn't. Ooh, I hate this uncertainty.

Although she had agreed to become part of the rebellion when the boy she fell in love with was killed, she has never been certain she's the right person to reunite their war-ravaged world. Before she commits to such an important role, she needs time to adjust to the changes in her life—and time to mend her broken heart.

Unable to bear the constant sympathy of her family and friends, Basia had jumped at the chance to travel back in time to learn a little of how the politically savvy females in the early twentieth century had developed as they fought for women to get the vote.

Running away now would not solve her problems, and it won't bring Allan back. Squaring her shoulders, Basia lifts her chin and whispers to herself, 'I will find a way to help heal our world, and in the process, I might heal myself.'

'What was that?'

'Nothing,' Basia pants, concentrating on placing one foot after another as she follows Izzy up the narrow stairs. 'Just wondering how much further.'

'We're here,' Izzy says, stopping on a small landing.

Basia joins her, trying to catch her breath while Izzy searches for her key.

'Isolde, is that you? I did not expect you back so soon. Did you get what you needed for the story?'

Izzy leans over the banister, and Basia follows suit. 'Hello, Mrs Gardiner. Yes, I did. I am just here for a quick change of clothes before taking my notes to the paper to see what they can do with it.'

'I see you have a friend with you.' The tall, black-clad woman peers upwards, trying for a better look at Basia, who takes a step in behind Izzy so the woman won't notice her strange clothes.

Izzy half turns, a questioning look on her face. Shrugging, Basia thinks, *Don't ask me. I have no idea how best to explain why I'm here.*

'Ah yes, this is… um… my friend Barbara from school. I bumped into her on the train back.'

'Ah, another of you girls taking up a new life in London.' The woman catches Basia's eye. 'I am afraid I have no spare rooms—'

'It is all right, Mrs G. She can stay with me for a few days until she finds her feet.'

Mrs Gardiner frowns, shakes her head, then says, 'Mmm, just for a few days, mind, and you will pay extra if she joins us for meals.'

'Of course.' Izzy turns and bundles Basia back into the shadows before opening the door behind them.

Basia is surprised to find herself in a well-lit attic room. It's clean and tidy, if sparsely furnished. In one corner is an old cast-iron double bed with a faded quilt on top. Under the dormer is a desk covered in a shocking explosion of books and papers. Behind the door is a large wardrobe with drawers at the bottom. The only thing in the room that isn't strictly essential is the large multicoloured rag rug on the floor.

Once the door is firmly closed, Basia turns and asks, 'Barbara? Is she made up or a—'

Izzy places a finger over her lips to silence her, opens the door a smidgen,

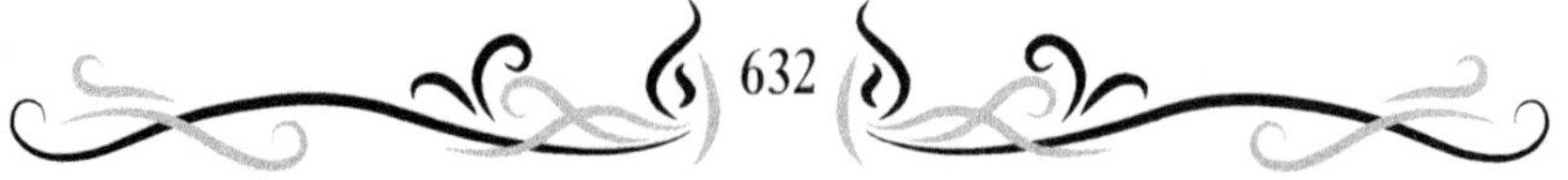

and listens at the gap before closing it again. 'Mrs Gardiner is a great landlady, but she does like to snoop.'

She strides to the wardrobe, opens it, and starts rifling through clothes. 'Basia is a name that would raise questions, and we don't want to draw attention to you. I had a friend at school called Barbara. The name is close enough to yours, and your accent is pretty generic English, so it should work.'

'Okay, that makes sense.'

Izzy isn't finished. 'Also, you need to not talk too much. You know far more about many things than is right for a girl in this day and age, so your saying little is our best option. Also, speech in this time period is a little more formal than you're used to.'

'I've read lots of books, so I think I can wing it,' Basia says, more than a little put out.

Izzy barks a laugh. 'Only lower-class people use contractions like "I've", and "wing it" is not a concept people will know. Fortunately, Barbara was a fairly shy, quiet girl, and I commented on this a little to my friends in London, so no one will be surprised if you don't say much.'

'Am I to be invisible?' Basia's brows draw down into a frown. 'How am I supposed to learn anything if I'm in the background?'

Izzy's shoulders rise in a shrug. 'You're asking the wrong person. It's a shame Bruno—I mean Sigma isn't with us. He maintains that a Time Guardian taking animal form can learn more than one appearing as a human because they can listen and observe without anyone noticing them. I can't change you into an animal, but we're fortunate that I came from a time when it is not unusual for a girl to be shy and retiring.'

'All I can do is try.' Basia sighs, not in the least certain she will be able melt into the background.

Izzy drops some clothing onto the bed, and Basia picks through it, shaking her head as she imagines trying to wear such strange things. Finally, she asks, 'What are these?'

'Underthings.'

As she holds one piece up, Basia's eyes go wide. 'Is this a corset? Do I have to be tortured into it?'

'Of course not. It's laced to support you like a bra. It doesn't need to be tight.' Izzy adds shirts and a skirt to the pile, then rummages around for boots.

Glancing sceptically at Basia's foot, she hauls out a pair of black boots right from the back of the closet. 'These belonged to the girl who had the

room before me. She forgot them when she packed up. I don't know why I kept them, but now I'm pleased I did.'

The next half-hour is spent helping each other into appropriate clothing, and then Izzy finishes by styling their hair into loose buns. As Basia pulls on the surprisingly comfortable and not too badly fitting boots, Izzy retrieves two short jackets out of the wardrobe, handing one to Basia.

'Right, we're ready,' Izzy says.

'For what?'

'I have some savings, but we need some more money if we are to eat while you're here. I seem to remember having left some articles behind that I had written. If the newspaper will take them, that should tide us over for a while.'

'THE NEWSPAPER,' BASIA repeats. 'You work for a newspaper? How exciting.'

Izzy shoves some pages from the mess on the desk into a leather satchel. 'No. No newspaper would ever employ a woman. I work for the NUWSS, writing pamphlets.'

At Basia's blank expression, she expands, 'The National Union of Women's Suffrage Societies.'

'Ahh.' Basia nods. 'If you work for them, why are we going to the newspaper?'

'Because the NUWSS doesn't pay enough for a soul to live on, what with prices in London being so high. I do some ghost writing for a journalist friend to make ends meet.'

Basia tilts her head to the side. 'So you *do* work for a newspaper?'

Before Izzy can answer, Basia stands, takes a step, then wobbles precariously.

'Are your boots too big?' Izzy asks, pausing for a moment as she surveys the footwear.

'No, they fit okay. I'm just not used to the heel.'

'Here, let me look.' Izzy drops to her knees and checks Basia's shoes before tightening the laces. 'Try again.'

Basia takes another couple of steps and manages to move a little more gracefully. 'Better, but I prefer my hiking boots.' She looks mournfully at her footwear abandoned by the bed.

Izzy nods. 'Me, too, but we would stand out too much.' She returns to the papers, searching through them for something in particular.

'So, you didn't answer properly… about the newspaper work.'

'Ah. Got it.' Izzy shoves the new page into the satchel with the others. 'I have a friend who oversees freelancers writing for a couple of newspapers. He throws some stories my way sometimes and will also take some of the pieces I write about the suffrage movement. Of course, he prints them under his name. With two of us to feed, I'm going to need a little more work from him.'

'I can do something to help,' Basia offers. Having fought for her independence these last couple of weeks, she isn't keen to give that up.

Izzy raises an eyebrow, and Basia's cheeks heat up. 'All right, I probably can't do much, but I could help write a couple of articles, or maybe check your work. Or I could clean up that desk for you.' She sends Izzy a cheeky grin.

A smile twitches Izzy's lips as she holds Basia's gaze for a second, then nods. 'Actually, you probably could write things up from my notes, but you would need to be careful not to include any spoilers from the future. If you did that, it would free me up to take on some more work and cover any additional costs.'

Feeling a little less like a burden, Basia folds their clothes and leaves them in a pile on the bed while Izzy shoves their boots into the back of the wardrobe. 'Put those clothes in there too,' she tells Basia. 'It wouldn't do to have anyone walk in and see them while we're out.'

While Basia hurries to hide their modern-day clothes in the back of the wardrobe, Izzy lifts the mattress on the bed and takes out a coin purse. She shakes it, making it jingle.

'For emergencies,' she says. 'Room and board are included with the job, but I'll need to pay extra for food for you. Also, if we're to be here for any length of time, you'll need your own clothes. But before we spend, let's go and see if we can make some money.'

After slipping the purse into her bag, Izzy ducks her head through the satchel strap and leads the way out of the room, making sure to lock the door behind her.

As they descend the stairway, Izzy tries to remember how much money she has in her stash. Enough for maybe a few items of clothing and a week of food—then things will get desperate. With the Time Fixers providing everything she needed for so long, she had forgotten how hand-to-mouth her existence in London had been. Now, with an extra mouth to feed and clothe, they would have to be careful with their coins.

The front door opens directly onto the street. The two girls pause for a moment before exiting, making sure the coast is clear. Checking the busy

street, they find no sign of the boys who'd followed them. With their change of clothes and hair, Izzy and Basia will blend in with the rest of the Londoners and will be unlikely to draw additional attention to themselves.

As they step out, Basia stumbles, bumping into a gentleman walking by.

'Sorry. I—' she starts to say but is silenced by the glare he directs down his nose at her.

Izzy slips her arm through the other girl's. 'Best we walk together until you get used to your new footwear.'

'And this cursed long skirt. The corset may not be tight, but I feel like I'm walking with a rod up my back,' Basia complains. 'How did people wear this all the time?'

Izzy strides past the alleyway and is surprised to see a couple of their pursuers camped out by the gate. One of the boys catches her eye, but he doesn't make a move towards them or show any signs of recognition. Izzy relaxes and answers, 'They do not know any better.'

As they stroll through Spitalfields towards Fleet Street, Basia starts to lag behind. At first Izzy thinks it's because of her boots but soon realises it's actually because she's gawping at everything that moves. Her face shows every reaction to the bustling early twentieth-century London street, and people are beginning to notice.

'Basia,' Izzy whispers. When the other girl doesn't respond, she jerks her arm, and Basia slowly turns her head. 'Basia, get a grip. You look like you just landed in London from outer space.'

'I feel like I have,' Basia whispers back, unable to stop herself from turning to follow every new sight. 'This is not at all like I expected it to be. It's so… dirty… and run-down. Not at all grand like in my novels. And the women—they look so tired, not glamorous at all.'

Izzy chokes out a bitter laugh. 'Most women alone in London can not afford to live the high life. Spitalfields is not, shall we say, the best part of London. It's all I can afford, given it comes with the job. And in spite of how the area might look, Mrs Gardiner runs a respectable house.'

It's Basia's turn to chuckle. 'I knew the books I read showed a more upper-class way of life, but I had no idea so many people lived like this.'

'This is not as bad as some areas. And there are some great things about living around here, like the local teahouse,' Izzy reassures her. 'But you must try to blend in. A woman who looks lost in London is a target for all kinds of bad people.'

'Oh, yes, sorry. It's just….'

'I understand. Your first few hours in a new time period can be overwhelming. And I guess London is not the easiest place to drop into.' Izzy pats her hand reassuringly before leading them onwards.

Basia manages to keep up this time, and, without the need to check on her friend, Izzy imagines what it would be like to see London through Basia's eyes. The sheer number of people must be scary and, at the same time, quite exciting. Then her eyes latch onto the things that had made her discontented when she had lived here before: a man striking his wife and no one bats an eye; the gaunt woman selling flowers, wearing a dress more patches than fabric, her eyes lowered to the ground so no one sees her shame.

Then there are the less obvious things. The fact that there are more men than women out and about because men have business to take care of and women should be at home, the way men walk the streets as if they own them, and the way women move out of their way as if in acknowledgement of the fact. Her chest tightens with anger, but experience has shown her there is little she can do to change any of this.

As they draw closer to Fleet Street, the number of women decreases, and those they see are dressed substantially more elegantly. Their dresses swish in the way only expensive fabrics do, and their heads tilt with confidence, showing off their ornately decorated hats. Izzy tries to ignore them, but she remembers that not so long ago she walked like that, assured of her superior place in society.

Fleet Street itself is a little quieter, but the air is vibrant with activity, and for a moment, Izzy allows herself to dream about what it would be like to actually work here. To go into the newspaper office, receive her assignments, then head down to the cafes or pubs with the other journalists when her work was done.

She sighs. It will be years before women are admitted to respectable newspapers as reporters, and many more before they'll be allowed to report on anything more than society events or bake-offs. She should be grateful her work is published, even if it is under someone else's name.

STOPPING OUTSIDE THE door of a particular establishment, she waits until she catches the eye of the porter. He recognises her and calls to one of the runners lazing on a bench just inside the door. 'Go find Mr French for the lady, and be quick about it.'

The porter turns back to her. 'Shall I tell him you will be in the usual place, miss?'

Izzy nods, and the porter smirks. He believes their liaison is of a romantic nature, and he's happy to help them sneak about. Perhaps he even believes she's married and is meeting Lionel on the sly.

She wonders briefly if he would be so quick to get Lionel for her if he knew theirs was mostly a business relationship, and that a love affair with a woman was the furthest thing from her childhood friend's mind.

Her grey mood lifts at the look of sheer delight on Basia's face as she leads her into a teahouse a little further along the street.

'Izzy, this is delightful. This is exactly what I imagined London to be like. I feel like a heroine from one of my books.'

Basia's eyes sparkle as she scans the cake display, and a smile pulls at her mouth as she studies the women and a smattering of men seated at the tables. Izzy doesn't have the heart to tell her this isn't even one of the better places to take tea.

Gently pulling Basia behind her, she finds an empty table, and they are already seated with tea and cakes ordered when Lionel enters.

'Lee?' Basia whispers quizzically as Izzy stands to accept Lionel's kiss on her cheek.

'Lionel, this is my friend Barbara, from school. Barbara, this is my oldest friend and benefactor, Lionel.'

'I guess from that introduction that your father still has you cut off and I am paying for tea,' Lionel says as he takes Basia's hand and raises it to his lips. 'I am delighted to meet you, Barbara. Isolde has told me absolutely nothing about you, but then, she never tells anyone anything. However, I am not going to let that stop us from becoming the best of friends.'

He takes a seat as Basia continues to stare at him. Izzy kicks her under the table.

'Ah, yes. Isolde has mentioned you, and I am pleased to finally put a face to the name.'

Lionel's eyebrows rise. 'She told you about me? I wonder why.'

Disaster is averted when their tea arrives, and the trio busy themselves with drinks and food. When the waiting staff departs, Lionel appears to have forgotten his chagrin over having been discussed. 'I am afraid I am unable to stay for long. I only came because I have the perfect assignment for you, and I need you to start on it today.'

'First things first,' Izzy says. 'I need to know if you can use any of these.' She reaches into her satchel and draws out some pages.

Lionel briefly reads through the pile. He holds on to one and gives the others back to her. 'This one on the conditions of women pieceworkers I can use alongside another I have on the tailor's guild complaining their income is being reduced by the increase in clothing factories.'

'Lionel!' Izzy's tone is threatening. 'No. It will take away the focus from women doing piecework for pennies.'

'Trust me, Isolde, I will not show the women in a bad light. I simply wish to better highlight how changes in the garment industry are affecting a number of the working poor.'

Izzy relaxes and asks, 'The usual rate?'

Lionel nods, and she takes a sip of tea before pulling out a final piece of paper from her bag. 'I have this. It is an exclusive.'

As Lionel reads it, he turns white. 'Isolde… I… you know I….'

'I was there, Lionel. This is a true eyewitness account.'

Lionel sighs, runs a hand through his hair, then pushes the page back towards Izzy.

'If you had come to me a week ago, before other papers printed the official version, I might have had a chance of convincing my editor. If this is really the truth—that Emily Davidson tripped and was trampled to death—then this is a great tragedy.'

'It is the truth. I swear it. The version the papers are running—that she threw herself in front of the prince's horse during the Derby—is a lie. It is propaganda designed to malign the masses against us.'

Lionel reaches for the paper, then draws his hand back. 'If it were up to me, I would publish it. But you know the editor will never let it through. Perhaps you could rewrite it. Make it lean more towards a… more of a "what if she had tripped"….'

Izzy's lips purse, and she opens her mouth to argue.

Lionel reaches out again, and this time he takes Izzy's hand in his. 'You and I both know we need to pick our battles, and I am telling you, there is no point in fighting this one.'

'But—'

'Besides, the new piece I want your help with is really important. So much so in fact, the paper is prepared to pay expenses as well as a modest fee for your work.'

Her disappointment at her inability to alter the narrative about Emily Davidson's tragic death is overwhelming, but Izzy forces herself to ask, 'What is it?'

'The Women's Pilgrimage is due in Hampshire this week, and my editor

would like someone to write about it—and he chose me.'

'How does that affect me?' Izzy asks automatically, still working on how she might convince Lionel to take her Emily Davidson story.

'I have some things to tidy up here before I can move on to this, so I need someone to do some background research for me on the local suffragette movement. I thought perhaps… you might be ready to… go home.' Lionel changes his face to appear beseeching.

Izzy freezes. 'Lionel, you know I cannot go back. I cannot face…. You know what I left.'

Before Lionel can respond, Basia sits forward and says, 'But, Isolde, I thought you wanted to see if you could fix things.'

Izzy catches her bottom lip between her teeth. Basia is right. She'd asked the Time Fixers if she could go back to her own time to see if she could remake her life here, and part of that had been to see if she could repair her relationship with her family… and maybe Jo too. Still, this was all happening too quickly.

Her disappointment over the treatment of Emily Davidson's death combined with the mess of her own life had led her to join the Time Fixers in the hopes she could nudge civilisation towards a better world. When she realised her work had done little to change history, she thought perhaps she could take up the reins of her old life. And, yes, that would mean facing her family in Winchester sooner or later, but she had hoped for later.

Lionel takes her silence as agreement. 'Good, that is settled, then.' He reaches into his pocket and produces an envelope. 'Here are your expenses for the trip and a little something extra just in case. As you will not have time to let me know what hotel you are staying in, I will call in at your aunt's the day after tomorrow for the first draft. Now I must be off. I will settle up on the way out. Nice to meet you, Barbara.'

Seconds later he is gone, and Izzy is still frozen in shock, staring at the spot Lionel just vacated, when she feels a gentle hand on her arm.

'Izzy, are you okay?'

It takes a moment for the words to penetrate the fog of her thoughts. 'Um, yes. I… um, guess we should get going, too, if we are to travel to Winchester today.'

Out in front of the teashop, Izzy hails a cab. The journey back to her lodgings passes in a blur. She only fully comes out of her head when they're back inside her room.

'Was that Lee?' Basia asks, taking a seat on the bed. 'I mean, like I was the

reincarnation of Lee's sister, is Lionel someone who becomes Lee in the future?'

'What? Um, yes, I guess. I had never really thought of Lionel in that way, but he might be. Though, he and his cousin Stanley are very similar, so I am not sure.... Perhaps Stanley becomes Lee.'

Basia frowns. 'So there's someone in this time who will become me?'

Izzy kneels, pulls a valise out from under the bed, and begins packing clothes inside.

'Izzy?'

'Mmm.'

'Pay attention. Will I run into an earlier version of myself? And won't that cause some sort of... anomaly?'

Izzy pauses. 'Possibly.' She stops what she's doing for a moment. 'Actually, to be honest, I've never seen two versions of the same person together in all my five years of time travel. So I guess time or history must do something to keep the different versions apart.'

Basia swings her feet as Izzy finishes packing. 'You talk about time as if it's a living thing.'

'What? Yes... it sort of is. I know it isn't alive as such, but it does sometimes act as though it's a sentient being. There are rules to time travel, and if you don't follow them, you will find yourself kicked back to your own time.'

Basia falls silent, and Izzy senses she wants to ask something else. When she finally does, Izzy is prepared for it.

'So, we'll see your version of Johan, my brother, in Winchester?' she asks.

'Most likely.'

'And are you intending to make things up with him?'

With her, Izzy says in her head, but she answers with a noncommittal 'Maybe.'

'What's he like, this Jo?' Basia presses.

'Josephine is serious and committed to her family, kind of like your brother,' Izzy says as she closes the travel bag.

'YOUR JOHAN, JO, is a she? Oh.' Basia's legs stop swinging, hesitating for a moment. 'And that's not good, is it? Not in this time period. And not for some time into the future.'

'Can we talk about this later?' Izzy asks, the clasp of her bag clicking to accentuate her request. 'The last train to Winchester leaves in just over an

hour, and we still need to buy you some clothes.'

Basia is aching to ask more questions, but she appreciates now is not the time for a heart-to-heart. They've only been back in Izzy's timeline a few hours, and her friend must be overwhelmed with everything happening so quickly.

'Have we enough money for clothes?' she asks instead.

Izzy opens the envelope Lionel gave her and counts the money inside. She closes her eyes, and her mouth moves as if she's calculating. She sucks in a breath and opens her eyes. 'We will be fine if we can stay with my aunt rather than at a hotel… and if we just buy the basics. You can borrow something of mine for evenings…. Yes, we should have enough.'

'Evening dress? Surely we won't need anything like that.'

Izzy's mind was somewhere else, and she didn't respond. 'Come on. If we hurry, we'll have time to go to a second-hand clothing stall I use in the Petticoat Lane Market.'

Before Basia can object, Izzy grabs her arm, pulls her off the bed, and almost drags her to the door. She keeps up her frantic pace as she takes them through a maze of back streets until they finally reach the market.

Izzy slows as she wanders along the street lined with stalls. She ignores the vendors' calls, clearly searching for a particular one. While Izzy takes the lead, Basia is overwhelmed by the crush of people and the array of goods on display. Izzy comes to an abrupt stop halfway down the street, and Basia almost bangs into her back.

She pushes Basia forward towards a mass of clothes piled up on a table. The stall is decorated with still more pieces hanging from ropes strung around the sides.

'I need a day dress and some skirts and blouses. Oh, and shoes for the dress, and boots. And that valise will do nicely.' Izzy points to an old brown leather bag.

The stall holder looks Basia up and down, then shows Izzy some garments. Izzy shakes her head or nods, and Basia stands there saying nothing, feeling as though she is some doll to be dressed up. The two haggle over price, Izzy adds some undergarments and another skirt and blouse, and the deal is done.

The now stuffed valise is shoved at Basia, and Izzy hauls her back through the crowd and searches for a cab. Once inside one, Basia slumps into the seat. 'I hate pink,' she says.

'That day dress will be very becoming on you. Besides, it was the only dress that went with the shoes.'

Basia humphs, unable to argue because Izzy's right. At least the light blue skirt and white blouses are more to her liking, and they'll mix and match with

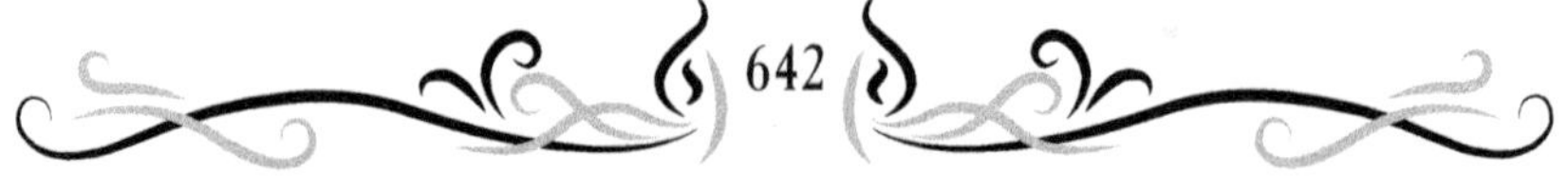

the clothing she's wearing. Perhaps she'll never need to wear the day dress.

Basia leans her head back to rest on the seat, wishing she could slide back into her jeans and T-shirt and get out of these layers of clothing that threaten to stifle her.

The cab pulls up outside a station near the river. Not just any river, *the Thames*. Basia sits up in her seat and stares out the window, doing her best not to gawp and fails. The bustle of people, actual steam trains billowing smoke, the Thames right there—it's easy to believe she's in a dream. Only Izzy's hand on the small of her back guiding her out of the cab and into the station keeps her on track.

'Quick now,' Izzy says as she exits the ticket queue. 'The train leaves in ten minutes, and it is the last one today.'

'That's plenty of time to make it to the platform, isn't it?' Basia quickly realises her mistake as they struggle through the crowds to the barrier. She clutches her satchel close to her chest as they push between bodies and bags.

A tall, suited man rushes past, catching Basia's shoulder and turning her around. When she's righted herself, she can't see Izzy anywhere. Panic tightens her throat until she catches sight of Izzy's frantically waving hand over by a barrier.

Taking a deep breath, she pushes her way through the crowd, determined not to get waylaid again. Blowing out a breath, she relaxes as Izzy takes her hand and leads her through the turnstile and onto the platform.

As the clock strikes three, a guard checks their tickets and assists them onto the back of the train with only moments to spare. If he had not helped them inside and passed them their bags, they wouldn't have made it.

Izzy leads them through the carpeted first-class section, and Basia glimpses plush seats and well-dressed gentlemen inside the cubicles. 'I could only afford second-class tickets,' Izzy says, opening the door to another carriage.

The corridor is wooden, and Basia struggles to stay on her feet. As the train curves out of Waterloo Station, she slips and grabs for anything to right herself, which happens to be a door handle. Her weight causes the door to slide open, propelling Basia into a compartment occupied by a young woman. Basia straightens herself, smiles, and makes out that she is exactly where she's meant to be before saying, 'Excuse me, do you mind if we join you?'

The woman raises her eyes from a book and looks over the top of her glasses as Izzy joins them. She shakes her head before returning to her reading.

Izzy slides the door shut, and they stow their bags in the overhead racks before taking a seat opposite their travelling companion. Basia sits by the

window and cannot take her eyes from the sight of Edwardian London as they pass through it.

'How long until Winchester?' she asks Izzy without shifting her gaze.

'About two and a half hours.'

More than two hours. Basia sighs and glances over to their travelling companion, wishing she could sink into a good book too. The woman is reading a battered edition of *The Return of Sherlock Holmes.*

A first edition! Her eyes widen with the realisation. She turns to Izzy, who is leaning back against the seat, eyes closed.

'Izzy?'

'Isolde,' Izzy corrects. 'It is best if you use my proper name while we are in Winchester.'

'All right, Isolde, then.' Basia tries to keep the frustration out of her voice. She has followed Izzy around for hours, and she wants to know more about where they're going and what they're doing, not another reminder that her speech is not what it should be. 'What is this Women's Pilgrimage thing you are going to Winchester for?'

Before Izzy can answer, the woman across from them says, 'My goodness, girl, where have you been living, darkest Africa? The march is almost all anyone is talking about.'

Placing her book in her lap, their travelling companion then reaches into a carpetbag on the seat beside her and produces a newspaper. She opens it and points to a section before handing the publication to Basia.

Scanning the print, Basia reads the advertisement calling for women to join a nationwide march to Hyde Park from all corners of Great Britain.

'I thought suffragettes were all about courting attention with violent displays and hunger strikes,' Basia says as she hands the paper back.

The woman frowns at her and snorts with disdain. 'That is why this march is so important. After what happened at the Derby, many moderates have turned away from advocating votes for women.'

Izzy inhales sharply before she snarls, 'Emily Davidson's death was a tragic accident.

'I am sorry, was she a friend of yours? I did not mean to offend, merely to state a fact. The newspapers have blown her death out of proportion and used the event to stoke the fears of moderates.'

Izzy relaxes a little, and the woman across from them sits up a little straighter in her seat. 'Look, this march is a chance for us women to explain

why we want the vote. Newspapers love to paint us as radicals, but we are not. For the most part, we are ordinary women who just want a say in how our country is run.'

'Are you a part of the Women's Pilgrimage?' Izzy asks, a glimmer of excitement twinkling in her eye.

The woman smiles for the first time since they entered the carriage. 'Why yes, I am. The lady I work for has been giving speeches along the way. She wanted her father to go through the address she is giving in Hampshire in a couple of days, so I took it to him in London. I am to meet her in Winchester in two days' time to go over the final version.'

Izzy leans forward on her chair and studies the other woman. 'I think I have seen you before. You are Miss Fielden's secretary, are you not?'

The woman blushes. 'I am, yes. Maisie, Maisie Ottaway.'

She holds out a hand, and Izzy shakes it. 'I am Isolde Fielding, and this is my friend, Barbara Trelawney. A pleasure to meet you. I am doing some background research on an article for the *Sunday Times*, and I would love to interview you about the march.'

Maisie withdraws her hand and shrinks back into the corner. 'In spite of having a female chief editor, the *Sunday Times* has not always been friendly to our cause.'

Izzy grimaces. 'No, it has not been. Like most papers it has tended of late to focus on the activities of the suffragettes—after all, sensation does sell papers. However, my friend is writing the article, and he promises me he will be sympathetic and will tell the suffragists' side of the story. Besides, I always write a second article for our pamphlets just to be sure.'

Maisie's eyes widen. 'Oh my, you are *that* Fielding—I have admired your work and own some of your pamphlets. Of course I will answer questions, but I must remain anonymous. Miss Fielden's father is in a precarious position with regards to the Pilgrimage… what with being a member of Parliament and all.'

Izzy takes the woman's hand in hers. 'You know you can trust me. I will not pass anything on that could hurt anyone who supports the movement.'

Maisie's shoulders relax, but before Izzy can pull out her notebook, the rattle of the tea trolley interrupts them. Izzy buys them all tea and cake, and then they chat, getting to know one another before the detailed questioning begins.

2

WINCHESTER

WITH THE TEA things cleared away, Izzy rests her notebook on her satchel and asks her first question. 'Why are you supporting the Women's Pilgrimage?'

Maisie's fingers twist in her lap, and the only sound in the carriage is the chug of the train as she appears to search for an answer.

Izzy waits patiently, then tries again. 'Let me put that another way—can you tell us why the women's movement is important to you?'

Maisie's fingers slow, and she tentatively says, 'It has been difficult for us moderates since the incident at the Derby, then the attack on Parliament. Those harridans—' Her hand rises to her mouth, and her eyes widen in shock. 'I am so sorry. I realise some of the women involved must be your friends.'

And they pay for my lodgings, Izzy adds but keeps it to herself because to get her story, she must keep Maisie talking. Instead she says, 'I think we can all agree the sentiments on the street have turned against all women in recent weeks—suffragettes and more moderate suffragists alike.'

'Well, yes, it has not been easy for any of us,' Maisie says primly as she smooths her skirt. 'Only the other day, my mother had rotten potatoes thrown at her by stallholders she had worked beside for years simply because she mentioned I was on this march.'

Beside her, Basia gasps.

'Oh, Miss Trelawney, not to worry. Some of the other stallholders stood up for her, and things are back to normal in Covent Garden Market now.'

'Of course, the march through England has been advertised in all the main papers and talked about at many meetings as well as in many homes for some time now,' Izzy says, trying to bring the conversation back to the topic at hand. 'Supporters of suffrage for women on equal terms to men are heading to London from six starting points around the country, and they plan to converge on Hyde Park for a rally. Is that so?' she prompts Maisie.

'Yes, we have been advertising in the main papers for months, trying to encourage people to walk at least part of the route with us. We aim to educate people along the way that most of us do not want a radical transformation of society—all we want is a voice in making the laws of the land.'

Izzy nods in encouragement, but Maisie doesn't elaborate any further. 'So, how did you become involved with the suffragists?'

Maisie beams, and her voice rings with pride as she answers. 'I am involved because I work for Miss Fielden. I started with her family as a maid. Much to my surprise, we became friends when Miss Fielden taught me to read better with her suffragist pamphlets.'

'That is an unusual thing for an employer to do,' Izzy says.

Maisie frowns, as if sensing some sort of trap. 'She did not brainwash me, if that is what you are thinking. She found me trying to read one of her pamphlets one day. Instead of reprimanding me for touching her personal things, she sat down and helped me read it. After that, every time she had a new pamphlet, she would lend it to me and told me to come to her if there was anything I could not understand.'

'Sorry, I meant no offence,' Izzy reassures her, silently applauding Miss Fielden for her philanthropy.

Somewhat mollified, Maisie continues. 'Some months later her work with the Women's Social and Political Union became too much for her, so she asked her father if she may employ me as a secretary, and here I am. She is a great woman whom history will remember as a staunch fighter for women's rights,' Maisie finishes up proudly.

Basia catches Izzy's eye and raises a questioning eyebrow. With her work in the future, Izzy well knows that Miss Fielden, in spite of the inspiring speech she would give in Haslemere in a few days' time, will end up a footnote in history, not one of the shining stars.

It's a fate many of the suffragists will suffer. Even Basia, who is relatively well read, had no idea the more moderate suffragists existed. Her sole insight into those who worked tirelessly for women's suffrage had been of the more radical suffragettes—who actually only make up a small part of those advocating for a women's right to vote.

Maisie turns to Basia. 'Are you a reporter, too, Miss Trelawney?'

'No, I've no job at the moment,' Basia responds. 'I'm taking a bit of a holiday with Izzy.'

As she spoke, Maisie's brow drew down into a frown, and Basia's mouth forms an "O" as she realises her mistake. This was why Izzy had asked the woman from the future not to speak.

'You will have to excuse Barbara. She has been volunteering in the slums up north and… well, her speech has become somewhat common, and she has picked up some unusual habits,' Izzy says, directing a pointed stare at Basia. 'I hope she will have fixed this by the time we meet my aunt.'

Chuckling nervously, Maisie pats Basia on the hand. 'I know how easy it can be to fall into bad habits when people around you speak differently. It always takes me a couple of days to adjust after I have visited my parents.'

'Barbara will not have that luxury,' Izzy says, and Basia squirms in her seat, clearly getting the message.

'Perhaps it is best not to say too much to people first off,' Maisie tells her. 'That is how I do it.'

Basia smiles her response, and Izzy relaxes a little.

'To answer your question, Barbara came to London from Manchester to decide her future. I had to come to Hampshire and cover the march, so she decided to travel with me.'

'Have you any idea what you want to do in London?' Maisie presses. 'There are so many opportunities for the modern woman.'

Beside her, Basia tenses. Izzy takes her hand. 'Is it all right if I tell Miss Ottaway?'

Basia nods, her shoulders relaxing with relief.

'I am sorry if I have made you self-conscious about speaking,' Maisie says to Basia. 'I really do not mind if you sound a little… common.'

Izzy squeezes Basia's hand. 'It is not that, Miss Ottaway, but more that Barbara still cannot believe she is here and not at home with her parents. You see, she risked a lot by not going back to her family after the charity work she did in Manchester.'

As if sensing a drama, Maisie inches forward on her seat. 'Oh, Miss

Trelawney, how very brave of you.'

'And she probably would not have had the courage to do it if she had not believed it is her future to do good works. When we return to London, she will apply to join the Nightingale Home and Training School for Nurses at St Thomas's Hospital.' The cover story rolls off Izzy's tongue with ease, and Basia sends her an appreciative glance.

'Oh my goodness,' Maisie gasps. 'I do so admire the Nightingale Nurses. I hope you do apply and get accepted. It is such a noble calling.'

'I am sure she will,' Izzy says. 'She has already had some training at home, working with a local nurse.'

'It must be difficult taking such a step when your family would no doubt rather you stayed at home and married instead of studying nursing in London. I dream of the day when having a career will be commonplace for us women.'

Basia draws her bottom lip between her teeth as a mix of emotions flashes in her eyes. Izzy can only guess at what she's thinking—that Maisie had inadvertently described her life.

Before the Time Fixers and Time Guardians' joint mission to save humanity from extinction, Basia's family had indeed wanted to keep her close to home, if not actually married off, for her own protection. It wasn't a surprise to Izzy that someone in that situation would choose to leave her home and run away on an adventure with Allan, an escapee from an underground city. He had been passionate about returning home to tell his people it was safe to live above ground.

Unfortunately Allan's actions had brought factions in post-apocalyptic Hampshire to the brink of a war that could have ended humanity. Before his death, Allan not only managed to get a commitment from Basia to carry on trying to bring above- and below-ground people together, but he also sacrificed his freedom on the promise that the two sides would hold peace talks

Appreciating her friend's discomfort, and knowing the complexity of the situation she was in, Izzy changes the subject. 'What are you able to tell us of the contents of Miss Fielden's speech?'

Maisie stiffens and starts plucking at the seam of her skirt. 'Oh, Miss Fielding, I cannot tell anyone anything about it, not even someone as respected as you.'

She hadn't expected an answer, but it had been worth a try if only to take the heat off Basia for a bit.

'That should be enough for my article. Thank you for talking to me,' Izzy

says as she returns her notebook to her bag.

With the interview over, the three women relax into a comfortable silence, retreating into their own thoughts. Basia leans her forehead against the window, watching the scenery pass by. Izzy allows herself to be lulled by the chugging of the carriage wheels and battles the urge to sleep.

Obviously tired from days of travelling, Maisie's eyelids begin to droop, and she is soon snoring gently. The charlady returns for their cups, and when they're alone, Izzy whispers, 'Are you all right?'

Basia nods, resting her head against the seat, but doesn't take her eyes off the scenery rushing by.

'Sorry about the slip-up,' she whispers. 'I will try to speak more like a heroine from a Jane Austen novel in future.'

'Or not speak at all.'

Basia chuckles.

Izzy leans in and, in a low voice, says, 'I am sorry about springing the background story on you. I tried to keep it as close to the truth as possible—that is essential for a good cover story.'

'No, you did well. It's just, it *was* quite close to the truth, and it reminded me why I came.'

Izzy smiles. 'There is nothing to say you cannot enjoy yourself a little while you are here—indulge your passions, perhaps.' She's referring to Basia's penchant for reading novels from the eighteenth and nineteenth centuries, and her country-manor view of the times. She's excited to see Basia's reaction when they reach her aunt's house. Instead of a hand-to-mouth existence in London, her friend would be thrown into her idealised view of early twentieth-century England.

'My aunt Augusta is part of the set in Winchester, and there is no reason you should not enjoy yourself with her while I work on the story for Lionel. Goodness knows she would probably enjoy the company.'

She doesn't add that it will take the pressure off her to spend time with her aunt. 'Once we are done here and are back in London, there will be time enough for you to be introduced to some of the WSPU leaders. Then we should be able to find a way for you to move things forward in your time without upsetting the balance and starting a war.'

'I'm not 100 percent sure I want to be one of the ones leading the change at home,' Basia whispers so quietly, Izzy almost doesn't catch what she says, but she does hear the sadness lacing her words.

Turning her head, she sees unshed tears in the other woman's eyes. They remind Izzy that in the space of a week or so, Basia found her soulmate, then lost him to the cause she was now expected to champion for him. She herself knows how hard it is to lose the love of your life, and how easy it is to channel that heartbreak into a movement for social change. Well, she thinks she knows.

'Are you having second thoughts about carrying on Allan's work?' she asks, keeping her voice low so as not to wake Maisie.

Basia shrugs. 'I promised to help in the heat of the moment. Now… I am not sure it is what is best for me, or for the people in both communities.'

'You should not take anything on until you are sure you can commit,' Izzy advises, drawing from her own experience.

When she first joined the WSPU, she'd been able to immerse herself in the cause. However, when their actions became increasingly violent, and people began turning against them, she had no longer been sure she was doing the right thing.

She'd been spiralling into despair when the Time Fixers approached her to join their team. With them, she had hoped to find a different way to make society better. Both ventures had altered very little for Izzy, or for women in general, if Basia's post-apocalyptic future was anything to go by.

'Still, I want to help our world heal—I can't leave it hurtling towards a war,' Basia says.

No, but can you actually do anything to prevent it? Izzy wonders.

She had gone to Basia's home on a mission to prevent humanity from wiping itself out. In the post-apocalyptic world, she found that the small above-ground settlements mostly valued women for their ability to breed and men for their skill in defending them. Hard-won equalities were stripped bare in the face of limited resources and a human population close to extinction.

Below ground, things were even worse. Women may have had equal status with men, but the totalitarian state had become corrupt in a way that reminded Izzy of twentieth-century communist Russia.

If being in Basia's time had taught her anything, it was that history really does repeat itself. She was now so disillusioned, she was back in her own timeline, trying to squeeze some happiness and meaning from the life she had been born into.

'Do you think one person can make a difference?' she asks Basia.

'Allan made a difference, I believe. So, yes, I think one person can make a big difference, but perhaps not everyone can. I think most people will end

up just doing the best they can to live what they believe to be a good life.'

Basia's words are wise. Once this jaunt to Hampshire is over, Izzy hopes she can return to London, forge a writing career that might make a slight difference, and perhaps find a small measure of happiness.

Before that can happen, though, events have conspired to force her into returning to Winchester and facing the demons of her past head-on—this was most decidedly not what she had planned when she'd decided to go home.

Basia wriggles beside her, and then an arm drapes over Izzy's shoulder. 'I guess we both have a lot to sort through, but perhaps we both can have some fun along the way.'

AS THE TRAIN pulls into Winchester Station, Basia catches sight of the clock. It is just after five thirty in the afternoon. Bathed in late-afternoon sunshine, the Victorian brick building is postcard picturesque.

The train shudders to a stop, waking Maisie. Still half asleep, she hastily shoves her belongings back into her carpetbag, dropping her newspaper on the floor as she does so.

Izzy is already on her feet and passing down their valises. 'Can I get your travel bag down for you, Miss Ottaway?'

The woman in question pauses and looks up from grabbing the newspaper. 'Yes, please.'

Moments later, a guard opens the carriage door to the platform, and Basia is the first to step into an English countryside she has only read about in books. Her heart beats faster, and she turns to Izzy with an enormous grin on her face. 'This is just perfect.'

'If you react this way at the station, what will you be like when we get into the city proper?' Izzy winks, taking the sting from her words.

'Oh my,' Maisie says at the number of passengers disembarking. 'I did not expect it to be so busy. How will I ever find a porter… and a taxi?'

'Follow me,' Izzy instructs, then takes off in the opposite direction from the crowd.

Maisie and Basia share a quick glance before following. Izzy stops at a wrought-iron gate at the end of the building, and when they catch her, they find she's talking to a man on the other side.

'Are you sure I canna be getting one for you, too, Miss Isolde?' the man asks.

'Thank you, Thomas, no. It is only a short walk to Augusta's place, and it is a lovely evening for a stroll.'

'Right you are.' The man's wrinkled face breaks into a grin, compressing the multitude of folds and revealing a gap-toothed smile. He opens the gate and allows the three girls through.

'Miss Ottaway, this is Thomas. He will help you find a cabbie to take you to wherever you are going.'

'Oh, thank you, Miss Fielding. I am ever so obliged. I am told the lady I am staying with has a house not far from the station, but I have never been to Winchester….'

'It is no bother, really. My aunt has an arrangement with Thomas.' She leans into Maisie and says, 'Just tip him a few pennies for his time. He is cheaper than a porter, and he will find you a trustworthy cabbie, so it is well worth every penny.'

Thomas already has Maisie's travel bag in hand, and she throws her thanks over her shoulder as she scurries after him.

'I hope you are up for a short walk,' Izzy says as she leads them past the front of the station.

'No,' Basia mutters under her breath as she totters behind in the unfamiliar heels. It appears the comment was rhetorical and that Izzy, in her determination to walk to her aunt's house, has forgotten Basia's inability to walk in the borrowed footwear.

Fortunately for Basia, it appears Izzy's aunt's place is truly not far from the station. Or at least she hopes that's why they've stopped outside the military college on Southgate Street and are staring at the houses on the other side.

When there's a break in traffic, Izzy grabs her arm and hauls her across the busy main road. She halts again at the bottom of some steps leading up to the porticoed entrance of a four-storeyed house.

'Here we are,' Izzy announces. 'Home.'

Basia's jaw drops. 'Oh my god, Izzy. This is a mansion.' She turns a suspicious gaze to her friend. 'Who the hell *are* you?'

Izzy laughs. 'I am a nobody, but one of my cousins is a duke—the Lord of Denbigh. My branch of the family has wealth and land but no title. Aunt Augusta, my father's sister, married a Northern industrialist. When he died she retired to Winchester and has been spending his money on charitable works ever since.'

'Does she have children?'

'Goodness no. Aunt Augusta never wanted to be bothered with kids. She's much happier bestowing her largesse on orphans and the oppressed than she would be spending it on ungrateful offspring—well, at least that is what she says.'

'Izzy!' Basia reprimands, shocked at her assessment of their potential hostess.

'It's the truth. I can't complain, though. She's always been good to me until.... Well, let's just hope she's forgiven me for the argument we had when I left for London.'

Suddenly Basia's stomach drops. 'Izzy, are you telling me we spent most of your expense money on clothes for me when you weren't sure we'd be able to stay with your aunt?'

Izzy had the good grace to appear a little apologetic. 'I was trying not to think too much about it. You see, before I left, my aunt found out I had been writing some pamphlets for the NUWSS, and to say she was angry is an understatement. She believes the militant suffragettes are actually preventing moderates from supporting votes for women, and she issued me an ultimatum—leave the NUWSS or leave home.'

'Clearly you chose to leave home,' Basia says dryly.

Izzy shrugs. 'It wasn't quite that simple. I'm a member of both the NUWSS and the WSPU—the Women's Social and Political Union, which is the NUWSS's more well-behaved cousin. To be honest, I'm not a great fan of some of the violent acts members of the NUWSS have carried out, but I didn't like being told what to do.'

'Izzy, this is not sounding good.'

'It gets worse.'

Basia cringes.

'I had just learned that I had lost Jo to another, and I was emotionally drained. I may have overreacted. I stormed out, telling her I would not have anyone telling me how to live my life—not my father and not her.'

'That was a bit melodramatic,' Basia laughs.

Izzy grins. 'It was, I guess. In all honesty, though, I left for London to hide away and lick my wounds.' Her smile falls away.

Basia places her hand on Izzy's arm. 'I'm sorry you didn't find love with your Jo here, but you can always come back with me, and I'm sure you and Johan… would that be allowed?'

Izzy takes a deep breath, and the tension leaves her shoulders. 'Let's worry about all of that after we find out if we have somewhere to stay tonight.'

With that, she marches up the steps and knocks firmly on the door. Basia

joins her as a tall, pasty-faced man with slicked-back hair wearing a formal suit appears in the crack of the doorway.

'Ah, Miss Isolde,' he says, not moving to let them in.

'Hello, Jensen. Is Aunt Augusta receiving?'

He peers down his nose at them, as if deciding whether he'll allow them to enter. Finally, he pulls the door wider. 'Come in. She is taking tea in the drawing room. Please remain here while I enquire as to her availability.'

Basia follows Izzy into the wood-panelled, checkerboard-floored hallway to find Jensen is still there and is staring pointedly at her.

'My friend is Miss Barbara Trelawney of the Northampton Trelawneys,' Izzy says as they place their bags on the floor by the coatroom.

'Very good, Miss Isolde.'

Jensen turns on his heel and disappears through the door to his right.

Basia half turns to Izzy. 'What was that about?'

'Jensen will announce both of us, and he needs your family connections in case Aunt Augusta questions him about you.'

Basia has read about the strictures of upper-class English society, but seeing them in action is a little odd. It's difficult to comprehend that, although she's Izzy's friend, that might not be enough to gain her admittance here—she has to be the right kind of friend.

She doesn't have long to dwell on this, though, as Jensen re-emerges through the door and opens it for the two girls to enter.

Basia has to control her excitement at being shown into an honest-to-god drawing room. She drinks in the Persian rug, the green-papered walls, and the William Morris print curtains before settling on the chairs grouped around the fire opposite them.

The red settee in front of the windows is empty, but one of the two matching chairs by the fireplace is occupied by a woman.

As she turns to face them, Basia almost stumbles. There is no doubt this woman with her dark violet eyes and greying black hair is related to Izzy. In fact, seeing her, Basia knows exactly how Izzy will look in twenty-odd years' time.

'Jensen, could you please arrange another pot of tea and two more settings, and perhaps some more cakes and sandwiches.'

'As you wish, ma'am.'

The door snicks shut behind him, leaving Basia and Izzy standing on the carpet in front of Izzy's aunt. Her stern demeanour causes butterflies to flutter in Basia's stomach. She feels like she's done something wrong and is

about to answer for it, but for the life of her, she can't think what it could be. Basia tries not to fidget as Izzy's aunt stares at them with a haughty scowl.

'So, Isolde, you have spread your wings, found life wanting, and have finally returned home where you belong,' the woman states, her piercing blue eyes raking over Izzy. Basia should be offended at being ignored, but, in truth, she just feels grateful the woman hasn't acknowledged her presence.

Beside her, Izzy squares her shoulders. 'No, Aunt Augusta. I have work to do in Winchester and have called to pay my respects.'

'Work?' Augusta snorts the question.

'Yes. I am writing a piece for the *Sunday Times* with Lionel.' Izzy tilts her chin as if daring her aunt to challenge her assertion. 'My friend, Barbara, has travelled with me to see some of the country before she begins nursing school in a few weeks. Miss Barbara Trelawney, my aunt, Mrs Augusta Hartfield.'

'Pleased to meet you.' Basia manages to force the words out through trembling lips, not keen to draw the attention of their hostess.

The room falls silent, only the crackle of the fire offering some respite. The butterflies in Basia's stomach began to dance—has she said something wrong again?

Finally, Augusta gestures towards the sofa. 'Please, girls, take a seat.'

Basia lets out a breath, happy to follow their hostess's direction. She's making herself comfortable on the settee when there's a knock, and then the butler follows a tray-carrying maid into the room. Jensen removes the tray from the table, and the maid places the new one down. It's all done so effortlessly and with such grace, it's like watching a dance.

When they're alone again, Augusta pours their drinks, and Basia waits for Izzy to move and show her how this all goes. Izzy's eyes flick to Basia, and leaning forward, she places a sandwich and a cake on a plate, then begins taking dainty bites. Basia follows suit as Augusta picks up her cup and sips thoughtfully.

'So you have found work in London, then?' Augusta asks, half turning in her chair so she can better see Izzy.

Izzy's chin tilts upwards a little. 'Yes, Aunt. I told you I could take care of myself.'

A grimace passes over Augusta's face before she schools herself back into mild interest. 'And you have found lodgings?'

Izzy pauses, her sandwich halfway to her mouth. She places the food back on her plate before answering. 'Yes, in a boarding house in Spitalfields. I do some secretarial work and write pamphlets for room and board.'

This time Augusta's face clearly transmits her distaste. 'If you had not been so obstinate, you could have stayed in your father's townhouse. Am I correct in assuming all this is being provided by the NUWSS?'

Izzy's eye flash defiance as she says, 'Yes.'

Augusta's face is thunderous. 'I told you when you left that I will not have a lawbreaker in my house. If you are a part of their violent protests, I will not have you here now. Not only is what you are doing illegal, but you are making it harder for us women to get the vote.'

Izzy's knuckles whiten as she grips her plate, and Basia wonders how much force the delicate china can take before breaking.

'I told you then, and I am telling you now, that while I do not condemn their actions as you do, I do not take any part in them either.'

Aunt and niece hold each other's gaze, as if they're each waiting for the other to back down. Finally, Izzy says, 'I want to focus on becoming a journalist, not getting myself arrested.'

Her aunt's face loses some of its hauteur as she accepts the olive branch. 'What story are you down here to write?'

'I am covering the Pilgrimage,' Izzy tells her.

Augusta relaxes. 'Now that is something I can support. Many of my friends are going to join the march when it reaches Portsmouth.' She turns to Basia, as if she's seeing her for the first time. 'My apologies for our rudeness, Miss Trelawney, but as you possibly know, my niece and I did not part on the best of terms.'

'Please, you do not need to apologise. We dropped in on you unannounced, after all,' Basia reassures her hostess before reaching for her tea, hoping Augusta will forget her presence again.

Turning back to Izzy, Augusta says, 'You have just missed your father. He only left for home yesterday. He kept hoping you would come back and agree to meet with Lord Rathrune's son to discuss your future.'

Beside Basia, Izzy stiffens. 'Lord Rathrune's son and I meet all the time, and we never discuss marriage. What is more, I have told Father I am not interested in marriage or in becoming someone's wife. I will marry for love or not at all. In the meantime, I will forge my own life on my own terms.'

For the first time since they arrived, Augusta's mask slips and her face softens. 'Ah, your mother still has a hold over you even in death. I know her marriage to your father was not a good one, but not all marriages are like that.'

'So many are, though, and times are changing. Not all people of our class are prepared to accept an arranged marriage. That is why I take my mother's

advice—not to settle for anything less than a love match.'

Augusta slowly shakes her head. 'I know it is difficult, Isolde, but sometimes the best we women can do is find a man who allows us to have our own life. I thought you and the lad could have come to an arrangement, especially as you are such good friends.'

Izzy's eyes drift down to the teacup in her hand. 'Lionel and I grew up together, and I am sure we could come to an arrangement… but….'

Basia stares in shock as she realises Lionel is the person Izzy has refused to marry.

Augusta sighs, places her cup back on the table, and reaches for Izzy's hand. 'You wonder why you should have to?'

Izzy nods, her face a mask of determination. In contrast to her niece, Augusta's face is a study in sorrow. 'Given where both your hearts lie, it would have been a good match, though your father suggested it for other reasons.'

Basia shifts uncomfortably in her seat, aware she's witnessing something rather personal.

'You know Josephine is to be married in two weeks,' Augusta says, and Izzy blanches, withdrawing her hand.

Izzy's cup clinks, her hand is shaking so much. Augusta takes it from her and places it on the table.

'So soon?' Izzy's words sound strangled.

'They saw no point in a prolonged engagement,' Augusta says. 'There are some pressing matters in Australia that Stanley needs to deal with, so they moved the wedding date forward.'

The room falls silent. Izzy's first day back in her own life is turning out to be quite eventful. Basia places her hand over Izzy's in a gesture of solidarity, telling her she's there if Izzy needs her.

BLOOD POUNDS IN Izzy's ears. The wedding is in two weeks. Does that mean she's too late to change Jo's mind, or just in time? No, she didn't come back to force Jo to change but to find a way to… to… be in her life. Still, a part of her must have hoped Jo would change her mind—otherwise, why had the news devastated her like this?

Her heartbeat is so loud, Izzy doesn't catch what her aunt is saying. Shaking

her head, she tries to focus.

'Isolde, are you all right?' Basia's voice is close to her ear.

'Um, yes, I am fine.' The words sound hollow, even to her own ears.

'Ah, Jensen,' Augusta calls, 'Miss Isolde and her friend will be staying with us a few nights. Can you please make sure the rooms are made ready?'

'Yes, ma'am,' he replies.

Izzy had thought she would have to beg her aunt to be allowed to stay, but her shock over how quickly things have moved in her absence has done the job for her.

'Perhaps you both need some time to rest before dinner is served. It must have been a tiring trip down here,' her aunt is saying, and Izzy nods in agreement, happy to go with the flow.

'I am sure we would both like to freshen up a bit and, um… compose ourselves,' Basia says nervously.

Izzy knows it is she who's supposed to be taking care of Basia, who is out of her depth in this timeline. But it's the other girl who helps her upstairs and into the hallway outside her old bedroom.

'Your room is here, Miss Trelawney,' Jensen says as he indicates the door opposite Izzy's room. 'The gong to dress for dinner will sound in an hour,' he adds before departing, leaving them alone in the hallway.

Basia wants to ask about dressing for dinner but instead leads Izzy into her room. 'Are you all right?'

'Yes, sorry. It's just….'

Basia pats her hand. 'You've had a shock. Perhaps we both need a bit of a rest and time to regroup before dinner.' She takes a tentative step backwards. 'I'll give you some time alone, but I'm here if you need me.'

Izzy doesn't move. She's aware of Basia hovering, and part of her hears Basia gasp, 'A four-poster bed, how gorgeous.'

Finally, she shakes herself out of her stupor. 'I'll be fine,' she tells Basia as she bundles the girl out of her room and shuts the door.

Izzy studies her bedroom. It's exactly the same as she left it. She sinks down onto the bed, then lies back, her legs dangling over the edge. She had almost asked Basia to swap rooms with her because this one holds perhaps the worst memory of her life.

It was here that she last spoke to Josephine. Here that she made one last-ditch effort not to have her life torn apart. She closes her eyes and tortures herself by replaying the scene in her head.

SHE PULLED JO into her bedroom and closed the door before clasping Jo's hands in hers and announcing triumphantly, 'I have told Father I will never marry Lionel, that I intend to remain unmarried until I find someone I love.'

Instead of appearing relieved, tears welled in Josephine's eyes. 'No, Isolde—tell me you did not turn down Lionel's offer.'

'It was not a real offer but one he was forced to make by his father,' Izzy insisted. Josephine's face remained stricken, so she continued, 'I cannot marry him when you hold my heart. I mean, I do love Lionel like a brother, and he would not be a bad husband. It is…. Well, I promised my mother never to be forced into marriage unless I love the person. I love you, and I cannot marry you—ergo, I will never get married.'

'Isolde, do not be so dramatic. The love you have for Lionel would be enough,' Jo admonished her. 'And, unlike some, he would allow you the freedom to live your life as you want.'

'True, I would be financially independent, and he would never stop me from doing anything, but society would treat me as his wife, not as Isolde. If that were not bad enough, I would have to give up my dream of becoming a journalist because no newspaper would employ a married woman.'

Josephine squeezed her hands, forcing Isolde to look at her. 'Would it really be so bad, though? You would live in London, and Lionel has such influential friends, you would be right in the intellectual thick of things. There would be plenty for you to write about—if you could not work for a newspaper, you could write pamphlets.'

Izzy shook her head, not believing the words coming from Jo's mouth. 'Do you want me to go away, to leave you alone here?'

'I will not be alone.' Jo's voice was barely above a whisper.

'What?' Izzy asked, then paused. 'Oh, Jo, what have you done?'

Josephine withdrew her hands. She tilted her chin, and when she spoke, her tone was defensive.

'Izzy, I am not like you. I cannot disappoint my father, and I do not want to be ostracised from my family and friends. I am going to marry Stanley and return to the family estate in Dorset.'

Izzy's chest tightened, and her head felt light, as if her heart had stopped beating. 'Jo, you cannot do this. You do not love him, and he does not love

you—he is only interested in your money. If he were going to inherit the family estate instead of his brother, he would not look twice at you.'

Josephine shrugged. 'I dare say that is true. In spite of that, though, we like each other, and we both know what we are getting into. Besides, Isolde, people like us cannot expect to marry for love, so I am at least lucky I like my future husband.'

Izzy paced the room in agitation. 'But why—*why* must we settle for less? You love me, I know you do—remember that first kiss under the apple tree and that day we spent by the river? Can you give that up so easily?'

Josephine grabbed hold of Isolde's arm as she passed and swung her so the two were face to face. 'If you marry Lionel, you can settle on your father's estate, and Lionel can move his valet in. We can be "friends forever." Nothing need change. It might even be better.'

'It will be different. I cannot write the types of articles I want to write in the country. Also, they are far more conservative down there, so we would be even more constrained by our husbands' wishes.'

'Oh, Izzy, that is simply nonsense,' Jo snapped impatiently. 'Both Lionel and Stanley are modern sorts of men. They would allow us to live our own lives—you know they would.'

Izzy smiled slyly. 'Would Stanley be happy with our arrangement? He is already talking about visiting your father's property in Australia. He wants a great adventure. If you go with him, nothing will be the same.'

Jo faltered. 'We would only be away for a few years—'

'Or forever.... Once we set our feet on different paths, we will have different things influencing our actions, and we will be pulled apart,' Izzy said, pleading her case, all the while knowing she was losing this battle.

Jo confirmed this when she straightened her shoulders and schooled her face into an iciness Izzy had never seen before. 'I have made up my mind.'

Izzy's stomach lurched, and she feared she may be sick. Ignoring the pain, she clenched her fists and defiantly said, 'Then so have I. I am going to London.'

'Izzy, you cannot. How will you survive?'

'I have been offered some work with the NUWSS, and I have the allowance my mother left me. I am sure I can get by.'

'Izzy, why go like that when you can go with Lionel as your husband and live in your father's house?'

Part of Izzy wanted to find a way through this. In her heart she knew Josephine would never defy convention, and yet Izzy would never break the

promise she'd made to her mother to only every marry for love. So she said, 'I want to make a stand. I want to show that women do not need husbands to have a good life. I want to do this so that in the future, women like us do not have to settle for less.'

IZZY OPENS HER eyes and stares at the rosette on the ceiling. *Was that truly only a couple of months ago in this timeline? I've seen so much since then, and it's been exciting and exhilarating, but also so very lonely. That loneliness smudges what once seemed black-and-white into grey.*

'I thought I could make things better, but I haven't changed anything, and it certainly hasn't been better for me,' she says, and her voice echoes in the heavy silence of the room. *What about Josephine? Is she happy? Will she be pleased to see me, or will I still be a problem for her to solve so she can have her cake and eat it too?*

The bell to dress for dinner sounds, and Izzy lets out a deep sigh before hauling herself off the bed. These questions certainly won't be answered tonight, and she owes it to Basia to introduce her properly to Winchester society.

Heading to the closet, she leafs through her clothes and extracts two evening gowns. She places them on the bed before taking a moment to push aside the memories she longs to forget. Tonight she must think of Basia first. She'll be excited about dressing for dinner and about living in one of her historical novels.

During the short walk to Basia's door, she plasters a smile on her face and calls brightly, 'Want to come into my room and dress for dinner?'

Basia flings open the door, her face an image of barely contained excitement. 'I thought you would never ask.'

DINNER TURNED OUT to be a rather stilted affair, with conversation limited to "please pass the salt". It seems Izzy and Augusta had said everything of importance at teatime. Fortunately Basia is happy enough to amuse herself with the novelty of being waited on for the first couple of courses. She even pinches herself to make sure she isn't dreaming when the maid in a black

dress and white apron appears to remove her plate.

The novelty soon wears off, and she finds herself unable to stand the tense silence any longer. Making conversation, she asks Augusta, 'Have you had a lot to do with the suffragist movement?'

Augusta smiles and turns to her. 'I have been campaigning for women's rights for as long as I can remember and have assisted with gathering signatures for many a petition to Parliament to extend the vote to women.'

'Have you met with members of Parliament yourself?' Basia is excited to be talking with another person who has a history in fighting for women's right.

'A few, yes, at political salons. Of course, I used to spend time with the Kensington ladies when I was younger, and I joined the National Society for Women's Suffrage in Manchester when I married.'

'Yes, Aunt Augusta is acquainted with all the great and the good in the suffragist movement,' Izzy says, her tone a little bitter.

As August's face hardens, Basia's hands clench in frustration. Izzy's comment is certain to return the tension to the room.

'And I know the suffragettes as well, young lady. Just because I do not agree with their violent tactics does not mean I have not worked with them in the past. After all, they also sponsor peaceful activities aimed at extending the vote to women.'

Izzy's cutlery clatters to the table. 'You sneer at their tactics, but what did your petitions and all those signatures achieve?'

'More than your friends and their throwing stones through windows and chaining themselves to railings ever have,' Augusta retorts. 'At least we won some important parliamentarians over to our side.'

Izzy's jaw juts defiantly. 'At least the suffragettes have everyone talking about votes for women.'

'And forced the undecided to become our opponents,' Augusta comments sourly.

Sensing a fight brewing, Basia knows she must tread carefully, for although the women seem to agree that females should have the vote, they clearly disagree on how to achieve that goal. Trying for a mutually safe topic, she asks, 'What do you think of the Women's Pilgrimage?'

If she expected an easing of tensions, she is disappointed. Augusta turns in her seat, deliberately blocking Izzy out, and says, 'I think it is a grand initiative. With public opinion turning against votes for women, I wholly support the idea of marching through the country, showing everyone that most of the women who want to vote are peace-loving citizens like they are.'

'But what will it achieve in the long run?' Basia asks the question before Izzy can, and with way less animosity.

'Perhaps not much,' Augusta concedes, 'but it is also a great opportunity for women to talk directly with people without the filter of the press. At least they will be able to set the record straight.'

Basia smiles, pleased she finally managed to change the tone of the conversation. 'Will you be marching at all?'

'Oh, my dear, I am far too old for that. Though I will be taking the train to London to join the rally in Hyde Park on the twenty-sixth of the month.'

Izzy's laugh sounds harsh in the quiet dining room. 'And you think the police will allow such a large group of suffragists to walk through the streets of London? There will likely be a riot. Already reports of locals attacking groups on the march are starting to filter through.'

Basia catches a brief look of pity on Augusta's face before she rearranges it into a haughty mask. 'Isolde, I know you think very little of us, believing we have accepted the slow pace of change. Even so, you should at least trust us enough to believe we will run an orderly march and that we have spoken with the correct authorities.'

'I do respect you and your ladies, Aunt, but you cannot deny many of those opposed to women's suffrage will stop at nothing to throw our cause into disrepute or to ensure we do not succeed.'

'On *that* we do agree,' Augusta say. 'Now, shall we take tea in the drawing room?'

Great, another torturous hour of this. Basia is exhausted from tiptoeing through the minefield of this family relationship, and it's taking the shine off her first experience of a life she's read so much about.

'If you will excuse me, I am tired and not the best of company.' Izzy stands, offering her aunt a tight smile. 'Good night to you both.'

It's all Basia can do not to heave a sigh of relief.

After Izzy's departure, Basia follows Augusta into the drawing room, smiling to herself at the delicious sound her sea-green silk skirts make as she walks.

For the next hour, the two women sit by the fire playing the exciting new game of gin rummy. When Basia wins the fifth hand in a row, Augusta exclaims, 'You have luck on your side tonight, Miss Trelawney.'

'Please, call me Barbara, and I do seem to be lucky at cards tonight,' Basia demurs, unable to tell her hostess that she's been playing the game for years with her family when it's only recently arrived in England.

'Another hand?'

Basia stifles a yawn and responds, 'My apologies, I am a little tired after the travel today.'

'Of course, my dear. Do you know the way to your room, or should I call a maid?'

'I shall be fine, thank you,' Basia says as she rises to her feet and heads for the door. As she reaches for the handle she turns. 'And thank you for a lovely evening.'

'Oh pish,' Augusta says, but the smile tugging at her lips shows she's pleased with the compliment.

3

FACING OLD HURTS

EVERYONE IS TURNING, distracted by some guy waving a gun around and yelling about the fall of civilisation. He is clearly a maniac. Her attention is still on Allan. His wound isn't healed, so she's come along to support him. Sweat beads on his forehead, and she's worried he has taken on too much. She's still watching when his eyes widen in surprise as a sharp crack fills the air followed by a red bloom spreading on his shirt. He sways and collapses as she reaches out to support him, but he drops to the ground in spite of her efforts.

'No.'

'No.' Basia sits bolt upright, the bedsheet clasped in her hands. It takes her a moment to realise she's in the guest room of Aunt Augusta's house in Winchester in 1913 and not watching Allan die yet again years in the future.

Finally, her breathing slows and the shaking stops. Her grief at the loss of Allan churns her insides. It's all that's left of him.

She lies back on the pillows. 'I should not have promised I would carry on your fight to bring the people of our world together.'

Although there's no one in the room to answer her, saying the words out loud is soothing, and the well of grief weighing her down doesn't seem so heavy. Trying to lighten it even more, she continues voicing all her fears.

'Perhaps we would have been better off allowing time to end, because it

will take strong, committed leaders to mend the rift between the people left above ground and those who escaped below.'

A tear slides down her cheek. 'I'm not strong enough to lead them, and I don't have the commitment and passion you did.'

Of course, no one answers and tells her it's all right to be scared. Still, there is something cathartic about speaking aloud the words she's held inside for so long, even if she's left feeling hollow and alone.

A soft knock at the door has her closing her eyes, hoping whoever it is will go away. No such luck. The door opens quietly. Whoever enters must be tiptoeing, as the next thing Basia hears is the click as it closes.

She opens an eye and finds a discreet maid has left a bowl of warm water and a fluffy white towel on the dresser. Sighing, she forces herself out of bed, reluctant to start the day. After the strained atmosphere at dinner last night, she's in no rush to make her way down to breakfast.

No doubt Izzy and her aunt will maintain a stoic silence interspersed with short, sharp exchanges, as they had last night. This morning, Basia will not make the same mistake of trying to thaw the chill.

Now dressed appropriately, she hopes, in a shirt and blouse, her hair in a plait, Basia pulls back the heavy curtains to find out what the day is like.

The street below bustles with people, carriages, horses and carts, and the odd motorcar. Watching them go about their lives is like seeing a scene in one of her books come to life, and she has to stop herself from clapping her hands like a small child. She can't wait to get out and about and immerse herself in the story.

She swiftly crosses the hall and knocks on Izzy's door. She opens it when she hears a faint 'Come in.'

She's happy to find her travelling companion dressed in a similar outfit to her own, but Basia bites back her exclamation of relief when she sees how pale her friend is and how listless and dark-rimmed her eyes are. Izzy looks like she hasn't slept a wink.

'Are you all right?' Basia asks.

Izzy attempts a smile. 'It's nothing a cup of coffee won't fix. Hopefully my aunt or one of her staff has remembered I prefer it in the mornings to tea.'

Feeling guilty about her earlier reluctance, she hooks her arm through Izzy's. 'Let's go and see, shall we?'

Downstairs, the breakfast room is blessedly empty. Izzy literally sighs with pleasure when she sees the coffeepot on the sideboard. She bypasses

the breakfast trays and pours herself a cup of the black liquid before taking a seat at the table and enjoying a long sip.

Lifting the lids of the hot dishes, Basia is faced with a difficult choice. Along with bacon, eggs, and sausages, one dish contains some odd fish and another something made with rice that smells faintly spiced.

'The fish are kippers, and the rice is kedgeree,' Izzy says, standing and making her way towards the food. Picking up a plate, she serves herself a little of everything before returning to her chair.

Basia is more circumspect, taking some sausages and egg and adding a little of the kedgeree to try. As she is about to sit, Augusta sweeps into the room with a bundle of black-and-white fur tucked into the crook of her arm.

'Good morning, my lovelies. And what a grand day it is too. I want you to meet Cuddles, my new companion. He arrived today.'

Izzy chokes on her food as she snorts a laugh. Augusta's frown forces her to pull herself together. 'You called your dog Cuddles?'

Ignoring the disdain in Izzy's voice, Augusta says, 'Yes, and a most apt name it is too. He only arrived this morning, and all he has done is cuddle with me.'

Izzy stops eating. 'He came today?'

Augusta continues to serve herself breakfast one-handed, then takes a seat with the dog settled in her lap before answering. 'Yes, the man who delivers our meat has been promising me a pup from one of his litters for some time.' She feeds the dog a morsel of sausage before starting in on her breakfast.

Izzy sends Basia a meaningful look. Basia shakes her head, not having the least idea of what Izzy is trying to tell her.

Izzy's voice sounds inside her head. *Sigma, is that you?*

'What are you doing?' she leans in and whispers close to Izzy's ear.

Izzy nods meaningfully at Augusta before answering in mindspeak. *Sigma said he might try to meet us here, and I'm pretty sure that's him.*

Basia stares at the dog sitting placidly in Augusta's lap. Sigma, the Time Guardian who helped save the world, could not get any further from his last animal disguise if he truly has taken the form of Cuddles. She had met him when he was Bruno—a German shepherd working as a tracker for the military.

She shakes her head as she takes in the now snoozing dog. 'I do not think that is him. Or maybe the Time Fixers stripped you of your powers when they sent you back.'

'You could hear me talking, could you not?'

Basia nods.

'Then I can still mindspeak.' *Sigma? Cuddles?* Izzy sends again. 'Maybe he does not want to upset Aunt Augusta by talking with us,' Izzy says when there's no response.

'What are you girls whispering about?' Augusta interrupts them, her tone terse. 'Isolde, you look dreadful. There are crow's feet forming around your eyes—it must be that London air.'

Or the fact that I'm five years older than I was when I left.

Basia wonders if Izzy knows she mindspoke what was likely meant to be internal dialogue.

'Isolde, perhaps you could do something with your day. Like taking Barbara for a stroll in the park.'

Basia almost leaps from her seat at the suggestion, but Izzy is slower to move.

'Come on,' Basia says. 'The fresh air will do us both some good.'

Izzy rises listlessly and makes eye contact with the dog in Augusta's lap. Cuddles raises his head expectantly, but Basia can't sense any mind contact.

Twenty minutes later the two girls arrive in the hallway, coats on, hatted and gloved. Jensen opens the door for them, his face impassive. Yesterday's animosity seemed to have disappeared when Augusta invited the girls to stay.

As Basia rushes down the stairs to the street, excited to get going, Izzy falls behind. She turns to find her friend in conversation with the butler. When Izzy rejoins her, she asks, 'What was that about?'

Slipping her arm through Basia's, Izzy says, 'Nothing important. Jensen was admonishing me not to hurt my aunt again or he wouldn't admit me back into the house—ever.'

'Wow, he's really protective of your aunt, isn't he?'

Izzy chuckles, and colour appears in her cheeks for the first time that day. 'You know, I always thought Jensen was sweet on Augusta, and he just confirmed it.'

Basia's free hand covers her mouth. 'You don't think they're….'

Another laugh escapes her companion. 'I wouldn't put it past Augusta. She's always been more egalitarian than most. However, I think that may be a step too far even for her.'

'Shame,' Basia says. 'Wouldn't it be nice if she were spending her time with someone she's close to when you're not here?'

Izzy wrinkles her nose. 'Jensen? No, I don't want to think about it.'

'He's not that bad,' Basia laughs.

'Come on, enough with the romance. Let me show you the famous Winchester Cathedral, followed by a visit to the most excellent teahouse in town.'

WINCHESTER HIGH STREET is a bustle of well-dressed people window shopping, walking, or stopping to talk with friends and acquaintances. Basia's head swings left and right until she becomes dizzy trying to take everything in.

It's not only the sheer number of people and the sense of having fallen into one of her favourite novels—it's also the experience of walking through a town that hasn't been devastated by nuclear bombs and seeing buildings left to rot because no one lives in them.

To say she's overwhelmed would be an understatement. That sensation only increases when Izzy leads her round the corner into the Cathedral Precinct. Winchester Cathedral itself is a stunning vision in creme stone outlined by a cloudless blue sky. It is beautiful and amazing and awe-inspiring. Basia gasps, but Izzy continues walking, unmoved, as if this is a building like any other.

Catching Izzy up, she asks, 'Can we go inside?' She's aware that she sounds like a small child asking for a treat, but she's so excited, she doesn't care.

Izzy doesn't alter her course, circumnavigating the park in front of the building, deftly avoiding the headstones dotted around. 'Maybe another time. I am a little tired for it today.'

Turning to her friend to object, she finds Izzy's pallor has returned, and she's looking more washed-out than ever. Making an effort to quell her disappointment, she takes pity on her friend and says, 'I know what will pick you up—a nice cup of tea.'

The smile Izzy forces at the mention of tea doesn't reach her eyes, and Basia begins to worry her friend is falling sick. No, her eyes are clear, and she isn't exhibiting any signs of a fever. Perhaps this is more a sickness of the heart than the body.

Izzy picks up the pace as they return to the high street, slowing down only to enter the teahouse. When Basia sees the cakes in the window, her eyes almost pop out of her head. The teahouse in London had been utilitarian compared to the confectionary delights on display here.

The shop is well lit but still dull against the bright sunshine outside. Basia grins when their waitress appears. She's dressed in a black ankle-length dress with a white apron over top, just like the maid last night. This will never get old. As the woman leads them through the room, Basia comments on how few people are sat at the tables.

'It is a little early for morning tea, miss. Are you sure you want to sit back here in the dark? A table is free by the window. Most people find it enjoyable to watch passers-by as they take their tea.'

'This will do fine, thank you,' Izzy says as she takes a seat. When the waitress tuts disapprovingly, she adds, 'I have a touch of a headache and prefer the dark.'

Basia runs her hand over the white lace tablecloth. It's been starched within an inch of its life and is so pristine, she hopes she won't embarrass herself by soiling it.

The waitress takes their order for English breakfast tea and two slices of their speciality—a spiced marble cake.

After the waitress departs, Basia angles her chair to get a better view of the shop. Izzy glares and shifts so her face is obscured from the rest of the patrons.

'What's the matter?' Basia asks. 'You snapped at the waitress, which is not like you at all.'

'Nothing is the matter. I am fine,' Izzy insists. 'Look, here are our drinks.'

They have their morning tea in an awkward silence. The cake is as special as Basia expected—the mixture of spices creates a taste explosion in her mouth. Having heard her mother talk of the spices they used in food before World War Three, it's a real treat to finally experience it.

She wonders how she will ever be able to go back to eating bland food when she returns home and opens her mouth to say so to Izzy. Then she promptly shuts it again when she sees the closed expression on her companion's face. It's not the time for idle chitchat.

Izzy pours them a second cup of tea, and Basia takes the opportunity to study the rest of the customers. The shop has become much busier since their arrival, with most of the tables occupied by women dressed in an array of colourful outfits, and the occasional man dotted here and there. Basia drinks in the sight, committing everything to memory.

'Would you like another pot?' Izzy asks when they've finished their drinks.

In spite of Izzy's reluctance to leave, Basia is itching to get back out into the world. 'No, I'm good. I wouldn't mind a walk around the shops if you're feeling up to it.'

'That should be fine,' Izzy responds without much enthusiasm.

Izzy calls for the bill, and when the formalities are done, Basia leads them back through the shop, only to have a gentleman step into their path when they're almost at the door.

Glancing up, Basia starts. 'Lionel?'

The man grins, and his green eyes sparkle with good humour. 'Not quite, but we do look rather alike. I am Stanley, Lionel's better-looking cousin. Pleased to make your acquaintance….'

Stanley has such a way about him, and he looks so much like Lee that Basia immediately feels like she's in the presence of an old friend, so she offers up the name Izzy chose for her without a second thought. 'I am Barbara, and my friend is—'

'Isolde and I have known each other since we were children. Nice to see you back in Winchester,' he says, looking over Basia's shoulder at Izzy.

Basia half turns in the small space between the diners to find her friend whiter than a ghost and frozen still, staring fixedly at the girl still seated at the table beside them. Recognition hits Basia like a lightning bolt—she needs no introductions.

She's Johan.

As the thought enters Basia's head, the girl's eyes flick up, slide over her, and lock with Stanley's. Something unspoken passes between them, and Stanley nods. He takes Basia's hand, tucking it in the crook of his elbow.

'Since we are clearly to be good friends, I wonder if you would do me the honour of taking a turn round the cathedral gardens with me?' He winks conspiratorially. 'I think these two have a lot to talk about, and we will just be in the way.'

'Um… Isolde?' She turns to seek her approval, but from the look on her friend's face, she's forgotten Basia is even here.

As Stanley leads her to the door, Josephine says, 'Take a seat, Isolde. I will order us a fresh pot of tea.'

Basia pauses in the doorway, waiting for some sign that Izzy is all right.

'Come, I promise you will be safe with me,' Stanley tells her, and she reluctantly lets him lead her away, sensing Izzy needs this time alone with her Jo.

FROM THE RECESSES of her mind, Izzy watches Stanley leading Basia away, and that part of her acknowledges that this is not right. Not just because she's responsible for Basia, but because Stanley has the knack of getting people talking, and she's worried Basia might let something slip. As they head down the street, she can already see they are deep in conversation.

I should follow them, make sure Basia is all right. A great idea, but she can no more move and leave the teashop than she can stop herself from breathing. She takes a seat opposite Jo, her eyes still firmly stuck on Basia's retreating back.

Finally, she allows herself to look at Josephine, and a tumult of feelings rushes through her: love, regret, hurt, and then finally, she settles on anger. With shaking hands, she pushes her chair back, intending to follow Basia, but Jo reaches for her.

'No, please do not run away again,' Jo entreats her, and the hurt in her voice freezes Izzy in place.

Uncertain of her next move, Izzy whispers, 'I am not sure we have anything to say to each other anymore.'

A waitress arrives with tea, and Jo busies herself pouring while Izzy resists the urge to drink in the sight of her. She loses the battle. Jo has attempted to tame her thick chestnut hair into a bun, but already bits are escaping and forming curls around her face in the humid air. Her dark brows draw into a frown as she concentrates on the task at hand.

Most people would find her face unremarkable—that is, until she turns her chocolate-brown eyes their way. When she looks up at Izzy, she's lost for a moment in those eyes, and all her fears melt away.

'I am sorry.' The words tumble from her lips before she realises she's saying them.

Jo pauses, the teapot hovering over the table. 'Sorry for what?' Her voice is strained, but she holds Izzy's gaze.

'I am sorry for running away. Sorry for not taking you with me. Sorry for.... Oh, I do not know... everything.'

Jo puts the pot down, then reaches across the table and clasps Izzy's hand. The touch is brief, the merest brushing of skin against skin, but Izzy shivers in response. Soon that hand is raising a cup to Jo's lips, and Izzy takes a sip of her own brew, desperate for Jo to respond.

'Where did you go?' Jo finally asks. 'Was it London?'

Izzy nods. 'Yes, I took up the position writing pamphlets for the NUWSS. I have travelled a bit too.' *You have no idea how I have travelled.* She wants to tell Jo everything. They had shared all their deepest secrets ever since they met when Jo's father purchased a manor in the same county.

Izzy's father, a member of the aristocracy, was at first disdainful of the new money from the North moving in. However, the two men soon found they had much in common and met frequently, allowing Jo and Izzy to get

to know each other. Of course, it helped that Jo's mother had come from 'good stock'—as her father put it.

'Have you been up to Manchester? I hear their branch has been quite active lately.' Jo's voice is maddeningly polite, giving none of her feelings away.

Izzy nods. 'Just the once.'

'Funny, we may even have been there at the same time, as Father took me up last visit. He decided I should start learning the business since I am to take over the reins.'

Izzy's eyes widen. 'I thought he would be training up Stanley.'

Jo's nose wrinkles. 'I am not sure Stanley sees himself managing a fabric and clothing factory. He is far more interested in the sheep producing the wool than how we turn it into cloth and then into clothing.'

'So you still intend to take over the factories and start improving conditions for the women and children who work for you?' Izzy tries to keep the surprise from her voice, but she can tell from the frown on Jo's face that she hasn't succeeded.

'Of course. Why would that change?' Jo's tone is guarded.

Because you're marrying Stanley. The unspoken words settle between them, and they fall silent, not quite able to find the old rhythm of their relationship.

They finish up their tea, and then they both rise as Jo places a few coins on the table before joining Izzy. In a last-ditch attempt to resurrect their friendship, Izzy threads her arm through Jo's as they leave the teashop.

Jo stiffens a little at her touch but doesn't remove her arm. 'Come, let us catch the others up,' she says.

With Jo close by her side, Izzy finally plucks up the courage to raise the subject that has haunted her since last night. 'Aunt Augusta said you are to be married in two weeks.'

Jo moves away a little, placing some distance between them. 'No point in waiting. Is that why you are back—to try and stop me?'

The question throws Izzy off balance, and she slides a look at Jo, trying to gauge how she should respond. 'No.... Yes.... Look, I do not know why I am back. I just know that I missed you. I—'

'Isolde, please. I am at peace with my decision. If you have come back to cause trouble, then we had best part ways here and now, and you can return to London.'

Izzy's stomach clenches, and she feels sick at the thought of being parted from Jo so soon after she's found her again. They walk along in silence for a bit, and Izzy considers whether the price of being friends with Jo might be

too high for her to bear after all.

Being her friend and nothing more. Always seeing her with Stanley. Is it enough? She had thought she wanted to come back to this, but perhaps distance made things look rosier—or perhaps she remembers Jo's feelings as having been stronger.

Taking a deep breath, she makes a decision—for today, a little bit of Jo is better than none. She can worry about the future later.

'What are your plans for after the wedding?'

Jo's step falters, and she glances sidelong at Izzy, as if trying to get a sense of her motivation. 'We will go down to Dorset for a while. I will open the house, and Stanley will see to the farm. Then, after a time, he will go to Australia and sort out some problems we are having with the sheep station. It has been left to a caretaker manager for too long.'

Izzy's world tilts on its axis. She doesn't want to ask the next question, but she also needs to know. 'And… will you go with him?' She dare not breathe while she waits for Jo's answer.

'I do not know…. There is so much to think about—the farm, the factory, our holdings in Australia—but I am considering it.'

But you don't mention what Stanley wants. Is this a marriage or a business arrangement? Izzy is wise enough not to voice her opinion.

'Ah, look—there is Stanley with your friend,' Jo says, changing the subject.

Izzy allows herself to be dragged along the path towards Stanley and Basia. All the while she wonders how it's come to be that she can no longer share her innermost thoughts with the person she was once closest to in all the world.

STANLEY CHATS AWAY, pointing out the sights of Winchester and telling Basia about some of the more colourful residents as he threads their way back towards the cathedral grounds. She finds him pleasant and diverting, and he's obviously well liked, going by the number of people who smile and say good morning to him.

'It was such good luck that we ran into you and Isolde at the teahouse this morning,' he says as they take a turn round the Cathedral Precinct. 'Josephine has sorely missed her friend since she went away.'

Basia isn't quite sure what to say. It isn't only that she's nervous about

talking to anyone in this time, but also because, although she knows how Izzy feels about this man's fiancée, she's unsure if Stanley is fully aware of their relationship. She decides to change the subject with a simple sentence even she couldn't get wrong. 'So, you and Josephine are getting married soon?'

'Yes, in two weeks' time, I shall be a married man.' Stanley sounds neither excited nor upset by the prospect. In fact, he could be talking about a business transaction for all the interest he shows.

Basia isn't quick enough to mask her confusion at his answer.

Stanley stops and takes her hand in his. 'Perhaps you think I am a cad because I do not love Josephine, or at least pretend to love her. Maybe you think I am only in this for her money. Or maybe you think she and Isolde are more suited?' His eyes twinkle with mischief.

'Um….' Basia chews on her bottom lip, unsure of how to answer such a direct question from a virtual stranger. She needs to be careful with her words and remember that he isn't a friend—no matter how familiar he feels to her.

Stanley isn't going to let her off the hook that easily, though. 'Maybe you wonder how I can bear to be around such an abomination… a woman who loves another woman? Or is it you cannot understand how I can marry a woman whom I know loves another?'

Stanley studies her, head cocked to the side, waiting for an answer.

'Well, more the second, I guess,' she finally replies.

Stanley smiles. 'It is true that many people will find the idea strange, which is why we only talk about such things with close friends. I am sure we can trust in your discretion.' An eyebrow rises in question, and Basia nods.

'Yes, you can trust me. I am great at keeping secrets.'

'Good.' He pats her hand, and they carry on wandering. 'You see, I have no interest in, um… that side of things—physical things between people.'

He pauses, perhaps waiting for a reaction from her, or maybe because that's all he's going to say. Basia opens her mouth to speak, but Stanley continues before she can utter a word.

'You appear to be good friends with Isolde, and I am sure you will hear the whole story sooner or later.'

Or perhaps not at all, Basia thinks, not sure where this conversation is going, or if she even wants it to continue.

Stanley appears unaware of her discomfort as he continues talking. 'And at least you will hear it from me. I have read about it in books, of course, and

some of the chaps have talked about different things, but it is all alien to me. I do not know whether it is because I am yet to find the right person, or perhaps I am not built that way… the way you need to be to feel physically attracted to someone.'

Basia isn't sure where to look.

Stanley finally seems to remember she's there. 'Ah dear, I did not mean to tell you all of that…. It is perhaps because you are one of those rare women who listens more than they speak.'

He stares at her as if expecting a response. There's so much going round in her head, she's unable to form a single coherent thought. Although she had come across studies on asexual humans while learning medicine from her mother, she's never had such a frank conversation with anyone about their sexuality. She understands the theory that some people are asexual from birth, but her sampling of humanity has been so small, she hasn't come across anyone quite like Stanley before.

'Oh dear, have I horrified you?' Stanley's face is a study of concern, and she almost falls over her own words in her effort to reassure him he hasn't.

'No, no! Of course not.' She pats his arm. 'It's just, I've never had someone speak so openly about their sexuality before. But I'm okay with it… with you, I mean.'

As the words leave her mouth, she realises her mistake—she's answered as Basia, not Barbara. Her eyes widen with dismay as Stanley's brows draw into a frown.

Closing her eyes, she sighs inwardly, wishing Izzy were here to help. She isn't, though, and Basia is going to have to use her own wits to get out of this. Opening her eyes, she lowers her gaze to show her dismay.

Offering an apology to the real Barbara Trelawney, Basia invents an excuse straight out of one of her many books.

'Oh, Stanley, please do not say anything. I am from the wrong side of the Trelawney family, and we are not quite proper. Although I was at school with Isolde, it was only because my uncle paid the fees. Sometimes I forget where I am and drop back into my regular speech. I have to be careful because we are staying with Isolde's aunt, and she would not have me in the house if she knew where I really came from.'

Stanley studies her, as if trying to assess the truth of her words.

Please be the true gentleman I believe you are, Basia prays.

He nods once, as if her words have convinced him.

'It seems you and I are both to hold each other's secrets. We really are best of friends now.'

He places her hand back into the crook of his arm, and they continue walking. Then he carries on talking as if her slip had never happened.

'Of course, once Josephine and I are married, I will do the right thing and father an heir. It is my duty and all that, what with Josephine being an only child. All part of the deal, really. After that, I suspect we will both fill our lives in other ways. Society will be appeased and will let us get on with our lives in peace, and we will both find some measure of happiness in this arrangement.'

While Stanley continues talking about his plans, Basia grows quiet and more than a little sad. Like Stanley, she had grown up in an age where same-sex relationships, nonbinary, and asexual people were frowned upon. At some point in history, the world had begun to accept people's differences, only to have that tolerance disappear when faced with the prospect of human extinction.

Procreation is at the heart of societal norms in both times. Here they protect bloodlines and inheritances, while in the future, they ensure there are enough people for humanity to survive.

Suddenly they stop walking again, and Stanley appears to be waiting for her to speak.

Unsure of what he'd asked, she fumbles for something appropriate to say. 'It is nice you have found a solution that works for you and Josephine.'

'But not for Isolde.' Stanley shakes his head slowly. 'She wants to take on the entire world and change it. I am afraid it is all or nothing for her, and that is what saddens Josephine the most.'

'And you would be happy to have Isolde in your lives?' Basia asks, not really believing someone would be all right with sharing their partner.

'If it makes Josephine happy…,' Stanley chuckles. 'Even if it did not make Josephine happy, I enjoy Isolde's company. I am not sure she likes mine so much, though.' He appears genuinely saddened by that thought.

Part of Basia wants to agree with Stanley, that leading a good and peaceful life is something to aspire to. Then she remembers how stifled she'd felt before Allan arrived and opened her eyes to the possibility of change. 'But surely Isolde is right to challenge things. How else will anything ever get better?'

'Challenging is all right, but expecting radical change?' Stanley shrugs. 'People's minds and their beliefs are not that easily altered, especially those who have a death grip on power. Besides, society has to have rules, you know, or we would descend into chaos.'

Basia stares at Stanley, unable to believe he's prepared to accept that he must hide his real self. 'But do you not long to be who you are, for people to accept you?'

Such a look of sadness crosses Stanley's face that Basia immediately regrets speaking so forcefully. Then he nods towards a couple across the park. The thin, darkhaired young man is arguing earnestly with the dainty blonde woman.

'There are worse things than marrying for friendship and position. Take my friend Nathanial over there. He is head over heels in love with Hannah, and they have been betrothed for more than a year. Every time he even suggests getting married, she comes up with another reason they should wait a little longer.'

Intrigued, Basia watches the couple as their fight becomes more animated. They both have a look of hopelessness about them, and it pulls at Basia's heart.

'Why does he not simply give her an ultimatum? "Marry me or I will find someone who will"?' Basia asks.

Stanley sighs. 'Because he loves her, and he cannot imagine himself happy without her in his life.'

A single tear escapes Basia's eye as sadness presses down on her—she empathises with Nathanial. She had met her soulmate in Allan, and then he'd died so soon after. The world is not as rich a place without him.

'Oh dear, I did not mean to sadden you. I mean, really, it is not as bad as all that. Come, I will introduce you,' Stanley blusters as he steers her towards the couple. 'I will prove to you I was exaggerating to make a point.'

His panic over her lone tear is sweet, as is his wanting to make everything right. Basia wipes the tear away, her mood a little lighter now.

As they approach, Basia can't help but overhear the conversation between Stanley's friends.

'Is a month too long to plan for? And we can still meet our commitments while planning a wedding. It does not have to be anything too spectacular. In fact, from my perspective, the quieter the better,' Nathanial is saying, almost begging.

Hannah places her hands on her hips. 'Are you suggesting we put ourselves before our duties? As educated people, we have a responsibility to help those less fortunate.'

'So, what, we put our own lives on hold indefinitely—oh, hello, Stanley.' Nathanial turns to them, his face red, but Basia can't tell whether it's from his anger or embarrassment at someone overhearing their private conversation.

'I am so sorry, old chap, I did not mean to interrupt,' Stanley apologises, although from his tone, Basia thinks he intended to do just that.

'No, no problem, simply a bit of a misunderstanding,' Nathanial says, trying not to look at his fiancée.

Hannah plucks at something on her floral-patterned skirt, studiously not meeting anyone's gaze.

'Nathanial, Hannah, I would like to introduce you to a friend of mine, Barbara. She is newly arrived in Winchester and is staying with Isolde Fielding.' In contrast to the tension surrounding the group, Stanley's voice is friendly, as though he thinks he can single-handedly clear the air.

'Does Josephine not mind you walking around with lovely young women?' Nathanial asks as he shakes Basia's outstretched hand.

Stanley runs a finger nervously around his collar. Basia wonders how many of these everyday comments he must endure and if it ever annoys him, living up to society's conventions.

'Um, well, Isolde's close friend Barbara and I are out for a friendly stroll in public, so there is nothing for her to worry about. Besides, she knows she can trust me.'

Hannah's skirt suddenly seems to be fixed, and she raises her eyes. 'Of course she does. Nathanial, leave him alone. He clearly only has eyes for Josephine. I mean, have you ever seen him spend more than a moment with another woman in the whole time we have been in Winchester?'

Basia flushes with embarrassment on Stanley's behalf as an awkward silence falls over the group. It's broken by Hannah before it's allowed to become too uncomfortable.

'We must make our apologies, Stanley, Barbara. We are expected for lunch with my parents. We should have dinner soon, Stanley, before the wedding.'

'Yes, we must. I will mention it to Josephine,' Stanley agrees as Hannah slips her hand into Nathanial's and virtually drags him away.

When they are well out of earshot, Stanley says, 'See? He is madly in love with her, and she leads him round like a child.'

Basia's lips curl into a smile. Stanley's defence of his friend is heart-warming. 'He seemed to be holding his own when we arrived,' she says, because she feels someone should be standing up for Nathanial. Though, in truth, she agrees with Stanley.

'He would jump into the jaws of hell for her, and she would let him. I much prefer the arrangement I have with Josephine. It is an honest bargain,

and I still get to be my own man.'

As she watches the couple cross the common, she wonders if she had felt empathy for Nathanial because she's so like him—following the one she loved even if it wasn't in her best interests. When she was with Allan, she had lost sight of her own goals.

Of course, she truly believes uniting the disparate groups in future Hampshire is the best way to prevent another war. What she worries about is whether or not she's the best person to lead people towards that goal, in spite of her deathbed promise to Allan.

'Barbara? Are you all right? You have come over all pale. Have we overdone it? Shall I find us a place to sit?'

Basia pulls herself back to the present to find a concerned Stanley clasping her hand. Unable to explain her scattered thoughts, she's relieved to see Izzy and Josephine approaching.

'I am fine, Stanley, and here is your fiancée and Isolde.'

With the others joining them, Stanley is so distracted, she doesn't have to explain her sudden sadness. As they return to Aunt Augusta's, she happily follows the others. Her excitement at being in the world where some of her favourite authors penned their stories has been washed away by the intrusion of her real-world problems.

4

SIGN OF THE TIMES

WALKING ARM IN arm with Josephine, Izzy begins to relax. They may not be talking, but their silence is at least companionable. Izzy catches sight of Basia and Stanley across the park.

'They are over there.' She points, but Jo is distracted by the couple who rudely brushes past them, heading for the high street.

'They do not look very happy. I wonder what is wrong now?' Jo comments.

Izzy squints, trying to get a better look at the pair, but can't place them. 'Do we know them?' she finally asks.

Jo's laugh tinkles. 'Goodness no, they are friends of Stanley's. Hannah's family have taken a house down here for the rest of the year while her father does something with the local regiment.'

'Oh.'

'We had them over to tea last week, and they did nothing but bicker,' Josephine says. 'Stanley wants me to invite them for dinner, but I am not sure… though I guess I should for his sake.'

Izzy raises an eyebrow. 'Perhaps you should invite them to the theatre with you. They cannot argue while a show is on.'

Josephine chuckles. 'Isolde, you are naughty. Still….'

'Hello, you two,' Stanley says before Jo can finish her thought.

'Did you invite Nathanial and Hannah to dinner with us?' Jo asks as she releases Izzy and links her arm through Stanley's.

Stanley's face flushes. Not a good look for someone with pale skin and fair hair. 'No, I did not think.... Besides, they had to rush off for lunch.'

'Good,' Josephine says, 'because Isolde has given me a much better idea. Speaking of lunch, though, we should head back.'

A cheeky grin crosses Stanley's face as he catches Izzy's eye. 'I rather thought we would invite ourselves to lunch with Augusta. She always enjoys our company, and I am sure you and Isolde still have a lot to talk about.'

Jo sends him a thunderous look, but Izzy can't help but grin back at Stanley. In all her angst over losing the love of her life to him, she'd forgotten what fun he could be. It's difficult to stay mad at him for long.

'I warn you, she was not in the best of moods this morning. Then again, you always could charm her, Stanley.'

Jo glances from her friend to her fiancé and sighs. She knows when she's beaten. Basia, on the other hand, looks like she would rather be any place but here.

'Are you all right?' Izzy asks Basia as they follow Stanley and Jo.

'Mmm.'

Izzy places a hand on her arm. 'Basia,' she whispers, 'is something wrong?'

Basia shakes her head slowly, almost as if she isn't quite with them. Izzy's worry eases a little when her friend says, 'It's just.... Let's just say my conversation with Stanley was a little unsettling. He raised some ghosts I'm not yet ready to face.'

Izzy slides her arm around Basia's waist and gives her a swift hug. 'We travelled such a long way in time that it is easy to forget you only lost Allan a few days ago. You need time to mourn and to find a new path for yourself. Don't force it.'

Basia closes her eyes for a moment, then whispers, 'I feel like a fraud, missing him so much.' She wipes a tear from her eye. 'We were only together for such a short time. I don't feel I have the right to be this sad.'

Giving Basia another hug, Izzy leans her head on her shoulder. 'Love and loss have no time limit. If you are sad, go ahead and be sad. There is no right or wrong way to mourn a death.'

Basia leans into her for a moment, as if drawing some extra strength, before pulling away and giving her a tear-laden smile. 'How did it go with Jo?'

'Ah, changing the subject, I see,' she chuckles. 'I have the opposite problem to you. I've had time to consider what I want from Jo, but it's only been a few weeks for her, and she's still angry with me.'

'But you two seemed okay when you joined us, and she *is* coming to lunch.'

'If Stanley hadn't suggested it, she would have been more than happy to leave us.' Izzy can't keep the pain from her voice. It hurts her that Jo is coming to please Stanley and not her.

As they turn the corner into Augusta's street, Basia chuckles out of nowhere. 'Um, I guess I should warn you, Stanley thinks I'm not as well-bred as I ought to be.'

Izzy's eyes widen in shock. 'What did you do?' she asks as a dour Jensen opens the door.

Basia is saved from answering as he ushers the group inside, saying in his tartest voice, 'You are late. Madame is already in the dining room.'

They remove their outdoor wear and hand it to a maid under Jensen's watchful eye.

'Can you please set two more places, Jensen? Stanley and Josephine are staying for luncheon,' Izzy says.

A flicker of annoyance crosses Jensen's face, but he is too well schooled to speak out. 'As you wish, miss.' His words are more clipped than usual.

Normally she wouldn't have been so high-handed with the butler. Although her aunt won't mind her asking Jo and Stanley to lunch, in the past, Izzy would have waited for her to issue the order for more settings herself.

It seems she can't strike the right note with anyone. Five years with the Time Fixers have changed her enough that she can't slot back into being Isolde.

When Jensen opens the dining room door, she almost bolts. With the tension between her and Jo and Basia still making slip-ups, she's uncomfortable enough as it is. She doesn't think she can sit through a meal with guests.

'Isolde, do not hover in the doorway,' Augusta orders, and Izzy obeys, letting the others pass by her into the room.

'Oh, Stanley, such a pleasure. Are you joining us? And you, too, Josephine. The more the merrier,' Augusta carries on, not noticing Izzy's reticence.

Before Izzy can make her excuses and leave, Augusta says, 'For goodness' sake, Isolde, come in and take a seat.'

Augusta sits at the head of the table with a thin birdlike woman of around her own age on her left. Izzy has met Mrs Trimms a number of times, as have the others. Stanley takes a seat beside the older woman and immediately

begins charming her.

On Augusta's left is a familiar face, but it takes her moment to recognise Maisie Ottaway from the train. Basia is quicker off the mark and takes the seat beside their travelling companion.

Josephine and Izzy wait for Jensen to lay the additional places before sitting opposite each other. She and Jo have spent many hours at this table with Augusta, discussing politics and imagining a different future. Sitting across from Josephine now, all of that old camaraderie has gone.

As if sensing her discomfort, Augusta's new companion pokes his head out from under the table. His fluffy body brushes against her leg as if to give her comfort. Leaning down, she picks Cuddles up and places him in her lap, absent-mindedly stroking him while the first course is served.

Sigma, is that you? I hope it is. I need your help. I've no idea why I came back. Nothing here has changed, but I have. I missed Jo so much, and I had hoped she missed me, too, but she's moved on with her life. If you were here, you would tell me to take my time and get to know everyone again. Why won't you talk to me and tell me yourself?

'Isolde, what are you doing? You are almost choking poor Cuddles. Here, bring him to me.'

The room slowly comes back into focus, and Izzy realises everyone is looking at her. She glances down at the dog, and he stares back at her with loving but vacant eyes. Slowly she rises to her feet and hands the dog to her aunt.

'What is wrong with you?' Augusta hisses.

'Nothing,' Izzy mumbles before returning to her seat. Perhaps Cuddles is not her friend Sigma in animal form after all. The very thought that he isn't here leaves her even more alone.

After the second course is served, Izzy tries to pay more attention. Mrs Trimms brings up the Pilgrimage, and it sets off a lively conversation.

'In our day it was all petitions to Parliament, Augusta, but this march through England is such an inspired idea.'

'Do you really think people will change their minds about women getting the vote by listening to speeches?' Stanley asks, and Izzy silently applauds him.

Mrs Trimms's eyes narrow. 'Are you against women having the vote, young man?'

'Me? Goodness no,' Stanley laughs. 'I think we would all be better off with women running the show. Well, they could not make a worse job than we men have been doing.'

Again Stanley has smoothed over a wrinkle, and Izzy wishes she didn't

like the man so much. In truth, the only thing she has against him is that he's going to marry Jo.

Basia moves into the seat next to her. 'Isolde, do you think we could join the march? It goes through Portsmouth. Or perhaps we could meet it at Petersfield or Haslemere? Maisie says Miss Fielden is to deliver her speech at Haslemere.'

'I see no reason why we should not go and hear Miss Fielden speak,' Izzy says and is instantly rewarded with a beaming smile from Basia.

Reminded that she's actually here in Winchester to do a job, Izzy leans around to catch Maisie's eye. 'Do you think Miss Fielden would speak with me if we went to the rally in Haslemere?'

Maisie winces. 'I am not sure. She does not like to speak to the press because they often twist her words. If I tell her how kind you have all been to me, perhaps it might convince her to talk to you.'

'Thank you, Maisie,' Izzy says. 'When do you go and join her?'

'I shall be staying with Mrs Trimms for two more days yet. I received a telegram today that Miss Fielden has some additions to her speech. They should arrive by post tomorrow. Once I have the notes, I must write a clean copy of the new version and have it ready for her when she arrives in Haslemere.'

'She is lucky to have such a diligent secretary,' Augusta says, patting Maisie's hand. 'Now, shall we have tea in the drawing room?'

Stanley's expression is rueful as he says, 'I am sorry, but we must refuse. Josephine and I have an appointment at the solicitors that we simply cannot be late for—another time, perhaps.'

Izzy hopes her relief isn't too obvious as she watches Josephine and Stanley take their leave.

'You two are family and are always welcome,' Augusta says as she bids the two farewell.

'I am afraid I must be excused as well,' Izzy says once Stanley and Jo have left the room. 'Lionel will be here tomorrow, and I have very little to give him on the march that he would not be able to find himself from the newspapers.'

'If I may suggest,' Mrs Trimms said, 'you might start by talking to some of the shop assistants on the high street. They have been quite active in our local suffragist group.'

Izzy already knew this information, but Mrs Trimms was only trying to be helpful.

'Thank you, Mrs Trimms. I will take your advice. Barbara, would you like to join me?'

Basia glances up from her conversation with Maisie. 'If it is all right with you, I would prefer to stay here for a while. I find myself a little tired.'

Izzy shrugs. Catching Augusta's frown, she interprets it as 'Girls of breeding do not make such common gestures.'

Are you all right? she sends.

Basia gives her a slight nod. *I'm still feeling a little sad after this morning. Besides, I would just be hanging around while you ask questions. At least here I'll be able to talk to Maisie.*

'Of course, Basia. Coming with me would be boring for you, and you must be tired after this morning's activities.' She turns to her aunt, and in an attempt to make amends for her unladylike behaviour, she says, 'I will be back in time for tea, Aunt Augusta.'

BASIA SETTLES ONTO the sofa and accepts a cup of tea from Izzy's aunt. While the others chat away, she stares into the crackling fire, surprised at how weary she is after the emotional turmoil of the morning. She'd done very little compared to a normal day on the family farm, but she's finding it difficult to concentrate on what the other women are saying.

Sipping her tea, she marvels at the smoky taste. It's unlike anything she's drunk before. When there's a pause in the conversation, she asks, 'What type of tea is this?'

'Why, just common old Darjeeling,' Augusta tells her. 'Although I have to say, my supplier does have the best quality tea in all of England. Do you not have it at home?'

'I don't th… I do not believe so. It is delicious,' Basia stutters, holding her breath and hoping Augusta didn't notice.

Fortunately Izzy's aunt simply flushes with pleasure. 'Before you go, I will give you my supplier's details so you can pass them on to your mother.'

'Thank you' is all Basia says because she can't say, 'Tea and spices are severely limited in the future, where I come from.'

Taking another sip of tea, Basia decides she's going to stop wallowing and make the most of everything before she has to return to her time—even if it means she won't be able to fit into her clothes when she gets back. With a renewed sense of purpose, she focuses on what Augusta and Mrs Trimms are talking about.

'My dear Augusta, because you run your poor dead Harold's business affairs, you are treated differently to us mere wives and mothers. Men respect your opinion, whereas it never occurs to them that I would have one at all,' Mrs Trimms is saying.

'And as I have said more times than I can count, if you do not stand up for yourself and make yourself heard, how will men ever consider that you want to have a say in politics, let alone a vote?'

Mrs Trimms's eyes narrow, and Basia senses she's ready for a fight.

Before she can speak, Maisie sits forward in her chair and says, 'We do have to be careful, though. Those Pankhurst women and their followers have gotten men so scared of a violent overthrow, any time a woman stands up for herself, she is tarred with the same brush.'

Augusta snorts. 'We must not let those women speak for all of us, yet we must not be cowed into the shadows either.'

'What do you propose we do, then?' Basia asks, genuinely interested.

Augusta's head tilts slightly as she considers her answer. 'We simply must not stop pushing for the vote, but perhaps for a time, we must not push quite so hard. The Pilgrimage is an inspired idea. We must find more ideas like this.'

'And you do not believe the more radical women are helping by keeping the issue forefront in everyone's mind?' Basia presses.

'An interesting question,' Augusta says, sending Basia an approving smile. 'Although I cannot condone civil disobedience and lawbreaking, I can understand why they choose to take direct action. And, if I am honest, they have gotten people talking.'

Maisie sits forward, her eyes blazing. 'There is no excuse for their behaviour.'

'Ah, the convictions of youth. My dear, I have been a part of this movement for a long time, and I know change has come slowly—too slowly for many. And it is that snail's pace that has driven women to violent acts.' Augusta looks into the fire. 'Many of my old friends have not been well treated by the authorities. I shudder to think how demeaning being force-fed must be.'

Maisie's lips form a line, and she clearly wants to say something. Eventually she can hold it in no longer. 'If they did not break the law, those women would not be in prison. If they were not in prison, they would not need to go on hunger strikes to make a point.'

'And then they would not need to be force-fed. I understand your argument. However, many of them have been sentenced under the flimsiest of pretences. I think perhaps their biggest mistake is not the violence or the unruly protests

but more that they have not recognised that their actions are creating a reaction of fear which affects us all.'

'And that fear is causing men to hold on to what they have with an iron fist,' Mrs Trimms says. 'Which slows the pace of change even more. Ah, it is a vicious circle.'

The room falls silent as the four women follow their own thoughts. Basia can't guess what the other women are thinking, but she's pretty confident their paths are miles from hers.

From her study of history, she knows it will take a world war before a small number of women get the vote in England and another war before women are allowed into many professions—although they will soon be pushed out of those jobs once the men return home. It has her wondering if it will take another war for people to work together in her time.

No, she can't let that happen. The population is barely holding on as it is. They can't afford to lose good people to senseless fighting. There has to be another way.

'Well, this has been an interesting end to a lovely lunch,' Mrs Trimms says as she stands to leave.

'Perhaps a reflection of the times we live in,' Augusta replies as she pulls the bell.

As they wait for Jensen to come and show the guests out, Maisie says, 'Barbara, I would love to meet with you and Isolde tomorrow if you have time. I am sure Miss Fielden would be interested in what she has found out from the local women.'

'I will see what we can arrange,' Basia prevaricates. She would enjoy seeing Maisie again, but Izzy had been in such a strange mood over lunch that Basia can't predict what her response to the invitation will be.

In fact, Basia would bet her life that Izzy's need to go out is less about writing her story for Lionel and more about dealing with her feelings after spending time with Josephine.

PLACING HER PEN on the bureau, Izzy stares at the words on the page. They had flowed from her hand as if someone else were directing her. Having heard the lofty ideals of the leaders of the Women's Pilgrimage, she's been brought back to earth by the words of the local working women.

Like everyone else involved with the march, they hope to sway enough hearts and minds to support another 'votes for women' petition to Parliament.

However, they're more pragmatic than the movement's leaders and believe there will need to be many more such marches before public opinion swings their way and politicians are forced to vote for change.

They're also questioning the timing of the Pilgrimage while so many are angry at the actions of the suffragettes. Already, accounts of women being attacked on the march have been coming through, and they report being afraid for their welfare when attending local meetings.

At first they had been reluctant to talk about it. Winchester is a small community, after all. However, with a little prompting, and promises of anonymity, they admitted that a group of men had started lying in wait for them to leave the meeting hall.

Some were bold enough to follow them home, taking note of where they lived. They threatened women and their families with violence if they continued with their wicked ways, and the threat has been escalating in both intensity and frequency.

'I tell you, our meetings are only half the size they once were since they started hanging around,' one shopgirl had told Izzy. 'Some of us have young children, and others have not told their husbands what they are doing, and so it is easier not to come.'

The girl sounded apologetic, almost guilty, that some of her friends had put family over the cause. Izzy won't stand in judgement of them, though. She knows all too well that there will be more violence and more fear before women get the vote.

'Everyone must do what is right for them,' she had agreed. 'Those who are unable to openly support the cause can assist in other ways, I am sure.'

Izzy knows the fight for equality will only ever move forward in small, hard-won steps. Once women have the vote, there is still the fight for other forms of equality, like equal pay for equal work. History shows that they don't meet this goal before the world falls into its last and final war. It all seems so futile.

Flopping down on her bed in a way that would give her aunt conniptions, Izzy stares at the ceiling. Writing an article in support of the march is advocating for social change, but she's become used to taking more direct action.

She can't remember when she had last gone more than a couple of days without being thrown into a difficult situation while trying to set the world

on a better course of action—one that would see all people treated with respect and would not end in the horrific holocaust of World War Three.

Now that she's back home, she's frustrated both at the lack of direct action and at the hope many hold about future change. Has she always been this pessimistic, or is this the result of five years more experience and a knowledge of the future?

A tap on the door sees her shoot upright. Straightening her clothes, she attempts to hide her surprise as Jo slips into her room.

'Jo, what are you doing here?'

'I have not got long. Stanley is waiting for me downstairs,' Jo starts but is unable to continue.

Izzy holds herself still, not wanting to frighten Jo away, but she's unsure of how to help her.

Jo takes a deep breath, and the words rush out. 'Why did you come back, Izzy? If it was not for my wedding and to wish me well, and it was not to ask me to give Stanley up, then why?'

'Because—'

'Because I was starting to get over you. Now… now I am confused.' Jo's hands are tying themselves in knots, and she fixes her gaze on the carpet as if waiting for a blow to descend.

Izzy sighs. There are so many things she could say. She should tell Jo something that will cut their ties and allow her to move on, but she hasn't come back to live a lie. Perhaps this last time, she'll tell Jo how she feels.

'I missed you. The world is not so bright without you in it.'

Jo doesn't move. 'Is that it?'

All or nothing, Izzy thinks. 'And, if I am honest, I hoped you missed me.'

'And?'

Does Jo truly want me to say the last words out loud? The room remains silent. Izzy guesses she must. 'And that because you missed me, you had changed your mind about Stanley.'

Jo raises her head. Tears glisten in her eyes. 'Isolde—'

'I am aware it is selfish and self-serving, but you asked for the truth.'

'Isolde, I told you about our arrangement, and you still rail against it.' She takes a step towards Izzy but stops herself.

'I know, I know.' Izzy tries to keep the impatience out of her voice but fails. 'Marry, produce an heir, go your own ways.'

'I owe my father that, Izzy. He deserves an heir to pass his business on

to. Unlike you, I have no brother to take up that burden, and I do not have the luxury of holding out for a love match as you insist you must.' Her eyes silently beg Izzy to understand.

Izzy starts to reach for Jo, but then her hand drops to her side. 'I understand your reasons, but I cannot bear the thought of Stanley…. I just can't—'

'We all have responsibilities, and my love for you does not wipe those away.' Jo takes another step, and Izzy thinks her heart might burst from her chest.

The two women stand an arm's-length apart now. Izzy wants nothing more than to cross that void and take Jo into her arms, but so many things hold her back.

In all the years she's been a Time Fixer, she never found out what happened to Josephine and Stanley. Did they survive the war? Did they have a child? Was there actually a way for her to fit into this world if she stayed? Or would she simply be ruining Jo's life?

'Jo, I want so much for the two of us to be together. You believe you have space for both of us in your life, and I do not see anywhere for me to fit. I miss you so when I am not here—' Her voice catches, and she swallows down the lump in her throat. 'Perhaps I should not have come back.'

As the words spill from her, Izzy's chest tightens, making it hard to breathe. *Is this it? Is it truly the end?*

Jo closes the gap between them, taking hold of both of Izzy's hands. 'There is a way forward for us, a way that should be acceptable to everyone if you can only move past that one little hitch.' Jo leans forward, her lips grazing Izzy's cheek. 'Can you think about it… for me?'

Their eyes meet briefly, but before Izzy can answer, Jo dashes from the room as the tea gong sounds.

Taking a deep breath, Izzy tries to centre herself before appearing downstairs, but she can't shake the feeling that she doesn't belong here anymore. She quickly checks herself in the mirror and is not surprised that she looks every one of her twenty-four years. A part of her knows she should use some concealer to hide the fact that she isn't the nineteen-year-old who left home, but she's too shattered to care.

Of course Augusta has to notice she isn't herself when Izzy joins her and Basia in the drawing room.

'Isolde, you look positively ancient today. You have certainly lost the bloom of youth while living in London. I will ask Jenkins to pour you a tonic before dinner.'

'Thank you, Aunt,' she mumbles, wishing she had taken the extra time to get ready before coming down.

Basia shoots her a sympathetic glance, and her mood lightens a little.

Izzy has no idea how she manages to make it through afternoon tea, let alone dinner that night. Basia's presence certainly helps. She manages to keep up a conversation with Augusta and then to include Izzy in the teatime conversation when she asks how her research had gone that afternoon.

For the first time since arriving home, Augusta's attitude towards her thaws a little, and she even asks to read what Izzy has written so far. Izzy takes her notes down at dinnertime, and much to her surprise, her aunt even comes up with some ideas on how to improve the content.

Still, it's like someone else is going through the motions while she watches from within. Finally, dinner concludes, and she's free to retreat to her room without seeming rude, using the excuse that she wants to update her work before Lionel arrives tomorrow.

She's almost finished her amendments when someone knocks tentatively on the door.

'Izzy, it's only me.' Basia opens the door a crack and pops her head in. 'Are you okay? You seemed a little… off today.' Basia hovers in the doorway, her face pinched with worry.

'I'm getting there.' That's all she intends to say, but the sadness in Basia's eyes is her undoing, and the words come of their own accord. 'I still have some things to work through, but at least now I'm almost sure I don't belong here anymore. My mind's telling me this. I just need to get my heart on board.'

'Oh, Izzy. I'm so sorry.'

She takes a deep, calming breath and offers her friend a small smile. 'It's okay, Basia. Time will mend my heart.' It's as if saying everything out loud has freed her, and suddenly, as if she's laid down a heavy load, she is lighter. However, she's said enough, and it's time to stop being so self-absorbed.

'What about you? How was your day?'

Basia's smile is tremulous. 'I'm loving this world. The sights, the sounds, the tastes…. It's like a fantasy come to life, but, like you, I don't fit in here. I can't show how I'm really feeling, and it's exhausting being someone else all the time.'

'Yes, isn't it?' Izzy agrees.

'I believed it would be worth it, though. I mean, Sigma was so sure I would find the answers I need here. I thought so too. Now I'm not so sure.'

Izzy chuckles. 'Mmm, he was sure, wasn't he? And he hasn't even had the good grace to turn up and help us, or at least let us tell him how wrong he was.'

A look of understanding passes over Basia's face. 'That's what you were doing with the dog at lunch, wasn't it? You were convinced Cuddles was Sigma, and you were trying to get him to speak with you.'

Izzy nods sheepishly, and the two girls burst into laughter. When they finally settle down, Izzy says, 'Sigma may not have turned up in person to help, but that laugh at his expense did the trick.'

'For me too,' Basia agrees, a genuine smile on her face. The weight on Izzy's shoulders lightens even more. 'Sleep well,' Basia says, closing the door behind her.

5

GOING BACKWARDS TO GO FORWARD

A LOUD SNICK tells Basia the maid has left the room. She rolls onto her back and stretches her body, resisting the urge to curl up and go back to sleep. Through a gap in the curtains, she can just make out the crimson sky. It's almost dawn, too early to get up yet.

At home she would be up and inside the barn, milking the cow by now. Mum would be in the kitchen, making porridge for breakfast, and her father and Johan would be preparing for the day's work—either getting ready for a hunt or hauling out farm implements. She doesn't miss the early wake up or the work, but boy, does she miss her family.

Glancing over at the steaming bowl of water, she sighs. Here she might have the luxury of a maid bringing her water to wash in the morning and food she's never eaten before, but nothing is familiar, and she can't be herself. Hell, she can't even speak normally. It's time she returned, but to what?

Not to the role Allan wanted her to take up, and also not to her home in the country where she would be expected to find someone to spend the rest of her life with.

It's a big decision giving up her promise to Allan—to be a leader in the movement uniting their people. She mentally shakes her head. No, she isn't giving it up—she'll merely approach it from a different angle. If there's one thing she's learned from Maisie, Augusta, and Mrs Trimms, it's that not all change is brought about by confrontation or by great leaders. Societal change can also be effected by small acts by a number of individuals.

Word will spread in the underground town, Portsdown, of the changes in the world above. Many will want to leave, and she'll work with her local communities to ensure they have somewhere to go.

She won't be at the centre of it all, and it won't be as exciting as running away from home with a boy hunted by soldiers from Portsdown. What she will have, though, is a real purpose in her life, and she'll still be close to her family, who she's sure will support her.

Suddenly full of energy, Basia is keen to embrace the day. She throws back the covers, and the cool morning air hitting her skin wakes her more fully. She quickly washes and dresses—well, as quickly as she can in Edwardian clothing. Now that she's made up her mind, she's impatient for Izzy to take her home.

Unfortunately her momentum is stalled when she enters the breakfast room to find herself alone. Heaping her plate with food from the heated silver salvers, she takes a seat at the table and picks at her breakfast.

Where is Izzy? Should I go and wake her? She's convinced herself to do just that when the door opens and Izzy herself appears. Although she's impatient to get going, she waits until Izzy is sitting with a cup of coffee and some toast before she broaches the subject.

'I am ready to go home,' she states.

Izzy raises dull, lifeless eyes to her and nods. 'I am meeting with Lionel to give him the story at two. We can leave after that.'

Basia wants to ask why they can't leave now. Surely Jensen can arrange for Lionel to get the piece for the newspaper. Then she takes a closer look at Izzy.

Last night Basia had sensed her return home had not been all she wanted it to be. Now it seems the experience has taken a bigger toll on the woman than she first thought. The strong, confident woman she first met has turned into a lost little girl.

'Izzy, are you okay? Do you want to talk about it?'

From across the table, Izzy's eyes stare blankly at her. Slowly they focus,

and Izzy smiles wanly. 'No, I am not okay, and I do not think I have been for some time.'

She takes a sip of coffee, and Basia wonders if she'll say more.

Izzy puts her cup back down and continues, 'I have been running away from something painful, and yesterday I finally faced up to it. So, while I am not all right, I believe now I have a chance to be.' Her hands tremble as she picks up her coffee again.

'Are you coming back here once you take me home?' Basia asks.

Izzy shrugs. 'No, probably not. I do not think I belong here anymore. Maybe I will go back to the Time Fixers. Perhaps Cynthia and Beta will find a place for me in their new—'

The door bangs against the wall as Augusta flies into the room, Cuddles tucked under one arm and a sobbing Mrs Trimms hooked through the other. 'You sit down, and I will fix you a nice cup of tea, Minnie.'

Augusta leads her friend to the seat beside Izzy and plonks Cuddles on her lap. Mrs Trimms absently strokes Cuddles, and the dog curls into her as if sensing her distress. Over the clatter of cups, Izzy asks the distraught woman what's wrong.

'Mai… Maisie went to a… suffragist meeting last night…. She thought she could encour… encourage some of the girls to join the march.' Mrs Trimms sniffs, fiddles round in her pocket for a handkerchief, and then dabs at her eyes before continuing. 'When I awoke this morning, I was informed she did not return last night.'

Mrs Trimms dabs at her eyes again, then in a woeful tone adds, 'And I cannot find the copy of the speech she wrote for Miss Fielden. I know it was on her writing desk yesterday….'

Izzy and Basia lock eyes. *This isn't good,* Izzy sends.

Augusta places a cup of tea in front of the crying woman and takes a seat on the other side of her. 'All will be well, Minnie—'

'But it will not, Augusta. Some of the girls have been followed home and subjected to abuse after the meetings….'

'Now, now, please do not upset yourself.' Augusta pats her friend's hand. 'It is likely she got talking, realised how late it was and that your house would be locked up, and elected to stay with one of the girls.'

Basia catches Izzy's eye. Izzy had spoken with some of the local suffragists yesterday, and Basia now wants to judge her friend's reaction. Izzy is white as a sheet, and when her eyes meet Basia's, it's clear she thinks something

bad has happened to Maisie.

'Perhaps we should check the hos—'

A glare from Augusta stops Izzy midsentence.

'Just in case something is not quite as it seems, I have had Jensen call for the police. I am sure they will be able to track her down if she has not yet returned to your home, Minnie.'

Before anyone can say anything more, the door opens, and Jensen enters. The four women turn expectantly, but Maisie isn't with him.

'Miss Josephine and her young man have arrived. Shall I tell them the timing is not convenient, ma'am?'

'They are family, Jensen. Please show them in,' Augusta says.

Izzy's knuckles turn white as she grips her cup more tightly, and Basia guesses her friend would rather not have Jo and Stanley around this morning. After a sleepless night and with her decision to leave just made, Basia is sure Izzy doesn't want her goodbyes to be said like this.

'No, wait,' Augusta says, and Izzy relaxes a little. 'Show them to the morning room. We will join them in a moment—and please arrange fresh tea and coffee.'

'As you wish, ma'am.'

The door closes behind the butler, and Augusta's eyes sweep the table. 'I am sure no one feels like finishing their meal,' she says.

Basia looks down at the bacon and eggs that had earlier seemed so appetising, but now her stomach is churning so much, she couldn't eat another mouthful.

'I think I am done,' she confirms.

When they join the others in the morning room, a chintz-inspired affair with a large mahogany desk directly opposite the drawing room, they find Stanley has disappeared. Josephine is sitting by the empty fireplace, a cup of tea in hand.

As they arrange themselves, Stanley returns, followed by Nathanial and Hannah. The latter's pursed lips tell Basia she is none too happy to be here.

'Look who I saw wandering by,' Stanley says and is surprised by the cold response from most of the room.

'Stanley, now is not the time for visitors,' Augusta says tartly. 'Not when Mrs Trimms's house guest has gone missing.

'What?' Stanley splutters at the same time Nathanial gasps, 'Pardon?' and the room erupts into a cacophony of questions and explanations.

More tea and coffee are brought in, and amongst all the chaos, Izzy leans

in to Basia and whispers, 'I have decided to leave my article with Jensen. I am ready to go when you are.'

Basia almost drops her teacup. 'We cannot go yet. Why are you all right to save complete strangers in my world yet leave Maisie, whom you have met, to her fate in yours?'

Izzy's mouth forms a hard line. 'You and I cannot interfere anyway because we might be changing history. I mean, we are not even sure Maisie is not meant to disappear. Besides, she must be returned safe and sound because I am pretty sure Miss Fielden gives her speech.'

Basia's jaw drops. 'What is wrong with you?' she hisses. 'You know Maisie. How can you just abandon her? The Izzy I followed here was prepared to do anything it took to do the right thing—no matter what.'

Izzy stares into the fire and says, 'I thought you wanted to go home.'

'I do, but I cannot abandon a friend, even if you can.' Izzy picks up her tea and takes a sip. *Ah, I might have a way to convince Izzy to stay.* 'What if our being here changed the timeline somehow, and that meant Maisie was taken or hurt in some way she would not have been if we had not come?'

Beside her, Izzy's blank look is now replaced with a flicker of interest. 'That is a possibility, but unlikely. If this is an abduction or a murder, it would require direct intervention, which is not allowed. And I do not believe either the Time Fixers or the Time Guardians would send operatives out while I am here—especially as our presence would already have caused small ripples.'

Basia stares at the dog sitting in Augusta's lap. *If only you were Sigma, you would know how to jolt Izzy from her apathy.* The dog returns her gaze with liquid brown eyes, and in that moment, Basia makes up her mind. Izzy can do what she wants, but she isn't the type of person to walk away from a friend when they're in trouble.

She stands and joins Stanley by the window in time to see a man walking up the steps. Her stomach drops and her head swims. He looks so much like Allan, it's painful.

'Barbara, are you all right? You have come over quite pale.' Stanley cups her elbow and leads her to a chair.

She wraps her arms around herself and resists the urge to rock. Perhaps staying isn't such a great idea after all.

IZZY SITS WRAPPED in a cocoon of her own misery. Having made her decision to leave last night, she thought the actual departure would be easy. This time she even planned to say her farewells before leaving. Then she saw Jo again, and her resolve crumbled.

All the hours of loneliness and of missing her soulmate crashed down on her, and she wasn't sure she could go back to her solitary existence. In typical Izzy fashion, though, instead of revisiting her decision, she decided to double down and leave earlier than planned.

When Basia had questioned her about ripples in history, Izzy had been pretty sure Maisie would have spent the night out in the original timeline… or had she? When an operative returns to their time, there's bound to be some small changes. Because of this, permission to return is only granted on rare occasions. Perhaps it *is* their fault that Maisie didn't go home after the meeting last night?

Stirring from her self-imposed exile, Izzy considers her options. If she and Basia caused this, then it' up to them to fix it. If they didn't cause it, then they will leave as planned.

Before she can act on her decision, the door opens, and Jensen slips in.

'Ma'am, a Detective Barker is here.'

'Well, show him in,' Augusta snaps, and the room falls silent, waiting for the detective.

Jensen holds the door for the policeman to enter. Izzy's first thought is that he is younger than she expected. Everything else about him screams early twentieth-century detective, though—from his well-made but inexpensive woollen suit, to his immaculately shined shoes, and to the trilby that sits on the top of his head.

As Jensen takes his hat and coat, she does a double take. He pushes his jet-black hair out of green eyes, and her mouth falls open. It's Allan.

Izzy's eyes slide past him to Basia, and the shock drawn on her pale face tells Izzy she's already noticed the resemblance.

Izzy's concern for her friend is temporarily put on hold as the significance of who is present in the room becomes clear to her. She taps her index finger against her lips. All four of Sigma's team are here—Jo, Stanley, Basia, and now Allan. Time would not have brought their reincarnations to this place unless it was important. Is there something more going on here than a girl staying out for the night?

She turns to study her aunt's dog. *If you're not Sigma, then where is he? Or am*

I reading something into this situation that isn't there?

As Izzy's attention returns to the room, the detective is taking a seat beside Mrs Trimms.

'Now, tell me in your own words what happened,' he says in a deep, soothing voice.

At the sound of the detective's voice, Basia releases a small whimper but quickly hides it with a cough. Izzy wants to go and comfort her, but she also doesn't want to draw attention to the woman's distress.

Mrs Trimms appears a little calmer now, but her voice is barely more than a whisper as she repeats her story.

'With the unrest caused by the Women's Pilgrimage to London, I am a little surprised you let a young lady go out unaccompanied,' the detective says after Mrs Trimms has finished speaking.

This apparent criticism affects Mrs Trimms more than everyone's concern had. She straightens her back and says, 'Young man, Miss Ottaway is from London and travels by herself around the country all the time. She is no wilting flower needing to be chaperoned everywhere.'

'Still…,' the policeman muses.

Every woman in the place leans forward, seemingly about to give the detective a piece of their minds, but it's Augusta who gets the first word out.

'Perhaps you should consider not blaming the potential victim,' she snaps, her face screwed into a scowl. 'If a lone woman is attacked by a male, it is not her fault for being alone but the man's fault for attacking her.'

The young detective shifts uncomfortably in his seat as Augusta continues. 'And are you sure you are old enough to be a detective? You hardly look to have left school.'

Red starts to creep up from under the man's starched collar. 'I must confess, I am newly appointed to my position, but the captain is not going to send a seasoned man out to check on a woman who did not come home last night.'

Augusta nods her approval, and Izzy smiles. Testing new people's mettle is one of her aunt's favourite pastimes. Augusta can't bear to be around people who won't stand up for themselves.

Having taken back control, Detective Barker says, 'Now, it is likely Miss Ottaway stayed with a friend last night because it was too late to walk home, is it not? I mean, you said she is a sensible girl.'

Mrs Trimms nods, but Izzy's unease has been growing as time has been marching on. It's almost morning teatime, and no one from Mrs Trimms's household has arrived to say Maisie has returned.

'That was our original thought,' Izzy says, 'but the suffragists Maisie met with were mostly shopgirls or in service of some kind. They would have left for work early this morning, and it is unlikely Maisie would not have reached home by now.'

The detective's cool green eyes bore into Izzy as he considers her words. Nodding once, he reaches into his pocket and takes out a notebook, writes for a moment, then asks Mrs Trimms, 'Have you spoken to your neighbours? Asked if anyone has seen her?'

Izzy cringes with embarrassment. If she hadn't been so wrapped up in her own misery, she would have thought of this already, and they would be well on their way to finding Maisie.

'No,' Mrs Trimms says. 'I was all in a fluster, and I came straight here because I knew Augusta would know exactly what to do.'

'Where do you live, Mrs Trimms?'

'On Clifton Road, looking over the park. It is close, not five minutes' walk away.'

'All right. You and I shall return to your home and start by questioning the neighbours.'

He stands to leave, and Augusta rises to her feet. 'I will come with you, Minnie. You should not be alone.'

'Wait,' Stanley says. 'We cannot just stay here and do nothing.'

Detective Barker takes the group in and dismisses them. 'These things are best left to the professionals, sir.' He turns to help Mrs Trimms from her chair.

Izzy is not to be put off. 'I spoke with some of the suffragists yesterday. Basia and I are going to go talk with them to see what we can dig up. Jo and Stanley, how about you go and see if you can find out anything from the morning cathedral walkers.'

'What about us?' the girl Stanley introduced as Hannah asks.

Izzy had forgotten about them, or perhaps had disregarded them, as they aren't part of Sigma's team. Still, many hands make light work.

'Perhaps you and Nathanial could talk to people on the high street and see if that turns up anything.'

'Hold on now,' Detective Barker says. 'This is a police matter. I cannot agree to your all becoming involved.'

Izzy is now sparked up, and she isn't going to let anyone tell her what she can or can't do. 'Little more than a minute ago, you were prepared to write this

off as a woman staying with friends. Now you want the police to handle it?'

Detective Barker blinks a couple of times, as if he can't believe Izzy is speaking to him like this. Before he forbids them to become involved, she adds, 'What is more, we can cover far more ground if we all pitch in. After all, I believe the first few hours after someone has been abducted are critical, are they not?'

Detective Barker holds her gaze, and she gets the sense that he's still going to refuse their help.

'You are not trained to ask questions. How will you know whether you have something useful or not?'

Izzy's eyebrows rise. Allan's reincarnation has always been the brains of the group. 'You cannot be serious. We are generally intelligent people. We can ask questions without causing a catastrophe and are more than capable of sifting the wheat from the chaff.'

'This is all getting out of hand,' the detective says, running a hand through his hair.

Jo steps forward. 'How about we gather what information we can and then meet back here in… say two hours to share everything with the detective.' She pauses, waiting for the others to agree. 'Then you can decide how best to proceed, Detective.'

Izzy mouths a thank you to Jo, who smiles back.

Detective Barker studies the two of them, a thoughtful expression on his face. 'That plan is acceptable. But be careful. And please, if you find something, do not act alone.'

With that admonishment, he leads the ladies from the room, followed closely by the other teams. Izzy is left alone with Basia, who appears to have been frozen in her seat since the detective entered.

'Basia, are you good to do this?' Izzy asks.

Basia turns to her. 'It's Allan,' she says, amazement colouring her voice.

'Yes it is. But not your Allan,' Izzy tells her gently, then regrets her words when a tear slips from Basia's eye.

'I know,' she says, 'but it's difficult because he is so like him.'

Izzy wraps her arms around Basia and gives her friend a hug, wishing she could take away the pain of her loss.

After a few minutes, Basia pulls away and wipes the tears from her eyes. 'Come, let's go find Maisie.'

As they retrieve their outdoor clothes, Izzy sends a thought to Sigma. *Where are you? I could really use your help with whatever the hell is happening here.*

VIVIENNE LEE FRASER

AS BETA SCROLLS through the report on the tablet, a frown forms between his brows. He takes a seat on the orange leather sofa and again marvels at how Cynthia has furnished her place in 1960s retro. Only it probably isn't retro to her, as she was recruited from the '60s.

He waves the tablet in the air, thinking of how it isn't nearly as satisfying as waving a paper report. 'And they're sure of this?' he asks Cynthia.

Today she's dressed in capri pants, a white button-down shirt, and ballet flats. With her hair teased into a beehive, she so completely fits into the room he can't help but smile.

Her lips purse, as if he's criticising her rather than trying to clarify the situation. He's still an outsider in Time Fixer headquarters, so he needs to choose his words more carefully until he gets the lie of the land.

'As sure as they can be without having someone on the ground,' she tells him.

'The report says there are usually some minor changes when agents go back to their original timelines. Are we able to confirm we don't have an incident on our hands without sending someone in?'

Shaking her head, Cynthia says, 'I don't believe so. What do your guys say?'

'They, too, are reporting minor anomalies that are not part of the historic timeline. So far they haven't affected any major events, and they're taking a wait-and-see approach.'

Beta reaches forward and places the tablet on the coffee table. Leaning back in his chair, he closes his eyes to better process what he's read. Opening them again, he studies Cynthia's face. She's projecting a calm demeanour, but there's a tightness around her lips that suggests she isn't comfortable with something and, knowing her, he'll have to prise it out of her.

'What are you not telling me?'

Her smile is distracted. 'Nothing for you to worry about.'

'Now I'm even more concerned. If you don't let me in, I can't help.'

'The Council was discussing whether to bring Izzy back or not?'

Ah, now they've reached the crux of the matter. When Izzy returned home from her last mission, she had requested a visit to her own timeline.

Unlike the Time Guardians, who train their operatives during many lifetimes and ask them to join at the end of their life cycle, Time Fixers recruit their agents from any time or at any age. They also allow occasional returns

to their lives to keep in contact with family and friends, giving agents a chance to reaffirm their commitment or return to their lives.

Although this process is controlled, it does cause some disruption. Agents are monitored to ensure they don't make too many waves and are immediately pulled out if they might cause too big a disruption.

'What did they decide?' he asks.

'To monitor and meet again tomorrow and decide whether or not to intervene,' Cynthia replies.

He studies her again, this time noticing her posture has still not relaxed. He reaches out and takes her hand. 'What is it?'

'Something doesn't feel right about this. The potential Time Guardians you've had working with Sigma are all there. That has me anxious.' Her fingers squeeze his. 'I don't want Izzy pulled out, but….'

'But you think the situation will turn bad?'

She nods.

He considers their options. With Sigma on a well-earned sabbatical, the only Time Guardian he would trust to treat this with the delicacy it requires is Theta.

Although his new position allows him to contact other Time Guardian councillors' agents without going through them, Theta is close to Alpha and would likely report her assignment to him. Then it would be goodbye to the gentle touch.

A sigh escapes his lips. 'You knew when you brought me that report that the only option was to ask Sigma to come back to work early, didn't you?'

'Harold, he is the only one I would trust in this situation and the only one Izzy would too,' she confirms. 'Besides, his team is assembled and waiting for him.'

Cynthia speaking his real name throws him off balance for a moment, and he wonders if she had meant to do just that. Or has he become too cynical from working with the Time Guardians for so many years?

'Well, it seems neither of our people are going to get the time they need to recharge. I hope this disruption doesn't turn them off coming back to us after their respective breaks.'

When Cynthia doesn't respond, he says, 'All right, leave it with me.'

6

YOU CAN'T ESCAPE TROUBLE

WITH ONLY A couple of days left until the Women's Pilgrimage passes through Portsmouth and Haslemere, the streets of Winchester are bustling. Supporters from outlying areas are gathering in the city to take advantage of the buses the local WSPU organised.

In general the atmosphere is festive, at least among the women and their male supporters, but Basia notices a few disgruntled faces as she and Izzy walk to the high street. A couple of men are outright hostile, jostling women and calling them names even Basia has never heard in mixed company. The anger and aggression send a shiver of unease down her spine, and she stays close to Izzy.

In spite of keeping a low profile, one of the hooligans jostles Izzy and snarls, 'Think yer better than us, do yer?'

Izzy's fists clench, but before she can take action, a constable moves between them and the man. 'Move along, you, and leave the ladies be.'

The man thrusts his chest forward, and for a moment, Basia thinks he's going to refuse, but the constable bustles him away. Before they can voice their thanks, he goes to help another policeman break up a scuffle across the street.

'With all this activity, I am surprised the police were able to send anyone to investigate Maisie's disappearance,' she says to Izzy as they duck into the doorway of a clothing store.

'He said he is only newly appointed, so perhaps they did not mind sending him,' Izzy replies as she opens the door, sounding a lot calmer about the situation than Basia.

A bell tinkles, calling a figure from the back of the store. When she sees who's entered, a look of alarm crosses her face before she schools it into the mask of a professional saleswoman. 'Good morning, ladies. What can I assist you with today?' she asks, her voice bright and chirpy.

Izzy frowns. 'I was in here yesterday—'

'Ah, yes, I remember. You were looking for a new blouse.' The young woman moves to a rail by the door. 'It was this one that took your fancy, was it not?' She takes an apparently random piece of clothing from the rail and walks towards them.

When she's close by, she whispers, 'The owner is in today. You will lose me my job if I am caught chatting with you on her time.'

Izzy nods her understanding and plays along. 'Yes, it was. I brought my friend along for a second opinion.'

'I think it would look lovely on you, but a friend's opinion is always best. What do you think, miss?'

Basia reaches for the blouse, feels the fabric, then holds it up to get a better look. The simple white shirt doesn't require a second opinion, but she pretends anyway so Izzy can talk with the shop assistant.

'It is a little plain for your tastes, Isolde. Let me see if I can find something a little more suited to you.'

She slips past Izzy and the assistant and moves to the rack of blouses. Placing herself between the back room and the two girls, she begins flicking through the clothing, all the while keeping up a constant inane prattle to cover their voices.

'No, this is too big, and this one is too fussy. This one, the cotton is too… stiff. Ah, I like this one. It is much nicer than the other one.' She holds up a blouse with a Chinese collar and pin tucks down the front. 'What do you think, Isolde? Do you not think it will go nicely with your blue serge jacket?' she asks just as the gap in the curtains widens and a thin, stern-looking woman with a pair of pince-nez perched on the end of her nose joins them.

'That is one of our most popular styles,' she says in a dry voice and with little enthusiasm.

Izzy peers around the shop assistant and says, 'I knew I was right to bring you with me today, Barbara. I will take it. Could you please wrap it and send it round to Mrs Augusta Hartfield? I believe she has an account here. The address is—'

'I know the address, thank you,' the woman interrupts, peering down her nose at them. 'She is one of our most valued customers. I believe I have seen you with her before, although not for a while. You are her….'

'Niece,' Izzy provides. 'Yes, I have been in London for a bit, but I am back now.'

'Ah. Daisy, do not stand about gawping like a fishwife. Get that package wrapped and sent around to Mrs Hartfield's.'

'Yes, Mrs Mirth. Right away.'

Daisy's heels click on the wooden floor as she takes the blouse, and Basia bites back a laugh. Mrs Mirth! That woman was anything but mirthful.

'Thank you, Daisy. You have been most helpful,' Izzy says, looping her arm through Basia's and leading her out of the store while saying, 'Come, Barbara, there is the most adorable hat in a shop just up the road, and we still have time to buy it before we are expected for luncheon.'

Still chuckling to herself, Basia follows Izzy as she threads their way through the crowd. They stop for a minute in the entrance of a side street to regroup.

'What a dreadful woman,' Basia says. 'Did you manage to learn anything useful from Daisy?'

'Yes. She said Maisie left the meeting with a girl named Alice. She works in a hat shop at the other end of the high street,' Izzy says.

'Let us hope we do not have to buy anything there to get information, or else Aunt Augusta might not be too happy.'

Izzy grins. 'Do not worry, Augusta will charge my father for everything I buy. And, so long as they are items to make me pretty and more marketable as a bride, my father will pay up without a murmur.' She winks, then laughs. 'So it is a good thing none of my contacts work in bookshops, or I would be out of pocket.'

Izzy's laughter sounds hollow, and Basia squeezes her arm in sympathy. At least her own parents have always been happy for her to be who she wants to be—the people in their community, not so much. They want her to fit into the mould of wife and mother, whether she wants to or not.

'Come on, we need to move. By the time we work our way through the

crowd, we will not have much time to talk with Alice before we have to head back.' Izzy takes hold of Basia's hand, pulling her through the ever-growing throng of people.

They enter the small millinery shop ten minutes later to find a tiny black-clad woman run off her feet. Pinning some stray stands of grey hair back in place, she can't keep the exasperation off her face when Izzy asks to speak with Alice.

'I am sorry, Alice is not in today.'

She moves to serve someone else, but Izzy places a hand on her arm. 'Is she ill?'

'Are you a friend of hers? I have not seen you in here before.' The woman eyes them suspiciously.

'I am a member of her women's group, and some of us were worried. Another member has gone missing.'

'Dear me,' the woman gasps, a hand flying to her mouth. 'It is all so dreadful. Her younger brother popped in to say she had been attacked walking home from her meeting last night. I told her no good would come of joining those—'

Basia grips Izzy's arm, but her friend maintains a professional demeanour as she interrupts the shop owner. 'Do you know where she was attacked?'

'Yes, I believe it was near Clifton Terrace, by the park there—the one with the historic whatnot in the middle.'

'Oram's Arbour,' Izzy offers, turning white.

Basia's stomach churns, and what little breakfast she'd eaten threatens to come up. While she tries to keep everything down, Izzy asks, 'Do you have Alice's address?'

'Oh, I am sorry dear, I am unable to give out that sort of information, not to a complete stranger. I am going round to her place as soon as my sister arrives to take over here, so I can pass on your good wishes if you would like.'

Basia expects Izzy to take offence, or at least argue vigorously. Instead, she says, 'Thank you. Tell her Isolde Fielding asked after her, and if she needs anything to send a message care of Mrs Augusta Hartfield.'

'I will, dear. Now, if you are finished, I must attend to my customers.'

Izzy leaves the shop at speed, and it takes Basia a while to catch her up. When she does, she says, 'I thought you would put up more of a fight. I mean, do you not want to talk with Alice?'

Izzy stops and turns to Basia, her face showing a determination previously missing. 'We know Maisie and Alice left the meeting together and that Alice was attacked near Mrs Trimms's place. Something bad has happened to Maisie.'

'Yes, I get that. But we need to talk to Alice so we can find out exactly what happened during the attack,' Basia presses, unsure why Izzy doesn't feel the same sense of urgency.

'I agree we need more details, but I think our detective friend might be able to find them more easily than we can. I mean, he has to be good for something. Come on, we should go back to Augusta's and set him off in the right direction.'

Half an hour later, after Jensen lets them in and then guides them to the morning room, Basia becomes less certain about coming face to face with the detective again. Fortunately, they're the first back, much to Basia's relief. Jensen leaves them alone after advising coffee and tea would be arriving soon.

Basia takes a seat by the window so she can watch for the others' arrival, but Izzy can't settle. She paces the room and only sits down when the maid brings in the tea tray.

Stanley and Josephine are the next to return, followed minutes later by Nathanial and Hannah. Both groups have nothing to report other than tensions seem strained in Winchester with the influx of suffragists.

When Basia begins to tell them what they found, Izzy shoots her a warning look. 'We should wait until Detective Barker comes back before we share. After all, we only want to tell it once,' she whispers as she hands Basia some tea.

Izzy then returns to the table to get herself some coffee, and Nathanial joins her in the window seat. Basia places her teacup on the table to hide her surprise. The two times she had met the couple, Nathanial had been glued to Hannah's side, almost as if he thought that if he left her alone, she would disappear.

'I thought I might help you keep watch for everyone,' he says, a shy smile forming on his lips. 'I have a feeling that when they arrive back, things will really take off.'

Basia searches his face. He looks like Nathanial and sounds like Nathanial, but something is definitely off about him. She wonders if he and Hannah had another fight, and this time one of them had said something that had altered their relationship forever.

Through her lashes, she glances over at Hannah, studying the girl as she talks with Stanley and Jo. She appears engrossed in the conversation, but every now and then, she sends questioning glances Nathanial's way. He continues to sit with his back to her, completely oblivious.

Interesting, Basia thinks, but she's distracted by the appearance of Augusta swooping down the street with Detective Barker striding in her wake.

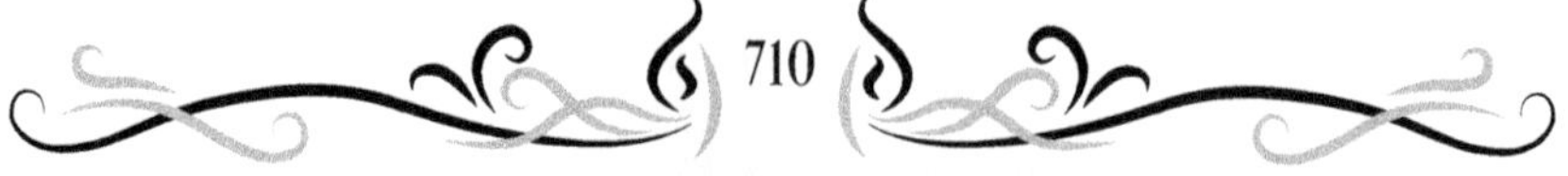

'APOLOGIES TO YOU all for being tardy, but we stumbled on some interesting information as we were on our way back,' Augusta blusters as she blows into the morning room.

'Where is Mrs Trimms?' Jo asks before Izzy can get a word in.

'My dear, she is so dreadfully upset, I left her at home. She has taken a tonic, and her housekeeper is sitting with her while she rests. Oh, is this tea still hot? I am parched.'

Izzy tries to hide her impatience as Augusta pours herself a cup of hot tea, then sits beside Jo on the settee.

Before her aunt has a chance to settle in, she starts, 'Basia and I found out—'

'Isolde, manners, please. I was in the middle of explaining why we were delayed.' Turning to the room, Augusta carries on speaking. 'On our way back here, we ran into Mrs Joyce, who owns the millinery shop just off the high street.' She turns to Izzy. 'I bought you that dear little hat from there before you left for London.'

Izzy nods, willing her aunt to move on so she can tell everyone what she and Basia had learned.

'Well, she was all in a fluster. She was on her way to visit one of her girls. Someone attacked her last night as she walked home from a meeting. Well, that set off Mrs Trimms, who almost fainted, so we had to take her home and make sure she was all right before we came back here.'

Augusta pauses to take a sip of tea, and Izzy uses the break to jump in with her news.

'We spoke to Mrs Joyce, too, in her shop, and to Daisy, another friend of Alice's. Basia and I found out that Maisie left the meeting last night with Alice, the girl who was attacked, and we believe it might all be linked.'

She spoke so fast, it takes a moment for her words to sink in with the others. She watches as their faces change from mildly interested, to concerned, to genuinely worried.

'You are right. It is linked.'

Izzy turns to see Detective Barker standing in the doorway, a manila folder in his hand. 'I sent a runner to the station to get the police report of the incident and bring it here. According to this, Miss Ottaway and Alice were walking together when they were attacked by two men. Alice was

knocked unconscious, but she was pretty sure she saw Maisie being dragged away before she completely passed out.'

'So your people are already following up?' Izzy asks.

The detective shakes his head. 'With so many constables assigned to keep the peace in and around town, we have not had the resources to do anything other than search the park to make sure Miss Ottaway has not been left lying injured somewhere.'

In her head, Izzy is putting all the pieces together, but they aren't adding up. Her mind is sluggish from a restless night, and she can't make out what's missing until Basia says, 'Why was Alice attacked and Maisie taken away? It does not make sense.'

'A good question,' Detective Barker says, beaming at Basia as though she's a star pupil.

Although Basia is finding it difficult to look the policeman in the eye, his praise brings a small smile to her lips. *Interesting,* Izzy thinks as she turns to hide her own smile.

As the detective leafs through the report again to see if there's something he missed, Basia joins him, reading over his shoulder. He moves so she can get a better look, and Izzy half turns to hide her smirk. There's obviously a budding attraction between the two of them, and they look so right together.

Basia reaches over and points at something, and Detective Barker asks, 'You think that may be important?'

'Everyone has been talking about it, so maybe,' Basia answers.

The detective shuts the file. 'According to Alice, as they were walking, Miss Ottaway was complaining to her about the number of versions she had written of the speech her employer, Miss Fielden, is to give in Haslemere.'

'That seems an odd thing for the two women to be talking about,' Nathanial says.

'Not so odd given she had taken a draft speech for the women to read. Some of them wanted to add comments, and Miss Ottaway was worried she would now have to give two versions to Miss Fielden so she could choose which one to use,' the detective informs them.

'And you think she was taken because she had the speech with her?' Jo asks. 'That is a little far-fetched. I mean, surely they would just take the speech.'

'She had obviously copied it many times. Maybe they need Maisie to locate all of them,' Hannah says.

Basia frowns. 'Perhaps, but Mrs Trimms said she had seen the speech in

Maisie's room earlier in the day, but it is not there now—which is odd.'

The cogs in Izzy's mind have finally warmed up. 'Maybe it is not only about the speech. Although there might be many copies of it floating around, only Maisie knows where and when she is to meet up with Miss Fielden to hand it over. Delay her long enough, and Miss Fielden will have nothing to deliver to the crowds in Haslemere.'

'One speech in a small country town cannot be that important,' Stanley laughs.

It is, Izzy thinks. In the future, Miss Fielden's words and how they inspired onlookers is one of the few things reported from that day. Perhaps her speech motivated people to support the march or changed their minds about giving women the vote.

Only she can't say any of these things because she would have to explain too much. Would they even believe her if she told them she had travelled to the future and seen how altering one little thing like this could change the course of history? It's more likely they'd think she's going crazy.

She rises to her feet and paces around the room. *Why was Maisie taken? There must be a reason.* If the group here couldn't understand how a minor change could affect the future, nor could Maisie's kidnappers. So why would they have abducted her rather than beat her like they did Alice?

Could the Time Fixers be involved here? It can't be the Time Guardians—they're sticklers for protocol and would never do anything to alter history.

Basia joins her on her circuit of the room. 'What is it?' she asks, keeping her voice low so the others won't hear.

'I am not sure,' Izzy whispers. 'Miss Fielden's speech is spoken of well into the future, which raises the possibility that her inability to give it may have a very real impact on women getting the vote in England.'

Basia's brow furrows. 'Okay, I see it is important to find Maisie and make sure she delivers the speech to her employer, but how does that help us find her? I mean, her abductors are not able to see into the future.'

'No, they cannot, but there must be a reason they chose her. Maybe they are trying to sow the seeds of fear by abducting one of the people from out of town who have arrived here to support the Pilgrimage. Or they may even know about her connections.'

Izzy and Basia both start at the voice. Neither of them had realised they'd drifted towards the window until Nathanial joined their conversation. Izzy looks to Basia, whose wide-eyed surprise tells her she's worried too—how much had he overheard?

'Of course, that is the most likely explanation,' Basia says, perhaps louder than necessary, as if trying to cover their earlier conversation. 'They probably overheard her London accent and decided they would cause more mischief and fear by taking her rather than Alice.'

'A sound analysis,' Detective Barker says as he approaches them.

Basia's cheeks pink at his words, and Izzy fears a full-on blush will soon appear.

Leaving her friend to the detective, she turns back to Nathanial. If he had indeed heard their entire conversation, he seems completely unaffected by them discussing the future impact of Miss Fielden's speech.

Nathanial meets her gaze and raises an eyebrow, and the corners of his mouth twitch as if about to form a smile—or a smirk.

'Shall we join the others, Izzy, and see if we can find our Miss Ottaway?'

Before she can react to the use of her nickname, Nathanial has joined the others. He waits patiently for a break in the conversation and asks, 'Detective Barker, Alan, how many men can the police assign to the search for Miss Ottaway?'

'Nathanial, what are you doing?' Hannah asks, her tone conveying surprise.

She isn't the only one startled by Nathanial's actions. He had called her Izzy, and he called the detective Alan, even though the man hasn't told anyone that's his name.

Oh Lord, he has the same name as Basia's Allan. She searches for her friend, who's listening intently to the conversation. The only sign she gives that the detective reminds her of her dead lover is the way her fingers are wrapped so tightly together, her knuckles are white. Basia smiles wanly, acknowledging Izzy's glance of support.

'I am looking out for someone who needs our help, just like you have always wanted me to,' Nathanial responds to Hannah's question as Izzy's focus returns to the group.

He turns back to the policeman, missing the shock on his fiancée's face, but Izzy doesn't miss it.

What's happening here? Who is Nathanial, and why did he call me Izzy?

The door swings open, and two maids enter carrying trays with more tea and coffee, Cuddles close at their heels. Izzy follows the dog as he pads around everyone, sniffing them and cataloguing their scent.

If only you were Sigma. We could do with some Time Guardian help about now.

You thought I was the dog? That dog? How long have you been trying to talk to him—I mean me?

Izzy's eyes fly upwards to meet Nathanial's amused smile.

You? You're Sigma? You're taking human form now? Wait. Where's the real Nathanial?

Nathanial simply stares at her and waits for the penny to drop. Izzy fights the urge to palm her forehead.

You were Nathanial? Then Hannah is… will become Theta. Oh…. Still, that doesn't explain what happened to Nathanial.

Nathanial shrugs. *I'm not quite certain. I seem to have… integrated with him, or maybe I've boxed him away somewhere. I can't really tell. Beta sent me here on short notice, and my best option to place myself in the middle of things was to come as me. Beta assures me Nathanial will be fine when I leave.*

Izzy glances at Cuddles, then back at Nathanial.

If Cuddles was here, why not come as him? It would be less messy.

It would be too weird being here and interacting with myself. Besides, Cavaliers are home dogs, and I need to be out and about if I'm to be of any use.

Hannah steps between them, momentarily obscuring Izzy's view of Nathanial.

'Nathanial, we have lunch with my parents, and there are enough people here that they no longer need us.' Hannah's voice holds an undertone of command.

'I cannot leave now, Hannah. Things are only just starting to get exciting,' Nathanial tells her. 'You go ahead, though, and please give my apologies to your parents.'

Hannah's head swivels, and she glares at Izzy, instantly making her the cause of Nathanial's defiance. 'No, I will stay too. We will ask Jensen to send a message to my parents.' She links her arm through Nathanial's, and he follows her out to search for the butler.

Izzy moves to the table to pour herself some coffee. She's sipping it thoughtfully when a maid enters and hands Detective Barker a note. He reads it, nods once, then calls them all to order.

TAKING THE SEAT closest to Detective Barker, Basia sends a questioning glance to Izzy as her friend takes the seat opposite. Something has been going on between her and Nathanial. Hannah may think they're flirting, but Basia knows it must be something else. "Later," Izzy mouths, and Basia nods.

'So, my captain informs me he cannot spare anyone else to look into Miss Ottaway's disappearance—I am instructed to investigate on my own.'

'But that is outrageous.' Stanley stands. 'I shall go and have a word with him.'

Josephine smiles indulgently and reaches out an arm, pulling Stanley back down beside her. 'Let the detective finish before you go charging off,' she tells him.

Detective Barker smiles at Jo, and Basia's heart literally flutters. What's going on here? Her head knows this man isn't her Allan, but her heart is taking time to catch up, and her physical reactions—well, that's a whole other level.

Perhaps it's that her loss of Allan is so recent. She would give anything to look into his green eyes one last time, to hold his hand and tell him how much she misses him. This must be a stage of grief —yes, that must be it.

Detective Barker starts, 'Since—'

The door opens, and Nathanial and Hannah return. Nathanial is actually smirking, but by the set of Hannah's lips and the storm brewing in her eyes, she is furious. Izzy catches Nathanial's searching gaze and drops her head to hide her chuckle.

Putting on her best schoolmarm face, Basia glares at Izzy. "Stop it," she mouths, and Izzy attempts to look chastened. Basia glances from Izzy to Nathanial and wonders what the two of them are up to. She doesn't have time to work it out, though, as the detective has started talking again.

'Since you were all so helpful this morning, I am hoping you will agree to assist me in the next step of the investigation,' he continues.

They all murmur their assent except for Augusta. 'I am afraid I must return to ensure Mrs Trimms is all right. Besides, I am told I can be a little… off-putting. I would not like to hinder your efforts.'

Basia's lips curl into a fond smile at Augusta's words. The woman is certainly a force to be reckoned with, and Basia can see how people might be a little intimidated by her presence.

'What would you like us to do, Detective?' Jo asks.

Just like her Johan, Jo is the one keeping them to task—the glue holding them together.

'Pretty much what you have been doing already—asking people if they saw anything unusual last night. This time, however, we will be a little more targeted because we are pretty certain Miss Ottaway was taken from the park. We will be questioning people who live around the streets near Clifton Avenue, and those who are walking in the park itself.'

'That sounds pretty straightforward,' Jo says. 'Will we be in the same pairings as before, Detective?'

'Probably—'

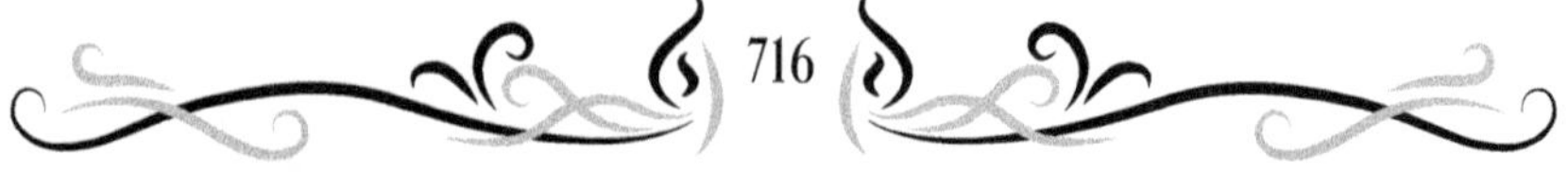

'Before you go, Jensen has set up a light lunch in the dining room. You will need sustenance before you tackle this new round of investigation,' Augusta adds.

And a toilet break, Basia thinks, unable to remember when she's had so many cups of tea in such a short time.

Arriving in the dining room after the others, she loads her plate with dainty sandwiches and pastries before finding there are only two empty places at the table.

One is beside Hannah, who seems to be haranguing Nathanial between mouthfuls of food. Basia seats herself beside Detective Barker and begins to eat self-consciously, all the while hyperaware of how close the detective is to her.

'Miss… um—'

'Oh, please call me Barbara.'

He smiles. 'And I am Alan.'

Of course you are, Basia thinks.

'So, Barbara, how is it you are staying with Mrs Hartfield and her niece?'

An odd question. Then again, perhaps being a detective, he likes to know how everyone fits in.

'I have a little time before I start my nursing studies in London, and when Isolde decided to come to Winchester, she asked if I would like to accompany her,' Basia tells him, outlining the cover story Izzy had created for her.

'Fascinating. So you want to be a nurse? And are your parents supportive of your choice?'

Is this what it's like to be interrogated? Should I tell him they would rather I became a doctor, but that road is as difficult in my time as it would be now? How would he react?

Suddenly she doesn't want to know. If he is one of those men who wants a woman at home rather than working, her attitude towards him would change. It's selfish, but she's enjoying how his presence soothes her battered soul too much to want this budding friendship to end. *Still, this attraction isn't real. It's simply a spillover from losing Allan so recently,* she reminds herself.

'They are happy for me to find my own way in the world,' she said. 'How about you? How did your parents react when you told them you wanted to become a policeman?'

He chuckles. 'Surprisingly well. I am a younger son, and I always knew the money my grandfather left me would never be enough to live on. My father would have preferred I took a commission in the military, but I have

always been intrigued by solving mysteries.'

Basia could easily imagine the serious man as a child curled up with Sir Arthur Conan Doyle's latest offering, imagining himself as Sherlock Holmes.

'When I announced my intention to join the police, my uncle introduced me to the captain here in Winchester, and he took me on to repay an old favour, I believe.' Alan's eyes drop to his food, and Basia wonders if he's finished speaking. 'I aim to make sure he has no cause to regret that decision.'

Alan says these last words with such intensity, Basia is a bit taken aback. She decides to lighten the tone. 'So are you enjoying being Sherlock Holmes?'

Alan smiles wryly. 'I am afraid I am more of a Dr Watson. I still have much to learn before I make Sherlock status.'

Basia nods and fiddles with her sandwich as she considers how useful this newly minted detective will be in the search for Maisie.

Alan chuckles. 'Ah, I see you are now wondering how much help I will be in finding your friend. Or perhaps you are thinking the captain sent me here today so I would keep out of the way of the main action.'

'No….' She turns towards him, eyes wide, worried she'd offended him.

'And that is fine. I believe it is probably true. I only joined the force last week, so my police training is rather limited. I suspect the captain sent me here to appease a lady whose name carries a lot of weight in this town.'

'But—' His words don't inspire confidence.

'Oh, do not fear. I aim to show the captain that assigning me this case was the right thing to do by finding your Miss Ottaway. Sometimes a man who has something to prove can be more effective than one who does not.'

Basia sends him a shy smile. 'Then I hope we can help you achieve your goal.'

A slight frown furrows his brow as he answers, 'For some reason I am even more sure of succeeding with all of you helping.'

Of course you are. With you here Sigma's team is all assembled. If only the Time Guardian were—

It hits Basia like a punch. She raises her head to find Nathanial staring straight at her, a cheeky grin on his face.

'Why is it you have smiles for everyone else but me today?' Hannah complains, her tone more angry than hurt, and Nathanial is pulled back into whatever battle the two are having.

Before the argument becomes too heated, Alan rises to his feet and addresses the group. 'If you are all finished, perhaps we can get started.'

7

THE GANG IS HERE

BASIA TRIES NOT to let her disappointment show. Before they left Augusta's, Detective Barker split them into two groups to cover more ground and also so they would remain safe.

It wasn't being split up that disappointed her, but more the fact that he sent her off with Josephine, Stanley, and Hannah. They're to proceed up Clifton Hill and follow the line of houses round until they meet up with the others on Clifton Road.

It was obvious the detective separated Nathanial and Hannah so their constant arguing wouldn't interfere with the afternoon's work. Nathanial had readily agreed—perhaps too readily. Hannah hadn't said a word, but the sour expression on her face spoke louder than anything she might have said.

Meanwhile, Basia is brooding. Why had the detective not wanted her with him? Not that she's too bothered either way, but it would be nice to know.

Stanley drops back and falls into step with her. 'I think our young detective is quite sweet on you,' he teases.

Heat rises from Basia's collar. 'What makes you think that?'

A smirk pulls at his mouth. 'Perhaps the way his eyes always seek you out first when he walks into the room and how he always manages to be close to you.' He nudges her gently with his elbow as Jo half turns to join the conversation.

'I think what clinched it, though, was his sending you along with us instead of Isolde,' she adds.

Basia doesn't want to rise to the bait, but she can't help herself. 'How does that show he likes me?'

'Why, because if you are with us, he can concentrate on doing his job,' Stanley says, a twinkle in his eye and a chuckle in his voice.

'I am sure I have no idea what you mean,' Basia responds a little too tartly, causing Jo to smile knowingly and sending Stanley off on another bout of laughter.

'Of course you don't.' He winks conspiratorially.

It's hard to stay annoyed with Stanley—he's just so likeable. Besides, it's such a beautiful day, and the world is a happy place now that she no longer feels the sting of rejection.

If only Stanley could work some of his magic on Hannah. Basia turns to the girl following them silently, dragging her feet, and clearly not engaged. When they questioned passers-by, she had stood to the side, her eyes wandering, saying nothing.

Basia racks her brain for something that might lift Hannah's spirits, but she doesn't know her well enough, and Hannah has been rebuffing her efforts at conversation with terse, dismissive replies.

After an hour of disappointment and no new clues, they finally meet up with the others in the centre of the park. When she finds they have nothing unusual to report either, dread seeps its way into Basia's bones.

Although she has always felt that there's something untoward going on, she's now beginning to fear something more sinister happened to Maisie. Coming to a stop by Hannah, Basia listens to the intense conversation as the others argue over what to do next.

'That nurse has been pushing her pram around for a while,' Hannah comments.

Basia follows her gaze. 'The poor woman looks half-asleep,' she sympathises.

'Yes.' Hannah taps her chin thoughtfully. 'Almost like she has been walking that child around for hours.'

Without saying another word, Hannah strides off purposefully towards the nurse. Basia drifts along in her wake, interested to find out where this is going.

'…notice anything unusual today?' Hannah is saying as she catches her up.

The nurse scrubs a hand over her tired face and studies Hannah wearily.

'A friend of ours has gone missing, and we are searching for her,' Basia says. 'You look like you might have been around the park for a while. Perhaps

it is something you do quite often? Maybe if you noticed something, even if it is just little, you might be able to help us find her.'

A wail comes from inside the pram, and Basia leans over to find a newborn baby screwing its face up, readying itself for a good scream.

Standing up, Basia says, 'Come, let us help you. We can walk a while and let the baby settle while you think.'

Basia places her hands on the handle of the pram, guiding it onto the path. The nurse drops her arms with a sigh of relief, and Hannah, to Basia's surprise, slips the woman's hand over her arm.

As soon as they're on the move, the baby's eyes begin to flutter and are soon closed.

'Is the baby always this unsettled?' Basia asks conversationally.

'Always, and it's worse after she's been fed. She screams and is forever sicking up. She's such a fussy one. I hardly sleep at all, and I'm out walking her all hours of the day and night. If I'd known she was going to be this difficult, I would never have taken the job.'

'I have seen many babies with similar problems. They have what is called reflux. Maybe this little one is one of those,' Basia says.

'Naming it don't help much,' the nurse grumbles.

Basia smiles at her grumpy reply. 'No, it will not, but there are some simple things you can do to help. Here, I will show you.' Basia reaches out and adjusts the mattress in the pram until the baby is a little propped up. 'If you keep the baby gently raised up, she will be a little more comfortable. Also, stirring a teaspoon of ground wheat into her milk to thicken it should help a little.'

As Basia adjusts the baby, her face relaxes, and in a couple of minutes, she's already looking more contented. Basia stands to find the nurse and Hannah staring at her in amazement.

'I help my mother out, caring for newborn babies. This is more common than you would expect.'

'Still, I'm grateful,' the nurse says as the three of them start walking again, this time in silence.

Perhaps it's the mention of her mother, or perhaps it's the peace and quiet of the common, but Basia's thoughts are pulled home, and a wave of longing sweeps over her. She had been on her way back when all this started, and now she's stuck here until they find Maisie. In this moment, trying to prevent the end of the world in her time is not as daunting as trying to find the

missing suffragist here.

'You know,' the nurse says, interrupting her thoughts, 'I do recall something odd from this morning. When the policeman asked me earlier nothing came to mind, but now that the baby has settled, and I can take a moment to think….'

'Do tell. It may not appear important to you, but it might help us,' Hannah encourages.

'Well, grumpy Mr Parsons down the road is forever yelling at me when I'm out early. He says the baby crying wakes him up. So rude, he is. Lulu was especially noisy this morning, and I didn't hear a peep from him.'

'That is interesting,' Basia says, not sure how this is relevant but pleased to have something from their efforts this afternoon.

Hannah, however, has a glint in her eyes. 'And you are sure that it was not because he has gone to visit relatives or is too poorly to leave his bed?' she asks.

The nurse shakes her head. 'He has a nephew who comes and visits, but only at Christmas. My mistress says it's only because he hopes the old man will leave him something in his will. And he's too curmudgeonly to get sick. Besides, I'm sure he's home, because I saw two men go inside just before midday, and he opened the door for them.'

For the first time that day, Hannah's mood brightens. 'Where does Mr Parsons live?'

The nurse points across the park. 'Over there, at number 54. The big, creepy house with the overgrown garden.'

'Thank you so much. I am sure this will help.' Hannah smiles. 'Come, Barbara, let us rejoin the others.'

'THERE IS NOTHING more we can do at the moment,' Alan says for the umpteenth time. 'Not until we have some new leads.'

'There must be something. We cannot just leave her to fend for herself.' Izzy doesn't try to hide her frustration, which is being fed by the growing fear that something is very wrong here.

She catches Nathanial's eye, and he shakes his head. *Does he also think this is a wasted effort, or does he want to lose the detective and strike out on our own? No, he can't want that because Alan is a part of that team.*

Izzy tries again. 'Perhaps we could—'

'Leave everything up to the police. We are the right and proper people

to investigate this,' Alan tells her before she can outline her plan.

'Yes, Isolde, we should leave it up to the police,' Stanley says.

Clenching her fists, Izzy stares at each of them in disbelief. She had at least thought Nathanial would support her efforts to continue the search.

'Let us go back to Augusta's and have some tea,' Josephine suggests. 'A bit of distance might give us a new perspective.'

Under the weight of their objections, all the fight goes from Izzy. 'I guess that is almost a plan.'

'Wait,' Hannah's voice rings out. 'Hold up.'

The group turns as one towards the sound to find Hannah practically running towards them with Basia close behind.

'We have a lead,' Hannah says to Alan. 'Tell me, did your group question the owner of number 54?'

Alan takes his notebook from his pocket and flicks through the pages. 'Um, yes, let me see. A Mr Parsons, who reported nothing unusual in the street.'

'Of course he would say that.' Hannah turns to Basia, who nods approvingly. 'It appears our Mr Parsons has been hiding something.'

'According to a local, he has some guests staying, which is very unusual, and he has not been out bothering the neighbours as he normally would,' Basia chimes in.

'How does that help us?' Stanley asks. 'So he has guests, and he is not harassing the locals. They should be grateful.'

Hannah's eyes capture Nathanial's, and Izzy senses she's looking for some softening there, perhaps even his support as she argues her case.

'It seems he is not the type to have visitors. And he usually complains about any noise in the street, but he was strangely quiet this morning,' Hannah explains, relaying what the nurse had told them.

There is a heavy silence once she finishes, and Izzy fears she hasn't convinced anyone this is indeed a lead. She's about to voice her support and suggest this warrants a follow-up when Nathanial slowly nods his head. 'If it is strange behaviour for him, then perhaps we should look into it.'

Stanley sighs. 'If we must, let us go over now and ask him what is going on. The sooner we clear this up, the sooner we can have some tea.'

'Whoa, wait a moment there.' Josephine places a hand on his arm. 'We cannot just go barging in, asking questions. If he does have Maisie, then he has already lied to the police, and he is not likely to tell us anything.'

Stanley puffs out his chest. 'Then Nathanial, the detective, and I will

force our way in and demand to look around.'

'We will do no such thing,' Alan tells him. 'We do this by the book or not at all.'

'If we do it your way, then we might not get anywhere,' Izzy says, unable to keep the frustration from her voice.

Nathanial holds up his hands in a placating gesture. 'Surely we can find a middle road.'

Even though Alan might be the authority figure here, the Time Guardian is still the one galvanising them as a team and leading the way.

'And that would be?' Alan asks.

'We need to watch the house for a bit to see if we can find if anything unusual is going on there,' Nathanial outlines.

'What, all of us?' Stanley asks. 'It will be a little obvious, do you not think?'

Izzy bites back a sigh. Stanley is a lovely guy, but he really wasn't blessed with great intelligence. 'If we take it in turns, it will not look suspicious. This is a popular place for walking and picnicking, so I suggest we pair off and plan some surveillance.'

'I am not sure this is a good idea, all of you getting involved like this,' Alan worries.

Basia moves close to him and asks, 'Do you not need to go back to the station to update the captain?'

The detective holds her gaze for a moment, and his whole body seems to soften as he contemplates her words, or perhaps Basia herself. In response, Basia leans towards him and adds, 'A walk together would be pleasant. And, if you are not here, you can turn a blind eye to what the others are doing.'

'And we will not do anything stupid, like storm the house, until we have spoken with you,' Josephine assures the detective.

'But—'

'Stanley, I want your word,' Josephine says, confronting her fiancé. 'No heroics.'

'I suppose,' Stanley mumbles, sounding so much like a thwarted child that Izzy chuckles under her breath.

Now that Stanley has been tamed, all eyes turn to Alan, who's staring at the ground as if it might provide him with a solution. 'But if something happens to you… to any of you….'

'Nothing is going to happen to us. Best case, a crazy old man has some unexpected guests and there is nothing going on. Worst case, Maisie is being held

in that house, we confirm it, and meet back this evening at Augusta's to formulate our next steps.' Izzy's gaze rakes over the others, begging them to agree with her.

'We promise not to do anything without talking with you first,' Stanley says.

The others nod their agreement.

'I suppose when I leave, you are just going to do what you want to anyway,' Alan says, almost defeated.

They all have the sense not to answer.

'I guess what I do not know….'

Basia places her hand on the detective's arm and says, 'Come, you can walk me to Aunt Augusta's on the way back to the station.' Basia quickly smiles over her shoulder at Izzy as she steers Alan away.

Izzy admires how deftly Basia dealt with the detective, leaving the rest of them to plan how best to observe Parsons's house without anyone noticing—not that it was any hardship for her if that glint in her eye was anything to go by.

'Nathanial and I will take the first turn,' Hannah says before anyone else can offer.

Given the tension between the two of them this morning, Izzy expects Nathanial to object. Instead he says, 'I think that is a perfect idea. Shall we stroll?'

He holds out his arm, and Hannah takes it, leaving Izzy with Josephine and Stanley.

'Well, Stanley, I think you and I should have a picnic tea in the park later this afternoon,' Josephine says.

Stanley smiles. 'Always happy to oblige when food is involved.'

'Aunt Augusta's cook can sort something for you, I am sure,' Izzy tells them.

'Will you join us?' Stanley asks.

Izzy shakes her head, and Stanley's face droops in disappointment. 'You are not still holding a grudge against me, are you?'

To Izzy's surprise, she finds she isn't. 'No, Stanley. It is just, if I picnic with you, who will accompany Basia when it is her turn to take watch?'

'Perhaps we will already know what is going on by then,' Stanley says before his eyes twinkle at another thought. 'Or perhaps the charming policeman will accompany her.'

'Come, you two, we do not need to decide now. Let us return to Augusta's and plan in comfort.' Josephine links arms with both Stanley and Izzy and leads them back through the park.

In spite of the gravity of the situation and her worry for Maisie, for the first time since she returned home, Izzy feels like she belongs.

VIVIENNE LEE FRASER

IT'S A BEAUTIFUL day for a walk, and Nathanial would be enjoying being back in his normal time, enjoying the scenery, if only the years between didn't weigh so heavily on his shoulders. Then again, it's hard to relax when Hannah's nervous energy is radiating off her in waves with such intensity that Nathanial imagines he can actually touch them.

He wants to reach out to his fiancée and reassure her that he's just excited about the adventure they're on and that everything will return to normal once Maisie is found. The problem is, there's a gulf between them, only Hannah is blind to it.

This Hannah has no idea that in a few months, they'll meet the Time Guardians Alpha and Beta. Or that in a little over a year she'll decide to become a Time Guardian herself, ready to abandon him if he doesn't join her.

He sends a sidelong glance her way. Even with her lips pursed, she is beautiful, and his heart skips a little.

As if sensing his attention, she turns and catches him watching her.

'What?' she snaps.

'Nothing. Well, I know you are upset with me. Why not tell me what I have done wrong, and I will apologise and try to fix it.'

He sighs inwardly. Falling back into old patterns is so easy. She's always taken the lead in their relationship—why change things now? He steels himself, waiting for her to outline his latest list of transgressions.

'Oh, Nathanial, and here I was, thinking you had grown a backbone today,' Hannah whispers almost as if to herself.

What? His toe hits a protruding tree root. He stumbles, rights himself, then catches Hannah up. They carry on walking as if nothing happened.

Had he heard her correctly? He can't have. She's mad at him for making decisions without consulting her, and for talking to other women, and for perhaps a hundred other little things he doesn't know about.

Is she actually implying she approves of his behaviour? He chews his bottom lip thoughtfully. Had he gotten it wrong all those years ago? In trying to be exactly who Hannah wanted him to be, had he pushed her away?

They complete a circuit of the park, and Nathanial's mind is still in turmoil, questioning the actions of his younger self. He'd fallen hard for Hannah when they first met—no doubt about it. It took time for him to convince

her to actually consider him as a serious suitor, and even more time for her to accept his marriage proposal.

He'd tried to change himself into the man she wanted, but it never seemed enough. Had he altered himself so much that he pushed her away? If he'd been true to himself, would things have turned out differently?

Hannah's hand on his arm interrupts his thoughts. 'Nathanial, did you see that?'

'Sorry, no, I was… elsewhere.'

A frown creases her brow. 'If you are not going to take this—'

'Hannah, I lost focus for a moment.' He knows his tone is terse, but this isn't the right time for one of her lectures. 'Why not just tell me what I should be looking at.'

She turns to face him, taking his hands in hers as if they're having an intimate moment, and looks into his eyes. 'There are two men walking towards us, heading across the common in the direction of Parsons's house. Something about them is not right—I am pretty sure they do not belong here.'

Nathanial raises her gloved hands to his lips as if to kiss them while at the same time turning his head slightly to get a better look. As he does, his breath catches in his throat.

Straight away he sees what had alerted Hannah. One of the two men has a military-style haircut but is dressed as a day labourer. The other has the look of a thug—perhaps he's hired muscle. At a quick glance, they appear to be labourers, perhaps employed in one of the houses around the green.

It isn't just the unusual haircut of the military-looking one that makes him question what he sees. It's more the fact that they're walking through the park in the middle of the day, one of them carrying what looks to be a bag of groceries, when any real labourer would be working.

The pair draw closer, and it's only Nathanial's training that prevents him from dropping his fiancée's hand, stomping over to the man with the military haircut, and punching him in the face. Anger bubbles inside him. How could he be here after everything he's done?

As they walk by, Nathanial forces his gaze back to Hannah. 'My love, I know you want to carry on walking, but I think we should return home, else your parents might believe I have kidnapped you.'

Hannah's mouth opens as if to snap a snarky retort, but she bites it back as he turns to follow the men's retreating backs. Not taking his eyes off them, he releases one of her hands as he slips the other into the crook of his elbow.

Arm in arm, they follow the strange men.

'But, Nathanial,' Hannah simpers, and the oddity of that tone coming from her lips almost has him stumbling again. 'I am so enjoying our stroll. Maybe we might stay a little longer?'

He realises she's playing along with the ruse and says, 'I would love to, my sweet, but I have some business I must attend to this afternoon. Besides, we will be together again at dinner tonight.'

'Of course you must visit with your lawyer, but I shall miss you so.' Hannah pouts prettily, and it's all Nathanial can do not to snicker. This performance is so the opposite of his independent, confident fiancée.

For a brief moment, he wonders if things would have worked out between them if she were more like she's pretending to be now. No, the thing he admires most about her is her drive and her independent nature. He wouldn't put up with someone who bent their will to his.

Then it hits him like a sock to the jaw. He'd be frustrated by a woman who puts his needs first all the time… yet that's exactly what he's done with Hannah. Is that why she's grown increasingly terse and distant with him?

He shakes his head. This is not the time for deep soul-searching. He needs to keep his mind on the job.

They've only walked a couple of paces when the larger of the two men swings round and stalks back, stopping only when he's standing toe-to-toe with Nathanial. His eyes are ice cold, and menace wafts off him. Hannah gasps but stands her ground.

'You follow'n us, pretty boy?' His voice is rough and raw, and Nathanial has to force himself to swallow the lump in his throat before answering.

'I have no idea what you are talking about. My fiancée and I are simply returning home after our walk.'

The man turns his head to look at Hannah. With her face obscured by the hat she wears, he contents himself with raking his eyes up and down her body, leering lasciviously, before focusing back on Nathanial.

'Well, y' keep yer distance if you want to keep that pretty face for your luscious lady.'

Hannah's grip tightens on his arm. The thug still holds Nathanial's gaze even after speaking, his looming presence causing Nathanial's heart to pound. Still, the man keeps his attention on him rather than on Hannah.

'Come on, Barry, leave the locals alone. We have business to attend to.'

The voice carries the tone of command, and its familiar sound sets

Nathanial's teeth on edge. In spite of the physical threat from the man in front of him, it's the owner of that voice who scares him more.

'Huh. Can't a man 'ave a bit of fun?'

The thug lifts his arm and pokes Nathanial in the shoulder. 'I'm a-watching you,' he almost purrs before turning on his heel and catching up with his mate, who's almost at the edge of the common.

As the men walk away, Nathanial calms his racing heart, squares his shoulders, and pulls Hannah a little closer. 'Shall we continue?' he asks.

'But…,' Hannah starts, and he senses her gaze on his face. Perhaps it's the determination she sees there that stops her from finishing what she started. 'Of course.'

As they reach the end of the common, they're in time to catch the men entering Parsons's place as expected. Rather than going round the rear to the servant's entrance, they boldly walk up the steps and open the front door.

If their threatening manner hadn't confirmed that these men are not part of the normal social scene of Winchester, their entering the front door of the house does.

'Come on, we must report back to the others,' he says to Hannah, leading her away from the house and towards the centre of town.

When he glances down at her, surprised by her acquiescence, a small smile plays across her lips. Is she actually enjoying his taking charge? Or is this reaction because he hadn't backed down when threatened? His heart is racing again, and this time it's from joy rather than nerves.

Before the house is completely out of view, he chances a quick glance back and starts in surprise as a face appears at one of the upper windows. He stops and half turns to get a better look. A woman seems to be trying to pull the window open, but it's well and truly stuck. Her face twists in fear, and she backs away as the thug fills the space, pushing her back into the room. Moments later he's replaced by a familiar face, who reaches out and pulls the curtains shut.

Nathanial quickens his pace. This is not good, not good at all. He must contact Beta and find out what the hell is going on, and then Izzy and Basia need to be warned.

8

LOOK WHO'S BACK

BETA DUMPS THE papers he's been reading onto the table and reaches his arms above his head, stretching out his spine. There are certainly some advantages to being back in a body, but the aches and pains he could do without.

Standing, he stretches again, then paces the room. He isn't just trying to loosen his muscles but is also trying to force his jumbled thoughts into some semblance of order.

The reports he spent the morning reading were proposals for the second joint Time Guardians and Time Fixers mission—their second attempt to nudge humanity away from a future war that would set it on course for extinction.

It's against his training and beliefs to interfere in history, but their recent success in stopping a major war had highlighted the potential benefits of limited intervention. As Cynthia had pointed out on more than one occasion, history would not let them change anything too drastically without removing them from the timeline and using someone else to redress the balance.

Still, choosing where to make changes is fraught with pitfalls he hadn't had when planning his missions for the Time Guardians. Trying to keep history on track is black-and-white, whereas amending it is too many shades of grey for his liking.

Sighing, he has to admit he needs Cynthia. Not only is she more experienced with planning these types of missions, but she would also see problems he couldn't even imagine.

Beta?

He stops pacing. He only put Sigma in place this morning. Surely he wouldn't have anything to report yet.

Sigma, what is it?

You should have told me Jason was at the heart of this mess before you sent me in.

Jason? Jason is in Winchester with the others?

Are you sure?

Of course I am. I've seen him with my own eyes.

Sigma sounds angry. Surely he doesn't believe they sent him to Winchester knowing full well Jason is around?

Is Jason meant to be here? I mean, is he from this time?

What? No! Jason is from twentieth-century London.

Okaaay.

There's silence as the two Time Guardians reflect on the situation. Sigma breaks the silence first.

Beta, before we proceed, I need to know if I'm working for the Time Guardians, limiting a Time Fixers mess, or am I working for this new combined agency, and I'm somehow supposed to be helping him?

Beta's head spins. As far as he knows, Jason had been placed under house arrest until he decided whether to retrain or leave the Time Fixers. He isn't supposed to be anywhere near 1913 and definitely not on an assignment.

Umm… I can assure you that Cynthia and I have not chosen our next mission. I'm not sure—

So Jason is working for the Time Fixers. I thought all but essential missions had ceased until you and Cynthia finalised the new agency set-up. And Izzy is here. Don't they have some rule about that?

Beta stares out the window, his head pounding as he tries to make sense of Sigma's report.

Beta?

I'm here. Just give me a moment.

Beta, you sound a bit… if you don't mind me saying… uncharacteristically woolly brained.

Sorry, Sigma, but this information is as much a shock to me as it is to you.

How do you want me to proceed?

For the first time in his afterlife, Beta not only has no idea how to advise

his agent, but he also doesn't know where to start to find the answers. Nothing makes him angrier than having someone on the ground he's unable to support.

Beta, are you still there?

Ah, yes. Let me think. You need to brief Izzy, of course, and try to hold off from taking any further action until I can clarify the situation. And under no circumstances are you to confront Jason.

Beta, he's the one holding the young woman captive. What happens if we believe her life to be in danger? I mean, Jason is hardly the most stable of characters.

Obviously, if you fear for her life, you must intervene immediately, but please try and hold off doing anything, and I'll try to get answers as quickly as I can.

Please do. I would like to wrap this up as soon as possible. Not only for Maisie's sake but also because people have started to notice I'm not quite myself. I'm not comfortable with this whole "being me" situation.

Beta chuckles, enjoying Sigma's discomfort. This is his first mission in a human body, and time constraints had forced him to take over his own. It must be quite the distraction for him.

Yes, of course. I'll do the best I can, but I must proceed with some delicacy, as our agency isn't exactly meant to be running missions yet.

The connection winks out, and Beta strides to the door to his apartment, trying to remember where Cynthia said she would be this morning. As he marches through the corridors to her office, his anger grows. *What in god's name do the Time Fixers think they're doing, running a mission in the same timeline Izzy has returned to?*

Flinging open the door, he launches himself towards Cynthia's desk. 'Why on earth did you guys send Jason to 1913 with the others? I mean, *Jason*? And a mission in the same time period as a returning agent?'

As he says the words, he realises how ridiculous he sounds, and Cynthia's stunned expression tells him she thinks he's lost the plot too.

'What nonsense are you accusing us of now?'

Her voice chills him to the core, and his heart sinks as he realises he may have damaged their relationship with his accusations. He needs to remember that Cynthia is not his Time Guardian nemesis, Alpha, and that not everything with her has to be a battle.

Taking a deep breath to calm himself, he also takes a seat. Leaning forward, he rests his arms on his knees and starts again. 'I'm sorry, Cynthia. I just had some disturbing news, and my imagination ran off on me.' He gives a self-deprecating laugh. 'I guess this trust thing between us will take some getting used to.'

Cynthia's stony face doesn't soften as he had hoped it would, but her voice when she answers him is a few degrees less chilly. 'Your apology is accepted. Now, please explain what's going on.'

'Sigma—Nathanial—just informed me that Jason is the one who kidnapped the suffragist. It's him causing the timeline variations.'

Cynthia blanches and clasps her hands in front of her, and he senses it takes quite a bit for his partner to control her reaction to that piece of news. She rises slowly to her feet and, in clipped tones, says, 'If you will excuse me, I have to go make some heads roll.'

THE MURMURINGS OF the others intrude on Basia's calm as she stares out the window, not exactly waiting for Alan to return but hoping he'll arrive soon. Life is so much brighter with him in the room. *Goodness, Basia, you're acting like a lovesick girl from a romance novel. Get a hold of yourself. Alan is not your Allan, and it's unfair to him for you to treat him as though he is.*

She forces herself to turn around and sit on the window seat. Jo and Izzy are talking animatedly, and Stanley lounges in his chair, watching them, a self-satisfied smile on his face.

What's he up to? Basia rises and wanders to the tea trolley to refill her cup and to eavesdrop.

'What is the point of getting the vote if all we are able to do is vote for men? Why must men always represent us?' Josephine's voice is tight with frustration.

'Because society does not change with great leaps forward. It takes small, incremental steps,' Izzy argues.

Josephine's face breaks into a triumphant smile. 'Yet you would have them leap to accepting same-sex relationships when they cannot even countenance women governing.'

Izzy is wide-eyed and stunned into silence as she realises Jo has trapped her. The atmosphere is heavy. Almost as if the entire room is holding its breath, waiting for her response.

'Well, you walked right into that, Isolde,' Basia says.

Izzy turns to her, then laughs. 'I guess I did. Well played, Josephine.'

Stanley regards his two companions fondly, and in that moment, Basia is able to imagine the three of them building some sort of life together.

She hopes for Izzy's sake that she'll come to see it, too, because she's a better

person when she's around Jo and Stanley. Besides, it seems to Basia that there's as much, if not more, for Izzy to focus on changing here in her own timeline as there would be traipsing back and forth at the beck and call of the Time Fixers.

If only her own dilemma were as easily resolved. Walking back to Augusta's with Alan had been enjoyable. It's clear he admires her, is perhaps even attracted to her. She also has to admit that, in spite of the recent death of her Allan, the attraction is reciprocated.

This disturbs her, not least because she can't work out whether she's falling for Alan himself or if it's because he's so like her Allan, it's uncanny. Then again, one of them is a reincarnation of the other, so does it matter?

Either way, she needs to take a step back because she isn't staying around. Or… is it possible she can stay here a little while longer and see where this is heading? No, that wouldn't be good. One or both of them would inevitably get hurt because she can't stay here forever.

Not only does she have a life to get back to, but there would always be the risk that she might overstep and inadvertently change something, and then history would dump her back home, not caring how or where, and that might cause her and Izzy problems explaining things.

Also, at some stage, she and the person she's the reincarnation of might end up in the same area. From what Izzy had said, that might change history as time worked to keep them apart.

History? Oh no. A hand flies to her mouth as her brain catches up with her ramblings, and she turns away so the others can't see her face. Next year, these young people will be embroiled in a war themselves, and not all of them will survive—perhaps not even her detective.

'Barbara, are you all right? You have gone quite pale,' Stanley says from her side. When had he moved?

'Yes, I am. I just thought of….' She doesn't know what to tell him, but fortunately she's rescued from having to say anything at all as she glimpses two figures rushing down the street.

'Nathanial and Hannah have returned early, and they do not look very happy,' she says, drawing Stanley's attention to the approaching couple.

'I hope they have not had another fight,' Josephine says as she joins them.

As one, the four people head out into the hallway to meet the Nathanial and Hannah, arriving just as a maid is closing the door behind them.

'Whatever is the matter?' Izzy demands before they have a chance to even catch their breaths.

Nathanial glances around, taking in the maid as well as the butler emerging from the morning room. 'Perhaps we should find somewhere a little more private to talk.'

Izzy turns to Jensen. 'We shall be in the library. Please show Detective Barker up when he arrives.'

'As you wish, miss. The fire has been lit. Would you like any tea or refreshments?'

Izzy takes in how distressed Nathanial is and says, 'Thank you, Jensen. If you could bring up some tea and perhaps a decanter of claret. It looks like we might need some fortification.'

'Very good, miss.'

Izzy leads the party up the stairs to the first floor. As she opens the door to the library, she asks, 'What was wrong with the morning room?'

No one answers until everyone is inside and the door is firmly closed.

'Nathanial is being a bit overdramatic,' Hannah says. 'I believe this is his attempt at complete privacy. Although why we need it is beyond me. All we have to report is that we saw some suspicious men, followed them, and, as we suspected, they were headed for Parsons's home. As we were turning to leave, a distressed woman appeared at the window—we believe it may be your Maisie Ottaway.'

A stunned silence follows Hannah's words, and then everyone talks at once. Nathanial holds up his hand for silence. When he has it, he says, 'There is more to the story. Hannah, I did not tell you that when I was in London last week to see my lawyer, I believe I was in the same teahouse as Isolde and Barbara.'

Hannah eyes him suspiciously, but he explains, 'I did not recognise them at first, and when I tell you the whole story, you will understand why.'

'All right, go ahead,' Hannah tells him, arms firmly crossed in a defensive position over her chest.

Butterflies erupt in Basia's stomach, and she leans forward, eager to hear what Nathanial has to say. *Because I'm pretty sure I wasn't in London last week. I was hundreds of years in the future, attending a peace conference, so this should be good.*

'I had tea in a shop on Fleet Street and was paying the bill when a ruckus started up outside. A man was yelling and shouting and waving a gun, threatening to kill another man. The gun went off, and the victim fell to the ground. I was quite disturbed by the whole thing, and I decided there and then not to share the incident with you.'

'And seeing Barbara and Isolde?' Hannah pressed.

'Well, it was only when I saw that man again today that it must have jolted

my memory. I believe the two women sitting at the table by the window last week were Isolde and Barbara,' Nathanial explains.

Basia stares blankly at the Time Guardian. What is he talking about?

Nathanial returns her gaze, and his eyes widen, as if he's willing her to do something—but what? A man with a gun? Last week? Then it dawns on her—last week, one of the Time Fixers shot her Allan. Was he saying that that man was here—in this timeline? She looks from Nathanial to Izzy and back again.

'Yes, I believe we were there,' Izzy confirms, sending a look to Basia that says, 'Please back us up.'

'We were,' Basia says somewhat hesitantly.

Nathanial nods and continues. 'Well, you would have seen the wild cast of his eyes and heard the nonsense he was spouting. He was unhinged and very dangerous.'

'But… but the authorities got him,' Izzy says. 'Surely he is not here. He cannot be.'

'Perhaps he escaped.' Basia's voice is barely above a whisper. 'I mean, it's… it is the only explanation.

'I hope that is what happened,' Izzy says, her voice crisp. 'One cannot be too sure about where the authorities sit on this.'

'Isolde, of course the authorities will be on the right side of the law,' Stanley almost bellows. 'How can you think otherwise?'

Josephine places a hand on Stanley's arm. 'You have such a good heart, Stanley, but even you must see how the police have been manhandling and arresting suffragettes—even those who have not broken any laws.'

'But… but…,' Stanley splutters, unable to conceive that those who keep law and order might not be perfect.

He's still coming up with a response when Alan enters the library.

'I see I have arrived in good time to hear you denigrating my fellow officers.' Although his tone is stern, it's softened somewhat by his good humour as his eyes rake over the room, falling finally on Basia. He sends her a warm smile before turning to the others. 'Am I guessing correctly that you at least have something to report?' he asks.

The gong to change for dinner sounds as Nathanial quickly fills the detective in, including their suspicions that one of the men might be a wanted criminal.

'I must say, Nathanial, I have not read any reports of escaped prisoners, or indeed of anyone apprehended for a shooting in London,' Alan protests. 'Are you all quite sure the man from London is in fact the man you saw today?'

'I am completely sure,' Nathanial says.

Heat rises to Basia's face, and she's sure she must appear guilty of something as she struggles to come up with a way to support Nathanial's story.

Izzy, however, is quite at ease with lying—a skill she's no doubt honed on her many Time Fixer missions.

'Of course, I cannot say anything about the man Nathanial and Hannah met today. What I can tell you is last week, I watched one man shoot another man. He was yelling and raving, and the crowd in the street went wild. Because of the ensuing chaos, I cannot swear that he hit his victim, but I can assure you, everyone in the teashop had a good view of the gun wielder's face. We also saw the policemen who led him away. If Nathanial says it is the same man, then I believe him.'

It would be difficult for anyone to question Izzy's firm assertions, but Alan is not so easily mollified.

'Well, I can assure you, no one has escaped custody. We would have had a report and been directed to be on the lookout for him. So it cannot be your man.'

Before anyone can further argue the point, Nathanial steps in. 'Does it matter whether he is the man from London or not? We have discovered where Miss Ottaway is being held. It is likely that, whoever her captors are, they are armed and dangerous, and we should take that into account when we go rescue her.'

'Well said, Nathanial.' Stanley raises a glass of wine to his friend.

Alan is not so supportive. He takes the glass of claret Izzy hands him and has a small sip before saying, 'Identifying the location of the missing girl has been most helpful of you, but now it really is time to let the professionals take over, gentlemen. Not only do we have the experience, but we also have the numbers.'

'The six of us here stand ready to help you. Do you really believe the police force will release enough officers today, given everything going on in Winchester?' Izzy asks, and Alan's eyes widen in what Basia thinks can only be shock.

'But… but you cannot possibly mean to…. I mean, you women cannot be involved in any rescue.'

'Piffle,' Josephine snorts. 'I am a better shot than Stanley. No one can punch harder than Isolde. And I warrant you, Barbara and Hannah have some hidden talents as well. Detective, write us off as feeble women at your peril.' The look on Josephine's face challenges Alan to deny their usefulness.

Alan opens his mouth as if to respond, then closes it, almost as though he knows this is not an argument he can win. When he does speak, it's to reiterate that they should leave this to the police now.

'When do you think you can get someone organised to retrieve Miss Ottaway?' Stanley asks.

Alan frowns again, and he appears reluctant to answer. 'Well, um, rather a large number of people have been misplaced in Winchester today, so the captain doubled patrols this afternoon in light of Miss Ottaway's disappearance.'

'So more women have been abducted,' Josephine gasps.

'I am sorry, I should have chosen my words better under the circumstances. With the number of visitors in the city, people have lost members of their groups. We have more constables out and about to provide directions and try to reunite stragglers with their friends.'

'Oh, thank goodness. I thought things might have escalated beyond our ability to help.' Josephine breathes a sigh of relief. 'So, when will the constables be freed up to rescue Miss Ottaway?'

'Perhaps later this evening, but more likely tonight,' Alan answered.

Nathanial, who was shaking his head before the detective had even finished speaking, says, 'Not only is that too long to wait, but if their captors are smart, they will be expecting a night-time rescue by the police.'

Izzy nods. 'Yes, and if we go in now, perhaps with a frontal approach to throw them off-guard, we might succeed. Josephine and Hannah will be the best to send in as decoys. No one will expect two women looking for their friend to be part of a rescue attempt.'

'Good thinking,' Basia says. 'And the chap from London will not have seen them before and so will not be suspicious—'

'Except when I was in the park this morning, they walked right past me,' Hannah butts in. 'But if I change my dress and hat, I will seem like someone completely different to all but the most observant of people.'

'Yes, you could borrow something of mine,' Izzy agrees. 'We are much the same size.'

'So, while Josephine and Hannah are at the front door, causing a scene over—' Stanley starts, and the entire group except for the detective forms a circle, bandying around ideas. Alan turns from one to the other as they speak, a look of bemusement on his face.

'Asking about the disappearance of one of our suffragist sisters, of course,' Josephine interrupts. 'That should get them aggravated enough to drop their guard.'

Alan places his wine on the table, clearly not comfortable with the runaway plan but seemingly not sure how to stop it. Basia wishes she could say

something to include him, but Maisie must be rescued as soon as possible, and this plan is coming together nicely.

'But, my dear, what if they try to abduct you too?' Stanley's face creases with concern.

'Then you will be inside, having come through the back door, ready to help,' Hannah says, a smile on her lips.

As Hannah speaks, Nathanial rises to his feet and excuses himself from the table. 'Please carry on. My stomach is just a little upset,' he says as he rushes from the room.

WHAT IS IT, Beta? Nathanial asks as soon as the door closes behind him.

You still sound angry, Sigma.

Sorry, I had to make an excuse to leave the room. I'm with people who have no idea Time Guardians exist, let alone ones who can mindspeak.

So you couldn't have just gazed out a window?

Hannah already thinks I'm acting strangely enough, and I don't want to give her any more reason to think I'm not her Nathanial.

Nathanial is annoyed, and though he's pretty certain the interruption isn't the cause, he is not quite certain what has gotten him so het up.

Of course, it could be because he was taken from this first ever holiday during which he'd been trying to get some perspective on life so he could make some serious death decisions. Or maybe because he's been dropped into a situation that appears to be going from bad to worse. Or it could be because he doesn't like cleaning up someone else's mess—and that someone else should definitely have cleaned Jason away some time ago.

If he was being honest, though, what's gotten under his skin is the fact that Hannah appears to like this new version of Nathanial far more than the old one. It has him questioning his whole past life, and one does not need a life crisis in the middle of a mission.

How he wishes he were back in the holiday simulation, lazing on a beach, reading books, and drinking ice-cold beer.

Well, it's never easy going back into your own timeline, Beta says, and his holiday vision recedes.

A little less of the pop psychiatry, if you please.

All right, I have an update for you.

Beta is being his usual chatty self and taking time Nathanial does not have. *I thought as much, but please make it quick. I've excused myself to use the facilities, so I can't be away for long.*

All right. Cynthia's investigations found Jason has escaped from house arrest and is hellbent on ruining Izzy.

Izzy? Why not all of us? Nathanial asks.

The enquiry into his actions last week caused some doubt over his past performance. They reopened the investigation into the mission he went on with Izzy, and some judges are thinking perhaps her version of events may be closer to the truth. So now Jason blames her for everything that's happened to him.

That is nonsense. Izzy wasn't even involved in his decision to interrupt the peace talks.

Beta's sigh is clearly audible. *You can't argue with crazy, and this guy has definitely lost the plot. Unfortunately for us, there are enough supporters of his family who are prepared to listen to his nonsense, including his parents themselves.*

You mean there are Time Fixers helping him? Nathanial asks, sure his shock has transmitted through to Beta.

He was under house arrest, which means he had a bracelet preventing him from portalling anywhere. Someone must have removed it or opened a portal for him if he's in Winchester.

Unbelievable.

And that's not all. He's spun some yarn about needing to go and clean up Izzy's mess because she's been taking action contrary to Time Fixers protocols.

But that's nonsense. Izzy had barely arrived.... Ah, you mean by bringing Basia here.

Exactly.

It was my suggestion, though.

But Izzy agreed to take her.

Nathanial runs a hand through his hair. Could he have brought this mess down on everyone because he tried to help Basia?

Don't beat yourself up, Sigma. Jason would have found another excuse to attack Izzy if this one didn't exist.

He's sure Beta is right, but it doesn't stop him feeling somewhat responsible anyway.

So, what now, Beta?

We—Cynthia and I—have taken responsibility for Basia being with you. However, all this debating has created delays on our end.

Delays?

Yes. The Time Fixer Council wants to send a team to extract Jason, Basia, and Izzy before they cause any damage to the timeline. However, Jason's parents and their supporters

have called for a full Council session to debate the mission and clearly define its parameters. There are some who are prepared to argue that Jason's actions will improve the timeline.

You can't be serious. How would delaying women getting the vote improve the chances of stopping the world ending? No, don't tell me. I don't have time, and it'll only make me angrier. So what now?

Cynthia is about to leave to attend the Council session, and I'm off to Time Guardian headquarters to see if they're prepared to send an extraction team for Jason. They've been strangely silent on the matter, so I'm not sure I'll gain any support.

So, what do we do in the meantime? We can't leave poor Maisie with Jason—he's clearly unhinged.

I will leave that up to you and Izzy. You need to decide what's more important—her future with the Time Fixers or saving the girl.

Not much of a choice, Nathanial says.

Whatever you decide to do, remember that Jason is no longer considered an agent of ours, as he was stood down. His actions will be considered unsanctioned until the Council votes to approve them, Cynthia's voice cuts in, her tone terse.

Has she been listening this whole time? He knows Beta trusts the Time Fixer, but Nathanial hardly knows her. He quickly reviews the conversation to work out if he had said anything he didn't want her to hear. Fortunately, he hadn't opened up too much about the awkward situation between him and Hannah. Happy he had kept things professional, he turns his mind back to Cynthia's statement.

So you're saying the sooner we get to Jason, the better for Izzy's future? he clarifies.

Exactly. Now I must be off, or I'll be late.

The silence drags out, and Nathanial wonders if Beta has gone as well until his mentor says, *I am afraid she's angry with me because I didn't trust her enough when I found out about Jason. And she's beyond angry with the Time Fixers for not telling her Jason escaped and that they were trying to find him. This new unit…. Well, it's new, and we have a few teething problems.*

I don't think anything about this situation is good for anyone, Nathanial sends. *In fact, I'm surprised that history hasn't removed Jason from the timeline for taking direct action.*

Well, we believe that's because anti-suffragette sentiment is running so high, meaning his actions are not as extreme as they first appear.

Nathanial considers this for a moment and wonders how he hadn't noticed the depth of anger towards women seeking the vote when he lived through this time before. Had he really been so wrapped up in his own life that he hadn't seen the signs that were so obvious to him now? Or was it simply

because he'd been viewing the world through a male perspective? Was it any wonder Hannah had been so disparaging of him?

Sigma, if we've finished, then I must go—the Time Guardian Council awaits. Any ideas on what I should tell them?

Still caught up in his own self-reflection, it takes a moment for Nathanial to redirect his thoughts. Everyone in the room next door appears intent on taking action. The Time Fixers are procrastinating, and the Time Guardians are unlikely to become involved.

Do you think you can persuade the Guardians not to react for a day in order to see how the timeline looks and whether history intervenes?

I can probably swing that, but what do I tell them about you and Izzy?

Do they even know you asked me to come here?

Not exactly. In my new role, I have some autonomy….

At first Nathanial doesn't know how he feels about that. It's as though he's going against the Time Guardians. Having only ever stretched the rules before, he isn't sure he's up to breaking them. Then again, not being required to follow their rules gives him a feeling of freedom.

Sigma? Whatever happens, this is on me if it goes wrong.

Nathanial's laugh is hollow. *Thanks for your support.*

No, what I mean is, I sent you to deal with the situation—you've done nothing wrong.

So why does he feel like he's about to? Putting his misgivings aside, he sends, *Right, so rescue Maisie it is!*

It's Beta's turn to laugh. *All right, my friend. In that case, I believe you have a day at the most to resolve this before one or the other of the sides chooses to intervene.*

Understood.

At the creak of a door hinge from behind him, Nathanial quickly turns and steps forward as if he's returning from the bathroom just as Hannah emerges from the library.

'Ah, there you are. I wondered if you were all right.' She smiles tentatively at him, but the question remains in her eyes, the same one that had appeared when he replaced his earlier self.

'I am fine. Just a small stomach upset.'

Her smile broadens. 'Good, because it is getting out of hand in the library, and I am sure they could use some of your newfound organisational skills.'

She takes his hand and leads him back to the fray.

9

DANCING AROUND

HANNAH'S DESCRIPTION OF what's going on in the library is woefully inadequate. Everyone is talking over top of everyone else. Voices are raised, hands are busy gesticulating, and no one is listening.

Nathanial watches for a moment and decides there's nothing else for it—he whistles. It's as if he's stunned the room's occupants. They stop talking and immediately turn to him.

'We are not going to get very far if we behave like a group of street thugs,' he tells them.

Big mistake, because they all start talking at him. He sighs, wondering if he is the right person to lead this group. Then again, who else is there? Izzy? She's too distracted by Josephine, and this reincarnation of Alan is too young and green, as is Hannah—although he knows she'll go on to be a formidable Time Guardian. Basia is sitting quietly by the fire and appears to have opted out of whatever is going on. So, it's up to him.

He holds up his hand for silence, and it takes a few moments, but they all eventually quieten down. When he's positive they're going to stay that way, he speaks, keeping his voice low so they will all have to concentrate or risk missing out on what he's saying.

'When I left only a few minutes ago, I thought we had agreed to rescue Miss Ottaway and were forming a rather decent plan—something about Hannah and Josephine approaching the front door as a distraction. What happened in that small amount of time to cause this chaos?'

Everyone opens their mouths, and he holds up his hand again. 'One at a time, please.' He points at the detective.

'We should not do this. We should wait for the authorities,' Alan says, predictably.

'We have gone past that point. We are going to rescue Maisie. All we need to decide is how,' Nathanial says, dismissing the detective's plea. He points at Stanley, the other person who has some misgivings about this rescue.

'I think the women should not be so directly involved. We should gather some chums and let the men take care of this,' Stanley says. 'Of course, they will need to be there to help Miss Ottaway once we have taken out her captors, but there is no sense in placing them in harm's way.'

'And I think you are being a pompous idiot,' Izzy says without waiting for Nathanial to point at her.

'Isolde, do not talk to Stanley like that.' Having admonished her friend, Josephine turns to her fiancé and says, 'And you should have more faith in us. We are perfectly capable of taking care of ourselves.'

Basia rises to her feet, frustration written on her face. 'I cannot hear this another time. We should all be thinking about what is best for Maisie, not going round in circles with this constant bickering. I shall be in my room when you are ready to plan sensibly.' With a swish of her skirts, she leaves them.

The silence following her departure is heavy. 'I am not surprised she is annoyed with you all. You do rather sound like squabbling children,' Nathanial says, smiling wryly, and the others laugh, breaking the tension.

'Look, if we want Miss Ottaway out of that house, we are going to have to work together.' He pauses for a moment, searching for agreement on the faces in front of him. They give him nothing.

Taking a deep breath, he continues regardless. 'That will mean each of us bending a little. For instance, Detective, perhaps you could send a runner and ask for a constable or two to be dispatched to help us out. You could use them to make up a team to lead a charge through the back once the ladies have distracted the men out front.'

'I guess I could do that,' Alan agrees reluctantly.

'But—'

Nathanial does not allow Stanley to complete his sentence. 'And, Stanley, maybe you could remain hidden at the front of the house to ensure help is at hand if something happens to Hannah or Josephine.'

'Well, yes, I guess that could work,' Stanley concedes.

'And if I wait with you, we four could make our way through the front door when the others enter from the back,' Izzy adds.

Stanley grins. 'Catch them in a traditional pincer movement.'

'Exactly.' Izzy grins back.

'And that leaves Nathanial and Barbara joining the fray from the rear,' Hannah finishes.

Nathanial relaxes. 'It looks like we have the beginnings of a plan. Perhaps someone should find Bas… um… Barbara so we can finish our planning? And maybe we could have some more refreshments?'

'I will find her,' Josephine offers.

'And I shall organise more tea—that is if you do not mind, Isolde,' Hannah adds.

'That would be great, thank you. And could you please ask Jensen to hold dinner? I fear we may be a while yet,' Izzy says as the two women leave.

Everyone's playing nice again. Nathanial is pretty proud of himself until Izzy pulls him aside and says, 'You should know that while you were out, Stanley and Hannah were talking about the change that has come over you today. Perhaps you should be a little less Sigma and a little more Nathanial for a while.'

Nathanial's lips curl into a smile. 'I rather thought Hannah liked the new me.'

Izzy's eyes sparkle. 'I think you are right, but what mess are you leaving for the Nathanial who has to stay behind?' Her eyes widen. 'Or are you thinking of staying here as well?'

Seizing the opportunity to change the subject, Nathanial says, 'So have *you* decided to stay?'

'I am not letting you off the hook that easily. Answer my question—are you thinking about remaining here after this is over?'

'No, of course….' Nathanial had been about to give a vehement no, but he realises he would be lying. 'That was not my intention when I arrived, but I have to admit, I am kind of enjoying being the new me in this old time.'

Izzy's eyes narrow. 'I understand you find the rules around being a Guardian difficult, but I kind of thought you might join Beta's new team.'

'I was struggling with that decision while I was on leave—trying to decide whether to allow my soul to slip away, or wondering if I had the energy to

continue and effect some real change in humanity's timeline,' he admits, running a hand over his jaw. 'But I feel alive here, for the first time in a long time—and before you say it, it is not just because I am back in a human body.'

Izzy chuckles. 'I must say, it is unusual to talk to you face to face like this, but please, do not get carried away by the excitement… or by Hannah's admiration.'

'So, it is all right for you to decide to stay but not me?' Nathanial doesn't mean to sound petulant, but he can't help it.

For the first time in a long time, he feels like he's being true to himself, and for some reason, he'd hoped Izzy would be happy for him. After all, over the past few months, he and the Time Fixer had become close, even working on missions together, and she of all people should understand the conflicts he faces in his job. Even so, why is he so bothered by her negative reaction?

'Nathanial, you are my closest friend, and—'

'Sorry?' he says, ready to stop her. Friends? Then he reads the concern in her eyes, and he realises she *is* his friend, or at least the closest thing he's had to a friend for some years.

'Please hear me out, Nathanial.'

He nods for her to continue, but he's only half listening, as part of him is still processing this new revelation.

'I want you to find your place in the world almost as much as I want to find my own, but your staying has such different consequences. As much as I want women to be treated the same as men, the reality is that we will not be when war comes next year. By staying here, you could be placing your life in danger.'

'War?' he reacts, suddenly paying attention. Of course, the war to end all wars is almost upon the world.

'Yes, the war in which Britain's male population is decimated. Now, it may be that Hannah will make a different decision with her new and improved Nathanial, but are you willing to take that chance only to be drawn into fighting a war that will, like as not, result in your being shot in a trench somewhere in Europe?'

It was as if she'd thrown cold water over him. 'What a grim picture you paint, Isolde.'

It had been so easy for him to be drawn into his old life, renewing his attraction to Hannah, and thinking perhaps he had found a way to make a life with her that didn't mean joining the Time Guardians. Combined with the excitement of searching for Miss Ottaway, he had totally forgotten about the war looming over the horizon.

As Great Britain spiralled towards conflict, he and Hannah had become despondent, worried about the future of mankind. They both opposed Britain going to war and worked tirelessly for peace. Hell, he'd even been leaning towards becoming a conscientious objector.

Not long after, Hannah had changed. She'd become distant and would go missing for hours on end, offering no explanation. Finally, he forced her hand, and she introduced him to Alpha, and Beta, and the Time Guardians.

She was so excited, believing she'd found a better way to stop warring factions in the world. When he questioned her some more, she asked him to come along on a mission.

He feels a hand on his arm. 'Nathanial, I am sorry. I did not mean to dredge up unhappy memories. Especially not when we should be focusing on Maisie and how to get her away from Jason. You join the others, and I will go and see what is happening with the refreshments.'

A part of him notices Izzy's departure, but he continues replaying the scene between him and Hannah after their first two missions together.

'I am going to join them, Nathanial. They say I am ready, that I have helped them in past lives, and I can now ascend.'

'And what about me? About us?' he'd asked.

'The good news is that they are happy for you to come with me. It seems it would be cleaner if we both died in an accident. Our families would find some peace, knowing we were together in death.'

The shock he felt at how she calmly planned their demise is still as raw today as it had been then.

'Beta said most guardians ascend at the end of their natural lives,' he'd countered. 'I am happy to wait until my life ends naturally.'

Her anger had surprised him. 'Of course you would be. It is not you who would be left alone for years, grieving for me.'

'What? I do not understand.'

'Alpha has explained that in the coming war, so many men die that I will likely be left a widow. So, chances are you would be given the option to ascend within the next few years. I will likely live out the rest of my life alone, without you.' Hannah's words were laced with a bitterness that cut him deeply.

He was not so ready to jump to his own death. 'If there is only a chance I might die, there is also a chance I might live, and that we will grow old together.'

The scornful look she'd turned on him cut him to the quick. 'Even your optimism cannot remain in the face of the scale of this war. I have decided.

I will ascend next week. Alpha has planned the accident. I want you to join me, but if you decide not to, I hope you live a happy life.'

Turning on her heel, she'd left him standing alone in the deserted park. He reached out, trying to call her back, but he couldn't form the words. What would he say to her? What would convince her to stay with him?

Now, standing in the library in Augusta's house, his feelings of loss and betrayal return in full force. With his new knowledge, could he actually influence Hannah enough to change her mind, to have her try for the slim chance of a life together? Knowing the decision she'd been capable of making once before, does he even want to try?

As if she materialises from his thoughts, Hannah appears beside him. 'Nathanial, do you want to join us?'

The Hannah from the past wouldn't have asked. She would have assumed he would always want to be by her side.

They move to the circle gathering around the fresh pot of tea, Hannah making sure he's cut off from Izzy, and he finally sees it.

The potential future he'd seen for them was a fantasy of his own making, a vision he's holding on to, has indeed been longing for, during the years since they ascended. It's time to let it go and start making decisions for himself.

He pulls Hannah's arm through his as the other Nathanial would have done, hoping to reassure her everything is all right, but his mind has already returned to the problem of rescuing Maisie.

BASIA RETURNS TO the library with Josephine after the woman promises everyone is now playing nice. As she takes a seat by the fire, she studies the group, and they do indeed appear to be getting along. She's barely had a chance to sit when Alan joins her, offering a cup of tea.

'Thank you, but no. If I have any more to drink, I think I will burst,' she tells him.

'You are quiet this evening,' he says, taking the seat opposite, the cup still in his hands.

'All this arguing and fussing is really not my style. To me, it is clear-cut. Maisie is being held by some not very nice people. The sooner we get her out of there, the better.'

Alan looks at his tea so intently, it's as if he's searching for something in the bottom of his cup.

'Extracting her will be dangerous. Surely you should leave saving her to the professionals.' The words explode from his mouth as if he's been trying to keep them in, but they have to be spoken.

Basia bites back a snort, but she can't keep the scorn from her voice. 'If it were not for us, you and your professionals would have no idea where she was being held, or by whom.'

Her companion has the good grace to colour at this. 'I have to admit, you have all turned out to be most helpful—'

'And we will also be helpful in extracting her from their clutches.'

Alan continues to study the tea, then takes a sip and places the cup back on the saucer. 'I would prefer it if we had more men. I have sent a runner to the station, but by the time they get here, it will be late, and it will be dark.'

Basia doesn't understand why he's so concerned about darkness falling when he'd been perfectly happy to wait before. 'You see that as being a problem? I thought we would be able to hide better in the dark.'

'True, we will be able to hide more easily, but if these men are professional criminals, they will know that too. If they can reasonably guess what we will do, they will be prepared—if not for our exact plan, then for something to happen.' He raises his head and looks her in the eyes, almost as though he's willing her to understand.

'That sounds logical. When would you suggest we go?'

Alan shrugs. 'If it were completely up to me, I would go in at first light. One of the captors will not be quite awake, and the other will be tired from guard duty.'

Basia nods, understanding his argument but not really liking it. She wants to say she can see his point, but they need to get Maisie out now. Alan is gazing so earnestly at her, she hasn't the heart.

'It sounds like early morning might be a better time. And I guess it means everyone can get into position under cover of darkness and be ready when Josephine and Hannah make their entrance at first light.'

The smile Alan gives her causes her heart to skip a beat. 'You know, if they let women on the force, you would be quite good at this.'

'Will they not be suspicious about women being out so early?'

Basia had been so focused on Alan, she hadn't heard Stanley approach.

'If we were truly worried about a friend, we would be up bright and early

looking for her,' Josephine says from the other side of the room.

'I am still not completely comfortable—' Stanley starts, but he's interrupted as the door opens.

Izzy enters, followed by Jensen pushing a tea trolley loaded with cakes and sandwiches. 'Refreshments,' she announces.

'I am going to need to get a whole new wardrobe when I get home,' Basia sighs as she eyes the delicious offerings.

Izzy catches her ogling and says, 'I had forgotten how Aunt's cook likes to feed everyone.'

'I have no problem with the amount of food she sends up,' Stanley says, placing a cake on a plate. 'She is a superb cook, and I will show my appreciation by eating whatever she serves.'

With the food having distracted Stanley, Alan presents his objections to the current plan. They take very little persuading that his option has a better chance of success with a couple of tweaks. Once they've agreed, he outlines it again to make sure everyone is on the same page.

'At around five thirty tomorrow morning, Nathanial and Isolde will take their place in the bushes in front of Parsons's house. Barbara and I, with hopefully two constables, will take up a position in the back garden with easy access to the back door. Then, as the sun rises, Josephine and Hannah, escorted by Stanley, will knock on the door and question whoever answers about their missing friend.'

'So far so good,' Stanley says, helping himself to another cake.

'When we are certain the household is distracted, those of us at the back will enter. Hopefully this will cause whoever is answering the door to return inside. After which, those at the front will be able to enter the house and head upstairs to find Miss Ottaway.'

'What then?' Basia asks. 'I mean, how will they get her out?'

Alan shrugs. 'Obviously the optimal solution would be to retreat the way we came in, but we cannot predict where people will be in the house, how many of them there are, or how they will react.'

'Should I stay at the bottom of the stairs or go up with the women?' Stanley asks.

'A good question,' Alan tells him. 'I guess that depends on how many different voices you make out downstairs when you come in. If all the action is there, you might need to stay on the ground floor with Nathanial to ensure no one goes up to disturb the getaway.'

'Understood.'

'It sounds like we have a plan,' Alan says and waits for agreement.

'I am not comfortable leaving her there for another night,' Basia says, not quite able to give up on helping the young woman escape from her prison this evening.

The faces the others turn towards her show they disapprove. Only Nathanial is nodding in agreement. 'That thug who threatened me seemed like a bit of a brute, and I certainly did not like the way he looked at Hannah. I am not sure Miss Ottaway will be safe with him in the house.'

'You do not think they would….' Hannah's voice trails off as she contemplates what might befall a young woman alone in a house full of men.

'No one is saying that.' Izzy steps forward, hands on hips.

'Perhaps when I return to the station, I will find out if one of the trainee officers can watch the house for the night,' the detective offers.

'What good would that do?' Basia asks.

'He would raise an alarm if he hears anything untoward. It is not much—'

Basia's spirits lift at Alan's gesture. 'Thank you. It may not be much, but it would make me feel better.'

Jason may be many things, but he wouldn't let anyone defile a woman.

Basia is sure the comment was meant for Nathanial. Nonetheless, she's a little more settled knowing Izzy thinks Jason incapable of assaulting a woman—although he did appear to be okay with killing a man.

He may not be able to control his hired muscle, Nathanial sends.

I know how Jason works. If he's worried about what the man might do, he'll most likely take the night watch himself to ensure Maisie is safe.

Izzy and Nathanial lock eyes, and Basia watches them, waiting for Sigma's lead that he believes it'll be okay to leave Maisie where she is until the morning.

That's what I would do in a similar situation, so maybe it's all right to wait until tomorrow.

'Nathanial,' Hannah hisses, startling Basia. 'Stop staring at Isolde. It is beyond rude.'

Basia can't help smirking. Hannah is obviously jealous of Nathanial and Izzy. Of course, she has no idea the two are actually friends or that Izzy's romantic interest lies elsewhere.

Nathanial turns away from his fiancée and says, 'All right, the morning it is, then, unless you still have concerns, Barbara?'

Although she hates the thought of Maisie spending another night alone, she understands why a morning rescue has a better chance of success. 'I

guess this is the best plan we have.'

'Good, then let us meet at the station at five o'clock. We can then proceed in small groups to our places around Parsons's house.'

It's comforting how easily Nathanial moves into his Sigma role of directing the troops. Alan and Hannah eye him uneasily. Alan probably because he believes he should be in charge, and Hannah because she isn't used to seeing Nathanial like this.

Sensing Alan's discomfort, Basia positions herself beside the detective. This plan will only succeed if the two men work together, and she has an idea on how she might achieve that. 'So, Alan, you will obviously be coordinating our entry from the back. Perhaps it might be useful to have Nathanial take the lead in the front.'

The detective looks at her, a frown drawing his brows together.

'I mean, you will be supervising the two constables and me as we capture the kidnappers. It would be difficult to also lead the rescue from the front.'

Maybe it's because he sees the sense in her plan, or maybe it's because it's her making the proposal, but whatever the reason, Alan says, 'What a good idea, Barbara.'

'Good. If we are all agreed, Nathanial and I are due to join my parents for dinner,' Hannah says, linking her arm proprietarily through Nathanial's as she glares at Isolde.

'That is, if there is nothing further to discuss,' Nathanial adds, clearly not as keen to leave as his fiancée.

'No, I think we are good,' Alan tells him, and Basia wonders if he's hoping to remove the threat to his control of the situation. Then she quickly admonishes herself for thinking badly of Alan.

Once Nathanial and Hannah have departed, Stanley decides to help himself to more tea and yet another cake.

'Stanley,' Josephine chides him, 'you will not fit into your wedding suit if you carry on eating like that.'

Stanley turns to her, sending her his best puppy dog eyes as he holds another bite-sized sweet halfway to his mouth. 'I am unable to resist them. They are truly delightful. I have no idea how Augusta is not three times the size she is, having such an amazing cook.' Stanley returns to the vacant chair by Josephine and Izzy, cake still in hand and grinning contentedly.

The three begin talking quietly, and Basia wonders if they're doing their best to give her and Alan some privacy. As if confirming her suspicions, Alan

moves in closer and takes her hand. For a moment she freezes as her mind is overwhelmed with conflicting thoughts. The touch draws her closer to Alan, and yet at the same time, it reminds her of the Allan she lost.

Completely unaware of her internal conflict, this Alan speaks. 'Um, Barbara, I was wondering if perhaps you would join me for supper, as you now have nothing on?'

Basia's first thought is to pull her hand away and respond with an adamant no. It's too close to Allan's death, and although this Alan is so like her love, he isn't him. Besides, she isn't sure she wants to spend an intimate evening with a man calling her Barbara—it's difficult enough to remember to respond under normal circumstances.

Still, her hand tingles from his touch, and a warmth spreads across her cheeks. Maybe she could let herself enjoy an evening with the detective. He's so handsome. She likes the way his eyes twinkle, and the smile that often plays around his lips causes her heart to flutter. He'd been good company on their walk back to Augusta's earlier, talking on a wide range of topics: his family, the current political situation, and his role as a policeman.

Yes, she would enjoy an evening getting to know him. Perhaps it might even end with a kiss.

She shakes her head. Tempting though the thought is, she shouldn't toy with Alan's affections like that. In a few days, she'll return to her own time, and she doesn't wish to do so knowing she left behind a broken heart or perhaps taking one with her.

'I am sorry, Alan, but with such an early start tomorrow, it would not be such a good idea.' She allows her all-too-real disappointment at turning him down to ring through her words, hoping to soften the blow.

'Ah, I see. Yes, that is certainly sensible. Maybe after this is over?'

'Maybe,' Basia agrees, feeling guilty that she doesn't have it in her to be strong and completely reject his attentions.

'It is a shame, though, because I had hoped to spend the evening convincing you to stay at home tomorrow morning. Now that I have changed the time, I am sure I can find another officer to replace you.'

Basia's sympathy for the detective disappears at these words. Withdrawing her hand, she says rather primly, 'If you thought that, then you have completely the wrong impression of me.'

A familiar smile plays around his lips. 'No, Barbara, I think I am beginning to know you quite well. I said I would try. I was pretty certain I would not succeed.'

He stands and announces it's time for him to leave, as he needs to organise his men for tomorrow. Basia barely hears a word he says, as she tries to regain control of her emotions after their teasing interplay. Dammit, she wants to ask him to stay for dinner, to spend more time with him, and perhaps have the evening end with that kiss she imagined.

Instead she rises and calmly says goodbye to him, and then Stanley and Josephine, who have also decided to have an early night. The room feels empty after their guests are gone, and Basia gravitates to the round window nestled between the bookshelves and follows Alan's retreating form until he disappears from sight.

Jensen comes to clear away the tea things and advises them that Augusta would be staying with Mrs Trimms that night.

'Would you like dinner in the dining room now?' he asks.

'What do you think, Barbara?'

'Um, pardon?' Basia pulls her gaze from the window and turns her attention to the butler. 'Ah, I think I might retire to my room, if that is all right with you, Isolde?'

Izzy's gaze holds concern for her, but she doesn't say anything. Instead she instructs Jensen that they will both take trays in their rooms.

Basia follows the butler out before heading upstairs, needing some time alone with her thoughts.

FOR THE THIRD time that night, Izzy crosses the corridor and stands outside Basia's door. There had been little sound from within when she checked previously. This time, though, she thinks she hears pacing.

She raises her hand to knock, then drops it back to her side. Earlier, Basia had appeared distant and… well, sad. Although she and Basia have become close over the short period of time since they met, she doesn't know her well enough to feel certain the other girl would want to confide in her—or would want her help.

'If you're going to come in, just come in,' a voice calls from inside.

Does that mean she wants me to come in, or is she just letting me know she knows I'm here?

Turning the knob, she opens the door, all signs of prevarication hidden behind the confident demeanour she normally presents to the world.

'I wasn't sure whether you were asleep or not,' she tells Basia's back. 'Since you're awake, I have something to show you.'

Basia turns from staring out the window. 'What is it?'

Her voice shows no interest at all, but Izzy ignores that. 'You have to come with me.'

She leads Basia back into her room, where she'd laid two sets of women's trousers and tailored jackets out on the bed.

'I wouldn't normally wear these in Winchester, as they attract too much attention. But I think they'll do fine for tomorrow and will give us better freedom of movement.'

Basia stares at the outfits on the bed, and Izzy wonders if she's even seeing them.

Reaching out a hand, she touches the other girl's arm. 'Basia, I think the ones on the left will be perfect for you, as they're cut to accommodate someone with more curves than I have. You'll have time to tack the trousers up a little so they fit better.'

'Yes, of course.' Basia reaches for the clothing, ignoring Izzy's hand. 'I'll get right on it.'

Turning, she carries the garments back into her room. Izzy follows. There's something wrong with her friend.

'Basia, did things go all right with Alan? You two seemed happy enough this afternoon, but… well… now you seem a little sad.'

Basia drops onto the bed, facing Izzy, the clothes resting in her lap. 'He's so charming, Izzy, and funny and serious and… and, well, he's everything my Allan was, but he's not, as well. I can't tell whether all these feelings I have are for him or if I'm simply missing my Allan.'

Izzy sits beside her friend and wraps an arm around her shoulders. 'It must be so difficult. I can't tell you how many times I've fallen for my Josephine's reincarnations—loving that person but knowing full well they aren't the one I truly want to be with. And at the same time knowing I can't fully be with the one I love more than life itself.'

Turning slightly to face her, Basia says, 'How do you cope with it, Izzy?'

'I'm not sure I ever really have,' Izzy responds, speaking from the heart. 'I mean, look at me. I came back here hoping I might salvage something with my Jo. At the moment I'm thinking it's better to be with her some of the time than with someone else all of the time.'

Izzy's eyebrows draw together. She hadn't known she was going to say that. The words just flowed from her mouth, bypassing her brain and coming straight from her heart. Now that they're out there, she recognises them for the truth they are.

'I'm pleased you've worked out what you want, but it's not so simple for me. Allan won't be there waiting for me when I return home. And you of all people know I can't stay here.' Basia sounds as though the weight of the world rests on her shoulders.

Izzy curses inside her head. Why is life so difficult for Basia and the many versions she's met of her old nemesis Barabal?

'You know, Basia, Sigma and I first met you in medieval England. You were called Barabal then.'

Basia smiles. 'I know. Sigma told me that was the only timeline he'd come across where I ended up with Allan, only he was called Alain then.'

'Sure, and they had many babies, and yet Barabal was a political force to be reckoned with in her time. I always thought it was because women were of no consequence, and she used every skill she had to make sure she mattered, and Alain respected her enough to just let her get on with it.'

Basia stood, clutching the clothes to her chest. 'I'm not sure why you're—'

'I'm telling you because not one of your incarnations I have met since then has been as confident defining their own future while still having a relationship with their Allan.'

Izzy isn't sure whether or not to go on. As Basia hasn't moved, she decides it's worth a try to get her message across.

'I next met Bebe. She was so focused on her career that when she met her Allan, she had no room for him in her life.'

Basia sits on the bed, places her hands on top of the clothing in her lap, and stares at Izzy. 'And how would you describe me in this reincarnation loop?'

'I would like to be able to say that you're the one who found her calling… and love as well.'

'But…?'

'But at the moment, you're the one who fell in love and allowed Allan to mould your future.'

Basia's shoulders slump, and Izzy wonders if she's gone too far. In an attempt to bring Basia back, she asks, 'Who are you, Basia?'

The other girl blinks a couple of times. 'Sorry?'

'No, seriously—who *are* you, and what do you want? If Allan hadn't turned up on your doorstep, and the last two weeks had never happened, who would you be?'

Basia is motionless beside her except for the teeth gnawing at her bottom lip. Izzy allows the silence to lengthen, forcing Basia to speak next.

'I'm… I'm not sure I can answer that. I'm not the same person I was before Allan came, and I don't think I can go back to thinking like farm-girl Basia.'

Again Izzy resists the urge to fill the silence.

'What I can say for certain is, when I return home, I will no longer allow people to define my life by my ability to have children. I refuse to put off my dreams until I've contributed to repopulating the world.'

Izzy can't hide her surprise. 'You don't want to have children?'

Shrugging, Basia answers, 'I don't know. I might, one day. I've never been allowed to think of it in terms of want. If I do, though, I'm determined that having children will be my decision, not an expectation.'

'Well, good on you,' Izzy says and mentally high-fives Basia. 'That's a step in the right direction.' But it's still not enough. She needs to ignite something in her friend, something to knock her from her dreamlike state and give her a reason to take her life into her own hands and move it forward.

Sigma had believed bringing Basia to this time would show her anyone can fight for what they believe in and that women are more than capable of leading the charge.

After a few days with Basia, Izzy now believes that in the wake of Allan's death, it's more important for Basia to find out who she is and what she wants from life.

'You were ready to go home today. Did you want to go back to your parents? Pick up from where you left off before Allan shook things up? Or did you have something else in mind?'

Basia laughs. 'Going back to the farm is not an option. I had already outgrown that girl before Allan appeared, I just hadn't admitted it to myself.' Basia's voice drifts off. She sits still for a moment, then rises to her feet, the trousers and jacket dropping to the ground.

Izzy picks up the discarded clothing from the floor as Basia paces the room.

'I thought I followed Allan to Portsdown, and I guess in some ways, I did. What I hadn't realised until now is it was my choice to go. If Allan hadn't come along, I would have found some other reason to leave.'

She paces a little more before adding, 'I think I may have been as attracted to the opportunity for adventure, for change, as I was to him.'

'Are you saying—'

'Oh no, he was definitely my soulmate, and I wish more than anything I could spend the rest of my life with him, but—'

'He was the icing on the cake, not the cake,' Izzy finishes for her.

Basia's laugh tinkles 'What a lovely way to put it. Stanley *would* approve.'

Izzy chuckles at this and relaxes a little. Lying back on the bed, she allows the sense of crisis averted to sink in.

Basia flops down beside her. 'Now I just need to decide what it is I want to do from here.'

Izzy reaches out and curls her fingers around Basia's. 'And in the meantime, you know it's perfectly acceptable for you to have a bit of fun with a certain handsome detective.'

Basia sighs. 'After talking with you, I've gone off that idea a bit. He's not Allan….'

Izzy rolls onto her side and smiles a teasing smile. 'But he is handsome… and here.'

'So, are you actually thinking of staying?' Basia asks, changing the subject, and Izzy lets her, happy to finally tell someone about her change of heart.

'I'm still in two minds. Yesterday I thought I might return to the Fixers. Well, at least to Cynthia's new group, and I was kinda hoping Sigma would too. After today, though, I can see how a life with Stanley and Jo wouldn't be too bad. Still, what would I do with my life if I stay here? I would miss the adventure and trying to keep the world in line. And there's the problem of Josephine's attachment to Dorset. I'm certainly not going to spend the rest of my life stagnating down there.'

Basia squeezes her fingers. 'It's a good thing neither of us have to make up our minds right now, isn't it? Perhaps we should just concentrate on saving Maisie for the moment, and maybe things will fall into place for us when we're not trying so hard.'

Izzy's lips form a wry smile. 'You're such a sensible girl.'

'Not so sensible.' Basia sighs dramatically. 'I've just realised I don't have a sewing kit, so taking up those trousers could be a bit difficult.'

Laughing, Izzy forces herself off the bed. 'Come back through to my room. We can work on them together.'

10

THE GAME'S AFOOT

THE MORNING IS still shrouded in darkness when Nathanial arrives at the house Hannah's parents have rented in Winchester. As he waits for her to appear, he paces the sidewalk, wondering what he'll do if she doesn't turn up soon. After all, he can hardly knock on the front door and request to see her at this early hour.

He's about to give up when the squeak of the side gate shatters the silence of the deserted street. Hannah appears, dressed plainly and carrying a reticule, something she doesn't usually do. Noticing his interest in her purse, she says, 'It has one of the smaller irons from the laundry inside. You never know when you might need a bit of an advantage, especially if I encounter that brute from yesterday again.'

Nathanial wants to smile at the thought of her swinging that iron at someone, but the tone of her voice tells him his behaviour the evening before has not been forgotten or forgiven.

To say that the air between Hannah and Nathanial is strained during their walk to the station would be an understatement. The increasing tension almost has Nathanial apologising, but he stops himself before the words leave his mouth. He hadn't been at fault. Well, not totally.

Hannah had been quiet through dinner. Then, as they left the dining room, she had said, 'I do not appreciate you paying so much attention to Miss Fielding and Miss Trelawney. It is not done for an engaged man to spend so much time with single women.'

Although she mentioned both Izzy and Basia, he was sure it was Izzy she was most concerned about. Perhaps she sensed they were more than casual acquaintances.

Hannah had always been the jealous type. Even the old Nathanial knew that. Then again, old Nathanial wouldn't have dared talk to other women when he was with her, and so this fight would have been avoided.

When he patiently explained that they only talked about the missing suffragist and that she was overreacting, Hannah had exploded. After a full dressing down, she finished with 'Your behaviour is not that of a man devoted to his fiancée but of a cad about town.'

Years of pent-up resentment broke through his thin hold on the old Nathanial facade, and he'd met her accusations head-on.

'You are turning nothing into something and blaming me for it,' he'd told her, trying to keep his voice low as they followed her parents to the drawing room. 'Your jealous nature is the problem here, not my actions.'

'Is it too much to ask for you to pay attention to me rather than courting every other young female in the room?' she'd asked haughtily.

It was her tone that did it. It told him she believed she was right and that he should apologise and do better.

'I believe you would prefer it if I were a puppy dog following at your beck and call,' he spluttered. Leaving her side, he took his own hat and coat from the stand in the hallway and let himself out, without even taking leave of her parents.

He had immediately regretted his actions but wouldn't lose face by returning. Instead he spent the next couple of hours wandering the streets of Winchester, partially to allow his temper to cool but largely because his memory of where he stayed on this particular visit was a little hazy.

Around midnight he'd stumbled upon the boarding house, and then he spent a restless couple of hours trying to sleep before giving up and reading for a while.

This morning he finds himself in a bit of a quandary. His anger hasn't abated, but he has to admit it had been fuelled by his knowledge of the future rather than the incident yesterday. He knows what Hannah would do, and he's aware he is a changed person because of her actions. Still, even without that

foreknowledge, the way his fiancée treated him does not sit right with him.

Yet he's older and wiser now, and he sees how the role he was playing has allowed her to dictate the terms of their relationship. It wouldn't hurt him to smooth things over without taking the blame on himself if at all possible.

As he opens his mouth to speak, Hannah gets in first.

'Nathanial, you have changed these last two days, and you cannot be surprised that I think it is because of another woman. I mean, the only thing that has changed has been Isolde and Barbara arriving. Now, Barbara is clearly taken with the detective, so I can only assume that you have become, um, distracted by Isolde—'

'I am not—'

'Therefore, you cannot blame me for believing your relationship is more than that of casual acquaintances. The looks you share are too intimate.'

'As I was about to—'

She holds up a hand to stop him from speaking. 'No, please do not deny it. Instead, I have a question for you. Well, perhaps two. Do you still love me? And do you still want to marry me? And before you answer, let me say that I am aware that people in our position do not always marry for love. So I am quite prepared for you to say you no longer care for me but still wish for our marriage to go ahead. It would be awkward for both of us to continue on in society if we were to break our engagement now.'

Nathanial is stunned into silence. This is not the conversation he expected to be having with Hannah this morning. The cool tone of her voice is shocking, like being doused in ice water, and the way she's been speaking of their upcoming marriage as if it were a social transaction hurts. It has him wondering if Hannah ever really loved him or if it's always been a marriage of convenience for her. Had the old Nathanial been so besotted that he hadn't seen the signs?

Old Nathanial was pliable, well connected, and would inherit the family estate when his father died. He would have made the perfect partner given her social aspirations, so he shouldn't be surprised. Then again, should any of this matter? They are where they are, and Hannah deserves an answer.

He needs to be careful, though, because he hasn't decided whether to release this body back to old Nathanial or to integrate the sleeping part of him and carry on using the body himself.

'Nathanial? Did you hear me?'

'Yes, sorry, I was thinking. There *is* a lot we need to talk about, Hannah,

and as we are nearly at the station, I suggest we leave it until after we have rescued Miss Ottaway.'

His neck prickles as he feels her eyes bore into him, almost as if she's trying to search is soul. Had she expected him to apologise and reaffirm his commitment to her? Probably. He meets her gaze, making sure to keep his face neutral.

When she realises he isn't going to back down, she purses her lips and says, 'Of course, you are right. This has been an odd few days, and perhaps these questions are best left until things have settled down. But do not think you have dodged a bullet today. We *will* talk about this.'

I'm sure we will, Nathanial thinks as they approach the station. Hushed voices cut through the predawn air as they draw closer to the group assembled by the main door.

'It is hardly the done thing, Barbara. I mean, a woman wearing trousers. Well, not in Winchester, at least,' the detective is saying, at which point Nathanial realises it isn't a man talking to Alan but indeed a woman in trousers.

'I say, sir, my Doris always wears trousers when we are at my parents' farm. She says it is much easier to do some things without skirts getting in the way,' one of the young constables with them says.

'I agree, sir. If she is coming in with us, her skirts might hinder her, or us, in a confined space,' the other adds.

'If there is a possibility she will get in the way, perhaps she should not be coming with us,' Alan says under his breath, but the others appear not to have heard. 'I guess I have been outvoted,' he says a little louder and somewhat sourly.

Izzy's voice comes from behind Basia. 'If that is settled, then, now that we are all here, we should move.'

'Yes, it will soon be dawn, and we will lose the chance to hide without being seen,' Stanley adds, stepping out under the station light.

'Of course.' The detective holds out his arm to escort Basia. She ignores him and strides off, followed by the two constables.

'Leave it a couple of minutes, then head out,' Alan instructs Nathanial before rushing to catch up with the rest of his team.

'You know,' Izzy says when he's out of earshot, 'for all his planning, he has not even suggested how we might let them know when we are in place, or for them to let us know where they have hidden.' She smirks.

'And I guess you have that covered?' Hannah says tartly.

'Of course. Basia and I have sorted out some signals.' She smiles. *Good*

thing we can all mindspeak, she adds for Nathanial's benefit.

He bites back his own smile, not wanting to aggravate Hannah any more than he has already.

When the first group have disappeared around the corner, Izzy asks, 'Shall we go now, Nathanial?'

'Give it a few more minutes,' he tells her. 'We want to allow them enough time to get in place before we arrive.'

Izzy taps her foot impatiently. Hannah glares at her and moves closer to Nathanial. Stanley catches his eye, grinning wickedly as he sums up the situation.

Josephine punches Stanley's arm. 'Keep your mind on the job,' she tells him.

That only makes Stanley's grin even wider.

'Time to go,' Izzy says, 'before Stanley causes a riot.' And with that she strides off into the darkness.

'It is fine, old chum. Off you go. The ladies and I will follow as the sun rises.'

'Good luck,' Nathanial says to them all as he heads off, not catching Izzy until the corner, a few houses down from Parsons's place. As he does, he spots a familiar figure. The nurse they spoke to yesterday is pushing her young charge along the footpath. For once the baby is silent.

Her eyes widen in recognition as they approach, then track from the trouser-clad Izzy and back to him. Nathanial puts a finger to his lips, hoping she understands to keep quiet.

As they walk past, she whispers, 'You're part of the group from yesterday. Have you found your lost miss?'

Nathanial nods.

'I knew there was something going on at old Parsons's place. Lulu will be quiet this morning, sir. It's me that wanted the air after feeding her. So we won't be waking no one who should be asleep at this hour.' She winks conspiratorially and walks on.

Nathanial and Izzy stop at the house before Mr Parsons's. Before they break cover, Izzy speaks to Basia. *Is it clear for us to come through?*

There's a light on in the back, so someone is up. We didn't notice any activity at the front, but check the top windows just in case. Oh, and there's a huge rhododendron to your left as you come round. That should cover the two of you.

Thanks, Izzy sends.

Nathanial leans around and checks the second- and third-storey windows. All the curtains are drawn, and there are no lights on.

All clear.

The gravel of the driveway crunches under their shoes no matter how careful they try to be. Although it sounds loud to them, it doesn't appear to disturb anyone inside as the curtains don't twitch once. They make it to the gigantic bush and crouch behind it, finding a spot with views of both the door and the street.

We're in place, Izzy sends to Basia.

The ground is damp beneath Nathanial's knees, and after a couple of minutes, the cold begins creeping through his bones. He hopes they don't have to wait for too long because if they do, he might be too stiff to move. As the sun peeks up from the horizon, he shifts a little, trying to keep the blood circulating in his legs.

'Stop fidgeting,' Izzy hisses. 'You'll give away our hiding place.'

He sends her a meaningful look, telling her to quit nagging, but she ignores him. Shivering from the cold and damp, he listens for footsteps on the pavement. Nothing. Then a crunching of gravel heralds the arrival of the rest of their party. Finally. They're almost in sight at the bottom of the steps when he feels a tug on his consciousness.

Sigma, whatever you're going to do, you need to do it soon. Someone is leaking information to Jason, and he knows you know where he is.

Nathanial's heart starts pumping, and he rises to his feet to stop the others as a loud bang fills the early morning air followed by another as Hannah knocks on the door a second time. It's too late to call things off.

Rubbing his now sweaty palms down his trousers, Nathanial steps back behind the shrub, accepting that all great plans are only good until you engage the enemy. Then you have no option but to wing it. All they can do now is react to what's happening and hope Jason hasn't had too much time to prepare for them.

What is it? Izzy asks, but Nathanial is too intent on watching the door to the house to respond.

Jason answers, and he opens the door wide, a grin plastered on his face. Nathanial's stomach sinks. Jason has recognised his team and looks like a man who knows he has the upper hand.

Nathanial is about to step out and call everything off when Jason's face turns pale. He swings round and rushes inside, just as they'd planned.

THE GUARDIANS OF TIME: SUFFRAGETTE

THROUGH THE MISTY morning air, Basia makes out Hannah's and Josephine's voices as they speak with whomever opened the door. She turns to Alan, and he nods, letting her know they're ready whenever she gives the word.

Josephine's voice carries through to her. 'Sorry to disturb you so early, but we are going house to house, trying to find out if anyone has seen our friend.'

There's silence for a moment, and Basia suspects whoever answered the door is now talking. Alan had said to wait either until the others are about to be let inside or are being turned away before giving the signal to move.

'Of course the police are looking for her, but we are really worried and decided to help.' Hannah's voice holds just the right amount of anguish.

She should have been an actress, Basia muses.

The response is somewhat mumbled, but Stanley's next words are not. 'I say, old chap, that is a bit uncalled for. These two are only trying to find their friend, and language like that does not make their job any easier.'

'Look, if you are not able to help…'

As Josephine speaks, Basia turns to tell Alan their forward team has almost reached the end of their usefulness, only to find the space beside her empty.

Glancing around the yard, she finds Alan beside the back entrance, whispering fiercely to his constables. Of all the nerve! When he'd asked her to monitor what was going on at the front and let them know when to go, she believed it would help. Now she realises it was a distraction to keep her occupied so he and his men could move without her.

Leaving her hiding place and sticking to the shadows, she reaches the three men as the two constables are shouldering the door, breaking it inwards. Alan follows the constables in, unaware that Basia is coming in behind him.

She walks through the entrance, deftly avoiding the door swinging on its hinges, and steps into a scullery or perhaps a laundry—it's difficult to tell in the early morning light. Striding forward, she makes it into the kitchen in time to see a large, thuggish man drop his teacup, stand, lift the heavy wooden table he was seated at, and launch it at the two constables.

Fortunately, they're nimble on their feet and split off in opposite directions. The table misses them. As she and Alan step back, the piece of furniture skids to a halt, blocking the doorway, wedging itself in place, and preventing them from assisting the two constables.

The kitchen's occupant is more than a match for the two younger men, and Alan struggles to move the table out of his way to go help them. Basia joins him, and they manage to swing the piece of furniture around far enough for the detective to squeeze through, leaving Basia to fend for herself.

A wave of anger threatens, and she resists the temptation to give the detective a piece of her mind. No, she won't give him the satisfaction. Taking a deep breath, she surveys the scene, wondering how she might be of use.

The thug stands in the doorway leading into the main house and is using a poker from the fire to fend off the three policemen. He doesn't seem interested in doing anything other than keeping them in the kitchen. It's a stalemate.

Searching the room, she looks for anything that might throw the man off balance and tip the scales in their favour. On the bench she spies exactly what she needs. Slipping through the gap between the table and the door, she grabs the sugar bowl and moves in behind one of the young constables.

'Hey, you,' she shouts, and all four men turn her way. As they do, she throws the contents of the sugar bowl at the thug's face before allowing the bowl to drop to the ground.

'What the—' The man stumbles forward, momentarily blinded, and the three policemen take the opportunity to close in on him.

When a gap opens behind the kidnapper, she slips past the others and runs through the doorway. If the police don't want her, she'll help with getting Maisie out of the house.

She finds herself in a dark passageway she hopes will lead to the main entrance. Tentatively moving forward, she yelps as a hand reaches out of the darkness and swings her round. Before she has a chance to react, her attacker twists her arm behind her back and pulls her in close. She shivers as cold steel presses into the soft part of her throat under her chin.

'I killed your boyfriend, so you know I'll do the same to you if you don't do exactly as I say,' says a male voice close to her ear.

Her insides turn to jelly as she recognises the voice of the man who shot her Allan in cold blood.

'What do you want?' she asks, hating the fact that she sounds as fearful as she does.

'Hold still,' Jason instructs as he forces her back towards the kitchen.

As they move through the doorway and stop, Basia is frozen in place. Her head screams for her to do something, telling her, *You'll never get back home if you don't,* but fear has robbed her of even the most basic movement.

Jason shifts the gun to her temple and takes another step into the kitchen. 'Step away, or Basia dies.'

Basia takes in the scene before them. One of the constables is standing

by the sink, a bloody towel held to his forehead. The other backs away from the man lying on the floor, hands held up in surrender. Alan looks up from his position on the thug's back. Jason's accomplice appears to be out cold with his hands now behind him in cuffs.

'Come now,' Alan says as he pushes himself to his feet. 'Your friend is no help, and at best you will be up for kidnapping, which is a prison sentence. If you hurt Barbara, then you might be looking at the gallows.'

'Barbara?' Jason shifts around, dragging Basia with him. 'He doesn't have any idea who you are, does he, Basia?'

Alan's brows draw together. 'Basia? Who is Basia? Barbara, what is going on here?'

Jason's laugh rings hollow. 'What a hoot. They have no idea, do they? You've wrangled some unsuspecting local yokels into this, and they really have no idea.'

'Jason, it's over. Put the gun down, and let Sigma take you back home,' Basia says, trying to do her best to keep her voice calm.

'Sigma's here? I didn't see any animals. No, you're trying to trick me.' Jason pushes the revolver harder against her temple. 'Don't do that, or I might just kill you for fun, and won't that screw up the timeline?'

Basia freezes, silently begging Alan to calm Jason down before he loses it completely. Instead the detective stands in the middle of the kitchen, his eyes going from her to Jason and back again, as if trying to understand what's going on.

'You know this man?' he asks, the hurt in his eyes cutting through her. 'All this time you knew him, and you said nothing to me. Instead you came up with some half-cocked story about an escaped convict. Are you all in on it?'

'She's taken you for a fool, mate,' Jason crows, shuffling back towards the hallway they'd entered through.

'Whoever he is to us, don't forget he's kidnapped Maisie. The rest I can explain, will explain, after we—'

A sharp pain courses through Basia's skull. She sways and crumples to the ground. The last thing she sees before blackness overwhelms her is Alan stepping over top of her in pursuit of Jason.

AS SOON AS Jason disappears, Josephine pushes the door open and peers inside. Izzy and Nathanial are across the lawn and climbing the five steps to the entrance in a flash, catching up with the others at the bottom of the stairs.

From the back of the house, the sounds of furniture moving and grunting suggest a fight is in progress. Nathanial and Izzy turn almost as one to check out the stairs. There's no sight or sound of Jason that way, so he'd likely headed for the kitchen or is already upstairs with Maisie.

'Should we go and help them?' Stanley asks, an excited gleam in his eye.

'No.' Nathanial is decisive. 'Our task is to secure the release of Miss Ottaway. We should wait at the bottom of the stairs and stop anyone following the women up. They can call out if they need us.'

Stanley's shoulders slump.

Nathanial claps a hand on his shoulder. 'Do not be so glum, Stanley. The fight may end up out here yet.'

'Come on, ladies.' Izzy hooks her arms through Josephine's and Hannah's. 'Let us not waste any time getting Maisie out of here.'

At the top of the stairs, Izzy takes a moment to orient herself. She need not have bothered, as Hannah has it all figured out.

'The window we saw the woman at is along this way.' She turns to her left, pulling the others behind her.

The corridor is dark and lined with closed doors. Hannah walks past them all, stopping in front of the one at the end. A key is sticking out of the lock, and Hannah reaches for it.

As the lock clicks, Josephine turns to Izzy. 'Perhaps you should stay out here and keep watch. You might upset her, dressed like that.' She gestures down Izzy's body, indicating the male clothing.

Izzy grimaces. She'd only thought of ease of movement when she dressed, not of how Maisie would react to the appearance of another strange man. She allows Josephine to slip past her and peers into the dark room, her eyes following Hannah and Jo.

A single bed is tucked into the far corner, its occupant curled into a ball under the blankets. They've been so quiet, the person in bed doesn't even appear to know they're there. Hannah clears her throat, and the figure reacts immediately, sitting bolt upright, then cowering against the wall, blankets pulled up under her chin.

The sound of a door banging downstairs reminds Izzy she's supposed to be lookout, and she reluctantly turns her back on the room but keeps an ear out, listening to the conversation.

'Maisie, it is all right. We are here to take you home.' Hannah has pitched her tone low so as not to distress the young woman.

THE GUARDIANS OF TIME: SUFFRAGETTE

She's really quite good at this, Izzy thinks as she peers along the gloomy hallway. Did something move down the far end of the corridor? As her eyes adjust to the dim light, she scans back and forth, trying to pick out a potential threat. If there is anything down there, she can't find it. It must be the dawn light playing tricks on her.

Distracted by the moving shadows and lulled by the sound of the soothing words coming from the room, she jumps when Josephine's voice comes from just behind her.

'Isolde, we need your help. Maisie is terrified and unable to move. She knows you. Maybe you can gain her confidence.'

With one last glance down the hallway to reassure herself that she was probably imagining things, Izzy enters the bedroom, leaving Jo to stand guard. Someone opened one of the curtains, flooding the room with early morning light, making the figure crouched in the far corner of the bed easier to see.

Izzy gasps, then stifles the sound, realising it won't help Maisie to know how frightful she looks. She's dressed only in her undergarments, and her hair has worked its way free from the neat bun she normally keeps it in, forming a knotted halo round her face. Though it's the bruises on her arms and the swelling on one side of her face beginning to colour purple that upsets Izzy the most.

With her arms wrapped protectively around her body, Maisie has forced herself as far back into the corner of the bed as possible. The eyes that peek out through her hair are frantic, and Izzy fears their dawn raid has scared her beyond reasoning.

Spying Maisie's outer clothes on the trunk at the end of the bed, Izzy fumbles for her coat before approaching.

'Maisie, you remember me. I am Isolde, Augusta's niece. We met on the train. Mrs Trimms is worried about you and sent us to find you. Come now, put this coat on you, and we will take you to her.'

As she speaks, Izzy reaches out her hand and waits patiently for Maisie to respond. Finally, trembling fingers reach for hers, then grasp her hand with surprising firmness. Izzy pulls the other girl into an embrace, nose wrinkling at the smell, and then she drapes the coat over Maisie's shoulders.

Hannah comes to help button the garment while Izzy holds Maisie upright. They're almost done when a voice from behind echoes through the nearly empty room. 'And what do you think you are doing?'

Maisie trembles in her arms and moans softly. Izzy half turns to find an elderly man standing in the doorway. He's obviously been woken from his sleep, as his thin white hair stands out in tufts, and his spindly white stick legs poke out from under a nightshirt. She would have laughed at his challenge except for the fact that he has a shotgun pointed directly at them.

'You young women, you think you can do anything you please. Well, not in my house.'

The gun wavers a little, as if it's too heavy for the man to hold. This makes Izzy even more worried. What if the shaking causes him to tug on the trigger? He might shoot them all without meaning to.

Then she realises that the man is so focused on the three of them, he hasn't seen Josephine, who stands less than a step behind him, chamberpot raised above her head.

'I am so tired of men telling us what to do,' Josephine tells his back as she brings the porcelain pot down towards his head.

Turning, Mr Parsons sees the danger too late to move and can only watch in dismay as the pot descends.

As the old man crumples to the floor, Josephine's anger disappears. 'Oh, I did not expect that. Have I killed him?'

'Feel for a pulse,' Izzy instructs.

Josephine bends a knee and places a couple of fingers on the man's neck before looking up and grinning. 'Still strong.'

'Good. Now take that gun of his, and Hannah and I will get Maisie out of here.'

As she and Hannah walk Maisie towards the door, Josephine picks up the weapon. A country girl at heart, she's no stranger to guns. She pushes the lever to the side and breaks the gun open. With the weapon made safe, she leads the others out of the room.

As they reach the stairway, a crash reverberates through the house. They wait at the top of the stairs as Nathanial and Stanley move to block someone from coming up.

'It is over, Jason. Put down the weapon, and we will take you back home,' Nathanial says in an even voice.

Izzy peers down at the figure in front of the Time Guardian. He's shaking, and his eyes are erratically scanning the room. Finally, they return to the two men keeping him from the stairs.

'Who are you? I don't know you. Out of my way. I have to finish what I started.'

Jason sounds unhinged, and the thought turns Izzy's blood cold. Always excitable, in this state Jason might do anything.

'Does Nathanial know that man?' Hannah asks.

'Shh,' Izzy tells her without taking her eyes off the scene below. 'I want to hear what he is saying.'

'Ah, Izzy, I see you. Bring the girl down, and no one else needs to get hurt.'

No one else? Where are the detective and Basia? 'You know I will never do that, Jason.' Izzy moves so she's in front of the quivering Maisie.

'Please… do not let him have me,' she whispers between sobs.

'You know him, Isolde?' Josephine asks, stepping one stair down and in front of the group as she closes the shotgun, making it ready to fire. 'I hope you are not friends, as I would hate to shoot someone you hold an attachment for.'

Izzy cannot help but chuckle in spite of the tension in the room. 'Feel free to fire away.'

'I only want the girl,' Jason says, moving back and raising his pistol.

'And we have already said no,' Josephine responds, raising her own weapon.

Nathanial takes a step towards Jason, hands out in front. 'Put the gun away, Jason, and perhaps we can talk about this.'

'Don't take another step.' The gun moves from the women at the top of the stairs to Nathanial. 'I *will* shoot!'

'Halt and place your weapon down. You are under arrest for kidnapping and assault. Do not add murder to your charges.'

The tension in the room snaps like a rubber band. Izzy flings herself at Maisie and Hannah, forcing them to the floor as gunfire fills the room.

11

FALLOUT

JASON IS BECOMING increasingly more erratic. Sweat is beading on his brow, and the gun shakes in his hand. Nathanial is doing all he can to keep the Time Fixer's attention on him, but Jason fixates more and more on the women at the top of the stairs.

If only Nathanial were able to talk to the man as Sigma, he might be able to calm him down. Jason obviously doesn't recognise him as a Time Guardian in human form, and for the first time ever, he regrets his penchant for undertaking his missions as an animal.

A movement from the back of the house catches his eye and Jason's as well. At least it takes his attention from the women. With Jason looking elsewhere, Nathanial takes a step forward, but the man isn't as distracted as he thought.

'Don't take another step,' the rogue Time Fixer says.

Nathanial stops, not wanting to push his luck. He's now close enough that he might be able to disarm Jason if there's another distraction.

At that moment Alan chooses to stride forward and command, 'Halt and place your weapon down. You are under arrest for kidnapping and assault. Do not add murder to your charges.'

The fragile balance in the room is broken, and it's as if time slows for Nathanial.

Jason's finger begins to squeeze the trigger as he launches himself at the Time Fixer. The thunder of guns discharging blasts through the room, and Jason falls to the ground. Nathanial hits the floor beside him. Thrown onto his side, he looks up to find a tumble of women falling down the stairs.

Utter confusion follows. Stanley is bellowing for Josephine, who's leaning against the banister, a patch of red blooming on her dress. Alan is helping the other women untangle themselves as Izzy yells at him.

'What did you think you were doing?'

'Taking control of the situation as I was trained to do,' Alan responds.

'You threatened him, you idiot. You pushed him over the edge, and whatever happens now is on you.' Izzy's voice is stern and steely underlined with a touch of fear.

Nathanial pushes himself up on an elbow. He readies himself to tell Izzy it isn't Alan's fault, that Jason was so out of his mind, anything could have set him off, but something moves beside him. He turns to find Jason reaching for his gun. He drags himself across the floor towards the weapon, the wound in his leg leaving a bloody path behind him.

Nathanial pushes himself to his feet and rushes for the gun. Kicking it away, he does something he's been wanting to do since he met the Time Fixer. He pulls back his arm, leans down, and punches Jason square on the chin. It's satisfying to watch his head jerk back, and even more satisfying when it cracks on the tiled floor, and Jason's eyes lose focus.

Hannah's shocked voice comes from behind him. 'Nathanial, what are you doing?'

Unable to deal with her for the moment, he bends at the knees and hauls Jason's limp form over his shoulder in a fireman's lift.

Alan rushes forward. 'I will take him now.'

'You have done quite enough!' Izzy says as she joins them.

'I already told you, it is how we are taught to deal with such situations,' Alan protests again.

Izzy puffs out an impatient breath. 'Common sense should have told you Nathanial had it under control. How about you give him a pair of cuffs, and then you head upstairs and deal with the old man we left up there. He had a bit of an accident with a chamberpot, but he should be coming around soon.'

'Cut him some slack, Izzy. We all rely on our training when under pressure, and it is not Alan's fault his training has been inadequate,' Nathanial says as he shifts Jason's body to a more comfortable position.

He holds his hand out to Alan, and for a moment, he thinks the detective is going to protest. Perhaps it's because he sees sense, or maybe it's because Nathanial defended him, that he reaches under his coat and hands a pair of handcuffs to Nathanial.

'Thank you,' Nathanial says as the detective moves off to help Stanley.

'Go on, do what you must,' Izzy says, opening the door for him. 'I will keep the others busy in here.'

Nathanial steps outside, and before the door closes behind him, he hears Izzy's voice rise in panic as she shouts, 'Barbara? Has anyone seen Barbara?'

'Oh my god, Barbara,' Alan's voice responds just as the door slams, cutting off all noise from inside.

He drops Jason onto the steps and kneels beside him. After placing a cuff on the closest hand, he rolls Jason so he can cuff both hands behind his back. Then he pushes him none too gently back against the house and takes a couple of deep breaths before opening his mind.

Beta?

We're here, Sigma.

It's done. Maisie Ottaway is safe, and I have Jason ready for pick-up. We're outside, and no one else is around, so I can say he jumped me and took off.

Well done, Beta says.

Umm, about that pick-up, Cynthia adds. *No one here can decide exactly what to do with Jason, so I suggest you let the local authorities take him until they do.*

'Are you all right, sir?'

Nathanial looks down the steps to find one of Alan's constables staring up at him, concern written on his face. Considering the nasty gash on the constable's forehead, and the fact that Nathanial himself only has a couple of bruises, the question makes him smile.

'Thank you, yes. I brought our friend out here while everyone sorts themselves out inside.'

'Detective Barker sent me to fetch a doc and transportation for the prisoners and the wounded, but I can help you take him round to the kitchen with the others if you like.'

Sigma?

Wait a moment.

'No, thank you, I can manage. You go ahead and do what the detective asked.'

'As you wish.'

Nathanial waits until the young man disappears through the gate and has

had time to walk well down the street before resuming his conversation.

Cynthia, are you sure you want to leave him here? Prisons can be quite brutal in this time.

Quite certain. In fact, it's a shame they stopped sending convicts to the penal colonies.

Nathanial chuckles.

'Wasso funny?' Jason mumbles from beside him.

Gotta go. Will give a full report later.

Nathanial closes his mind and turns to his prisoner. 'Come on. If you can speak, you can walk.' He hauls Jason to his feet.

'Where to?'

'Inside with your accomplices to await transportation to the cells.'

'Hold on, where's the extraction team?' Jason asks, now more alert.

'No extraction team for you, mate. It seems you have annoyed quite a few of the Time Fixers, and they have decided you will face local justice.'

Jason went white, his eyes wild with fear. 'No, they can't do that. Won't it screw up the timeline, or… history? The Time Guardians… they won't let that happen.'

Strangely, Nathanial finds no joy in Jason's fate. Used to being pulled out by the Time Fixers, the self-centred man had wreaked havoc in a number of time periods. Because he'd always been extracted by his organisation, he never faced the consequences of his actions. That he'd face justice now did little to make up for what he'd done, here or in the past.

Hauling the reluctant time traveller back into the house, Nathanial finds the hallway empty. Voices drift in from one of the rooms to the side, but Nathanial ignores them and heads to the kitchen.

Alan is settling an elderly man into a chair, his hands tied behind him with a silk scarf. The man is grumbling about unnatural women and the state of the world. He glares at Jason as he comes in.

'You said we would have our revenge on them, put them back in their place. And look what that got us.'

Jason turns to Nathanial. 'Take me back outside, please. If I have to spend another minute with that nasty curmudgeon, I won't be held responsible for my actions.'

Nathanial pushes him into a chair. 'He is all yours,' he says to the detective and walks away before he does something he won't be proud of.

ON THEIR ARRIVAL at Augusta's what seemed liked hours ago, Izzy's aunt had gone into organisation mode. She'd allocated the two guest suites on the first floor for use as an infirmary for Maisie, Basia, and Josephine.

Although still a little woozy, and with blood seeping through the makeshift bandage on her head, Basia had instructed a maid to bring hot water and towels. By the time the doctor had arrived with his nurse, she had Jo's bleeding under control.

Hannah and Nathanial, after seeing they weren't required and ensuring the patients were comfortable, had left to clean themselves up, promising to return later to give their statements to the police.

Detective Barker had taken the prisoners to the station and had agreed that everyone could give their accounts later from the comfort of home. Izzy still hadn't forgiven him for what happened to Jo. However, he'd been so distraught and so aware of how his lack of experience had almost caused a fatality that she'd at least stopped haranguing him.

Stanley had been clearly quite shaken and, after carrying Jo up to the guest room, would not move from her side. After ensuring Jensen would look after things in her absence, Augusta left to tell Mrs Trimms the good news and bring her back to see Maisie.

So, Izzy now finds herself alone in the dining room, picking listlessly at some scrambled eggs. Unable to force the food down, she pours herself some coffee and returns to the table.

Staring out the window, she attempts to calm her mind. She keeps replaying the moment the bullet hit Jo. Any wound in the stomach area is not good news, not in this time and not in the future. Finally, she admits it's no use staying down here. She heads upstairs to the makeshift infirmary and knocks on the door.

A maid answers, poking her head through a small opening. 'Doctor says no one is to be let in, miss. Sorry.' She closes the door.

Izzy raises her fists to pound out her frustration but stops short, realising that won't help the patients. No doubt they will let her in soon, and she'll be here waiting.

Pacing along the carpeted hallway, she tries counting her steps. Then she runs through song lyrics. Nothing is working. Nothing calms her growing fear that Josephine isn't going to make it.

She had lost a lot of blood after the rescue, and when Stanley carried her up the stairs to the guest suite, she'd passed out. Although medical science has

been making great strides, people here still die from things that could be easily cured in later years. Izzy is about to contact Cynthia to have Josephine moved to Time Fixer headquarters for treatment when the infirmary door opens.

She spins on her heel, hope blooming, only to be quashed when Basia, not Josephine, appears. Of course it wouldn't be Jo—she'd passed out less than an hour ago.

Still, Basia doesn't look so good either. Although her head wound has been more professionally bandaged, she's pale and a little shaky on her feet. When she turns towards her, Izzy can see the edge of a black stitch peeking out from the white cloth that mostly covers the purplish bruise above her right eye. Moving swiftly to her side, Izzy allows the girl to lean on her.

'Where are you going?' Izzy asks, alarmed she's wandering around so unsteady on her feet.

'To my room. The doctor says I have a concussion and I need to rest, and there aren't enough beds for me in there.'

'Surely you shouldn't be alone. I'll help you upstairs and stay with you.'

'Oh, Izzy, don't look at me like that.'

'Like what?'

'Like I'm about to die. The doctor couldn't find any sign of internal bleeding, and my skull appears to be intact. He gave me aspirin for the pain and told me to rest for the day. His nurse will pop up and check on me every hour or so, but I should be right as rain tomorrow.'

'Are you sure? Head injuries can be quite tricky, especially when there's no way to x-ray or monitor what's happening inside.'

Basia chuckles. 'Izzy, you forget, I've treated many such injuries myself, and I'm not showing any signs of brain trauma.'

Izzy sighs. 'The moment you do, I'm taking you to Time Fixer headquarters where you can get some more modern treatment.'

Basia says nothing and allows Izzy to lead her to her room. She even lets Izzy help her into a nightgown and pour some water into a glass on the bedside table in case she gets thirsty.

'Do you need anything else?'

'I'm hungry. I wouldn't mind some tea and toast.'

Izzy smiles. 'That's a good sign. I'll go find Jensen and have something brought up.'

When Izzy returns a few minutes later, Basia has a bit more colour in her cheeks. Izzy helps place some pillows behind her head and finds a book for

her to read should she become bored.

'Is that comfortable? Breakfast shouldn't be far away.' Izzy is torn between taking a seat on the bed and flying back downstairs to wait on news of Josephine.

As if sensing her mood, Basia says, 'Sit for a minute, Izzy. They won't be finished with Jo and Maisie for some time yet.'

'But Stanley is with her. Am I destined to spend any crucial time in Jo's life relegated to the sidelines?'

Basia chuckles. 'Don't you think we've had enough drama without you adding to it?'

Izzy grimaces.

'Would it help if I tell you that even Stanley isn't allowed in with her? He's been in the room next door, waiting on the outside, just as you are.'

Izzy sinks onto the bed. 'I know it's petty, resenting his being at her side, but.... Now, tell me how Maisie is.'

'Maisie is fine. Actually the doctor spent most of his time with Jo when he arrived. It was his nurse who questioned the both of us, then had Maisie strip down and take a bath before she saw to her. The maid your aunt assigned helped her bathe in the downstairs bathroom while the nurse stitched me up.'

Izzy flinches. 'That must have been painful.'

'Yes, it still is. What I wouldn't have given for some local anaesthetic. While I recovered, I listened to the nurse and Maisie. She's battered and bruised and hasn't eaten for a couple of days, but other than that, she's physically unharmed.'

'She was lucky.'

'Yes, she was. Last I heard, the nurse was going to fix her a sleeping draught before putting her to bed. Just after, the doctor popped in, checked my head again, then ordered me to bed.'

'And I should be letting you rest.'

Izzy makes to stand, but Basia puts a hand out to stop her. 'Don't go. You're not tiring me, honest.'

'All right, but tell me if you get tired. Oh, I almost forgot. Did you find out anything about the missing papers?' Izzy asks. 'Did we find Maisie's satchel?'

'I don't think we did, but it didn't matter. The speech she took to the meeting was an old draft. The final copy was in her room at Mrs Trimms all along. She'd hidden it under her mattress to keep it from prying eyes.'

'Ah, cunning. How will they get it to Miss Fielden? She needs it for

tomorrow. Will Maisie be okay to take it to her?'

'The nurse wanted Maisie on bedrest for a couple of days, which upset Maisie, as she was determined to take the speech to Haslemere. She calmed down when the maid assured her she would tell Mrs Trimms where the papers are if Maisie is asleep when she arrives, and that your aunt and Mrs Trimms will make sure the speech gets to Miss Fielden in time.'

She relaxes a little with the news that Maisie and Basia are fine, but Izzy still can't settle. Still running on adrenaline, she needs to move or take some sort of action. *What on earth is happening with Josephine?* She should be with her.

As if sensing the reason for Izzy's restlessness, Basia says, 'She'll be fine. The bleeding had stopped by the time the doctor arrived, and we both agreed the bullet didn't break any bones or go through any major organs. As soon as the doctor removes it, she should be fine.'

Izzy is so wound tight with worry, she can't let go of her fears that easily. 'She lost so much blood, though.'

'I'm not saying her injury isn't traumatic or that she won't need to be careful for a while, but there's no reason why she shouldn't make a full recovery.'

'I almost lost her once, Basia. I can't lose her again.' Izzy's voice trembles as she acknowledges her greatest fear.

'And you won't.' Basia pats her hand. 'I guess you've made up your mind, then?'

'I guess I have. I had better get used to waiting outside while Stanley is with her.' A sad smile pulls at her mouth.

Stanley appears in the doorway as if thinking of him had called the man. 'Ah, there you are. I thought I heard voices.'

Finding Basia in her nightclothes, his eyes go wide, and colour instantly stains his cheek up to the roots of his hair. His hand goes to his eyes, and he turns away, not knowing what to do with himself. 'Ah, um… I am sorry, um….'

At the sight of Stanley so awkward, Izzy bites back a laugh, something she would have thought impossible just moments ago.

'It is all right, Stanley. I am decent. What do you want?' Basia clearly does not feel the need to hide her amusement at Stanley's antics.

Turning back around, Stanley grins at the both of them. 'The nurse sent me out so Miss Ottaway can rest. She said the doctor is almost finished with Josephine and that there will be a few minutes before the sleeping draught takes hold when I might talk to her. So I came to find you, Isolde, so we can both go see her together.'

12

A NEW DAY

HAROLD ISN'T COMFORTABLE having guests in his new home, and in human form too. And he certainly isn't comfortable with them calling him Harold instead of Beta, regardless of Cynthia's advice that it would make him more approachable.

Cynthia enters from the kitchenette, carrying a coffee tray, and, as if sensing his discomfort, smiles at Nate and Izzy, who were still standing by the door.

'Goodness me, take a seat, both of you. Make yourselves at home. Harold, will you pour the coffee while I get the cakes?'

He fidgets while he waits for everyone to eat and drink. Harold has no idea why seeing Izzy and Nate in person has thrown him so off kilter. Over the years, he's spoken to them both so many times, they're almost family. Perhaps it's this face-to-face thing. It's going to take some getting used to. It's so much more… personal.

When everyone has finished and the small talk dies down, Harold leans forward in his seat, resting his elbows on his legs in what he hopes looked like a casual pose.

'Hem, ah, thank you for joining us this morning. Cynthia and I want to

try a less formal way of closing off cases and thought meeting like this might be the trick. Well, we'll see how it goes.'

'Although, perhaps not so informal given your current dress.' Cynthia smiles at Izzy and Nate's turn-of-the-century clothing.

In spite of their efforts, the atmosphere in the room remains stilted, and Harold has to admit that changing the formal review process might be more difficult than he thought. Sighing inwardly, he says, 'All right, let's get started. Nate, where do things in Winchester stand now?'

'Well, Beta... um... Harold, Jason is being held in the local jail, pending formal charges being laid. They're still questioning him, but I understand Mr Parsons's evidence is quite damning. He claims Jason met him on the street at an anti-suffragette rally and convinced the man he needed to take positive action or he would be personally responsible for the breakdown of god's natural order.'

'Interesting,' Cynthia interrupts. 'We had wondered why history didn't eject him from the timeline. I should have guessed he was able to suggest a course of action to a local, and I'm sure there was no shortage of people prepared to go along with him.'

Nate nods. 'If it hadn't been Mr Parsons, he would easily have found someone else. Jason even provided the muscle. He met his co-conspirator in London before heading to Winchester. Barry needed to get out of town fast, as the police were looking for him. Jason facilitated his escape in return for help with his plan. Although, to be honest, I think Barry would have helped just for the fun of it.'

'What do you mean?' Harold asks.

'The police were looking for him with regards to some rather violent attacks on women. He's already on his way back to London to face those charges,' Nate expands.

Izzy shudders, perhaps imagining what a man like that could have done to Maisie had she been left there any longer.

'Izzy, where is Maisie now?' Harold asks.

'She's still at my aunt's house. When she's well enough, Augusta will take her back to London and see her safely settled back with her parents.'

'And the papers?' Cynthia prompts.

'They're being delivered to Miss Fielden as we speak, so she'll be delivering her speech today, as history recorded. Do either of you have any idea why this speech in particular was so important?' Izzy asks.

Cynthia shrugs. 'We're still not quite sure. We can't trace any particular historic movers and shakers to having heard it. We believe it may have influenced some local members of Parliament, but that's pure speculation. Or it might have some influence on a future event. We found references to it in some books, and it can easily be found on the internet, so maybe it has an impact on someone hundreds of years later. Or maybe Jason chose his victim simply because she knew you, Izzy.'

Izzy catches her bottom lip between her teeth. 'I would hate to think Maisie went through that nightmare because of me.'

'Whatever his reasons, you are not responsible for Jason's actions,' Cynthia reassures her.

'Definitely not, Harold says. 'Now, just one final thing before we're done. What about Alan? I understand Jason told him you all knew him from before?'

Nate smiles. 'It seems when Alan questioned Jason at the station, he was going on and on about time travel and that Basia was from the future. Of course, Alan wrote that off as hysterical rantings, and we didn't have to explain anything.'

Cynthia leans forward. 'What about the fact that Jason said he knew you?'

'Basia covered that. She said she might have met him when she was working with the poor up north, and he must have gotten her name wrong,' Izzy explains. 'Oh, and we told him that when I told Nate he could take Jason outside and do what he needed to do, I meant he should keep him out of Stanley's way by handcuffing him. It was a good thing there was no extraction or Alan would have really had something to be suspicious about.'

Nodding, Cynthia asks, 'So we don't have to fix a cover story or anything?'

Nate and Izzy shake their heads.

'Good, good, a most satisfactory outcome in the end,' Harold finishes off.

With the report complete, the room falls silent. No one wants to be the first to bring up the elephant in the room. As if avoiding the subject, Izzy asks, 'Do you know what will happen to Jason in the long term?'

Cynthia blows out a slow breath. 'Yes, well, that's a tricky situation. His parents are lobbying for his extraction from the timeline, but the Council is arguing that he's now too embedded in it to be removed without creating chaos. I suspect it's more that they want him to face the consequences of his actions for once.'

Nate rubs his chin thoughtfully. 'I hope his staying hasn't put your new venture at risk. I mean, you already have Alpha lobbying against you. Won't

Jason's parents cause you even further problems?'

Cynthia turns and catches his eye, and he gets the message. Nate is too good to let go. However, he knows they'll have to tread gently if they want him on the team.

'It's true, they have been pretty active in trying to put up barriers for us to jump over, but we can handle them.' Harold shifts his gaze to Izzy. 'From our perspective the important thing is to keep Jason locked up for as long as possible.'

Izzy smiles. 'I second that. I hope they let him rot in prison for a long, long time. It'll save a few Time Fixer careers to have him sidelined for the time being.'

Aware she speaks from bitter experience, Harold says, 'I'm sure there are many agents who agree with you.'

'Speaking of careers, what now for you two?' Cynthia segues, finally getting to the real reason the two were invited here in person.

Izzy and Nate look at each other as though each is willing the other to speak first.

Nate is the first to break eye contact, although he can't look his old mentor in the eye. With his gaze firmly fixed on the ground, he starts.

'If I'm honest, I'm still not sure. I had thought to remain in this body, but I can't be the man who Hannah once spent the next two years with. I've changed too much, learned too much, and it wouldn't be fair to her.'

Harold doesn't want to ask the next question, but in his experience, all things are better out in the open. 'So you will choose to expire rather than return to the Time Guardians?'

Nate nods slowly. 'That's the way I'm leaning. I no longer believe what they're doing will benefit humankind. Besides, I was never really cut out for the hit-and-run lifestyle. Dropping into a time period, fixing things, then walking away doesn't suit my essentially homebody nature. So, I think it might be for the best.'

When it's clear Nate has finished speaking, Izzy takes over.

'I'm leaning towards leaving the Time Fixers and staying in my own timeline. However, I want to talk with Josephine and Stanley first and discuss whether what I have in mind will work or not.'

Cynthia raises an eyebrow. 'You would do that even though you know there's a war coming?'

'Yes, and perhaps my decision is all the more important because there *is* a war coming. We all have so little time together, and humanity seems to want to hurtle towards its own ending regardless of what I do to thwart it. If they continue ignoring warnings to change their ways, then all any of us can do is grab what happiness we can while we can.'

Perhaps we've lost her regardless of what we say next, Harold sends to Cynthia.

I haven't given up on her yet.

'We have something we want the both of you to consider,' Harold says. 'You're aware we've been setting up a new joint taskforce. I'm sure you both expect to be invited to join, and we're inviting you now.'

Nate shuffles in his seat before turning to Izzy. Harold is sure that look is meaningful, but he can't decipher it.

Nate speaks for himself and Izzy. 'I'm not sure there's anything you can say to change our minds.'

'Please, hear Cynthia out before you make your final decisions. I think you will be pleasantly surprised by what we've worked so hard to get agreement on. Cynthia?'

Cynthia stands and hands out the booklets she had stashed under her seat.

'The details of what I'm about to tell you are in there. They're the operating guides for the new unit. In a nutshell, though, we won't be overseeing joint Time Fixer/Guardian missions but setting up a new team that Guardians or Fixers can apply to join.'

Seeing both Nate and Izzy about to speak, Harold holds up a hand. 'Let Cynthia finish.'

Cynthia smiles at him and continues. 'Both our organisations have always been limited by what we're able to achieve because if we interfere too much with the timeline, history will eject us. So, we want to place operatives in a time and let them live their lives as normal.'

Cynthia stops talking and waits for a reaction. Neither Nate nor Izzy speaks, and Harold once again can't read what they're thinking from their faces. This is a once-in-a-lifetime opportunity, so why aren't they more excited?

He rises to his feet and begins pacing around the room, unable to contain his enthusiasm in an inert body.

'There will be none of this dying and living outside of the world. We will no longer be limited to having to work through people living in a time period, because our agents will be a part of whatever is happening.'

'How does this change anything other than that we'll be able to act as individuals rather than through others?' Nate asks.

Finally, a reaction. Even if it is negative, it's better than being stonewalled. Harold has been expecting this criticism and is prepared for it.

'Well, that's where you're wrong. Though we'll still follow Time Guardian strictures on not removing or killing anyone critical to history—'

'And we won't fundamentally tamper with agreed key historic events,' Cynthia adds.

'What does that leave?' Izzy asks before Harold can finish the pitch.

'Ah, now this is the fun bit.' Harold is truly excited about his new team and unable to keep that feeling inside. 'We have identified key moments in history where the tide of human thinking almost changed but got stalled. We aim to place operatives in key positions to ensure those ideas gain traction.'

'Won't that change history?' Nate asks.

'Potentially, so we'll have to monitor it closely. What we're aiming for is that key events still happen, like the collapse of civilisations or the rise of leaders, no matter how much we abhor their actions. Underneath all of that, though, we want to have a groundswell of change that grows through the centuries so that after the war that leaves humanity's future in the balance, we end up with people left in key countries still working for a better future. People who want to destroy their weapons rather than turn them on one another. People who support diversity while they rebuild for the future.'

Harold turns his back to the window and faces the two agents he hopes to be the first two members of his new team. Cynthia sends him a nod of encouragement, but he's waiting on tenterhooks.

Izzy is the first to react. 'Okay, I get the big picture, but how will this work day to day?'

'Let's take you as an example, Isolde,' Cynthia says, making her pitch to win Izzy over. 'You would return to your original timeline in 1913 and continue to work as a journalist, and we would use our contacts to get you assigned to one of the less-major dailies. The idea we believe you could push forward is the rights of women. Women getting the vote and moving toward equality is a precursor for all minorities being accepted. If we can nudge the timeline even a little, we project that by the time World War Three comes along, equality will be so entrenched in human consciousness that it will simply become a part of the post-war world.'

'And a breakdown of the data shows this small shift will make it easier for the disparate communities to get along after the war,' Harold adds.

Izzy sits forward in her chair. 'So you have actual analysis that shows the

acceptance of women as equals models the way for other marginalised groups in society to find their own voices?'

'Yes,' Harold tells her. 'And if we also get enough resources to nudge at the edge of racism and acceptance of different sexual identities, look to find commonalities rather than differences, who knows what impact that may have on the future—we may even be able to prevent World War Three.'

'Prevent it?' Izzy asks. 'But it's an historic event.'

'Apparently not,' Harold tells them. 'There is some debate on whether it's a fixed event or not.'

'Okay. And if I'm back in my own time, I can still try and work things out with Jo and Stanley?'

Cynthia smiles. 'Yes, so long as you're able to take up the journalism job we sort out for you.'

Izzy asking questions is a good sign, and a spark of hope blossoms in Harold, but Nate is still not engaged. Time to draw him in with his own new life option.

'And you, Nate. We would like to place you into the 2010s. The rise of the Me Too Movement, along with Black Lives Matter in the United States, goes hand in hand with the rise of extreme right-wing politics and the rise of nationalism.'

Nate laughs. 'You want me to go in as a white liberal in one of the most volatile times in world history?'

'Not exactly. Well, yes, exactly that. We would like to place you in an organisation called Hope Not Hate in the United Kingdom. It has an interest in cleaning up social media to prevent the dissemination of misinformation.'

For the first time, there's a tiny spark of interest in Nate's eyes, but Harold doesn't want to celebrate yet.

'You would want me to live in that time because there would be no incarnations of me, because I officially died in 1914. Right?'

'Yes,' Cynthia says, 'but it would be a place and a time where you could set down new roots if you wished.'

Nate draws his bottom lip between his teeth. Finally, he says, 'You've given me a lot to think about.'

'Given us both a lot to think about,' Izzy says. 'Although, if I go down this path, I will miss working in other times.'

Cynthia smiles. 'Oh, we're not ruling out agents needing to help one another out from time to time if situations become volatile.'

Izzy grins. 'This is almost too good to be true. Let me talk with Stanley and Josephine. If I can get Jo to meet me halfway by moving to London, then I'll be able to be with them and also still work for you.'

I think we have her, Cynthia crows.

But not Nate. Harold is somewhat desolate that he might have lost his protégé after all these years working together.

THE TRAIN IS rocking back and forth, and Basia struggles to keep her eyes open. It had been an early morning start from Winchester to catch the bus to Portsmouth Harbour, then a short wait for the connecting train to Petersfield, where she and Alan will join the Pilgrimage for Women's Suffrage as they walk to Haslemere. Both trains had been packed with suffragists of both sexes and all walks of life, and it's quite a party atmosphere.

Glancing sideways at Alan, she chuckles. He's well out of his comfort zone with this group of people. In fact, Basia had been surprised when he offered to escort her when he found out she was intending to go even though Izzy couldn't accompany her.

Knowing he struggles with the idea of modern women, she had politely refused. He insisted.

'You have had a nasty bump on the head, and it is a long journey. It may not be my cup of tea, but as I feel somewhat responsible for your injury, it is a way for me to make things up to you.'

After self-consciously raising her hand to her bandage, Basia had assured him there was nothing to make up for. Then she explained that it would take more than a hit on the head and a couple of stitches to keep her from such an historic event.

Then Izzy had jumped in. 'Barbara, you really should not go alone, and Detective Barker does seem quite keen to take you.'

Too tired to argue, Basia gave in, and they agreed on a time for him to call the following morning. The detective had then taken his leave, as he wished to visit Josephine before heading home.

'I must apologise to her,' he said, 'although I have no idea what I can possibly do to make amends for causing her wounds.'

Izzy had widened her eyes as he closed the door, but Basia had forestalled any teasing.

'Don't say a word. He's doing his best to make up for his mistakes.'

'He's sweet on you,' Izzy sang.

'I need an escort, and he's offered. And that's all there is to it.'

Izzy had winked and responded, 'Of course it is,' and she'd been conspicuously absent when Alan called early this morning.

When the train stops, and they finally alight at Petersfield, he resolutely slips her hand through his arm and hangs back behind everyone else as they walk to the village square.

'Barbara, I have wanted to… that is, I feel I should formally apologise to you for my actions yesterday,' he says, nerves causing his hands to shake. 'It was my first time leading such an operation, and I did not cover myself in glory.'

A bit of an understatement. Basia is still a little annoyed at his attempt to leave her behind when they entered the house, as well as the fact that once everything was over, it had taken him a while to remember she'd been knocked unconscious and was left lying on the floor. In fact, it had been one of his constables who'd helped her up and into the sitting room. Instead of voicing all this, she tells him, 'You could have handled it better, I am sure.'

'Yes, well, I have been reflecting on my actions, and I am afraid I allowed my insecurities to get the better of me. I was uncomfortable with Nathanial taking charge, and I acted without considering all possible outcomes. I have made a list of things I need to work on for next time.'

Unsure about how she's supposed to respond to such an honest accounting of his behaviour, Basia simply says, 'We all make mistakes, Alan.'

Something in the tone of her voice, or perhaps the set of her face, alerts Alan to the fact that she hasn't totally forgiven him.

'And I must atone for mine. I have apologised to everyone else, and now I must make amends to you in particular.'

A small smile begins to form at the edge of Basia's mouth. He's so earnest and so intent on making everything right, it's difficult to stay mad at him.

'I am pleased you have taken responsibility for your actions, and I am sure everyone has forgiven you. However, I do not think any of them will be letting you take charge of anything any time soon.' She nudges his arm and laughs, trying to lighten the moment, but Alan appears intent on vilifying himself for yesterday.

'They may have offered their forgiveness, but I am yet to forgive myself. If it were not for me, Jo would not have been injured.'

That's true, but there's no point in going over it again. Besides, they're coming

up on the square, and Basia doesn't want to miss a moment of the march. As the square comes into view, it hits her that she's going to experience a bit of history first-hand. There is no way she's going to let Alan spoil this for her.

She turns back to Alan, and his face is sombre. She forces conviction into her voice and says, 'Maybe she might have, or maybe not. We have no way of knowing. I always think what is more important is learning from our mistakes, and maybe in the future, you will take time to read the room before acting.'

Basia hopes that will be the end to it, as women are spilling into the square from all sides, and someone on the back of a horse and cart is speaking through a megaphone. She steps forward, excitement racing through her, straining to hear the words and join the crowd. However, Alan stands firm, determined to get everything out in the open, and forces her to stay with him.

'If I am being totally honest, Barbara, I was already off balance when I entered the fray. You had been hurt, and I was angry at Jason for hitting you as well as at myself for not protecting you better.'

She knows she should say something placating, or even just say, *Can we talk about this later*, but history is happening around her, and she's becoming increasingly more impatient to join the march. Biting back a sigh, she makes herself speak calmly but forcefully. 'Remember what I said about reading the room—now is not a good time to discuss this. Besides, I neither wanted nor needed your protection yesterday.' The stricken look on his face causes her to pause a moment and add in a lighter tone, 'What happened to me was on my own head—excuse the pun.'

Even the attempt at a joke doesn't remove the hurt from Alan's face.

'I am sorry, Alan. I did not mean that to come out the way it did.'

'Gosh, I really have misread things. I thought we were getting along well… that perhaps we had… and I have gone and completely mucked it up.'

Guilt washes over her. Basia lets out a slow breath before turning to Alan and reaching out a hand to clasp his. 'We were… are getting on. I like you, and if I were staying in Winchester, I would probably want to get to know you better.'

He takes her other hand and raises hopeful eyes to meet hers, searching for something more—something she knows she shouldn't give.

'What I was referring to was your assumption that I would look to you for protection and to look after me. The world is changing, Alan, and although there will always be some women who look for that in their partners, I am not one of them. I intend to make my own way in the world, and anyone I choose to be with will need to understand that.'

As the words leave her lips, she realises she really means them. She's ready to go home and decide her next moves without the weight of Alan's expectations or her parents'. She isn't quite sure yet what that will look like, but she is sure she won't decide that hiding here in this make-believe existence.

'So you have made up your mind? You are heading back to London?'

It's time to be fair to them both and put an end to this… whatever it is. 'Yes, Alan, I am.'

'Are you sure I cannot tempt you to stay? Perhaps if we started over again?'

The way he looks at her with such intensity sets her heart racing. It would be so easy to say yes, to allow him to wrap his arms around her. To kiss those lips. She mentally shakes herself.

'Tempting though that offer is, this is not where I am meant to be.' Staring into his eyes she knows she could get lost in, she wills him to let her go as she's been forced to do with him. 'We can still be friends and enjoy today, can we not?'

'Ah, the friend gambit. There is no coming back from that, is there?' Alan says, doing his best to put on a brave face. 'If that is what you wish, we can try,'

As it turns out, enjoying themselves is easier than they expected. The atmosphere of the march is joyous, and the speeches are rousing—especially Miss Fielden's, although that may be because they know what Maisie had gone through to make sure the speech was perfect.

Basia sleeps on the train on the way home, allowing her head to drop onto Alan's shoulder. Something about their being together feels so right, and as he walks her back to Augusta's, her sadness grows.

This is the last time she'll be with Alan, and it would be so easy to let temptation take over logic, to rebel against what's right and let her desire take over, to at least have this one night with him.

He rings the doorbell, and as they wait for Jensen, he lowers his head and presses his lips to hers. The first touch is gentle, sweet. Then, as she responds, the kiss deepens, and a familiar fire begins to glow deep inside her.

At the sound of the locks being released, he draws back, and his green eyes meet hers. 'Goodbye, Barbara. If you ever change your mind, you know—'

'Where to find you,' she finishes, a smile hovering on her lips.

He tips his hat and jauntily walks off down the stairs, taking a piece of her heart with him.

13

EVERYONE IN THEIR PLACE

IZZY STANDS IN the hallway, staring at the door. *I can do this!* No, she can't. Turning on her heel, she walks back towards the stairs, sucks in a breath, turns, and walks back to where she started.

It's time to face the music. Time to talk with Josephine and Stanley and find out once and for all if they could plot a way forward—together.

She takes a deep breath and knocks. When Josephine tells her to enter, she walks in, head held high, a smile on her face.

Josephine is propped up in bed, a book lying open on her lap. Stanley is sitting in his shirtsleeves in the chair by the window. A newspaper open to the finance section lies on the floor beside him, and his jacket is slung over the empty chair.

She falters at the domestic sight. 'I am sorry, you were talking. I did not mean to interrupt.'

'Nonsense,' Stanley tells her. He rises, pulls on his jacket, and brings the other chair in the room closer to the bed. 'Sit. Stay with us a while.'

Izzy perches on the edge of the chair, not quite knowing where to start. 'Ah, that is just it. I do not have much time. I have to pack, as I am going away for a couple of days, and I just wanted to check whether or not you will be here when I get back.'

Jo's brows draw together in a frown. 'Are you sure you are not running away again? Or that you are checking when we are leaving to find out when it is safe to return?

'Now, Josephine, give Isolde a chance,' Stanley says, patting Jo's hand.

Izzy sends him a grateful smile. 'I really do have to go. Barbara has to return to London, and it is only fair that I accompany her given that I dragged her all the way down here, then got her tangled in… everything.'

'Fair enough.' Jo tilts her head to one side. 'When are you planning to be back?' Her dark eyes flash a challenge, and Izzy resists the urge to look away.

She runs her sweaty palms down her dress, 'Well, that sort of depends on you…. Well, you and Stanley.' She glances from one to the other, then closes her eyes, trying to find the right words. When she opens them, the words just flow. 'I would like to attend your wedding, and I would like to stay as part of your lives, but I will not marry to make this work.'

Stanley's face breaks into a wide grin. 'You know where I stand. I always wanted you to be a part of our family, damn convention.'

Jo sighs. 'As always, it comes down to me, and I will not fly in the face of convention. That is not in my nature.'

'I do have an idea—a way this might work for all of us,' Izzy says, 'if you will hear me out.'

'Go on,' Jo prompts.

'Aunt Augusta is going to approach my father and ask him if he will allow me to open his London house. She thinks she can convince him it is a good way to bring me back into the family fold.'

'I do not see how that helps,' Jo says, looking from Izzy to Stanley, then back to Izzy.

'Well, Lionel is due any moment now to pick up my story for his paper.'

'I thought he was meant to get it yesterday,' Stanley interrupts.

'He was, but he was late for his train and ended up staying the night in Guildford. Jensen informed me of the new arrangements this morning.'

Jo shifts in the bed. 'And how does Lionel fit into this? You have already said you will not marry him.'

'I thought to ask him if he would like to move out of the dump he is living in and move in with me.'

Jo's eyes sparkle with a flicker of amusement before she carefully schools her face again.

'That will cause a bit of a scandal with both of you being unmarried,'

Stanley says, grinning as though he relishes the thought.

'So you will not marry him, but you will allow people to think you are living in sin?' Jo's voice is prim.

'Not exactly.' Izzy smiles. 'If you two move into the master suite once you are married, you will be suitable chaperones for us. He can continue to bring his men friends home, and I can continue unmarried and still be chaperoned… and we can all be together.'

Jo cocks her head to the side, studying Izzy with an unconcealed intensity. 'Why not move into your father's house in Dorset, or into ours, for that matter?'

Izzy takes a deep breath. She knew this would be a stumbling block. However, part of her feels if she can accept Jo marrying Stanley, then Jo can meet her halfway and move to London. Besides, if she isn't in London, she can't work for a newspaper, and she can't be a part of Cynthia and Harold's new agency—and she would really like to do that.

'Oh, Josephine, you know I could not do that. You have your family's business interests to keep you occupied, but what would I do in the wilds of Dorset?'

'You could write for the local newspaper,' Jo offers.

'What, you want me to write about bake sales and fetes and the latest fashion? I would die a slow death.' Izzy shudders at the thought of it.

'Or you can be badly behaved and shock the local gentry like you used to,' Jo chuckles.

Izzy joins her. 'Still, Josephine, it is not a job.'

'London is not so bad, Josephine. There are shows and soirees, and you know you enjoy pitting your wit against Lionel's cronies,' Stanley says. 'You can run the business from anywhere, and Isolde can get on with her newspaper things. Besides, Dorset is but a train ride away. We can go back and forth anytime.'

Izzy stares at Jo, beseeching her to understand she's shifted on letting Stanley into her life, and she now needs Jo to move a little, but she won't lose her over this. 'If you insist, then I will give up London.'

Jo's eyes widen. 'You are sure about this?' Her voice isn't particularly enthusiastic, and Izzy's stomach clenches as worry worms it way through her. She nods her answer, not trusting herself to say anything, lest she say the wrong thing.

'Well, you have given us something to think about,' Jo says, still scrutinising Izzy. 'How long—'

She's interrupted by a knock on the door.

'Come in,' Stanley says.

The upstairs maid pops her head through and searches for Izzy. 'Begging your pardon, miss, but Mr Lionel is in the morning room. He asked for you to join him immediately as he is on his way to catch a train.'

'I guess I will leave you to discuss my proposal, then,' Izzy says, relieved to leave the room.

After quickly slipping upstairs to retrieve her article, Izzy heads for the morning room. Her stomach is still churning, but she hopes she's schooled her face to hide her inner turmoil as she enters.

'My darling Izzy, whatever is the matter?' Lionel asks as he kisses both her cheeks.

Guess I'm not as good at hiding how I feel as I thought. Izzy smiles at Lionel. Then again, she has known Lionel far longer than she has Jo, and they have so much more in common, both living on the fringe of acceptable society as they do.

'Nothing… everything. Lionel, I am thinking about returning to London, and Aunt Augusta has said she will try and talk Father into allowing me to open his house.'

'Bravo. I never did like that boarding house you were in.'

'It is perfectly respectable,' Izzy responds, rising to the bait. 'Still, if Father says yes, and I can find a way to keep the gossips happy, would you like to come live with me—in your own room, of course?'

'Are you serious?'

'Yes. I mean, there is really only the Sewals to do for us, so it would be pretty basic.'

'Oh, poppet, you have seen where I am living. Tell me when you are moving in, and I will join you, gossips be damned.'

Relief rushes through her, making her light-headed. Even if Jo turns her down, Lionel will be there for her, helping her mend her broken heart.

Izzy flings her arms around him. 'Lionel, you know if I were ever to marry a man, or decided to let my mother down and marry for convenience, you would be my first choice.'

'You *are* a silly thing. Now, I must be on my way, or I will miss my train. Telegram me the details of your arrival. Oh, and in the meantime, I expect a thousand words on your adventure with Miss Maisie Ottaway. My editor says he will print it under your name, and, if it is any good, he will consider a regular column.'

Her breath catches in her chest. He can't be serious. 'Lionel, this is too cruel if you are teasing me.'

Lionel's Cheshire-cat grin splits his face. 'All totally above board, my pet. It seems your recent notoriety has made you marketable. Now, really, I must be off, or I will miss my return train.'

Izzy sees her friend out and heads back upstairs, her heart radiating such pure joy that her fear of what Jo and Stanley might say does little to dim it. She finds Jo alone in her room.

'Stanley has returned to the library to give us a moment alone.'

Izzy's stomach drops. Jo is so serious, Izzy knows what she's going to say, and she steels herself to take it without breaking down.

'You broke my trust when you ran away, and my heart as well. You will always be the love of my life, but….'

Here it goes. Be brave now, Izzy.

'…trust is everything to me. You need to earn that back before I can make a commitment to you being in our lives permanently.'

Izzy does a double-take. Is Jo turning down her offer or not?

'I am not sure what you mean,' she finally says.

'Stanley and I will move into the house in London with you—that is, if your father can be brought around—but it will only be a temporary arrangement.'

'What Josephine is saying,' Stanley says from the doorway, 'is that we will return to London after our honeymoon, and we will stay with you for six months. That is when I plan to leave for Australia to check on Josephine's father's holdings.'

'I had toyed with the idea of going with him because there was nothing keeping me in England,' Jo adds. 'If things work out, though, I may then decide to remain here while he is away.'

'Or maybe you will be so tired of the Big Smoke that we might all set out on an adventure together,' Stanley says, unable to hide the gleam of excitement in his eyes. 'Do you not think it would be great fun to take on the New World together, just the three of us on safari in the Australian outback?' He walks towards her, rubbing his hands together like an excited child.

Izzy knows she's grinning deliriously. She hugs Stanley, then Jo, then Stanley again. 'I will not let you down, I promise.'

'All right, enough of this mush,' Jo says. 'I need my rest, and, Izzy, you have a train to catch. The sooner you go, the sooner you can get everything organised for us.'

This time she's reluctant to leave Winchester, but Izzy walks upstairs to her room on a cushion of air, safe in the knowledge that her future will be waiting for her when she returns.

VIVIENNE LEE FRASER

NATE IS ABOUT to knock on the door to Basia's room when footsteps on the stairs have him ducking into a doorway. Cook had allowed him in via the back door to say his farewells on the understanding he wouldn't compromise either lady's reputation. Actually, she made him promise on pain of death.

Now he's trapped and has nowhere to go. The door in front of him opens, and Basia's head pops out. Finding him cowering in the doorway, she sends him a "What on earth do you think you're doing?" look.

He straightens himself up and brushes down his suit.

'Are you coming in, or are you going to stand out in the hallway all day?' Basia asks.

'I … um… shouldn't….'

'If you're worried *I* will say anything about your being in a lady's bedroom, then you're mistaken,' Izzy chuckles as she joins them. 'Besides, it's almost respectable, now I'm here to chaperone you.'

'You're in a good mood,' he says, trying to hide his very Nathanial embarrassment.

'I am, aren't I?' Izzy says as she virtually pushes him into the bedroom before closing the door behind them. 'To what do we owe the pleasure of your visit without the lovely Hannah?'

'I heard on the grapevine that Barbara is returning to London, so I thought I had best come and say goodbye to Basia before you return her home,' he tells them. 'Although I'm surprised you're leaving so soon. I thought you might want to take a couple of days to enjoy Winchester before heading back.'

Basia grins. 'I think it would all be too quiet for me after the excitement of the last few days.'

'Besides, if she stays any longer, she'll be back to fighting off an amorous detective,' Izzy chuckles.

'Yes, I'm not sure I could let him down gently a second time.'

'You mean you might rip his clothes off and do something you might regret later,' Izzy teases, mischief gleaming in her eyes.

Rather than joining in the fun, Nate studies Izzy closely. She'd been but a shadow of herself the last couple of weeks, and it's heart-warming to see the old Izzy again.

'What?' Izzy says, catching him staring at her.

'Nothing. It's just, you're different. You're Izzy again.'

Her smile lights up her face. 'Yes, I am, aren't I? I'm staying in my world, and I'm going to take up Cynthia and Harold's offer. I finally feel like I'm where I want and need to be.'

'You know, with spending most of your time here rather than in headquarters, you'll start ageing again,' Nate teases.

Izzy contorts her face into one of mock fear. 'Oh no, I guess I'll have to give all this up.'

Basia laughs along with Izzy, but Nate can barely manage a smile.

'You, on the other hand, seem even more sad and detached,' Basia says, placing a hand on Nate's arm. 'You may not want to hear this, but it would be a shame for the world to lose you. I wouldn't have any life to go back to if it weren't for you—and I bet there are many other people who feel the same way.'

Izzy is nodding. 'I chose to work with you more than once, Nate, even though our organisations were at loggerheads. It would be such a shame for you to melt out of existence. You deserve better than that. Besides, I shall miss you, even if we won't see each other as often.'

He looks from one woman to the other, and a sigh escapes his lips. 'A part of me is proud of what I've achieved, I really am. It's just, I'm….' He stops, unsure of how to put his feelings into words.

'You're not happy,' Basia offers.

He considers this for a moment, then nods. 'Yes, that's exactly it. I'm not happy, and I'm not sure I can even place a finger on when I last was.'

Now it's Izzy's turn to study him, and tears come to her eyes as they find the bleakness in his. 'You know, Nate, if I have learned anything these last few days, it's that happiness does not just happen. Life is full of chances and opportunities to be happy, but sometimes you have to be prepared to take a risk and reach for those opportunities when they present themselves.'

Nate's brows drop into a frown. 'I'm not quite sure what to say to that, Izzy.'

'Oh, Nate, you goose. I'm saying that for so long, you've bound your happiness to Hannah, and when she stopped making you happy, you didn't know where to look next. Now you've finally let her go, you should take the time to find out what truly makes you, Nate, happy. Only to do that, you have to be brave and take the first step.'

'And what would that look like, in your opinion?' he asks with a touch of curiosity.

Basia moves to stand beside Izzy. 'It doesn't look like staying here with Hannah.'

'Nor perhaps returning to the Time Guardians, where you'll more than likely run into Theta,' Izzy adds.

'Exactly,' Basia chimes in. 'You need a fresh start.'

'If you don't like the one Cynthia and Harold offered you, negotiate another.'

'But don't simply allow yourself to blink out of existence before you've even tried,' Basia finishes up.

Nate holds his hands up in front of him, but he's smiling, really smiling, for the first time in days. 'Whoa, guys, I get the picture.'

'Good,' Izzy says, 'because I, for one, cannot bear the thought of not ever seeing you again.' She wipes a tear from her eye before it has a chance to fall.

Nate finds she isn't the only tearful one. He hadn't realised how strong his bond to Izzy had grown. Somehow, throughout their adventures, they've become friends, and the thought of her not being in his life saddens him.

'All right, I'll think about it. That's all I can promise. Now, I have very little time, as an operative is being sent to restructure Nathanial's memories to integrate my takeover with his life. Then I… I mean *he*—considering I'll no longer be inside Nathanial—has a lunch with Hannah to discuss whether the new and improved Nathanial still wants to be with her.'

'And will he?' Basia asks.

Nate shrugs. 'I have no idea. The original Nathanial would have fallen at her feet and begged forgiveness. However, he'll retain some memory of what happened and his role in the rescue, sans the Time Guardian bits, and that has to have changed him. So, anything might happen.'

'And when you're released from his body?' Izzy asks.

'I'll return to Time Guardian headquarters to finish my sabbatical. Then it's decision time. And before you say it, I will take your thoughts into consideration.'

The two of them smile at each other.

'Then our job is done,' Basia says, leaning over and kissing him on the cheek. 'Thank you for saving my world, and for being… well, for being you. I'll miss you.'

'And I shall miss you too,' he tells her.

'No you shan't,' Izzy says, 'because whatever time you choose to live in, the original Barabal—or Barbara or Bebe or Basia, whatever reincarnation is in that time—will gravitate towards you, and so will the others.'

He frowns at her, and her face takes on a belligerent set.

'Don't you look at me like that, and don't you dare say goodbye, because we *will* see each other again.'

Before he can answer, she gives him a quick kiss on the cheek and storms from the room.

BASIA PUSHES HERSELF through the dark, filmy gauze of the portal, fighting for her breath as the diaphanous film clings to her face, fighting her way to the future—her future. As if sensing a part of her is reluctant to return home, travelling back is more difficult than leaving had been. It's as though time is holding on to her, giving her a chance to change her mind. She stumbles, struggling to find her footing as the gateway spits her out behind a building in the Portsmouth dockyards.

'Wasn't that fun?' Izzy says, grinning. 'Well, welcome home.'

Basia's stomach roils as she surveys the dockyard, pinkish in the early morning light. 'How long have I been gone?' she asks.

'We left last night. As promised, only Johan knows where you've been, and he covered for you to make sure no one interrupted your sleep.'

'And you're certain no one can see my stitches?' Basia tugs at the headband Izzy had given her before touching the now yellowish bruise around her eye. Izzy had concealed it with make-up, popping the tube into her pocket for Basia to use until everything healed.

'You look fine. Grab a hat and keep it low, and no one will notice.'

'And Lee? Is he still here?'

'Of course. Theta will come and get him in one month. That ought to give him time to get fixing this world out of his system.'

'That'll be odd, now that I've met her as Hannah. Hey, will she remember having met me before?'

Izzy frowns. 'I have no idea. I've never been around to see how altering someone's timeline affects them in the future. You'll have to find some way to let me know.'

Basia laughs. 'No worries. I guess that will be the least of the odd things I face. I mean, I've been through so much, it seems strange coming back here where nothing has changed at all.' As she speaks her stomach churns, and she's not sure whether what she's feeling is excitement at returning home, disorientation at having been away, or trepidation over what's to come next.

'I wouldn't quite put it that way,' Izzy tells her. 'It was a busy night here in Portsmouth. The Commander and his Council have been up all night, working to find a way to defuse tensions between Portsdown and the outlying communities. Last report was that he was almost at his wits' end.'

'And what about Portsdown?' Basia asks.

'Theta is probably still there, trying to keep things calm and talking them down from using the weapons they've stockpiled in their bunker, or trying to convince the Time Guardians not to call her back until things are more settled.'

Izzy's eyes cloud over, and as she communicates with someone, Basia sighs. The gulf between the peoples seems as insurmountable as ever, and the plan she's been working on in her head will take time to implement and take hold. Would it be enough?

Izzy's gaze refocuses. 'Beta said Theta is still here. The timeline is still in the red, so it'll be some time before they can release her. Are you sure you want to stay? I can always take you back to your detective.'

Basia laughs, as she was sure Izzy intended her to. 'No, I'm where I'm meant to be, and I think it's time for this reincarnation to find a life away from Allan. Besides, I have some ideas that I think might work to help bring things out of the red.'

'Ah, so you've been inspired by the leaders of the suffrage movement as Nate thought you might be.'

Basia shakes her head. 'No, quite the contrary, and it isn't because I don't want to be a leader of a great movement. It's because I think we've put too much emphasis on leadership, and the Commander here has shown me there's another way—change by consensus. I like the way he talks, and listens, and builds a solution along with the people who follow him.'

'So, if you don't want his job, what do you want to do?'

Basia grins. 'I still want to be what I always wanted to be—a healer… a doctor.'

'What about what Allan was working for?'

Sadness seeps its way into Basia's heart. Being back home brings the raw hurt of her soulmate's loss back to the forefront of her mind. She doesn't want to let him down, but she's her own person, and she can't take on his fight. At least not in the way he would, and she has to believe he wouldn't want her to.

'Not only do I not want to lead and inspire people, but I have learned that great people and big ideas aiming for a shift in society can sometimes create fear. And that fear often alienates people who might otherwise have

supported what they're working towards.

'Look at the difference between the suffragettes and the suffragists. They both worked for the same end, but suffragettes ended up polarising people, whereas suffragists worked on bringing everyone along with them.'

'So you're saying the suffragettes were wrong to aim big and push hard?' Izzy asks, frowning.

'Yes… no. I'm not sure. All I know is, here and now, in this time, we can't afford to polarise anyone—the stakes are too high. Perhaps we need to learn to walk together for a while before we start pushing for radical change.'

Izzy nods, a thoughtful look on her face. 'Funny, over the past week, I've been thinking very similar things myself.'

Emboldened by Izzy's support, Basia stands taller. 'I think if we can build some communities of interest to share ideas, then that will be a step in the right direction. Allan's growers could work with our farmers. Portsdown's medics with our healers. Even their soldiers with militia. My hope is that as we share ideas, understanding and friendships will grow, and then we might find we're more alike than we are different.'

'And with understanding maybe will come change for the better.'

'Thank you for everything, Izzy. I wouldn't be here, literally physically or emotionally, if not for you.' Basia sniffs and wipes her eyes.

Izzy's face softens with a look of quiet pride. 'You would have gotten here eventually.'

Basia throws her arms around the Time Fixer who's become her closest friend and hugs her tight. 'Who knew saying goodbye would be so hard? I will miss you, Izzy.'

'And I you.' Izzy's voice chokes.

'Not so much, I think,' Basia gives Izzy one last squeeze. 'You have a new adventure to start. You'll soon forget me.'

'Never,' Izzy swears, wiping the tears from her eyes.

'Basia, you're back.' Johan's voice cuts through the morning air, preventing the scene from getting even mushier than it already is.

Her brother pulls up when he realises Izzy is still with her, and he grins. 'You're still here. Does this mean you're staying?'

'I'm sorry, Johan, but no. I have somewhere I must be.'

The sadness in his eyes batters Basia's already tender heart.

'I thought…,' he starts, then trails off.

Izzy reaches out and takes his hand. 'Once, I may have taken you up on

that offer, believing it may have been enough. But I know for sure your true love is out there somewhere, as is mine. You just need to be patient and not settle for anything less.'

Their eyes lock, and the emotion running between them is tangible enough for Basia to believe she could reach out and touch it. She turns away to give them a little privacy as fresh tears trickle down her cheeks.

'Come on, Johan. Izzy has things she has to do, and you need to help me find the Commander. I want to talk to him about something.'

Reluctantly her brother steps away but stops by Basia's side, not taking his eyes from Izzy until she's opened her portal and returned home. Reaching for Johan's hand, Basia gives him a squeeze of support.

With his other hand, Johan brushes the tears from his eyes and clears his throat. 'All right, Basia, tell me what's so urgent. I hope you're not thinking of taking off on another harebrained adventure.'

His face is back to his normal mix of bossy with a faint smile. Basia chuckles. It's good to be home.

EPILOGUE: AGENCY HEADQUARTERS JUST TO THE LEFT OF TIME

HAROLD CURLS HIS legs underneath him on the sofa and wraps an arm around Cynthia, who drops her head onto his shoulder.

He takes a sip of whiskey and sighs. 'Well, that was a trial, wasn't it?'

'One day you'll have to stop expecting Alpha to treat you with anything but disdain,' Cynthia says, giving his thigh a squeeze to take the sting out of her words.

'You're right. It'll never happen, no matter how many millennia we live for. The only consolation is that now, no matter what he says when he goes back to the Council, it will change nothing. Everything is finally signed and sealed.'

Cynthia clinks her glass to his. 'Cheers,' she says.

'As of now we're operating independently of day-to-day oversight by either Council, unless a major incident appears on either of their horizons.'

Cynthia raises her head, then swings around to face him. Has he said something to upset her? No, she isn't frowning. There's a gleam in her eye, like she's excited.

'I was going to wait until after dinner, but I just can't. I had the techies rush through the monitoring feeds on our first two recruits, and they set up a link so we can see what's happening from here.'

A frisson of excitement fills the room. He so wants to look at the feeds, but first he wants to thank Cynthia for… well… being her. He leans forward and touches his lips to hers. 'Thank you,' he says. 'This is the best present ever. Well, apart from you.' He kisses her again. 'You surprise me and challenge me, and I'm so lucky I found you.'

She returns his kiss, then pulls away. 'Yes, you are lucky to have me, and I want you to hold that thought until after we test these links.' A frown line appears between her brows. 'Is that bad? To put snooping on our agents first?'

He leans over, pecks her cheek, then picks up the vid control. 'If it is, then I'm bad too. Let's see what we have.'

He presses button one, and the picture enlarges to show Izzy sitting in a room across from a man, who has his back to them.

'Is that—'

Cynthia chuckles. 'What timing. Izzy is on one of her three monthly visits to Jason.'

'Ooh, she doesn't look happy. I guess she won't be sending a report telling us he's taken responsibility for his actions and is ready to be extracted.'

Somehow the thought of Jason spending another three months in a turn-of-the-century British prison does nothing to bring his mood down. In fact, he would be perfectly content if Jason was never to return.

'I had hoped to see her at home,' Cynthia says. 'Josephine and Stanley should be returning from their honeymoon any time now.'

'Oh well, we get what we get,' Harold says. 'I mean, normally we'll only be watching if an anomaly occurs, once we've thoroughly tested the feeds.'

'Testing could take a little longer than expected, though,' Cynthia says. 'Not that I want to spy on anyone, and obviously, I wouldn't watch any intimate moments, but Izzy is like a daughter to me, and what mother doesn't want to make sure their child is all right?'

Harold laughs. 'Every parent, I should imagine, but you'll just have to limit yourself to watching anomalies and those times agreed on with Izzy.'

Cynthia sighs dramatically. 'I am so lucky to have you to help me follow the rules.'

'Shall we test the feed to our other operative?'

'Of course.'

THE GUARDIANS OF TIME: SUFFRAGETTE

Harold presses button two, and the screen opens up on a room full of people. Some are dressed in civilian clothes, and others are wearing what could only be described as hospital scrubs.

'There she is.' Cynthia points to a woman standing at the front of the room, talking as a slide is projected onto the wall. 'Is she doing a talk on medicinal plants? I can't quite see without my glasses.' Cynthia leans forward, squinting at the screen.

'You know, your glasses make you even more attractive. You should wear them more often.'

Cynthia chuckles. 'Flattery will get you nothing unless you tell me what you see.'

'Yes, she's talking about medicinal plants. And if you had your glasses on, you would be more interested in the doctor sitting to her right. He can't take his eyes off Basia, and every now and then, she catches him watching. I can't be sure, but I think she's blushing.'

'Oh, how exciting.' Cynthia says. 'Are you sure you don't want to check in on the sly a little to see how that romance might go?'

'Cynthia!'

'Just asking.' She smiles, then reaches over and takes the controller from him. 'You are a true rule follower, but I'm doing this, and I'm doing it for you. He hasn't fully agreed to join us, but I had them set up the feed just in case.'

The picture shifts to a young man sitting in an office across the desk from an older man. A file between them seems to hold their attention. A young woman enters the room, the three speak for a moment, and then the young man rises to leave. The woman appears to be encouraging him to stay, but he shakes his head.

As he opens the door, the image flickers, and a crackle of static comes from the speakers.

'Oh, how exciting. They have the sound up and running,' Cynthia says.

'Shh, we might miss something interesting.'

'…toy with him, Minnie. Nate is good with the kids, and I can't afford to lose another councillor. We're struggling to keep our funding as it is, and I don't want to have to go back to Dad and beg for help.'

The girl is still looking at the door, a dreamy smile on her face. 'Who's toying, Charles? I think this one might be a keeper.'

ABOUT THIS BOOK

HOW MUCH IS fiction and how much is real?

Many years ago I studied Women's History in the late nineteenth and early twentieth century. Since then I've been interested in how women have been sideline and treated as wives and daughters throughout the centuries. It was no surprise to me when that of them fought physically to be treated as individuals when they were constantly denied their rights.

Like Izzy in Suffragette I have never been comfortable with what they did, but I can understand why they did it. How frustrating must it have been to be told your voice did not matter. That frustration is being voiced again with many groups around the world today, and I can only hope we have learned from history, and that they will not need to resort to violence to be recognised and valued.

Although I drew heavily on historic records for Suffragette, all the main characters in this book are fictional, and most of the events described did not happen—except for in my imagination that is.

The suffragette and suffragist organisations mentioned did exist, and The Women's Pilgrimage was real. A Miss Fielden did give a speech at Haslemere, but her secretary, Maisie Ottaway, is definitely fictional.

THE GUARDIANS OF TIME: SUFFRAGETTE

I could find very few details about Miss Fielden and believe she may have have been the daughter of a member of Parliament who supported the movement to give women the vote. If I have this wrong it is simply because Miss Fielden leaves very little trace even with all the data in the internet.

Emily Davidson was also a real figure, and was considered a martyr by suffragettes when she threw herself in front of a horse on Derby Day 1913. Recent research has questioned whether or not she may have tripped, turning her death into a tragic accident rather than a political protest. I have chosen the second version of events for the purposes of this book.

The Fielding family do exist, and I came across them when trying to track Miss Fielden when I mistyped her name into a search engine. They were part of the peerage and a politically well connect family. I hope they don't mind me inserting Izzy into their family tree for the purposes of this story.

I have attempted to make this story as historically accurate as possible, and I apologise for any glaring mistakes, or maybe they aren't mistakes but simply history correcting the timeline.

THE GUARDIANS OF TIME

ACKNOWLEDGEMENTS

FIVE YEARS AGO in a hospital room this series shouted at me to be written. This series of books more than any other is rooted in my family and in my early love of writing and history. I'm saddened to be finishing the series with *Suffragette*, but I'm sure you noticed I've given myself the option of resurrecting some of the characters should the urge take me.

In all of the *Guardian's of Time* stories I have borrowed heavily from my family and our history and, indeed, from some of my actual family members. I want to thank them for allowing me to do that, and for not mentioning it at family get-togethers.

Apart from my dad who inspired these books, I also have to thank my uncle, Stan, for giving me the starting point for Stanislaus. To all the Williamson women who inspired Barabel, Bee and Basia, it has been a privilege to be related to so many strong, independent, powerful women—aroha nui. To my Southampton family, I would never have found the setting for these books if it weren't for you.

A special call out to Sandy and Margot, the first readers of my first ever book that was transformed into *Soldier*. I'm sure I've learnt a lot since that early, hand-written story.

VIVIENNE LEE FRASER

A special call out to the animals from the books. Lala the lamb was based on my son, Sam's favourite baby toy. Trouble is actually our Spoodle dog. Bruno is in fact Sam's big gruff teddy bear, and Cuddles is the name Trouble would have been landed with if Sam had his way.

I always say it takes a community to turn a story into a novel and it does. Apart from my family, the fact that you have read these as cohesive stories is due solely to the editing team who supported me in getting the books out. Heather Bosevski, who edited Swagman and helped me find my voice as a writer. Lauren McKeller from Creating Ink, for editing Alchemist—this is still my favourite book of the series. Sali Benbow-Powers from the Creating Ink Team, thank you so much for challenging me and especially for helping me find Basia's voice.

McKinley Hellenes Krantz and Kristen Scarce from Hot Tree Editing, for your commitment to details. Honestly, no one would read my books if it weren't for these lovely editors.

A special thanks to Kim Last from Kila Designs. She not only set me on my self-publishing journey, but produces incredible covers and interior designs for my books. Thank you so much - ngā mihi.

No acknowledgement would ever go out without a thank you to Jim and Sam who always support me by feeding me, bringing me drinks, and keeping the house going so I can meet editing guidelines.

And thank you to you for reading my stories. I'm always amazed and humbled when someone enjoys what I write.

ABOUT THE AUTHOR

VIVIENNE HAS BEEN writing books since she was fifteen years old, but only friends and family were allowed to read them. Forced to give up work because of family commitments she was encouraged by friends and family to finally put some of her writing out there for others to read.

In the real world after leaving university with a BA in History and Politics she worked as a Personnel Officer, an Office Manager, a Project Manager, a DBA and IT Manager then as a Business and Data Analyst, adding an MSC in Information Systems along the way. In her world she continued to write.

Born in Invercargill (New Zealand), she has lived in; Dunedin (New Zealand), London (England), Petersfield (England) and currently lives with her husband and son, their dog Trouble and kitten Lola in Sydney (Australia).

If you are interested in her future releases, or simply want to find out more about her books, you can find Vivienne at **www.viviennelfraser.com.au** or on Facebook at **www.facebook.com/vivienneleefraser**

www.ingramcontent.com/pod-product-compliance
Lightning Source LLC
Chambersburg PA
CBHW070824020826
48982CB00014B/455

* 9 7 8 0 6 4 5 5 1 5 7 9 4 *